A TRUTH UNIVERSALLY ACKNOWLEDGED

E.B. NEAL

Cover Art by
MYA SARACHO

To J—
For teaching me that love looks with the eyes
as well as the mind.

FOREWORD

When it comes to historical accuracy in fiction, it is impossible to please everyone. However, I believe that when writing in a particular era, certain fixtures, figures, and details should be included to preserve a degree of authenticity. To this end, I have adhered to historical accuracy where it serves the story, and set it aside where it does not. These choices were made with deliberation and care, and to the end of guaranteeing a better fate for the characters of this narrative, a fate that may not have always been available to their historical counterparts.

This story features potentially triggering content, including but not limited to: body image issues, mild food restriction, referenced sex trafficking of minors, and attempted assault.

A playlist to accompany this story can be found on my Instagram.

CHARACTERS

THE BAILEY HOUSEHOLD
 Sir Ian Bailey, the Royal Physician
 Rosaline Bailey, his daughter
 Lisette, Rosaline's *au pair*

THE PRINCE HOUSEHOLD
 Hieronymus Prince, the Earl of Devon
 Lady Charlotte Prince, his daughter
 Mrs. Randolph, a governess

THE GENTLEMEN
 Harold Cunningham, the Duke of St. Albans
 Edward Lightfoot, the Earl Cadogan
 Lord Lawrence Martel
 Captain Ronald Morris
 Lieutenant Callum McGrath

Lord Roden, a Toad
Lord Crawley, a Toad
Mr. August Heath

THE KNIGHT HOUSEHOLD
Mr. Richard Knight
Mrs. Edwina Knight
Lucas Knight, their eldest son
Katherine Knight, their youngest and only daughter

THE JOHNSON HOUSEHOLD
Maximus Johnson, the Earl of Alwyn
Anneke Johnson, Lady Alwyn
Rebecca Johnson, their youngest

THE CUNNINGHAM HOUSEHOLD
Lord Marcus Blackwood, godfather to Harold
Randall Merrywether, the estate manager
Mr. Brooks, the butler
Mrs. Andrews, the housekeeper
Elsie, a maid

Madam Kensington's High Society Papers,
No. 22

Bonjour, my darlings, and welcome to another riveting season here in London! The streets echo with the promising rattle of carriage wheels as the realm's finest families descend upon their summer residences, and our windows vibrate with the calls of a hundred merchants trying to catch the eye of the Empire's flashiest jewels. Like you all, I find myself sitting with bated breath, desperate to see which fresh-faced blossom will catch the Royal eye — and which sad, unaffected daisies may yet wither beneath its unforgiving stare.

Not that there is a shortage of blooms — on the contrary, it appears that this season will feature a selection unlike any other that came before it. True, like you, my darling readers, I was captivated by the diverting delights of last year's matches — who could forget the tender-footed dance between a certain dark-haired Beauty and the quiet, beseeching Raven always hovering at her shoulder? Or, dare I say, a wedding reception that left half a crate of fresh Parisian glass unceremoniously shattered beneath the bridegroom's chair? Or Lady Plumhurst's masked ball, which had too many dark corners and not enough candles? Yes, my dears, last year's season was a cataclysmic force to be reckoned with, a delicious standard to which each coming year must be held against and appraised, like a fine piece of art.

But it seems that this coming season truly will not disappoint. Already, the town's most exclusive tailors hurry, their thimbles catching at their gaping mouths, to order an excess of ten thousand yards of silk, muslin, and tulle to tend to the whims of their most excitable clients. Already, the town's finest jewelers polish their new arrivals, each one desperate to outshine the other. Already, butlers and chefs order pounds upon pounds of flour, butter, and sugar pulverized into crystals finer than sand. What better reward, one wonders, than to have the Star of the Season place a slice of candied pineapple on her innocent, pink tongue, smile demurely, and call it delicious?

Indeed — a Star she shall be, and from what a variety may she emerge! A Baron's eldest daughter, with hair like spun gold and an ear for secrets; an Earl's twins, with their bottomless eyes and predilection for giggling; a Dowager's fresh-faced redhead; a certain merchant's youngest, who is perhaps more suited to a ship's deck than a grand ballroom; and even an Earl's little fairy, her hair as white as the sun and her mind as empty as air. This, my dear readers, is the wide, uncompromising variety from which we spin our futures.

But what of the opposite sex, you may ask? A young Hound, fresh from battle; a handful of nubile Lords, their ears ringing with the yells of Parliament; a fossilized Baron, a curdled Earl, a venomous Viscount, and a floppy-haired young Pup — they all descend upon our dear little town, ready and panting for the coming weeks ahead.

And now, my dears, for the most compelling news of all — it seems that a certain Famous Recluse has been poked and prodded into the light of fine society, bringing with him a cold, closed countenance and a five-figure income. The Hound raises its head, scenting the chase; a brave Pup steps forward, sword in hand; and from the Continent, a fresh, rose-scented wind begins to blow...

❦

ROSALINE GLANCED OUT THE WINDOW AT THE TRIM HOUSES and tidy parks of Kensington and let out an unrestrained, inelegant sigh.

"*Ma chère*," cooed Lisette, not even looking up from her mending. "There is no need to be so glum. I am sure you will find London quite diverting, in spite of your best efforts."

"It lacks imagination, Lis," Rosaline replied. "Imagination and... and spark, and vivacity, and— did you see the state of the wharfs?"

"Mademoiselle will not be anywhere near the wharfs, as she already knows."

Rosaline huffed, sitting back against her cushion, then winced as they went over a large pothole. God, she was fed up with traveling, with the noise, the heat, the dust, the endless motion, the heave-to of the tide, salt in the back of her throat, and—

This neighborhood was actually quite serene, especially in comparison to the thick, clotted neighborhoods clustered around the city center. She looked out the window again, frowning. "What do you suppose they do for fun here? Trim hedges and snort about the weather?"

"I am sure they hire servants for the hedges and find plenty more than just the weather to snort about." Lisette did look up then, her unusual amber eyes far too keen and knowing. Most people found her gaze unsettling, but Rosaline did not — she found it challenging, engaging. "And I am sure you will find much diversion during your stay at Lord Devon's residence. Enough that you need not concern yourself with such triviality."

In spite of herself, Rosaline grinned. "Would it be terrible, to prefer triviality to parading about in a room full of bloated suitors and sneering mothers?"

Lisette bit her lip, barely restraining a smirk, and swatted at Rosaline. "*Ma chère*," she said, the words tight in her throat. "You must make the best of the situation. You know all too well that there is nothing you can change, and the people you mock today may be your allies tomorrow. They are not yet worthy of your scorn, or your inattention. In fact, it may be easier to bear if you find things to enjoy, and do not decide to dislike everything as a matter of principle."

Rosaline's grin had evaporated like dew in the warm spring air. "I know, Lis." Irritation simmered under her skin, and the sensation was nothing new. Well, nothing new to the last few weeks they'd spent traveling to London from the south of France. But before that, Rosaline's life had contained very little irritation at all, and she still was not wholly used to its presence.

I do not wish to be here, she wanted to say. I would rather be up a tree, at the end of a cliff, dangling from a crow's nest, anywhere. Not here. Not now. But she couldn't say that, so instead, she said, "I know nothing of the Earl. I have very little idea of what to expect."

Lisette shifted, putting aside her mending, energy zipping through her slight frame. Gossip — her strong point. "An eccentric figure to be sure. He has some strange habits, but he is kind, friendly, and good to his servants. And, you forget what we ourselves already know." She swept a hand through the air, gesturing to their surroundings. "We know that he has good taste, refined taste, but not extravagant. This carriage is well-made and elegant, and its driver does not take liberties with traffic." She leaned forward now. "And there are whispers, *ma chère*, that Lord Devon is the secret publisher of a magazine devoted to... the working man."

Rosaline blinked in surprise. "Well," she managed, quickly

revising her assumptions about Lord Devon, "I'm sure he'll provide much entertainment."

Lisette hummed, her eyes sparkling. "To say nothing of his daughter."

"Yes." Rosaline's glance slid to the window once again. They were turning onto a quieter, hidden court away from the main flow of traffic. She knew Lisette was poking her for information, but in all truth, she had very little to give. She hadn't seen Charlotte since they were quite young, when they both had mothers and better manners. "A little more of a mystery."

Because that was what Charlotte was, in truth. Certainly, they had been close when they were girls, but those memories were clouded, flimsy. And it was easy to be friends with someone when your parents threw you together, when you were the same age and ran in the same social circles. And Rosaline knew how loss could change a person. Make them shrink, make them fold a part of themselves away from everyone else. She had no idea if Charlotte, with her quiet, benevolent joy, would be the same now as she once was.

They had written, of course, over the years. Charlotte's letters had drawn a portrait of a soft-spoken, watchful young woman with a piercing intelligence and a weakness for the unproven. Rosaline couldn't even remember the number of times Charlotte had mentioned the "discovery" of a fantastic new species of flora or fauna in her back garden, devoting many subsequent lines to the various possible health benefits of said discovery. Rosaline had somewhat suspected, and now strongly suspected, this to be indicative of her father, Lord Devon's, influence. Charlotte's mother would never have entertained or encouraged such nonsense, she was sure.

But, flaws aside, Charlotte had been a quiet, steadfast companion, even from afar. Enough so that Rosaline was actually looking forward to arriving at Prince Manor, to having a friend, a real friend, help her endure her first season. Because she was dreading it, and that was no secret. In fact, she was certain that half of Provence had heard her heart shatter on that night, that horrible night when she'd opened the letter from her father and read—

—we are going back to London for good, Honeybee. It's dreadful, I know, but I must be within calling distance of the King, and, I am afraid, it is time for you to debut.

Debut. A horrible word, even if it was French. A short word, but it held so much — weak promises, rippling anxiety, simpering looks and false starts. Immediately, her brain had spun through each and every option, but no matter how she'd looked at this equation, this balancing act called her future, each solution had ended at the gates of marriage, at the last place on this earth that she wanted to be.

She had tried to fight it, of course. To argue her way out of it as best she could using only pen and ink, her stained fingers flying like crows above the parchment. She'd overwhelmed her father with pages upon pages of treatises and debates and negotiations and, finally, outright pleas, but none of it had worked.

You are the daughter of the Royal Physician, he'd written to her, and she could hear the apology beneath the words. *Even the Queen asks after you, wanting to know details of your arrival. There is no other way. To turn your cheek now is to turn your back on the Crown.*

At least he'd made her a promise. *Just one season*, he'd written. *You need only debut once, of course, and after the season is over, we can discuss what happens next.*

"What you'll do with me, you mean," Rosaline had said aloud, her tone dripping with a venom he did not deserve. And she was correct — her father did not deserve her anger; after all, he was not the one who had invented this debuting nonsense in the first place. And the last thing she wanted to do was to jeopardize his new position at court, the very position he'd dreamt of his entire career.

So, even if marriage was the last thing in the world Rosaline wanted, even in the sense of entertaining it as one would entertain an unwelcome guest, she could do this. She could go through the motions, carry herself the way she was supposed to, and she could get through the season without creating so much as a wrinkle. She owed it to him to try.

After leaving Provence, after packing up her dearest possessions, after saying goodbye to her favorite tree in the garden, after driving away from the house that had been her home for the past decade, Rosaline and Lisette had spent ten days in the Paris house buying everything she would need for the London season.

"Isn't this a bit... superfluous?" Rosaline had asked, her eyes huge as they skated over a dozen new dresses laid out on her bed. In the corner, the modiste was humming away over a set of elbow-length gloves.

"Not at all, *ma chère*," Lis had said, shooting her a sheepish glance. "And this is just the beginning. This is only your daytime wardrobe, your dress for your presentation to the Queen, and a few dresses suitable for balls. Once you are in London, you will need to have a new dress made for each *soirée*. Every party, every picnic, every ball must have its own unique ensemble."

Rosaline's eyebrows had scaled her forehead. "Surely you jest, Lisette—"

"She does not, *Mademoiselle*," the modiste had said, approaching her with those infernal gloves. "And we will need to fit you for new stays."

Rosaline's spine had gone rigid, and Lisette had looked away, embarrassed. Stays were not a topic often raised in her household, and for good reason.

After that, it had been a hurried handful of days on the road — first, the carriage to Beauvais, then to Amiens, and finally to Calais, then from Calais to the boat — then the boat to this carriage, and all Rosaline could think about now was a pile of cake and a fresh pot of tea. Well, that, and perhaps getting to crack the spine of her new collection of Shelley's works, a conciliatory gift from her father.

A part of Rosaline wished more than anything that she would be staying at their own home, at the house that had remained the fixture of so many memories, the house she hadn't seen since they'd last left England. But her father had sold that house in a fit of guilt and grief and pain — it was gone, and he'd purchased a new one just a few days before her arrival. It was older, more run-down, and would require a lot of work before they could move in, before her father could hire a fleet of servants and fill the library. There was doubt it would even be ready by the end of the summer; there was every likelihood that Rosaline would get through the season and return to Provence for the winter without spending a single night under their new roof.

And yet another part of her did not want to see the new house at all. Rosaline wanted to remember London as the hazy, warm maze of her childhood dreams. She wanted to remember picnics in their garden, fresh raspberry jam streaking across her fingers and sticking in the corner of her mother's smile. She wanted to remember quiet, snow-filled nights when she pretended to be asleep, curled up against her mother's side as they waited for the crunch of her father's shoes on the frost-covered steps. She wanted to remember afternoons lost in the museums, and Fortnum's tearoom, and Hyde Park, her mother's hand warm and firm against her arm as they strolled under the trees and spoke in iambic pentameter, the words falling like liquid from their lips.

A part of Rosaline worried, always worried. That the moment she crossed the threshold of the new house, those memories would crack and fade like plaster.

Now, the carriage slowed and pulled into the front drive of a large, elegant manor painted a bright, sunny yellow. An untamed, flourishing garden full of butterflies spilled from the sides of the house into the front; some wild, pink roses even hovered above the edge of the gravel drive, close enough to threaten thorns at one's ankles. The house itself had tall, forgiving windows, pale cream curtains, and a dark oak front door.

Rosaline couldn't help herself — she stared as she took the footman's hand and stepped out of the carriage, feeling the gravel settle beneath her new, uncomfortable shoes. She batted a stray piece of hair out of her eyes, wondering what on earth would happen now, when suddenly, the front door flew open, and an ethereal woodland sprite descended the front steps to greet her.

Rosaline blinked. But of course — this was not some fairytale creature. "Charlotte?"

Charlotte beamed, her wide blue eyes crinkling with merriment. "Rosaline!" She rushed forward, appearing to skim across the ground, her long white-blonde hair flowing through the air behind her. She pulled Rosaline into a close hug, forgoing every pretense of decorum, and pressed a kiss to her cheek. "Here you are, arrived at last!"

Utterly at a loss, Rosaline hugged her in return. "Indeed, Charlotte! And what a warm reception!"

"Of course!" Charlotte pulled away but linked her arm with Rosaline's. "The least I could do for my dearest friend. How was your journey? I hope the roads and the seas were not too rough."

Her mind still stuck on the words 'dearest friend,' it took a moment for Rosaline to reply. "Not in the least, we had very good weather."

Charlotte gave her an elegant, leisurely nod. "As I suspected. I saw it predicted, you know, in the chestnuts. From the garden. But they are very rarely wrong."

Oh, my Lord. "Of course," said Rosaline, offering a smile.

Charlotte's gaze drifted to Lisette, who had been waiting patiently by. "Oh, you must forgive my manners!" She offered her free hand to Lisette, who just stared at it. "I am Charlotte, and you must be Lisette, of course! Rosaline's steadfast ladies' maid and constant companion!"

"Ah," said Lisette, recovering a little, "yes, Lady Prince—"

"I can see the reception proceeds without me!" barked an imperious, officious voice, and to Rosaline's surprise, an older woman in a terrible brown dress with a square jaw and a no-nonsense bun marched out of the house. Her bosom was heaving with disapproval. "And I can see the young Lady Prince has forgotten her manners, once again!"

"Not forgotten them, Mrs. Randolph," said Charlotte, smiling her enigmatic smile. "Just temporarily put them aside in the face of long-standing familiarity and friendship."

Mrs. Randolph appeared to swell. "Might I suggest we move this touching reunion to the drawing room? It does not do for young ladies to cluster in the drive."

"Very well," said Charlotte, turning to Rosaline. "Will you take refreshment?"

"Yes, absolutely."

"Perfect." Charlotte gave her a gentle tug, guiding her towards the house. "I've had our cook prepare your favorite, honey cake with strawberries."

Rosaline blinked, taken aback. How on earth did Charlotte remember something like that? "Oh, really, you have gone to far too much trouble—"

"Not at all!" Charlotte sang as they crossed the threshold into a bright, tasteful foyer. "And this is only the beginning, of course—"

A loud, incredulous sniff came from Mrs. Randolph, who had followed them inside. "You will both be following a moderate diet over the coming months, Lady Charlotte. Best not to become too attached to certain items that are more of an indulgence than a necessity."

"Yes, Mrs. Randolph," said Charlotte, unruffled, "but I believe cake to *be* an absolute necessity after such a long and tiring journey."

Rosaline was having a very hard time trying not to laugh as a cheerful young footman took her traveling cloak. "Thank you," she murmured to him, and he inclined his head in return.

"Come," Charlotte continued, guiding her to the right. "We shall take our tea in the Blue Room. The drawing room is so stuffy, even on lovely days such as this one. And you must join us, darling Lisette," she added, and Mrs. Randolph seemed to swell again. "The tea has already been laid for three, after all."

"I would be honored, Lady Prince," said Lisette, dropping into a quick curtsy. Rosaline could've sworn she flashed Mrs. Randolph a smirk before following them into the next room, and she bit the inside of her cheek to keep herself from doing the same.

The Blue Room was light, airy, with its gauzy drapes fluttering in the breeze. Its furniture was simple, tasteful, and, much to Rosaline's relief, looked like it had actually been used at some point. An open book had been abandoned on an end table; a chess board showed a game mid-play; and a box of ribbons was spilling its contents across half the sideboard. Between the sofas, a low table was filled with all the makings of an excellent tea.

Unfortunately, Mrs. Randolph had followed them in like the creeping shade that she was. Rosaline wondered if this was her habit. "Well, Miss Bailey," she said, flashing an insincere smile, "Prince Manor is considered to be one of the better examples of high-end residences here in London. I do hope our furnishings are suited to your more... cosmopolitan tastes. Though I must admit..." She cast a shrewd, sharp glance up and down the length of Rosaline's body. "You look a tad more provincial than I'd expected."

Rosaline felt Lisette bristle beside her, but she kept her expression flat, pleasant. "Perhaps, Mrs. Randolph. You forget it has been many years since I have found myself in company as highly esteemed as your own. Perhaps I am simply unprepared."

It took a moment for her sarcasm to land, then Mrs. Randolph's cheeks flushed an ugly shade of puce.

"You may leave us now, Mrs. Randolph," came Charlotte's

calm intonation. "We have much to discuss, and I'm sure such trivialities will only bore you."

Mrs. Randolph gave her a curt nod. "Miss." And with that, she marched out of the room, closing the door behind her.

"*Mon Dieu*," Lisette swore under her breath. "A dragon, if I ever saw one."

"Yes," said Charlotte, her expression still infuriatingly enigmatic. "One must be careful, or one finds oneself burnt by her mere proximity."

"She is beastly, Charlotte!" said Rosaline, sinking onto one of the couches and toeing off her detestable shoes. "Wherever did she come from?"

"A recommendation from an old governess of mine," Charlotte replied, sitting down beside her as Lisette took the seat opposite. "She is a social coach, of sorts, specializing in difficult cases. Apparently, there were some concerns about my ability to comport myself in public."

"Were there?" said Rosaline, biting the inside of her cheek once again. A glance told her that Lisette was doing the same. "I can hardly imagine. And where is your father? I cannot see him approving of the dear old Dragon."

"She is quite saintly in his presence, I'm afraid. And business has kept him in town today, but he shall return for supper, along with your father."

Rosaline groaned. "Oh, excellent. And I assume Mrs. Randolph will have something to say about our attire this evening?

"Does the mockingbird sing?" Charlotte replied, leaning forward to uncover a platter full of sliced honey cake with chunks of strawberry baked into the top. "Unfortunately, she is to be something of our chaperone this season, especially when Papa cannot attend the events."

Rosaline's stomach, which had jumped at the sight of the cake, now began to sink to her knees. Her dismay, she was sure, was written plain on her face. "Charlotte..."

Charlotte shot her a sympathetic look, then began to pour the tea. "She is not so terrible, especially if you listen to her once in a while. But in her words, given that you and I are poor motherless whelps, we cannot be expected to know how to behave like proper young ladies, and therefore require her constant tutelage."

"Constant?" Rosaline repeated, sharing a look of horror with Lisette.

Charlotte shot her a mischievous glance. "Only when she can find us, that is. Milk or sugar?"

Rosaline found herself smiling in reply. "Both, please." This was shaping up to be a most diverting summer, indeed. "Pray tell in what areas, precisely, do we require improvement?"

Charlotte handed her a cup of tea. "Dancing, curtsying, wooing, simpering, and..." She reached under the sofa and unearthed a small basket. "Memorization." She dropped the basket of miniature portraits next to the tea service, and the china rattled with fright.

Rosaline stared at the piles of eligible, mostly-young men, their faces glazed and frozen in the diffused sunlight. "Oh my," she managed. Lisette put her hand to her mouth, her shoulders trembling with suppressed giggles.

"Quite. Milk or sugar, Lisette?"

"Just milk, Lady Prince, thank you."

"She will also see to our appearances, of course," Charlotte went on. "Not a single hair can be out of place." She passed Lisette a cup of tea and considered Rosaline. "But I quite like your hair as it is. All wild and untamed."

Lisette's giggles turned into hiccups, and Rosaline fought off a blush. "Would you believe," said Lisette, "that it was quite tame, this morning?"

"Was it?" said Charlotte, fixing her own cup. "What happened to it? Was there an accident?"

"Rosaline's hair swallows its own pins," said Lisette, wiping at her eyes. "It is quite beyond the reproach of any hairdresser in Paris."

"Lisette," said Rosaline, her cheeks now flaming. "You exaggerate."

"I am not sure she does, my dear." Charlotte smiled. "Fair warning, Mrs. Randolph will certainly consider it her main project."

"How delightful," Rosaline replied, reaching for the cake. "Now, Charlotte, tell me what you've been reading."

"It just," Mrs. Randolph gritted out, her mouth pursing blood-red around the pins between her teeth, "refuses to cooperate—"

Rosaline swallowed a yelp as Mrs. Randolph gave another fearsome tug, sending a bolt of pain across her scalp. Tears threatened to spring from her eyes but she gripped the edge of the vanity, trying not to move an inch. This was the one area in which her new stays were quite helpful — she felt as though she could hardly breathe.

"Madam," Lisette said, for the third time in as many minutes. Her voice was hard but low, unrelenting. "I have been attending to Miss Bailey's hair since she was a young girl, I am sure I can offer some assistance—"

"Tenure does not speak to ability, you impudent thing." Mrs. Randolph huffed, reaching for a brush. "The state she was in when she arrived this afternoon! She looked fresh out of a barnyard, an association we should dispel at all costs, given her... complexion."

A cold, seething anger rose in Rosaline's belly and she gritted her teeth. She could hear the meaning beneath the words. *A black,*

Mrs. Randolph wanted to say. *Who would think a high-born lady would ever marry such a tar-rag of a man? And now look at their offspring—*

Mrs. Randolph attacked, dragging the bristly brush through Rosaline's hair, pulling it back into a tight handful, then let out a squawk as the hair seemed to expand in size.

"Madam," said Lisette again, sharp as a knife. "You must not use a boar's hair. It will only unravel her curls, and—"

"I will listen to your opinion when I ask for it!" Mrs. Randolph spat, giving another fierce tug. Pain rippled down Rosaline's back and she bit her lip to keep herself from whimpering. Reflected in the mirror, she could see Mattie, Charlotte's ladies' maid, watching with an expression of unchecked horror.

"Mrs. Randolph." Charlotte stepped in, her expression demure. There was a cold fire burning in her eyes that was not betrayed in her voice, and she reached for a loose section of Rosaline's hair. "Perhaps two pairs of hands would be better than one. I shall assist you."

"I assure you, Lady Price," Mrs. Randolph replied, now attempting to twist the hair. "I do not require any such assistance, which is inappropriate for you to offer in the first place—" She lashed out suddenly, snatching the section away from Charlotte and yanking hard enough to bring a fresh wave of tears to Rosaline's eyes. "Mattie! See to Lady Charlotte's hair, at once. Ensure that it is brushed properly and pinned into a bun. I don't want to see a single flower anywhere near that child's head."

Rosaline had a sudden recollection of Charlotte as a child, running through the garden with daisies braided into her long, untamed hair, and almost smiled, in spite of the pain.

Mrs. Randolph took a deep breath and straightened, squaring up to Rosaline's head. "Now," she said. "To war."

An hour later, Rosaline picked at a plate of chicken and potatoes, her neck aching with the weight of her hair and the effort of not turning her head. Her hair had been so tightly pinned —

"There must be two pounds of metal hidden in there," Lisette had whispered — that it felt as if it had been drilled into her skull, and the slightest movement sent white-hot bolts down her back and shoulders. Her skull throbbed, ached, and she had no idea how she was going to make it through this dinner, let alone the season, if this was what awaited her each night and day.

They were in the dining room, seated at a relatively informal table. She'd been laced into one of her more formal dresses, a light turquoise that stood out in this austere room made of dark wood. Charlotte was beside her, dressed in pale pink. Lord Devon sat at the head of the table, and across from her, her own father looked at her with a careful eye, his expression one of bemusement and amazement.

Their reunion had been somewhat muted, considering her relative inability to move. He had given her a kiss and a hug, demanding details of her trip, and she'd been so relieved to see him she had almost forgotten how angry she was at him for forcing her to do this, to leave the only home she'd known for almost a decade and succumb herself to torture by hair pins.

"I do believe," her father said now, his gaze sparkling with mirth, "that my daughter has been replaced by a young lady."

Rosaline tried to take a deep breath, her ribs pressing against the stays.

"Quite," said Lord Devon, in that hazy, dreamy way of his. "I cannot help but express the same sentiment regarding my own daughter."

"How odd," Sir Ian went on, "to find our daughters replaced by strangers."

"Is that not a natural part of growing older?" said Charlotte. "That one can no longer recognize one's own children?"

Sir Ian looked at her in surprise. "How apt. It seems that you share my Rosaline's keen eye for the evident but unstated."

Charlotte gave a delicate laugh, and for a wild, absurd moment, Rosaline hated her, hated that she could be so good at this, at putting up with the stays and the hair and the dress, at putting aside part of herself to become someone else entirely. "I can only aspire to share an ounce of Rosaline's intellect, Sir Ian. That would be more than enough for any one person, I am sure."

"Again, most aptly put." Sir Ian leaned forward, smiling. "And I do believe a certain philosopher had quite a bit to say on the topic of children, did he not?"

The corner of Rosaline's mouth twitched. This was one of their oldest games. Quotes and mottos over dinner. "Plato," she said. "Do not force your children into your ways, for they were created for a time—" In her excitement, she moved her head, and let out a small gasp as pain ricocheted down her neck.

Then, she was aware of a small, warm hand on her leg. Charlotte's.

Sir Ian's smile had melted into a frown, and Lord Devon was looking at her with an expression of mild concern.

After a lengthy pause, Sir Ian spoke. "My dear, are you... all right?"

"Yes," she managed, feeling a little dizzy. "Yes, of course."

"Rosaline has a headache," said Charlotte softly. "Her beautiful hair is a heavy crown to bear."

Something flashed in Sir Ian's eyes — understanding. She could only watch in surprise as he placed his napkin on the table, stood up, and made his way to her side. "A common malady, to be sure," he said, reaching for her hair. "A condition I have seen amongst the finest of ladies, both old and young."

Rosaline felt a peculiar grinding sensation, then a wave of startling relief as a large chunk of her hair fell out of her bun. She barely had time to recover before it happened again — a grind, a *clink*, then another section of hair cascading down in her peripheral vision. The relief was acute, unlike anything she'd ever experienced, and she had to keep herself from closing her eyes in bliss.

"May I ask," her father said next, steadily building a pile of hair pins beside Rosaline's plate. "Who tended to my daughter's hair this evening?"

"That would be Mrs. Randolph, Charlotte's tutor," said Lord Devon. He was watching, unperturbed, his expression showing only the faintest interest.

"I see," Sir Ian replied, his tone still friendly, nonchalant. "Can she be fetched?"

Lord Devon gave a nod, and Rosaline heard a door behind her open and close. Mere moments later — she must have been standing outside the room — Mrs. Randolph came in, still flushed from her battle with Rosaline's hair. Rosaline's stomach flipped and she forced herself to swallow, unable to guess what would happen next.

"My lord," Mrs. Randolph said, dipping her head. Her gaze fixed on Sir Ian's hands. "How can I be of assistance?"

"Mrs. Randolph," said Sir Ian. "I hear you insisted upon taming my daughter's hair this evening. Is this correct?"

"It is, sir," she replied, clearly thrown but trying to hide it. "May I ask—?"

Sir Ian pulled out the last hair pin, dropping it on the table with an ominous finality. "You will find, Mrs. Randolph, that her hair — our hair, since she inherited it from me — does not respond well to your more traditional methods."

Then, he did something he had not done since Rosaline was very, very young — a hazy time, between maids, perhaps. He pushed his fingers through her hair, shaking it out into its full, astonishing size, then took the top section of hair, his fingers gentle against her tender scalp, and divided it into three strands. Rosaline felt a soft tug, then he began to braid. "It responds best to braiding. Brushing will only make her curls frizz and expand, whereas braiding will keep them tight and neat."

Rosaline could practically hear the servants' jaws hitting the floor. Mrs. Randolph looked as if she'd been struck across the face. She could only stare as Sir Ian braided his daughter's hair at the Prince dining table, an event that, at any other moment, would surely have been beyond the imaginable. But it was happening, much to Rosaline's hidden delight.

"I can understand your confusion," Sir Ian went on. "You are not the first to be stymied by this particular beast. But it is perfectly possible to tame, given the time and the correct effort." He separated the next section of hair and began integrating the strands into the main braid, guiding it in a slant across the back of her head. "My sisters had the same hair, you see, and my mother had very little time to see to it. I learned how to do this before I learned how to write. Hours spent in front of our little fireplace, and my hands would ache afterwards. I had four sisters, so it was a lot of hair. A lot of happy memories." Rosaline could hear the smile in his voice and her heart gave a twinge of sympathy — she knew these recollections were bittersweet.

He moved onto the final section, twisting a few of the strands before he worked them into the main braid. "I can assure you that once you look for it, you can find an infinite variety. For example, when Rosaline was younger, she wore it braided on one side, like this, but loose at the end. Now that she is older, perhaps it would be more appropriate to pin it up." Accordingly, he gathered the end of the braid, gave it a twist, and spun the whole thing into a low bun just behind her left ear. He reached for a pin, then slid it through the bun, just barely grazing her scalp, and did this again with a second pin.

"And there." Sir Ian stepped away, and Rosaline couldn't keep herself from smiling. Charlotte was beaming at her, and Rosaline blushed, giddy with relief and something akin to victory.

Her father was still looking at Mrs. Randolph, his expression one of mild distaste. "I am sure," he said, "that what you just witnessed was nothing short of what you may call shocking and inappropriate. So before you spread incessant gossip, allow me to remind you that I only braid my daughter's hair because my wife cannot. And she would have been deeply insulted by the treatment you have forced upon our daughter this evening. Take care to ensure it does not happen again."

Cowed, Mrs. Randolph ducked her head. "Yes, sir."

"Try braiding," he added, going back to his seat. "Lisette is more than able to assist you."

"So am I," said Charlotte at once, still beaming. "I wear braids all the time, so I will consider it my next great challenge."

"Excellent!" Sir Ian took his seat and replaced his napkin.

"You are dismissed, Mrs. Randolph," said Lord Devon, with just a hint of amusement.

Mrs. Randolph curtsied and left the room. Rosaline fancied that she could almost see steam coming out of the woman's ears, then hoped that there would not be a price to pay later.

"So remind me, Hieronymus," said Sir Ian, slicing through his piece of chicken. "What is required of us poor, humble fathers, tomorrow?"

"The girls' presentation is scheduled for one o'clock," replied Lord Devon. "We should arrive at the palace no later than twelve thirty, I believe."

"Then a brief break," Charlotte chimed in, "before the opening ball at Whitehill Manor."

"Ah, yes. Lord Alwyn's home, is it not?"

Lord Devon nodded. "Correct. Then, as they say, it is off to the races."

Everyone laughed, and Rosaline dug into her potatoes, feeling much more content than she'd expected to.

⚜

"Altogether," murmured Lisette, "a rather interesting day, was it not, *ma chère?*"

Rosaline smiled, her eyes skimming over the pages of her Shelley. "Perhaps an understated characterization, Lis. I think that might have been the most overwhelming day I have ever had."

Except the funeral, neither of them said.

The air was thick with the clean, light scent of the rose-hip oil Lisette was working through Rosaline's curls, and Rosaline let her eyes fall shut for the briefest moment, allowing herself to imagine that they were in her bedroom at the old house in Provence. It would be a midsummer night, one of her favorites, and the scent of jasmine would drift in through the window, mingling with roses, sage, and lavender, as well as something darker, earthier. She could almost hear the crickets and the cicadas, the lulling splash of the pond in the garden and the low, throttling grunt of its amphibian residents. She would be hazy from a bottle of wine she and Lisette had snuck out of the kitchen, and Lisette would be singing while she crocheted, a book open on Rosaline's lap as she curled into the window seat and looked out into the smooth blue night, content to sit in the stillness of the moment, but waiting, yearning, for something—

Her breath caught and her eyes opened. She heard the faint, distant clatter of late-night carriages on the road, smelled the musty, coal-laced bitter air of London, and felt, for a brief, startling moment, that she was lost, adrift.

Lisette's hands stilled, then continued their work, twisting oil into hair. A fresh wave of roses spilled over Rosaline's shoulders and she shivered. "You are tired, *ma chère*. It will be easier, tomorrow."

Rosaline gave a brittle smile, not that Lisette could see it. "Will it? I fear it will be much the same, just with royalty and every eligible man and woman in London crammed into a single room. I am hardly a physicist, but even I would consider that a risk of explosion."

"You know the rules."

Rosaline sighed. "I do. But I cannot believe I have to spend my whole summer doing this."

Lisette's finger, poking her waist. "Perhaps you will find something to help you pass the time. Something... or someone."

Heat flooded Rosaline's neck and she ducked her chin. "Do not be ridiculous."

"I am not ridiculous," Lisette said. "I am a romantic. I believe, *ma chère*, that every person is given a chance at love, and a young woman? Three chances. So you are well past your due."

"Oh, hush," Rosaline mumbled, pulling her comforter up over her knees.

"I am almost finished, *ma chère*." Lisette's voice was smug, pleased. She separated Rosaline's hair into two sections and began to weave them into two loose, simple braids. "Your father. He has much courage."

"Yes," Rosaline said at once. She played the image over in her mind again — a black man, braiding his daughter's hair in one of the finest dining rooms in all of London. Even though they'd been in the company of old friends, it had been quite a risk. Rumor was likely flitting through town on her winged chariot, spreading whispers of the audacious new Physician. "He did not have to do that."

Now finished, Lisette's hands came to rest on Rosaline's shoulders, and she gave a light squeeze. "Yes, *ma chère*, he did." Lisette slid off the bed and picked up her candle. "And now, you must rest. I have something spectacular planned for your hair tomorrow."

Rosaline smiled. "Yes, Lis. Thank you."

Lisette smiled back and dipped into a small curtsy. "Of course. Sweet dreams." With that, she slipped out of the room, leaving Rosaline sitting in relative silence.

Rosaline glanced down at her book and shut it with a sigh; if she did not stop now, she would be up all night from sheer nervousness. She tucked it under her pillow, then slid beneath the warm, luxurious covers, and paused with her nose in front of her candle.

Every night, she did this. It felt strange, facing a different nightstand, a different wall. But a tradition was a tradition.

"I wish," she breathed, making the flame flutter, "to survive tomorrow, regardless of what may come. And," she added, thinking of what Lisette had said, "I wish to have fun."

With that, Rosaline blew out the candle, plunging herself into darkness.

❧ 3 ❧

"Lord Crawley," said Charlotte, smiling down at one of three miniatures in her hands. "He has such a kind chin. I wonder if it is where he keeps his secrets."

"Lady Charlotte," said Mrs. Randolph, her voice strained with the effort of unleashing this rebuke for the third time in as many minutes, "if we could focus on—"

"But why should we?" said Charlotte, holding Lord Crawley up to peer down upon them all. "The attributes of his estate are only of immediate, material concern, but what of his humor, his voice? Can he make a clever joke, can he actually ride a horse, the proper way?"

Rosaline rolled her eyes as Mrs. Randolph swelled. She had had enough of this cat-and-mouse. "He has five thousand a year, a younger sister he will have to support since she is ill and unlikely to wed, and prefers to spend time at his country estate. He is of reasonable, though not startling, intellect, but cannot hold a political opinion to save his life, and has a particular fondness for pear tart."

An echoing silence followed this speech. Mrs. Randolph stared at her in equal parts shock and reluctant admiration, while

Charlotte gave her a simple, but knowing, smile. "Well," Mrs. Randolph said eventually. "It appears that someone has been paying attention."

"Of course I am paying attention," Rosaline said, managing to keep the edge out of her voice. "We have been studying these for hours." She ached for a good novel.

Mrs. Randolph had marched into her bedroom at only a few minutes past seven, flung a dressing-gown at her, and said, "Blue Room. Ten minutes. Be ready to work."

And work they had. The past four hours had been a non-stop parade of court etiquette, dancing practice, and, finally, an attempt to memorize the personal history of each and every eligible bachelor within fifty miles.

"It is a good thing you have," Mrs. Randolph snapped at her now. "I was warned you were unprepared for the demands of social life here in London, but the situation is far worse than I expected. If I'd had a week with you before your presentation, we might have whipped you into reasonable shape, but we will have to make the best of what we do have. You are a quick learner, at the very least."

Rosaline took a deep, careful breath, not betraying an inch of the anger seething under her skin. *Quick learner*, she thought bitterly. *You think this challenges me? I can name every bone in the body. I can name every visible constellation in the night sky, no matter the season. I can perform Euclidean geometry in seconds, I can write mathematical proofs without batting an eye. I can recite most of Shakespeare's soliloquies and nearly all of his sonnets. I can debate you on the finer points of Classical philosophy and tell you exactly what Jefferson got wrong. I can tell you the most important events of Roman history, conjugate French and Latin verbs, and write a hundred-page paper on modern poetry, all while you gape at me and try to remember, precisely, why you tried to take the upper hand.*

"In the meantime," Mrs. Randolph went on, oblivious, "you know enough to survive today. But you must remember all we have reviewed, Miss Bailey — memorizing personal income will only get you so far, especially when a gentleman expresses a wish to dance."

Dancing. Not her strength. Unlike Charlotte, Rosaline lacked the ability to float over the ground, keeping each turn of her head and each lilt of her arms perfectly attuned. But at least she didn't fall over or injure herself.

"Now." Mrs. Randolph nodded at Charlotte. "On to the next, please."

"Richard Thomas, the Marquess of Reading," said Charlotte, holding up the portrait of a handsome, if lanky youth. Rosaline felt an odd flutter of pride — like her, he too had darker skin, and unlike her father, he wore his hair a little longer, several inches above his scalp. But it was tidy, combed, and it made him look rather rakish. She could almost hear Mrs. Randolph's frown. "A bit of a cad, apparently," said Charlotte, "but he has an estate in Berkshire and a good income — four thousand a year. A good education, a sister married to a Prussian noble, and a particular interest in athletics. He plays polo, he wrestles, and he hunts. A life with him would never be boring, I am certain."

"Indeed," said Mrs. Randolph, with some reluctance. "Perhaps we should focus on the cream of the crop." She crossed over to Charlotte's couch and picked up the basket of miniatures. She spent the next few minutes sifting through them, making little noises of approval and disapproval, slowly building two piles of faces.

"There," Mrs. Randolph said at last, putting aside the basket of rejects. "I think you should keep an eye out for these gentlemen in particular at the ball this evening. They are the strongest prospects, to be sure, and well worth the attentions of two such high-ranking ladies." She handed each of them a pile of miniatures and stepped back, almost glowing with satisfaction.

A small part of Rosaline wanted nothing more than to trade her pile with the basket. *But*, she thought, *perhaps I have tested the*

Dragon's patience enough for the morning. So she sat back, took a breath, and started looking through her cards.

She knew all of them already, of course, and, in truth, they meant very little to her. For all her faults, Mrs. Randolph did have a keen eye — she'd left out anyone over five-and-thirty, and all of the men were of excellent backgrounds and reasonable appearance. As Rosaline looked over the flat, frozen faces, she sifted through all the facts she could remember about each of them. At least, that was what one part of her mind did — the other part started scrolling through Prospero's soliloquy.

Ye elves of hills, Rosaline thought, feeling the words echo down through her fingers as she flipped from Lord Russell to Lord Wetherby, *brooks, standing lakes and groves—*

She smiled, her fingers pausing on the next card. "Charlotte," she said. "I see your kind chin and raise you a set of dimples and a warm gaze." She held up the card and turned it around so that the wide grin of Edward Lightfoot, the Earl Cadogan, faced Charlotte.

Charlotte smiled in return, then tilted her head to one side. "You are correct. He looks quite happy, frozen in aspect though he is."

"What do you think?" said Rosaline. "Custard tart or fruit?"

"Fruit," said Charlotte at once. "And two sugars in his tea." Then, to Rosaline's surprise, she reached forward and took the card, brushing her thumb across the line of Lord Cadogan's jaw. "It is a shame," she said, even though her tone said the opposite, "that he be saddled with such a unique moniker."

"Not a name to be sneered at," Mrs. Randolph chimed in, "though a fresh arrival, to be sure. A strong prospect, ladies, but his ascendancy is new and therefore not quite as stable."

That pricked Rosaline's interest. "Really? How did he make his fortune?"

Mrs. Randolph sighed a little, as if loath to admit it. "He is something of a natural scientist by hobby, Miss Bailey. He patented several new plant hybrids, I believe, and profited handsomely from it. He is now quite the businessman and purchased his title just last year."

Rosaline could see why Mrs. Randolph hadn't wanted to mention Lord Cadogan's interests. Charlotte's eyes were quite aglow.

"But," Mrs. Randolph hastily added, "he is sure to be the talk of the town, if only for the sake of his appearance. Every young lady within a mile of him will do her best to snatch him up."

"Indeed," said Rosaline. "Who could blame them, at eight thousand a year?"

Charlotte was still smiling. "Such money," she said, "for one so unconcerned with it."

Every part of Rosaline wanted to point out that there was no way for Charlotte to know such a thing, but she held her tongue. She went back to the faces in her own hands, feeling as if she were playing some elicit game of faro, then reached the last card and paused as a pair of brilliant blue eyes stared up at her.

She did not remember this gentleman. In fact, she was certain she had never seen him in the dreaded basket, nor even heard his name. *Harold Cunningham, Duke of St. Albans*, she read, rolling the Christian name through her mind. It was almost a common surname, but there was nothing common about this man.

His face was wide, square, with a sharp jawline and a chin to match. His portrait was somewhat strange — unlike the others, it was dim, almost blurred, leaving nearly half his face in shadow. He had a straight nose, dark, thatched hair that looked like it had never seen a comb, and, somewhat to her surprise, those startling eyes, blue as a cornflower. His mouth, which was narrow, with a romantic plushness to it, was pulled into a slight grimace, as though he were uncomfortable with even a sole painter's scrutiny. His body, what little of it she could see — shoulders, some of his chest — was alive with energy, and she almost expected him to leap out of the painting, his hand hot and insistent on hers as he grinned and said, "Shall we escape?"

Rosaline shook her head as if to clear it of cobwebs, trying not to blush. Quite apart from every other absurd aspect of such a fantasy, this man would never grin. He did not seem capable. But his moodiness was not broody, or self-indulgent — he simply did not like attention, or scrutiny. And that was something Rosaline could understand all too well.

For a brief, frightening moment, she realized she was doing exactly what Charlotte had done. Alarmed, she dropped the miniature, and it landed on the cushion with a faint *thud.*

"It appears Rosaline is quite taken with one of our prospects," said Charlotte, not even glancing up from Lord Cadogan's miniature. "She nearly flung him across the room."

"I did not," Rosaline muttered, but it was too late — Mrs. Randolph came over, standing behind the sofa to look down at the abandoned miniature.

"Ah," said Mrs. Randolph, giving them a smile that was both astonishing and frightening. "Very good instincts, Miss Bailey. He is perhaps the most sought-after of them all."

"Is he?" said Charlotte, with only the faintest hint of interest. "Why?"

"A Duke, Lady Charlotte, is the best prize a young lady of any rank could hope to win, especially when he is as young and handsome as this one. And this Duke has a particularly affluent estate, and no family to share it with."

"No family?" Rosaline echoed, feeling a pang of sympathy.

"No. Supposedly, that is why he keeps so much to himself — one can hardly remember the last time he appeared in London, except on very official business. It is quite a shock that he is attending the season at all." Mrs. Randolph turned to Rosaline with a glimmer in her eye. "Why, Miss Bailey — has our notoriously reclusive young Duke managed to capture your interest?"

Rosaline was saved from a reply by a knock at the door. "Good morning," said Lord Devon as he walked in, then he looked at the girls in surprise as they jumped up from the sofas and curtsied. "Heavens, are you still at work? You are not even dressed."

"We were just finishing, my lord," Mrs. Randolph replied. "It is time for the ladies to begin their preparations."

"Preparations?" Lord Devon repeated, frowning. "Are they not joining me for a spot of tea and a hot breakfast?"

Rosaline's heart leapt at the idea — she and Charlotte had only been given a small meal of tea, bread with butter, and fresh fruit, and her stomach was almost empty. But her heart fell just as quickly as Mrs. Randolph shook her head. "No, my lord," said Mrs. Randolph. "We do not have the time, I'm afraid."

With that, Rosaline and Charlotte were ushered upstairs and into Charlotte's bedroom, which was larger than Rosaline's. Their dresses were already laid across the bed, along with their stays and other accessories. The vanity was covered in every hair and beauty tool imaginable, and in the middle of it all, Lisette and Mattie stood ready, smiling.

"First," said Mrs. Randolph, with the air of a conductor stepping onto their podium, "Lady Charlotte's hair and Miss Bailey's dress, then you will switch. I am afraid it will be all hands on deck for Miss Bailey's hair."

If Charlotte heard the sneer hidden beneath those words, she did not acknowledge it. She clapped with delight, squeezing Rosaline's arm. "The season is truly starting!"

Rosaline tried to smile. If it was an act, Charlotte was quite the performer. "Yes, it appears so." And with that, she stepped into Lisette's welcoming arms, already dreading the coming day.

"I cannot do this," she whispered to Lisette as she went behind the changing screen. She shrugged out of her dressing gown and nightdress, then reached for her chemise. "Lisette, I cannot do this. I do not know why I ever thought I could—"

"Yes, you can," Lisette hissed back, slipping her hand behind the screen. In it was a raisin scone, and Rosaline snatched it from her with surprising speed. "You will see, once you have your audience with the Queen, everything will—"

"—fall into place?" Rosaline whispered back through a mouthful of scone. She chewed furiously, her mind awhirl with a low-burning panic. "It is not that simple — look at Charlotte. She will surely be the most popular debutante of the season, I won't have any chance of escaping notice—"

"Why should you?" Lisette pressed, her hand reappearing behind the screen. This time, it was half a ham and butter sandwich on brown bread. Rosaline had no idea how Lisette had managed to hide it in her apron. "You are a beautiful woman, *ma chère*."

It took Rosaline a few moments to finish inhaling her food. She swallowed thickly, then said, "I am not here to marry. I am here to survive."

Before Lisette could reply, Rosaline marched out from behind the screen and squared up with her gown, summoning what was to be only the first of many bouts of courage.

"Stop fidgeting," Charlotte whispered. She herself was as still as a statue, ethereal in her pale, radiant beauty. Mattie had brushed the softest hint of rouge across her cheeks, making her look windswept, demure. Her hair, gathered and twisted back into a simple, high bun, glowed above her like a halo.

By comparison, Rosaline felt like a clot of earth. She could hardly breathe in her stays, which dug painfully into her ribs, and her hair — though deftly braided into a half-crown that cascaded in a long, intricate plait down one side of her neck — was heavy. At least she looked more like herself, or as close as she could get, given the circumstances.

Lord, she thought, glancing at the other young ladies behind her, *what fools these mortals be!*

"Come now, my dears," said Lord Devon, his voice low beneath the dim chatter of the crowd, "the best way to tackle an enemy is to square up to him, head-first."

Charlotte let out a quiet, musical chuckle. "How droll, Papa."

It would be a lot easier, thought Rosaline, *if I had a sword—*

But she didn't have time to say it, because there came a loud thud from the other side of the double doors, followed by a ringing proclamation:

"The Lady Charlotte Prince and Miss Bailey, presented by the Earl of Devon."

Her heart skipped a beat, but there was no time to process it, because the doors swung upon and her instincts took over. Rosaline stepped into the throne room and began to approach the throne at its opposite end, where the Queen sat in all her glory, staring down at them.

When you walk into the hall, came Mrs. Randolph's voice, clear as a bell in her head, *you cease to be human. Every pair of eyes in the room will be watching you, expecting you to glide without a hint of mortal clumsiness, to hardly make a sound as you whisper across the floorboards—*

Whisper! Rosaline thought frantically, becoming aware of her shoe pinching her pinky toe, and the dozens of courtiers staring at her and Charlotte— *Glide!*

Do not plant your weight on your heels. Walk on your toes, if possible. Keep your chin up, your neck elongated but not stretched, which will appear unseemly, and whatever you do, do not look Her Majesty in the eye—

She could feel Charlotte beside her, moving with all the grace and ease expected of a young lady. Rosaline's next step faltered and wobbled, but she recovered just as they reached the throne. She sank into her deepest curtsy, dropping her gaze to the pale wooden floor.

Complete silence. Then—

"Lord Devon." The Queen gave him a stately nod. "As always, a pleasure to see you."

"The pleasure is all mine, Your Majesty," he replied, straightening from his bow.

"And what a delightful young lady you brought with you today." The Queen shifted, her dark eyes flickering over Charlotte. "Come closer, my dear."

Charlotte rose from her curtsy, offering a small, becoming smile as she took a step closer to the throne. Her gown and gloves looked creamy, peachy against her lily-white skin, and her eyes were twin globes shining a deep, clear turquoise in the sunlight.

The Queen remained seated, but she reached for Charlotte, taking her hand. "Yes," she said. "The spitting image of your mother. Perhaps, I think, even more striking."

Charlotte beamed.

Then the Queen's attention shifted, and Rosaline's heart skipped another beat when those dark eyes fell on her. *Why?* she had the capacity to think as her thighs burned from holding the curtsy. *Why is she—?*

"Miss Bailey." The Queen looked her over, impassive. "Such a shame your father could not join us this afternoon."

Lord Devon cleared his throat in a quick cough. "Indeed, ma'am. He assured me it was perfectly appropriate to present his daughter on his behalf—"

The Queen flitted this remark away with a wave of her hand. "I am aware that he was called away. It is of no importance."

Rosaline noticed that she did not mention it was to tend to her husband.

"Child. Please, stand."

She did, and she met that dark, piercing gaze head-on. Her heart either restarted or stopped beating entirely.

"I have heard much of you from your father. And your mother was once a dear friend of mine." The Queen's gaze narrowed. "Your father has told me of your education. And it so happens that your old tutor, Mr. Al-Hakim, has been to court."

Rosaline had no idea what to say to this, so she remained silent.

"You are quite the mathematician, I hear. And an authority on Shakespeare."

Heat flooded Rosaline's body, and a cold sweat broke out on her lower back. Lord Devon nodded at her, and she knew then that she had to say something. "That is correct, Your Majesty."

Then. Just the barest flicker of a smile. "How unique. I do like a young woman with a mind of her own. You inherited some of that from your mother, you know, along with her looks." Her attention drifted back to Charlotte, and she leaned forward.

"I think," said the Queen, raising her voice loud enough that it rang through the hall, "that I am in the presence of a few precious gems." She looked at Charlotte. "A Star." She turned her head to look at Rosaline. "And a Sapphire."

With that, she sat back in her throne and gave a nod. "Thank you, Lord Devon."

"Thank you, Your Majesty." Lord Devon gave another bow, then he led Rosaline and Charlotte out of the limelight and into a side hall, where, her head spinning, Rosaline slumped against the wall, only vaguely aware of Charlotte grabbing her arm.

"A sapphire, Rosaline!" Charlotte whispered, her excitement electric. Her father gave her a rare grin. "What an honor!"

"Yes," Rosaline managed, her imagination filled with that piercing, dark gaze. "An honor."

4

Several hours later, Rosaline stepped onto yet another gravel drive and stared up at the enormous manor house. It was easily twice the size of the Princes' and surrounded by numerous gardens and porticos. Each window gleamed orange in the rapidly-falling dusk, and from within came the strains of an orchestra, followed by a cacophony of laughter and exclamations of delight.

She took as deep of a breath as she could, her body straining against the stays, steeling herself as two more carriages rolled up to the house.

Charlotte's hand, light on her arm. "It will be wonderful, I promise." She glanced at Rosaline. "And even if it is terrible, I swear I will tell no one if you sneak away to read whatever work you have stashed in your petticoat."

Heat flooded Rosaline's cheeks. "You are a true friend, Charlotte."

"As are you."

Lord Devon stepped forward, beckoning to the house. "Come along, my dears. We might as well walk straight into the lion's mouth."

The interior of the house was even more ornate and over-whelming. Rosaline stared at the portraits, the furniture, the decoration, absently cataloging the various exits in case she needed to make a quick disappearance. And then, a prickle of unease crept up her spine, because, for the first time in her life, people were staring at her.

This was not to say that people had never stared at her before — they certainly had, but for a different reason. Before, they had regarded her with expressions of surprise, disgust, mingled with apathy and irritation. But now... these people looked at her with envy. With spite.

Rosaline tried to take a breath, wishing Lisette were here. But Charlotte had noticed as well; she, too, was receiving these looks of jealousy. She met them with a placid, almost unsettling smile that brooked no protest, and Rosaline did her best to copy it, her heart thudding in her ears.

"Charlotte," she muttered as they passed from the foyer into a room decorated in pink and gold, "why are they—?"

"Something to do with the way we shine, I think." Charlotte flashed her a cheeky wink.

"Pay no attention, ladies," Lord Devon murmured, then he paused beside a table covered in what looked to be scraps of paper. "Aha!" He handed them each a scrap, and Rosaline realized that they were actually cards, with a piece of ribbon attached. "For your intrepid suitors. And what luck, I do not believe the dancing has started yet."

"Yes," Rosaline managed, staring down at the dance card, wondering if the earth would swallow her at some point soon. "How lucky."

"I hope there is a treacle," said Charlotte. "It encourages light-ness of the feet, you see."

Before Rosaline could even begin to reply to that, Lord Devon approached a cluster of people — their hosts, Rosaline suddenly realized. "Lord and Lady Alwyn! An honor, as always."

Rosaline felt a flicker of surprise as she took in the couple before her. Like Rosaline and her father, these people were black. Lady Alwyn wore her hair in a high, elegant twist accented with gems, and Lord Alwyn's beard was neat and trim. They had guarded but friendly faces; Rosaline realized that, like her, they were always ready for the worst.

Lord Alwyn inclined his head. "Lord Devon, a pleasure. The town is quite abuzz about your daughter. Seems she caught the highest level of praise from our dear Queen."

Lord Devon waved an airy hand in dismissal. "You flatter us, sir. My daughter, Lady Prince, and Miss Bailey, who I present on behalf of her father, Sir Ian Bailey."

Rosaline and Charlotte curtsied as Lord and Lady Alwyn inclined their heads. "A pleasure," said Lord Alwyn. "May I present my own daughter, Lady Rebecca Alwyn."

He stepped to the side, revealing a tall, striking young woman with simple hair and remarkable cheekbones. She looked exactly as Rosaline felt — as if she'd rather be anywhere but here. But she curtsied, a quick bob in place, before turning away with a scowl.

In spite of this chilly reception, Rosaline took an instant liking to her.

Lady Alwyn cleared her throat, then smiled. "My eldest, Geraldine, is married to Lord Cawdor, and my second eldest is married to Lord Dashwood of Kent."

Ah, thought Rosaline. *Poor Rebecca.* She, too, would be expected to make such an excellent match.

"Do enjoy yourselves," said Lord Alwyn. "There is plenty of food and drink, and I am told the orchestra is quite unequaled."

As they passed into the next set of rooms, Rosaline realized that people were staring at Charlotte even more than they were staring at her. But Charlotte seemed not to care in the least; she floated along, and as they came to a stop just outside the ballroom, the crowd shifted. Suddenly, there seemed to be more young men nearby than was physically possible, and Rosaline fought the urge to recoil from all the faces she had memorized.

"Lord Devon," she managed. "I find myself quite parched." And with that, she turned tail and hastened to the other side of the room, where a table of refreshments groaned under its own weight. People looked away as she passed them, and she hoped they did not notice that she was flushed, unnerved.

The punch was sweet and ice-cold, much to her relief. As she sipped it, she felt her heart slowing, her stays loosening. Just as she began to look over the food, a shadow fell over the *vol-au-vents*.

"Miss Bailey, I presume?" came a lilting, chilly voice.

Rosaline looked up and found herself facing a cluster of young women. At the front stood a short, buxom woman with honey-blonde ringlets and a sharp nose. She was flanked by a pair of twins who looked on with wide, dark eyes that instantly reminded Rosaline of the Queen. "Yes," she managed to reply.

The young woman looked her up and down. "Miss Brown," she said, and Rosaline guessed it was an introduction. Her gaze was sharp, ruthless. "I do not believe we have ever had the pleasure of your acquaintance here in London."

"No," Rosaline said. "I am new to court."

Miss Brown smiled, but there was no warmth to it. "Precisely. A fact which, I think, you would do well to remember." And with that, she turned and walked away, the twins on her heels.

"Pay little heed to her," came another voice. Friendly, amused. "Her mother is a heavy-handed cow, and your Royal reception this afternoon left many of your peers feeling quite... overlooked."

Rosaline glanced at her new companion. A tall, thin young woman with a shrewd expression and a simple dress. "Indeed, Miss—?"

"Miss Knight." She inclined her head. "You will find, I think, that you are the object of much envy. Do not be afraid to return fire with equal persistence. And if I were you, I would be wary of any... demonstrations of friendship."

"Indeed." Rosaline took another breath. "Then what is this conversation, Miss Knight? A declaration of war?"

Miss Knight gave her a small, enigmatic smile. "For that to be the case, Miss Bailey, I would have to have a passing interest in the opposite sex." She dipped into a brief curtsy. "Excuse me. I found a hiding spot in the garden and must claim it before someone else does." Before she left, she glanced over her shoulder, at the room and everyone in it, and added, "Feel free to join me, if you need fresh air. Behind the southern trellis, near the fountain."

"Thank you," Rosaline managed, feeling a rush of gratitude. And for a moment, that was all she wanted to do — hide herself in the garden, stay there until the sun crested the horizon and she could declare the day over — but then she turned, and saw Lord Devon beckoning her back to where he and Charlotte were standing. Well, she could only see *him* — Charlotte was obscured by a thick crowd of suitors. Their eagerness was... tangible.

Rosaline swallowed a groan and knocked back the rest of her punch. *To war,* she thought.

Only a few heads turned as she rejoined Lord Devon, much to her relief. She slipped in beside him, watching as Charlotte smiled and spoke to every single one of the young men, regardless of what Mrs. Randolph would have said. Rosaline found it impossible to shake the image of a cluster of panting dogs begging for attention.

And then—

"My lady."

A pause. Then the crowd parted, the young men looking disgruntled as a very familiar face surfaced from the sea of admirers. The Earl Cadogan stepped forward, his miniature not doing his smile justice, his dimples on full display. He was practically aglow, and Rosaline could tell that he was blushing as he looked at Charlotte, all but breathing her in.

She glanced at Charlotte. Charlotte was still smiling, but now, she was radiant, beaming from the inside out as she offered the Earl her hand.

"Father," Charlotte said. "Won't you introduce us?"

Lord Devon cleared his throat, and Rosaline swore he knew exactly what was happening. It was obvious to everyone with a pair of eyes. "My lord, this is my daughter, Lady Prince. Dear, this is the Earl Cadogan."

"Lord Cadogan." Charlotte bent her head like a swan. "An honor."

"I can assure you the honor is all mine, my lady." Lord Cadogan produced a pencil. "Might I request a dance?"

"Certainly, my lord." But when she lifted her card, her smile disappeared. "Oh, dear, it seems to be quite full—"

"Ah." Lord Cadogan appeared to be somewhat on the back foot — clearly, this had been his only idea. "Perhaps another—"

"But there is plenty of time between dances," said Charlotte, looking up into his face once again. Her frown had disappeared, and Rosaline was quite certain that the rest of the world had fallen away from Charlotte's periphery. "And in the meantime, my lord, you may escort me into the ballroom and make pretty commentary about the pictures."

Lord Cadogan's face broke into a grin. Mrs. Randolph had been right — he was quite handsome. "I would be delighted, my lady." He made an aborted movement, as if to offer her his arm, but then he stopped, glancing over his shoulder. "Good God, where are my manners! I do apologize, ladies, allow me to introduce—"

Lord Cadogan reached behind him, grabbed onto someone, and pushed him to the front of the crowd. The man stumbled, barely catching himself before he fell over. "My very good friend, the Duke of St. Albans!"

The Duke straightened, tugging his jacket back into place with a poorly-concealed scowl. He glanced at Charlotte, and when he turned his head, he met Rosaline's gaze.

Blue, she thought, her mouth going dry and her lungs squeezing shut. *Very blue.*

After what felt like a short eternity, the Duke broke eye contact with her and glanced at Lord Devon. "A pleasure, my lord," he said, his voice deeper, richer, than she'd expected. And it had an undeniably sharp edge. It seemed as though the Duke did not want to be introduced to anyone at all.

"Your Grace," said Lord Devon, inclining his head as Charlotte and Rosaline both dipped into a curtsy. "An honor. I believe I know your godfather, Lord Blackwood."

A muscle twitched in the Duke's jaw. "There are very few who are not acquainted with him."

"Prongs!" said Lord Cadogan loudly, clapping a hand on the Duke's shoulder. "Come, we must accompany the ladies into the ballroom!"

"Oh, must we?" The Duke glanced at Rosaline again, just a fleeting look, and his voice was as dry as a bone. "I am sure they have a keen enough sense of direction."

There was a loud *thud* as Lord Cadogan's shoe met foot, and the Duke restrained a grimace. Lord Cadogan merely grinned, but there was a manic edge to it. Rosaline fought the urge to laugh. This was absurd. This was—

"Certainly," said the Duke, a beat late. "Ladies."

Charlotte fell in step beside Lord Cadogan, slipping her hand into the crook of his proffered elbow. Within moments, they bent their heads together, chatting quietly, and Rosaline allowed herself a soft, singular smile as she and the Duke likewise made their way towards the ballroom. Everyone was staring, she noticed, in open surprise and revulsion. The Duke and the Unknown? What scandal!

The Duke was mere inches away, but the space between them

felt like miles. He had not offered her his arm, and his gaze was fixed on the back of Lord Cadogan's head — planning his death, she guessed.

They passed into the ballroom, where the orchestra was playing a light, jaunting tune. The dancing had yet to begin, but the room was already packed, the air stifling. Rosaline fought the urge to yawn. She would, soon enough, if the Duke did not—

"Are you a Lady Prince as well, then?" the Duke said.

Rosaline blinked, then realized that they'd never finished the introductions. "No, Your Grace. A Miss Bailey, though I suppose Charlotte is indeed like a sister to me."

"Bailey," the Duke repeated. They were carving a slow line into the crowd, and the guests parted around them like water. The mothers were watching him like hawks. He glanced at her, and God, those eyes— "Your father is Sir Ian Bailey, the Royal Physician?"

Two surprises, now. "Yes, Your Grace."

"I was not aware he had a daughter." Another flinty glance. "You are not French?"

She smiled. "No. But my mother was."

It took a moment. Then a third glance, but this time, he lingered. Rosaline fought off a shiver. "I am sorry," he said, his voice quiet. "For your loss."

Yet another surprise. Rosaline wondered if this conversation would ever become predictable. "Thank you, Your Grace."

He looked at her for another moment, and where his gaze was piercing, his face was as rigid as stone. Expressionless. Then, he looked away. "We seem to have become part of the décor."

Rosaline followed his line of sight, then smiled at the image of Charlotte and Lord Cadogan standing together, utterly absorbed in one another. It was impossible to tell what they were talking about, but it did not matter. "Indeed. But a minor complaint, in the scheme of things."

"Is it?" He did show just a flicker of surprise then, but then it was gone. "I assumed an enthusiasm for the first ball of the season. For dancing, for drinking."

"An assumption without proof, Your Grace."

Another shrewd look. "How, then, shall we divert our attentions?"

Rosaline let out a sigh, trying not to grin. In spite of his abject rudeness, he could play along quite well. "You could make a passing comment about the wallpaper or the portraits. Then, I could say something about the dresses, the shoes, the violinist's wig—"

"Which, I believe," said the Duke, "is about to sit up and recite Marlowe."

"He that loves pleasure, Your Grace, must for pleasure fall."

"So he must." Then he glanced at the orchestra. "I am afraid that if we do not move now, we will be flattened by the most eager heels in all of London. And you, surely, must surrender to some heavy-footed suitor or other."

Rosaline's heart leapt into her throat, but she managed to shake her head. "No, Your Grace." And she held out her blank dance card as proof.

His gaze, again. Cutting right through her. "I see," he said, but then before he could say anything else, Lord Cadogan was clapping a hand on his shoulder and saying—

"Come on, Prongs—"

And then, to her absolute astonishment, Rosaline found herself pulled onto the dance floor by none other than Charlotte herself, her face shining with delight. She managed to school her expression into something other than horror, stumbling into line beside the other young ladies, and there was Charlotte's hand again, squeezing hers, and the Duke's eyes, meeting hers across the crowded floor, and then the music, the music—

Later, Rosaline remembered very little of this excruciating moment. It was a reel, of course, because it *had* to be the dance that made her the least comfortable, but she did not fall, or knock into anyone else, as a few other ladies did. The Duke only looked her in the eye twice, not that she was counting, but she was more aware of his hands on hers, warm and firm through the fabric of her gloves, and he gripped her with a surety that was breathtaking, overwhelming—

The music ended with a *bang*, and the room erupted into cheers. Charlotte was laughing, and she truly was a Star, then, in that brilliant moment, when she seemed to reflect every light in the room and magnify it tenfold. She had the attention of everyone in the room, and Rosaline could practically hear the gentlemen counting down the dances until they'd have a chance to snag her.

From across the floor, Rosaline met the Duke's gaze. He was looking at her, his hair even more tousled than it had been before, his chest heaving a little, and she felt the moment stretch between them, gossamer-thin. But before she could even begin to imagine what would happen next, a hand seized the Duke by the shoulder, and he turned—

"Prongs! Heard you'd come up to town, you old beast—"

It was Lord Russell, she realized, even as she fought off a wave of dizziness. She could only watch as he steered the Duke off of the dance floor and into a crowd of other young gentlemen, who greeted him with a shout of delight.

A recluse, Mrs. Randolph had said. But a recluse with plenty of friends, apparently.

"Miss Bailey?" Another young man appeared in front of her. He had piles of blonde hair and a wide smile. "May I—?"

"Apologies," she managed. "I require... fresh air."

And with that, she turned and left the dance floor, doing her best to melt into the crowd.

When she was little, Rosaline developed a talent for hiding in plain sight. This talent served her all too well when her mother's family came to visit, or when she had no inclination to attend a tea party. It was instinctual, but after all those wonderful years in

France, she was out of practice, and it also went against one of Mrs. Randolph's dearest maxims—

Do not find yourself unsupervised, unaccompanied, or in any way unattended. Your virtue must be beyond question.

Rosaline rolled her eyes at the figures flickering on the lawn below her. She was perched in the corner of a wide window-seat on the second floor, looking down upon the garden, the fountain, the party. She'd kicked off her shoes, and was steadily making her way through the small pile of *vol-au-vents* she'd managed to sneak from a refreshment table. Her well-loved copy of *A Midsummer Night's Dream* lay open on the seat beside her, half-lit by a cluster of nearby candles.

She could hear the music — the orchestra had been playing for several hours now, and it seemed, finally, to be on its last legs. Perfect timing, since she could see the pale, pinkish fingers of Dawn stretching along the edge of the horizon. Soon, she would have to find Charlotte, and Lord Devon, who was no doubt asleep on a chaise somewhere, or lost in the library.

But she still had a few moments to herself. She chewed, looking out at the few remaining stars in the milky indigo sky, and thought about the Duke.

He had been brusque, unfeeling, careless, offering only an attempt at politeness and decorum. The kindest description of his behavior would be *rude*, and yet. He'd said sorry, about her mother. And danced with her.

When he was forced to, Rosaline reminded herself, rolling her eyes again as she brushed stray flakes of pastry from her lap. No, the Duke was hardly worth any consideration, let alone another moment of her sympathy. It was clear that he loathed crowds and hated attention, which was most unfitting for a man of his status, his wealth. But perhaps that was why he behaved as he did, cold and indifferent, mildly entertaining the conversation of an acquaintance — he was, in reality, quite far above it all. He had every freedom; why should he concern himself with this, the only diversion sure to end in shackles?

Perhaps he is lonely, Rosaline thought, before she could stop herself, but she dismissed that explanation almost as soon as it had surfaced. It was clear, from the brief moment she had seen them together, that Lord Cadogan was somehow responsible for the Duke engaging with the public tonight. There had been a forced hand quite literally behind every moment, dealing some form of repayment, perhaps, or an old favor. No, she was certain that Cadogan had something to do with it. What else would push the Duke into the light of day when, according to the entire town, he preferred to slip through the shadows?

With a sigh, Rosaline stood up and put on her shoes. It was not a simple task; her skirts were rather larger than she'd thought, and she nearly fell. Scowling, she grabbed her gloves and her book, pausing to tuck it back into the hidden pocket of her petticoat (which came courtesy of Lisette and her thimble). Best to end this night before it ended itself.

She made her way back through the darkened house, paying little heed to the quality of the furnishings, the paintings. She'd snuck up here via a small staircase tucked in beside the kitchen, and she retraced her steps with ease, making note of everything she'd seen on her way up. The orchestra had stopped, and the loud rumble of voices rose like a tidal wave to greet her. Something clenched in Rosaline's stomach, but she forced herself to continue onward, slipping down the shadowy, hidden staircase like a ghost. A golden beam of light illuminated the doorway to the ground floor, and she braced herself as she neared it, and then—

She collided head-on with someone tall, dark, and broad. She stumbled, heard something drop to the floor, and nearly fell over herself, but then a hand, warm on her bare elbow.

"Miss Bailey." The Duke stared at her, and somehow packed outrage, surprise, and confusion into those two short words. A brief, electric moment, then his hand disappeared and he stepped back, the golden light cutting his face in half. He looked like a sprite, alien and ethereal.

Mortified, she could hardly meet his gaze. "Your Grace. Please forgive me, I did not realize that you were—"

He bristled and looked away. "Not at all. It was I who surprised you." Then, in the space of a moment, curiosity seemed to get the better of him. "What were you doing?"

Rosaline's heart thudded in her ears. "Taking the air."

"On the second floor?"

"Yes." She tried to take a breath, embarrassment still hot on her face.

A beat passed, then another. "Indeed," said the Duke, and she could have sworn she heard amusement simmering beneath the word. "Well, I must take my leave—"

"Goodnight, Your Grace." She bobbed a quick curtsy, desperate to flee. She did not like this, this feeling— unsettled, wary... yearning.

He took another step away, but then his foot bumped into something on the floor with a soft *thud*. They both froze, and in that moment, Rosaline's hand flew to her petticoat pocket, which suddenly felt very, very light.

Her mouth dry with horror, she could barely watch as the Duke bent down and plucked her book from where it lay on the floor. He held it out, and when she met his gaze, she was shocked to find the corners of his eyes crinkled, as if he were smiling.

"I believe," he said, "that you dropped something."

She could not breathe. She took the book from him, mute.

He inclined his head. "Goodnight, Miss Bailey."

And with that, Rosaline fled.

᠀ 5 ᠀

Madam Kensington's High Society Papers,
No. 23

ell, my darlings… What a spectacular opening night to the season! I could hardly have imagined an evening so succulent, so teeming with intrigue and tension. And where on earth to begin? I suppose the Royal presentation is as good a start as any, in more ways than one!

None was more surprised than I to see a Fairy step into the sunlight and transfigure, as if by unseen and mystical powers, into none other than this season's Star. No one had expected a light-headed, whimsical little figure to be the center of such high regard, her delicate beauty notwithstanding. Indeed, she cuts a fine profile, but what on earth could possibly reside in her cloudy, peculiar mind? This writer overheard her bending a young suitor's ear about the supposed healing properties of something called a Thumbleroot — perhaps, ladies, your mothers were correct; looks really can get you everywhere in life.

And what of her companion, this so-called Sapphire? A virtual unknown, but truthfully, there is none like her anywhere in

London, perhaps in England (although one could make that pronouncement based upon her hair alone). Her looks are unique, and her temperament thoroughly unpredictable — it seems that this Sapphire is quite the enigmatic, fleeting creature; after the night's first dance, she all but disappeared. Surprising, perhaps, when one considers that she caught the attention of even our famed Recluse...

ROSALINE WOKE TO THE LOUD *BANG* OF HER BEDROOM DOOR flying open, and mere moments later, there was a thin tearing noise before her room was flooded with sunlight.

She sat up, squinting against the bright light, and something landed beside her in bed.

"Get up!" barked Mrs. Randolph, marching over to the next set of curtains, which she flung open with an enthusiasm both frightening and amusing.

Still foggy with sleep, Rosaline glanced at the clock on the mantelpiece. She'd only fallen into bed some six hours earlier, and her brain thumped at the idea of going anywhere. But before she could say anything, the weight beside her on the bed turned into a person.

"Look, Rosaline," said Charlotte, sliding onto her stomach, her feet kicking in the air. She was still in her nightgown, her braid was mussed, and she smiled down at something in her hands. "I woke to find a visitor on my windowsill."

Rosaline blinked a few times, trying to take in what she was seeing. It was a small, brown snail with an impressive shell and a shiny back. He was slithering along Charlotte's palm.

"And," Lisette added as she made her way to Rosaline's closet, "a special delivery." She flung something small and made of paper onto the bed.

Mrs. Randolph made a poorly-concealed noise of disgust. "That," she said, "is nothing more than a filthy rag."

Rosaline reached for the small pamphlet. The paper was thick and heavy with the smell of fresh ink. She found herself intrigued, and she thumbed through it, taking note of the illustration on the front — a large feather quill, with its point morphing into the blade of a knife. "Madam Kensington," she read aloud, her voice cracking. "Who is she?"

"A malicious busy-body with too much time on her hands." Mrs. Randolph was standing by the vanity, a statue of disapproval.

"And the most watchful pair of eyes in all of London," said Charlotte. "There is nothing she does not see or hear about. And she is completely anonymous — no one knows who she is."

Her interest piqued, Rosaline flipped back to the front page. An anonymous female writer with a steady, enthusiastic readership? Impressive, to say the least. "What makes her different from all the other gossip rags?" She'd heard about society papers like this, but had never seen one before.

Lisette shrugged, bringing out one of Rosaline's dresses. "Madam Kensington is correct, *ma chère*. Always. And she hears things that most would assume to be private."

Rosaline's heart thudded once in her throat, and she looked down at the clean, sharp words. Almost unwittingly, she began to read, and what she read made her heart catch once again, made her reach for Charlotte's arm. "Charlotte... she wrote about us."

"Unavoidable, I think." Charlotte kept watching her snail, unperturbed.

"Yes, but..." Rosaline had no idea what to say. She could only continue reading, horror mounting in her chest. She'd never imagined that her association with Charlotte would bring her this much notice, this much criticism. The mothers and daughters had been difficult enough to withstand the night before, but now, when she featured as a literal cover story?

This is a nightmare, Rosaline thought, almost wondering if she was still asleep. *An absolute, inescapable nightmare.*

"Now!" Mrs. Randolph clapped her hands together. "Visiting hours begin shortly, ladies, and we must be ready."

Rosaline's heart once again leapt into her throat. "Visiting hours?"

"Indeed," said Charlotte, now watching the snail slither up her index finger. "Apparently, we will be receiving admirers."

Definitely a nightmare, Rosaline thought. "But... why?"

"To be read poetry and generally wooed." Charlotte shot her a glance that was far too cunning for this early in the day. "We must give them biscuits in return."

Rosaline caught the scent of cheddar and chive, oddly mixed with buttery shortbread. The kitchen was working hard.

"That means best foot forward, ladies," said Mrs. Randolph, now busy sorting through a pile of hair accessories. "This will set the tone for all future social encounters, you know. If you are kind, and generous with your time, you will never want for dance partners, or for companions when you are promenading."

"Promenading?" Rosaline asked Charlotte in a horrified whisper. Charlotte did not react.

"And in time, you will determine which suitor, among the many I assume you will collect, might serve as the best partner, the best lifelong companion," Mrs. Randolph went on.

Rosaline stared at her bedding. The floral pattern swam before her eyes. "I am going to be sick," she muttered, mostly to herself.

"What an exciting time, ladies!" Mrs. Randolph was getting quite worked up. "Who knows how many gentlemen callers will come today! I gather you made a rather favorable impression at court, and at the ball." The edge in her voice was unmistakable — she envied not being there herself. "It is entirely possible that you will find yourselves occupied until supper."

"Supper," Rosaline repeated, with just a hint of hope. "Does that mean— there are no events this evening?"

"No," Mrs. Randolph replied. "There was an invitation to a small dinner party at Lady Graham's, but that did not merit your attendance. No, this way, you will not appear in public until tomorrow evening, at the Denisons' ball. And as we all know, absence makes the heart grow fonder, does it not?"

"Perhaps," Rosaline said, catching Lisette's eye. She would need another ham sandwich, if she were to make it through the afternoon.

An hour later, she and Charlotte were in the drawing room, tucked into their dresses and seated on couches opposite each other. Rosaline glanced around the room; she had yet to come in here, and it was quite different from the Blue Room. More austere, less lived-in, less colorful. There were several paintings on the walls, of impressive landscapes and Princes from centuries past. It was personal and impersonal all at once.

At least she was allowed to read. They had to be occupied, according to Mrs. Randolph, or at least give the appearance of being occupied, when the suitors came in to call. Charlotte had a small embroidery hoop in her hands, but she was paying it little attention. Her gaze kept wandering to the window, where bursts of birdsong were interrupting the relative silence of the morning.

Rosaline shifted where she sat, frowning as the stays dug into her ribs. She'd hoped, perhaps stupidly, that she could avoid wearing them until the following day, but no. At least her hair was somewhat simple — the top half had been braided into three separate sections, then joined with the rest of it and pulled into a loose bun. It was a far cry from her hair the night before, which had taken Lisette almost half an hour to unravel.

She glanced at Charlotte, wondering what she was thinking, what she was feeling. They hadn't yet had a chance to speak, at least not about the events of the previous night. A part of her wanted desperately to know what Charlotte thought of Lord Cadogan, if the deep, keen interest she had seen in the young man's eyes was reciprocated. Charlotte did seem more distracted than usual, but perhaps that was because she was tired, or overwhelmed, or even bored. She could be difficult to read at the best of times, and Rosaline longed for the evening, when they might be alone, when she might be able to pull Charlotte aside and demand to know the truth.

There came a sudden flurry of noise from the front door, and Rosaline's spine straightened. Mrs. Randolph, who had occupied a large armchair near the windows, quivered with anticipation and clapped her hands like a giddy toddler. "Girls!" she hissed. "Brace yourselves!"

Rosaline's stomach twisted with nerves, but she forced herself to sit still, even with every instinct telling her to fling herself out of the window. She gripped her book hard, sending a silent apology to the front cover, and looked up as Benny the footman appeared, followed by a trail of eager young men, their hands full of bouquets and sweets.

"Lady Prince," said Benny, facing Charlotte. "May I present Lord Crawley?"

"Indeed." Charlotte put aside her embroidery and smiled up at the newcomer. "How do you do, Lord Crawley?"

"And Miss Bailey," Benny continued, "may I present Lord Roden?"

Rosaline blinked, staring at her caller. He was several years older than her, her height, pale as a pile of snow, with a weak chin, poorly-trimmed whiskers, and a thick neck. She had never seen him before in her life.

"Certainly," she managed, putting down her book. "How are you, my lord?"

"All the better for having made your acquaintance, my dear." His voice was as slick as oil, and she held in a wince as he swept into an officious, unnecessary bow.

"You flatter me, my lord," she said, glancing wistfully at the window. *Too late now.*

He leered at her, then handed her a small posy of wilting yellow tulips. "You charming little creature. I was wondering if I might be permitted to regale you with a selection of Casanova's finest verses. He is my personal favorite, you see."

Charlotte, meanwhile, was being offered a large bouquet of fresh pink roses and a small box of chocolates. She smiled and blushed, and Lord Crawley melted like a pat of butter.

Rosaline glanced at Lord Roden, whose leer had only deepened. "Certainly, my lord," she said, almost wishing she were back at the Opening Ball.

Anywhere was better than here.

"Careful, *ma chère*," Lisette said, handing over the steaming mug. "*Il fait très chaud.*"

"Thank you." Rosaline cupped her hands around the mug, grateful for its heat in spite of the mild evening air. After Rosaline's horror-show of an afternoon, she and Charlotte had taken a very pleasant supper with Lord Devon, and now, they were sitting in front of the wide bank of windows in Charlotte's room, which opened on the back garden.

"This is delicious, Lisette," said Charlotte. She took another sip of cocoa and smiled. "Perfect, even in summer."

Lisette smiled and sat down between them on the window seat. "You are too kind, Miss Prince. And take care not to drink it too quickly, or you may find yourself wavering."

Rosaline smirked at Charlotte. "Lisette has a heavy pour."

"Oh." Charlotte looked from Lisette to Rosaline and back again. "You mean to say there is liquor in this?"

Lisette's smile turned into a grin, her eyes flashing with impish delight. "I would never suggest such a thing, Miss Prince."

Charlotte brightened and she took another sip, savoring it. "Rum?"

Rosaline took a sip herself and recognized the oaky bite. "Scotch."

"Scotch," Charlotte repeated, as if tasting the word. "I have never had Scotch before."

Lisette hummed. "And you had never known adoration personified until you met Lord Cadogan."

Rosaline choked on a laugh and Charlotte gasped, unable to hide her smile as she grabbed Lisette's arm. "You wretch!" Charlotte squealed. "Oh, how dare you—!"

"She dares, Charlotte," said Rosaline, "because she is quite correct. And you are undoubtedly taken with him, unless I have the most flawed pair of eyes in all of London."

"So what was he like, *ma chère?*" said Lisette, leaning in and giving Charlotte's arm a squeeze. Her tone was reverent, secretive, and Rosaline loved her for it — Lisette was making herself Charlotte's friend, sister, confidant, and doing so with such beautiful ease. "Was he every bit as charming as his portrait suggested?"

For a moment, Charlotte simply smiled at her, but then something inside her cracked, and she blushed, going radiant and shy all at once. "Every bit," she said, "and more."

Rosaline almost squealed, stolen by the giddiness of the moment. Barely two days into the season, and here they were, with Charlotte on the precipice of what was sure to be a great love. "What of your conversation? Was he engaging, curious? Or was he only full of petty compliments and other such pieces of nonsense—?"

Lisette smacked her on the arm. "Such things are not always nonsense!"

"He did ask me many questions," Charlotte said, as if she were divulging some momentous secret. "And he listened quite keenly to each answer. And he was most diverted by my observations about the toadstools at the foot of the garden—"

Lisette stared at Charlotte. "*Ma chère*, that is hardly—"

"—and he told me about himself. The most engaging, rapturous details. Did you know he is an orphan? That is why he inherited his title so young, just like the Duke."

Rosaline blinked, the Scotch making her head spin. "The Duke is an orphan?"

"Yes, but his parents and Cadogan's parents were close friends, you see, so they grew up together. But now all Lord Cadogan has is his great aunt, a formidable woman, if the stories are true. And he simply adores gardening, you know. His estate features a large greenhouse, where he conducts all sorts of experiments. He has a new variety of hyacinth he plans to unveil next spring."

"How..." Lisette was clearly struggling to come up with the right words. "But, *ma chère*, did you speak of love? Did you trade sweet nothings, and did he compliment your beauty, your wit?"

Still smiling, Charlotte just looked at her. "No," she said at last. "I do not believe those topics arose."

"*Ma chère*," said Lisette, her voice thinned by exasperation. Rosaline put her hand to her mouth to hide her smile. "You must speak of these things, if you are to make a match. And from what I hear, the two of you — you have such a connection, such a spark. It would be a pity to overlook it, even if it is not... what you intended to get out of the season."

But these words seemed to slide off of Charlotte like water off a duck's back. "I am sure we will, eventually, if that is the path we are destined to follow," she said in her dreamy, lilting voice.

Lisette sighed a little and Rosaline took a sip of her cocoa to avoid giggling. "Very well," said Lisette, and, much to Rosaline's horror, she turned and gave Rosaline a sly look. "And what of the Duke? You have been far too quiet, on that account."

Heat crept up Rosaline's face and she gripped her mug tight. "Have I? I can hardly— Lis, we did not even spend five minutes together—"

"But that is more than enough time to make an impression,"

Lisette pressed. "I wish to know if the rumors are true."

"Rumors?"

"The rumors that the Duke is ill-mannered, bad-tempered," Charlotte chimed in. "And he never gives the time of day to anyone he thinks is beneath him."

"And that he is gorgeous," Lisette purred. "Handsome in a dark, roguish sort of way—"

"I suppose," Rosaline managed, "that you could call him handsome, yes, but every fool with a pair of eyes could tell you the same—"

"And what of his person, his conversation?"

"I suppose he was rather rude," Rosaline said, and it was true. "It was evident that he had no wish to be there, and he only deigned to speak with me because Lord Cadogan—"

"Rude in what way?" said Charlotte, tilting her head to one side. The Scotch had given her skin a delicate flush.

God. Rosaline tried to swallow. "Distant, or disengaged. He was neither courteous, nor attentive, and he spoke to me as if I were no more interesting than a piece of stone."

Not true, chimed in the small, treacherous voice from the back of her mind. *Your mother. The dancing. Your book.*

"Huh." Lisette was looking at her, something knowing and distant in her gaze. "Very well."

"With any luck," Rosaline went on. "I shall never have to endure his presence again."

"Indeed," said Charlotte, with a smile.

Later, when she was in bed and staring down the last remaining candle, Rosaline leaned in towards the flame and felt its heat wash over her nose.

"I wish," she whispered, her heart thudding, "to learn something about the Duke. Something... that perhaps no one else knows."

Her last thought, before she plunged into darkness, was of his hand, warm and surprisingly soft, on the bare skin of her arm.

6

Rosaline stared up at the remarkable edifice of Denison manor with a distinct sense of foreboding. Three days into the season, and she was already fed up with all of it — the simpering, the curtsying, the hair, the stays, the shoes, the gowns. *And*, she thought, meeting Miss Brown's ferocious glare, *I am fed up with the ladies.*

"Come along," said Lord Devon, lifting a hand to help Charlotte out of the carriage. She looked ravishing, a vision in pale blue, with a line of diamonds around her neck. Rosaline, who had paid little attention to her own appearance that evening, was dressed in pink, with her hair in another intricate braid pulled back into a bun.

"The Denisons," Charlotte remarked, coming to stand next to Rosaline. "A friendly enough family, I think."

"You know them?" said Rosaline.

"A little," Charlotte demurred. "Their daughter once called me a fanciful half-wit, but I hear she has grown more charming with age."

"Ah." Rosaline stared at her. "Lovely."

And with that, Lord Devon led them up and into the house.

Inside, it was remarkably similar to the Alwyn manor. It was, perhaps, a touch smaller, though, and as they walked up to their hosts, Rosaline could see that Lord Denison was all too aware of it. He wore his insecurity like a second skin, and gave them all a haughty, unamused look.

"Lord Devon," he said. "Ladies."

"A pleasure," said Lord Devon. He began the small-talk and the introductions, but Rosaline's attention wandered, then snagged on a cluster of young ladies in the next room.

They were all crowded around something, fluttering with excitement, and she caught the flurry of overlapping conversation, gasps and coos snaking through the air. Just as she began to wonder what was going on, one of the ladies ducked her head, and, at the center of it all, Rosaline saw none other than the Duke of St. Albans. He was surrounded by debutantes, pressed against the wall, and his expression, though flat and unamused, betrayed just a hint of panic. He glanced around, completely ignoring Miss Brown's attempt to engage him in conversation, trying to find a way out.

In spite of herself, Rosaline grinned. *Serves him right*, she thought, though she wasn't sure why. And then, before she could turn away, his gaze landed on her.

She froze, but just for a moment. There was something overpowering, stupefying, about his eyes. She relaxed, and let her grin turn into a chuckle, relishing the way the Duke's gaze tightened with irritation. *Good*, she thought, turning back to Lord Denison just in time to curtsy.

As she and Charlotte made their way into the thick of the party, Lord Devon following them at a distance, Rosaline let her gaze wander over the crowd, taking note of the people she knew and the people she did not know. They were all dressed within an inch of excess, as they had been two nights before — Rosaline had never seen such dresses, such coats, such accessories and jewelry. She knew she looked much the same, but this did nothing to dampen the effect of seeing luxury in real life, paraded about as if it were nothing more than commonplace or typical. This world was still so foreign to her; she felt a prickle of unease, but hastened to bury it. She must appear totally in control, engaged and yet removed from the world around her. Disinterested, and yet present. *Like the Duke*, she thought, then rolled her eyes.

Once again, the crowd parted as Charlotte cut a path through the room. Dozens of eyes landed on her and flitted away before she could acknowledge them. Charlotte was still the center of attention, then, as Rosaline suspected she would be for the entirety of the season. Envy, regard, disregard, even outright hatred — Charlotte seemed to receive each and every emotion in equal measure, but she did not appear to care. In fact, she did not appear to notice anything at all. She wore a faint smile as she looked around, making a beeline for a table set against the opposite wall.

Rosaline closed the distance between them, frowning. "Charlotte?" she said in a low voice. "What are you—?"

They had reached the table. "Dance cards," Charlotte replied, handing one to Rosaline and looping another around her own wrist. "I am sure we will be in high demand, as we were before."

Rosaline smiled, tempted to tear up the card without any delay. "As *you* were, Charlotte. You may recall that I made myself scarce in order to avoid this very situation."

"Ah, yes." Charlotte turned to her, still smiling that faint smile. "I do not understand why. Even if you claim to dislike a jig, I know you enjoy waltzing."

"Correct," Rosaline admitted, "but not with strange gentlemen. I do enjoy waltzing with you." She recalled her first morning in London, before her presentation to the Queen — leading Charlotte around the drawing room, giggling as she spun Charlotte into a turn, Mrs. Randolph scowling but clapping along to the count.

"Most of the gentlemen are strange," said Charlotte, nodding, "but some of them are quite lovely. I am sure at least one or two of them would refrain from stepping on your feet."

"What a ringing endorsement, dear," her father chimed in, winking at them both. "That would not have been such an issue, back in my day."

"Your dances were easier, Papa. The standards have shifted, and the gentlemen are still catching up."

"We do our best," came a voice. A pleasant, familiar voice. "Good evening, my lady."

Charlotte spun around, breaking into a genuine smile as she turned to face Lord Cadogan. "My lord!" She curtsied, and he inclined his head in return. "What a timely arrival. We were just discussing the importance of dancing."

"And its difficulties, if I heard correctly." He smiled back at her, and Rosaline saw an unmistakable light in his eyes. He was smitten. "I must admit, it is not my strength."

"Not at all, my lord!" Charlotte replied. "From what I saw the other night, you present no more than a passing danger to ladies' feet."

"You are too kind, my lady. But perhaps you would be brave enough to test such a claim sometime this evening?"

Charlotte's smile widened. "Certainly." She held out her dance card. "You may take the first slot, and the third."

A delightful blush spread across Lord Cadogan's cheeks, and Rosaline hid her smile with a quick cough. "You are generous," he said, leaning forward to pencil in his name. "Are you certain you wish to commit so much of your time, when you have yet to sample my efforts?"

Charlotte twinkled at him. "I am in the mood to take risks this evening, Lord Cadogan. And, three is my lucky number."

"Mine as well, I think." His gaze landed on Rosaline and he startled a little, as if surprised by her presence. "Miss Bailey, Lord Devon. Good evening to you both."

"Good evening, my lord," said Lord Devon, amusement lacing

his words. "Though you seem to be lacking a shadow this evening. You have only one, instead of two."

"Oh, yes." Cadogan frowned and he looked around, scanning the crowd. "The Duke arrived a few minutes after I did, and I could have sworn he was just behind me. I cannot think where he got to."

"He is stuck," Rosaline said, surprised that she was saying it at all. "Near the other door. It seems that every young lady in London wishes to gain his attention, and he is struggling to escape."

"Oh, yes!" Cadogan grinned at the sight of the trapped Duke, then cut her a knowing look. "Every young lady, apart from you."

Before Rosaline could do more than choke on a reply, her face heating with indignation, Charlotte laid a hand on Cadogan's arm and said, "Oh, we should rescue him! Yes, do let us rescue the poor Duke!"

"What an excellent idea!" Cadogan let Charlotte slip her hand into the crook of his elbow. "Miss Bailey, would you join us? Two is hardly enough for a rescue party."

Rosaline bit her tongue and looked to Lord Devon for help. But he gave her an enigmatic smile just like Charlotte's, the picture of demurral. "Very well," she said, and turned to follow Charlotte and Cadogan through the crowd.

By the time they'd reached the Duke, the group around him had grown distressing in size. Cadogan grinned, clearly enjoying the sight. "One moment, ladies," he said, and he pushed his way to the front of the crowd, dodging fans and feathers as he went. "Come along, Prongs! I require your assistance at once!"

Cadogan resurfaced a moment later, a disgruntled Duke in tow. "You took your time," the Duke snarled to him under his breath. His collar was crooked. "I was accosted as soon as I—"

Cadogan cleared his throat pointedly. "Ladies," he said, "might I once again introduce—"

"Oh, for Christ's sake, Ed," the Duke burst out, "they know

who I am!" He gave Charlotte and Rosaline a passing glance. "Good evening, Lady Prince, Miss Bailey."

"Good evening," Charlotte replied as she curtsied, far too delighted by this development.

Mute, Rosaline copied her. The Duke looked even more ruffled this evening, but he was as handsome as ever, and as he glared at the people around them, she felt something inside her stir in response to the unbridled energy in his face.

"We were just discussing dancing," Cadogan went on. "Lady Prince has kindly agreed to accompany me." He glanced at Rosaline. "Perhaps you would do Miss Bailey the honor of your company as well?"

The Duke's gaze landed on her, and Rosaline's mouth went dry. He still looked angry, his jaw tense and his eyes flashing, and he seemed on the verge of saying no. But then he glanced at Cadogan, at the pleading look on his face, and seemed to relent. "Very well," he said, looking at Rosaline once again. "If Miss Bailey will have me."

Before Rosaline could reply, there came a blast of music from the adjacent ballroom, and the crowd roared with delight. Heart thudding, she was all too aware of the Duke taking her hand in his and leading her onto the dance floor.

His grip was firm but not tight, and he shot her another look as she held her chin high and matched his pace. "You are quiet this evening," he said, under his breath.

"Not quiet," she replied, the words leaving her mouth before she could think about them. "Merely attempting to escape your ire."

He seemed almost amused by this. "My ire," he said, leading them to a vacant bit of floor, two couples behind Cadogan and Charlotte, "is reserved for those who provoke it."

Rosaline dared to glance at him. "And for those who prolong it?"

"Well," he replied, "a far worse fate than this." And to her astonishment, he spun her into frame, taking her right hand and resting his own just below her left shoulder blade. His eyes drilled into hers, alight and enigmatic, and she tried to swallow, heat sweeping up her face.

Then, he looked away, the music began, and they were dancing.

Rosaline's body reacted on instinct, responding to the subtle shifts in the Duke's frame. He was a skilled dancer, and he led them around the floor with a fluidity and ease that was unlike anything she had ever experienced. Their bodies, she realized, after a minute, were close — closer than, perhaps, they should have been. She could not escape the heat of his chest, the line of his shoulders. In a flagrant disregard for technique, he kept his gaze averted, fixed on some distant point, and did not once meet her eyes. Instead, Rosaline stared at the lapel of his jacket, the gold buttons that shone in the bright candlelight, noting the craftsmanship, the fine stitching. Anything to distract her from the way his fingers pressed into the edge of her spine, holding her close and guiding her with an ease that was almost frightening.

He was not a simple dancer, either. The Duke led her through turns, chassés, promenades, and even a heel turn that took her breath away, all without once knocking into another couple. Surprise was mixing freely with the unease and embarrassment already churning in Rosaline's stomach, and it was enough to pull her focus away from the way he was making her feel — untethered, boundless. Beautiful.

The music ended, and the Duke spun her out of frame before sinking into a deep bow. Rosaline curtsied back, wobbling a little as she straightened, and suddenly realized that almost everyone in the room was staring at them, at her and the Duke, and some of them were smiling, astonished by their performance.

Because that's all it is, Rosaline told herself as the Duke straightened. *A performance.*

"Another?" she asked him, before she knew she was asking it.

The Duke looked at her, and she shivered. "You flatter me, Miss Bailey," he said, stepping away. "But I am afraid I have had enough of dancing this evening." With that, he turned and was gone, melting into the crowd.

Rosaline immediately did the same, knowing that if she lingered, people might guess what had just happened, the insult she had just suffered. Her face burning, her stomach twisting into knots, she made for the nearest exit, pausing only to snatch a glass of punch from a nearby tray.

"Enough," she snarled under her breath. "Enough, now."

Once again, her feet carried her where her brain could not, and she found herself on the terrace in the garden. It was nice enough, though planned within an inch of its life. There were a handful of couples out here, and a small quartet playing beside the fountain. Still struggling to catch her breath, Rosaline made for the arcade, which was covered in climbing roses. No one would see her there.

At least, that was what she had thought. But when she stepped into the cool, earthy shade, she was shocked to find herself face to face with—

"Miss Knight," she blurted, forgetting to curtsy. "Please excuse me—"

"Not at all, Miss Bailey." Miss Knight gave her an inquisitive sort of look. "We meet again. I assume you need a place of refuge?"

Tension leaked out of her, and Rosaline slumped onto a nearby bench. "Correct."

"Then you are my guest." A smile, or something close to it. Miss Knight produced a small plate piled with *hors d'oeuvres*, and a half-empty bottle of wine. "Here. Join me."

The food settled Rosaline's stomach and made her feel more steady, less likely to be flung off the edge of the earth. She sipped at the wine, feeling a pleasant rush in her arms and legs, and smiled at Miss Knight. "You have yet to ask what induced me to flee."

"That is because I already know," Miss Knight replied, licking a spot of mustard off her thumb. She met Rosaline's gaze. "A man."

Rosaline sighed, slumping against the bench. "I want nothing more than to go to bed."

"Don't we all?" That almost-smile again. "And you have had the poor fortune of catching the Queen's eye. You would do better if you were unremarkable, less wealthy. Like me."

"You are hardly unremarkable," Rosaline replied. "You are clever, sneaky. And pretty."

Miss Knight snorted, taking a swig of wine. "And unsuited to marriage. A mother's dream."

Rosaline looked at her, really looked. "Are you in love, then?" she said, testing the invisible boundary that hung in the air between them. "With someone who returns your affections?"

Miss Knight sighed, and for a moment, something small, something hurt, showed in her face. "Yes, I am. But she is likewise being made to suffer the slings and arrows of this ridiculous farce. We can hardly steal a moment together."

Rosaline felt a twinge of sympathy. "I am sorry. I would not wish that upon anyone."

Miss Knight looked at her, her eyes soft. "I think," she said at last, "you should call me Katherine."

"Katherine," Rosaline repeated, but before she could say anything else, voices filtered in through the roses, and Katherine pressed a finger to her lips, her hand gripping Rosaline's arm. They both froze, desperate not to be found.

"—you are being thoroughly disagreeable, and I will not accompany you if you insist upon being an absolute brute to every young lady within spitting distance of London—"

A snort. "By all means, I am more than happy to remain at home—"

A groan of frustration. "You cannot be happy alone, you know that as well as I—"

"And, what, the solution is to find me a wife?"

Katherine stared at her, her face ashen, and Rosaline could only stare back, her heart thumping in her ears. For she knew those voices. Cadogan, and the Duke.

"Yes!" Cadogan retorted. "Or, at the very least, for you to entertain the idea."

"I find nothing entertaining about the idea." The Duke's voice was dry, indifferent. "And I will not continue to pander to your whims. If you wish to woo the Prince girl, then fine, but leave me out of it. Find someone else to occupy her friend."

"Her friend," said Cadogan, heated now, "is as diverting and charming as Charlotte herself, you cannot hope to convince me that you—"

"Diverting?" the Duke repeated, sardonic. "Charming? She can barely keep a conversation, and there are a dozen prettier girls in the ballroom alone. Besides, apart from a passing familiarity with literature, she has few other skills to commend her."

A few beats of silence. Then:

"You are wrong," said Cadogan. "You are very, very, wrong."

"I doubt that," the Duke replied, then the sound of footsteps. He was going back to the house. "And I expect to be proven right."

Silence followed, save for the sound of the fountain. A few minutes later, Cadogan left as well, with a huff of lingering exasperation.

Her throat thick, Rosaline could hardly begin to string together a coherent thought as Katherine stared at her. "Well," she finally managed, with an attempt at a smile, "at least I will not have to suffer his presence any longer."

Katherine offered her a weak smile in return, and they went back to their meal, though the food, Rosaline realized, was now tasteless.

SEVERAL HOURS LATER, ROSALINE GRITTED HER TEETH AND summoned every last remaining scrap of her patience. Lord Roden leered at her, his hand sliding precariously low as he led her down the dance floor. *Thank God*, she thought, *for slow waltzes.*

"I do enjoy big game hunting, you see," he went on. "Last I was in France, I managed to bag a bear as well as a boar. Their heads are mounted, quite beautifully, if I may use the word, in the drawing room of my country estate. Which is very large, as you may recall."

"Indeed, my lord," she replied, wincing as he stepped on her foot.

"Gorgeous creature, the boar. Mad as anything, but all the more fun to watch it struggle out of a trap, you see."

Much to Rosaline's relief, the music ended before she had to respond. She stepped away from Lord Roden and curtsied. "A pleasure, my lord."

His leer broadened and his gaze went directly to her chest. "But not one that has to end, Miss Bailey." Then, his attention was drawn to something over her shoulder and his leer turned into a frown. "Oh, and what, I suppose you've come to steal her away?"

Rosaline's heart throbbed once in her throat, then she looked over her shoulder to find the Duke, halted mid-step at the edge of the dance floor, staring at Lord Roden with unchecked outrage.

She had not known the Duke long, but seeing him even once after hearing what she'd heard was enough to make her skin tingle with anger.

"Hardly," she said, before the Duke could say a word. "The Duke can make no pretensions to my favor or my time. He is not so fortunate, or so entertained."

She could feel his gaze on the back of her head, but she

ignored it. Now Lord Roden was staring at her, surprise over-ruling his presumption for the first time that evening.

"If you'll excuse me," she went on, "I would like a glass of punch." With that, she fled.

After locating a dimly-lit corner in the next room, Rosaline slumped against the wall and allowed her eyes to slip shut, her ears throbbing with the sounds of a party kicking into high gear. By this point in the evening, the punch was warm and syrupy, but she gulped it down regardless, fighting the urge to sneak away.

"Miss Bailey?"

She opened her eyes and took in the young man before her.

He was handsome enough to be smug about it, with dark hair, bright eyes, and an uneven smile. He looked at her chest before he looked her in the eye, and she fought the urge to smack him.

"Lord Cornwall," he said, making an attempt at a bow. "Might we dance?"

Rosaline gritted her teeth, then imagined what she would have to endure once Mrs. Randolph found out she'd turned down a dance. "Yes," she said, and let him take her hand.

He was almost, but not quite, as bad as Lord Roden. He stepped on her toes, bragged about his land, his staff, his estate, and claimed that his tenants bowed to him in the street.

It took far too much effort for her to smile and nod, to act charmed instead of revolted, and when the dance was finally over, Rosaline made an excuse without hearing it and fled properly this time, slipping through the crowds until she stumbled onto a veranda at the side of the house, her mind reeling. The veranda was empty, surrounded by a lawn and bordered by hedges, and she made her way to the railing, fighting for air.

Gasping, Rosaline braced herself on the stone railing and squeezed her eyes shut, trying not to cry as a small section of hair fell out of her bun, grazing her cheek. It was too much, all of it. She'd never thought it would be this bad, this unendurable, that she would have to suffer their leers and their stares, to let them touch her—

"Miss Bailey."

An all too familiar voice, this time. She tipped her head back in exasperation, letting her eyes fall open and take in the stars above. "Please leave."

"You are upset." A statement, not a question, and he approached her. She could hear his steps on the stone. "I have, perhaps, insulted you in some—"

"Your Grace," she bit out. "I have no desire for company."

"He is a toad. Lord Roden, I mean. And Lord Cornwall a tadpole."

This threw her for a moment. When she recovered, her confusion was replaced only by anger, and she spun around to face him. "You have no right," she spat, "to even attempt at expressing an insult on my behalf."

The Duke's face was impassive in the half-darkness. "I do not?"

"No, Your Grace. You are not my ally, my friend. And I cannot see what you might wish to accomplish by cornering me in this manner, but I demand that you stop at once."

A beat of silence. Then he took a step closer, producing a handkerchief. "You are crying," he said, his voice low.

"Is it any wonder?" she spat at him, snatching the handkerchief out of his hand.

"You will not match with them," he said. "Roden and Cornwall, I mean."

Rosaline tried to take a breath, dabbing at her face. The handkerchief was soft and, she noticed, embroidered with the initials 'H.C.' in the corner. "I will not match," she managed, her voice shaky, "with any of them."

Another beat, longer than the first. "You will not marry?" said the Duke, betraying only a hint of surprise.

"No, Your Grace." Her voice was low, vehement. "I would only marry if it would get me into a University, but even God Himself cannot work that miracle."

The surprise showed on his face now, and he took a step closer. "You are..." he said at last. "Very unexpected."

"What a pronouncement," she said, the words hot on her tongue. "Here I thought I had few skills to commend me, let alone good looks or the ability to hold a conversation."

This seemed to rattle him and he stared at her. "You heard me."

"Indeed, Your Grace." She pushed the handkerchief into his open hand and gathered her skirt. "Which is why we no longer need entertain this farce. Besides, I have two pieces of slime that would probably like to corner me into another dance, and I cannot dream of insulting them."

"Miss Bailey." His jaw worked. "Allow me to apologize."

"I will not," she replied. "Because I do not think it would be genuine."

"You cannot—" The Duke seemed to swallow his own words, and something flashed in his eyes. "What if you did not have to endure them? The suitors?"

Rosaline stared at him, at a loss for words. "What on earth do you mean?"

"I mean." The Duke cleared his throat, and if she did not know any better, a blush seemed to color his cheekbones. "We could pretend... to form an attachment."

This was such an abrupt turn that for a moment, Rosaline felt quite dizzy. She continued to stare at him, hardly able to believe what she was hearing. "You are mad."

"I am not," he returned. "My title, my status. They would protect you. If the other men knew... if I set my claim to you, then they would..." He winced. "Fall into line."

It was a horrifying and yet tantalizing idea. Such an attachment would please Mrs. Randolph beyond measure, and Rosaline would never again have to endure a waltz with the likes of Lord

Roden. But there was something— "You would not ask," she said, her mouth numb, "if you would not benefit in some way, as well."

A brief pause, then the Duke ducked his chin and nodded. "I likewise have no desire to marry," he said, "or any desire to entertain the matchmaking efforts of every mother in London. If we were... then I would be free, as well."

Her heart thudding, Rosaline's mind whirled through the idea, spinning it in every direction she could imagine. Perhaps an arrangement such as this *would* work, and she would be able to escape the season with little injury to her pride or her sanity. *What better way*, she thought, *than to pretend with someone I could not love, and who could never love me?*

"Yes," she said, before she knew she was saying it. "Yes, Your Grace."

The corner of his mouth twitched. "Then we are agreed, Miss Bailey."

"We should have some rules," she blurted. "Guidelines."

He cocked his head to one side. "What do you suggest?"

"We must be seen together at every ball, and attend at least three semi-public events every week, whether they be promenading or a picnic or a tea." Her heart thudded again. "You must send flowers, and come to call on occasion."

His smile was growing into a smirk. "Very well."

"And," she added, "we should dance together. Frequently."

The Duke pocketed his handkerchief and closed the distance between them. His eyes were amber in the reflected light of the manor as he offered her his arm. "Then I suggest," he said, "that we begin at once."

Rosaline tucked her hand into the crook of his elbow and, to her own surprise, returned his smile. "Yes," she said. "Let's."

7

Madam Kensington's High Society Papers, No. 24

What a ravishing night! Truthfully, I, along with the rest of London, did not hold any sort of high expectation for a ball at the noble and stuffy House of D, and its laudable qualities were certainly not to be found in the passable refreshments, the mediocre music, and tasteless wine. But the guests, the entertainment! Oh, my dears! Where on earth to begin?

It should likely come as no surprise to any of my readers that I must first comment about the endearing, light-footed game of blushes and flattery occurring between the Star and a young, handsome Pup. One is perhaps surprised to see such a display, when one considers the wide variety to which she finds herself quite entitled. But the Pup is not alone, and nor is he the first to catch the Star's eye. Only time will tell which, of many, she might find herself drawn to.

And now, for perhaps the most shocking piece of news. Our favorite Recluse has surprised all of England by stepping into the light with none other than a Sapphire, who shone ever-so-brightly as she took his hand and stole the breath from everyone in the ballroom. Who would ever have imagined that such an Unknown, with only half a lineage to recommend her, could aspire to one of the highest titles in the land? It certainly makes one wonder what enticing, mysterious qualities may linger beneath her finely-cultivated veneer, just waiting to be uncovered...

ROSALINE DID NOT HEAR LISETTE COME INTO HER ROOM. SHE did not hear the curtains, the birdsong, the faint clatter of the tea tray. But she jerked awake when she heard—

"You have some explaining to do, *Mademoiselle!*"

Rosaline sat up, the room spinning a little as she remembered, all too quickly, how much she had had to drink the night before. "I—" she somehow managed. "Lisette—"

"You!" Lisette snarled. She was like a cannon in full battle mode, and she hurled herself at the dresser, seizing a handful of small objects. "You!" She threw a wooden figure at Rosaline's head. Rosaline ducked, just barely avoiding it. "You dance not *once* —" she now threw a comb— "not *twice*—" a bonnet— "but *three times*—" a small box— "with the *Duke*—" something metal, which bounced off the footboard— "and you do not mention it the *moment* you walk in the front door?!"

"Lis," Rosaline tried, her hands raised in defense as she crouched on the bed. "Lis, I was going to tell you—"

Lisette made an extraordinary sound, somewhere between a shriek and a growl. Next, she lunged for the vanity, and Rosaline grabbed her largest pillow, holding it aloft like a shield.

"Not a single *word*—" another comb— "for your *steadfast companion?!*" Now a mirror, which Rosaline managed to deflect with the pillow. "The woman with whom you have shared every *secret*—" a spool of thread— "every *dream?!*" A comb, plated in pearl, bounced off Rosaline's hand. "What am I to you?" Lisette spat, a small Bible held aloft. "Am I just a shade, a ghost? Someone who does not deserve the *truth?!*" With that, she flung the Bible at Rosaline's head. Rosaline let out a shriek and ducked just as the door opened and a pale figure appeared.

"Have you finished killing each other yet?" said Charlotte, unfazed by the scene before her. "You sound like two cats in heat."

"She is a *wretch*," Lisette snapped, her chest heaving with emotion as she glared at Rosaline. "How dare she! How *dare* she! A Duke, and she says nothing!"

"Come now," said Charlotte, stepping in and closing the door behind her. "Rosaline has not said a word to me about her apparent association with the Duke, either. If that merits me a projectile, have you one to spare?"

"Certainly." Lisette passed her a hairbrush. "Now that you are here, we could hold her down and tickle her, she will have to confess eventually—"

Rosaline stared at them, still hiding behind her pillow. "I haven't even had a cup of tea."

Charlotte seemed to consider this, then she turned to Lisette. "Perhaps we should let her have a cup of tea. As a gesture of faith and goodwill."

"For God's sake," Rosaline burst out. "There is nothing to tell!"

Lisette frowned, and Charlotte raised an eyebrow. "We do not believe you," said Lisette.

"The Duke," Rosaline said, conscious of the heat crawling up her face, "simply wished to dance with me, so he did."

"Did you not hear me?!" cried Lisette. "Not once, not twice, but three times! That is not wishing to dance, that is wishing to give you flowers and children and the finest jewelry in the world! Not to mention one of the largest estates in all of England!"

"You exaggerate," Rosaline hissed at her, brandishing the

pillow once again as something flashed in Lisette's eyes. "We found ourselves... well-matched. In terms of height. It was pleasant to dance together, so we continued to do so."

"Well-matched," Lisette sneered. "A likely story."

"They do dance very prettily together," said Charlotte. She was watching Rosaline, her expression thoughtful. "And the Duke did not seem well-disposed to any of his other partners, in the rare occurrences that he deigned to dance with them."

Rosaline met her gaze, swallowing thickly. Unspoken, in the air between the two of them, was a shared knowledge. They both knew the truth — that the Duke had not danced with any other woman. Had not even looked at another woman.

"Is it any wonder?" Lisette demanded, flinging a hand at Rosaline's general person. "Look at her, she is perfection! No, no, this is not what upsets me—"

"I did not tell you because I did not think it mattered!" Rosaline blurted. "It was only dancing, it was hardly proclamations or— Lisette, you must believe me! And I was so exhausted last night... even if I had something to tell, I was going to tell you this morning."

Lisette clutched her heart... "To think that *ma petite fille... ma compagne...* danced half the night with a *Duke*, and she would rather I heard it from *Madam Kensington* before I heard it from *her!*"

Rosaline felt a wave of dizziness, and she gripped her pillow. "Madam Kensington?"

"*Oui!*" Lisette marched over to the tea tray, then flung the pamphlet at her.

Rosaline caught it midair and fell upon it with unladylike haste. She had forgotten, she was so *stupid*— she had forgotten about Kensington, had forgotten that people would *notice*, apart from the mothers and the suitors—

To her surprise, her mention was tame. Much more flippant than she would have expected. *But it is early yet*, she thought, then felt another wave of dizziness as she imagined what it would be like in a week or two.

"Ladies!" A disgruntled Mrs. Randolph appeared in the doorway, and she took in the scene before her — Rosaline hunched on the bed, Lisette scowling at her, Charlotte cooing at a robin through the window — with a frown. "Do come downstairs, it is getting late! You have received a deluge of tokens and I cannot be expected to—"

The air in the room changed. Rosaline dropped the pamphlet and turned to meet Charlotte's gaze, her pulse beating in her ears like a drum. Lisette put her hands to her mouth to stifle a squeal, and Charlotte gave Rosaline that small, cheeky smile of hers. "Tokens," said Charlotte, then she grabbed Rosaline's hand and pulled her out of bed, down the hall, down the stairs, and into the drawing room, Lisette hot on their heels.

Hardly able to breathe, Rosaline could only stare as an entire greenhouse seemed to erupt before her. Every surface, even the couches, was covered in a seemingly endless variety of flowers and greenery, interrupted by small parcels of what appeared to be sweets. The air was thick with every floral scent imaginable. She tried to swallow, but her throat was clogged, and she hardly noticed Charlotte reaching for the nearest bouquet — which also happened to be the largest — and taking a card out from between the carnations, roses, and peonies.

Charlotte beamed, her whole face lighting up. "This one is from Lord Cadogan."

Rosaline managed a smile. "That is not surprising, Charlotte."

"Perhaps, but it is generous of him." She bent her head and closed her eyes, breathing in the flush, delicate scent.

"*Ma chère,*" came Lisette's hushed voice from behind Rosaline. She sounded shocked.

Frowning, Rosaline turned, and what she saw made her heart plummet to her feet.

The card table had been all but swallowed by the largest

bouquet — basket? — of roses Rosaline had ever seen in her life. It dwarfed every other bouquet in the room; it was practically a planet, in its own right. Red, white, and pink all crowded together, and they seemed to stretch out to her, beckoning, inviting her in. As she stepped towards the bouquet, she was hardly aware of Lisette reaching out to pluck a card from between the thorns, a card that had her name on it.

Her hands shaking for some ridiculous, indefinite reason, Rosaline unfolded the card, pausing just for a moment on the way her name was written — *Did he write this?* she thought, *Did he write this card himself?* — and read its contents with surprising composure.

To say the truth, reason and love keep little company together nowadays.
Is this enough flowers?
H.

Rosaline read the words twice more before she lowered the card to stare, once again, at the roses. "He has a heavy, untidy hand," she murmured, and this small observation was enough to keep herself from sinking to the floor, because flowers were one thing, but an unnecessary bit of Shakespeare was quite another.

Why? she thought, as Lisette pounced on her and snatched the card from her limp hand. *Why include the quote?* Then, once Lisette had let out a dramatic gasp— *To sell it, I suppose.*

"I CAN UNDERSTAND WHY YOU DO NOT ENJOY THE promenading," said Charlotte the following day, "but you must admit it is lovely to be in the fresh air. Does wonders for the humors, you know."

Rosaline had to smile at her. "Yes, I know." She looked around them, at the wide lawns and the flowers slowly stretching out of their long hibernation, and thought that Kensington Gardens was certainly one of the better parts of London. She looked around again, but now, her gaze caught on the pairs and clusters of other young ladies, and the chaperones trailing dutifully behind them. It reminded her that Mrs. Randolph was just a few feet away, and to hold her tongue accordingly.

She sighed a little. "How long must we do this, again?"

"Until we catch an eye or two," Charlotte replied, "or long enough that we secure a deluge of dance partners for the ball tomorrow evening."

"Another ball?" Rosaline groaned. "Good Lord, I've barely slept enough as it is."

Charlotte hummed. "We both know that that has less to do with the social agenda and more to do with the fresh tomes I caught Lisette sneaking into your room yesterday afternoon."

Heat rushed to Rosaline's face. "I do not know what you mean."

"It is a lovely day, is it not?" Charlotte went on, spinning in the middle of the path. "Perfect for tadpoles. If there were a creek, we could go hunting."

Rosaline smiled at that. "*You* could go hunting, Charlotte. I, for one, am in no hurry to make a fool of myself in public."

"The season is still young, Rosaline. There is time enough yet."

They wandered back to their picnic blanket near the pond, where Lisette was waiting under a small canopy with a light meal. She was surrounded by a plush collection of cushions and rugs, and, in all honesty, it looked quite splendid.

"This is exceedingly pleasant," Rosaline admitted a while later, when she was slumped into a cushion, shuffling the deck of cards. "Certainly more pleasant than a ball."

"If only," said Mrs. Randolph, her lips pursed, "you would sit up straight."

Rosaline smiled at her. "Come, Mrs. Randolph. Such a thing is impossible when one is perched on the side of a hill."

"I, for one," Charlotte chimed in, "am quite impressed that I have yet to roll onto my side."

"You are *ladies*." Mrs. Randolph sounded pained now. "Not... beetles."

"Are you certain?" said Charlotte, examining her reflection in a silver spoon. "I seem to be sprouting antennae."

"It is a shame you are made of legs and not luck, Charlotte," said Rosaline, dealing the cards. "Otherwise, you might have a sporting chance at winning back your losses."

"I still cannot believe," hissed Mrs. Randolph, "that you are playing *casino*. In *public*." She glanced around furtively, as if worried that they were about to be arrested or worse, spotted by one of the mothers.

"And I cannot believe," said Rosaline, "that you are such a terrible player, Charlotte."

Charlotte shrugged, smiling as she took up her cards. "I have no mind for strategy."

Rosaline shot her a grin. "Remind me never to partner you at whist."

Then—

"Good afternoon, ladies! It seems we are interrupting quite a party."

Rosaline did not bother to look up; she knew that voice.

"No party," Charlotte said to Lord Cadogan, "merely Miss Bailey thrashing me at cards."

"What a grim pronouncement for such a lovely day!" He halted at the edge of their camp and inclined his head. "I take it that you have already been for a walk?"

"Call it a stroll," said Rosaline, putting down the deck. "It is only a walk when there are hills and mud and fields of sheep."

"What an intriguing definition," came a second, all too familiar voice. A voice that twisted her stomach and made her mouth go dry.

Rosaline looked up and met the Duke's piercing gaze. He was dressed in his usual dark, trim manner, and his hair was an absolute disaster. *He is wealthy enough to own a mirror,* she thought, *so it is likely that he does not care.* "It is a definition informed by a lifetime of experience, Your Grace."

His expression was stoic, but his voice was warm with mirth. "I am sure it is, Miss Bailey."

"Might we join you?" said Cadogan, his dimples twinkling in the sunlight. Behind her, Rosaline could practically hear Mrs. Randolph's heart palpitating and Lisette drooling.

"Certainly," said Charlotte, and as the gentlemen sat down — Cadogan beside Charlotte, and the Duke by Rosaline — she flashed Rosaline an excited little grin.

For a moment, Rosaline had to work very hard not to grin back.

Here, on the fresh sunny lawn, it was almost difficult to remember the circumstances leading to her present truce with the Duke, and to reconcile his flat, open expression with the grim determination from two nights before. The warmth and the birds made it easier to forget the things she had heard him say, to forget the poorly-concealed insults he had passed about her character, her appearance. *Truthfully*, she thought now, *I would not have toyed with his pride if he had not slighted mine, unwitting though it might have been.*

Rosaline knew she would likely never forget those words, and not just because the person who had spoken them was a high-ranking member of society with the ear of every peer. No — it was because he had felt, for a brief period of time, like an ally. An unwilling ally, granted, but an ally nonetheless. And he had voiced every insecurity, every worry she had ever had about herself. An uncanny bit of luck, that.

But together they had passed the rest of the evening in a pleasant, if unsteady, atmosphere. Granted, they had been much distracted by the dancing, the drinking, the chatting to other inconsequential lords and ladies; but there had been a few moments, a few keen, pressing moments when his touch had lingered, when he had spun her into an unnecessary turn, when Rosaline had felt every pair of eyes in the room raking over them with an almost greedy appetite. Most of it now felt like a blur to Rosaline; the only constant, apart from the heavy, but not unpleasant, weight of the Duke's hand on her back, was the piercing, flashing blue of his gaze as it found her own, over and over again. She had had a fleeting thought between waltzes that perhaps, with time, she would get used to it. But now that he was here, and glancing at her in that pleasantly bright, open way... *Perhaps*, she thought, *I will never get used to it.*

"Gentlemen," said Charlotte. "May I introduce our chaperone, Mrs. Randolph? Mrs. Randolph, the Earl Cadogan and the Duke of St. Albans."

"A pleasure," said Cadogan, giving Mrs. Randolph a nod. The Duke copied him.

"I can assure you, gentlemen," came Mrs. Randolph's surprisingly breathy reply, "the honor is all mine."

"It appears that we've interrupted a serious game here, Prongs," said Cadogan, mock-frowning as he peered at the cards. "What is the score?"

Charlotte sighed. "Rosaline, eighteen, and I, only four."

"Not a very fair fight," said the Duke, and he looked right at Rosaline.

She fought off a shiver, reaching for the dealt cards. "No matter. We can put them away, and find something more diverting to amuse ourselves."

A hand, warm and firm on Rosaline's wrist, stopping her. "Deal us in," said the Duke.

"Very well." As she did, Rosaline glanced at Cadogan, then at the Duke. "Meanwhile, Charlotte and I should thank you both for your very kind gestures yesterday morning."

"Not at all," said Cadogan, then his brow twisted a little and he looked at his friend. "What does she mean, 'both?' Prongs, does this good lady imply—?"

"No implication," said the Duke, and when Rosaline looked up, he was looking right at her. "Merely a simple truth."

"Which is?" Rosaline managed.

"That a beautiful woman should receive equally beautiful flowers." With that, he captured her gloved hand, and, his eyes boring into hers, brushed a kiss to her knuckles.

Behind her, Rosaline heard a thud, and supposed that Lisette had fainted clean away. Meanwhile, half of the people in the park had turned to stare at them. As she held the Duke's gaze, Rosaline felt a slow smile creep upon her face. *It is working*, she thought.

For all his faults, the Duke was an excellent card player.

"My goodness," said Charlotte as they were tallying the score. "Eight points in a single round, Your Grace! Perhaps you have a better mind for strategy than even our Miss Bailey."

"Perhaps," the Duke said, sifting his cards into a single pile. "Though I must admit, strategy is one of very few areas in which I excel."

Cadogan scoffed. "Modesty does not suit you, Prongs. He is a dab hand at riding and boxing as well."

"Boxing?" Rosaline asked the Duke a few minutes later, as they were taking a walk together around the pond. "What an odd pastime, Your Grace."

He cocked his head to one side. In the sun, parts of his hair were almost chestnut. "Is it?"

"For one of your standing, yes. Is it not a tad... vulgar?"

"On the contrary, I find it quite thrilling." He shrugged. "There is a certain equality to it. Titles do not matter when you are in the ring. What matters is your strength, your speed. Nothing that is predestined by virtue of birth."

"I see." She wondered what would happen if she took hold of this sensitivity of his — this insecurity about his own status — and poked at it. *Behave*, she told herself. It was easier to be cordial with him now that they had found this new, slightly more even footing — the common ground of shared conspiracy. He was different, now. More relaxed. "Can I ask... why does Lord Cadogan call you 'Prongs?'"

For a brief second, his face did something very complicated — something between a wince and a grin. "A family tradition," he said, "for the male heirs. Our coat of arms has a huge stag at the front of it, and the antlers..."

"How..." She fumbled for a good word. "Creative."

"Not at all, really." He shrugged. "That was what the previous Earl Cadogan and Lord Blackwood always called my father, so once I got old enough, I just inherited the nickname along with the title. In all honesty, I cannot remember the last time Ed called me by my actual name."

She glanced at him. "I must admit, Your Grace, I do enjoy your friendship with Lord Cadogan. It is quite endearing to see two such close friends."

"Do you know," the Duke said, stopping abruptly and meeting her gaze. "Now that we are... attached... you need not address me with my title."

Before she could stop herself, Rosaline grinned and raised an eyebrow. "Very well... Prongs."

The Duke did wince then. "Good God," he said, while she could only laugh, "please, I beg you, refrain from doing that again—"

"Not if it creates a reaction as brilliant as this," she managed, clutching her stomach.

"Hal," he said, pained. "You may call me Hal."

Rosaline raised her eyebrow again. "Harold."

"You," said the Duke, as she dissolved into giggles, "are a menace."

"Truce, truce," she choked out, swatting at him in a very unladylike manner. "Hal."

He met her gaze and gave her a rare, cheeky smile. "Rosaline."

8

Something unhelpful swooped in Rosaline's stomach and she looked away, clearing her throat. None of this felt very funny, now. She continued walking, and after a moment, the Duke did the same. "I meant to tell you, Your— Hal. We made a very positive impression the other night."

"Did we?" His voice was neutral, but she caught the teasing edge.

"At least, according to Madam Kensington. But hers is the most important voice in London, apart from the Queen's, so do not discount her opinion."

"Madam Kensington," the Duke repeated. "Enlighten me?"

"A gossip-monger." Rosaline slipped her hand into her pocket and pulled out her rumpled, creased copy of issue No. 24. She handed it to him. "She sees and hears everything, and has yet to be proven wrong."

"Ah, yes. I had almost forgotten about your mysterious hidden pocket." The Duke unfolded the pamphlet as she fought off a blush. "Lose any more Shakespeare?"

"No," she bit out, then cleared her throat. "Our mentions have been quite tame, so far, but that may change as the season progresses and tensions rise."

"I can handle a bit of juicy slander," the Duke replied, scanning the front page. "She certainly does not mince her words."

"Not in the least," Rosaline replied. "No one knows who she is, either. But she must be someone of note, because she is privy to details that only a peer would know. And she makes money hand over fist — each of these costs half a shilling, and hundreds of them are distributed throughout London almost every day of the week. She has an entire underground empire, and need not betray a whiff of her identity to rule it."

The Duke looked up at her then. "You envy her."

Rosaline's veins flooded hot and cold, and all she could choke out was, "No!"

"You do." The Duke looked smug, almost triumphant. He folded the pamphlet and handed it back to her. "You need not pretend otherwise, Rosaline, and you forget that you are in confidential company. Secrets do not a happy attachment make."

She overcame her shock in order to laugh. "Now that was an excellent jest!"

The Duke lifted his chin with exaggerated seriousness. "What do you mean?"

"It is a jest," she said, "because you are probably the most reticent, guarded person in all of England. I cannot imagine that such a quality would suddenly change, even in the face of an association born of shared conspiracy."

He was looking at her again. "This speech is brutal evidence," he said, "that you certainly do not neglect your Shakespeare."

"An artful dodge, Your Grace. I shall make no mention of the fact that you ignored my reply, and all the implications it carried."

"I did not ignore anything," he replied.

"Where does this leave us, then?" Rosaline said, almost smiling. "In terms of secrecy?"

The Duke stopped walking, still looking at her. His expression was flat, but the corner of his mouth twitched. "I suppose," he said, after several moments' pause, "that our situation will likely result in us becoming quite acquainted with one another. If we are going to spend all this time pretending to everyone else, the least we could do is not pretend with each other."

For a brief instant, Rosaline felt a bolt of fear. It rattled her, but she did her best to ignore it. "I suppose so."

His expression clouded over slightly, like a sudden storm over a field of wheat, and she knew then, in that moment, that, regardless of what he might say, or what he might agree to, a part of the Duke would always remain hidden from view. He looked away, across the pond, where Charlotte and Cadogan were chatting under a large oak.

Rosaline cleared her throat and tried for a smile. "They do enjoy each other's company."

"Indeed." Then the Duke turned his back on the oak, the pond. He was restless; she could tell. "Perhaps we should return, and discuss our plans for tomorrow."

"Tomorrow?" she echoed, before she remembered. "Ah."

"No need to sound so excited," he said, but his voice was grim. They began walking back the way they had come. "Did you hear the Queen will be in attendance?"

Rosaline nearly stumbled, but she managed to catch herself in time. "I did not."

The Duke nodded. "She has a keen eye, as I am sure you've noticed, and you can be certain that she, too, subscribes to Madam Kensington. We must dance the first two dances together, but greet her separately. If we greet her together, then it will be seen as—"

"An implication," Rosaline finished for him, fighting yet another blush. "What about before the ball?"

"I am afraid I will be occupied." He cut her an amused glance. "Though I can certainly send flowers."

She smiled. "It seems almost a shame, you know. Just how many blooms need to suffer for our art."

"Really? What would the good lady have me send instead? A bouquet of books?"

Rosaline had never heard of anything more perfect, but— "That would turn too many heads, Your Grace. A bouquet of fruit, perhaps?"

He gave her a proper look now, his eyes narrowed. "Fruit?"

"Fruit," she confirmed, enjoying this little joke. "Pretty and practical. Besides," she added, "it would be helpful to have some food that was small enough to hide in my petticoat, so I could sneak it into my room. Mrs. Randolph keeps us on a very strict diet. Lisette has become a master of subterfuge just to hand me the occasional ham sandwich."

This time, when he looked at her, there was something sharp about it. "A diet?" he said, his voice brittle. "I cannot think of anything less necessary—"

Rosaline looked back at him, a little lost. "Really, Your Grace?"

"Yes, well." Something was happening to him. He looked like he'd been clubbed over the head. "Your figure. It is very..."

He stopped walking, so Rosaline did so as well. He stared at her, she stared at him, and at his back, the pond splashed quietly at his heels. The silence was astounding.

After a few painful, eternal moments, the Duke cleared his throat and kept walking, dropping his gaze to the ground. He was slightly flushed. "What have you planned for this evening?"

Rosaline, too, continued walking, wondering what on earth had just happened. "Nothing terribly exciting. We have a visit from the modiste, and Mrs. Randolph has promised to overwhelm us with dining etiquette."

The Duke shook his head, still not looking at her. "I do not like this woman."

"Then you would be in the majority," Rosaline told him.

"Why must you put up with her?"

She sighed. "When mine and Charlotte's social abilities were analyzed by anyone who claimed to be an expert, we were found to be somewhat lacking. She has been installed to turn us into proper young ladies."

"Good Lord." The Duke seemed appalled. "How horrendous."

"It is quite a relief to hear you say that," she said, and it was the truth. "I have become accustomed to regarding her as a person of consequence."

Then, finally, he cut her another glance. "Has she been unkind to you? Needlessly?"

"Not since my first night here in London," Rosaline said. "My father... corrected some of her behavior."

The Duke gave a nod and looked away once again. "You know, you have not yet mentioned... why you summer with the Princes, and not your father."

Rosaline blinked, a little surprised by this turn in the conversation. "My father and I are new to London, and by the time he was looking to purchase, most of the good houses were gone. Ours will need several months of work before it is habitable, and he spends most of his time at the palace. Quite apart from concerns of practicality, he did not relish the idea of me sitting alone in some empty, stately house."

Something twitched in his jaw. "You are... close."

"We are. Out of choice as well as necessity." Rosaline smiled, then glanced at him. "And what about you, Your Grace? Do you have—"

"Hal," he said, with a bite of impatience. "Call me Hal."

"Hal," Rosaline acquiesced, the name still foreign on her tongue. "Do you—?"

"Miss Bailey." He stopped abruptly, then gave her a quick, stilted bow. "Forgive me, but I must be on my way."

She hastened to drop into a curtsy, trying to hide her confusion. "Of course—"

"Good afternoon." With that, he turned and marched off, not

in the direction of their picnic, but towards the main path. Within moments, he was slipping back into the streams of promenaders.

Rosaline stared after him, utterly bewildered. What had happened? Had she said something wrong? Had she—?

She glanced across the pond, and saw, again to her surprise, that like her, Lord Cadogan was watching the Duke's departure. Even from this distance, she could tell that his jaw was clenched. A moment later, he bade Charlotte farewell and walked off, following the Duke's line of exit.

When Rosaline arrived back at their picnic area, Lisette looked at her with a question in her eyes. Rosaline could only shrug. "I have no idea."

❦

ROSALINE FROWNED AS THE MODISTE SLIPPED THE MEASURING tape around her waist and pulled it tight. "Charlotte, surely you must have discussed something beyond the life cycles of tulips—"

"The Earl is so knowledgeable," Charlotte replied. The tone of her voice told Rosaline that she wasn't listening at all. Rosaline glanced over her shoulder. Charlotte was reclining on the chaise in the corner, wafting a huge yellow feather — courtesy of the modiste — through the air. "He learned so much of what he knows from his great aunt, you see. Plants and flowers have been a lifelong passion for his family, but he is the first to turn it into a business."

Rosaline was beginning to share Lisette's worry. Carefree, sweet, enigmatic Charlotte might well drive Cadogan away if she did not make her own sentiments — which hopefully extended beyond the bounds of plant life — known. "He seems a very agreeable dance partner."

"Yes," Charlotte sighed happily. Perhaps she *was* listening. "He does occasionally step on one's toes, but he has such enormous feet, I think he can hardly avoid it."

There were far too many things for Rosaline to say to that, so as the tape measure slipped from her waist to her hips, she settled on, "At least he knows his manners. Lord Roden cannot claim the same."

"Bite your tongue," Mrs. Randolph snapped, choosing that perfect moment to come into the room. "Lord Roden is as acceptable a match as any. The fact that he is paying you any attention at all is quite the compliment."

Rosaline did indeed bite her tongue. Mrs. Randolph had not taken kindly to the Duke's sudden departure earlier that afternoon, and had decided that Rosaline must have done something wrong to cause it. The carriage ride home had been an awkward one, to say the least.

"But Lord Roden is too old for us, Mrs. Randolph," said Charlotte, and Rosaline again bit her tongue to keep from smiling at the way Mrs. Randolph's eye twitched. "And he does not share our sense of humor, or her passion for literature. I, for one, cannot fault Rosaline for wishing he would keep his distance."

"If Miss Bailey continues to repel all her suitors," Mrs. Randolph said imperiously, "then it is possible that Lord Roden may give her the best offer she can hope for. Sapphire or not, you are not guaranteed a single thing if you do not make yourself an attractive option."

For a brief, delightful moment, Rosaline imagined Puck flying into the room and giving Mrs. Randolph a pair of donkey's ears and a tail to match.

"Madam D'Amboise," said Mrs. Randolph, and the modiste looked up in reply. "Have you an estimate of how long it will take you to complete a new gown for Miss Bailey? Lady Prince has several more she can wear, but Miss Bailey's wardrobe is surprisingly lacking for a young lady fresh from Paris."

A hat, Rosaline thought savagely. *A little red hat, and a bell around her neck*—

"Give me two days, madam," said the modiste. Her French accent was light, lilting, not as thick as Lisette's. She was several years older than Rosaline and Charlotte, but her eyes sparkled with an undeniable vivacity. "Perhaps less, if she is happy to wear not such a complicated pattern."

"Yes," Rosaline began, but Mrs. Randolph swelled.

"Miss Bailey's gowns cannot be seen as any less intricate than the Lady Prince's." For a brief moment, Rosaline was surprised by this concern, then realized that Mrs. Randolph was only worried about how such a supposed disparity between the Star and the Sapphire might reflect poorly on Lord Devon. "I suppose two days is acceptable. Miss Bailey can borrow some of Lady Prince's dresses for the Queen's tea party and the opera, but she will continue to need dresses, Madam D'Amboise, both formal and informal. Please," she added, "spare no expense. And do not hesitate to use plenty of beadwork. Miss Bailey needs all the help she can get."

"Absolutely, madam." Madam D'Amboise dipped into a curtsy. Mrs. Randolph gave her a nod and left the room, her steps echoing in the hall.

Once Madam D'Amboise straightened, she flashed Rosaline a knowing look that Rosaline was all too happy to return.

"*I feel I should apologize for her manners*," Rosaline said in French. "*She does not actually speak for me, though she thinks she does.*"

"*I understand, Mademoiselle*," Madam D'Amboise replied, likewise in French. She knelt down to take Rosaline's inseam. "*It seems she is not too fond of you, huh?*"

"*I am not her true concern*," Rosaline replied. Speaking in French again — with someone other than Lisette — felt oddly cleansing, like a weight dripping off of her back. "*And she has some perplexing ideas about fashion.*"

"*Beading*," Madam D'Amboise repeated, spitting out the word.

"*She reminds me of my grandmother, which is not a flattering comparison.*" Then, she looked up, her bright eyes fixing on Rosaline's with a kind of determination. "*They dress you quite modestly, no? In silly little whites and pinks and blues?*"

Rosaline nodded, bemused. She gestured to the open closet, where they could see the evidence. "*Why do you ask?*"

Something resolute crept across Madam D'Amboise's features. When she looked up at Rosaline again, her gaze was alight. "*Mademoiselle, you deserve to be dressed like a woman, not a little girl. I will make that happen.*" With that, she stood up, snaking her measuring tape into a thin, tight bundle. "*Give me two days. You will see.*"

"*I look forward to it,*" Rosaline replied, trying to sound very normal and controlled when, in reality, her stomach was exploding with butterflies. *Dressed like a woman?* What on earth did she mean by that? How else was there to dress?

Madam D'Amboise packed up the remainder of her things in a few quick, efficient movements, and swept into a final, deep curtsy. She flashed Rosaline a conspiratorial grin. "It has been an honor, Miss Bailey, Lady Prince. Take care."

༺❀༻

AT SOME POINT DURING SUPPER THAT EVENING, LORD DEVON looked up from his potatoes and said to Rosaline, "Well, my dear, it seems that you and the Duke are the talk of the entire town. I can hardly walk three feet without someone asking me about the two of you."

She tried, a beat late, to smile. "Really? How extraordinary, I cannot think of anything less newsworthy than—"

"Quite the contrary, I am afraid." Lord Devon flashed her something that might have been a smile. "Is there any chance I could glean something of import?"

She couldn't help it; she stared at him. "Can I ask, my lord, what you mean?"

He waved a noncommittal hand. "Well, you know. Was it love at first sight? Are you merely doing a bit of cat and mouse, before you see what your options are? Come, there is hardly any need for secrets. I can certainly promise you that anything you may mention will be kept in the strictest confidence. One only wonders at these things because of the Duke's reputation, you see."

"Reputation," Rosaline repeated, her mind spinning. "Well, my lord, seeing as it has only been a few days, I do not think we can attach any particular motivations to my actions, or the Duke's." She attempted a carefree shrug. "We are at the beginning of the season, after all. Why should we bother to commit ourselves to any one feeling or person?"

Lord Devon shook his head but gave her a smile. "Spoken like a true modern woman. I can tell you, in my day we never had any of this dancing around. Well, perhaps, but it was more—"

On and on he went, oblivious to the seething turmoil in Rosaline's stomach. She stared down at her half-eaten food, and realized that if she had any hope of making it through her arrangement with the Duke with any of her sanity, pride, or heart left, there was something she had to do.

Several hours later, Rosaline looked up at the sound of Lisette's quiet knock and said, "Enter."

"*Me chère*," Lisette breathed as she slipped into the bedroom. She took in everything with a glance — Rosaline's petticoat, left hanging over her screen; the open windows, welcoming in a gentle breeze; the desk in the corner, covered in books and papers, far messier than Rosaline usually liked to keep it. And then there was Rosaline herself, curled into a chaise she'd dragged in front of the windows. "You have already changed," Lisette said, somewhat surprised, then made her way to the desk. Again, all it took was a glance, then her gaze snapped to Rosaline. "What is the matter?"

Rosaline tried to take a steadying breath, but it did not work. "I wanted to undress, but... my stays, I could not—"

Lisette was by her in an instant. She went to work on the laces, which were half-undone and had tangled into a large knot. "Tell me," she said, simple, not pressing. She tugged the laces open and Rosaline took a grateful gulp of air.

"*I have to tell you the truth,*" Rosaline managed, in French. "*About me... and the Duke.*"

Lisette stilled. Her hands went to Rosaline's shoulders, and she leaned forward enough to make eye contact. "*What truth?*" she said, her words even sharper in French.

Rosaline squeezed her eyes shut, hating herself for the hot, prickling tears that threatened to break free. "*It is not real,*" she said, hating the way her voice shook. "*None of it. Our attachment is a pretension, a farce.*"

A ringing silence. Lisette's hands dropped from Rosaline's shoulders back to her laces. "*How did this happen?*" Lisette said, her voice softening.

Once Rosaline began to speak, everything spilled out of her like a flood. It felt almost Biblical — emptying her heart to the cooling air, staring out at the stars behind the trees, feeling Lisette's warm hand on her arm, a soft encouragement, a reminder that she could find moments of safety even in a place like this. Around her, the world continued to shift, to spin, to slip towards dawn, but here, in this moment, it was just Rosaline and the Duke, staring at each other across the darkened hall, his face half-lit as he looked at her and said, "Goodnight, Miss Bailey."

By now, her stays were a crumpled mess on the floor, and Lisette was sitting beside her on the chaise, looking out into the throbbing night. "*My dear,*" she finally said, breaking a long silence. "*This is a very strange situation. He is helping you, but to protect himself.*"

Rosaline almost smiled. "*I know.*"

"*He insulted you, but he respects you. And he trusts you.*"

Rosaline nodded. "*I know*." The Duke's trust was the thing that unsettled her most.

"*You are helping each other, yet toying with the possibility... of hurt.*"

Rosaline sighed now, dropping her head into her hands. "*I know. But I would be more worried if I thought that I could fall in love with him.*"

When she opened her eyes, Lisette was looking at her with something akin to surprise. "*Really?*" said Lisette. "*You do not think you could love him?*"

"*No.*" The word was heavy in Rosaline's throat.

Lisette's gaze shifted into something knowing, something clever. "*So when he walks into a room, you do not feel every light dim, feel a weight in your stomach that settles deep, pulling you towards him even when you know it shouldn't?*"

Rosaline blinked a few times. "*No.*"

"*You do not find yourself looking for him, even when you know he is not there? You do not dream of his hands, his eyes, you do not long to hear his laugh, to see him look at you even when he is speaking to someone else? You do not wait to see if he smiles, before you do?*"

"*No,*" Rosaline said, vehement now. Her face was hot.

"*When something happens, you do not want to tell him right away, to see the way his face changes when you speak, to see if he watches you, as much as you watch him? You do not wonder what he dreams of at night, what he thinks while he reads, what he sees in the stars?*"

"*No, Lisette.*" Rosaline rubbed her face, trying to will away the butterflies roaring in her stomach. "*What you are talking of... it does not exist between us. It never will. Besides, I hardly know him.*"

"*Of course,*" said Lisette, but she sounded smug. "*Now, you hardly know him, but in a few weeks...*" Then, she leaned forward again, giving Rosaline a final piercing, warning look. "*Do not let him hurt you, my dear. No matter the cost.*"

Later, when Rosaline was staring down that solitary flame, she looked into its bright, flickering depths, and whispered, "I won't."

9

The next day, Rosaline woke slowly from a deep, uninterrupted sleep to find that her bed was occupied by another pair of legs apart from her own.

Frowning, she stretched out her foot and nudged Charlotte's calf. "Charlotte," she hissed, to no effect. She had to push away a chunk of the covers before she uncovered Charlotte's angelic face, tucked in against a pillow.

Rosaline paused for a moment, reluctant to wake her. But no. A glance at the windows told her they had slept quite late — sunlight beamed in brilliant cracks and seams around the curtains. She tapped Charlotte on the forehead. "Charlotte," she said. "Wake up."

It took a few moments, but eventually, it worked. Charlotte blinked up at her with those brilliant blue eyes and stretched into a yawn. "Rosaline! Good morning."

"Morning. Charlotte, dear, why are you in my bed?"

"Oh!" Charlotte stretched again, reaching her hands up towards the ceiling. "I had a nightmare. I came to see you, but you were so blissfully asleep I could not bear to wake you. I resolved to lie down for a few moments, and here we are."

"A nightmare, Charlotte? What about?"

"Oh," Charlotte sighed. "It was about the ladybirds in the garden. A dreadful wasp was hunting them, and they were forced to flee to another garden in London."

Rosaline stared at her for a moment. She honestly could not tell whether Charlotte was being truthful. She knew that if Charlotte had had a nightmare about something serious, about her mother, perhaps, that she would not admit it. "Sounds awful."

"Indeed, but it is all over now!" Charlotte sat up, tossing her braid over her shoulder. "We have quite a day ahead of us. We must not dally for even a moment!"

"Charlotte," said Rosaline. "You cannot honestly tell me that you are looking forward to this ball. It is our third this week alone."

Charlotte shrugged. "No, but the Marchbanks family has one of the best pastry chefs in London." She grinned suddenly. "And I must admit I am quite excited to see a certain someone."

Rosaline smiled. "Lord Cadogan?"

"Lord Crawley," Charlotte replied, wistful, but before Rosaline could react, her bedroom door opened and Lisette marched into the room.

"*Bonjour, ma chère!*" Lisette sang, but she halted when she saw that Rosaline's bed was occupied by one more person than usual. "Charlotte! What are you—?"

"She had a nightmare, Lis," said Rosaline. She could hear a set of running footsteps, getting louder and closer until Mattie crashed into Rosaline's room—

"She's gone!" Mattie burst out in a horrified whisper. She wobbled, barely catching herself on a nearby chair. "My Charlotte is gone!"

"Not at all, Mattie," Charlotte piped up, waving at her. "I am here."

Lisette tsked while Mattie collapsed into the chair, half-faint. "You girls," said Lisette, throwing open a set of curtains. "If you aren't giving us heart attacks, you are making us lose hair. Now." She glanced at the door, which was cracked open, and, satisfied that no one was approaching, said, "Quickly, before she sees—"

Lisette pulled a crumpled paper bag from the depths of her apron and threw it at Rosaline, who caught it midair. She upended it onto the bed, and out rolled half a dozen hot cross buns, still warm from the oven.

"There is a baker," Lisette hissed, "two streets over, who makes them during the whole summer. Apparently, *ma chère*, you are not the only one who likes them out of Lent."

"Thank you!" Rosaline whispered, pushing three of them towards Charlotte. "Quick, Charlotte, this is our best chance at solid food before this evening—"

"You are too kind!" Charlotte immediately bit one of them in half and threw another at Mattie. It landed in her lap. "Eat, Mattie, you've gone a very funny color."

Mattie took a half-hearted bite, then began to eat with more fervor.

"Lisette," said Rosaline, through a full mouth. "How is she today?"

Lisette held up her hand in a so-so gesture as she went over to the next set of curtains. "Her temper is no shorter than usual, though she was displeased to find that there were even more tokens delivered to the drawing room this morning." She flung the curtains open and more sunlight poured into the room.

Rosaline scoffed, sharing a look with Charlotte. "She is a piece of work. She wants us to attract suitors, but not too many—"

"And Heaven forbid the suitors demonstrate their interest," Charlotte added. She cocked her head to one side. "I do wonder what made her temperament so disagreeable. I shall have to consult the toadstools."

Rosaline and Lisette's eyes met for a fraction of a moment before they had to look away for fear of giggling. "Tokens?" said Rosaline, working on her second bun. "How many?"

"Quite a few," said Lisette, smug as anything. "We should bring some of them upstairs. Oh, and—" She turned and flashed Rosaline a grin. "Your father is here."

Rosaline let out a strangled gasp, dropped her bun, and rolled off the bed, nearly turning her ankle as she lunged for her dressing gown.

"Be careful!" Lisette admonished, but to no effect — dressing gown hanging off one arm, Rosaline tore out of her bedroom and down the hall, almost crashing into Mrs. Randolph.

"Sorry!" Rosaline gasped, but she didn't stop, not even when Mrs. Randolph cried, "We do not stampede like wild animals, Miss Bailey!"

Rosaline nearly fell down the stairs, but she managed to catch herself when she reached the first landing. She ducked an oncoming tray of silver as she tumbled onto the ground floor, tugging her dressing gown into place. The door to the drawing room was open, and she burst in, taking little notice of the growing piles of flowers—

There he was. Standing by the fireplace. Sir Ian turned, surprise overtaking his features as he looked at her. "Rosaline—" he began, but then she charged at him and flung herself into his arms.

Her father let out a wheeze but caught her all the same, and she could feel his shoulders shaking with suppressed laughter. "My," he managed. "Good morning to you, too."

"I've missed you," she whispered, burying her face in his shoulder. He was wearing one of his newer, fancier coats, freshly-pressed, and it smelt of his favorite tobacco.

"And I you," Sir Ian replied. After a moment, he gently shifted away, taking her hands in his own, and looked her in the face. "I came because I wanted to see how you were doing. I've had reports from the Queen and from Hieronymus, of course, but I wanted to hear it from you."

"I am fine," Rosaline said, and for a moment, she worried that he could see everything, the truth of it all, written plainly in her eyes. After all, her response was a vast understatement of everything she was feeling at the moment, and her father always knew when she was lying. "Truly, Father. Charlotte and Lisette are wonderful companions, and they are making everything much easier to bear."

"Good." He squeezed her hands and led her over to a couch. "Now, you must tell me everything. Spare no detail." Sir Ian nodded to the nearest table, where a huge pot of tea sat beside a plate of sandwiches, cakes, and deviled eggs. "We have provisions."

Rosaline passed a very pleasant hour doing just that — telling him everything that had happened since he last saw her, only leaving out the more personal details about the Duke. Her father laughed, grinned, and even cringed at all the right moments, and for a while, she glowed with it — with the joy of sharing her life with him, of having him here as her friend as well as her parent.

She was also quite happy to eat as many sandwiches as she liked. She was licking a stray bit of butter from the edge of her thumb when he cut her a look and said, "When last we spoke about the season, you were treating it as something to be endured. You spoke as if you wanted to travel in shades and fogs, avoiding attention at any cost. But, it seems as if you have done the opposite."

Rosaline rolled her eyes but smiled. "*You* try avoiding attention when you are next to the most beautiful girl in the room. You can thank your friend the Queen for that one."

"I see your point," he replied, raising his teacup to gesture at the piles of flowers. "I can tell you have caught many an eye." His eyes sparkled. "Anyone... worthy of your interest?"

"Not in the least," she said. "That is not what I am here for."

He seemed to soften. "I know." A beat of silence. "So it really is nothing? Your..." He winced. "Flirtation... with the Duke?"

Her face burning, Rosaline put her teacup down with a clatter and stood up. "You could not have possibly used a worse word, Father."

He winced again. "I know... it sounded better in my head."

"The Duke and I are nothing." She turned, facing her huge basket of roses from the other day. More of them had opened, and their scent was resplendent. She traced one of the blooms with her finger, and felt a part of herself yield. "Well... not nothing. We have more in common than I would have thought. Which is why it is a little easier for us to spend time together."

A very telling pause. Then, "You get along?"

Her father's voice was almost toneless, and she had to admire his ability to conceal a reaction. "We do. We have a shared sense of humor." *And a shared sense of survival,* she didn't say.

"I see," he replied. "I am... glad you've found that. I have to admit, I was concerned. About you spending time with the young gentlemen of London."

She turned, letting her surprise show. "Really? Why?"

The corner of Sir Ian's mouth twitched. "Because you and your intellect can dance circles around them, and too many men do not like women with minds of their own."

Before Rosaline could reply, there came a knock at the door. Sadie, one of the maids, appeared and curtsied. "Miss, there is another delivery of flowers. May we—?"

"Certainly," Rosaline said at once, stepping back. "Bring them in."

Sadie pulled open the door, and a small trolley came trundling in. Benny's eyebrows were just visible over the sea of blooms as he guided the trolley into the nearest corner.

"Goodness," Rosaline said, feeling a little unsettled. She wasn't even dressed yet. "I do hope most of them are for Charlotte."

"They are, Miss," said Sadie, with just a flicker of a smile. But then she nodded at a huge bouquet of white roses and camellias interrupted by purple clematis. "Except for that one."

Something pricked at Rosaline's stomach and threatened to

crawl up her throat. She took a quick breath, then approached the trolley with a distinct sense of foreboding. There was a small card nestled between two camellias and she unearthed it with deplorable haste.

Love looks not with the eyes, but with the mind.
My secret lies beneath the stems.
H.

Unbidden, her heart skipped a beat. Rosaline blinked, looked up at Sadie's sly face, then looked back down at the card. He wouldn't. Would he?

She shoved the card into the pocket of her gown and, with a distinct sense of foreboding, pushed her hand into the depths of the bouquet. After a few moments, her fingers brushed against something stiff and rough to the truth. Frowning, she gripped it, and yanked it out of the flowers.

Half of the bouquet collapsed, but it did not matter. Bewildered, Rosaline stared at the small, burlap-wrapped parcel in her hand. It was misshapen, lumpy, though uniformly packed.

"What is it?" said her father, breaking the relative silence.

"I have no idea," she replied, bringing the parcel over to the couch. She sat down, tugged at the knotted twine holding it together, and could only stare as the burlap unfurled and revealed its hidden treasure.

A beat passed. Then two.

"Is that," her father finally said, "a meat pie?"

"And tomatoes," Rosaline said, her face on fire, unable to keep herself from grinning.

FOR THE FIRST TIME SINCE HER ARRIVAL IN LONDON, ROSALINE stepped out onto a gravel drive, looking up at the massive house before her, and felt a distinct sense of calm. She smiled up at the glowing windows, at the streams of people flooding into the party, and linked arms with Charlotte. "Don't let's dally. I want a drink."

"You are in a good mood," Charlotte replied with a smile of her own. As they approached the house, Mrs. Randolph hovering behind, people turned to look and curtsy. For once, it did not make Rosaline feel unsettled. Instead, it made her feel powerful. "Is there any particular reason, perhaps a title that rhymes with 'Luke?'"

"Not in the least," Rosaline replied. "I suppose I am getting used to this. The parading, the curtsying, the smiling. The sooner we get it over with, the sooner we can leave."

Charlotte squeezed her elbow. "Wait, I know why you've cheered up! You had all those sandwiches this afternoon, you lucky beast—"

Rosaline shot her a fretful, sheepish glance. "I am sorry I didn't manage to sneak you one." It had been difficult enough to smuggle the meat pie back into her room. "*Someone* had them whisked right back to the kitchen when she realized what my father had done."

"It is no matter, Rosaline," Charlotte replied as they began to ascend the stone steps. "I managed to charm a cold chicken leg out of Katherine, the kitchen maid."

Rosaline blinked at her. "A *cooked* one, I hope?"

Charlotte gave a pretty, delighted laugh that turned several dapper heads. "Not at all, Rosaline, I make a habit of eating raw meat. Does wonders for one's complexion."

Rosaline was just thankful they were too far out of earshot for anyone — even Mrs. Randolph — to hear them. It was impossible to tell whether or not Charlotte was joking. They passed through the front entryway, and she couldn't help herself — she glanced around for a familiar face, a familiar shock of hair. But no. The Duke did not appear, and she refused to feel disappointment of any kind.

Without Lord Devon, their introduction to their hosts was pleasant, mindless, and Rosaline made her way into the ballroom feeling as if she had dodged a bullet. Mrs. Randolph melted into a nearby crowd of mothers, but gave both of them a sharp, warning look. Miss Brown, she noticed, was keeping her distance with her usual gaggle of followers, and there was no sign of Katherine.

"Have you promised any dances to Earl Cadogan?" said Rosaline, picking up the train of thought where she had left it earlier that day. "I am sure he is eager to see you."

"Yes," said Charlotte, smiling again. "The second and the fifth."

"Oh." Rosaline did not bother to hide her surprise. "What about the first?"

"Lord Crawley," Charlotte replied, with something of a sigh. But not a jaded sigh. A wistful sigh. "He is a marvelous dancer."

"Lord Crawley," Rosaline repeated, staring at her now. "Why him?"

This, in turn, seemed to surprise Charlotte. She paused, turning to Rosaline. "What do you mean, why? He is a lovely gentleman, and—"

"Charlotte." Rosaline found Charlotte's gaze and held it. "You cannot be serious."

Charlotte stared at her for a moment, then took a step away, unlinking their arms and flashing Rosaline her best Delphic smile. Rosaline stepped back as well, feeling as if she were warding off a blow. "I am perfectly serious," said Charlotte, her tone betraying only a hint of coolness. "And now, I must see if I can find my partner before the music starts." With that, she turned and made her way across the room, the crowds parting around her like the Red Sea.

❧ 10 ❧

It took Rosaline several long, bewildering moments to compose herself, long enough for people to notice that she was standing alone. As people — as *men* — turned to stare at her, her pulse began to throb in her ears, and her stays seemed to tighten around her ribs. Then, she caught a dreaded glimpse of Lord Roden through the crowd. He stopped, looked right at her, and began to make his way—

"Miss Bailey," came a deep, disinterested voice from behind her. "Can I offer you a glass of punch?"

She spun around, nearly colliding with the stranger. He stepped back just in time, a muscle in his sharp jaw twitching with irritation as his dark eyes fixed on her face.

"You are too kind," she managed, dipping into a curtsy. "I am afraid I do not know you, sir, I have not made your acquaintance—"

"Martel," he said, the French word brittle in his mouth. "Lord Martel. Your... friend, the Duke of St. Albans, asked me to look after you, should you need rescuing." He frowned a little, glancing at the people around them. It was the minutest of expressions; his chiseled, pale face had hardly changed at all. "Mind you, it looks as if he was right, for once."

Her head reeling, Rosaline could only stare up at him. *Tall,* she thought. *And thin.* "You are... friends... with the Duke?"

His head twitched a little, and his silvery blond hair shone in the candlelight. His irritation seemed to grow. "Not... friends, so much as comfortable enemies."

"Enemies?" she repeated, her stomach giving an unhelpful swoop. "Then why are you—?"

"Punch?" he said, and with that, he took her hand and led her into the next room.

Rosaline couldn't help noticing the way people seemed to shrink from Lord Martel's presence as he made his way through the crowd. It was the exact opposite of being with the Duke. "my lord," she said, once they were within sight of the punch bowl, "I am afraid I don't understand—"

"The Duke is delayed," he said, passing her a glass of punch. His hand, its knuckles heavy with silver rings, hovered over a platter of *vol-au-vents* before he seemed to think better of it. "He is arriving later than he'd intended, and he asked me to keep an eye on you. Seems you're having trouble with a few overenthusiastic suitors."

For some reason, this explanation did not help in the least. Rosaline's head continued to spin and she sipped at her punch. It was watery, unimpressive. *The Duke,* she thought. *The Duke tasked someone who is barely his friend to... what, protect me? Keep me company? Why would he do that? And what else did he tell this man?* "What about Cadogan?"

Another minute expression flitted across his face — this time, a sardonic grin. "Ah," said Lord Martel. "Cadogan is likewise delayed."

"Is he," she replied, her voice flat. *Damn,* she thought, knocking back the rest of her punch. She was sure Charlotte would forget Crawley in an instant once she saw Cadogan again. "I don't suppose you can tell me why?"

"Ah," he said again, taking her empty glass and sliding it onto a tray. "Not my honor to impinge, I'm afraid, as much as I would like to. But fear not, he should appear before long. As is his way."

Curiosity roared through her like a fire. She fought the urge to grab him and shake him until he gave her a straight answer. "So," she said, "how are we to pass the time?"

"In near silence, I would hope." He flashed her a real smile this time, or something close enough to it.

Rosaline reminded herself that she could not smack him. "No," she replied. "I think, at the very least, you could tell me what your connection is to the Duke, and to Cadogan. What is it, childhood rivals?"

Lord Martel gave a very put-upon sigh. He led her to a nearby empty corner, and she leaned against the wall with some relief. "You are correct, Miss Bailey. We were at school together, and we never seemed to get on."

She raised an eyebrow at him. "I cannot see why."

He ignored this. "It's in our blood. His family and mine have never been allies. In fact, some years ago, things got quite dark and dramatic, and while the Duke and I are back to our uneasy truce, our families still prefer to keep a comfortable distance. But, of course, ours is a small world, so butting heads with the Duke was somewhat... written in the stars. He could avoid me no more than I could avoid him."

"What was he like at school?" Rosaline said, before she could help herself.

Martel shot her a glance. It was quick, observant. "Utterly infuriating, to tell you the truth. He's quite clever, when he wants to be, and a bit insufferable about it." Then, to her shock and delight, he actually rolled his eyes. "And he was good at sport."

This was too brilliant. Rosaline leaned in a little. "And?"

"And," Martel acquiesced, "he had a habit of playing the hero."

He glanced at her again. "Which, I suppose, explains our present circumstances."

Unbidden, a blush fluttered across Rosaline's cheeks and she looked away. "He told you."

"I guessed." Martel seemed to conjure a glass of wine from thin air and he sipped at it, contemplative. "He's been very clear about his intentions. I did not imagine he would ever change his mind, even in the presence of such..." He gestured to her entire person, an echo of Lisette.

Rosaline did not know how to defend herself, and more importantly, she did not want to. "We are helping each other."

He sighed in a disinterested sort of way. "So bloody noble. My wife would find this most entertaining, though perhaps not in a way that would flatter you."

"Wife?" Rosaline repeated, not bothering to hide her shock.

"Indeed," he replied, twitching the ring finger of his right hand. A silver ring, heavier and more ornate than the rest, caught the light. He inclined his head to the far corner, where a group of women hovered around a card table. "The one in green."

Rosaline followed his gaze to a short, thin woman with a sleek profile and hair as black as a raven's. Her ballgown was lavish and understated all at once, cut in just the one shade of deep emerald with light beading along the *décolletage*. Her hooded, dark eyes landed on Rosaline, and the plush curve of her ruby-red lips twisted into something of a smile. Then, just as quickly, she looked away, dipping her head towards one of her companions.

"Oh," Rosaline said. "She is very beautiful."

"Perhaps," Martel replied, to her surprise. "Our pairing was determined at birth, so I suppose we must think of each other as, at the very least, passable. Makes for a healthier marriage, you see."

"At birth?" Rosaline repeated. "Really?"

"All the old families do it," he replied, like this explained anything. "But we are uncommonly well-matched. Perhaps our parents were on to something, back then. I lead my life, and she leads hers. And we do throw a spectacular supper party."

"Supper party," Rosaline said, because apparently, that was all she could do. Cling to the wall and try to fathom the reality playing out in front of her. "You do not—?"

"Love her?" Martel finished for her, and he almost shrugged. "Love is a consequence, a choice. Even if it is something you fall into by accident, you first have to be clumsy enough to lose your footing. Though I suppose we do have a very special... regard for one another. We live together quite happily, which must mean something." He took a swallow of wine. "Perhaps that is just a result of knowing one another for our entire lives. Very few surprises, when you've caught someone sneaking a cigar and a whiskey from your father's hidden stash."

Whiskey, Rosaline thought, taking another glance at Martel's wife. She was impressed, in spite of herself. "Why are you telling me this? Surely the town would have a fit if they knew the truth. To say nothing of Madam Kensington."

There. A flint, a spark in his eyes. "Because," he said, raising the glass to his mouth, "there is no better person to keep a secret than one with a secret of their own."

It took a few moments. She stared up at him, feeling mutiny curl under her skin. "You wouldn't," she said, her voice in a low throttle.

"I wouldn't," he agreed, twitching an eyebrow. "Without reason."

Rosaline stared at him some more. "You are protecting him," she said at last, surprise once again overtaking her. "The Duke."

"He is a good man," Martel replied, an edge to his low timbre. "One of the best I know. I will not stand to see him hurt, especially by someone who has known him for all of five minutes."

"Your enemy," she pointed out. "The man you claim you can hardly stand."

"Yes." The muscle in his jaw twitched. "Him."

For a moment, the air between them only thickened, tension pulling them along a wire. Finally, Rosaline leaned back, smiling a little. "I wonder how he would react if he happened to hear the details of this little... *tête-à-tête* of ours."

Then, to her delight, a smile cracked Martel's features and he raised his glass. "I can see why he tolerates your company." When she grinned in reply, he shook his head. "And to think I was worried about how we would pass the time."

"How unfathomable," she said, dry as a bone. "Do you read, my lord?"

"Not if I can help it."

"Shame. There is a remarkable new economic treatise from Denmark, by a gentleman with the name of Jacobsen. I was up for half the other night working through some of his equations. They are quite diverting." When he only stared at her, expressionless, she added, "What are your interests, then?"

"The official line is pheasant-hunting, billiards, and terrorizing my tenants."

"And the unofficial one?"

For all his earlier frankness, now he seemed to hesitate. "Wine," he said, lifting his glass as evidence. "Endless variety and indulgence. The perfect hobby."

"Oh?" She nodded at his glass. "And what do you think of tonight's sampling?"

Lord Martel made an elaborate show of sniffing his wine, taking a long, gurgling sip of it, and giving a resigned shrug. "Absolute swill, darling."

Rosaline burst into a laugh, but before she could recover, Lord Martel stood up straight and schooled his expression. A smooth, Scottish voice behind her said, "I would ask if he was troubling you, my dear, but I believe I already know the answer to that question."

For the second time that evening, Rosaline turned and met the gaze of a stranger.

She was an older woman with large, penetrating eyes and a regal posture, dressed in a sumptuous dark blue that was almost black in the dim lighting. She leaned on a thin cane with a golden handle, and her graying hair was done up in an intricate bun with a small feather cascading over her part. And she looked Rosaline over with a keen gaze, the corner of her mouth twitching.

"Lawrence," the woman said. "Won't you introduce us?"

Lawrence? Rosaline thought as she dipped into a curtsy. *That was too good to be true*—

"May I present Miss Bailey," Martel said, his voice stiff. "Miss Bailey, this is the Dowager Countess McDunn."

"My lady," said Rosaline, bowing her head. "An honor."

The Dowager chuckled, a small, throaty chirp of a sound. "Goodness me. I can see why you are the center of so much attention, Miss Bailey."

Rosaline's face prickled. "You flatter me, my lady."

"Not in the least. When and if I flatter you, you shall know it." The Dowager shot Lord Martel a sharp look. "Is he behaving?"

"So far, my lady."

"I should hope so." The Dowager arched her brow. "He required a firmer hand when he was younger, but I think you are up to the challenge, should it become necessary."

Delight overcame Rosaline and she could not keep herself from smiling. "You knew my lord when he was a child?"

"Of course I did," the Dowager replied. "Just as I knew everyone who crossed my godson's path. Though, of course, this one left more of an impression than others."

"The Dowager Countess," said Martel, "is the Duke's godmother."

"Oh!" Suddenly, things made a lot more sense. "I had no idea. Apologies, my lady."

She spun her cane in reply, knocking Rosaline's words out of the air. "None needed. Even though it is common knowledge, you are new to court, and the uncommon and the common rarely meet." A brief pause, during which she scrutinized Rosaline with her bright, pale blue gaze. "I understand you have caught my godson's eye."

Something caught in Rosaline's throat and stayed there. "Perhaps," she managed. "I would never attempt to speak to the Duke's inclinations."

The Dowager gave her a sharp grin. "What a diplomatic reply." She turned to Martel. "Lawrence, fetch me a glass of wine."

"Are you certain?" he said, looking down at his own wine and wincing a little. "I myself would not indulge in a second glass—"

She rapped him on the leg with her cane. "Lawrence!"

"Very well." With that, Martel headed for the refreshment table, but not before shooting Rosaline a warning look.

"Tell me, Miss Bailey." The Dowager stared her down again, an enigmatic smile playing about her mouth. "Where were you educated?"

For a moment, Rosaline could only stare back at her. "Educated?"

"You think I do not know a good mind when I see one?" The Dowager shook her head. "I have heard whispers of your intellect."

"Then you must know that I would never admit to such a thing in the present company." Rosaline shot a meaningful glance around the room. "Doing so would leave me open to ridicule, or worse."

The Dowager sighed. "I suppose." She leaned in closer. "Though perhaps you could give me a hint? I myself have a particular fondness for the Greek tragedians. Always so delightfully bloody and full of metaphor." After glancing behind her, her voice dropped to a whisper. "I even learned to read Greek. It was easier than trying to find copies of translations."

In spite of herself, Rosaline was impressed. She leaned forward as well, whispering, "I myself learned Latin to read the *Aeneid*.

Greek," she added, "is my next project. I just cannot seem to find a suitable tutor."

The Dowager nodded, thoughtful. "There may be someone," she whispered. "I shall have to see if he is still in retirement. But who knows, perhaps the right entreaty might convince him otherwise." She cocked her head to one side. "The *Aeneid?*"

"And Ovid. Herodotus, Livy, Tacitus." Rosaline shrugged. "Anything I could find, really."

"Ah, yes. You grew up quite alone, I gather?" At Rosaline's nod, the Dowager gave her another thoughtful look. "In a life of solitude, you turned to books. In contrast, my godson turned to the outdoors. There was hardly a day he did not come home with a new creature in his pocket, or an owl following his shadow. And then, of course, there was always Lightfoot — or, I suppose, the Earl, as you know him."

"Yes," Rosaline said, still processing everything she'd just heard. "Owls?"

"Indeed." The Dowager stepped back, resuming her poised stature in time to accept her glass of wine from Martel. "Thank you, Lawrence, though you certainly took your time."

"Not at all, my lady." Martel raised his refilled glass to her before he took a sip.

"I don't suppose you know when my godson will deign to show his face?" she went on. "When he does, he must have an explanation for abandoning Miss Bailey for such an extraordinary length of time."

"He and the Earl are delayed." Lawrence seemed to relish saying it. "He should be along soon." He glanced at Rosaline. "It is still strange, referring to them by title. For years they were just Lightfoot and the Prat."

"Lawrence!" The Dowager thwacked him once again with her cane, and Rosaline stifled a giggle as Martel staggered and winced, nearly spilling his wine. "Manners!"

"That was *not* necessary" he hissed, straightening up. "They're the ones who are late, which makes them far more deserving of your ire."

The Dowager's eyes flashed. "You know better than most, my dear boy, what may come of telling me where to direct my frustration."

Martel bristled, but before he could reply—

"Come now, Lady McDunn, there is no need to be so vindictive." The Duke stepped up to their little cluster, a smile threatening to break through his impassive expression. "Besides, it is too early in the season for mysterious disappearances."

Rosaline looked right at the Duke, taking in his appearance with a glance. He was rumpled around the edges, as if he'd gotten dressed in a hurry, and his hair, though messy as usual, was damp. His tie was crooked, and he hastened to straighten his shirt cuffs before he met her gaze. His eyes were bright, warm. This, she realized, was the most relaxed she had ever seen him.

The Dowager seemed to be thinking along similar lines as she considered her godson. "You look as though you've just rolled off a vegetable cart. Where on earth have you been?"

"Ask me no questions," said the Duke, "and I'll tell you no lies."

"Incorrigible," said the Dowager, though it almost sounded fond. "I was just saying to Lawrence what a pity it was to see Miss Bailey all but abandoned by you, Your Grace."

"You seem to imply that Miss Bailey is not more than capable of holding her own," he replied. He was still looking at Rosaline, and Rosaline did not quite know how to handle it.

"Holding her own, yes," the Dowager allowed, "but one cannot dance by oneself." Her eyes sparkled as she looked at Rosaline. "Unless Miss Bailey knows something I do not."

Rosaline smiled back at her. "I do not think that is possible, my lady."

The Dowager chuckled and turned back to her godson.

"Please ensure that she has a most pleasant evening. Come along, Lawrence, let us leave them to their sweet nothings."

Lord Martel seemed thoroughly repulsed by the idea of sweet nothings, but he nodded. "Miss Bailey, a pleasure." He met Hal's gaze. "Prat."

"Rodent."

And with that, Martel turned and escorted the Dowager into the next room. Rosaline watched them leave, still smiling.

"I am truly sorry for my lateness," the Duke said. "It was not my intention to leave you feeling abandoned."

"Not at all, Your Grace," Rosaline replied, then at his warning look, quickly added, "Hal." The name still felt so peculiar in her mouth. Too personal, too real. "I enjoyed conversing with them. Lord Martel certainly is of singular character."

"That is a generous way of putting it," the Duke replied. He was still fussing with bits of his clothing. "I should have known that she would corner you. She has a habit of being obstinate and... well, nosy."

"I suppose she has a right. She is your godmother, after all."

"Yes, she's always been somewhat protective."

Rosaline filed that information away for later thought. "Now, if I ask after your appearance, will you give me the honest answer you could not afford your godmother?"

For a moment, the Duke almost smiled. "Perhaps," he said. He was looking around the room, taking stock. "I did not answer because I knew she would not approve. I was boxing."

Rosaline wasn't sure what she had expected, but it wasn't that. "Boxing?"

"Sparring," he clarified, plucking a glass of champagne from a passing tray. "It lasted rather longer than it was supposed to, and I became separated from my driver. Edward and I had to make our way through half the East End before we were able to hail a decent cab and get back to my house. God, I'm parched." He took a gulp of champagne and pulled a face. "Ugh, that's awful."

"The East End?" she repeated, having trouble imagining it.

"Yes," he replied, like it was nothing. The Duke swallowed the rest of the champagne, winced again, and traded his empty glass for a full one from another passing tray. "I had to rinse off and change." Which explained his damp hair. When he took yet another swig of champagne, his face caught the light. It was then that she noticed the dark, blotchy area along the left edge of his jaw.

Rosaline's mouth fell open and, before she could stop herself, she reached out to grip his arm, her nails digging through her gloves and into the fabric of his jacket. "Surely I am imagining things," she hissed. "Surely that is not a fresh bruise on your face!"

To her utter amazement, the Duke did smile then, cheeky and sheepish. "Dean has a mean right hook," he said, by way of answering her. "And usually, he aims below the collar."

"What?!" she bit out, then, again before she could stop herself, she darted out a hand and shoved him in the ribs. "Like that?!"

The Duke hunched into the blow, letting out a strangled wheeze. His champagne tipped dangerously close to the edge of his glass. He shot her a glare even as he clung to her arm, trying to remain standing. "That," he bit out, "was uncalled for."

"This is unacceptable!" Rosaline hissed, anger flaring under her skin. It was taking all of her willpower not to throttle him, or worse, walk away from him entirely. "We have to dance! We have to mingle! You cannot do all that while nursing a set of cracked ribs—"

"Bruised." His eyes flashed as he struggled to draw breath. "Not cracked."

"Do you wish to test that hypothesis?" She glared at him, her good mood evaporating like wax from a candle. "I thought you were taking this seriously."

Her words seemed to unnerve him. And it unnerved *her*, this still-new privilege of seeing actual emotions on his face. "I am," he managed. "I did not think—"

"That much," she spat. "Is clear."

"Rosaline," he said, in a low, pleading tone she had never heard him use before. It turned her veins to ice, freezing her in place. It was the only reason she did not leave. The Duke — *Hal* — looked at her, and his gaze bore into her own. In spite of herself, she shivered. "Would you rather I had not come at all?"

"We had a deal," she said, because if he did not give her real answers, she would not give them to him, either. "We had a deal, and you—"

"I *know.*" There it was. Frustration. He heaved a great breath and forced himself upright and out of her grasp. "Trust me, none of it went according to plan."

She scoffed, some heat returning to her body. "And yet you allowed it to happen anyway." Rosaline shook her head, her gaze drifting to some of the nearby guests. They had taken little notice of her and the Duke; dim corners had their benefits, she supposed. "Perhaps we were foolish to think this was possible."

"Rosaline." Pleading, still, but with an edge of rebuke. "It has only been a few days. It is far too soon for either of us to give up, and odds are, we will have to weather much worse than this if we are to make it through the entire season."

She closed her eyes for just a moment. "I suppose." When she opened them again, she looked right at him. "Please do not do this again."

She had not realized how much was in that sentence until it was hanging in the air between them, heavy and full. The Duke — *Hal* — looked back at her, and he nodded. "I will not."

Then, right at that imperfect moment, Cadogan decided to appear, a glass of wine in one hand and his tie in the other. Like Hal, he was rumpled, his clothing creased and somewhat messily put together. "Miss Bailey!" he said, delighted. "I have found you at last. How is your evening?"

Rosaline managed a smile. "Lovely, thank you. The Duke has just been telling me of all your adventures this afternoon."

Cadogan's ears went bright red, though his expression did not change. Rosaline wondered if that took practice. "Yes, uh— a most splendid, if infuriating time though it was." He sort of laughed. "Forgive me, I am still playing catch-up — where is Lady Prince?"

"I am not sure," Rosaline replied. "We were separated shortly after we arrived. She may be in the ballroom, waiting for the dancing to begin."

"Good God," said the Duke. He was leaning against the wall now, nursing his champagne. "I'd almost forgotten about the Queen."

The music would not start until she arrived. "Me too," said Rosaline, and for a moment, she could not feel more different than she had when she'd arrived. She no longer felt excited, ready, confident. Instead, she was tired, and anxious to get it all over with. She looked up at Cadogan, at his eager face, and realized that she had to tell him something. "Though... I am afraid Charlotte has already promised her first dance to someone else."

Something flickered across his face and was gone. "Has she? No matter." He took a sip of wine. "I arrived late, after all. I cannot expect her to wait for me."

"I suppose," Rosaline said, because she wasn't sure what else to say. Charlotte was rather a mystery to her at the moment, as well.

Thankfully, she was saved by a blast of sound — a fanfare, to announce the Queen's arrival. It was as if lightning had hit the manor. Everyone flew into a flurry of excitement, abandoning their drinks and their cards as they flocked to the entrance hall, desperate to be the first to see her.

Cadogan's shoulders straightened and he drained his glass. "Looks like we've been summoned."

"You go ahead," said the Duke, somewhat to her surprise. "We'll be along in a minute."

If Cadogan was taken aback by this, he hid it. He merely

nodded, gave Rosaline a smile, and followed the crowds into the next room.

When Rosaline turned, the Duke was looking at her in that uncanny, piercing way of his. "Only waltzes," he said. "And slow ones at that."

She almost smiled. "Yes," she agreed. "That seems fair."

"One other thing," he said. He pushed himself away from the wall, put down his empty glass, and made his way over to an open window, where the night air poured in. "I cannot begin the evening with the taste of champagne in my mouth." The Duke paused with his hand on the windowsill. "I hope that is what we can do. Begin again."

Every part of her wanted to shake her head, to deny him this bookend to his apology. But then, she said, "Yes. We can."

He gave her a nod. "Good." With that, he nearly threw himself out the window, leaning out far enough to grab something and pull it back in with him.

Rosaline could only watch, mute with confusion, as he crossed the empty room, closing the distance between them and holding out a bundle of leaves and flowers. "Honeysuckle?" she said.

The corner of his mouth twitched. "Indulge me?"

"I—" For a moment, she did not know what to say. "I haven't... not since I was a child."

"Go on, then," he said, teasing. The Duke pressed a few blooms into her gloved hand.

Rosaline looked down at the flowers, sumptuous and golden yellow in the low light, and felt a part of her resolve give way. She gathered the flowers together with their blooms in her palm, pinched the ends, pulled, and bent to drink the nectar.

It was sun-warm, sweet, far more delicious than any punch. Rosaline could not hold back a smile as the Duke copied her, a drop of nectar catching in the corner of his mouth.

"See?" He almost grinned. "Much better."

"It is," she agreed, reaching for more flowers. "How did you—?"

"The house is covered in it," the Duke replied. "I supposed that we may as well make the most of it."

A small part of Rosaline thrilled at the way he said *we,* the nectar sliding down her throat in a way that felt almost forbidden. "Well then," she said. "Let's go see the Queen."

"Yes," said the Duke, flinging the spent blooms onto a nearby table. He offered her his arm and the corner of his mouth twitched. "Let's."

**Madam Kensington's High Society Papers,
No. 25**

I believe it was my mother who once told me, "If you've seen one, you've seen them all!" — and I am afraid that turn of phrase is all I can offer you, dear readers, regarding the sullen, lackluster events of last night's ball. (My mother, of course, was talking of something else entirely!) True enough, the surroundings were splendid, the food passed muster, the wine potable though not enjoyable. The only real saving grace to the entire evening was the arrival and presence of Her Majesty — a fact of which, I am sure, she was all too aware. What else could explain the curl of complacency about her Royal mouth? (Though, perhaps it was the unmistakable whiff of young love floating over the dance floor, especially when a certain couple waltzed past...)

What a relief it is, knowing that we shall have a break from these terrible Balls for at least one evening. *But Madam Kensington,* you may say, your hand to your chest in shock, *nothing interesting ever happens at the opera! What on earth will you write about?* To that, my dear readers, I only say what is true — there is always plenty going on around you. You must simply open your eyes — or whip out your opera glasses — to see it.

And what shall we see? The Unknown and the Recluse, edging ever-closer to one another, trading glances and smiles when they think none of us are watching? Or perhaps the shining Star herself, who seems to have set aside her initial infatuation in favor of courting her options? This, my lovelies, was perhaps the smartest choice she could have made. A choice which I would, at one point, not have imagined her capable of making. But then again, what is a season without its surprises?

❧

"MISS BAILEY!" HISSED MRS. RANDOLPH, RED SPLOTCHES growing on her cheeks. "Will you stop fussing at your dress!"

Rosaline fought back a scowl but obeyed. Charlotte's dress did technically fit, it was just... a rather more daring cut than she was used to wearing. "I can assure you, it will be no small miracle if, somehow, the seams do not burst before the tea arrives."

"Hush!" Mrs. Randolph's eyes flashed. "There is hardly any need for such dramatics. You should show some gratitude to your friend for allowing you to borrow her beautiful dress."

Rosaline took a breath — as much of a breath as she could take, in this dress — and turned her attention to Charlotte, who was sitting opposite her in the carriage. Charlotte met her gaze, something like mirth dancing in her bright blue eyes, though her expression remained flat and serene. "Charlotte," said Rosaline, hoping that her friend could hear the sarcasm. "Thank you ever so much for allowing me to borrow the dress that Mrs. Randolph insisted I wear."

"Not at all," Charlotte replied, over Mrs. Randolph's choke of outrage. "You wear it far better than I ever have."

Rosaline rolled her eyes at the compliment and shot her friend a genuine smile. "You indulge me," she said, just as the carriage rolled to a stop. The door popped open, and Rosaline vaulted out of her seat.

It was just as well that she had a diligent footman. The sight before her nearly bowled her over completely.

Rosaline had heard, of course, about Kew Gardens. Mrs. Randolph herself had foamed at the mouth about it, and even Charlotte had told her that it was sure to be a wonderful, magical place teeming with diverse life and beauty. But nothing could truly have prepared her for the sight that greeted her now.

"Breathtaking, isn't it?" said Charlotte beside her. Her hand found Rosaline's and squeezed it. "I know, I could sit out here all day."

"And ruin your complexion," Mrs. Randolph muttered as their carriage rolled away. "Come."

They followed another footman along a wide gravel path, surrounded by towering hedges and dense flowerbeds overflowing with blooms. One end of the land dipped into a wide, low pond, and at the other, a dense collection of trees promised shade and wildlife. Butterflies swam in the air, and the trees roared with birdsong. They were approaching a huge, vaulted glass building, which Rosaline supposed to be a greenhouse. She was proven correct as they stepped in and found themselves enveloped by a musky, humid air.

"The Queen is receiving visitors on the terrace," said their footman as he led them past an overwhelming collection of orchids. "But feel free to wander the gardens as you please."

The terrace was bright and a welcome change from the stuffy air of the greenhouse. Tables and chairs were arranged in neat clusters, groaning beneath the weight of cakes and pastries and what looked to be half the Royal silver. The Queen was standing by the fountain, dressed in a resplendent canary yellow, and she gave Rosaline a sharp look as she curtsied, the hem of her dress brushing the Queen's.

"Child," the Queen said. "What on earth are you wearing?"

Behind her, Rosaline could hear Mrs. Randolph stifle a faint choking noise. She offered the Queen her best placating smile and said, "I had to borrow an old dress of Lady Prince's, Your Majesty. Apparently, I did not pack enough dresses prior to my departure from Paris."

"I imagine it is difficult to prepare, without a mother's guidance." The Queen's gaze had not shifted an inch. "Have you heard from her family at all, now that you have returned to England?"

For a brief moment, Rosaline felt as though she'd missed a step. Her stomach swooped and the previously warm, delicious air suddenly felt stifling. "No, ma'am," she said. "I have not." *And do not expect to*, she did not say.

A brief pause. The Queen just stared at her, that dark gaze drilling into Rosaline's own. Then, the moment broke, and she turned to Charlotte. "And look at you, my Star. You are magnificent. Far beyond any comparison I could possibly hope to make."

Charlotte curtsied like a doll, the sunlight beaming in her hair. "You are too kind, Your Majesty."

"I've heard you have your pick of suitors," said the Queen, and the pride in her voice was unmistakable. "Have any stood out more than others?"

"Perhaps one or two, ma'am," Charlotte replied. For a moment, Rosaline looked at her enigmatic little face and could only envy it.

"Well, the cream will rise in time, my dear." The Queen gave them both a nod. "Do enjoy yourselves. The *éclairs* in particular are indulgence manifested."

They curtsied and stepped away to allow the next guests an audience. "*Éclairs*," Rosaline hissed to Charlotte. "We must—"

"I think not," Mrs. Randolph snapped, happy to be sharp now that they were out of the Queen's earshot. "It is never a good idea to attend the opera on a full stomach."

Rosaline snorted. "*Così fan tutte* is hardly a bloodbath. What, are we expected to swoon in the stands like fathers in a birthing room?"

"Hold your tongue!" hissed Mrs. Randolph, her eyes flashing. "If you cannot keep a civil word in that mouth of yours—"

"I would be more inclined to do so," said Rosaline coolly, "had I not been squeezed into a sausage casing this afternoon."

"Come, Rosaline." Charlotte linked their arms. "I would like to try the peach tea."

With that, she swept them across the terrace, leaving Mrs. Randolph wheezing with anger. "You did that on purpose," Charlotte breathed to her, once they were a good distance away.

Rosaline hummed, smiling at a cluster of ladies. "Well, my gentle nature is in short supply today, Charlotte."

Charlotte's smile was sparkling. "Bold to assume you ever had one at all."

"You fox," Rosaline chided as they reached a free table. A few footmen appeared and helped them into their chairs. She did not fail to notice the way the men's eyes stuck to her figure like glue, and fought the urge to throw a chair at them.

The peach tea was indeed delicious, but Rosaline stared mournfully at the small platters of food. She'd been joking earlier, about her seams bursting, but now, under the hot sun and a dozen stares, she was actually quite worried about it happening. A single cucumber sandwich could make or break this dress.

"Rosaline!" came a voice laced with surprise. "You're here!"

Rosaline looked up to find Katherine, dressed in a surprisingly pink dress, smiling at her. "Katherine!" she exclaimed, managing to stand up and give her a hug. "Well met indeed, just when the party threatened to list into dullness."

Katherine gave a chuckle. "You flatter me, as usual." She leaned forward and dropped her voice. "I am only here thanks to my aunt's forceful hand. Please, do not let me alone."

"Miss Knight!" Rosaline said loudly, pulling her down into a chair. "You must join us!"

"It is so lovely to make your acquaintance," Charlotte said to Katherine. "Rosaline has told me such wonderful things about you."

For a moment, Katherine could only stare at Charlotte like a complete idiot, transfixed.

"I know," Rosaline muttered to her behind her raised teacup. "I would say you'll get used to it after a while, but you don't, really."

"The—the pleasure is all mine, my lady," Katherine finally managed. "It is an honor—"

Charlotte gave a light, trilling laugh. "Oh, you are sweet. You must have one of these strawberry tarts, they are divine."

All three of them then proceeded to spend a very delightful hour talking and gossiping about everything and nothing. Rosaline learned even more details of Katherine's life — she had three older brothers, who had given her a competitive streak a mile wide and particular knack for arm-wrestling. Katherine enjoyed riding horses more than almost anything else, and even, to Rosaline's shock, had been taught how to hunt and track.

"Really?" Rosaline whispered to her, agape. "You've killed an animal?"

Katherine smirked. "Three best stags in my father's collection, thank you very much."

Even Charlotte, who Rosaline would've expected to blanch at this topic, was transfixed. "Does anyone know?"

"No one outside the family," Katherine replied. "Well, except for you two." She winked at them, and Charlotte giggled with delight.

They were drawing a lot of attention, Rosaline realized. Other young ladies had begun hovering near their table, inclining their heads, hoping to snatch a piece of conversation, or, perhaps, an invitation. Even the mothers and chaperones were looking their way, with raised eyebrows and cautious, even jealous, expressions. For a moment, a surge of *something* went through

Rosaline's body — something that felt a lot like satisfaction. Like winning.

This feeling only deepened when she saw Miss Brown standing beside a table at the far end, flanked by those twins, her expression thunderous. The abandoned sets of plates and teacups told Rosaline that she had recently lost quite a crowd of supplicants — those who now hovered by Rosaline, Charlotte, and Katherine. Something was happening, here. Something was changing. Shifting, like the sands beneath the sea.

With that, Rosaline's gaze drifted to the nearest group of debutantes and she smiled. "Miss Harris, Lady Stuart, Lady Ednam. Won't you join us?"

"Oh, yes!" Charlotte chimed in, eagerly turning to the young women behind her. "Lady Linley, Lady Wolmer — you must take some tea!"

All the ladies beamed with delight, and a general chaos ensued as the footmen stepped in to push several tables together to make sure everyone had a seat. Rosaline watched everything unfold with a distinct sense of pleasure, chatting happily to Lady Stuart about the good weather, all too aware that she had never imagined she'd feel this way during the dreaded season — in control, powerful. Ruthless.

Perhaps it is silly, she reflected as she sipped at a fresh cup of tea. Charlotte, Lady Ednam, Katherine, and Lady Linley were now having a very good-natured argument about something or other, but Rosaline had tuned them out. *Perhaps it is silly to care about this sort of thing, about who sits where, about who listens to whom, about who has the most friends.*

Then again, she thought, stealing another glance at Miss Brown, who was looking more agitated by the moment. *Perhaps it isn't.*

"—they are severely misguided, look what happened at Bautzen—"

"—Liverpool does not seem to care, he has a clear agenda—"

Rosaline frowned, her awareness circling back to the conversation happening in front of her. This was the last thing she'd expected these women to be talking about.

"What do you think of it? Wellington going to the peninsula?"

"I hardly know what to think. I can see the reasoning — it is closer to Britain, so we might have more of an advantage. But attacking Napoleon in his home country—?"

"That might be just what he needs, a visitor on his front doorstep. It will rattle him—"

Just then, Rosaline glanced over her shoulder and saw a cluster of mothers approaching. In seconds, they'd be within earshot.

"Yes, Lady Linley," she said, loudly enough that half the ladies flinched. "I do agree with you, those tassels were too much for Countess Ramsay, they swallowed her figure and were entirely the wrong shade of blue."

For a moment, they all stared at her, speechless. Rosaline gave them a pointed look, and saw the recognition flicker in their faces.

"Oh, yes," said Lady Linley, picking up her teacup. "Tassels were all the rage, what, ten years ago, but we must keep up with the times—"

"That was very artful," Charlotte said to Rosaline later, when they were strolling by the edge of the pond, a short distance away from the terrace. Katherine was with them, looking more relaxed and happier than Rosaline had ever seen her. "The way you evaded the oncoming attack."

"As always, Charlotte, you are too kind. I merely happened to see it in time." Now that it was just the three of them, Rosaline bit her lip and took the leap. "I must admit, I was rather surprised... at the turn the conversation happened to take."

Charlotte cocked her head to one side, and even Katherine shot her a glance. "Why is that?"

Rosaline's face went hot. "They were talking of... politics. The war. And strategy."

"And?" Charlotte pressed. When Rosaline remained silent, she smiled. "I see. You are surprised to find that someone other than you has a brain."

Rosaline could cook an egg on her forehead. "No," she tried, "I just did not expect—"

"Of course they are interested in the war, Rosaline," said Katherine. "It affects everyone, even those of us in glass houses. We all know someone in the army, some of us even have military men in our families." She shrugged, but Rosaline caught the tension in her shoulders. "And France is only a short boat ride away."

"No, I—" Rosaline tried again. "I did not mean—"

"I am sure you didn't," Charlotte said lightly, giving her hand a squeeze. "But do not worry. You have us all quite beat when it comes to literature and mathematics. I still cannot comprehend those colossal sums to which you devote your time, and doubt I ever will."

"I just did not think," Rosaline went on, "that it was common. For women to be educated, in England."

Katherine and Charlotte shared a look, a look that Rosaline could not begin to comprehend. "We are not," said Katherine. "Not really. Not the way you were. But most of us find a way to steal our father's morning paper, to sneak into the library in the middle of the night and read the books no one has touched in years. And we share it, all of it, with each other. And we steal moments, when we might discuss these things with those who might share our perspective. As you just saw."

"Goodness," Rosaline breathed, looking out across the glassy, slippery pond. She felt a little dizzy, and not just because of her damn dress.

"This is not to say," Katherine went on, "that we *all* share this concern for current events, for politics. Not everyone has the... curiosity."

Then, as if following this invisible cue, there came a burst of noise from along the bank. A snarl of frustration, loud enough that Rosaline, Katherine, and Charlotte could all hear it.

A slow smirk spread across Katherine's face, and she beckoned to the others, guiding them behind the branches of a nearby weeping willow, just out of sight for anyone approaching from the other end of the bank. Breathing in the sweet, dusty scent of the willow, Rosaline's eye found a gap between the feathery branches, and she watched, anticipation knotting in her stomach.

She did not have to wait long. Within moments, their new point of interest came into view, golden curls flying around a red, angry face.

"—cannot stand to even look at her, that— that— witch!" Miss Brown spat, giving a very unladylike stomp into the soft earth. Her chest was heaving and she spun around to face — the twins, of course, who else? "She comes in here, simpering and waltzing around as if she owns the place, when she hasn't been so much as *glimpsed* in this country for nearly ten years, and what, we're all supposed to fawn over her and fall to her feet?! I bloody well think not!"

Beside Rosaline, Katherine shoved a gloved hand over her nose and mouth, stifling a bolt of laughter. Charlotte was grinning, drinking in the scene with something akin to triumph.

"She's not even that pretty!" Miss Brown went on, a savage edge to her words. "She looks as though she's rolled in a bit of dirt and slapped on a diamond necklace to make up for it! And that dress — *oh*, did you see that dress?! She looks like a harlot! Fresh off the streets of Soho, not even worth half a shilling—!"

"Did you hear that?" Rosaline whispered, grinning. Katherine trembled with suppressed laughter. "I am not even worth a measly shilling—"

"Who *does* she think she *is?!*" Miss Brown was becoming quite hysterical. The twins were starting to look nervous as they hovered. "Trying to steal all my friends, flashing those tits and those hips, it's no wonder the Duke only has eyes for her, she's probably already let him—"

"Miss Brown," said Rosaline, stepping out from behind the willow. She cleared her throat, biting her tongue to keep from smiling, and wished she had a painter beside her at that moment. She would've loved to have a record of Miss Brown's expression to outlast them both. "As riveting as this is, I feel it is my duty to tell you that you sound quite ridiculous."

Miss Brown seemed to rally, though one of the twins looked ready to faint. "I was being honest," she spat. "Not ridiculous in the least."

"Really?" said Rosaline. She heard the branches shift and knew that Charlotte and Katherine had stepped in behind her. "Then I am sure the other guests would be happy to hear the unimaginative, petty vitriol you would use to spoil such a pleasant afternoon."

To her surprise, Miss Brown marched right up to her, seething at her with an anger that was almost laughable. "The other guests," Miss Brown snapped, "would agree with me."

"Would they?" Rosaline said, glancing at the terrace. A small audience was forming, drawn by the noise. "Refresh my memory as to what, precisely, they would agree with?"

"That you are an incessant social climber with a half-baked lineage and the face of a second-rate charwoman!" cried Miss Brown. "That you put on airs and graces far above your station, and have bewitched the Duke into keeping your company!"

Rosaline did laugh then. "If you think the Duke of St. Albans susceptible to such a trick, you truly have no grasp of reality at all."

"Nor do you!" Miss Brown heaved a great breath. "You think you are so special, but everything you are is just because your mother condescended to accept your pathetic father!"

Something ice-cold settled into Rosaline veins and she stared down at Miss Brown. "Do not," she said, "speak a word against my parents!"

Miss Brown let out a scream of laughter. "I can and I shall!" She took a step back, not noticing that she was stepping directly into mud. "I shall say whatever I—!"

The world seemed to slow. One moment, Miss Brown took another step back, and the next moment, she was gone, swallowed by the pond and replaced by a terrific splash.

A stunned silence fell over the party. Rosaline could only gape as there came a muffled burble, then Miss Brown's face, red and puffy, surfacing from the water. She thrashed like a caught fish, and great waves of water and mud surged into shore.

"Miss Brown," Rosaline cried. She reached out. "Let me help you!"

Miss Brown locked gazes with her, and reached out in return. Then, she gave a hard pull, and Rosaline found herself flying through the air and into the ice-cold, muddy water.

It hit her like a wall and she gasped and gagged all at once, hitting the bottom of the pond. Shuddering, it took enormous effort for her to kick out and stand up, spitting out half a lung's worth of water. By the time she shoved her hair out of her eyes, she realized that the tea party crowd had descended upon the pond and the shore erupted into utter pandemonium.

Skin numb, ears ringing, Rosaline let herself be pulled into Charlotte and Katherine's warm embrace, just as Miss Brown was heaved out of the water by the twins. The mothers were shrieking, the footmen were swarming, and just when she thought things couldn't get any worse—

"What on earth is this nonsense!" boomed a very deep, Royal voice. The Queen came marching through the crowd, the guests scattering around her. She stared at Rosaline, then at Miss Brown. "Never have I seen such a display from two such refined young ladies!" She took a great breath, then continued in a low, deadly voice. "I would consider this matter resolved at once. If I hear so much as a whisper of you two arguing, I shall make my displeasure known." The Queen gave Rosaline a final cut-throat look, and Rosaline could only stare back at her. "And someone get this child a shawl, half the footmen have already forgotten their own names."

And then, to Rosaline's astonishment, the Queen shot her a tiny, sharp smile.

"Charlotte," Rosaline gritted out, snapping her fan shut. "If you do not stop talking at once—"

"No, truly." Charlotte was grinning and fluttering her lacy lilac fan across her face. "That is why they are all staring—"

Rosaline gave a humorless laugh. "Oh, really? I thought it was because my tits and my hips could stop traffic—"

Charlotte seemed to consider this. "Well, they could, but news of your spat with Miss Brown has traveled far and wide. Most versions claim that you pushed her—"

A blush flooded Rosaline's face and she pulled Charlotte aside. They were in the foyer of the Theater Royal in Covent Garden, and the air was tense with summer heat. There was enough of an excited crowd that their presence was not too obvious, but heads still turned to stare at Rosaline, and she could practically see Rumor flying through the room on her shining chariot. It did not help that Rosaline's dress — another borrowed from Charlotte — was just as if not more daring than the first. "Charlotte," she hissed. "I cannot be expected to sit through—"

"Good evening, ladies."

Rosaline looked up at Cadogan and the Duke as they approached. They were dressed quite splendidly in formal suits, and the Duke's hair was almost neat. "Oh, yes, hello," she said, then turned back to Charlotte. "What was I supposed to do, let her flounder around like an idiot—?"

"Seems we are interrupting a most intriguing conversation," said Cadogan, genial as ever. He inclined his head. "A pleasure as always, Lady Prince." He turned to Rosaline. "Miss— Bailey!" The word turned into a squawk as he finally looked at her, and his face went as red as a tomato. "You both look," he went on, his voice half an octave higher, "lovely!"

Rosaline sighed as Charlotte smiled and curtsied.

"Prongs?" Cadogan squeaked, then he cleared his throat and tried again. "Prongs, do greet the lady—"

The Duke said nothing. He'd gone a very funny color and he was looking, quite resolutely, at Rosaline's face.

"Prongs," Cadogan hissed, closing the distance between them. He muttered something in the Duke's ear and gave him a bit of a shake. Rosaline caught the barest edge of the words — "pull yourself together—" and for a moment, almost smiled.

The Duke seemed to rally. He cleared his throat and stepped forward, not looking anywhere lower than her chin. "Miss Bailey," he said, his voice deeper than usual. "How are you—?"

"Do not ask," Charlotte said as Rosaline groaned and slumped against the wall.

"Why?" managed the Duke, but then, the bells began to ring.

"Oh, dear," said Rosaline, standing up and looking towards the entrance. "I'm not sure my father made it in time—"

"He will be here," Charlotte assured her, patting her on the arm. "Come, let's find our seats."

"Where are you sitting?" said Cadogan. He fell into step with them as they made their way to the main doors, swallowed by the crush of people.

"Up in the grand tier, with my father," said Charlotte.

"That is where we are sitting as well," said Cadogan, delighted. "May we escort you?"

"Certainly." Charlotte beamed at him, and Cadogan beamed in return. Rosaline hid a smile, then noticed that the Duke had fallen in step beside her.

"I gather," he said in an undertone, "that you had an interesting afternoon."

"Don't," she hissed back. "I will not even speak of it."

Something played about on his face. Now that he was closer, she could see the faint shadow of the bruise on his jaw, darker now than it had been the night before. "How I wish I could have been there to witness it. Miss Rosaline Bailey, dripping wet and ready to kill."

"Behave!" She thwacked him on the arm with her fan. As more and more people joined the crowd, she and the Duke were pushed closer together and Charlotte and Cadogan were pulled further away. "It was all Miss Brown's fault; you should have heard the things she was saying about me. What was I supposed to do, ignore her?"

"No," he returned. "And while I am certain that you did not push her, I rather wish you had."

Rosaline stared at him. "You do?"

The Duke met her gaze, a haze of red still along his cheekbones. "Yes."

"Your program, Miss," came the usher's voice, and his leer met her chest. Scowling, Rosaline snatched the bit of paper from him and shoved her way past, barely noticing the Duke following her. Some way ahead, she could see Charlotte's shining bun and Cadogan's dutiful ear. With a huff, she turned in the opposite direction, away from the crowd of guests, and made her way along the hall.

"How on earth am I meant to make it through this evening?" she threw over her shoulder, certain that the Duke would catch it. "I already draw enough attention as is, and now half the peers think I tried to drown a girl—"

"Trust me," he replied. "It is a miracle that Miss Brown has survived unscathed thus far."

"To put it gently." They'd reached her target. Rosaline closed in on the footman, swiped a glass of wine from his tray, and downed it in a series of gulps.

"Well done." The Duke's words were warm, amused. He leaned against the wall, content to watch her test the limits of her own reputation. "That is certainly one way to pass the time."

"If I am to face half of London," Rosaline replied, taking a great breath before she traded her empty glass for a fresh one, "I shall need more than a little courage."

"Good point. Though I do hope you managed to eat something after they fished you out of the pond?"

Rosaline polished off her second glass and snorted. "What do you think?" she said to the footman, who was younger than them and had far too innocent a face. "Do you think the seams on this dress could survive my consumption of even a mouthful of food?"

The footman turned an alarming shade of puce. "My— my lady— I do not—"

"Point made," said the Duke, taking her by the elbow and steering her down the hall. "No need to traumatize the servants."

Rosaline's body thudded from the alcohol, and for a moment all she could think about was the place where his thumb caught the bare skin of her arm. "Do not patronize me," she hissed back. "You have no idea—"

"Yes, yes, you can berate me later." He guided her towards the stairs. "Did you manage to enjoy the tea at all, apart from its conclusion?"

"Hardly." She gathered her skirts with a huff and began to ascend the small, steep steps. "I did not get to eat any of the pastry, though I suppose the conversation was passable enough." Rosaline glanced around, making sure they were alone. "There was talk of Bonaparte."

The Duke shot her a glance. "I am not surprised. The situation is tenuous."

"What I would give," she said, heaving the biggest breath she could manage as they mounted the second flight, "to see it for myself."

The Duke shook his head. "Of course. Show her a war, and she runs toward it."

"Can you blame me?" Rosaline countered. They stepped out onto the first floor, where streams of people were finding their seats in the grand tier. Happily, she noticed several footmen bearing trays of wine. "When the height of my entertainment is ill-fitting dresses, Miss Brown, and *Così fan tutte?*"

The Duke frowned at her as they drew even, his eyes gleaming in the reflected light of the stage. "Rosaline, the opera tonight is *Le nozze di Figaro.*"

The world seemed to tilt, and it wasn't just the alcohol. "What?" she managed, her stomach giving a sickening jolt. Rosaline wrenched open her crumpled program and nearly swooned at the sight of those fateful words, printed in large, bold letters. They seemed to throb on the page, growing larger and larger as she stared at them, dizziness threatening to overcome her.

It took her several moments to realize that the Duke was looking at her, his brow creased as his mouth moved, as he said—"Rosaline. Rosaline, are you well?"

"Fine," she managed, even offering a weak smile. *Figaro. Figaro.* She crumpled the program again. "My stays are rather tight this evening. Perhaps I came up the stairs too quickly."

The Duke did not seem convinced. "Do you need a glass of water?"

"No, thank you." She caught a glimpse of her father, standing beside Lord Devon and waving at her. "My father is here. If you'll excuse me—"

"Of course," he said, but she was already gone.

The grand tier was packed, and it looked as though Rosaline was not the only one helping herself to the wine. She side-stepped a handful of ladies, a very old man, and a woman with a strong nose before she drew even with — "Father," she said, relief seeping into her voice as she reached him. They could not embrace in public, but he squeezed her hand and smiled at her. He looked tired, weathered. "I am so glad you could join us this evening."

"As am I," he replied. Because they were surrounded on all sides, they were being watched. Sir Ian seemed to be conscious of this; he squeezed her hand again, and his gaze sharpened. "I was not aware of tonight's program."

"Nor I," Rosaline said. She watched him digest this, saw the flicker of his concern, and squeezed his hand in return.

Sir Ian looked at her for another moment, then he gave her a nod. "You and Charlotte are in the front row. She is already seated."

Rosaline was barely aware of herself as she curtsied and smiled at Lord Devon — *Figaro* — as she squeezed her way past unhelpful lords and ladies — *Figaro* — as she sank into her seat and said something to Charlotte. *Figaro, Figaro, Figaro.*

Four acts, she told herself, staring down over the edge of the balcony at the empty, curtained stage. The candles roared in front of it, and the orchestra rattled their instruments. *Four acts, and you can leave.* Her eyes slipped shut for just the briefest moment. *You can do this.*

After several long minutes, there came a sudden silence. Then a whirring trickle of conversation, then silence again. The crowd held its breath, watching the stage with gleaming eyes. The conductor rose, tapping his baton on his music stand. Instruments up, then the violins.

A cascade of muted strings, then the burr of gentle winds. A blast of sound, and Rosaline's heart leapt into her throat, a fierce thought pounding through her head — *Control yourself.*

The music built, and demurred, and built, the sound reverberating off the walls. Around her, her peers quivered with anticipation. Charlotte's excitement was electric; she was staring at the stage with huge, brilliant eyes, and she was smiling her real smile. Rosaline almost smiled herself, her heart whirring along to the strings, and when the curtain opened, she felt ready.

The first act was easy enough. The wine still throbbed in her veins, and Rosaline lost herself in the comedy of the stage, enthralled by the soprano, something in her squeezing tight to the notes she knew so well, though had not heard in almost a decade.

"Is it not dazzling?" Charlotte said to her at the first intermission, while Rosaline helped herself to another glass of wine.

"Absolutely." Rosaline took a healthy sip, her gaze skimming over the crowd. A short distance away, she caught Cadogan speaking to someone. Beside him, the Duke glowered as usual, but then he looked right at her. She turned away.

The second act passed just as quickly. Rosaline learned to ignore the weight of her stomach, the thick beating of her heart in her ears. The wine helped her to overlook the memories swimming to the surface of her mind, as did her father's gaze, which she could feel on the back of her head. Onstage, Susanna snuck into the closet, and the ghost of old linen drifted over Rosaline's face. She shivered, burying the echo of her mother's laugh, the gleam of sunlight shining in through the crack in the door.

When the intermission bells rang, Rosaline sighed and stood up to stretch, feeling tense, feverish. She turned, and saw, to her shock, that her father's seat two rows behind her was empty. Her gaze darted to Lord Devon, who gave her a sympathetic look.

"My father," she said to Charlotte. "He is gone."

"Oh, no!" Charlotte turned to confirm it for herself. "He probably had to tend to the King, Rosaline."

"I am sorry, dear," said Lord Devon a few minutes later, after he'd pressed through the loitering crowd to check on them. His eyes were glassy in the damp heat of the theater.

Rosaline offered him a smile and reached for a fresh glass of wine. "It is of no issue."

By the time the third act began, the harpsichord and the negotiation echoing in the theater, Rosaline's heart was roaring in her ears, and she was fanning herself as quickly as she could without drawing attention. *Breathe*, she told herself, to little effect.

Figaro, Bartolo, and Marcellina embraced, and something pricked at her eyes. Susanna slapped Figaro in the face and something caught in her throat, leaving her unable to laugh along with the rest of the audience. And then, then.

The stage, empty except for the Countess. Her sharp, regal profile shining above her rich magenta dress as she looked to the heavens and sang, "*Susanna non vien!*"

Rosaline's stomach rolled, and something inside her fractured. Heat swept up her neck and unbidden, fiercely hot tears sprang from her eyes.

Managing a shaky breath, Rosaline slowly stood up, dipped her head, and slipped out of her row. Thankfully, the audience around her was so enraptured by the tender voice filling the theater that no one seemed to notice her departure.

Head spinning, heart pounding, Rosaline staggered out of the theater and down the empty hall, slumping onto a bench below a wide, unflattering portrait of some anonymous, swollen aristocrat. Tears poured down her face in tandem to the echoes of the Countess's questions, carrying the scent of dust and hot chocolate, the warmth of familiar skin, the exultant look on her mother's face when she—

"Stop it!" Rosaline hissed, curling into herself, wiping furiously at her cheeks. The air seemed to disappear, her lungs squeezing around nothing as she tried to stifle a sob.

A throat cleared in a quiet cough. "Are you all right, my lady?"

Rosaline looked up, and blinked at the blurry figure in front of her. "Do I look all right?"

It was a gentleman. Tall, broad, with a playfully handsome face and wavy blond hair parted to one side. His right arm was in a sling, but he carried himself in a sure, unrepentant manner. His bright eyes found hers, and something inside her seemed to stir in response. He gave her a sheepish, lopsided grin and held out a handkerchief with his good hand. "I suppose that was a rather an idiotic question. Allow me to make up for it."

In spite of herself, the corner of her mouth twitched. "Thank you." Rosaline took the handkerchief and began to dab at her face, sneaking another look at the gentleman. He was finely dressed, but in a simple, mended sort of way. *Money*, she thought, *but not much of it.* "Might I know the name of this handkerchief's owner?"

He smiled again, and Rosaline felt a flicker of warmth. "Lieutenant McGrath, my lady."

"Not a lady," she returned, stifling a hiccup. The tightness in her chest seemed to unravel a bit. "Merely a Miss. But you are on leave, then, Lieutenant?"

He nodded. "Not much use for me until I finish healing. And I am only here thanks to a pity-invite from one of the higher-ups." He pointed to the space beside her on the bench. "May I?"

Rosaline nodded before she thought about it, and when she did, her heart throbbed again. *I am alone*, she realized. *With an officer.* "America, or the Continent?"

"The Continent," he replied, then held out his injured arm with a sigh. "It was a stupid mistake — I have never been one to enjoy sitting still. Although..." The Lieutenant cocked his head to one side as he looked at her, playfully speculative. "I have to admit the present company is most helpful in that regard."

Rosaline did smile then. "You flatter me, sir."

"I hope so." Now his smile was cheeky. "A beautiful woman deserves flattery, I think."

She took a shuddering breath, still smiling. "If this is your attempt to stop me from crying, I believe you have succeeded."

"Not a short-lived victory, I hope." He was still looking at her, but his teasing seemed to ebb away. "May I inquire as to the nature of your upset?"

Rosaline snorted, then sighed. She balled up the handkerchief. "Simply a bad day. Not nearly as dramatic as you make it sound."

"I see. I was hoping it was the result of an overzealous gentleman, so we could get ourselves some real entertainment."

She gave him a mocking look. "Why, sir, do you not enjoy the opera?"

"Why do you think I am wandering the halls with a pocket full of handkerchiefs?" he countered. "No, almost anything would be more interesting than this."

Rosaline shook her head. *The wine*, she thought. *That is why I am humoring him.* "You remind me of another gentleman I know."

"Good God, I hope not. I am handful enough on my own." He grinned as she laughed. "There, see? Tears forgotten."

"It appears so." And they were. Rosaline felt warm, soothed. Her skin prickled. "I do not know how I will last through the rest of this."

"You will," he said at once, without a hint of doubt. When she looked at him, he caught her gaze and held it. "I know we only just met, but not every young lady would be brave enough to speak to a Lieutenant alone, let alone endure his abhorrent company." With that, he stood up. "And now, I must be on my way."

"Oh." She blinked, surprised. "Must you?"

The Lieutenant shook his head as he headed for the nearest exit. "I've had my fill of arias for this evening." Then he winked. "Keep the handkerchief."

With that, the Lieutenant disappeared down the stairs, and Rosaline leaned back against the wall, trying to figure out what had just happened. A part of her wondered if she had imagined it all. And why on earth was she grinning?

"Rosaline. Are you all right?"

She looked up and met the gaze of none other than the Duke. He was standing not two feet in front of her, but she had not heard him approach. *Two in one night*, she thought. *Mrs. Randolph would have a heart attack.* "Yes," she said. "Yes, I am fine, thank you." She cleared her throat, then frowned. "What are you doing here?"

To her amazement, that red haze appeared on his cheekbones again, and he looked away. "I saw you leave," he said. "You seemed... upset."

For a brief moment, Rosaline wanted nothing more than to pretend otherwise. But then— *the wine*, she thought— "Yes," she said. "I was, a bit."

His gaze snapped back to hers. "Because of the opera?"

"Because I had a terrible day, Your Grace." Which was technically true. Rosaline shrugged, trying to play it off. "It is getting late. I am tired, uncomfortable, and homesick." *True again*, she realized, but a beat too late.

When she'd first met the Duke, Rosaline would have expected a speech such as this to make him roll his eyes and leave. To her surprise now, he did neither. "I understand," he said, his voice low. "And I must admit, this is my first time at the opera in years. I had forgotten how warm it gets."

She smiled, shaking her head. "I do not know how you survive, wearing those jackets."

"I'd take a jacket over stays any day," the Duke countered, with half a smile. Then, he held out a handkerchief. "May I?"

"That is all right." Rosaline held up her handkerchief in reply. "I brought one from home." The lie was quick, easy, like a reflex. But still, she wondered why she did it. "I thought I might cry at the end."

"And I think," said the Duke, pocketing his handkerchief, "that when the time comes, you will be early to your own death."

"A macabre, back-handed compliment." She stood up with a stifled groan. These shoes really were awful. "Good to know we are back to normal."

A rich baritone boomed down the hall, and Rosaline's breath caught in her throat. The double wedding was about to begin.

The Duke seemed to notice. "It is only a few minutes until the intermission," he said. "We could remain out here, rather than disturb the audience."

Rosaline nodded, feeling a flood of relief. Then, her brain caught up, and she shot the Duke a look. "You know this opera."

He almost smiled. "Of course I do."

She shook her head. "You are rife with contradiction."

"Glad to hear it," he replied, and around them, the music swelled.

❦ 13 ❧

Madam Kensington's High Society Papers,
No. 26

R arely, my dear readers, am I ever proven wrong. Did I not promise that an evening at the opera would be full of surprises? Though even I can admit that much of the evening's delicious tension rested on a certain... shall we say, *confrontation*... that occurred during a very Floral afternoon. A writer such as myself could not possibly comment about the impropriety and admitted violence of certain actions, thrilling and deserved though they might have been. No, like everyone else, I must simply frown, stifle a giggle, and say, "Oh, yes, well... let us hope it does not happen again."

The opera itself was divine, and a winning choice for a season with an unmatched selection of eager Ladies and reluctant Lords — Marriage hangs in the air like a friendly spider, ready to draw us into her web. Even the Queen herself was seen laughing and smiling on more than one occasion, though she was understandably outshone by our favorite Star, whose brilliance glimmered even in the stuffy orchestral air. She certainly seemed to enjoy the evening more than our Sapphire, who appeared to disappear between the acts...

ROSALINE GLANCED ACROSS THE ROOM, WHERE MATTIE WAS IN the middle of doing Charlotte's hair. She watched as an artful, golden length of hair was pulled through another loop and pinned behind itself. Charlotte herself was distracted, smiling down at a scrap of paper. It had to be a letter, though from this distance, Rosaline could not tell if it was written in Cadogan's hand.

Unbidden memories from the last ball floated to the surface of Rosaline's mind. She remembered Charlotte's sudden cold manner, the way she had turned and left when Rosaline expressed her surprise at Charlotte's choice of dance partner. True, Charlotte had been her usual self at the gardens and the opera, but still, Rosaline had no idea what to make of Charlotte's sudden reluctance towards Cadogan. Had something happened between them? Had Cadogan passed some sort of insult? It was almost impossible to imagine such an intelligent, deferential gentleman such as himself making a mistake of that kind. Surely, if something like that had happened, Charlotte or even the Duke would have told Rosaline about it. And Cadogan had seemed so disappointed by Charlotte's absence, even if he did his best to hide it. He must care for her quite deeply — what else could explain such a reaction?

What on earth did Lord Crawley have to offer that Cadogan did not? He was good-looking enough, Rosaline supposed, but dull as a post. Crawley did not have Cadogan's ingenuity, his creativity, and certainly not his sense of humor. No, Crawley was much more reserved, with a quiet amiability that was pleasant but not memorable. What was Charlotte doing, toying with Cadogan's emotions? Rosaline never would have imagined her capable of playing such games for the sake of amusement or enjoyment, but perhaps she was. Perhaps that was how she thought of the season — a game, rather than a test of endurance. But was that not a cold, callous, unfeeling outlook? Could sunny, delightful, caring Charlotte really be so heartless?"

Lisette had evidently followed Rosaline's gaze. "*I do not know,*" she said in a low murmur, "*what that girl means, by trifling about with the Earl as she does.*"

"*I know,*" Rosaline murmured in reply, not letting an ounce of emotion show on her face, just in case Charlotte looked their way. "*A part of me wonders if she realizes she is doing it.*"

"*If she is not careful,*" Lisette went on, separating a new section of Rosaline's hair. "*She is going to lose him. He is a sensitive man, but a clever one. He will not entertain heartbreak for long.*"

"*I cannot think why she would wish to deter him.*" Rosaline spun the pin again. "*He is a gentleman of the highest order. Any woman with a half-decent brain would accept him.*"

"*Yes, but...*" Lisette met her gaze in the mirror. "*Do you know if Charlotte even wishes to marry?*"

Rosaline blinked, taken aback. "*No,*" she said, surprised by her own ignorance. "*I never asked her, and she has never mentioned it.*"

Lisette clucked her tongue. "*It is possible that, even if she truly has feelings for him, she is trying to spare him heartache by encouraging him to turn his affection elsewhere.*"

"*Wouldn't she just tell him, if that were the case?*" Rosaline let out a huff. This was all getting far more complicated than she ever could have imagined. "*And if she had feelings for him, what would be the point of denying him and herself the greatest happiness?*"

Lisette shrugged, moving on to the next small braid. "*You know her far better than I. If you are confused, then I am confused.*"

Rosaline glanced at Charlotte again. "*She has told me very little. But she did seem insulted when I implied that her attachment to Cadogan was a given.*"

"*Then she would not be the first woman who disliked other people making assumptions about her.*"

"*I suppose.*" Rosaline's attention drifted back to her own hair. "What on earth are you trying to do, exactly?"

Lisette was tugging at the left side of Rosaline's head, her lips pursed in concentration. "A half-coronet," she replied. "The braid will wrap around the back of your head, join with the other braids, then wrap into a large bun up here." She tapped the back of Rosaline's head. "It will be quite heavy, I'm afraid."

"Delightful," Rosaline replied. "I am assuming this is to match my new dress?"

"Of course." Lisette seemed surprised. "Have you not seen it yet, *ma chère?*"

"No," Rosaline confessed. "In truth, I wanted to spare myself any possible disappointment. Judging by Charlotte's dresses, Madam D'Amboise does fine work, but I do worry that my expectations will not hold against reality."

Lisette grinned suddenly. "I do not think," she said, "you will have to worry about that."

And she was correct.

As Rosaline stepped out from behind the screen, Charlotte let out a squeal and started clapping like a lunatic. Lisette was beaming, and even Mattie grinned and squeezed Lisette's elbow. But Mrs. Randolph's face became a blank mask of horror, and all the color drained away from her cheeks.

"Rosaline!" gasped Charlotte. "You look wonderful!"

"Like a true woman," Lisette added, unruffled by Mrs. Randolph's glare. "Just wait until the Duke sees you."

"Quiet!" snapped Mrs. Randolph. She looked ready to throttle something. "How— I must— why— why did that *woman* think that this would be suitable attire for—?"

"I can hardly see anything inappropriate about this dress, Mrs. Randolph." Charlotte gave Rosaline an overly careful, scrutinizing look. Rosaline swallowed a laugh. "The length, her straps, her neckline — all are quite fashionable. In fact, her dress is in the same silhouette as mine. The only real difference is the color."

"The *color*," spat Mrs. Randolph, "is the least of our concern—"

"Why is it a concern at all?" countered Lisette, much to Rosaline's delight. "It suits her."

"I agree," added Charlotte, flashing Rosaline a smile. "After all, a Sapphire should look like a sapphire, shouldn't she?"

❖

To her surprise, when she stepped out of the carriage and onto yet another gravel driveway, Rosaline had to swallow a wave of nerves.

Charlotte noticed, of course. "Don't be silly," she said. "You have nothing to worry about."

"Of course I do, Charlotte." Rosaline tried to take a breath. "I am showing up in a dress that screams at people to look at me."

Charlotte hummed, straightening her gloves. The feather in her hair — white, of course — bobbed gently. "It is not so terrible, if you do not meet their eye."

Rosaline shot her a frown. "Pardon?"

"Look past them. Behind them. Or at a point on the wall." Charlotte smiled. "Find something utterly mundane, and fixate upon it. If you distract yourself, their attention means nothing, because you are not there to receive it."

Suddenly, some of Charlotte's behavior — *floating on a cloud*, Lisette had called it — made much more sense. "Does it work?" she found herself asking, her voice hushed.

"It does." Charlotte linked her arm with Rosaline's. "Come, let's go in."

Just as Rosaline had feared, people did indeed turn to stare at her as she and Charlotte passed through the scattered crowds around the exterior of Rosier Manor. It was a bleak, dull building with little character or forethought, so its guests stood out in stark, unrelieved contrast. She heard, but tried to ignore, the wave of whispers that spread among the guests, traveling from ear to ear before it crashed and broke at her feet. Her heart was thundering painfully fast in her chest, but Charlotte's advice did have some merit to it — looking at the hedges, the front steps, the imposing front door made the collective attention, the collective shock, easier to bear.

Rosaline's dress was sleeveless, and the straps were made of intricately braided beads in a rich shade of lapis that offset the deep, supple blue satin. The beads trailed along her *décolletage*, met in a sharp point, then shattered across her skirts, where they would catch and wink in the light. Her skirts themselves were staggered, giving her a small train, and were layered in different shades of deep blue. The final layer, a dark turquoise, showed only when she turned or gathered her skirts to one side. Rosaline had never seen anything like it before, and it made her feel untouchable.

The color was perhaps the most daring thing about this dress. It was almost unheard of for a woman to wear such a dark shade during the summer, but Rosaline loved the way this blue made her skin glow with warmth. She was sure this was part of what drove the gossip through the crowd — a woman with dark skin wearing a dark dress was not a common sight in London society.

As she and Charlotte reached the top of the steps, Lord Devon, who was a few paces behind them, spoke up for the first time since their arrival. "To the right, ladies. This house is a goddamn maze. If you're not careful, you will go missing for a week."

Upon entering, Rosaline saw that Charlotte's father was quite correct. For all its exterior mundanity, inside the house was sprawling, counterintuitive, hunched in on itself like it was guarding a secret. The walls were paneled and painted in a dark near-black, with matching steely-gray fixtures, and she fought off a shiver of foreboding. Nothing about this residence was welcoming, an impression that was confirmed by its occupants.

"Lord Devon." Earl Rosier gave him a cursory, unimpressed look, and his attention merely flickered over Rosaline and Charlotte. Behind him, his tall, thin wife loomed like a shade, her hooded eyes betraying not even an ounce of emotion. "My wife, Lady Rosier."

"Charmed," Lord Devon replied. "And this is—"

"My son is already in the ballroom," Lord Rosier went on. "He is quite popular, you see, among a... certain crowd." His reptilian gaze, cool and uninterested, once again grazed over Rosaline and Charlotte. "Enjoy yourselves."

With that, Lord Devon steered them out of the room. Rosaline, trembling with repressed anger, barely took stock of where they were going.

"I forgot to mention," Charlotte breathed. "The Rosiers are intolerable, in more ways than one."

"That much," Rosaline gritted out, "was clear."

"Take care this evening, ladies." Lord Devon glanced over his shoulder as they passed two closed doors, a massive stuffed bear, and a seething, dark portrait. He looked quite sinister in the dim, cold light of the hall. "Perhaps you should..." He glanced around at the guests, some of whom Rosaline did not recognize at all. They looked almost foreign, with olive skin, dark eyes, and haughty chins. "Stick together."

"Come." Charlotte took Rosaline's hand. "We could do with a glass of wine."

"Or three," Rosaline muttered, but she allowed herself to be steered away.

Even though Charlotte had admitted that she had never before set foot in the Rosiers' residence, she moved through the jumbled, identical rooms with a surety that was at once impressive and worrying. She seemed to know exactly where she was going, dodging clusters of young ladies and mothers alike, ignoring furtive looks from would-be suitors and the leers of ineligible men.

Then, a hand on Rosaline's arm.

"Katherine!" Rosaline let out a breath she hadn't known she was holding. She immediately latched onto Katherine's arm and pulled her along, both of them following in Charlotte's wake. "Thank goodness, I almost—"

"Rosaline—" Katherine was staring at her, agape. "You look—"

"Yes, yes, I know. It is a new dress." There was no time for this. "Katherine, you must do me a favor, I shall not ask you again—"

"Of course—"

"If Lord Crawley appears," Rosaline said in an undertone, "distract him."

It took a moment, but then a flicker of recognition passed over Katherine's features. "It is no trouble," she replied. "Quite honestly, you could ask me to charge Bonaparte himself, and I'd say yes, so long as you were wearing this dress—"

"Do not be ridiculous," Rosaline sniffed. "You would go just for a chance to kick him in the balls."

"That is true," Katherine conceded, but then they drew to a halt. Charlotte had found the refreshment table.

"There we are!" Charlotte passed a glass of wine to Rosaline, and beamed at Katherine. "Oh, hello! I had not realized you joined our parade!"

"Any port in a storm," Katherine quipped, stealing Rosaline's glass and taking a healthy sip. "You look lovely tonight, Charlotte."

"Thank you, but we both know I have nothing on Rosaline." Charlotte twinkled and passed Rosaline a fresh glass.

"You both are ridiculous," Rosaline replied. At least the wine was good.

"Are we?" said Katherine. "Perhaps. But I shall reserve my final judgment until I see the Duke's reaction. What do you think, Charlotte?"

Rosaline looked from Katherine to Charlotte. "What does the Duke have to do with anything?"

"Rosaline," said Charlotte, patting her on the arm as one would a senile aunt, "he nearly fainted when he saw you at the opera."

"Because my dress left nothing to the imagination and he is a man with a fully functioning pair of eyes! You cannot possibly—"

"Oh," said Katherine, "but we *can* possibly."

"This," Rosaline seethed, "is ridiculous."

"Good evening, ladies," came a friendly, unfortunately familiar voice.

Rosaline paused to wince before she turned and smiled at—"Lord Crawley. A pleasure."

"Likewise." He bowed, and all three of them curtsied in return. "Lady Prince, I wonder—"

"Lord Crawley!" Katherine blurted. "I hear you hail from Yorkshire."

He gave her a look of blank surprise. "Well, yes, that is where—"

"Well," said Katherine, closing the distance between them, "my brother is looking to purchase land in that area, and since my mother's family—" She guided Lord Crawley to the side, spewing details about her great uncle, and shot Rosaline a wink.

Rosaline winked back, even as Charlotte frowned, but did not have time to relish her victory.

"Well, Prongs." Cadogan looked even more vibrant than usual this evening, a splash of royal blue among the drab gray. He smiled at Charlotte. "It seems we are late to the party."

"Then we must try to make up for lost time." The Duke stepped up beside him, and something in Rosaline quivered at the sight of him — he was dressed in a simple, sleek charcoal, and his eyes gleamed in the low light. He took her in with a languid glance, and she noticed how his gaze hooked along the lines of her dress. "Miss Bailey. Very well met, indeed."

"Good evening to you both," said Charlotte, and Rosaline was pleased to see her smiling. "Though I wish it were under more colorful circumstances."

"Indeed," returned Cadogan. "One walks through the door, and all of summer seems to melt away, does it not?"

"How are you, Miss Bailey?" The Duke's voice was low, an undercurrent to Cadogan and Charlotte's chatter.

She tried for a breath and nearly made it. "I am well, Your Grace."

"Is not the truth," he said, capturing her hand, "the truth?" He pressed a brief kiss to her gloved knuckle. "Though perhaps I must declare this an understatement, because you look..." His pause hung like a rock in the air between them. "*Very* well."

Rosaline looked at him for a moment, then figured it out. "You are drunk."

A beat. Then two. "No," the Duke said. "Merely over-served."

"How convenient." Rosaline tried for anger and only managed a smile. She could see it now in Cadogan as well — the flush along his cheeks, the looseness of his body. "Do you at least have a good reason?"

"An excellent one," the Duke replied. "Celebration."

Charlotte, who had apparently caught on to his and Rosaline's conversation, piped up: "What were you celebrating?"

"A successful business venture," said the Duke. He clapped a hand on Cadogan's shoulder. "Cadogan here has been most obliging."

"Oh!" Charlotte beamed at them both. "Do you mean to say that you will be joining Lord Cadogan in his greenhouse business?"

"Not exactly," said Cadogan. "No, my lady, this is something quite different—"

"There is a match," said the Duke in a hushed tone. "On Monday next."

"A match?" Rosaline repeated with a frown. "What do you mean?"

"A boxing match." Cadogan really was blushing now. "Dean versus Flint."

"Dean." Rosaline looked to the Duke. "As in your friend who—?"

"Exactly!" There was a feverish glint in his eyes. "Odds are in Dean's favor, but he needed money to front the pot, so—"

"Are you talking," hissed Rosaline, "of *gambling?!*"

"Of course!" The Duke was completely unruffled.

Rosaline anxiously glanced around, seeing if anyone had overheard them. "That," she snapped, "is entirely inappropriate and in very bad taste—"

"I believe I've been summoned." None other than Lord Martel appeared next to the Duke, smirking like a diabolical cat. "Do tell me what I am interrupting."

"Piss off, Rodent," said the Duke, without missing a beat. "Go and bother someone else."

Martel sighed dramatically. "No, I do not think I will. You owe me a favor, Cunningham, and it is your fault that I enjoy Miss Bailey's company."

Rosaline could only stare at the occupants of their little cluster, wondering when this had become her life. "You flatter me, sir," she said, dry as a bone. "The Duke was discussing his and Cadogan's investment in a local gambling pot for a boxing match."

For a moment, Martel just looked at her. She realized he was thinking quickly. "Actually," he said, turning to Cadogan, "that sounds quite good, who's fighting?"

"Dean and Flint," Cadogan replied, ignoring Rosaline's glare. "Good odds, low risk."

"Perfect. When is it?"

"Monday, four o'clock. The warehouse behind the Dog and Horse, out in Bethnal Green."

"Charming," said Martel, raising an eyebrow. "Though I suppose one does not attend these events for the atmosphere."

"Pray tell," said Rosaline, "why, exactly, *does* one attend them?"

"Entertainment," said Martel. "Not to mention the attraction of winning a handsome sum."

"But there must be more to it," she pressed, "than the simple lure of gambling?"

"Of course," said the Duke. He met her gaze. "One sees the grim detail of battle, the struggle and triumph of an ordinary man. One feels as if they, too, are in the ring, only a pair of hands and a hair's breadth away from loss or victory. It is intoxicating, riveting. An exhilaration borne of the unknown, unmatched by anything else on this earth."

A ringing silence followed this short speech. Then:

"My word, Cunningham," said Martel. "You *have* gone soft."

"He is right, though," said Cadogan. "He described the experience exactly."

"Odds favor Dean, do they not?" said Martel. At Cadogan's nod, he added, "That is unsurprising. He is a good fighter, quick on his feet."

The Duke smirked. "I believe that is the first time I've heard you pay someone a compliment, Lord Martel."

"Given that you make a habit of avoiding my good graces, Cunningham, that is entirely possible." Martel took a glass of wine. "Christ. My wife is glaring at me. Do excuse me, gentlemen, ladies. I shall be in touch regarding next Monday." With a final nod, he slid away, slipping through the crowd in an echo of his nickname.

"He was taller than I had expected," said Charlotte, and then Rosaline realized that they had made no introductions. Charlotte only knew who Martel was from Rosaline's — highly edited — recount of the other night. "And perhaps with thinner hair."

The Duke shot her a sudden smile. "My thoughts exactly, my lady."

Then, someone stepped into their little circle. Someone with irritation in the line of their shoulders. "Lady Prince," said Lord Crawley. "Good evening."

Charlotte smiled at him. "Good evening, my lord."

Rosaline bit the inside of her cheek and glanced over her shoulder. Katherine was standing alone in a nearby corner, looking worried and apologetic. "Sorry!" she mouthed, and Rosaline dismissed it with a wave of her hand. Katherine had done her best, after all.

Cadogan was staring at Crawley like he had been clubbed over the head. Crawley seemed not to notice. In fact, he ignored the Duke and the Earl entirely. "I was wondering," he went on, "if I might beg the honor of a dance with you."

"Certainly, my lord." Charlotte did not see the way Cadogan's face fell. "Shall we proceed to the ballroom? The music must be starting soon."

Finally, Crawley seemed to smile. "Splendid." He offered Charlotte his arm. She took it, and they made their way into the next room.

Cadogan watched their departure with a clenched jaw and a flash of hurt in his eyes. Rosaline glanced at him, then looked away, unable to bear it.

A light rustle of skirts announced Katherine's arrival. "I am sorry," she whispered to Rosaline. "I did try my best, but he was determined."

"You did a wonderful job, Katherine," Rosaline assured her. "Besides, Lord Crawley is a man with a mission." She cleared her throat, getting the men's attention. "Gentlemen, may I introduce my good friend, Miss Knight?"

The Duke gave her a nod, and Cadogan managed a smile. "A pleasure," said Cadogan. "I believe I know your brother, Lucas."

"Indeed, my lord." Katherine smiled at him in return. "He has spoken of you most favorably." She closed the distance between them. "In fact, he has some outrageous stories about a certain public house in Belgravia."

Cadogan's smile grew, and Rosaline felt a warm nudge of appreciation for Katherine. She'd handled that beautifully.

As Cadogan and Katherine drew themselves into conversation, Rosaline inched closer to the Duke. "Perhaps," she murmured, "we should take it upon ourselves to keep your dear friend in close company this evening."

"Yes," he said at once. "And we should do so in one location." He shook his head. "This house is a beast."

"A fair pronouncement. Besides, I believe we have earned a break from dancing."

"And yet you displayed none of this levity when I had a fresh injury." But a smile was playing about in the corner of his mouth. "I meant what I said, earlier."

Her heart gave a thud. "Your Grace?"

The Duke looked right at her, his eyes glowing with mirth and something else, something she could not name. "You look exceedingly well in that dress."

❧ 14 ❧

Rosaline was already awake when Lisette came into her bedroom. She watched Lisette open the curtains on a pale, watery, but sunny morning while humming a familiar tune under her breath. "I could do," she said quietly, "with a day to myself."

Lisette shot her a sympathetic look. "I would smuggle you out, *ma chère*, but we both know how a certain person would notice right away."

"This is true." Rosaline fell back onto her bed with a sigh. At least it was soft, luxuriant.

"Have you had enough of them already?" Lisette went on. "The men?"

Rosaline snorted. "Yes, I suppose I have." Unbidden, her thoughts suddenly turned to Lieutenant McGrath and the curve of his mouth. *Perhaps*, she thought, *I have grown tired of them all, except for one.*

"I find this surprising when I hear you were the center of attention last night." Lisette cast a sneaky glance over her shoulder, and lifted the corner of a familiar publication above the line of her apron pocket.

"Don't," Rosaline said at once. "I need a break from her incessant prattle."

"Harsh words for so fine a day."

"Perhaps." Rosaline frowned at the windows. "I wish it were pouring with rain."

Lisette tsked. "But then you would not be able to attend the finest flower show in the world. Tulips, petunias, lilies, and orchids as far as your pretty little eye can see." Even in English, her sarcasm was obvious.

Rosaline groaned, pulling her pillow on top of her face. "A whole afternoon," she said into the down. "A whole afternoon for *flowers*."

"I am actually quite looking forward to it," Charlotte said to her a while later. They were enjoying a rare moment alone in Charlotte's bedroom in the midst of getting ready — Mrs. Randolph had just flown out of the room in the height of fury, having heard that one of the chambermaids had improperly pressed Charlotte's dress, and Lisette and Mattie had run after her for a front-row seat. Rosaline and Charlotte were both sitting — slouching — in the middle of Charlotte's bed, fighting the inherent laziness of a summer afternoon. "Lord Cadogan's firm will be debuting a few new hybrids. He has nearly half a marquee to himself."

Rosaline looked Charlotte right in the eye, and some part of her waning patience prickled. Perhaps it was her half-finished hair, or the fact that she'd already been laced into her stays, but something pushed her past her limit. "You are... excited to see Lord Cadogan, then?"

There, for a moment — just the barest flicker in Charlotte's expression before she smiled. "Yes, of course I am."

"Intriguing," said Rosaline, still holding her gaze. "I thought you had tired of him. After all, you did abandon him quite rudely last night. He was very much looking forward to dancing with you, only to find himself rebuked and ignored."

These words seemed to settle at the edges of Charlotte's skin. She merely blinked, unaffected. "Well, Lord Crawley—"

"Is a dull, watery fool who would never make you happy and you know it." Rosaline took a quick breath to keep her temper at a low simmer. "Charlotte, what on earth are you playing at?"

"I," said Charlotte, with just a hint of coolness, "am weighing my options."

Rosaline scoffed. "At the expense of a good man's heart, at the expense of your own? Of all things Charlotte, I never would have believed you capable of such deliberate, unnecessary hurt."

"Really?" Charlotte stared right back at her, the corners of her eyes tightening. "Perhaps I overlooked the moment when you began to care about anyone's future apart from your own."

Her words hit Rosaline like a smack across the face, and she gaped at Charlotte, hurt welling in her stomach. "Of course I care, Charlotte—"

"Do you?" Charlotte snapped, finally, *finally* showing her emotion. She slid off the bed, turning her back to Rosaline. "We both had our ideas about what this season would mean. Each of us had our plans, our intentions."

"Well, yes." Rosaline swallowed, her ears still ringing from Charlotte's sudden ferocity. "But what does that have to do with—?"

"I did not mean—" Charlotte bit out. Her shoulders trembled. "This was not supposed to happen. You and I, we were meant to get through this together. A favor, a token to our fathers. A gesture of goodwill before we retired to lives of pleasant solitude."

"Yes." Rosaline was truly confused now. "But what—?"

Charlotte turned, and something in Rosaline broke because Charlotte had tears in her eyes. "This was not supposed to happen," she said again, her voice steady in spite of her emotion. "*He* was not supposed to happen."

Realization crashed over Rosaline like a wave. "Oh, Charlotte—"

"I did not recognize what was building between us until it was too late to stop it." Charlotte shook her head. "I cannot pretend to enjoy hurting him, but—"

Rosaline slid off the bed as well and closed the distance between them, taking Charlotte's hands in her own. "Charlotte, it is perfectly all right to fall in love. It is a wonderful, unique thing. Why would you ever try to keep it from happening?"

Charlotte squeezed her eyes shut and tears spilled down her cheeks. She leaned into Rosaline, but did not sob or shake. "I worry," she said. "That I am betraying myself."

Rosaline almost smiled at that. She tucked a loose piece of hair behind Charlotte's ear. "I would worry about that as well," she said softly, "were it any man other than Cadogan."

Charlotte said nothing, but a fresh wave of tears slid down her face.

"Charlotte, I could never have imagined a better partner for you." She squeezed Charlotte's hands. "I can understand being frightened. It *is* quite frightening to have your entire world shift on its axis, to suddenly find your values and your priorities changing when you never imagined they would. But you would never relinquish any part of yourself for this man, and nor would he want you to do so."

Charlotte took a deep, shaky breath and wiped her face. It was several moments before she said, "I worry it is too late. That I have pushed him to his limit."

Rosaline thought quickly. She had no idea if Cadogan's bruised feelings now outweighed his regard for Charlotte — like her, he could be quite guarded. "We still have plenty of time. There is no rush, Charlotte."

"Yes, there is." Charlotte opened her eyes and her deep blue gaze was fathomless. "He is arguably the most eligible bachelor in all of England. But I worry," she added, "about crowding him, or rushing him. I do not want him to feel obligated to me, especially if I have injured his pride."

"I understand." Rosaline sighed a little, her thumb tapping a rhythm onto Charlotte's hand. She had a brief thought of writing to the Duke for insight as to his friend's feelings, but dismissed it. "This week, there is only the Eventide Ball, and that's not for several days."

Charlotte sighed as well. "I do so hate attempting personal conversation at a ball, or even while promenading. One never knows who might be listening."

Rosaline raised an eyebrow. "Personal conversation?"

"Well." To her delight, Charlotte blushed a little and fidgeted. "Nothing *too* personal, you understand, merely... I just wish to apologize." She took a shaky breath. "If, you know, I can actually work up the courage to do so."

Suddenly, Rosaline had a wild, utterly improbable idea. "Charlotte," she said, her breath quickening, "you want to be alone with Cadogan, yes? To spend time with him without the concerns of etiquette and propriety?"

"Yes, I suppose." Charlotte frowned. "What are you thinking?"

"I am thinking," said Rosaline, her mind racing, "that we need an adventure."

⚜

TWO DAYS LATER, LISETTE WAS GRINNING. "TRULY, *MA CHÈRE*. It suits you."

"Hush, Lisette." Rosaline worried at her cap — beneath it, she could feel her hair threatening to break free of its meticulous braids. "And I am not going to ask where you found two pairs of trousers at such short notice."

Lisette shrugged, tucking the tails of Charlotte's shirt into the waistband of her trousers. "You have your friends, *ma chère*, and I have mine."

"I quite like them," said Charlotte, smiling. "Less of a breeze, but fewer layers. And no stays."

"No stays," Rosaline agreed, unable to keep herself from smiling in return. She still had to wear a length of fabric wrapped and tied snugly around her breasts, but it was a far cry from stays. "Now, Lisette, let's review the plan again."

"In five minutes, you and Lady Charlotte will take those piles of laundry and follow me down to the kitchen using the servant's staircase. You will climb into the baskets, and Sean, the kitchen boy, will cover you with laundry until it is safe to wheel you out of the house. Then, you will walk approximately half a mile, where Henry, the produce boy, will be waiting at the post office with his cart and horse to take you to Bethnal Green. You have to get home on your own, of course, but I am sure your *beaux* will be more than happy to oblige."

Rosaline paused for a moment, thinking it through. As far as she could tell, with her limited knowledge of smuggling operations, this plan was as good as it was going to get. "Come, Charlotte," she said. "Let us delay no longer."

Twenty minutes later, Rosaline and Charlotte walked out onto the quiet, pretty street and glanced back at Prince Manor.

"Well." Rosaline blinked. "That went a lot more smoothly than I'd imagined."

"I know. I half-expected for us to get caught and end up locked in our rooms for the next fortnight." Charlotte shrugged and turned away from her lifelong home. With her hair tucked tightly under her cap, she looked like a wide-eyed, innocent, high-born boy who had never seen the sun. "Let's go. I do not want to miss Henry."

"Wait!" Rosaline grabbed Charlotte's arm and tugged her to the side of the house, out of view of the windows. She knelt, took up a handful of damp earth from the flowerbed, and without a moment's hesitation, smeared it across her cheeks.

"Oh! I see!" Delighted, Charlotte copied her, rubbing a cloud of dirt across her face. Within moments, she had transformed from a cherubic adolescent to a rough-and-tumble farmhand on his first trip to the city.

"Your hands and arms as well," Rosaline told her, as she did it to herself. "Not too much, but enough that we do not stand out."

A few minutes later, Rosaline glanced over both of them and nodded. "We are ready."

Kensington was quiet, with pockets of liveliness scattered between the grand houses and shining carriages. Rosaline drank it all in with unceasing curiosity. The neighborhood had a quiet, enchanting beauty that nestled in the gleaming bricks and towering columns, but was not stuffy or overreaching in its enchantment. It had a plain, simple elegance that she had to admire, even covet.

Their path — meticulously written out and drawn on a scrap of Rosaline's note paper — took them out of the heart of Kensington and onto the High Street. Here, traffic was thick and lively, and the air rang with the shouts of merchants and hagglers. Rosaline had worried that, in spite of their apparel and their disguised complexions, she and Charlotte would be noticed, even exposed, in a second. But no one, not even the people within inches of their faces, seemed to realize or care that the two scruffy boys standing on the street corner were not boys at all.

Charlotte shot her a wide grin, her eyes shining with glee. "It is working," she whispered, and gave Rosaline's hand a brief squeeze.

Henry was their age, gray with exhaustion, and grumpy. His cart was overflowing with baskets of cabbage and lettuce, and Rosaline realized that he must have just completed a delivery. "You're late," he said, then barely gave them enough time to hop on the back of his cart before he started the horse. "Enjoy the fresh air while it lasts," he called over his shoulder.

An hour later, Rosaline realized this had been a vast understatement. Their cart had snaked into the middle of London, and the wealthy neighborhoods had gradually sunk into a clotted, overwhelming, seething mass of people and buildings. The dim, gray air stank of coal, smoke, rotting produce, stale spirits, and sewage. It only became worse whenever they drew to a stop, usually for Henry to unload a few baskets of lettuce. Rosaline's eyes would water from the fumes, but Charlotte remained completely unaffected by it all. She had her chin perched on her knee, and she stared out at the city like it was the most fascinating of all subjects.

"Is it not wonderful?" Charlotte murmured, staring up at the distant, looming edifice of St. Paul's Cathedral. "Is it not the richest tapestry of life?"

Rosaline said nothing, privately imagining Paris.

She had not thought the street and living conditions could get any worse, but their journey into the East End proved her quite wrong. The stench became overpowering, foul in its extremity and its pervasiveness. Now she saw, rather than just smelt, the raw sewage along the edges of the streets, the dead rats lying in plain view, the piles of rotting garbage wilting in the sun. She was grateful for her raggedy leather boots, then shuddered at the thought of having to wear her dainty little slippers in a place like this. The residents themselves were a haggard but lively people, boisterous, friendly, and confrontational all at once. They seemed content to air their personal woes, tragedies, and triumphs in plain view of the entire street. Many of them were miserable, she realized, but none of them were lonely.

Eventually, the cart pulled to a stop a short distance from a squat, dusty little building with a faded sign hanging above the door. It carried the lopsided profiles of a dog and a horse, and as Rosaline looked at it, her heart skipped a beat. They were here. This was happening.

"Thank you," she said to Henry, pressing two crowns into his hand.

"If I were you, I'd stay out of the pub. And try to slouch a little more." With that, he jostled the horse awake and rejoined the flow of traffic. In mere moments he was gone, another anonymous head in the crowd.

Charlotte's hand on hers. "Come on. Let's find the warehouse."

It was easy enough. The warehouse was behind the pub, a large, ramshackle, disused building that seemed to lean to one side. From within came a steady rumble of voices and heat — there was already quite a crowd — and at the doorway, a huge, surly man with stubble who reeked of gin and sweat glared down at them.

"Sixpence each," he grunted. "More if you want a punt."

Rosaline took out a shilling but held it in midair, then said a quick, silent prayer that her new voice, which she had spent most of the morning practicing, would hold up to scrutiny. "And if we do?"

A pause as he stared at her, rolling a toothpick between his teeth. "Go see Eddie," he eventually said. "He'll be standing near the front, red kerchief. Can't miss him."

Rosaline gave a nod and handed over the coin. With that, she and Charlotte stepped into the old, rickety warehouse.

The interior was brighter than she'd expected, and the air was thick with heat. She had already begun to perspire during their cart ride, and now a fresh haze of moisture erupted on her lower back. Charlotte, mute and practically vibrating with excitement, kept close as Rosaline led them through the thick crowd of men. The center of the open space had been enclosed with a chest-high wooden barrier, and risers had been installed in a loose circle around it.

Never in her life had Rosaline been so physically close to men that she did not know, or outnumbered by them to such a degree. Anxiety rippled through her, but she did her best to ignore it, just as the men were ignoring her and Charlotte, taking no more notice of them than if they were a pair of flies. Eventually, they reached a small break in the crowd, and Rosaline leaned against the wooden barrier of the ring, forcing herself to take a deep breath of the stale air.

Because even if she was afraid, Rosaline was alive with excitement as well. Every nerve, every hair on her body tingled with the forbidden delight of anonymity. She felt drunk and utterly awake all at once, almost unable to believe that she was here, seeing this for herself.

"Well, Charlotte," she murmured. "Shall we try to find our friends?"

"Yes," Charlotte replied, then, to Rosaline's surprise, tossed a handful of hazelnuts into her mouth. She offered Rosaline the small, crumpled cloth pouch. "Hungry?"

"I— no, Charlotte. Where did you get those?"

"The kitchen cupboard," Charlotte replied. "Sadie roasts them with sugar and salt." She crunched up another nut. "Do you see the Duke or Cadogan?"

Rosaline frowned, scanning the crowd. "Not yet." The faces blurred together, and most of them were rough, forgettable. There seemed to be hardly any peers at all, but there was still time before the fight. "If they are friends with Dean, perhaps they are helping him prepare." Then, her gaze landed on a familiar navy blue jacket and her heart leapt into her throat. "Or not."

"Where?" said Charlotte at once, and she followed Rosaline's nod to the risers opposite. The Duke, Cadogan, and Martel were clustered near the bottom row, just a few feet from a doorway that Rosaline presumed led to the pub. They were all talking together, and Rosaline's gaze lingered on the Duke's loose posture, his ready grin. She had not seen him since the Rosiers' three days before; he had been conspicuously absent from the flower show. The bruise on his jaw had vanished.

Charlotte tucked her bag of hazelnuts back into the pocket of her trousers. "What do you think? A direct approach?"

Rosaline smiled and pulled her cap down over her face. "Most certainly. Just be sure to follow my lead, dear Charlotte."

15

Rosaline once again led them through the crowd, keeping her head down and only shooting the gentlemen an occasional glance. Soon, she and Charlotte came within spitting distance of the man Rosaline presumed to be Eddie, red kerchief jauntily tied around his neck. He was chaffering with the men around him, and, on an impulse, she stepped in beside him.

"Five on Dean," she muttered, pressing the coins into his hand. He, too, smelt of gin.

His surprise only showed for a moment before he nodded. "Name?"

"John."

His grin was sudden. "Lots of Johns here tonight."

She grinned back at him without humor. "You'll remember me, I promise you that."

He held up his hands in surrender, and she shot Charlotte a glance over her shoulder. Together, they moved away from the ring. At the risers, the gentlemen carried on, oblivious, and she was surprised to see them sharing a bottle of wine. *Martel*, she thought, then rolled her eyes. It distracted her from the way her stomach seemed to float up into her lungs, buoyant with nerves.

Her instincts were screaming at her to rush towards them, to spoil the surprise with a shout and a gale of laughter, but no, she had to relish this moment, pull it like cooling sugar.

"Slowly," she muttered to Charlotte, and Charlotte smiled her agreement. They slid their way to the edges of the crowd, mere feet from the gentlemen, who were becoming more and more real the closer she and Charlotte got.

Cadogan was seated and Martel was leaning against one of the benches — only the Duke remained standing. If the gentlemen had noticed their approach, they did not show it. Martel said something, Cadogan laughed, and Rosaline saw her chance.

Swallowing painfully, Rosaline closed the distance between her and the Duke, silently slipping in beside him. She fixed her gaze on his shoes, crossed her arms against her chest, and said in her new voice, "I dunno, my lord, I think the odds are fixed. Flint's gonna come out ahead."

"Nonsense," he said at once, in an easy, sure way. He did not correct her use of the wrong title, and it floored her. "Flint's too slow on his feet."

"I hear he's got the heavier swing," Rosaline went on, her heart thundering a thousand miles a minute in her ears. "Better footwork."

The Duke scoffed, taking a pull of wine before passing the bottle back to Cadogan. "Dean's faster. And he strikes better nine times out of ten."

"Maybe," Rosaline conceded. "Still, I think Flint's gonna take the first round."

"I hope you don't have money on that. It would be a shame to witness two losses."

Rosaline sighed and switched back to her own voice. "Only the price of a new dress. Do you think that too much, Your Grace?" She finally looked up at him, meeting his gaze.

He had frozen in place and was staring down at her, just the barest hint of alarm showing in the lines of his mouth, the edges of his eyes.

Then, with perfect timing, Charlotte appeared at her side. "I'm afraid I already sunk half my dowry into the pot," she said, hitching her elbow up on Rosaline's shoulder and leaning into it. "Do you think it might be possible to get it back?"

"Yes, Your Grace," Rosaline went on. "Do tell us the procedures for such matters. You see, we are but humble women, and cannot be expected to control our lesser impulses."

The Duke was still staring at them, unmoving. After a few moments, he blinked several times, as if willing them to disappear.

Rosaline was beginning to worry that she and Charlotte had done some sort of serious damage. Cadogan, though, took the opportunity to save the day.

"—Prongs, come on, settle it for us, between Mendoza and Slack, who would win? Prongs?" When the Duke didn't reply, Cadogan turned, saw the cause for delay, and promptly fell out of his seat, spilling what was left of the wine.

"You great oaf, look what you've done—" Irritated, Martel glanced back at the Duke, saw Rosaline and Charlotte, and did a perfect double-take. After a moment, he recovered and stood up, his haughty expression unchanged. "Ah. This... complicates things."

"We are quite well, Lord Martel, thank you for asking." Rosaline smirked at him. "Any chance you gentlemen have room for two more?"

Martel made a quiet noise between a scoff and a laugh. "We are going to prison," he muttered to himself. "I do not know what for, but we are going to prison."

Cadogan had pushed himself up from between the seats and was staring at Rosaline and Charlotte, wild-eyed. "What are you doing here? What—? Why—?"

"You boys made it sound like so much fun," said Charlotte

with a smile. "We thought we'd join you and see what all the fuss was all about."

"Yes, but— but—" Cadogan was turning redder by the moment. "You're— you look like—"

"We had to sneak out somehow," said Rosaline. "Besides, we wanted an authentic experience. You can't have that in a silk dress and satin shoes." Her gaze returned to the Duke, who still had not moved. He was either mute with anger or thinking very quickly. "Your Grace?"

Then, *finally*, the Duke reacted, taking a step back and looking away. "Yes," he said, his voice rough but not brittle. "Come join us."

"Wonderful!" chirped Charlotte. "I have hazelnuts!"

Once they were all seated in the risers, the Duke gave Rosaline and Charlotte a shrewd look. "It really is uncanny," he said. "How on earth did you manage it?"

"Well, we already knew when and where the fight was taking place, thanks to you three," said Rosaline. "Lisette found us the clothes and helped us escape by smuggling us out in the laundry. Then we got on the produce cart and he delivered us here on his way to Hackney."

"How inventive," said Cadogan, with not even a hint of sarcasm. "But how do you plan to sneak back into the house?"

"Just as we snuck out," said Charlotte, smiling. "In the baskets of laundry."

"And where does Mrs. Randolph think you are?" said the Duke.

"In bed with hay fever, thanks to the flower show," said Rosaline. "Lisette and Mattie have even snuck into our rooms and let out great symphonies of sneezes and groans whenever they hear her walking past."

Cadogan was frowning. "Wouldn't she check on you?"

"Mrs. Randolph is quite lacking in maternal instincts," replied

Charlotte. "At the first sign of illness, any illness, she keeps a wide berth."

"Not that this isn't wildly engaging," said Martel, his tone suggesting the opposite, "but before we continue, I find myself quite parched." He let out a whistle, and a small, scruffy boy appeared out of thin air. "Boy, fetch us a pitcher of bitter and five glasses." He held up a shilling, just out of the boy's reach. "If you're quick about it, there's another shilling in it for you, and if you've got half a brain, you'll see that there's not an empty glass among us. Yes?" The boy nodded furiously, and Martel tossed him the coin.

"I hope," Rosaline muttered to the Duke as the boy sped off, "that Lord Martel does not have any interest in fatherhood?"

"Probably not," he replied, "though I do think he would take to it quite well."

Rosaline could not hide her surprise. The Duke caught it and added, "It is simple. He would only have to do the precise opposite of what his own father did."

"Oh." She let that sink in. "Oh, how awful."

"Yes, I suppose it is." He cut her a look, and her neck heated at the way his eyes raked up and down her body. "You know, I cannot get used to this. Rosaline Bailey, in trousers and a cap. And she apparently met the wrong end of a flowerbed."

"We needed to look authentic," she blurted. "If we were too clean, everyone would notice."

"I suppose there is some truth to that." He met her gaze and dropped his voice to a murmur. "Why are you here, Rosaline?"

She fought the urge to shiver, a fresh sweat erupting on her lower back. The others, who were in the midst of a lively conversation, did not notice the other conversation happening just behind them. "We told you. The fight—"

"Why," he said, "are you here, Rosaline?"

He is too clever, she thought savagely. *Too quick to notice.* She leaned closer, ignoring her own blush, and muttered, "Charlotte.

She wanted to spend time with Cadogan in a more natural setting, where they weren't under constant scrutiny."

If the Duke was surprised by this, he did not show it. "I see. And what about you?"

"Me?" Rosaline did smile then. "I wanted a day off."

He shook his head, and his face did something quite complicated, something between irritation, admiration, and amusement. "And what is your plan to get back to Kensington? Surely your produce boy would not oblige you twice in a single day."

"Oh, you and Cadogan will be taking us." She sounded much more confident than she felt, which was a relief.

"Ah." The Duke gave a slow nod. "Here I thought we would be having supper at our club. My apologies, Miss Bailey."

Rosaline quickly glanced around them, but no one in the steadily growing crowd seemed to have noticed. "Do not call me that," she hissed to him. "If you have to call me anything, call me Ros. And refer to Charlotte as Charlie — no one can hear the name Prince."

"All right." Heat flared in his eyes again. "Ros."

"Thank God!" The boy had reappeared with a pitcher and a tower of glasses in hand, and Martel stood up with a groan of relief. Within moments, he was pressing a glass into Rosaline's hand and filling it with a foamy, amber liquid. "Trust me," he said as he did the same for Cadogan and Charlotte, "the fight is nothing without the refreshments."

"Glad to hear such a frank assessment of your motivations, Rodent," said the Duke, accepting a glass.

Martel sniffed, sticking out his chin. "I'm sure I do not know what you mean."

Rosaline stared down at her glass, feeling a sudden rush of excitement at the thought of trying beer for the first time. She did not think about the way the Duke was smirking at her.

"It's the color of fresh honey," said Charlotte, holding her glass up to the light — Cadogan quickly put his hand to her wrist and lowered the glass back down. "Does it taste sweet?"

"Not at all," said Cadogan, but he was grinning ear to ear.

A sudden roar rose through the crowd, and Rosaline could only watch, fascinated, as two men entered the warehouse from opposite sides and made their way through the crowd towards the ring. Jeers and encouraging thumps rained down on their backs, and one, the taller, thinner one with hair the same color as the beer, raised his fist.

"Is that Dean?" she said to the Duke.

"Yes," he replied. The two men entered the ring, and she caught a glimpse of Dean's opponent — a thickset, towheaded man with appalling teeth. He looked out at the crowd and thumped his chest, yelling along with his supporters.

"How... civilized." Rosaline raised her glass to her mouth and took a cautious sip. The beer was warm, a touch bubbly, earthy and dry all at once. It was like nothing she had ever tasted before, and much easier to drink than Scotch. She took another sip. "How does the fight begin?"

"Is this how we are to pass the afternoon?" said the Duke, but the words were sharp with humor, not anger. "You pressing me with questions while the answers present themselves before your very eyes?"

"You did the same to me," she said, "at the Marchbanks'."

To her delight, he seemed to bristle. "I did not," he said, then took a swig from his own glass. She looked away as his throat worked. "That was entirely different."

Then, the two fighters turned to face each other, fists up, and the noise from the crowd rose to an astonishing roar. Rosaline's heart began to thud, and when Charlotte turned around to flash her a bright, excited grin, she couldn't help grinning back and letting out a cheer of her own. "Come on, Dean!" she yelled, getting to her feet. "Throw him in the dirt!"

Martel, Cadogan, and Charlotte all turned to stare at Rosaline in astonishment. "What?!" she yelled to them, still grinning. "Are we not here to support him?"

Charlotte looked at her for a moment, then stood up and cried, "Get him, Dean!"

Rosaline grabbed Charlotte's free hand and shook it with delight, her beer sloshing over the edge of her glass. She and Charlotte joined in the symphony of yells and cheers, and Rosaline felt her throat begin to tighten, but she ignored it as the fighters circled one another.

Then, Cadogan stood up and joined in. A moment later, with much rolling of his eyes, Martel did the same. Just as Dean took his first proper swing, Rosaline looked down at the Duke, who, unlike everyone around them, had remained seated.

He was staring up at her, looking as if someone had just hit him over the head. But there was something else there as well, something beneath the stupefaction — more amusement, perhaps, and even a flash of—

Ignoring the sudden surge of heat in her gut, Rosaline let go of Charlotte's hand and grabbed the Duke's wrist. His skin was warm and surprisingly soft in the close heat. She pulled him to his feet, leaned in, and cried, "He's your friend, is he not?!"

His face was mere inches away, and she felt like she could practically see the thoughts turning in his mind. For the first time since meeting him, Rosaline realized he had a light smattering of freckles across his nose. "Yes," he finally replied. "He is."

"Then show it!" With that, she let go of his wrist and returned her attention to the fight, which was well underway.

It was a lot like dancing, Rosaline realized, after watching Dean and Flint trade a few blows and evade each other's attacks. One would lead, and the other would follow. They would mirror each other, then one would break away and do something different, and the other would have to adjust, to predict what was coming next. Dean was clearly lighter on his feet, and more comfortable in his body — he moved with a natural fluidity, as if he already knew everything that was about to happen. Flint, however, was his polar opposite; he was heavy, flat-footed, unimaginative. Much of his style was rote, mundane, predictable. But, none was more surprised than Rosaline when Dean's fist flashed out like a snake and struck Flint square in the nose.

Blood spurted down Flint's face, dripping onto the dusty ground, and the crowd went wild. Flint let out a yell of fury and swung wide, but Dean was already darting away, his smirk visible even from this distance. *First blood*, Rosaline thought, taking a gulp of beer to steady her nerves.

"How many rounds?" She did not need to look at him to know the Duke was listening.

"As many as they need," he replied. "Until one goes down and stays down."

"Then we might be here a while." She nodded at the ring. "Flint looks ready to kill."

"Maybe," said the Duke, "but arrogance is a weakness, in this sport."

She watched as Dean landed another blow to Flint's ribs, then his kidneys. Flint managed to cuff Dean around the ear, but Dean was too quick for him, and he ducked away before Flint could do more damage. "Are there any rules at all?"

"They can use wrestling holds." The Duke had leaned in closer to her to make himself heard over the crowd, and only now did Rosaline realize that the confines of polite society did not apply to them in the least. She and the Duke did not need to keep a respectable distance, to refrain from touching each other outside the bounds of a dance floor. For some reason, her blood roared hot, then very very cold. His breath tickled her ear. "But they cannot grab each other below the waist, and if one of them goes down, the other cannot hit him."

Rosaline forced herself to nod. "What are the odds," she said, "that these two will keep to the rules?" Dean landed another hit to Flint's stomach and Flint fell to one knee with a grunt.

The Duke chuckled then, the sound dark and quiet, and her stomach turned to liquid. "Dean is a fair fighter, but Flint is not afraid to fight dirty."

She saw evidence of this moments later, when Flint suddenly ducked and tried to tackle Dean to the ground. At the very last second, Dean kicked out and sent Flint flying into the dust. The crowd exploded, and the whistles rang sharp in Rosaline's ears.

"This won't last long," Cadogan said to them, nearly deafened by his own applause. "It'll be quick, brutal."

"I'm not sure of that, my lord," Rosaline shot back. Martel had obtained another pitcher of beer and poured them a fresh round of drinks, sloshing it onto her boots. "Flint is angry, and anger can be a powerful motivator."

Cadogan smiled and shook his head. "Cooler heads always prevail."

Charlotte quirked an eyebrow. "Someone should tell Bonaparte."

As the fight went on, though, Rosaline saw that Cadogan had been correct. Flint fought like a bull, head down to the dirt, energy seething from his shoulders, whereas Dean was a little more mercurial, like a bird of prey. She noticed that he rationed his energy, tapping into it only when it was absolutely necessary, unlike Flint, who left everything on the table. He did not have Dean's endurance, his discipline. If nothing else, Dean could wait until Flint tired himself out.

Sometimes, though, Flint's unrelenting strategy did pay off. He caught Dean with a surprisingly powerful punch to the stomach, and Dean hit the ground with a wheeze. Then, to Rosaline's horror, Flint kicked him in exactly the same spot before retreating to his own corner.

Before she knew it, she was shouting along with the people around her, calling for Flint to be disqualified, castrated, unmade. Anger thudded in her body, loose and close to the surface, and she lost track of her surroundings. Rosaline lunged over Charlotte's head, her empty glass swinging wide, and was only prevented from launching herself into the dirt by a sudden, firm arm wrapped around her middle.

"Come on," grunted the Duke, pulling her away from the edge. His breath was hot on the back of her exposed neck, and she nearly elbowed him in the stomach. "Calm down."

"Calm down?!" Rosaline wheezed, struggling against his grip. Thankfully, their companions were too busy yelling down at the ring to notice what was going on behind them. "He could have a lacerated liver, someone should—"

"Don't worry." The Duke was stronger than he looked — his arm felt like a metal lance around her stomach, and he had practically lifted her off the ground. She kicked out into the air, but it didn't do any good. "He only did that because he knows he is going to lose."

Rosaline frowned, refocusing on the fight. Dean was up on his feet, and he looked surprisingly steady, given the circumstances. And something had changed. There was something new in his face. Something keen, something deadly. "Really?" she said, and did not notice when the Duke returned her to earth.

It did not take long — only two rounds. Then, Dean lashed out, again like a snake, his fists flying as he struck Flint in the stomach, the ribs, then the neck, the jaw, and finally—

Rosaline could only stare as Flint fell to the dirt, unmoving. The crowd went silent for a moment, then the noise began to build, from a seething murmur to a dull roar, and then to an overwhelming cascade of sound that made her head spin and her ears ring. But she remained silent, holding her breath, waiting for those thirty seconds to pass, and when they did, Dean looked up at the crowd and raised his battered, bloody fists into the air.

Rosaline let out a shriek, dropped her glass, and began jumping up and down, every nerve in her body exploding with triumph, and she did not have to worry about being discovered, because everyone around her was doing the same, and she was grabbing something, something solid and yielding all at once, and she met the Duke's gaze, and he was grinning, wild with delight, and something about his eyes, his face—

Their embrace was brief, overwhelming. His back felt surprisingly solid under her hands, and she was shocked to find that her head fit perfectly in the space between his chin and his collarbone. It lasted either a second or ten years. But then the shock of it overcame her and she stepped back, heat flooding her face.

The Duke looked every bit as panicked and embarrassed as she felt. His face flushed red, and he quickly turned away, his jaw clenched.

Before Rosaline could do anything other than stare at him, as confused by his actions as she was by her own, she was tackled by Charlotte. Rosaline quickly put aside whatever the past few moments had been and let out a shout of laughter, giving in to all of it — Dean's win, her and Charlotte's success, and the sheer freedom of an afternoon without a stitch of lace or propriety.

⚜

"I," said Martel, raising a very imperious hand, "have been over-served."

Rosaline giggled, shoving him up against the side of the carriage to keep him from falling over as they turned a corner. "I suppose that is one way to describe it, my lord."

"Consider yourself lucky," said Cadogan, with an easy grin. "Time has been kind to him. He is a much better drunk now than he was back at school."

"You—" Martel waved his hand in Cadogan's general direction — "are a turnip head."

"That is hardly an insult," Charlotte chimed in. Her face was red and shining underneath her cap, even filthier now than it was when they'd arrived at the fight, and still Cadogan looked at her like she was the sun to his moon. "Turnips are quite good for the humors. And for swollen elbows."

"Utter poppycock," muttered Martel, mostly into the upholstered wall.

"I much prefer this to a sober Martel," said Rosaline. "He seems quite pliant. Do you think we could convince him that he is actually a dog in a man's body?"

"Maybe," said Cadogan. "Though perhaps you would have more luck with a cat. Martel denies it, but the similarities are obvious."

"Excellent point." Rosaline looked up as the carriage pulled to a stop. She did not look at the opposite corner, where the Duke had been slouching and brooding ever since they had left the fight. He had not met her gaze even once on the long ride back to Kensington from the East End. The carriage door swung open, and Rosaline gave Cadogan a pointed look. "Perhaps, my lord, you could give my dear friend a hand?"

He caught on at once and nearly tumbled out of the carriage in his haste. But he recovered in time to straighten his jacket and offer Charlotte his hand. "My lady?"

She gave him a wide, genuine grin. "You are too kind, my lord."

Once they were alone on the street — Rosaline had told the driver to stop around the corner from Prince Manor, just to be safe — Rosaline finally glanced at the Duke and felt an odd tremor of disappointment when he did not meet her gaze.

"Do not worry, Your Grace." Her voice was quiet, toneless. "I shall be gone soon. I only wanted to give them a minute to themselves."

A few moments passed, but he did not reply.

"—'os-line," grunted Martel. His face was pressed flat against the wall, and his voice was oddly nasal. "I need... runner beans."

She nodded seriously. "Runner beans. How delicious. Cadogan will ensure that your cook receives the message."

He gave a sudden twitch, his brow twisting. "No— not cook—do not want— go home—"

"Don't be silly," Rosaline told him, patting his knee. "Home is where your wine is."

Martel finally cracked open a bleary eye. "Wine? Wine s'good." Before she could reply, he tucked himself back into the corner and began to snore.

Rosaline sat back with a sigh. And when she looked up, she realized that the Duke was watching Martel with a frown.

But still, he said nothing. And he only glanced at her for a moment, his gaze tight and relentless, before his attention returned to the floor.

She could not stand this— "Your Grace—"

"Miss Bailey." Cadogan's friendly face appeared in the open doorway. His blush seemed to have deepened. "Time to go."

Rosaline nodded, and spared the Duke one final glance before she climbed out of the carriage and jumped down to the ground. Charlotte was waiting for her beside a tree, and Rosaline joined her at once, offering her a smile.

"Well?" she said, keeping her voice low. "Was it worth the risk?"

Charlotte's grin was magnetic, unstoppable. "Yes," she breathed. "Yes, it was."

Rosaline took her hand and squeezed it. "Excellent."

"Good evening, ladies," Cadogan called, waving at them from the carriage.

"Goodnight!" she and Charlotte called back, and as the carriage pulled away, she turned her back on it, some small part of her not wanting to watch it go.

❧ 16 ❧

Lisette was either very happy or very angry to see them. It was difficult to tell.

"What did you do?" she grumbled, stripping Rosaline with clinical precision. "Roll around in *la connerie?*"

Rosaline scoffed. "Hardly. And if we looked clean, we would have only drawn more attention to ourselves—"

"You are too harsh, Lisette," Charlotte chimed in. Mattie was giving her the same treatment. "Rosaline is a mastermind, truly, I never would have thought to dirty our faces—"

Lisette let out a false laugh and spun Rosaline's filthy shirt through the air. "Oh, and what a shame that would have been. No, it was far better for you to give Lisette an entire pile of smelly laundry when she—"

Rosaline grinned at her. "*Stop whining,*" she said to Lisette in French. "*You loved seeing us in trousers, and you know what those places are like.*"

"*Oh, do I?!*" Lisette spat. "*And how, my dear, would I know what a gambling hall is like?*"

Charlotte sighed, smiling. "French is such a beautiful

language." She shucked her trousers and slipped into her bathrobe. "What a shame I never had a chance to learn it."

"But you did learn it, Charlotte dear," said Mattie. "With Miss Sanders, when you were twelve."

Charlotte seemed to be genuinely surprised by this. "Oh, well. Perhaps Rosaline should refresh my memory."

"And pay the old cow no mind," Mattie added, giving Rosaline a wink. "She's just jealous that she couldn't go with you herself."

Lisette, who was busy filling their tub with hot water, snorted hard enough that Rosaline had half a mind to check for loose bits of brain on the tile. "*And do you know what the old cow has to say to you, you mouthy little—*"

Rosaline could not help it — she laughed. "I do not know why I am the object of such ire. After all, I was not the one who had an unsupervised farewell with my beloved."

Lisette and Mattie both whipped round to stare at Charlotte, who turned a bright shade of red. "Rosaline! You promised you wouldn't!"

"I never promised anything, Charlotte," Rosaline replied, grinning as she fiddled with the knot for her chest wrappings. "Besides, I think you owe all of us some lascivious details. It is the very least you can do, after the extraordinary lengths we went to this fine afternoon."

"It was hardly *lascivious*." Charlotte fidgeted, uncomfortable for the first time since Rosaline's arrival. "I simply... clarified things for him."

"And?" Rosaline prodded. She gave up on the knot — Lisette could tackle it.

Charlotte somehow went even more red. "He was... most accommodating."

"Enough!" Lisette crossed the room and halted with her face mere inches from Charlotte's. She looked deep into Charlotte's eyes, her gaze unyielding. "Did he kiss you?"

Silence as Charlotte took a careful, shaky breath. Then, finally, she beamed and said, "Yes."

Lisette, Mattie, and Rosaline all let out a shriek of triumph, and within moments, they had tackled Charlotte, sweeping her into a huge, overwhelming embrace. Rosaline even forgot that she herself was half-naked, because none of that mattered. All that mattered was that Charlotte had told Cadogan the truth, and now was facing the greatest happiness of them all.

Later, when they were freshly scrubbed and still damp from their bath, Rosaline and Charlotte stretched out across Charlotte's bed in their nightgowns, waiting.

"I must admit," Rosaline was saying, "I am so impressed by your courage." She lifted a smudge of rouge from Charlotte's favorite pot and handed the pot to Charlotte. "I cannot imagine kissing someone like that in full view of the entire street."

"Well, nobody saw us." Charlotte's grin was unfaltering. She pressed two of her fingers into the pot. "The tree was quite helpful."

There, again, Rosaline felt it — a surge of ecstatic joy, and she squeezed Charlotte's arm with her free hand. "You did it, Charlotte. So what happens next? Wedding bells?"

"Not yet," Charlotte replied, dabbing the rouge onto the tip of her nose and her Cupid's bow. "Like me, he wants to be absolutely certain. We are in no hurry, and would like to enjoy the season as much as we can."

Rosaline reflected on this for a moment, pressing the rouge onto her own nose and upper lip, then at the corners of her eyes. "You are both mad. If I were in your position, I would march him to the church myself. Anything to get out of this ridiculous pageant."

Then, suddenly, the sound of familiar footsteps.

Rosaline swore and shoved the pot of rouge out of sight just in time for Charlotte's bedroom door to fly open and Mrs. Randolph to march in, her expression thunderous.

"Good evening, Mrs. Randolph," Charlotte managed in a thin, weak voice. She was slumped against the covers, looking very ill indeed. "Are you well?"

"I," snapped Mrs. Randolph, "have heard some ludicrous whispers."

"Whispers?" Rosaline croaked, squinting at her. "What whispers?"

"That some very suspicious parcels were taken away *and* delivered to our kitchen today, amidst some unusual comings and goings." Mrs. Randolph paused, finally giving them her full attention. Before her lay two meek, sickly girls collapsed in the same bed with raw noses and watery eyes, the very picture of pathetic lassitude. After a few moments, she took a step back, her lip curling. "But perhaps... I was mistaken."

"I do not know what you mean, Mrs. Randolph." Charlotte gave a very convincing cough. "We have been absolutely bedridden today. The pollen—"

"Yes, yes," Mrs. Randolph snapped, "I know about the pollen." She was backing away towards the door now. "Let us hope you are recovered for the Eventide Ball. It would be a shame for you to miss such an important event. I will see that you are sent some supper." With that, she marched out of the room, closing the door behind her.

Once her footsteps had faded into silence, Rosaline and Charlotte collapsed into gales of laughter, giddy with their final success. When they had recovered, Charlotte wiped the moisture from her eyes and said, "Are you looking forward to the Eventide? It promises to be one of the best balls of the season."

"I suppose." Rosaline rubbed the tips of her fingers together, watching with faint interest as the rouge spread and faded into her skin. "I do like my new dress."

Charlotte's grin had an edge of mischief. "I am sure the Duke will as well." When Rosaline said nothing, Charlotte gave her a careful look and said, "He seemed... quiet, after the fight."

Rosaline smiled in return. "Busy calculating his profits, I am sure." She herself had won a tidy sum, which was currently wrapped in a stocking and tucked behind a loose floorboard beneath her bed, in case she ever needed to make a quick escape.

Still, Charlotte was looking at her. "Did something happen between you two? Did you argue?"

"No, not at all." *Quite the opposite*, she did not say. "You know how he is. Perhaps he had a disagreement with one of his associates. Now, Charlotte." She sat up. "Let us plan your outfit."

THE EVENTIDE BALL WAS EVERY BIT AS MARVELOUS AS THE rumors had promised. Breathless, Rosaline walked through a foyer dripping in false icicles, the candlelight shining in dozens of suspended orbs made of pale, pastel glass. They stood out in stark contrast to the dark walls and bluish windows, which opened on a lavish, warm evening. She could see out onto the sprawling lawn, where burning torches illuminated thin circles of gaiety and laughter. The air even smelled sweet, like roses and sugar, and it seemed to froth with possibility.

Rosaline did not know why this tension hovered around her, sending an invisible thrill along her arms and down her back. The Eventide was no different from any of the other balls she had attended thus far, and she had no reason to anticipate anything apart from the usual suspects of wine, gossip, and the occasional dance.

Perhaps, she reflected, glancing at the massive landscape poised above the grand staircase, *it is because the Duke did not say goodbye.*

And it was silly, to carry that one, fleeting moment like an insult. Because it was not an insult, it was— it was—

That morning, he had sent a small posy of purple hyacinths, with an equally small card. A card that, for some reason, she had slipped into her pocket this evening, nestling it between the pages of *Antony and Cleopatra*. It was no more verbose than any of the others he had previously sent, and the handwriting had been even more cramped and rushed than usual—

> *And though she be but little, she is fierce.*
> *H.*

It was a reference to the boxing match, of course, and even from those scant few words, he did not seem angry or displeased with her. True, he was only fulfilling his promise, his obligation, by sending her flowers, but if his temper had been piqued, then would he have included a card at all? Her instincts told her that he would not, that the card itself meant more than it appeared — it was an olive branch, an apology without an apology. Wasn't it?

Finally, Charlotte's voice broke into her thoughts.

"Where are our hosts, Father?"

Lord Devon turned around, some surprise showing in his face. "My dear, I thought you knew. The Eventide Ball is famously anonymous."

Now *that* got Rosaline's attention. "What do you mean?"

"Each year, it occurs in a different location, on a different date. The invitations are sent out, the food, drink, and orchestra are booked, and the decorations installed, but never with any hint as to who might be signing the checks." Smiling, he walked over to a cluster of fake icicles and ran his finger along the edge. "People have tried for years, fruitlessly, to solve the mystery. It is almost as if the Eventide Ball itself were in charge of its own affairs."

"Well," said Rosaline, "surely the obvious culprit is the Queen?"

"Not at all," Lord Devon replied. "In fact, I would not even mention it to her. She seems quite irritated by those who outgun her, and our host has been doing that for years."

Charlotte spun in a slow circle, looking up at the audacious chandelier. "Then whose house are we standing in?"

"I believe this one is owned by Lord Stockton, who, incidentally, is not even in attendance," said Lord Devon. "He is in Scotland, on a hunt. We must assume our mystery host rented it from him for the occasion."

"Well, however it might have come to pass," said Charlotte, "we are fortunate to experience this magic." She took Rosaline's hand and led her through the nearest doorway. "Come, let us explore."

The rest of the house was much the same as the foyer — its original fixtures were rich, dark, and intimidating, but the sumptuous decorations gave it a pervasive air of whimsy. Large, foreboding chandeliers remained unlit and wrapped in lengths of pink, gold, and white gauze, tied off so that they cascaded to the floor in great waves, only to be swept aside by those passing through. Pillars of candles were poised in corners, creating great circles of light with edges that met and blurred, softening the harsh edges of the molding. Footmen dressed in a pale, tasteful gold and bearing trays of elegant finger foods wove silently through the crowd.

As they passed into the ballroom, Rosaline saw that the party was well underway, and the dancing had already begun. In spite of the distraction, she and Charlotte still turned many a head, and a sudden whisper swept through the crowd. Rosaline almost smiled. Charlotte was dressed in her most beautiful gown yet, a vision in pale pink with pearls scattered over her skirts. Beside her, Rosaline supposed she looked like Charlotte's devilish counterpart, dressed in a deep magenta gown, with a black gossamer overskirt dotted by silver beads. She quickly snagged two glasses of wine from a passing tray and handed one to Charlotte.

Watching as Miss Brown pranced past with some nameless youth, she said to Charlotte, "Did you and Cadogan plan to meet?"

"Yes," Charlotte replied. "He should be here any minute."

Rosaline smiled at her, then caught sight of a familiar face. As Cadogan approached Charlotte from behind, putting his finger to his lips in a silent plea, she said, "I am sure he'll be here soon." With that, she turned and left them to it, chuckling when she heard Charlotte squeal in surprise.

Rosaline had found, over the past few weeks, that the Duke's regard had done what he'd said it would — it had given her a shield, a cloak of invisibility, and though she passed through groups of suitors, none of them dared approach her; they seemed quite content to stare. She sipped her wine, departed the ball-room, and made her way to the grand terrace.

This house was seated in a private dip of land near the northern edge of London, before the polished streets gave way to the crowded dirt of the city center. The air was still fresh, still warm, and deliciously fragrant. It was a lovely summer night, which likely meant that it would rain tomorrow. She looked out on a thin, desperate cluster of trees, and a rose garden that was, in contrast, flourishing. Happily, the terrace was quite empty, since most of her peers were distracted by the dancing. Here, she could be alone, she could be quiet. She could read.

"I suppose," came a quiet, amused voice. "I shouldn't be surprised to find you like this."

Surprise rippled through her and Rosaline looked up from the pages of *Antony and Cleopatra* to meet the smile of none other than Lieutenant McGrath. "Lieutenant!" she managed, breaking into an unbidden grin. "What are you—? I mean, how are you?"

His chuckle was supple, indulgent. "Much the same," he replied, nodding to his arm, which was still in a sling. "And once again, I find myself at the mercy of a pity invite."

"Generosity, sir, not pity. After all, you are a man who sacrificed his well-being for King and country." Rosaline closed her book with a snap before he could see that she was using the

Duke's note as a bookmark. "And you are, I must admit, an altogether not unwelcome sight."

"I can see where you get your wit. The Bard is the best example of them all." His gaze flickered to the book. "Strange, to think I've only spent a few minutes with you, and yet seeing you here tonight, tucked away reading while the rest of London is dancing... Forgive me if I am too forward, but it feels somehow... correct."

Rosaline smiled, leaning back against the stone railing. "Perhaps you are simply a good judge of character. A quality I am sure is common to those in your profession."

The Lieutenant was watching her with a crooked smile. "I adore the way you speak."

For some reason, this compliment unseated her, threw her completely off track. Heat rushed to Rosaline's face and she looked down at the ground. "I— I—"

"No," he said quickly, "no, that comment was completely out-of-hand, I am the one who should be embarrassed, taking such liberties with a near-stranger—"

She looked up at once. "Not a stranger." A beat. "But rather more than an acquaintance."

"Am I?" His crooked grin threatened to break through. "Now that is a true compliment."

Suddenly, a shrill cry rang through the night air, and it seemed to originate from the ballroom. "Lieuuuu—tenant?! Where are you?!"

He winced. "My host's wife. She is... rather taken with me, I'm afraid, and I cannot afford to let her feel slighted." He took a step back, then shot Rosaline a private, hopeful glance. "Another time?"

"Yes," said Rosaline, a touch breathless. Her heart seemed to be going a mile a minute. "Another time."

The Lieutenant gave her a sparkling grin, a bow, then was gone, dissolving into the party.

Rosaline wobbled a little and found her wine glass. "Pull your-self together," she muttered, polishing off the wine in the hope that it would return her to reality. She was flustered. Why was she flustered? McGrath was like any other man, happy to spoil her with sweet nothings until she—

Not nothing, an unhelpful corner of her brain piped up. *Your voice. Your words.*

Grumbling under her breath, Rosaline shoved her book back into her pocket and made her way inside.

There was no sign of McGrath anywhere in the ballroom, and Rosaline cast only a cursory glance over the dancers — Charlotte and Cadogan were leading the charge — as she headed for the refreshment table. This ball had the best food she'd seen yet, and it was tempting to walk away with an entire platter. Sighing a little, she went for the wine.

"Miss Bailey." Of course. "I can see your evening is off to a strong start."

Rosaline met the Duke's gaze with a smile that hid her nerves. "I think it is too soon to make such a pronouncement. Although the wine is quite good."

He picked up a glass of his own. He was impeccably dressed, as usual, and his face betrayed none of the tension from their last parting. "Our friends seem to be in a world of their own."

"No surprise there. It will be a challenge to get them to part ways."

"I would not dream of it," he said, almost with feeling. His gaze found hers, then skittered around the room. "I must admit," the Duke went on, his voice dropping low, "this is... a lovely orchestra, but I find I have little patience for socializing this evening."

Swallowing a spike of worry, Rosaline only smirked and said, "You forget, Your Grace, that there is more to this house than a ballroom."

Twenty minutes later, they were creeping down a darkened,

cool hallway somewhere near the back of the house. It was quiet, empty. Even the sounds of the party were distant, muted.

The Duke took another pull off the bottle of wine they'd snuck from the refreshment table. The alcohol had eased some of the tension in his frame, but he still looked skittish, irritable. "I must award you some credit, Rosaline." He passed her the bottle. "This is mildly better than a jig."

"Hush." Rosaline took a sip of wine, then opened the nearest door. No luck — just another sitting room. "We will know what we're looking for when we've found it."

"How philosophical," he replied, dry as old sherry. "At least the wine has encouraged my patience. Otherwise, I would be quite intolerable."

"If you want to settle for a boring, stuffy sitting room, be my guest. I, however, have somewhat higher standards." On impulse, Rosaline crossed the hall and made for a small, recessed door that was easy to miss at first glance. It took a heavy push, but then it swung open, revealing a dim set of stairs receding into the depths of the house.

The Duke appeared at her shoulder. "Excellent," he breathed, and she did not shiver.

The stairs were narrow, cramped, and she followed him with a certain degree of trepidation. This had been her idea, combing the house for anything remotely interesting, and now, she felt a tingle of anxiety. Where would this lead them? Nothing good could be in the cellar, surely—

The Duke halted at the foot of the stairs, where a weathered wooden door begged to be opened. He glanced at Rosaline over his shoulder, and she could have sworn he smiled. "No going back now, Bailey."

With that, he pushed open the door, and they stumbled out into—

Not the cellar. A royal tennis court.

Battered, weathered, with a mysterious stain in one corner

and a long-disintegrated net, but a tennis court nonetheless. And they were not underground — the ceiling was quite high, and capped with vaulted glass, like a greenhouse. This offered them the only source of light, thanks to the full moon and the endless glow of the summer sky; the light was dim, but adequate. Rosaline guessed that they were somewhere at the rear of the house, in a sunken addition. Heart thudding in her throat, she crossed to the nearest wall and pressed her bare hand to the crumbling plaster.

"This must date back to the Tudors," she breathed. "When it was in vogue."

The Duke, meanwhile, was busy in a corner near the door. He was in his shirtsleeves, his jacket abandoned at his feet. "They say Anne was watching a match when she was arrested." He turned, a pair of dilapidated racquets in one hand and a filthy gray ball in the other. "Shall we?"

❧ 17 ❧

Rosaline let out a laugh, but put down the bottle. "You have unwarranted faith in my coordination." She went over to him and held out her hand. "I take no responsibility for any injuries sustained as a result of this exceptionally poor choice."

"Nonsense," said the Duke, but he did not give her a racquet. He was watching her intently. "I propose a twist on the game."

Rosaline quirked an eyebrow. "A twist?"

"Whoever loses the point must answer a question."

Her stomach flipped. She ignored it. "A question?"

"Nothing untoward, I assure you." He was inscrutable. "Merely a way to pass the time."

No, Rosaline's mind screamed. "Very well," she said.

The corner of the Duke's mouth twitched. "Good." Finally, he handed her a racquet. "Since we do not have the luxury of a net, I propose we make do with the far wall."

"And what," she said, kicking off her shoes, "take it in turns to hit?"

The Duke nodded. Together, they moved towards center

court. "Whoever fails to return the hit loses the point. Fair?" At her nod, he raised his racquet and said, "My serve."

The moment the ball made contact with the wall, it became clear to Rosaline that the Duke was taking mercy on her. She was certain that he could best her at this within seconds if he wanted to. But, she recognized that that would have made this entire endeavor thoroughly redundant, not to mention short-lived.

The racquet was gritty and heavy in Rosaline's hand, the floor cold against her feet. She kept an eye on the ball, then stepped forward and swung.

To her delight, the ball went flying through the air and hit the wall with a satisfying *smack*. Rosaline could not hold back her grin as the Duke returned fire.

So it went, until it didn't.

"Tell me," said the Duke, bouncing the ball once, twice. "Your three favorite books."

"Ovid," she said at once. "*Metamorphoses*. Descartes, *La Geometrie*. And— *Twelfth Night*."

He took this in with a nod, not seeming to notice her lie. "Of course. Maths." But he smiled, then tossed the ball into the air and sent it throttling towards the wall.

This time, Rosaline managed to hold her own, and she let out a cry of triumph as the Duke dove for the ball and missed. "And to you, good sir, the same question!"

"Damn," he muttered, shoving a hand through his hair. "*Crusoe. Gulliver's Travels*. And, I suppose..." He let out a gust of air. "The *Decameron*."

Rosaline tried not to let her surprise show. She never would have imagined— "The last one is not a common choice."

He nodded, spinning his racquet. "Blame my godfather. It is a personal favorite of his."

Rosaline itched to ask another question, but she couldn't, not without winning another point. So, she served the ball, and play resumed.

The Duke won the next point. "Which do you like better," he said, "Paris or Provence?"

She blinked, taken by surprise. "Neither. They each have their own strengths. But," she added, "it is difficult to compete with a Christmas in Paris, or a summer in Provence."

His gaze was unwavering, hollow in the dim light of the summer sky. "You miss it."

Rosaline took a breath, swallowing the familiar surge of longing. "Of course."

He won the next point as well. Rosaline shot him a scowl as she went over to the bottle of wine. "I am beginning to suspect that I've been duped."

"Perish the thought," he replied, easy and amiable. "Have you —?" He seemed to chew on his words. "Do you enjoy London?"

Rosaline took a sip of wine. "Yes," she landed on. "And no."

"Why?"

She smirked at him, taking another sip. "For that, Your Grace, you must win another point."

Thankfully, she took him by surprise this time. The Duke grumbled a curse and tapped the head of his racket on the ground. "Go on, then."

"Why does your godfather irritate you?"

The Duke appeared to be genuinely surprised by this. "He does not... irritate me. Really," he added, when she snorted. "He simply... He has a large personality, and a mischievous streak that threatens to outdo every whiff of propriety. It can be difficult, sometimes, to keep up."

Rosaline smiled. "I am sure the Dowager Countess gives him a run for his money."

The Duke smiled in return, then tapped his racquet on the ground again. "Your serve."

He took the next point with a savage hit that ricocheted well out of Rosaline's reach. She did not even bother to try. Instead, she put a hand to her hip and let out a huff of air. "This game is discriminatory," she said, "against players who wear dresses."

"Sounds like Henry VIII to me," the Duke replied, fetching the ball. "Why Shakespeare?"

She frowned. "Pardon?"

"Why Shakespeare?" he repeated. "As far as I can tell, you have committed much of his work to memory. Why?"

"Because," Rosaline said, without thinking, "his works are as simple and as complex as breathing. He creates joy from nothing, sorrow from ecstasy, and prosperity from ruin. And," she added, "his verses... they are like music. Overwhelming, intoxicating. Heart-breaking."

A throbbing silence fell as the Duke looked at her. Then, he turned away and hit the ball.

Somehow, Rosaline took the next point. She suspected this to be the result of lenience on the Duke's part, but did not contest it. "Tell me," she said, "what is your idea of a perfect day?"

"Good grief." The corner of his mouth twitched, impish. "You overestimate me. Nothing interesting, I can assure you."

"Try me," she said.

He gave her a look of exasperation, but it was coupled with a near-smile. "Up early enough to catch a ride in the dew, but not so early that I hate every second of it." His gaze darted away, as if this were somehow embarrassing. "A good breakfast, with plenty of bacon, then a few sparring matches. Not just me and Dean, but Ed as well, maybe even the Captain, if he was on leave. We'd find our way to the nearest pub, lose ourselves in a few rounds of pints, maybe get into trouble." The Duke tapped the head of his racquet on the ground again, the sound sharp and discordant in comparison to his low voice. "But I would be home in time for supper. In time to——" He broke off suddenly, then bent to pick up the ball. Before Rosaline could even begin to wonder what he'd stopped himself from mentioning, he'd sent a serve roaring at her head.

"This," she puffed out a few moments later, slumped against the wall, "is unfair."

The Duke almost smiled. "Go on, then. Your perfect day?"

It was not a difficult question to answer. "Waking early, perhaps early enough to see the sunrise. A walk in the garden, tea and scones on the porch. Then a tutorial, until I had conjugations and equations tumbling out of my ears. A game of cards, maybe, with Lisette or my father." She spun her racquet. "A light meal, and a fruit tart for dessert. I would spend the rest of the evening reading, and listening to Lisette's stories. We would laugh, and have a glass of wine, and I would hear the cicadas in the trees, knowing that the following day, it would all happen again. I would be free from observation, from gossip, from judgment." Rosaline looked at him, a fresh heat roaring under her skin. "Does that answer your question?"

For several moments, the Duke simply looked at her, still inscrutable. Finally, he nodded, and said, "Perhaps we should take a break. I apologize, I quite forgot that you were wearing stays."

In reply, Rosaline dropped her racquet and slid down to the ground. "You, sir, are a true gentleman."

The Duke gave a theatrical stumble, as if warding off a blow. "The height of insult," he said, and to her surprise, he sat down beside her, hardly more than a foot away. He picked up the bottle of wine, then seemed to think before he took a sip. "This dress... it suits you, as well."

Rosaline did not blush. "Thank you." She cleared her throat, feeling as if she were edging along a precipice. "Are we still...?"

The Duke's expression did not change, but she caught just a hint of red along his cheekbones. "We can, if you like." He passed her the bottle. "Why can't you make up your mind about London?"

Rosaline ran her thumb along the bottle. The exercise and the alcohol had been too much, perhaps, because she could not seem to control the surge of emotion in her chest. She could feel it, keen as a knife, and she could feel the silence of the room around them, and she could not understand why she was about to say— "London is my childhood, the first air I breathed, the first land I touched." Rosaline took a shaky breath. "But it is where I lost half my world. It is impossible to be here, and not to think of her."

The Duke glanced at her. "Your mother." It was not a question.

Rosaline nodded. "Yes." She took a swig of wine, and it steadied her. "We were inseparable. She taught me much of what I know; she is the reason I love Shakespeare and Latin and philosophy. She devoted every waking moment to me, to my father, and losing her... it felt as if a part of me had simply been cut away."

Something, some unnamed emotion, flickered across his features. "What of her family?" he said. "I know you have your father, but—"

Rosaline let out a dry, unamused laugh and passed him the bottle. "I have not seen my mother's relations since I was very young, certainly not since her funeral. The kind thing to say is that they did not approve of my mother's choice in husband. To them, my father and I are not family." Before the Duke could respond, before he could even hint at the sympathy, the pity, that she did not want to receive, Rosaline said, "And you, Your Grace?" She looked right at him, unyielding now in a way she had not been before, not with him. "What of your family?"

She watched as that nameless emotion flickered across his face again, and expected him to turn away, to say something or nothing and leave her, to crawl into his shell and push her away, just as he had done after their embrace. But then, to her surprise, the Duke put down the bottle, let out a sigh, and leaned his head back against the wall. It was a mark of acquiescence. Of surrender.

"My parents," he said, his voice low, "died quite suddenly, when I was a baby. There was a—" His throat worked. "An outbreak. Smallpox. It worked its way through half our village, and the two nearest ones. Ed — Cadogan, I mean — lost his parents as well." The Duke took a quick breath, as if to clear his mind. "Neither of us was even home. Our parents had sent us to the seaside at the first whisper of infection. Not that we remember it, of course."

Rosaline stared at him, her ears ringing with sudden pity. She could not imagine, could not even fathom—

"They left clear instructions. We were brought to the Dowager Countess, who looked after us until... until it was all over. It was some time before she felt comfortable sending us home, not that I can blame her." He almost smiled. "I suppose you could say that is part of the reason why he and I are such close friends. We were together from a very young age, in more ways than one."

"Yes," said Rosaline, a touch breathless. "Yes, you were. What of your godfather?"

The Duke frowned. "It was complicated, for him. He and my father were brothers in every way, except blood, and my mother was like a sister to him. It took a few years before he... found his way back to me. But once he returned, his commitment was absolute, unshakeable. He even moved into our family estate because he insisted that my parents would have wanted me to spend my childhood there, regardless of what might happen to them." He smiled suddenly. "He was rather the devil on my shoulder, growing up."

Rosaline smiled as well, restraining the urge to reach for him, to lay a hand on his arm. "He sounds like quite a remarkable man."

"I suppose he is." The Duke's gaze found hers, and his eyes were almost gray in the muted dusk. "Your mother. Is that why you were... upset at the opera?"

It is uncanny, she thought, her head spinning, *how much he sees*. And she could not bring herself to lie. "Yes." Rosaline tried to take a breath, but her throat was tight with emotion. "She was a singer. An amateur, in truth, but she was very talented. *Le nozze di*

Figaro was one of her favorites. We used to act it out together, just the simpler parts, you understand, and when she would sing the aria..." She brushed away a tear and cleared her throat. "The other night was the first time I'd heard it in years. To say I was unprepared for it would be an understatement."

"I see," the Duke said, and she could hear everything he was not saying, as well. She could hear the sadness, the empathy. "I understand, why you did not tell me at the time."

Rosaline tried to smile again. "Yes, I am not generally disposed towards maudlin self-pity. Perhaps that is one more skill to commend me."

She had meant it as a joke, but the Duke winced, pushed a hand through his unruly hair. He looked at her, and for a split second, she could see everything, all of the emotion in his eyes. "I cannot tell you," he said, his voice strained, "how much I regret what I said that night."

Rosaline blinked, heat surging up her neck. "No, I— That is not what I—"

"No," he said, a touch impatient. "I saw only what I wanted to see, which gave me an excuse to behave like an abominable ass. I have my own problems with the peerage, with this whole ridiculous farce, but I was wrong to project that anger onto others, especially onto someone as kind and as fearless as you." His gaze was bright, unfaltering. "I am sorry, Rosaline."

The corner of her mouth twitched, betraying nothing of the roiling emotion in her stomach. "There is no need for such histrionics," she murmured, "Your Grace."

He grinned suddenly, all impudence. "Hal," he said, and his face was close, close enough that she could count his freckles, if she wished. "Call me Hal."

Rosaline took a slow, steadying breath in a futile attempt to calm her roaring heart. Unbidden, her gaze dropped to his mouth, its teasing lilt daring her to move closer, or to pull away. She slowly returned her gaze to his face, and was astounded to find that the Duke had mirrored her. He was staring at her mouth, his eyes dark with—

"Very well," she breathed. "Hal."

His gaze snapped to hers, and Rosaline could feel it, could feel the air tighten and squeeze around them, pulling them together with a silent, inexorable power. Instead of fighting it, she surrendered, and stopped only a bare inch from his face, waiting.

She could see it again in his eyes, a flash of that unrelenting heat, and he reached for her, his hand slipping into the crook of her waist, and he was close, so close, that she could see the flecks of amber among the blue of his irises, and it was overwhelming, the weight of his hand on her body, the puff of his breath on her cheek, and she yearned for it, suddenly desperate, ready to fling herself into that infinite, enticing unknown—

BANG.

Rosaline jumped, whipping round to stare at the far corner of the tennis court.

CRASH. Then the sound of breaking glass, and a series of high-pitched shrieks.

"Shit," muttered the Duke, and he was on his feet in an instant. He offered her his hand. "Come, we had best see what that's about."

"What do you think happened?" Rosaline bit out, her heart going a mile a minute. She took his hand and struggled to her feet — her dress was stiff and heavy against her sweaty skin.

The Duke shook his head. He was not looking at her. "At this sort of party, anything is possible."

A minute later, they arrived at the ballroom, where a scene of general chaos was in full play. A crowd had formed around something near what had once been the refreshment table, but now was a pile of smashed glass and decimated food. Lying in the middle of it, a streak of whipped cream artfully splashed across her bosom, was Miss Brown, apparently in a dead faint.

"Ah," Rosaline muttered to the Duke. Apparently, their concern had been for nothing. "A well-timed swoon."

He nodded. They were standing quite close together, she realized, and panting for breath. "She chose her victim well. Looks like Rosier is ready to run for the hills."

Rosaline stifled a giggle, because this was true. Rosier, who was trapped with one arm underneath Miss Brown's torso, had gone very pale and sweaty. A part of her recognized that it was easier for her and the Duke to focus on this instead of what had happened — what had *almost* happened — down in the tennis court. Even now, her heart throbbed with lost possibility, which wasn't helped by the nearby heat of his arm. The Duke was still in his shirtsleeves.

"Out of the way!" Mrs. Brown shrieked, descending upon her daughter with a box of salts. "She is of very delicate constitution!"

"The only delicate thing about Miss Brown is her sanity," murmured the Duke, and Rosaline let out a very inelegant snort. She was not the only one who was taking amusement from the scene, and as she looked around the room, she made eye contact with none other than Lieutenant McGrath, who was by the doorway. He was smirking, and when he saw her, he winked.

Rosaline grinned, then, to her surprise, she saw McGrath's expression flicker and change. His gaze drifted over her shoulder, and his smile disappeared, replaced by a powerful scowl.

Shocked, Rosaline glanced over her shoulder, and saw that the Duke had met McGrath's gaze. His face was stony, unreadable, and when she looked back at McGrath, he had vanished.

"What a riot, eh, Prongs?" Cadogan appeared out of thin air, Charlotte beaming by his side. "Come, we should leave the tidying up to the professionals. There are fresh drinks in the garden." He clapped a hand on the Duke's shoulder. "What on earth did you get up to? There's plaster dust all over your back—"

"Join us, Rosaline!" Charlotte linked her arm with Rosaline's, then she noticed Rosaline's expression. "Whatever is it? Is something wrong?"

Rosaline gave her a quick smile. "Nothing, Charlotte. Nothing at all."

⚜

THE NEXT MORNING, ROSALINE WAS SHAKEN AWAKE INTO A DIM blue dawn. Her head heavy, her mouth dry, she could only blink as Lisette whispered, "Get up, *ma chère*, get up— He is here— the Duke—"

"What?" Rosaline mumbled. She was yanked out of bed and shoved into a dressing gown. "What on earth are you—?"

"He is *here*," Lisette hissed, tying the dressing gown shut. "He needs to speak with you, urgently. Oh my goodness, it is happening— Oh, just as I imagined— Well, maybe not quite as I imagined, there is no string quartet—"

"Lisette." Rosaline yawned widely. "You're not making any sense."

"Listen!" Lisette pulled her out of the room and into the deserted hall. "He came to the kitchen door, and thank God the cook was already up— The Duke said he had to see you right away, that it was a matter of the utmost importance." The stairs came next, and Rosaline had to cling to the banister to keep from falling down. Lisette let out a wistful sigh. "To think, *ma petite fille*, she is going to be engaged to a *Duke*—"

"Engaged?" Rosaline's brain chugged and caught up. "Lisette, you are out of your mind—"

"Why else would he be here?!" Lisette hissed furiously. "It is not yet dawn!"

"He does not love me," Rosaline hissed back, trying not to panic. "You forget, Lis, that he and I— we— none of it is real—"

Lisette snorted. They reached the bottom of the stairs, and the dark, gloomy hall felt like a mausoleum. "There is only so much you can pretend, *ma chère*, and he is not so good of an actor." She pulled open the drawing room door, squeezed Rosaline's hand, and said, "I shall be right here, if you need me." With that, she shoved Rosaline into the drawing room and closed the door behind her.

Her mind still reeling, her heart still pounding, Rosaline turned to face the Duke.

He was standing by the fireplace, dressed in a thick coat, riding trousers, and boots, his face gray with exhaustion. She could see the dull purple circles under his eyes, and realized that he likely had not yet been to sleep that night. She tried to remember how they had parted, mere hours before — his face had been ruddy, his mouth warm where it grazed her hand. She trembled and crossed her arms against her stomach.

"I am sorry," said the Duke, before she could say anything. "To wake you. I would not, were it not absolutely vital that I speak with you."

"Hal." She was too exhausted to see the way he shivered at his name. "What is it?"

"I have to leave. London, that is."

The words were tiny, simple. Devastating. She stared at him. "What?"

"There has been an attempted break-in at my estate," he went on. "The messenger arrived only an hour ago, and I must—" His jaw worked. "There are important things, valuable things, at the estate. I have to see the damage, work with the constable."

"Good Lord." Rosaline sank onto the nearest couch, suddenly feeling quite awake. "Was anyone hurt?"

"No," he replied, with evident relief. "But my staff are rather rattled, and we have to contain the news." He was looking at her. "I am sorry to leave you like this. It is not... It is not by choice."

"No, I—" She could not think what to say. "You must go. This, everything here— it is of very small concern, by comparison."

The Duke stared at her, then, to her surprise, he closed the distance between them and sat down beside her. He smelled of honeysuckle and river air, and he was so close, so pale in the dim light. She restrained the urge to put a hand to his arm, just to confirm that he was real. "I will only be gone a week," he said, his voice low, "perhaps two. And I will write to you."

Rosaline fought off a shiver. His gaze was relentless. "You do not need—"

"If you have any trouble," he went on, "with London's gentlemen, you must tell me. And Cadogan will keep an eye on you, as well."

She almost smiled. "That is very kind, but—"

To her utter astonishment, the Duke leaned forward and pressed a kiss to her temple. He rested his forehead against her hair, and her entire body exploded — she could feel the warmth of his skin, his breath against her cheek.

"I will write," he murmured. "Rosaline."

Her name was like a prayer on his lips, and she squeezed her eyes shut, wondering, yet again, if she was dreaming. "*Bon voyage*, Hal."

He pressed another kiss to her temple, and this time, she could feel his smile. Then he stood up and was gone, the drawing room door creaking open behind him.

18

Moment after moment passed as Rosaline sat in the cool, dim morning, unable to shake the conviction that she was still asleep, that everything — the Duke, his hand, his mouth, his voice — had been but a dream. It seemed impossible, now that he had vanished, to imagine him here, among the furniture and the wallpaper that she knew so well. The air hung still and quiet, undisturbed by its sudden visitor, by the turmoil of her thoughts. Until—

"*Ma chère?*" Lisette slipped into the drawing room, her face carrying all the hope and worry of a dozen mothers. "What has happened?"

Rosaline shook her head. She hardly knew herself. "The Duke has left London."

"*Quoi?!*" Lisette sat down beside Rosaline, put a hand to her knee. "*What do you mean?*"

"There has been some trouble at his estate." Rosaline did not feel able to parse the words into French, not when they felt so foreign on her own tongue. "Serious enough that he must go there himself. For at least a week, he said, but likely longer."

"*Mon Dieu!*" Then, a muffled cry came from the kitchen, and Lisette winced. "I must go, *ma chère,* I have my chores—"

"Yes, go," said Rosaline, and Lisette gave her a final look of concern before she ran from the room. Rosaline sank into the cushions, caught in a parody of wakefulness. Her mind dull and aching and sharp all at once, she began to replay each moment of their interaction, trying to understand when, precisely, she had begun to care for the Duke.

It was the only explanation for the way she felt without the surety of his presence — unseated, lost. When, Rosaline wondered, had her heart taken this leap without consulting her mind? And, was she drawn to him merely as the result of physical attraction? That odd, fateful moment the night before, when the lines between them had begun to shift, to blur, to transform into something new altogether — when she had been ready to step into the unknown, with little care for her heart, her sanity — had that been the result of *attraction*, of reckless daring and opportunism, or of something entirely different?

What would have happened? she asked herself, over and over again. *What would have happened if we had not been interrupted?*

Though she could not answer that question, Rosaline could understand her own behavior, to a degree. Attraction could, she knew, be involuntary. But affection was another beast entirely.

Perhaps this was all the natural result of her and the Duke's shared conspiracy, of an unlikely alliance, of too much time spent alone together. Too many conversations, too many unspoken decisions to chip away at the walls between them. When Rosaline thought back to the Duke on the tennis court, a touch sweaty and kinder than she could have ever imagined, then to the way he had kissed her temple mere minutes before, leaning into her as if she were the only thing in the world keeping him standing — she had to question when things had changed, when *he* had changed. Where was the man who had insulted her, ignored her, tolerated her with only the barest minimum of propriety? A part of her wanted nothing more than to go back to *that* version of the Duke. It had been so much easier to dislike him.

And what now? What would come of their separation, their distance? Would it stretch the invisible, tangible bond between them, until it snapped and was left to wither, untouched? *Or,* she thought, with a tremor in her belly, *will it strengthen the unsaid? Will it push us somewhere we never thought we would go?*

Rosaline returned to her room, too listless and agitated to sleep, and stood before her desk. Her proofs and pages of hastily scribbled French lay before her, an echo of what felt like another life, cheerful and unconcerned with matters of the heart. The sun began to threaten at the horizon; it would be several hours until Charlotte awoke from the revels of the previous night. What would she think of the Duke's sudden disappearance? What would she say?

Rosaline shook her head and shivered, reaching for her copy of *Julius Caesar*. If nothing else, perhaps the Bard could distract her.

The sky burst red and brilliant, and, following their cue, clouds began to descend from the east. A light rain broke shortly after eight o'clock, and the clock had just chimed ten when there came a soft noise from the corridor.

Charlotte appeared, yawning widely. Her braids were mussed, and she had a pillow crease across one cheek, but she looked as lovely as ever. "Good morning, dear. How dreary it is!" She made to join Rosaline in bed, but hesitated when she saw the tea tray, Rosaline's second of the morning. "Oh, I had not realized... How long have you been awake?"

Rosaline managed a smile, putting aside *Caesar*. "A while. Charlotte, I have news."

It took little time for her to relay the events of the morning, and Charlotte listened carefully, her hand on Rosaline's arm. "Gosh," she said, her eyes wide. "It sounds most serious."

Rosaline nodded. "He would not leave, otherwise." Suddenly,

her exhaustion seemed to catch up with her, rolling over her like a wave, and she slumped back into her bedding.

Charlotte's hand, still on her arm. "I know you must be very disappointed."

"Hardly." Rosaline offered her a thin smile. "He can be quite insufferable."

"Can he?" Charlotte's voice was light, unassuming. "You seemed to enjoy yourself last night. Or perhaps that was in spite of his insufferable nature, rather than in deference to it."

Rosaline blushed, caught out. The memories were still too fresh, too real, for her to face in the clear, if muggy, light of day. At least Charlotte had been kind enough not to mention Rosaline and the Duke's prolonged disappearance from the evening's diversions. "What are our obligations?"

"Very little, given the weather," said Charlotte. "There shall be no promenading, but we do have Lady Ednam's tea party this afternoon."

"No promenading," mused Rosaline. "Which means—?"

"Yes." Charlotte nodded. "Etiquette lessons."

Rosaline groaned into her pillow, and Charlotte grinned.

⚜

AT THE VERY LEAST, ROSALINE HAD TO ADMIT THAT LADY Ednam knew how to host a tea party.

It began quite normally. Silver and china, a light afternoon blend, cakes shining with peachy icing, a violinist in the corner. Twenty young ladies in total, seated around a ravishing table in a long, well-lit upper hall. The conversation was mundane — the same, repetitive stories about dresses and flirtations and ribbons and the weather. But then the mothers, who had been hovering in the corner, left the room, and Lady Ednam sprang into action.

"Ethel, Henrietta — the tables, quickly."

Within the space of about three minutes, the tea hall was

transformed into a gambling den, and Rosaline found herself facing quite the challenge at whist.

"Goodness me, Miss Bailey." A grin from Miss Harris, across a neat little trick. "You do play a very spirited hand."

Rosaline left with a few more coins in her pocket, her mind awhirl and her cheeks flushed from Lady Linley's secret bottle of gin. Charlotte was grinning like mad, stifling the occasional hiccup, and they clung to one another as they slipped back into Prince Manor. Mrs. Randolph met them at the door, offering little more than a disapproving glare, before she barked out, "Dining room in half an hour," and swept away.

"Just wait until she hears of the Duke's departure," whispered Rosaline as they shed their cloaks. "She will hardly be able to breathe for anger."

"Miss Bailey?" Benny offered her a silver dish with a smile. "The post."

Rosaline froze, staring at the little envelope with her name written on it. Written in a very familiar hand. "What?" she managed, her pulse jumping in her throat.

"The... post?" Benny's confidence seemed to wane. "The afternoon post, Miss Bailey. It arrived just ten minutes ago."

"No," she said. "No, that cannot be—"

"What on earth is the matter?" Charlotte joined her. "For Heaven's sake, Ros, it is only a letter—"

"A letter," Rosaline muttered, "from the Duke."

It took a moment, then Charlotte recovered. "But that's impossible—"

"No," said Rosaline. "Not if he posted it on his way out of the city." *But why?* she wanted to cry. *What more could he wish to say to me?*

"He must have urgent news," said Charlotte. Then, when Rosaline did not move— "Oh, for Heaven's sake, *I'll* open it—"

"No!"

Both Charlotte and Benny turned to stare at her, unnerved.

Rosaline quickly snatched the letter off the tray, stuffed it into her pocket, and said, "I will open it later."

"Very well." Charlotte shot her another quizzical look before turning to Benny. "Would you bring us some tea in the Blue Room? A few biscuits would not go amiss, either."

"Certainly, Lady Charlotte." Benny gave them both a nod and departed, shooting Rosaline a final, worried glance.

Rosaline empathized — she was quite worried about herself, as well. She had no idea why her heart pounded with a ferocity that echoed down her spine and settled in the bottom of her stomach, nor why her face burned and her hands quivered. *It has to be the shock*, she thought as she followed Charlotte into the Blue Room. *The shock of receiving a letter, when a part of me expected to never see him again.*

֎

THE REMAINDER OF THE EVENING PASSED AT A SNAIL'S PACE. IT was as if Time itself had decided to taunt her, cruel and merciless, for a sin unknown or as yet uncommitted. Rosaline had to force herself to sit still as she and Charlotte were grilled on dining etiquette, Mrs. Randolph's sharp eye following the slope of their shoulders, the height of their chins. *There are a limited number of ways to sip soup*, Rosaline thought, and just avoided knocking her spoon against the china. *Surely she cannot mean for us to master them all?*

They ate a proper supper with Lord Devon, who was in high spirits and attempted to cajole Rosaline into reciting Shakespeare aloud. She managed to escape with her dignity intact, and when she and Charlotte reached the top of the stairs, bid her friend a hasty goodnight. Charlotte merely smiled, not saying a word about the elephant in the room, and Rosaline loved her for it.

But, of course, the universe could not be so kind. Lisette was waiting for her by the changing screen, and questions burst from her mouth before Rosaline even managed to close the door.

"*I have been thinking, my dear — what if the Duke's departure is not so simple as it seems? He could have a lover in the countryside, and she has fallen ill, or...*" Lisette raised an eyebrow. "*Something worse.*"

Rosaline sighed, pausing beside her bed. "*If that were the case, he would not bother saying goodbye. Doing so might leave him too exposed to scandal, should the truth ever emerge.*" She toed off her shoes, then pulled her handkerchief out of her pocket and dropped it beside her pillow. The Duke's letter was hidden within it, and if Lisette noticed, she said nothing.

"*Do not underestimate him.*" For all the severity of her words, Lisette's voice was gentle. "*Men are capable of anything.*"

"Yes, Lis," said Rosaline, making her way over to the screen. "I am aware."

Perhaps her exhaustion was showing — Lisette said little more, and did not press the issue as she helped Rosaline to undress. Rosaline was beginning to feel her interrupted night; her eyes itched, then slipped shut while Lisette was braiding her hair.

Before Lisette departed, she glanced at Rosaline and said, "I am sorry that he left, *ma chère*. I know that you and he are... accustomed to each other's company."

Rosaline managed a smile. "It is all right, Lis." Anxiety, sudden and fervid, tangled in her stomach as she realized how close she was to reading his letter. "I wonder..." She bit her lip. "I am certain his absence will be the talk of the town soon enough. But in the meantime, might I count on your discretion, amongst the servants?"

For a moment, Lisette simply looked at her, then crossed the room and embraced her, planting a quick kiss on her forehead. "Of course, *ma chère*. You do not even have to ask."

Rosaline waited until the door had closed and Lisette's footsteps had faded down the hall before she gave in and darted across the room. She locked the door, blew out all the candles except for one, and flung herself into bed.

Here, in the sudden, brilliant glow of her solitary candle, she could stare at the Cunningham family seal and allow her excitement to surge, devilish and new. She was embarrassed to see her fingers trembling as they edged beneath the seam and broke the purplish wax.

The letter was longer than she'd expected — two sheets, covered front and back in that delectable, messy handwriting of his. Rosaline held the paper up to the light and began to read.

DEAR R.—

I write this to you in the fleeting moonlight, shortly before I depart London. I do not know whether I shall be able to bid you farewell in person — Does Randolph impose a nightly sentry at the gates? If so, I am about to make their acquaintance — and even if I am, I doubt that I will have the time or the presence of mind to say the right things, as I would like to say them. The circumstances of my leaving are frustrating and unavoidable — I must away to the country, even if all of my instincts tell me to remain in London and damn the consequences — and I find myself regretting that we were never able to finish our game of tennis. I believe, R., that it was your turn to ask a question. The serve is yours, and I need all the diversion I can get. Without the right company, the country can be quite dull.

I realize that my departure might compromise your standing in the eyes of London's leading men, and I assure you that Cadogan is well aware of the situation. If you would have him, he is quite happy to waltz you away from any unwanted admirers, and make it clear that in spite of my absence, my choice remains the same. It rankles me that we must take such measures, but I swore to you that I would protect you, and I am determined to keep my word.

My butler has come to the door to inform me that the horses are ready. He has a short temper, and I must not test it. But allow me to close by telling you that during my time away from London, I will think of little else besides your laugh, and our stolen Eventide moment before we found ourselves so rudely interrupted.

I can only hope that you might reply.

If we shadows have offended,
Think but this, and all is mended,
That you have but slumbered here
While these visions did appear.

Yours,
H.

Rosaline let the pages fall to her covers and noticed that her hands were still trembling. A fire had burst in her belly, and her face throbbed with too many emotions to name. Between this letter and the Duke's farewell visit, his mouth warm and soft on her skin, she hardly knew what to think. Why should he speak and write to her so fondly, with such abandon? When had his severity shifted, replaced by this unnamed but unmistakable tenderness?

What is happening to us? she thought. *What have we become?*

Rosaline did not know how long she sat there, staring down at the slanting, jet-black words. She ran her fingers over the paper, feeling where his pen had pressed, where it had flown, where it had scraped. He was a hasty writer, and seemed to care little for appearances. A reflection, in part, of his own character. She could feel the physical weight behind his words, and knew, as surely as she knew her own face, that he had written this with thought, and with care. He would not have said anything that he did not mean to say.

And to think — the Duke had taken the time to write this letter, and to post it, just on the off-chance that he would not be able to bid her farewell in person. What that meant, Rosaline could only guess.

A week before, she would never have imagined that she might exchange letters with the Duke of St. Albans. And now, Rosaline went over to her desk, gathered ink, quill, and stationery, along with her favorite dictionary, then climbed back into bed. Only once did she pause to wonder what she was doing, but then she dipped her quill into the ink and began to write, using the dictionary as a stable surface for her craft.

It was a simple, courteous letter, but towards the end, she paused, remembering the way the Duke had leaned into her, not just once but twice, the heat of his breath on her cheek. He had asked her for a question. Rosaline bit her lip, dipped her quill back into the ink, and wrote:

Tell me, do you dream?

With that, she signed the letter, resolved to seal it in the light of day, when she would not risk burning her fingers or, worse, the sheets. She tucked the paper beneath her pillow, her fatigue stealing over her like a shadow, even with her stomach still in tense, excited knots. Rosaline faced the small, trembling flame, and thought, *I wish to know what this is, between the Duke and myself.*

Then she blew out the candle, and knew no more.

ROSALINE FOUND BENNY FIRST THING IN THE MORNING, JUST outside the bustling, warm kitchen. She waited until no one was looking, then tugged him back into the outer hall. "Do me a favor?" she whispered, pushing the envelope into his hands. "Post this for me?"

He looked at her for a moment, wary, then nodded. "Of course, Miss Bailey."

"And Benny," she added, before she lost her nerve. "If there is a reply, please bring it straight to me. Do not..." Rosaline swallowed. "Do not include it with the rest of the post."

He nodded again. "Certainly, Miss Bailey."

And that, of course, was how it began.

❧ 19 ❧

A day later, the Duke's disappearance hit the society papers. Rosaline and Charlotte were sitting at breakfast with Lord Devon when Rosaline found a small pamphlet tucked under her plate. She waited until the Earl was distracted by one of his own stories, then slipped the pamphlet into her lap, nudging open the pages of *Madam Kensington's Society Papers, No. Twenty-Eight*.

As she read, Rosaline felt an invisible knot within her sternum unwind and pool beneath her bellybutton. *Thank goodness*, she thought, skimming the next two paragraphs. It was all speculation and wide-ranging hints, with none of the truth. She slipped the pamphlet into her pocket and returned to her meal, ignoring Charlotte's quizzical glance. There would be time for that later.

That afternoon, she and Charlotte promenaded with Cadogan, and Rosaline watched Rumor dart around the park, silver and shining in the brilliant sunlight, touching upon couples and mothers and sisters. She watched as whispers cascaded around her, followed by glances directed at the bare finger on her left hand.

Rosaline was an excellent mathematician; she could put two and two together. But it did not help matters when she and Charlotte returned to the carriage and found themselves faced with a red-faced, swollen Dragon.

"Is it true?" hissed Mrs. Randolph, glaring at Rosaline. "The Duke has left the city?"

"Yes, said Rosaline. "To attend to urgent matters at his estate. He will return to London within a fortnight."

"Will he?" Spit foamed at the corners of Randolph's mouth. "He had better. If I learn that you refused him—"

"Mrs. Randolph," said Charlotte, bright and friendly. "Have you seen the new roses at the front of the fountain? They are a delight!"

But distracting Mrs. Randolph would not work forever. When they returned to Prince Manor, she looked at Rosaline and said, "Given the Duke's absence, I expect you to be most accommodating at tonight's ball."

"Yes, Mrs. Randolph." Rosaline turned away, and collided directly with Benny.

Then Benny, who was one of the most steady-handed and sure-footed people Rosaline knew, dropped what appeared to be an entire tray of afternoon post.

"Good Heavens." Mrs. Randolph glared at him, askance. "Pull yourself together, Benjamin."

"Yes, ma'am, apologies." But he sent Rosaline a pointed look, and she immediately knelt to help him gather the envelopes. "That one," he whispered, pushing a letter beneath her hand.

"Thank you," she whispered back. "But perhaps we should find a more subtle way of conducting our business."

He gave a nod. "Understood."

All through her preparations, the carriage ride, and the ball itself, Rosaline thought of little else besides the unopened letter tucked beneath her pillow. *He replied*, she thought, over and over again, until the words lost their meaning, until they became loose and liquid in her mind. In spite of the Duke's promise to write to her, a part of her had doubted that he would actually do it. But it was her name on the letter, pointed and dark in his distinctive hand.

Rosaline barely noticed as she was spun around, handed glasses of wine, and made to laugh. Charlotte cut her one too many quizzical looks, but Rosaline ignored them all, thinking that at this point in the season, she could afford a little eccentricity. When they had finally returned to Prince Manor and unwound their hair, Rosaline once again locked her door, pulled out the Duke's letter, and held it to the candlelight.

Breaking the Cunningham seal felt like some kind of transgression, a way of teasing the Fates, and Rosaline savored the tendril of anticipation snaking up her spine. *Ridiculous*, she told herself, *it is simply a letter.*

Dear R.,

I shall not pester you with questions such as — How is London? How was the ball at Clearwater Manor? What is the weather? — because you and I both know you would dismiss me as quite an astonishing bore. Therefore, I shall begin by stating that the journey passed, as all journeys do, and I am thankful it is over, even if I do enjoy any excuse to be in the fresh air.

The damage to the house is minimal, thankfully, and it appears that the thieves took little, if anything at all. But they ruined a large antique window, which now requires extensive repair. As you can imagine, these events have caused quite a stir, and I have already had to entertain the inquiries of several neighbors who were "just passing." In truth, their solicitude makes me long for the city.

Upon returning to my library, I thought of you, and noticed that my collection of the Bard is rather lacking. You have inspired me, R., to refresh my memory of his splendid works. I shall have to pass the time somehow, waiting for the glazier — who is as fickle as a cat, to tell you the truth — to complete what he is now calling his magnum opus. What better way to amuse myself than to attempt to best you at the Sonnets?

Tell me all your news, and I mean all. Has Randolph taken kindly to my disappearance?

I do not often dream, though I will admit that of late, that has changed. But you will have to ask me another question to hear further detail, as I believe it is my serve.

What are your favorite colors? To see, to dress in, to touch?

'Tis almost fairy time.
H.

Rosaline was trembling once again, energy zipping through her body like a flea, dancing and hopping from limb to limb. She put down the letter and picked up the leaf enclosed within it — bright green, maple. Cold and smooth against her nose, with a clean, dusty scent. She imagined the Duke's fingers around the stem, and the blades resting in his wide, creased palm, fluttering when he brought the leaf to his face and smiled, pleased.

A shiver tore through her, followed by a wave of heat. It rolled over her back, down her chest, before pooling between her legs. Rosaline fidgeted beneath the covers, tugging her braid away from her neck, and reached for her stationery. As she composed her reply, she did her best to match his wit, wondering if she might make him grin.

How can I pick a favorite color, when they are all too beautiful to name? But I adore the mellow orange of a sunset, and the clear amber of fresh champagne. If I had to pick a favorite dress, I suppose it would have to be Madam D'Amoise's blue creation. After all, it is my namesake for the season.
Tell me, then — of what do *you dream?*

When she blew out the candle, her reply burning beneath her pillow, Rosaline felt as if she could see the distance between herself and the Duke shrinking, bridged by a delicate web of teasing, careful words.

❧

ROSALINE'S LIFE HAD TILTED AND SHIFTED, REORIENTING TO the rhythm of the post. Every other day brought a new letter from the Duke, and each of the days between she spent in a feverish state of anticipation. With each missive sent and received, she realized that they were further chipping away at the boundaries between them, unhampered by considerations of manners and propriety. It was like being back at the boxing match, but without the public audience. A part of her thrilled at their transgression, small though it was, and another part of her could not help but wonder what could happen if they were caught.

Benny became quite creative at passing her letters, usually with the excuse of bumping into her, or even when serving her tea. In turn, Rosaline became skilled in sleights of hand, making excellent use of her hidden pocket and, in one memorable instance, the front of her bodice.

Charlotte did not seem to notice a thing, and she and Katherine said little about the Duke, save for asking the occasional question about his health or the repairs at his estate. When the whispers and stares refused to abate, Charlotte had the brilliant idea of pinning a fresh red rose to Rosaline's *décolletage* whenever they went out into public, which seemed to dull the edge of scrutiny. Within a day or two, the tide turned, and people began to believe the story that was closest to the truth — that the Duke had been called to the country on urgent matters of business, and would return soon.

The season continued its inexorable, rolling orbit. Rosaline went to balls, suffered through the occasional dance with Lord Roden, attended stuffy tea parties that were nothing like Lady Ednam's, and did her best to escape Mrs. Randolph's ire. She watched as Charlotte and Cadogan continued their courting dance, drawing the eyes and attention of everyone in London. But they did not seem to notice — all they seemed to notice, in fact, was each other.

And all the while, Rosaline held on to her secret and clasped it tight.

Like her, the Duke seemed to have realized that their correspondence lingered somewhere beyond the bounds of propriety. With each letter, he seemed determined to tease her, to push her imagination further, darker.

I, he wrote, *have begun to dream of things within and without my reach. I tangle my hands in skirts I cannot see, run them along a stretch of warm skin. My fingers twist in long, curling hair, and my mouth catches at a smooth, supple neck. Of what do* you *dream?*

Her face blazing, her mouth numb, Rosaline knew she had to match him. This was still a game of tennis, after all. Her quill caught at her lip, leaving a splotch of blue ink before she lowered it to the paper—

Like you, I dream of embraces given and lost. A mouth beneath my ear. A hand at my waist, then at my ankle, sliding upwards. I dream of lying in a field with the sun on my face and a book at my hip. I dream of feeling the heat spill across my entire body, unhindered by stays or stockings. Tell me, what does one wear in the English countryside?

She wondered, ceaselessly, if her words ever unmade him just as his words threatened to unmake her. But perhaps none of this touched him in the same way, perhaps she was little more than a fleeting amusement. Rosaline did not often indulge in such cynicism — and she did not think the Duke capable of such malice. If he grew tired of her, he would simply cease responding. A game was a game was a game, even if it was no longer taking place on a tennis court. The setting had changed, but not the intent.

Will one of us win? Rosaline thought as she felt Benny sneak the Duke's latest response into her hands. *Or will both of us lose?*

Little more than a week had passed since his departure. Ten days of this infernal dance, of testing the invisible divisions that hung between them, as thin and clinging as a spider's web. Ten days, and she felt as if she were buzzing, bees caught beneath her skin, within her stomach, driving her to distraction. Rosaline knew what was happening, knew that his words, his invisible voice, were causing a slumbering part of her to rear its head and awaken.

And it was worse, somehow, to imagine how she might react to seeing him again.

At any rate, Rosaline thought, tearing open the familiar seal, *he need never know that he incites such a response within me.*

The Duke could never find out. Not ever.

As I write this, said his letter, *I look over the land beyond the house. I see it bursting with daisies, clover, and sweet grass. Have I told you that one of my favorite indulgences is to walk to a certain clearing in the woods and lie in the plush undergrowth? I look up into the sky, feel the sun on my face, hear the birds and the insects, and know a true peace. But perhaps this is fanciful — perhaps all I crave is privacy, a place where I might retreat to think and to read your letters.*

Truthfully, I know little of how a lady might dress for the country. It is difficult to imagine pearls mixing with mud and grass, but perhaps the gems are saved only for the most formal occasions. I tend to favor sturdy trousers and boots, as I often spend part of the day astride a horse. My valet berates me for returning my shirts with holes and dirt and marks from the grass, but in truth, I hardly notice. If the weather is hot,

I prefer to do without any shirt at all; like you, I crave the sun on my skin.

I must tell you, you drive me to distraction. I never imagined, dear Rosaline, that I might crave the diversions of London and the delight of an evening spent in your presence. Tonight, when I am alone in my chambers, I shall open a bottle of wine and think of you in your blue dress. What would you think about, over a glass of wine?

You do me mischief.
H.

Rosaline took a deep, trembling breath, and slowly lowered the letter to her desk. She noticed that her hands were quite steady, in spite of the turmoil seething through her body.

There was little doubt, now. The Duke had all but said the obvious. Yet another line had been crossed, left to wither in the fleeting dust, and Rosaline could not help herself.

Her imagination began to churn, almost without her permission, and she closed her eyes.

She could see the Duke — *Hal* — in his chambers, seated in an armchair, a half-empty bottle of wine at his elbow. A banked fire left him in lax, warm relief, with half of his face in shadow. He was partially undressed, as if he had been distracted halfway through his evening toilet, and his shirt hung open over a muscular torso hazed with dark, curly hair. She could even see where the hair gathered at the base of his stomach before dipping lower, between the open fastenings of a pair of trousers left to loll low on his hips. A quill dangled from one of his hands, and she imagined that as she watched, his eyes found hers, and a knowing smirk stole across his mouth.

Then the Duke shifted, and his trousers slid even lower, revealing more of his delicious skin. Heat rushed to Rosaline's face and neck, a tingling sensation pooled beneath her jaw, then began to trickle down her chest and her spine. She bit her lip, a hand tangling in her skirts, and tried to take a breath— she should not, not here, not now—

"Rosaline?"

The air caught in Rosaline's throat and she panicked. She fumbled with the locked top drawer of her desk, nearly snapping the key in half, then shoved the Duke's letter in with the rest of his correspondence. She locked it again in a flash, tucked the key into her pocket, and, praying that she was not blushing, called out, "Yes?"

A moment later, Charlotte, fully dressed, appeared in the doorway of Rosaline's bedroom and said, "Are you ready?"

Rosaline smiled and nodded. "Yes, of course." *Fool*, she told herself as she cast one last, cursory glance over her desk to ensure she had not left any damning evidence in view. *You should have opened it later.*

Frustration seethed in her stomach, replacing the other, more scandalous feeling from before. The Duke and his bare chest would have to wait until after supper.

৩৮৩

They were seated in Lady Linley's conservatory an hour or so later when Katherine took a sip of tea, shot them both a nervous look, and said, "I am expecting a visitor this evening."

As one, Charlotte and Rosaline frowned and turned to face her.

"My goodness," said Charlotte. "That does sound ominous."

"An unwanted visitor?" pressed Rosaline, trying to take a read of Katherine. She seemed fidgety, annoyed. "A family member?"

Katherine shook her head and glanced around the room. Once she confirmed no one else was listening, she leaned towards them and whispered, "August Heath."

Rosaline sat there for a moment, then traded a look with

Charlotte, who shot her a puzzled frown. Neither of them recognized the name. "Have we ever met Mr. Heath?"

"I doubt it," said Katherine. "As he is without a title, and has been abroad of late. In fact, he was not meant to return to London this season. He has business on the Continent. I met him through my brothers a few years ago — they went to Oxford together, and he came to stay at Christmas."

When she fell silent, Rosaline nudged Katherine's leg with her foot. "And?"

"Mr. Heath is... a perfectly nice gentleman. He has always spoken to me with respect and courtesy. And he is a marvelous partner at whist. But truly, I... I have no earthly idea why he might want to speak with me."

Charlotte looked at her for a few moments, then jolted upright. "Kath— Could he—? Could it be—?"

Rosaline inhaled sharply, catching on. "Oh, Katherine—"

Katherine went very pale, then very red. "That is precisely what I was afraid of—"

Rosaline glanced around again, then reached out and gripped her arm. "Kath, there is no need to be afraid, and you can always say no."

"Can I, though?" Katherine whispered. "I fear it is not so simple."

Charlotte sat down beside her and wrapped an arm around Katherine's waist. "There is no need to panic before you know his intentions, my dear. Now that you have debuted, he may wish to pay his respects as a simple courtesy to your family." She gave Katherine a squeeze. "You need only sit there and smile, my dear. And eat some biscuits, of course."

Katherine seemed to steel herself, and she nodded.

"Whatever should happen," Charlotte went on, "Rosaline and I are but a messenger or a brief carriage ride away, and we are always happy to lend a sympathetic ear."

Finally, Katherine managed a smile, and her eyes gleamed.

Charlotte changed the subject just as Lady Linley approached, but Rosaline's mind was elsewhere.

What if she found herself in Katherine's position? What would she say, what *could* she say, without irreparably damaging her father's reputation? Would she be asked to make a sacrifice, for someone else's sake?

☙❦❧

WHEN ROSALINE FINALLY LOCKED HER BEDROOM DOOR THAT evening, her candle had burned low, and a fresh wave of goose-bumps erupted across her arms and down her back. She turned, faced her desk across the shadowed room, and felt as if she were facing her fate.

How ridiculous, she thought, crossing the space and reaching for the key. *It is only a letter.*

Rosaline did not permit herself to look at the Duke's letter again until she was tucked into bed with the covers up to her chest. In the low, glimmering light of her candle, she unfolded the paper and began to reread the words that had haunted her throughout the day.

Unbidden, the earlier image of the Duke, lax with wine, half-dressed and slumped in his chair, sprang back into her mind. Rosaline's breath hitched as she traced his words with her finger-tip. *You do me mischief.*

He was enough of a gentleman not to paint her an explicit portrait, but the implication of his words was enough to make her shudder. Solitude, sunlight, thinking of her in her sapphire dress... he as good as confessed his own self-indulgence.

What if, she thought, sliding a hand beneath the covers, *I were to do the same?*

Rosaline let her eyes slip shut, and let her hand push aside the hem of her nightgown, her fingers grazing the bare skin of her warm thigh. The feeling was familiar and yet fresh — she had not done this since arriving in London, too intimidated by the prospect of discovery and too overwhelmed by her newfound life. But Rosaline was no fool, and she was no prude. Her education had been thorough in more ways than one, and her imagination was a force to be reckoned with.

She let out a breath, and let her mind unspool.

Before her, the Duke gave her that rich smirk again. The dim firelight sang on his skin, and her eyes sucked in every detail, every curve and dip of his exposed body. Now, his trousers were sitting sinfully low, as she watched, his hand went between his legs, his fingers trailing over the thin, curling hair and squeezing the thick, obvious bulge beneath the fabric.

"Is this what you want?" the Duke murmured, his head arching back and exposing the slope of his neck, the catch of his collarbones. "You wish to watch me?"

Rosaline's breathing hitched, and she trembled as she dragged her fingers over her belly, mimicking his movements. She felt as if she could smell him, earthen and warm, the scent that always clung to him at the end of a long night.

"You know that I think of you." His voice was a rich purr, and his hand skated up and down the length of his torso. "And now I know that you think of me."

She trembled afresh, her hand drifting across her breasts, worrying at the loose fabric over her nipple until it hardened beneath her thumb.

"I ache, Rosaline." The Duke rolled his head and let out a moan as his hand ghosted over his crotch. "I ache for you."

It was not enough. Rosaline dropped his letter and put her other hand beneath the covers, leaving one at her breast and using the other to tug her nightgown aside. She touched the edge of her sex, hesitant, and bit her lip when she found the skin tender and wet.

"Have you been waiting?" He smirked again, and his eyes

cracked open to pin her with a devilish look. "Have you been wanting?"

Rosaline stroked the length of her sex as she watched his hand slip into his breeches. He gripped himself hard and let out a moan, and the shining head of his cock crested above the edge of his trousers. She could see where his length strained at the fabric, rigid and relentless, and she shuddered at the thought of what it would feel like beneath her hand.

But she kept her own touch light and hesitant, skating over her folds and teasing her tender entrance. If she was to indulge, she was to do it properly. Rosaline slowed the hand at her breast, only allowing herself the occasional squeeze or flick as she watched the Duke stroke himself.

He, too, was in no hurry. He fisted his length at an agonizing pace, drawing a long, guttural moan out of his own throat. The sound made her shake and bite back her own, answering moan.

"Do not tease me," the Duke gritted out. "I want to hear you. I want to taste you. I want to feel you shake and I want to swallow your scream."

Rosaline gave a full-body shudder, drunk on the way he sounded, the way he looked — like a luxuriant god, at ease with his own pleasure and determined to be the champion of hers. Her fingers slipped and slid, moisture pooling along her inner thigh, and she surrendered, finally allowing herself to worry at the hard nub hidden between her folds. A groan tore out of her throat and she drove her face into her pillow, muffling the sound.

"Gorgeous." The Duke's hand stilled, and as she watched, he tugged his length fully out of his trousers, as if offering himself to her. He grinned. "Do you enjoy what you see, Rosaline? A man, driven to the edge of pleasure, throwing himself to your mercy?"

She pinched her nipple just as she circled her clit, and sparks flew up her spine. Light and heat began to pool in her belly, in the small of her back, and Rosaline knew that she would need little else to find her own edge.

"Tell me how you feel," he murmured. The Duke began to stroke himself again, his body trembling with every movement. He brushed aside his shirt and like her, pinched his nipple. "I wish to know every part of you. To lose myself and find you."

Rosaline abandoned her breast and slid two of her free fingers just inside her entrance, nearly shocked by her own wetness. Her face began to go numb, and she bit her lip, stifling another grunt of delight.

She had no idea how this part would feel — to take a man fully inside her, to stretch around him and to find her ease. But she could imagine, and for now, that would have to do.

He would be searing-hot and pulsing, thick enough that she would gasp to take him in. They would rock together, gentle and teasing, his fingers digging into her hips as he held her close and pushed in deep, relentless and determined and yet so very loving. Rosaline's fingers sped up, dancing across her clit, and she shook in tandem with her own pleasure, letting wave after wave of it wash over her.

The Duke grinned again as he watched her, then tipped his head back with a shudder. "Oh, Rosaline— Rosaline—"

She came with a muffled groan, burying her face in the pillows once again as her pleasure peaked and broke, overwhelming her in a single, heady rush. Her body twitched and arched with it, her hands going still. Wave after wave passed over her, gradually slowing and shrinking until she could catch her breath, her gaze blurry and her mouth fuzzy.

With that, her vision of the Duke vanished into thin air, and Rosaline glanced down at his letter, feeling a fresh wave of heat overtake her chest and her neck. She would reply to him tomorrow; perhaps the light of day would encourage her to mind her manners.

But then again, she thought, *this is a game a tennis, after all. It is only fair if I return fire with an enthusiasm to match his own. I cannot be the one to surrender, not now.* Rosalie swallowed. *Not when his return to London may be imminent.*

But that was a concern for another time, another day. She folded up his letter and tucked it beneath her pillow. It took all of her remaining energy to roll over and blow out the candle. "I wish," Rosaline whispered, "to fluster him, as he has flustered me."

20

Rosaline poured herself a fresh cup of tea and looked across the garden, watching as a pair of swallows dove through the air, chittering and squeaking at each other. Around them, the roses had exploded into full bloom, along with a sea of wildflowers and a thick carpet of luscious green grass, hugged by tendrils of snaking ivy. The garden was magical, in a way, full of a power and a beauty that was beyond her explanation.

She tapped her quill on the edge of the metal table. It would be mundane, surely, to write about the flowers. *I know a bank whereon the wild thyme blows*, she thought, *where oxlips and the nodding violet grows.*

Underneath the oak, Charlotte let out a cry of delight and dove for something on the ground. Beside her, Katherine grinned and leaned against the trunk of the tree, watching as Charlotte began digging up some kind of root.

Rosaline smiled and went back to her letter. *Things here are mostly unchanged,* she wrote. *Charlotte continues to seek out every form of plant life available to her, and Katherine indulges her, lending a ready hand whenever Charlotte should need it.*

She paused, took a sip of tea, and began writing again.

Summer feels quite different now. Indeed, the season continues — there is a ball tomorrow evening, a masquerade. Have you ever heard of anything so dull and overwrought? I, supposedly, will be something purple, with lots of feathers. She bit her lip, then frowned. *What would you wear, if you were here?*

Rosaline could not quite bring herself to be as forthcoming as the Duke had been in his previous letter. *Perhaps I lack courage*, she thought, and rolled her eyes.

Katherine had indeed received a proposal from Mr. August Heath. Before Charlotte and Rosaline had managed to temper their surprise, Katherine had quickly glanced around them, ensuring that they were truly alone in the Princes' garden, and said, "I was not fully honest with you both, when I spoke to you before. You see, Mr. Heath is like *me*."

The emphasis alone had been enough for Rosaline, but Charlotte had frowned in confusion. "He, too, is afraid of heights?"

Katherine had bitten back a grin and grasped Charlotte's hand. "No, Charlotte. Mr. Heath is in love with somebody else. With Lord Oswalt."

"Katherine," Rosaline had said, her voice low. "This is dangerous."

"I know." But Katherine's gaze had burned with possibility. "If I can convince my beloved to accept Lord Oswalt's proposal—"

Charlotte had straightened suddenly. "Oh, Katherine—"

"We might have a chance, Charlotte." To Rosaline's astonishment, tears had glittered in Katherine's eyes. "We could be together, you see."

"But surely that is not what you want. To marry and live with a man you could never love." Rosaline had met her gaze. "Not truly."

Then, a flash of anger. "Of course not. But it is what I must do."

And who were they to fight Katherine Knight?

Now, Katherine approached the table, a hand shading her eyes from the sun. Charlotte was only two paces behind her. "Any progress?"

"Yes!" Rosaline quickly pushed her letter to the Duke beneath the larger stack of papers and shifted the top sheet towards Katherine. "I have done all the sums, and I think you will find that it would come out most favorably for you both."

"Really?" Katherine's expression was a mixture of surprise and disappointment. She reached for the paper and began to read. "And would we have any—?"

"You would have approximately four pounds and twelve shillings left over each month, which is no small amount. Perhaps more if you found a way to come under your budget." Rosaline shrugged, leaning back in her chair. "You could do much worse."

"I suppose." But Katherine bit her lip and sat down at the table. "To be quite honest, I did not think that it would turn out this way."

"Katherine, dear," said Charlotte, flopping onto the wicker bench, "you cannot fault yourself for not wanting this."

"I know." Katherine shot them both a furtive look. "Is it horrible that I was hoping it would not be possible?"

"Not in the least!" Charlotte said. "Personally, I think that if you dislike the idea this much, you had better not go through with it."

Katherine rolled her eyes. "Charlotte, would that I were such a romantic." She looked at Rosaline. "What do you think?"

"I think," said Rosaline, "that this offer would be difficult to refuse. The numbers say it all, Katherine, and numbers do not lie. But," she added, "what you feel matters as well. Every contract comes with its emotions, its sacrifices, and this is no different. Apathy and discontent do not make a good start to a business relationship."

"Right." Katherine now appeared to be more conflicted than ever.

"You need not decide now," Rosaline quickly added. "You have a week, correct?"

"Yes."

"No hurry, then." Rosaline reached for her tea, hoping the others would not notice her blush. She thought of the letter hidden beneath her notes. "A lot can happen in a week."

Charlotte's eyes sparkled. "Do you speak from personal experience, dear Ros?"

"No," said Rosaline into her teacup. Perhaps she said it too quickly — both Charlotte and Katherine raised their eyebrows. "Merely a knowledge informed through careful study."

A weak excuse, but it tempered them. After helping themselves to cups of tea and a biscuit or two, Charlotte and Katherine went back to their diversions, chatting like the swallows that dipped and rose above their heads. Rosaline remained where she was, and once things seemed safe, she pulled out her reply to the Duke and wetted her quill.

Before her nerves got the better of her, she wrote:

Wine makes me think of long, luxuriant evenings, some of them spent buried in my bed. I think of being warm, of being touched, of indulgence and its many forms. I think of you, trying to best me.

Truthfully, very little of import has happened since my last letter. The constable continues to turn himself in circles, much to the irritation of the magistrate, whose involvement I still do not understand, given the utter lack of an arrest, or even a culprit. The few of my neighbors who have not descended upon London have made overtures at a tour of the grounds and a light supper, but I know the true reason behind their seeming sociability — they want to see the new window, which is undoubtedly the most interesting object within ten miles.

Rosaline could not stop herself from letting out a chuckle. She glanced up, and, satisfied that none of the few people on the veranda had heard her, continued reading.

Your letter, however, speaks to a very thrilling occurrence indeed. A masked ball? Surely there has never been a more entertaining diversion. I would likely find myself dressed in some horrifying color with a beaked mask to match. Please be sure to tell me what Cadogan turns up in; he would never give me the truth.

Now that the new window is in place, I should be able to return to London within the next few days. Unless, of course, some other part of the house starts falling down.

She let out a laugh then, a real laugh, and could not hide her surprise when—

"Only you could find something so amusing at a masked ball."

Rosaline quickly hid the Duke's letter behind her back as she turned to smile at McGrath. "Good evening, Lieutenant. Though perhaps I should inquire as to your methods of detection — how did you know it was me?"

"I have my ways." The Lieutenant was wearing a simple black mask, its edges embossed with a golden thread that flattered his shining hair. Beneath it, a coy smile lurked in the corner of his mouth, and his hooded eyes took her in with a sharp glance. "And I must admit, there is something about you that makes you stand out in a crowd."

She smiled, not blushing at all. "Apart from the obvious, you mean?"

He closed the distance between them and captured her gloved hand. She noticed that his sling was gone, though he still favored his left arm. "There is nothing obvious about you, Miss Bailey." With that, he pressed a kiss to her fingers, and her heart thudded against her ribs.

"You have learned my name, I see." Rosaline tried to take a breath.

"Indeed." In the dim, slanted light of the party, his face had a cunning line to it. "Daughter of the Royal Physician, no less. I am sure that made for quite an interesting upbringing."

"You are correct." Rosaline shifted where she leaned against the stone railing, and just managed to slip the Duke's letter into her pocket. Thankfully, the Lieutenant did not seem to notice. "One develops rather a strong stomach."

McGrath nodded. "Which must be quite an advantage at these gatherings."

"I notice you appear to have outgrown your sling. And, I assume, this explains your sudden absence this past fortnight?"

"Partially, yes." His mouth took on a teasing lilt. "A new surgical procedure, in Edinburgh. Seems I am a guinea pig first, soldier second. My surgeon rather warned me off the sling, once the stitches came out."

"Dr. Knox?" Rosaline said, then rushed past the Lieutenant's surprise. "Yes, there have been whispers of his new technique. He is known to be quite the risk-taker. How on earth did you manage to get on his books?"

"My Major knows him." He frowned at her. "And apparently, so do you?"

She shook her head. "By name only. My father keeps quite up-to-date when it comes to medical advances. Would you mind if I... if I saw his work?"

McGrath gave her a sudden, indulgent smile. "Not in the least." He was wearing an embroidered, fitted waistcoat and no jacket, so it took him mere moments to roll up his sleeve. "There you are."

Rosaline was not expecting the sight of his bare arm — tanned, she noticed, with a dusting of light hair — to cause her to blush. But she reached forward regardless, gently taking his forearm in her gloved hands.

The wound was scattered, unfocused, and spread from his elbow down to his hand. Its lines were a deep red, fresh but healing, and she could see where the stitches had been recently removed. She grazed a finger over the deepest line, along the rear of his elbow. "Shrapnel?"

"You have a keen eye. The field surgeon got most of it out, and I was healing quite well for a while, until I started having some trouble bending my arm. Dr. Knox went in and did something to the tendon, and he pulled out four more pieces of shrapnel while he was at it." McGrath shook his head. "He is a beast."

"You should consider yourself lucky, Lieutenant." She did not think about the close warmth of his skin, ready and inviting. "In terms of your life, and to be one of the first successful reconstructive surgeries on record."

"Luck, Miss Bailey, has little presence on the battlefield. Though I must give it some credit, for without it..." He met her gaze and held it. "I might never have met you."

Breathe, Rosaline told herself. "Does it hurt?" she said quietly. "Your arm?"

He smiled and slid his arm out of her grasp. As he rolled down his sleeve, he said, "Not much. It aches, sometimes, to warn me of rain."

"Well, I am sure you will make a full recovery, now that Dr. Knox has seen to you."

"Just in time for the joyful festivities of the London season." His sarcasm was heavy-footed — it trod through the conversation like a troll. "It seems that even the intoxicating mystery of a masquerade is not enough to hold your attention."

"Perhaps for the first half-hour," she admitted. "But I find that these events all run together. Each one is nearly the same as the last."

Something flashed in McGrath's eyes, though his smile did not waver. "Come now, that is not quite true. Unlike our last meeting, you are... unaccompanied."

Rosaline's stomach swooped and landed at her feet. But she managed a light, airy chuckle. "Whether I am or I am not is of little consequence."

This did not deter him in the least. "Have you known him long? The Duke of St. Albans?"

"Not at all," she replied. "I have only met him this season."

"And yet," he continued, "according to every report, you have bewitched him entirely."

"Every report," she allowed, "except my own."

McGrath leaned back a little, as if surprised. "If, then, I may be so bold as to enquire... What is the truth?"

"That I am promised to no one." Rosaline ignored the flood of heat to her face, which was borne of indignation more than anything else. "The Duke is merely a passing amusement."

"Really." But he did not seem convinced. In fact, he seemed smug. "You are a keen observer, Miss Bailey, and I am sure you did not miss the... exchange between myself and the Duke, at the Eventide Ball."

Something quickened in her heart. "I did not miss it," she said, not letting an ounce of curiosity show. "In fact, I found it most peculiar."

"There was good reason for it, and even if you claim that he is only a passing amusement, I believe you deserve the truth." McGrath glanced around them, at the scattered groups of people on the veranda. "But I should not discuss it here. The walls have ears."

Intrigue getting the better of her, Rosaline followed the Lieutenant down the veranda's steps and into the covered walk. Ivy curled above their heads, dotted with the occasional glimmer of a wild rose, and in truth, it was quite pretty. But she had little time to focus on that, for as soon as they were demonstrably alone, the Lieutenant began to speak.

"It may surprise you to know that the Duke and I have been acquainted with each other since birth. My father was steward to his father, and they were close, quite close. The Duke and I spent much of our time together growing up, and became good friends.

"The late Duke's death, and the death of the Duchess, were almost too much for my father to bear. But he remained in his post, and kept the estate running throughout the Duke's childhood, reporting only to his godfather, Lord Blackwood." Here a ripple of distaste crossed over McGrath's features, and Rosaline felt a tickle of surprise. "Lord Blackwood is the most... arrogant, self-indulgent buffoon to ever pretend at propriety. He fought my father on each and every decision, on minutiae that did not matter, had not mattered for years. After some time, it became clear that his concerns were of a personal nature — he seemed determined to undermine my father's authority, to imply that he did not know how to fulfill the requirements of the position he had maintained for almost twenty years."

"Goodness." True, Rosaline knew very little about Lord Blackwood, but perhaps this would explain the Duke's apparent embarrassment at their relation. "Did no one step in?"

"No." McGrath's voice was grim. "And as time passed, as I grew up, I made my intentions clear — that I would like to enter the clergy, and to take over the local seat near the estate. In fact, it had been my childhood dream. This request was met with little rebuke. The Duke's family and his godfather have never particularly cared for the church, or about the occupant of the local parsonage."

His pause was evident, telling.

"But?" Rosaline prompted him.

"But, when the time came, I was informed by the Duke and Lord Blackwood that someone else had already filled the position, and that I should look for employment elsewhere. They had felled my dream, my future, my income, with a single, decisive blow." McGrath's eyes were pinched, and his jaw was clenched.

"And to make matters worse, my father was asked to vacate the position of steward."

Rosaline blinked, unable to mask her surprise. "On what grounds?"

McGrath shook his head. "None that were legitimate, or even lawful. My father and mother were forced to leave the place that had been their home for two decades, abandoning their friends, their livelihoods, all for the sake of a bit of money." He cut her a glance. "You see, that is what it was all about. My father was known for being a generous, kind-hearted man. He had the ear of every tenant. He knew their woes, their difficulties, their triumphs, and he did what he could to help them. But this inclination did not agree with the Duke. When he became old enough to understand the income, the figures, he arrived at the conclusion that my father was too indulgent, and that the estate required a firmer hand if it was to turn the sort of profit he wanted to see."

Her ears ringing, her stomach churning, Rosaline sank onto a nearby bench.

"And they installed this new fellow as the steward, completely unheard-of, one of Lord Blackwood's many slippery friends. Someone called Merrywether, I believe." The bruised pride was evident in his voice. "And he has certainly changed the way things are done at Alban Hollow."

A fresh blush flooded her face. Hearing the name of the Duke's estate reminded her of the letter burning through her pocket. "I must confess, I find myself utterly speechless."

"I understand." McGrath sat down beside her. "It is a lot to take in." He sighed. "From what I have heard, Merrywether has very much cracked the whip. Several of the estate's oldest tenants have already left, and more will soon follow them, I think, if he continues as he began." He leaned back in his seat. "It has been most dismal, watching the Hollow of my childhood transform into something so grim and unrecognizable. I find it desperately sad."

"Of course." Rosaline turned to him, determined to find something, some scrap of the Duke she'd thought she had known. "And what of the Duke? You mentioned, before, that you were childhood friends. Surely you can't have burnt every bridge?"

McGrath's smile was grim. "We have not spoken since that fateful day. The Duke made his opinion of me quite clear when he effectively forced me out of the grounds. I have been forbidden, you realize, from ever returning."

For several moments, Rosaline could not bring herself to say anything, even a word of sympathy. As shocking as these revelations were, a small part of her conscience warned her not to take each claim at face value. She had only known the Duke for little more than a month, in spite of their correspondence, and the Lieutenant for an even shorter amount of time. The last thing she needed to become was a pawn in their game of chess.

So, she tried for a smile. "Well," she said, "I do appreciate you telling me. It speaks volumes to your character, and to the Duke's. Now." She stood up and held out her hand. "I believe there has been enough doom and gloom for one evening. Might I induce you to join me for a dance?"

A sudden, dazzling smile broke across McGrath's features, and he took her hand at once. "Miss Bailey," he said, brushing her knuckles against his mouth, "nothing would give me greater joy."

21

R osaline paid little attention to the glimmering houses and dark, abundant hedges passing outside the window of her carriage. This evening was like any other evening, in her opinion, regardless of her destination or the unexpected invitation that had arrived in the morning's post. Frowning, she trailed her gaze over the corded edge of the seat opposite, where she had been sitting when she'd caught her first glimpse of Prince Manor. Unlike that morning, now the interior of the carriage seemed dark, dull in the evening light.

Her mind was awhirl, just as it had been since her time with McGrath the night before. She had replayed their conversation over and over again, desperate to glean fresh meaning from it, to find some way of countering his version of the truth. But it was difficult, to say the least.

The Duke had been so reticent about his past, about his childhood, and he had never even mentioned McGrath, or McGrath's father. She was ready to believe that any man who adored the *Decameron* might harbor a petty mean streak, but perhaps Lord Blackwood was just another arrogant, over-interfering lord like any other of his peers, and his concern for his godson had simply manifested as a heightened attention to the management of the estate. It was equally possible that McGrath could not give a fair account of the situation, given his own personal stake in the matter — perhaps the Duke and Lord Blackwood had had good reason to offer the post to someone else, reason enough to spare McGrath the trouble and cost of obtaining the necessary education before he could assume a position as vicar.

And, as much as she was loath to admit it, it was possible that McGrath had spun her this story merely for the sake of his own fun, or for his chance at wooing one of the season's most eminent debutantes, pulling her away from the most eligible, sought-after bachelor in the country.

This, Rosaline reflected with a fresh blush, was a little more self-indulgence than she would normally entertain, but after spending a month in this never-ending climate of false flattery and social politics, it was a reality she had to consider. By associating with her, by being seen with her, McGrath was elevating himself above his station. He was gaining something by playing to her ignorance and sympathy, as guileless as he might seem.

Perhaps, she thought, a touch mournful, *he simply likes you.*

The idea alone was enough to make Rosaline shudder and fall back in her seat, her body alive with equal parts embarrassment and intrigue. This was new territory for her — she was used to passing through society as relatively unseen, unnoticed, and she had come to enjoy that invisibility, to relish it. The idea that her presence, her interest, was enough to change the status of another person, another *man*, was overwhelming, to say the least.

As if turning on a pin, her mind fell instead to matters of numbers — specifically, Katherine's offer of marriage. Even to an untrained eye, the union made very good and practical sense. Mr. Heath was a gentleman, and already carried the firm approval of everyone in Katherine's family. Katherine would have a stable income, a beautiful home, and the assurance of maintaining her hidden romance.

But Rosaline knew now, as she had when Katherine had first announced the proposal, that this marriage was not just a question of love, of doing whatever it took for Katherine and her beloved to escape notice. It was also a question of Katherine sacrificing a part of herself, to become somebody she was not. Even now, Rosaline could only think of Katherine's hands nervously turning the page of figures until it had become little more than a blur in the air. So much of her earlier conviction had vanished in the face of the union making financial sense.

Because it had become real, Rosaline thought now, finally glancing out the window as the carriage slowed and drew to a halt. *Before, it had only been a means to an end. But now—*

The carriage door opened, and a gloved hand appeared in midair. "Welcome to McDunn Manor, Miss Bailey. I trust your journey was pleasant?"

Rosaline gathered what little remained of her courage, took the hand, and stepped out onto a gravel drive. "Yes, thank you. Have the other guests arrived?"

"Indeed, Miss. They are in the drawing room."

The McDunn estate was nothing less than astonishing. It was one of the largest, most stately homes Rosaline had yet seen in London, and she was overwhelmed by the tasteful decorations, the splendid furniture, the regal portraits. She could so easily see the Dowager Countess sweeping through these polished halls, lifting them out of the faded past and into a balanced, modern age. The footman led her up a grand staircase, then along a wide hall. As they approached the drawing room, the low rumble of voices, laughter, and light music swelled in the air around them, and Rosaline took a quick breath before crossing the threshold, hardly knowing what to expect.

As she entered the room, several heads turned in response, and a cheer rose through the air. At the center of it all sat the Dowager Countess, smiling, glass of wine in hand.

"Well, everyone." The Dowager's voice carried enough to

silence the chatter. "It seems our final guest has arrived. Everyone, meet Miss Bailey. Miss Bailey, meet... well, everyone!"

A chuckle burst out of Rosaline before she could stop it, and she accepted a glass of wine from a nearby man dressed in a rich, deep purple. "Delighted to make your acquaintance!"

"We were just finishing our drinks," the Dowager went on. "Dinner will be served shortly. Best to mingle for a few more minutes, I think." She turned to the piano, where a woman was seated, her fingers hovering above the keys. "Play on, dear!"

The music started up again, and Rosaline turned to the man dressed in purple. "Do tell me your name," she said, "so that I might thank you properly."

"Reg," he replied. "Though my enemies call me the Marquess of Exeter." He gestured to the woman beside him — she was strikingly beautiful, with wide dark eyes. "And this is my wife, Margaret. We are most pleased to see a new face at one of these gatherings."

Rosaline nodded and smiled at the Marchioness. She was still taking in the scene before her — never had she seen such a wild mix of people all in one place. They were all of varying ages and skin tones, and they were all utterly at ease with one another. There was not even a whiff of formality, and one couple, she noticed, even slouched together in a single armchair. "I must admit to some ignorance," she said to the Marquess. "Do tell me what I have gotten myself into."

"The Dowager Countess hosts a dinner party once a month, and takes it upon herself to throw what she considers to be society's best and brightest into one room." His smile gave a wry twist. "You may be well assured, Miss Bailey, of more than one heated debate before the evening should conclude. But I promise it is all in the spirit of fun."

"I see." Rosaline took a sip of wine. "Tell me, then, who I ought to know."

The Marquess was ready to oblige her, and Rosaline was

unprepared for the array that unfurled before her. No less than two Ministers of Cabinet, several higher-ups from the Treasury, a diplomat, an American official, and a few women who apparently were the cream of London and Parisian society.

"And there," the Marquess concluded with a nod, "is Captain Morris. The youngest captain in a decade, and given the rank as a result of some astounding act of heroism, if the stories are to be believed. You might find his presence surprising, given that he is the only military man within five miles of this estate, but he has a long history with the Countess. Apparently, she has known him nearly his whole life, as he is good friends with her godson, the Duke of St. Albans."

"Really." Rosaline felt a wave of dizziness and blinding realization threaten to overtake her. She suddenly remembered the Duke's description of his perfect day; he had mentioned a Captain, but not given him a name. She stared at the man in question. Like the Duke, he was a couple years older than her, of medium build, lanky but muscular, with a frightful mop of ginger hair and a smattering of freckles noticeable at even this distance. He had a ready smile, and an easy demeanor. For a moment, she could easily imagine the Captain and the Duke as children, chasing after each other under the canopy of some forest. She took a quick sip of wine. "How intriguing."

It became quite apparent, as the evening progressed, that if anyone at the party knew of Rosaline's attachment to the Duke, they did not go out of their way to mention it. She was there, of course, not as the Duke's besotted, but as the young daughter of the Royal Physician, a new arrival with a brain built for equations of both the mathematical and social nature. Rosaline found herself passing between groups, at the side of the dutiful Marquess, laughing and telling stories of France under Napoleon.

When the time came for dinner, she approached a table dripping with silver and noticed, with a tingle of delight, that she was seated beside none other than Captain Morris.

It was going to take some effort, questioning him about McGrath without raising suspicion, or without seeming rude — if she appeared over-interested in the Duke, as she was sure most young women of London were, he would likely take offense or worse, dismiss her as silly. She would have to tread lightly, and pray that the Duke had not mentioned her even once.

The Captain sat down beside her and gave her a smile. "I do not believe we've formally met," he said, "though I feel I have heard enough about you that it almost feels unnecessary. Captain Ronald Morris, at your service."

Rosaline threw on a smile in an attempt to diffuse the panic screaming under her skin. *Well*, she thought, *there goes my attempt at anonymity.* "A pleasure, Captain. I do shudder to think what reports might have reached your ears."

"Given that you are well-acquainted with both of my sources, I am sure your imagination can do them justice."

"Perhaps," she allowed. "Though I must admit to some surprise at seeing a military man such as yourself in London, given Britain's determination to fight as many wars as possible."

His smile stretched into a grin as the first course arrived — soup. "You flatter me, Miss Bailey. I merely oversee the training at the camp nearby. So I am homebound, for the time being."

"Ah, training," she said, putting on a false, wistful air. "How delightful, to be surrounded by hordes of unwashed, unmannered young men."

"Well, when you put it like that..."

"If you remain near town, then I must ask why you have not seen fit to join us more often at the events of the season. You would be more than welcome, I can assure you. There is always a lady without a partner."

"I do not doubt that in the least. Though I must admit I find the prospect of a room full of eager debutantes somewhat... terrifying."

"I am sure your good friend the Duke would agree." Rosaline

tasted her soup — it was light, delicious. "He has made his reluctance in participating quite clear."

The Captain bit out a laugh. "I am sure he has. Tell me, has he been completely insufferable, or has he at least managed a modicum of politeness?"

"A bit of both," she replied. "Cadogan, in contrast, has been the perfect gentleman." She glanced at him, and took a leap. "When I first met the Duke, his reluctance was so astute that I could not help wondering if his presence in London was perhaps the result of... a forced hand?"

The Captain returned her glance, and it was sharp, gleeful. "He was right about you," he said, somewhat under his breath. "You do not miss a thing." He cleared his throat. "Our dear friend Prongs lost quite a bet with Cadogan. The price, of course, being his attendance at the London season, which he has previously avoided like the plague."

She chuckled, making a mental note to press Cadogan for more details. "How delightful."

"I did not think he would last a week. But I have been pleasantly surprised, on that score." He looked at her again, and she realized that his soup was gone — when he had managed to eat it all, she had no idea. "I almost feel a need to apologize on his behalf. You have been quite coy, I think, in your description of his behavior."

Rosaline gave an elegant shrug. "Truthfully, I take little notice of his behavior." A lie, of course, but it fortified her facade. "It is a passing amusement, if nothing else."

"Is it?" The Captain's expression was placid, but she rather got the feeling that he was seeing more than he let on. Then he cleared his throat, and the moment passed. "Tell me of your family."

As their conversation progressed, Rosaline learned quite a lot about Captain Ronald Morris. His parents were lifelong tenants on the Duke's estate, and he was one of six children — the youngest boy, and the second-to-youngest sibling. Rosaline felt a bit dizzy at the idea of being part of such a big family — the dinner table alone must have been *insane* — but it did explain why the Captain had chosen to go into the military. He had a better chance of making money, of having an actual career wholly separate from his parents' legacy.

"Do your siblings help on the farm, then?" Rosaline asked him over the meat course.

A funny sort of spasm crossed his features. "Yes and no. Unfortunately, my parents raised a brood of singularly-minded individuals who were all determined to forge their own path. My brothers all have their own unique careers, and they encouraged me to do the same, especially once it seemed that dear old Bonaparte would not take a hint. Much to my mother's disappointment, she found herself with an empty nest far sooner than she'd hoped. Except for my younger sister, of course, but she is determined to marry as quickly as possible, and preferably not a farmer. She says she has had enough of soil and manure for five lifetimes."

Rosaline smiled. "I can understand that. What of your father?"

The Captain waved an airy hand. "Oh, he could not care less. He claims to have always known exactly who his children were, that it is impossible for any of us to surprise or disappoint him. Once he decides to retire, they will likely move to a cottage in Devonshire, where my mother's family hails from."

"How lovely." She glanced at his hands, noting the absence of a certain ring. "I must admit, Captain, I find it surprising that such a well-seated man such as yourself remains unattached."

His grin was bright, biting. "No, Miss Bailey, I have not been so lucky in that regard." He sat back in his chair, took a sip of wine. "Though if you happen to run into any young ladies with a fondness for a good fry-up, who would not care if their husband came home reeking of mud and old socks, do send them my way."

She had to chuckle at that. "I will be sure to do so, Captain."

After supper, the whole party moved back into the drawing room for cigars, brandy, and in the Dowager Countess's case, a glass of porter.

Rosaline watched in fascination as several of the ladies, along with the men, trimmed and lit their cigars. The room soon filled with the rich, earthy scent of good tobacco, and a small part of Rosaline could not help feeling a tingle of intrigue — what did it taste like?

"Here you are, my dear." The Dowager handed her a glass of brandy. Her glance was shrewd. "I trust you are enjoying yourself?"

"Very much," Rosaline replied. She swirled her brandy in its glass, its smoky scent washing over her face. "This is unlike anything I have ever experienced."

The Dowager gave her a sudden, glittering smile. "A tremendous compliment, to be sure. I noticed you passed a very pleasant meal with Captain Morris?"

"I certainly did. He has lived a most colorful life. I cannot imagine being one of six."

"Can any of us?" the Dowager returned. "No, he has matured quite well. There was a time when it was unclear whether he would hone and cultivate his sense of self, or become lost in the crowd of his siblings' personalities. But he has done very well, I think, very well."

Rosaline glanced at her, and decided to take the risk. "I had no idea that the Duke and the Earl Cadogan made such close friends with the other children on their estates. It paints a rather lovely, bucolic image."

The Dowager nodded. "And a unique one. It is not a common practice, at least not among the families that I know. No," she continued, "I believe it is rather the result of the Duke's own character. He has always been like that, determined to seek out others who might feel overlooked."

Rosaline took a slow, careful sip of her brandy. It did nothing to calm the fluttering in her stomach. "Do you know why he is predisposed to ignore such conventional barriers?"

The look the Dowager gave her was soft, but knowing. "Because, my dear, he has always been determined to rebuild what he has lost. His family."

Rosaline managed a shaky breath. "I see."

"Do you still sing, Miss Bailey?"

Rosaline's heart thudded in response to the abrupt turn in the conversation as well as the revelation that— "How do you know?" she managed. "About my singing?"

The Dowager's smile was enigmatic in the extreme. "I have a good ear for whispers."

"I—" Rosaline forced herself to swallow. "I do not sing in public."

The Dowager took this in with a nod. "Do you play the pianoforte?"

"A little, and I must admit to being quite out of practice."

"Then, Miss Bailey, there is no time like the present." The Dowager nodded at the instrument in the corner. "Go ahead."

Rosaline gritted her teeth and curtsied, then made her way over to the piano, irritation boiling under her skin. How on earth did the Dowager know? Charlotte did not even know — she had made sure of that. Who could possibly—?

She sat down at the instrument with a faint grumble, plunked down her glass of brandy, and launched into a bit of Handel, which was one of the few things she had committed to memory.

"Goodness me." His voice was friendly but wary. "Did this instrument insult you?"

Rosaline managed to smile at the Captain. "The insult is all mine, good sir. For I have no one but myself to blame for my lack of practice."

"Well, in my opinion, you sound entirely adequate."

She laughed, some of the tension in her belly unspooling. "What a compliment!"

The Captain smiled in return. "May I join you?"

"Certainly." She shifted over on the bench. "In fact, you might even be able to help."

He scoffed and sat down beside her. "Not in the least. I am quite useless when it comes to music. And to dancing."

"And now the true reason for your reluctance in joining the season becomes clear. The big, brave Captain is afraid of a waltz."

"You are remarkably combative towards your allies, Miss Bailey."

"It is a singular talent, I think." She glanced at him. "I did so enjoy your stories of your childhood in Alban Hollow, Captain. Though I must admit to some lingering curiosity, for I did not hear you mention a Mr. McGrath."

His gaze snapped to hers, but his voice was low, even. "McGrath?"

"Yes." Her heart was in her throat, though she managed to keep playing. "I believe he grew up on the Duke's estate, did he not?"

"He did." The words were thin with reluctance. "And where did you get this report?"

"From the man himself." She risked a glance at the Captain. His face was brooding, impassive. "He is in London at present."

"Is he?" Here, now, was the first hint of emotion — and it was anger. "And what else did Lieutenant McGrath care to mention?"

Rosaline's heart skipped a beat — so the Captain knew McGrath, even knew that he was in the army. "Not much," she said, careless enough to hardly admit even a passing interest. "Though it seems that he and the Duke have an unfortunate history."

For several long moments, the Captain said nothing. Then, he stood up, glass in hand. "Miss Bailey," he said, "would you excuse me for a few minutes?"

She blinked in surprise and missed a note. "Of course, Captain."

Rosaline did not see him again until the end of the party, when she was saying her goodbyes to the remaining guests. She felt a jolt of apprehension when the Captain appeared, though his expression was open, friendly.

"Miss Bailey." He took her offered hand and bent his head to it. "A pleasure."

"Likewise," she managed, hardly able to think because he had pressed something into her palm. She closed her fingers around it and curtsied. "I do hope we meet again."

His smile was small but genuine. "I am sure we will."

Rosaline did not allow herself to so much as glance at the note — for it was a note, folded into a tight, compact square — until she was alone in bed, nose-to-nose with her candle.

Miss Bailey—

I will not speak to matters on which I am sworn to secrecy, for the sake of friendship as well as loyalty. But I believe you deserve the truth, or something close enough to it.

My eldest brother, William, is a Bow Street Runner. Write to him at the address below, and ask for records pertaining to a Mr. Adrian McGrath. He will be expecting your correspondence.

I would ask you to withhold your judgment on the matter until you receive his reply. And I need hardly mention the requirement of your absolute discretion — a certain mutual acquaintance of ours would be most aggrieved to learn of any such details coming to light, especially in the eyes of one whom he holds in such high regard.

Yours Most Sincerely,

Cap. R. Morris

❦ 22 ❧

**Madam Kensington's High Society Papers,
No. 33**

W ell, my dears, here we are — the midpoint of the
season is upon us, and only a few engagements have
rippled the fairly calm waters of the ton. Perhaps
this is surprising, when we consider the indulgent, delicate
courtships playing out before our very eyes — most of us would
have expected some of the Rare Jewels to shine a little more
brightly, instead of fading somewhat into the background and
allowing their duller counterparts to step into the light. It is
possible that our Jewels could just be very generous, even circum-
spect, and determined to consider each and every option before
them before they make that ultimate, unquestioning
Commitment.

But now that half of the season is over, already beginning to
fade into memory, it is possible that some of our favorite varietals
will find themselves a little more accommodating and a little less
frivolous when it comes to what they might require of an ideal
partner. I, for one, love a match borne of exasperation and resig-

nation — they so often make for the best wedding receptions, and the most scandalous marriages. It is my prediction, my dears, that we shall see several of these matches in the coming fortnight.

It would truly be such a shame if the season were to end before a certain Recluse found his way back to London. I — like many, I am sure — struggle to get through the day without a glimpse of his tremendous, ravishing jawline...

⚜

ROSALINE STARED DOWN INTO THE DEPTHS OF HER TEACUP, wondering if time had stopped entirely, or perhaps taken on the consistency of treacle. Nothing else could explain the way the afternoon had begun to stretch around her, relentless in its infinity—

"Oh, yes, Miss Bailey and I have passed many a delightful morning in our household garden." Charlotte smiled and beamed like the angel she was. The small white flowers poking out of her braided coronet only added to the illusion. "We pride ourselves on our bouquets, which we take great pleasure in sculpting." She shot Rosaline a pointed look. "Why, just this morning we built an exquisite creation of— what was it, Rosaline? Daisies?"

"Hmm?" Rosaline finally caught up. "Oh, yes, daisies, ivy, and baby's breath—"

"Lovely!" chirped the dear old aunt by Charlotte's elbow. She was ancient, sagging beneath the weight of her gown and her jewels. "Is that why your friend wears a rose?"

Charlotte let out a trilling laugh. "No. She does so in honor of her beau. They are separated at the moment, but they each wear a rose in the other's honor, so that they may be connected, in spite of the distance."

The old woman nearly swooned. She missed Rosaline snorting into her iced bun. "Oh, how romantic! I must go and tell my daughter, she would love to hear of such youthful adoration—"

"Do go ahead," Charlotte said, guiding her in the direction of the rest of the party. As the old woman tottered off, nearly losing her balance on the way, Charlotte shut her fan and used it to smack Rosaline in the arm. "Pull yourself together!"

"What?" Rosaline managed, through a half-full mouth. She was almost crying with suppressed laughter. "I did not do anything—"

"I do not know *what* is on your mind," Charlotte muttered, as close to angry as Rosaline had ever seen her, and yet she still smiled and gleamed at the nearby guests. "But you need to focus, Rosaline, I cannot steer this ship for the next two hours completely on my own—"

"Two hours?" Rosaline repeated, the fleeting joy of the iced bun now replaced with a sinking dread. "Surely you exaggerate—"

"Rosaline." Katherine appeared out of thin air, and for the second time that week, Rosaline found a small, tightly folded chunk of paper pressed into her gloved hand. "Are you well?"

"Sparkling." Rosaline slipped the note into her pocket and frowned at Katherine. Around the three of them, the garden party continued at its slow, inexorable pace, the clouds above lazily shifting them in and out of sunlight. Katherine was almost buzzing with nervous energy. "And you?"

"Delightful." Katherine shot her a look. "And you seem even more distracted than usual."

"Do I?" Rosaline gave a wan smile. "Think nothing of it."

"No," Charlotte interrupted. "Think *something* of it, Katherine. She has been like this ever since she got back from that infernal dinner party."

"Dinner party?" Katherine shot Rosaline a look of intrigue. "Do give us details."

Rosaline huffed. "There is nothing to tell, *Katherine*. It was like any other dinner party."

"With the Dowager Countess McDunn," Charlotte added.

"Who apparently carries the most exclusive invitation in London, apart from the Queen."

"You exaggerate," Rosaline chided her. "It was just a room full of interesting people exchanging ideas and opinions over a bit of food."

"That is not even the most exciting part," Charlotte said to Katherine, ignoring Rosaline completely. "She met a certain Captain Morris, none other than one of the Duke's dearest friends."

Katherine's eyebrows said far too much about *that*. "Really? I wonder, did she hear any stories about the good Duke of St. Albans that she would care to share?"

"No." Rosaline did not look at either of them as they giggled. "Truthfully, we talked very little of the Duke."

"Oh, I see." Charlotte truly had a knack for imbibing her sarcasm with the most believable sincerity. "Tell us, then, what you did speak of?"

Heat prickled at the back of Rosaline's neck. "Well," she said. "Well—"

Then, as if summoned by some great, cosmic force, Lieutenant McGrath appeared, offering Rosaline a smile as well as a bow. "Ladies." He twinkled at Charlotte and Katherine. "Might I be so bold as to steal Miss Bailey for a game of lawn billiards?"

"Yes," said Rosaline, with some relief, "you may." She shot Charlotte and Katherine a filthy look before joining McGrath and heading towards the other side of the party.

"You look exceedingly well today, Miss Bailey." His smile was easy, genuine. "I believe the sunshine flatters you, or perhaps it is the other way around."

She had to smile at that. *Cad,* she thought. "Your determination to compliment me is admirable, Lieutenant, though hardly necessary."

He gave her a look of false scrutiny. "I was under the impression that that was what one did when in the company of a beautiful woman. If this is incorrect, do tell me so at once."

"Correct when it comes to others, maybe, but you need hardly do so with me." They came upon the billiard green, where there were four rings laid out in the grass, and Rosaline reached for a cue. "Are we not quite beyond such trivialities?"

"As friends, perhaps." McGrath, too, reached for a cue, and it brought him within mere inches of her face, her body. He looked right at her, his gaze piercing, and said, "But not as something else."

Rosaline took a slow, steadying breath, and stepped away. "Have you done anything of import since I saw you last?"

"Hardly." McGrath retrieved two balls. "London can be quite tiresome, don't you think?"

No, thought Rosaline. "Have you much more of your leave, then?"

He glanced at her, and had she missed it, she would not have seen the flicker of apprehension in his face. "It is unclear at present," he said, his voice low, "if I will be returning to the Continent. In fact, whether I will be returning to the army at all."

She could not hide her surprise. "I see. Your injury has affected your abilities?"

"Not as such," McGrath said quickly. "Rather, it is just... time that I turn my prospects elsewhere." He glanced at her again. "Settle down, perhaps."

Rosaline swallowed a wave of trepidation. "Well," she said, with a small smile. "That, too, is an adventure in its own way."

"Indeed it is." McGrath swung his cue through the air, gave her an easy grin. "I must admit, Miss Bailey, I had my concerns about seeing you again, after the nature of our last meeting. I worried that it might have spoiled our acquaintance."

She smiled properly at him, and his grin widened. "How ridiculous of you. No, Lieutenant, if anything, it has done the precise opposite."

His expression was dazzling. "How glad I am to hear it." He fished out a coin from his pocket. "Heads or tails?"

⊙✷⊙

"THE POST," ROSALINE SAID, THE INSTANT SHE WALKED through the front door. "Benny, the post?"

Now accustomed to hearing this question several times a day, Benny was the picture of relief as he nodded and handed her— "Came just an hour ago, Miss Bailey—"

She snatched the letter from him, nearly taking off a chunk of his thumb — ignoring Mrs. Randolph's disapproving, "Miss *Bailey!*" — "Thank you, Benny," she burst out, and tore upstairs. At least Charlotte had lingered in the garden; otherwise, she would have been right on Rosaline's tail.

Once she was in her room, the door closed and locked behind her, Rosaline threw herself at her desk, the letter skittering across one of her books. She did not notice as something else went flying under her dresser, and stared down at her own name and address, scrawled in a hasty, though neat, and utterly alien hand. Her heart throbbed in her throat, and she knew, then, that this was one of the few moments in her life where everything could change in an instant.

Rosaline fumbled for her letter opener, almost slicing open her own pinky as she cut through the envelope. It was thick, stuffed to bursting, and a sheaf of papers spilled out.

The papers were a mixture of newspaper cuttings, some of them already yellowing with age, and copies of official-looking reports. Rosaline gaped as she sifted through them, quickly separating the papers into piles according to medium and chronology — she ignored the headlines, not wanting to form an opinion before she read William Morris's report. His letter was compact, neatly folded, and he had not wasted an inch of space. In fact, his writing was so cramped, so spidery, that Rosaline frowned at the window, then at the wall in front of her desk, and stood up.

It took a remarkable amount of effort and a few swear words for her to drag her monstrosity of a desk out from its corner and into the bright, sunny light of the windows. Rosaline slumped into her chair, caught her breath, and then finally applied herself to the matter at hand.

Bow Street, London

Dear Miss Bailey,

My name is Bill Morris, and I am pleased to make your acquaintance, even if from a distance. My brother speaks very highly of you, and anyone who has earned the Duke's friendship is sure to be a person worth knowing. I am very pleased to assist you in this matter, which, for the most part, is a part of public record, even though certain individuals have done their best to conceal it, for varying reasons.

Adrian McGrath was born in Ireland and came to London as a young boy. He grew up hard and fast, as many children of the city do, and was only saved from certain destruction by virtue of a gentleman's pity. This gentleman saw something in the boy, and so he helped Adrian, looked after him as one of his own, which, of course, was his first mistake. Adrian continued much as he began, and by the time he was eighteen, he had run up debts of historical size, been charged with a handful of petty crimes, including theft, and spent most of his time drunk as a skunk. But the gentleman excused this behavior, assured the magistrate that a good, strong dose of University would sort the lad out, and he was correct, to a certain degree. Adrian managed to scrape through his exams and find himself a position as a clerk for a transportation company. By all appearances, he had put himself firmly onto the straight and narrow, and he soon married the daughter of a local merchant. But his degenerate ways continued — he was always in debt, and at the time, no one at the company noticed the small amounts of money disappearing from the accounts.

He rose through the ranks of the company and soon found himself with the opportunity to become steward for the gentleman's friend, a young Duke who had recently ascended to his seat. They began on solid terms, and as time passed, Adrian proved himself to be an adequate estate manager. But, it would later come to light that he had taken advantage of the Duke's generous nature. The Duke and Duchess died quite suddenly, leaving their infant son to inherit the seat, and the estate was put into the temporary hands of the boy's godfather. As I am sure you are aware by now, I am talking of the seat of Alban Hollow, and the placement of Lord Blackwood as her, for lack of a better word, regent.

As time passed, Lord Blackwood grew suspicious of Adrian's solicitous nature and his determination to handle all financial matters of the estate. When questioned, he obfuscated; when confronted, he grew angry and cruel. Lord Blackwood began making discreet enquiries, and soon discovered that for years, Adrian had been siphoning a significant portion of the estate's profits into his own personal account in order to pay his creditors; his debts were constant and astronomical. He had also become involved in a rum smuggling operation based out of the West Indies. It goes without saying that this discovery was nothing short of devastating to the young Duke and his remaining family.

Lord Blackwood soon dismissed Adrian McGrath from his position and handed him — as well as all of the evidence he had uncovered — over to the constables. Further investigation revealed that McGrath's eldest son, Sean, was also involved in this subterfuge. And his second eldest, Callum, who had previously claimed an interest in presiding over the local parish, apparently had no interest of the sort — rather, he had planned to join his father and brother in their enterprise and, when enough funds had been raised, move the entire family to Barbados, where they would be beyond the reach of Adrian's creditors and, to a certain extent, the British law.

After the investigation and subsequent trials, Adrian was placed in a debtors' prison, where he will likely remain until his death. His son, Sean, was also convicted and sentenced, and will remain in prison for several more years. I feel it is also my duty to inform you that Callum McGrath is not entirely reformed; my sources tell me that, like his father, he is already in debt to several local merchants and creditors, and has appeared before *the magistrate on charges of petty crime. How he has managed to retain his commission is beyond my understanding — as is how he managed to purchase it in the first place — but these circumstances are more than likely the result of his willful, manipulative nature. I would advise you, from a professional standpoint, to limit your interaction with him, and should he cross any bounds of propriety or, Heaven forbid, ask you for money, send word to me at once. We would need very little evidence to charge him and help him to reunite with his father.*

I am sure that my dear brother has already gone to the trouble of telling you that your discretion is of the utmost importance. The Duke and Lord Blackwood have worked very hard to keep these matters separate from their family legacies, to protect themselves and especially their tenants from shame and ridicule. And, given what I know of the season, I am sure that news such as this would be nothing short of catastrophic were it to break in a dramatic, public manner (even if it is several years out of date). For your own sake, Miss Bailey, as well as the Duke's, I would urge you to keep your silence, unless absolutely necessary.

Yours Most Sincerely,
Const. Wm. Morris

HER HANDS TREMBLING, ROSALINE NOW TURNED HER attention to the cuttings and reports. Most of the newspaper articles consisted of reportage from the trials of Adrian and Sean McGrath, and the headlines alone spoke volumes —

FORMER STEWARD FACING CHARGES OF EMBEZZLEMENT, SMUGGLING

RUM SMUGGLERS CAUGHT RED-HANDED IN LONDON DOCKS

. . .

A. MCGRATH CONVICTED, FACING LIFE IN DEBTORS' PRISON

S. MCGRATH FACING CHARGES OF THEFT, SMUGGLING

RUM SMUGGLERS SENTENCED TO TWENTY YEARS HARD LABOR

IT DID NOT TAKE HER LONG TO READ THROUGH THE ARTICLES, her heart beating painfully fast, her ears ringing. As Rosaline read, every single one of Constable Morris's claims were reiterated and substantiated in succinct, unbreakable language. It was almost difficult to believe that such wanton behavior would occur at the highest levels of society, but Rosaline knew that opportunism and greed knew no bounds, answered to no moral code. And she fought off a shiver at the thought of Adrian McGrath's wife and only daughter, left to the mercy of the British public and any remaining generosity from their family members.

The reports showed her only the numbers. Rosaline saw, with perfect clarity, the raw mathematics behind Alban Hollow, saw the comparison of the accounts before and after Adrian had fiddled with them, completing — she noticed — a thorough, professional concealment of his own repeated theft. She saw where the money of the honest, hard-working tenants had been funneled into a nefarious criminal enterprise, turned into shipping supplies and large quantities of molasses, which in turn had seeped into the poorest streets of London, sating a constant itch, a constant need to dull the pangs of life, the pain of poverty. Rosaline saw where Adrian McGrath's original business partner, considerate enough to leave his half of the business to Adrian, had mysteriously and suddenly vanished in Barbados — an obvious cover-up, but, unfortunately, there was not enough evidence to support a charge of murder.

Rosaline also saw, with a touch of something a little too close to affection, where the Cunningham family had been lenient with their tenants during the bad years, and generous to them in the good. She saw that the land was well-tended, in spite of its troubled financial management; crops and grazing were rotated in and out as the soil needed, and every animal was put to good use. Her imagination began to churn, building a rich, stately home with huge windows that looked out upon a pond gleaming with lily pads and goldfish; a wide, sprawling lawn; a tangled, luscious rose garden; a forest, seething with oak and maple, vibrant with birdsong; a cheerful village, full of kind, joyful people who lived in the confidence of their livelihood, the resolute support of their landlord.

Rosaline sank back in her chair and tapped herself on the forehead, shattering the illusion and sweeping it under the rug. None of that mattered — Alban Hollow did not matter — all that *mattered* was that Lieutenant Callum McGrath was a liar, and a crook.

But what could she say? Nothing. Constable Morris's letter had made that quite clear, and if Captain Morris's reaction at the dinner party was anything to go by, Rosaline could not mention any of this to the Duke without provoking his ire.

And it would surely embarrass him, Rosaline thought, *to find himself so confronted by the past he is determined to forget, to outlive.* Even the thought of admitting to him that she knew some portion of the truth — no, it would be far too painful, for both of them.

Perhaps it does not matter, she thought then, a touch bitter. *He is not back in London, and will not return until God knows when. Maybe I shall never see him again, not in person. Maybe he will find another excuse, some other reason to remain in the country indefinitely.*

For she had not received a letter from him today, and it had been several days since his last.

Shaking off her momentary irritation, Rosaline returned her attention to her desk and went about gathering the contents of Constable Morris's letter. She collected them into a single, tight bundle, wrapped them twice in her best paper, then heated her wax and sealed the edges. When the wax was cool, she retrieved a spare bit of silk — from an old scarf, torn and fraying — and wrapped it around the entire package. This done, she got down on the floor, crawled under her bed, pried the loose footboard out of place, and slipped the parcel in beside her winnings from the fight.

A tad dusty and sweaty, Rosaline straightened up and began to brush off her dress, glancing out the window to see Charlotte dancing around beneath the oak in the garden. Then, her hand caught on something — Katherine's note, stuffed into her pocket, completely neglected. Rosaline gasped and hurtled over to her desk, where she wasted no time breaking the seal and scanning the contents.

Ros—

After much careful consideration, I realize I must once again make an appeal to your intelligence and your frightening aptitude with numbers. Please, my dear, if you are a true friend, would you examine the figures below and inform me whether they could, in any way, translate into a livelihood, enough to support two people? I promise this is the last request I shall make of you in this matter, and know that I will always be—Your dear friend, Katherine.

Her heart in her throat, Rosaline stared down at the list of numbers, her mind churning through the sums without her heart's consent. Within seconds, she knew what her answer would be, but she ignored it, surprised to find tears pricking at her eyes.

"Oh, Katherine," she murmured, folding the note shut again. "Oh, Katherine—"

Katherine's plan was obvious. She and her beloved had taken it upon themselves to explore the option of a life without the necessary husbands to steer them through it. It was a wonderful, beautiful idea, but— it would never be possible. Surely, Katherine had to know that, had to know that no matter how much money she managed to secret away, it would never be enough to mend her reputation, to repair her parents' and her siblings' broken hearts.

But how could Rosaline do it? How could she shatter the dream of a dear friend, someone like a sister—?

"There you are!" Charlotte sang, waltzing into the room on a cloud of fresh lilacs. She was smiling, until she caught Rosaline's expression. "Good heavens, what on earth is the matter?"

"Nothing, Charlotte," Rosaline said quickly, sliding the note into her top drawer and turning the lock. She slipped the key into her pocket and cleared her throat. "Did you enjoy the garden?"

"Tremendously. And Benny has just told me the most wonderful news — your father will be joining us for supper this evening!"

"Oh. Oh, how lovely." Rosaline's gaze drifted to the window, where a robin lighted on the windowsill and began to sing. She felt a sudden pang of nostalgia, aching for the simpler, easier days of the early season, when her biggest problems had been her new stays and Mrs. Randolph.

23

Supper was in the garden, lit by candles, and after dessert, drinks were served in the drawing room, accompanied by a spirited game of charades.

"My word," said Sir Ian, staring at Lord Devon flapping around like a lunatic. "Of all the things I never thought I would see—"

"It is quite a singular sight," Rosaline agreed, then took a sip of wine.

Her father shot her a look. "I must admit, my dear..." His voice dropped into a low rumble. "Perhaps this sounds a bit selfish of me, but I had expected my only daughter to be a tad more pleased to see her beloved father."

"Oh." Rosaline felt a prickle of guilt. Granted, she had seen him only a week before, but it had been a brief, stifled meeting. "Oh, I am sorry, Father—"

He dismissed her apology with a wave of his hand. "I merely wish to determine whether her distraction is the result of material or abstract concern."

She offered him a quick smile. "'Distraction' is probably too strong a term—"

"Do not try to dodge me, young lady." But his tone was teasing, light. "It has not worked since you were eleven."

"Sixteen," she corrected him.

"Be that as it may." Sir Ian's gaze was piercing, and, she realized, concerned. "Is it algebra, or something far more sinister?"

"Truly, it is nothing." But Rosaline could not lie to him. "The season is fraught with social drama. I seem to have overindulged."

"Counting your chickens before they've hatched!" cried Charlotte, and Lord Devon burst into applause.

"Well done, my dear!" Lord Devon squeezed Charlotte's shoulder and brushed a kiss to her head. "A dab hand, just like your mother!"

"Ah." Sir Ian nodded to Rosaline, ignoring them. "I assume that must have something to do with why you've been in contact with a Bow Street Runner."

It was as if she'd swallowed ice. Heart pounding, her mouth cold with shock, Rosaline could only stare at him as he offered her a smile and stood up.

"Come along, Ros, it's our turn."

"Yes," she managed, and put down her wine glass, ready to pay attention.

Her father squared up to the sofa, looked her in the eye, and held out his hands — together, palms towards his face.

"Book."

He nodded, then held up a single finger.

"One word."

He nodded again, and held up a single finger, again.

"First syllable—"

Then, somewhat to her astonishment, Sir Ian got down on his hands and knees and began shuffling about the floor, letting out a low series of grunts. His head twitched, as if turning over an invisible object with his nose, and he let out a grunt, then a squeal. Then, suddenly, he winced, collapsing onto his side and letting out another squeal, this time of surprise and pain. He flailed, he writhed, and finally, he fell still. Mystified, Rosaline watched as he popped open an eye and pointed at his own thigh.

"All right," she said reluctantly.

Sir Ian stood up, brushed off his trousers, and held up two fingers.

"Second syllable."

He stepped towards her, taking her hand. He looked her in the eye, squeezed her hand, then stepped back, releasing her hand — letting go.

"Let," Rosaline said, and realization charged past her simmering panic. "Pig—let. Hamlet!"

"Yes!" her father cried, while Lord Devon and Charlotte groaned — they were still two points behind. "Well done, Rosaline!"

"This is so unfair," said Charlotte, smiling ruefully as she picked up her quill and updated the points. "You both are far too talented at this. Almost professionals."

"We have lots of practice," said Sir Ian, and Rosaline felt a throb of nostalgia deep in her lungs. A thousand evenings materialized in her mind's eye, all of them with her and her parents in front of a roaring fire or a brilliant sunset, playing charades until they were breathless with laughter. She remembered one particular instance when her mother's foot had twisted in the rug, but before she could fall, Sir Ian had caught her and swept her into an elegant dip.

They did not have a chance to speak again until much later, when Charlotte and Lord Devon left them in the foyer to say their goodbyes. Rosaline met her father's gaze, unflinching.

"How did you find out?" she asked him. "About Bow Street?"

"Constable Scarlet," he replied, his voice mild, untroubled. But she knew that he was only so unaffected because he knew he had caught her like a fish on a hook. "An old friend of mine who happened to catch your address on a bit of his colleague's outgoing post." He raised an eyebrow at her. "Care to explain?"

"I would, but—" Then, to her utter astonishment and horror, Rosaline found her voice catching, her throat thick with emotion. "Father, it would betray a confidence..." Tears pricked at her eyes. "A confidence I hold most dear, and I would feel terrible if I had to—"

Concern, true concern, shaded his features, and he put a hand to her shoulder. "Rosaline, I had imagined this to be a bit of gossip at best and a prank at worst. But if you are this upset—"

"No," she tried. "Not upset, merely..." But the right word would not surface. She laughed a little, the sound wet and defeated. "Oh, gosh, I really am being ridiculous—"

"Rosaline." Sir Ian's tone was firm now, his gaze relentless. "If someone has hurt you—"

"No," Rosaline said again, pleading now. "No, I can assure you, it is nothing like that. The news was merely a shock, and dismaying, to say the least. It was... not what I had expected. My reaction," she went on, forcing herself to take a breath, "is one of sympathy for a friend, not distress for my own sake."

Her father looked at her for another moment, apparently seeking something in her face that would give him confirmation of her honesty. A moment later he nodded, with obvious reluctance. "Just..." he began. "Tread carefully, Rosaline. We are fresh meat in the busiest butcher's shop in the world. It would take very little for the blood to flow."

"Father," she admonished, with a smile. "How morbid."

The corner of his mouth twitched. "Maybe, but it is seriously meant." He squeezed her shoulder. "My position is a shield, yes, but it is by no means a guarantee. Your trust in others should be rare and carefully bestowed."

"I know," she replied, then was struck by a sudden thought. "Father, I know we have never had cause to discuss it, and I would not ask if it were not of serious import—" She bit her lip. "How much would my dowry be?"

His eyebrows threatened to ascend to the ceiling. "And why,

pray tell," he said, his voice rich with irony, "do you have cause to ask me such a thing?"

"Just—" she bit out, a blush burning her neck, "lay aside the theatrics. It is a question borne of natural curiosity, since Charlotte herself will soon be engaged."

If her father was surprised by this news, he did not show it. "Well," he began, "in the remarkable event that I would consent to some rake spiriting away my wonderful daughter, your dowry would likely be somewhere in the realm of ten or twelve thousand pounds."

The shock of this was so astute that for a moment, Rosaline feared that she would, for the first time in her life, slump into a faint.

"Of course," he went on, "this does not account for your inheritance from your mother."

"Of course," she parroted, her heart throbbing in her stomach.

"But that trust only passes into your possession on your twenty-fifth birthday."

"And is there a record," Rosaline said, "of my inheritance?"

He frowned. "Well, not yours, specifically, but wills are a matter of public record. Your mother's would have been published not long after her death, and the status of her family is widely known and acknowledged. Even if someone had not seen the contents of her will, they could assume her financial worth by her maiden name alone."

"I see." She could not breathe. It was all making sense now. "Thank you."

"You are welcome, I suppose." Sir Ian looked at her for another moment, then shook his head in bemusement. "As ever, you remain somewhat of a mystery to your poor father."

"My *dear* father," she corrected him, and pressed a kiss to his cheek.

Sir Ian almost smiled. "Go to bed."

"Only if you do as well." Rosaline pointed a warning finger at him. "And I don't mean sitting up and reading an anatomy book until you fall asleep at your desk."

He held up a hand in surrender. "Fine, fine." Sir Ian turned, opened the front door, and looked back at her, the cool night air swimming around his feet. "When did you get so grown up?"

Rosaline smiled. "It is anyone's guess."

⁂

THE FOLLOWING DAY, ROSALINE LOOKED ANXIOUSLY OVER HER shoulder as she, Charlotte, and Cadogan made their way over one of the fairy bridges — so called because they were minuscule, painted in charming pastel shades, floating above beds of lily pads — in Kensington Gardens.

Cadogan noticed. "Miss Bailey," he said, "are you quite well?"

"Yes, thank you," she replied, ignoring Charlotte's concerned glance. "Merely impatient."

"Oh." Charlotte smiled. "Fret not, Katherine should join us soon."

"Indeed." But Rosaline could not help glancing over her shoulder again. Her anxiety was twofold — first, that Katherine would not show up at all; second, that Katherine's reaction to Rosaline's news would not... do well... in a public setting.

I should have invited her to tea, Rosaline thought, a touch bitter. *Even the risk of being overheard by the Dragon or one of the servants would have been worth it, perhaps, to help preserve Katherine's reputation—*

"Are you ladies excited?" said Cadogan. "For tomorrow evening?"

"Oh, yes," Charlotte cooed, her face shining with glee. "All the whispers indicate that it promises to outdo even the Eventide Ball—"

"Difficult to imagine, is it not?" Cadogan grinned. "And such an interesting theme."

"Yes, black and white." Charlotte gave a little spin as she returned to solid ground. "Our modiste has been working quite hard these past few days, as, I am sure, has every clothier in London."

"It feels almost unfair," Cadogan went on, as they passed into the shade of a small copse, "that all we men have to do is show up in white tie, which requires but a single press."

"What riveting conversation," chimed a familiar voice.

Rosaline whipped round as Charlotte sang, "Katherine!"

Katherine smiled, curtseying to Cadogan's bow. "Good afternoon, everyone."

"Good afternoon indeed, Katherine," said Charlotte, grinning. "Rosaline was so anxious for you to join us."

"Was she?" Katherine did not show an ounce of surprise. "Then perhaps I should indulge her with my company."

They walked on, Charlotte and Cadogan wandering several feet ahead of Rosaline and Katherine. For several moments, Rosaline said nothing, waiting until they were out of earshot.

"Where is your charming Dragon?" said Katherine, glancing around.

"Asleep, under a tree across the pond." Rosaline would have smiled, had she the cheer. "Charlotte dosed her tea with an extract of valerian. We need a respite, sometimes, from her shadow."

"Indeed." Katherine looked ahead, and, seeing Charlotte and Cadogan immersed in conversation, halted and turned to Rosaline. "What is your news?"

"Katherine." Rosaline's voice dropped to a whisper. "I wish I had better tidings—"

Katherine's eyes slipped shut, and Rosaline saw a wave of grief pass over her face. "It is all right," she managed. "I should have known—"

An invisible hand clenched Rosaline's heart. "I am so sorry," she said, her voice catching, "but it just does not seem possible, as a long-term solution. And Katherine, it is so difficult to put a price on the destruction you would leave behind—"

Katherine's eyes snapped open, and anger flashed through her gaze. "Destruction?" she said, her voice low. "You think I *care* about my reputation, about what my family—"

"Yes," Rosaline said. "Yes, I think you would care, if not now, then in ten years, when your nieces and nephews can hardly be told of their aunt's existence, when you cannot watch your brothers become fathers, when you cannot watch their children's children take the helm of the family and steer it into the future."

"Rosaline." Katherine's voice was deep with pain. "There will always be a cost, and I must decide if the cost will be me and my happiness, my sanity, or theirs.'

Rosaline shook her head, then reached out, took Katherine's hand, and said, "Marry him."

Katherine's eyebrows scaled her forehead. "*What?*"

"Marry Mr. Heath, Katherine. And your beloved can marry Oswalt." Rosaline dug a bit of paper out of her pocket and pressed it into Katherine's palm. "Marry him, so that I may give you a wedding present."

Katherine frowned at her, disbelieving, then pulled away, tugging open the note. She stared down at the handwritten number, at the sum of Rosaline's winnings from the boxing match and what remained of her pocket money, and when her gaze snapped to Rosaline's, her expression was a mixture of fear and awe. "Rosaline— I couldn't— I could *never*—"

"Lucas," said Rosaline. "Your eldest brother. How much does he love you?"

Katherine frowned again. "Quite a lot, I suppose—"

"Go to him after you are married." Rosaline held her gaze. "And tell him that you wish to make an investment, separate from your husband's estate. If Mr. Heath is as good a man as he seems, he will not contest it."

"Rosaline—"

"I have done some research." Four hours with the property books in Lord Devon's library, she did not say. "This—" she tapped the note— "should be more than enough to purchase a seafront cottage in Cornwall, Devon, or Brighton. Or, even a modest townhome, should you not wish to be so remote. You can use the remaining amount to purchase all incidentals, pay your taxes, and even guarantee your servants' discretion."

Katherine went very pale, then very red. "Rosaline—"

"And with your combined allowance," Rosaline pressed on, "you and your beloved could be entirely self-sufficient, should you wish to be." She squeezed Katherine's hand. "You would have your own life, your own space. And your husband and Lord Oswalt would have the whole of their estates to themselves. You would not lose anything, Katherine, or anyone, and you would be safe."

For several moments, Katherine just stared at her, looking as overwhelmed as it was possible for a person to be. Tears shone in her eyes, and finally, she grinned, joy exploding across her face. "Yes," she managed. "Oh, Rosaline, you are too kind, I do not deserve—"

"Hush." Rosaline smiled and squeezed her hand again. "Don't you have a letter to write, and a proposal to accept?"

"Yes!" Katherine blinked, wiped away her tears. "Oh, yes, I must— I must go at once— Please, give the others my goodbyes, make up some urgent matter—"

Rosaline nodded. "Of course. Now go!"

As she watched Katherine speed away, she could not help but grin, satisfied that finally, something had gone right.

Rosaline could not sleep.

Perhaps it was the lingering excitement of Katherine's acceptance, or her inability to forget the contents of Constable

Morris's letter. She found her mind drawn to it more often than not, drawn to that inescapable reminder that someone she had trusted was no more than a base liar and a crook; the reminder that the Duke was humble, and wise as a result of suffering more loss and disappointment than most people would suffer in a lifetime.

She found her mind pulled again to the image of the Duke in the drawing room, stark in the gray pre-dawn light, smelling of dust and flowers and river damp, his mouth hot on her temple as he smiled and said goodbye. And something twinged deep within her, something warm and foreign and familiar all at once.

"Enough." Rosaline sat up, went to her dressing screen. There, she reached for her dressing gown, her mind set on a glass of milk or a measure of gin — whichever was easier to find — and then, she heard the first sound.

She froze, heart beating in her ears. There — again. Something like the wail of a baby. Mystified, Rosaline tugged on her dressing gown and went over to the window, looking out at the pitch-black night. She could see very little, and the rain pounded steadily at the glass. For several moments, all was silent. Then—

Rosaline tore out of her room, slipping through the empty, cold hall, down the stairs, along the corridor, through the dining room, and into the kitchen.

It was still too early even for the cook to be awake. All of the fixtures lay silent and dark, save for the banked coals in the massive fireplace. Her heart pounding, Rosaline dove for a candle, then bent at the embers, waiting for the wick to catch before she rounded on the back door.

The locks were sticky, but she eventually tugged the door open and stared out into the chilly, dank night, the rain a curtain before her face. Rosaline could barely make out the oak, the edge of the flowerbeds, the bench beside the roses. She waited, the candle sputtering in her hand.

Another howl. This one all the more mournful, resigned. And

then, she saw movement — a dark lump, shifting beneath a hedge.

Stifling a gasp, Rosaline abandoned her candle on the counter, pulled her gown tight around her body, and ran out into the rain. It soaked her through in an instant, biting cold and merciless against her skin, but in seconds she reached the hedge, got down on her hands and knees, the mud seeping into her clothing, and peered beneath the branches.

The lump turned, and Rosaline found herself face-to-face with a raggedy, soaking wet ginger cat with bright yellow eyes.

It stared at her, and she stared at it. Then, summoning her courage, Rosaline reached forward, wrapped her hand around the cat's middle, and tugged it out from beneath the bush.

The cat squirmed, then buried its face in her stomach. Panting, Rosaline clung to it and straightened up, running back into the kitchen and closing the door behind her.

She gently deposited the cat onto the draining board. It stared up at her, pathetic as anything, and she could see now, in the dim light of the banked fire, the fresh red scratches across its face. A stab of sympathy cut through her, and then she began to shiver. Rosaline looked down. A puddle had formed around her feet, her skin was frozen to the touch, and she was covered in mud. Even her hair was dripping wet.

"Lisette is going to kill me," she murmured, then she glanced around the kitchen, her gaze lighting on a fresh pile of laundry, ready to be taken upstairs. She looked back at the cat, who still had not moved, and was watching her, waiting for her to make a decision.

"*Alors*." Rosaline tugged off her dressing gown and reached for the hem of her nightgown. "*Allons-y*."

Twenty minutes later, she slipped back into her bedroom and gently shut the door behind her with her hip, candle in one hand and the cat tucked up in the other. The house was still silent — no one had heard her, or come into the kitchen. She'd left her wet clothing in a pile in the sink, along with the towels she'd used to dry herself and the cat. After she'd changed into a fresh chemise from the laundry pile, she'd set her sights on her new companion.

The cat had taken all of her ministrations in stride. He — a discovery she'd made after a quick examination — had allowed her to rinse off the mud on his paws and belly, wipe his cuts clean, and rub him dry, all without a single complaint. She suspected this to be the result of crippling fear rather than good humor; the cat had trembled the entire time, his eyes huge. Now, though, with his fur spiked and half-dry, his belly full of leftover trout, and his body warmed from being carried in her arms, he poked his head up over the curve of her elbow, taking in the sight before him.

"This is my room," she whispered to him, putting her candle down on her bedside table. "That's my bed. Over there is my vanity, my dresser, and my desk." She brushed a kiss to his damp head, then bent down and lowered him to the floor. "You can sleep wherever you like," she told him as he sniffed around, slowly making his way over to her dresser. "You need not join me in the bed, you might like to sleep beneath the window, or perhaps in the armchair." Rosaline huffed a sigh. "There will be quite an uproar in the morning. I cannot imagine Mrs. Randolph will be pleased to see you. But if you do not have an owner, I wouldn't dream of turning you out onto the street."

The cat paused, glanced at her, then continued sniffing. She watched as he stopped at the gap below her dresser; he sniffed for a moment, then stuck his front paw into the gap, trying to get at something she could not see.

Rosaline smiled. "What did you find? Is it a mouse?" She got down on her hands and knees beside him, and, seeing nothing, slipped her hand into the gap.

Her fingers brushed against something smooth, with a hard corner. Rosaline frowned, and pulled it out of the darkness.

It was a letter. An unopened letter addressed to *her*. Written in very familiar handwriting.

The cat pawed at it, and her body flooded hot and cold. It must have come with Constable Morris's letter the day before, and she'd dropped it in her haste. Rosaline stood up, sat down on her bed, and, her hands shaking, broke the familiar seal and opened the letter, holding it to the light.

R—

I find myself even shorter on time than I'd imagined, with hardly a moment to carve a proper word. But I had to inform you of the following — I am returning to London, and will be there two days' hence. Just in time to attend the Black and White Ball, I believe.

Save me a dance.
H.

Her mouth numb, her heart roaring, Rosaline stared down at the *H* she now knew as well as her own *R*, and tried not to panic.

In less than a day, she would see the Duke again. And what would happen when she did?

24

Rosaline woke later than usual to a flurry of activity. Head pounding, she could only look up at Lisette's face, which was a font of conflicting emotions. Excitement, irritation, worry — she could see it all.

"*Good morning.*" Lisette paused beside the bed, arms akimbo. "*Care to explain the pile of filthy, wet clothes and towels in the kitchen sink?*"

"*Certainly.*" With that, Rosaline pulled down the covers to reveal the cat, which was curled up against her stomach, dead asleep.

Lisette looked at the cat, then at her. "She is going to murder you."

Rosaline yawned widely. "Not over a cat, surely." She saw the way Mattie was hurrying around the room, opening the curtains and straightening up everything in sight — she was nervous energy personified. "Is something the matter?"

Lisette shook her head. "The opposite." She grinned. "The Earl Cadogan is in Lord Devon's study. He is here to discuss — well."

Rosaline sat up at once, ignoring the way her head throbbed.

She'd only managed to get back to sleep just as Dawn had poked her pink fingers over the horizon, but that hardly mattered now. "Where is Charlotte?"

"Downstairs."

"I must get dressed— Lisette, right away—"

Surely, Rosaline thought as Lisette was tugging her hair into submission, *dressing has never taken longer for any person, dead or alive—*

Some ten minutes later, she hurtled downstairs and skidded to a halt in front of Lord Devon's study. Charlotte was seated in an armchair near the door, placid as ever except for the wide, unstoppable grin on her face. "Oh, hello," she said to Rosaline. "Yes, I'd wondered when they would get you—"

"Why did you not come and get me yourself, you weasel?!"

"Well, I—" Charlotte glanced at the closed door of her father's study, and that was answer enough. "They've been in there for quite some time. Do you suppose—?"

Rosaline took her hand. "Charlotte, don't be silly. As if your father would begrudge you the most handsome, eligible bachelor in all of England. The fact that Cadogan is enormously wealthy and loves you to absolute bits and pieces is just an added bonus."

Charlotte squeezed Rosaline's fingers. "Then what can be taking so long?"

Rosaline waved an airy hand. "You know how men can be about money. Besides, who's to say that your father hasn't begun one of his speeches about radishes?"

"Oh." Charlotte's grin wavered, and she again glanced at the door. "Oh, dear—"

Then, suddenly, Benny appeared, looking quite uncomfortable.

"Yes, Benny?" said Rosaline, smiling at him. "Did you need something?"

He stared at her for a moment, then cleared his throat. "Miss Bailey," he said. "You have a visitor in the drawing room."

Rosaline's heart fell to her feet, then rocketed back into her chest, even as her brain reminded her that it would be all but impossible for the Duke to have gotten here so quickly. Perhaps it was Katherine — but, then, wouldn't Benny have said? "Have I?" she managed, then met Charlotte's curious gaze. "I have no idea —" But she stood up. "Very well."

As Rosaline walked down the hall, getting closer and closer to the drawing room door, she could not shake a sense of foreboding. Perhaps it was silly, but an unexpected visitor so late in the season was hardly a good sign—

Benny shot her a final, worried look before he took the handle of the drawing room door. He stepped into the room, cleared his throat, and said, "Miss Bailey, sir."

"Thank you," came the reply. Rosaline's stomach once again dropped to her feet.

She entered the room, first spotting Mrs. Randolph, who was seated by the card table. Her expression was impassive, but Rosaline caught the curl of distaste in the corner of her mouth. Swallowing thickly, Rosaline turned to face—

"Miss Bailey." Lieutenant McGrath's grin was blinding in the morning sunlight. She fought the urge to smack it off his face.

Rosaline managed a smile. "Lieutenant." She bobbed a curtsy. "What a lovely surprise."

"Yes, I hoped it might be." He gestured to the nearest sofa. "Join me?"

Rosaline felt a stab of repulsion. "Why, of course." She sent Mrs. Randolph a final, panicked glance before she sat down beside him on the sofa. Now that she was looking at him in the bright, direct light of day, without a single persuasion or barrier between them, she felt she could see the truth of his character in the sharp edges of his face, the pitiless depth of his eyes. But she kept her smile all the same — she had a part to play. "I do hope nothing is the matter, Lieutenant."

His chuckle was low, self-abasing. "Not so much the matter,

no, though I suppose it depends upon your perspective." McGrath's gaze caught on Mrs. Randolph and seemed to tighten imperceptibly before it landed on Rosaline's face. "I must confess, Miss Bailey, that ever since we met, I have found myself able to think of little else."

Merde, Rosaline thought, her heart stabbing in her throat. "Oh?" she said.

"Indeed." His hand inched towards hers, pausing a hair's breadth from her fingers. "You are like no woman I've ever known. You are kind, intelligent, generous, and friendly — these are just some of my favorite things about you, you realize, second only to— well." His gaze raked along the lines of her body before it met her own. "Well," he murmured. "It is no surprise that I find myself quite thoroughly in love with you."

The blush that rose to Rosaline's face was genuine, though borne of blinding anger as opposed to modesty. "Lieutenant, I—"

"No," he insisted, and he took her by the hand now, squeezing it tightly. "No, I must tell you, Miss Bailey, there must be an end to my madness—" With that, McGrath slid off the couch and onto a knee, facing her with the most beseeching expression she'd ever seen, outside of a spaniel. "Miss Bailey, would you do me the greatest honor of them all and... become my wife?"

One could have heard a pin drop.

After several painful moments, Rosaline realized she actually had to say something.

"Lieutenant." She tried for a smile and delicately extracted her hand from his. "You flatter me, you are too kind—"

Something in his face flickered, and his smile melted.

"But I cannot accept your most gracious proposal."

It was as if a storm had rolled across his features, turning what had once been calm into a battleground of the elements. His eyes flashed, and he set his jaw. "Why not?"

"Because it would not be right," she replied, "to lead you where there is no path."

McGrath rose to his feet, and for a moment, said nothing. Then—

"You love him." His voice was snide, cruel. "The blessed Duke."

A jolt of fear, real fear, hit Rosaline in the belly. "No, I—"

"Even after all he did to me? To my *family*?" McGrath snorted, his shoulders rippling with indignation. "To operate under the delusion that he would so much as look at you, *you*, a half-breed with a brain not nearly as large as her ego— I was doing you a kindness, a *favor*, you will get no better offer—"

Rosaline was on her feet before she knew it. "Allow me to elaborate, Lieutenant. My refusal was polite before, but it lacked a certain degree of honesty. I refused you not for the sake of another man, but because I could never love, could never so much as *entertain* such a spineless, conniving coward with so little regard, so little respect, for his fellow man." She took a breath. "Certainly not one so prone to egregious self-pity and insecurity. I can hardly think of anything less attractive in a suitor, let alone a husband."

For a moment, she really did think he would hit her. Then—

"Lieutenant." Mrs. Randolph's voice rang sharp as a whip across the room. "I believe that the time has come for you to depart."

McGrath threw Rosaline one final, wild look, and then he cleared his throat, buttoned his jacket, and stalked from the room. A few seconds later, the front door slammed shut.

Her heart throbbing, the fight bleeding out of her like a wound, Rosaline finally met Mrs. Randolph's gaze, and was shocked to see unmistakeable approval in her features.

"Well done." Mrs. Randolph gave a single nod. "I never liked him, anyway."

Rosaline could only nod in return, tucking a loose strand of hair behind her ear. She pressed a hand to her sternum, its weight calming her, and left the drawing room. There were better things to worry about, even as her instincts told her that McGrath would do his best to have the final word.

Rosaline watched with a smile on her face as Charlotte brushed her fingers against the new diamond necklace shining at her neck. Cadogan watched as well, smiling down at her, looking happier than any other man on earth. The necklace was certainly a divine engagement present — "Twenty thousand," Lisette had hissed while she'd laced pearls through Rosaline's hair, "it must be worth at least twenty thousand, look at all of them!" — and was tasteful enough that it did not appear gaudy or ostentatious. The other guests were already swarming around the newly-engaged couple; there was no better evidence of the speed at which news could travel in their small, envious world. One could only imagine the chaos that would unfold after the announcement appeared in the papers.

Rosaline had told neither Lisette nor Charlotte of McGrath's proposal, and somewhat to her surprise, Mrs. Randolph had likewise remained silent. Thankfully, no one had questioned Rosaline's sudden disappearance that morning, since they had all been so focused on Charlotte's news. She buried the secret quite happily, convinced that if she did not think about it, and if no one knew about it, perhaps it would simply cease to exist.

And, the excitement of Charlotte's engagement had prevented Mrs. Randolph from noticing the four-legged addition to the household. *Small victories*, thought Rosaline, though she was not sure how it had been avoided, given that Charlotte had tied a marvelous blue ribbon around the cat's neck and pronounced him her little lion.

"They make quite a handsome couple, do they not?" Lord Devon was wearing his usual enigmatic smile.

"They certainly do," Rosaline replied, sipping her wine. "Their children are sure to be the most gorgeous offspring on the entire island."

He glanced at her. "I suppose that you will be the one finding a husband next."

She grinned. "Why, Lord Devon, you say the most outrageous things."

"Perhaps." His voice was mild, unconvincing, and he slipped away to the refreshment table.

Rosaline glanced around the ballroom for the hundredth time that hour, searching once again for a familiar tangle of hair. But no, there was no sign of the Duke, and Cadogan had not mentioned him at all, swept up in the delightful chaos of his own engagement. It was getting to be too much for her, all of this waiting and hoping.

But what, precisely, was she hoping for? If Rosaline were being honest, she was not at all sure what she was expecting of her reunion with the Duke. Yes, they had remained in contact during his absence, but that was hardly ground-breaking. Their friend-ship was... their friendship. *But he kissed you,* came that treacher-ous, unhelpful voice in the back of her head. *He kissed you twice, and put his head to yours. That has to mean something. And whatever it meant when he left, it surely means more now, when you have hardly gone two days without contact. And when he told you—*

"Miss Bailey?"

Rosaline turned and stared, with some astonishment, at the newcomer. She dropped into a quick curtsy. "Good evening. I do not believe we've had the pleasure—"

The man almost smiled, and mirth flashed in his dark gaze. "Mr. Heath," he said, inclining his head, and a jolt of apprehen-sion wracked her body. "Might I steal you for a dance?"

"Of course, Mr. Heath," she said, and allowed him to lead her to the dance floor.

Once they were mid-waltz, with no danger of being overheard,

Mr. Heath glanced at her and said, "I understand that I have you to thank for the happy news of my own engagement."

Rosaline smiled. "You flatter me, sir. I played a very minor role. The decision was Miss Knight's, and Miss Knight's alone."

"Perhaps," he allowed, almost smiling again. He was quite handsome, she noticed, in a slight and dapper sort of way. "But I must express some gratitude. If not for your skills of persuasion, then for your unwavering support and discretion. Those are two qualities in short supply, Miss Bailey."

She took a steadying breath. "Again, you flatter me, sir."

"Then I shall close by saying this, and only this." Mr. Heath looked her right in the eye. "Without people like you, people like me and Katherine would find ourselves quite alone in this stilted and cruel world. I want to make it plain that you — and Lady Prince, of course — will always be welcome in our home, and if you should ever find yourself requiring assistance, in any matter, we would be most happy to help in any way we can."

Rosaline had to swallow past the thick emotion in her throat. "I find myself quite speechless, sir."

"A rare occurrence, from what I've heard." The music ended, and Mr. Heath stilled, stepping out of frame. He gave a small bow. "I hope to see you at the wedding, Miss Bailey."

"Of course, Mr. Heath." She curtseyed, smiled, and made her way back through the crowd.

After reuniting with a glass of wine, Rosaline took a steadying breath, her heart still soaring with the emotion provoked by Mr. Heath's speech. It seemed that Katherine's reports had been correct — he was a kind, honorable man with a direct manner and a fierce sense of loyalty. If Katherine had to marry, Rosaline could hardly think of a better man.

Charlotte and Cadogan had found their way to the dance floor, where they were dancing a jig, a vision of black and white. Rosaline smiled to see them, then made her way to the nearest window, which was open and inviting the most delicious breeze off the front drive.

It was there, as she sipped at her wine, that she first heard the voices.

"—see you've deigned to rejoin us—"

"And I see that time has granted you neither wit nor civility, though I cannot admit to any surprise over the matter—"

A cold laugh. "Oh, very well done, Your Grace, I find myself quite overwhelmed by the opportunity to be dignified by your insult—"

"Why are you here?" The Duke's voice was sharp with a poorly-hidden anger. "Of all the places in London, this can hardly be the most enticing option. I seem to recall, with perfect and unfortunate clarity, your fondness for brothels and public houses, of which this residence is neither."

"What, can a man not have multiple interests?"

A pause. Then, "You are drunk."

Another laugh. "Yes, happily. At least here, the booze is free."

"You should leave, McGrath. At once."

"No, Your Grace. Last I checked, we were not in Alban Hollow, and I have as much right to be here as anyone. You see, I find myself wanting a wife, and what better place to look for her than at this meat market?"

"You will keep a civil tongue in your mouth—"

"Will I?" came the taunt. "Perhaps, but not until it has become thoroughly acquainted with a certain Miss Bailey."

A chilling silence fell, and Rosaline gripped the windowsill, cold fear beginning to seep through her stomach. Around her, the ball continued.

"I would advise you," said the Duke, "to choose your next words very carefully."

"And I would advise you," returned McGrath, "to stay out of my way."

"If you continue to demean the young women of London, then I am afraid I cannot."

"Ah." McGrath was taunting now. "But I did not demean the young women of London, Your Grace. I merely expressed an interest in a certain debutante. What, surely the great Duke of St. Albans, the notorious bachelor, couldn't care less about the favor of an eligible woman, as enticing as she might be."

"You are not to speak with her." The Duke's voice was low, sharp. "You are not to so much as *look* at her—"

McGrath snorted. "And what would you say, Your Grace, if you knew that I had already done both, and worse?"

Another silence fell, and Rosaline's hands began to shake. She had known, of course, that McGrath might well try to seek his revenge, but even this was—

"You are a liar," spat the Duke. "She would never—"

"And what if she would? Is it any surprise, when her only other option is you, a man who has hardly even *touched* a woman, let alone fucked one—"

It was too much. Rosaline put down her glass and turned away from the window. Her feet moved of their own accord, carrying her through the crowd, across the room, and out onto the back veranda. But even there, with the fresh evening air in her face, she felt trapped, stuck, unhinged. Her heart roaring in her ears, Rosaline went down the steps, across the wide, sloping, lawn, past the rose bushes, and into an enclosed garden, where she was shrouded by a wall of hedges and finally enveloped by a welcome silence.

She stumbled over to a nearby stone bench and sat down hard, not caring how the dirt might show on her dress. What did it matter now, when she could hardly imagine walking back into that room, facing the Duke or even McGrath himself?

Rosaline's conscience screamed at her, telling her that it was impossible for the Duke to believe a single word out of McGrath's mouth, especially about her, but logic— cool, prevailing logic —

reminded her that she lived in a world where men listened to women even less than they listened to reason.

She had been careful, hadn't she? She certainly hadn't snuck away into dark corners and abandoned halls, like some of her fellow debutantes. But she had not been perfect, either. The opera. The promenading. The Eventide Ball.

Rosaline's mind raced, tracing back every moment she had been alone with a man, and she tugged off her gloves, dropping them onto the ground. If McGrath wanted to make a case, he had the evidence to do so. Charlotte and half the audience at *Figaro* had seen Rosaline abandon the third act; the only one who could vouch for her was the Duke, and he had not found her until a quarter of an hour later. There was a window. Enough leeway for any number of indiscretions. Enough to make the Duke doubt her, regardless of any attachment he might feel towards her. Because unlike him, she was expendable. She had no title, no seat, no land. Even her father's position did not offer immunity to scandal.

Rosaline was a cliché ripe for tragedy, and she had been stupid enough to trap herself in one.

Rosaline was not sure how long her mind whirled like this, in circle after circle until she was dizzy with panic, her throat thick with unshed tears. The garden around her grew dark, dimly lit by the half-moon above. She could see very little, and when she heard a twig snap, the sound like a gunshot in the silence, she stood up at once, facing the dark void of the hedges opposite.

Hardly daring to breathe, Rosaline stared across the enclosed garden, trying to discern movement among the leaves and branches. For a moment, nothing happened, and all was still. Then, she heard the sound of a footfall, a low chuckle.

McGrath stepped out from between the hedges and into the moonlight, a grin evident on his face. "How happily we are met on this fine evening."

Rosaline's heart began to race, and liquid fear pooled at her lower back. *I am too far from the house*, she thought. *They would not hear my scream above the music.*

He chuckled then, taking a few leisurely steps closer. She realized just how tall he was, how strong. She had little chance of outrunning him. "Come now, no need to be so reticent. We are old friends, after all."

Rosaline found her voice. "You," she spat, "are no friend of mine."

His forehead puckered. "Oh, dear. I can see that the Duke's poisonous words have done much to cloud your judgment." He tsked. "Poor thing. Though I suppose it cannot be helped — women are always so impressionable."

"Perhaps you're right," she fired back, with more conviction than she felt. "After all, I believed you to be a good man, once. Thank God I saw the error of my ways."

Something rippled in his face, giving it a mean edge. "After your ridiculous outburst this morning, I was inclined to give you the benefit of the doubt. I thought perhaps I had caught you at a bad moment, that the Duke had wrongfully called me a liar, or that you had temporarily taken leave of your senses—"

"I can assure you, my senses have never been sharper."

"You would do well," McGrath spat, "to hold your tongue. My temper, once provoked, is not readily put to rest."

"Your memory seems as weak as your temper is strong!" Rosaline took a step back, and he took a step closer. "You are forgetting, Lieutenant, that I rejected your proposal."

"And yet here we are."

"Yes," she bit out. "Here we are. And still, you playact and pretend."

He frowned, and the confusion seemed to slow him. "Whatever do you mean?"

"What I mean, *sir*, is that if you insist upon cornering me in this inappropriate manner, the least you could do is offer a degree of honesty." She took another step back. "You never loved me. You were only ever interested in my dowry, my inheritance."

McGrath's smirk was sharp, biting. And he was coming even closer. "Money was only part of it, Miss Bailey. Your open, easy nature was an added bonus." When she frowned, he added, "Come now, do not play coy with me."

Her mouth went dry, and Rosaline stumbled backwards. "I'm sure I do not know—"

"At the opera." He was close enough to touch, now. Close enough that she could smell the cheap liquor on his breath. "You knew exactly what you were doing. I was just gentleman enough to ignore it. Well." Another grin. "I am not ignoring it now."

McGrath lunged at her and grabbed her, his hands like vices around her arms, and Rosaline stumbled, a shriek dying in her throat, her right foot slipping on soft, muddy earth and down into a deep, tight hole— She wrenched her leg, desperate to flee, then felt and heard something crack — the pain was sudden, burning up her leg as she struggled against the weight of McGrath, shoving at him with all her might, but he had her, his nails raking down her arms, his mouth hot and insistent at her neck, his drunken weight bearing down on her—

Finally, Rosaline managed to wrest her arm free, and she reeled back, then slapped him across the face, but it did not matter — he fell upon her with a roar, tugging at her hair and clawing at her dress, and tears stung at her eyes, her body shaking with despair, her leg weak with pain, and Rosaline could not free herself, she could not—

Suddenly, something came bursting out of the bushes and tackled McGrath from behind, pulling him off of her. Rosaline collapsed to the ground, sobs wracking her frame, her hands clutching at her calf, her ankle still buried out of reach. McGrath stumbled, reeling up in time for his assailant — *the Duke*, Rosaline realized — to punch him clean across the jaw.

25

McGrath was taller than the Duke, and stronger, but he was drunk. He let out a growl and swung at the Duke, who ducked and landed a few punches to McGrath's ribs, his kidneys, the back of his neck. McGrath again tried and failed to land a hit, only for the Duke to deck him square in the face. McGrath went down like a brick of lead, and when he hit the ground, he remained there, motionless.

The Duke was beside her in an instant, and Rosaline thought that she might die, because here they were, they had not seen each other in weeks, and her foot was stuck in a rabbit den, snot was dripping down her face, and she couldn't seem to stop crying or shaking—

"There now, there—" The Duke's voice was low, and his arm was around her shoulders, warm and comforting, and he smelled of his soap and fresh dew, and all she wanted was to bury her face in his jacket and stay there. "It's all over now—"

"I—I—" Rosaline hiccuped, the garden swimming in her vision. "I tried, but I couldn't get away—"

"Yes, it's all right, it's all over now." The Duke was on his knees beside her, and he was rubbing her arm, and she could hardly see him in the moonlight, just the line of his lovely nose. "Are you all right, Rosaline?"

"No!" she sobbed, frustration taking hold of her. "My foot— it's caught in a fucking rabbit den—"

"All right, all right—" The Duke squeezed her shoulder, then shifted to kneel at her feet. He pushed aside the hem of her dress and flashed her a smile. "Language, sailor—"

"Shut up." Rosaline wiped at her face, probably smearing mud all over it, going by the state of her hands, the smell of wet earth in her nostrils. She glanced at McGrath and a fresh tremor of panic whipped through her body. "I wish you'd killed him."

The Duke snorted, busy digging at the mouth of the burrow. "Don't we all?" He shook his head. "No, unfortunately, he's something of a cockroach. And a Duke can get away with many things, but murder tends to stick."

She shook her head. "Your Grace, we... we did not even get to say hello."

The Duke paused, flashed her another smile. "Hello."

Something in Rosaline went weak. "Hello," she managed, wiping away a new wave of tears. "You fought very well, you know."

"You are kind. Though it is hardly a victory when your opponent has drunk half of Scotland under the table." Something collapsed above her foot, and she felt some of the pressure lessen. "Perhaps I should mention — you look quite beautiful in this dress, but I think it is rather—"

"Ruined, I know," she sniffled, then groaned. "I do not know why I am crying— I promise, this never happens—"

"I shan't hold it against you, I swear." His fingers, then, delicate against her skin, and she nearly jumped out of her own body. He eased her foot out of the hole, and now that her blood was unrestricted, a fresh wave of pain throbbed up her leg and she began to shiver.

"Th–th–thank you." Rosaline glanced at her ankle — it was

enormous already. "We— we have to get back—"

The Duke stared at her. "Are you out of your mind?"

"No." Her voice was firm, and she braced herself against the ground. Once the Duke realized what she was doing, he was at her side at once, wrapping an arm around her middle and taking the brunt of her weight as she stood up. "We have to— Everyone will think—" She put weight on her injured foot, and barely withheld a sob of pain.

"Rosaline." The Duke's voice was very close to her ear. "Forget what people think, you can hardly walk—"

"I am not you, Your Grace!" she burst out. "I cannot take any risk I like and walk away without consequences!" With that, she tried to hobble forward, and almost stumbled into another rabbit burrow.

The Duke caught her with a grunt. "This is not going to work. Let me go get help—"

"No!" It was almost a shriek. Rosaline put a hand to her face, overwhelmed, and forced herself to take a slow breath. It did very little good. "I just need to get back to the carriage, to the front of the house. No one will see us if we go through the garden."

The Duke sighed. "Fine. But it will go faster if I carry you."

Stunned, Rosaline could only blush. "Your Grace," she managed. "I think—"

"Enough thinking," the Duke bit out, and in a sudden, continuous movement, he bent down and swept her into his arms. His body was a warm, tight line against her own, his hands firmly tucked around her waist and her knees, and his face was just inches away, close enough that she could see the shadow of his stubble. He flashed her a smirk. "Much better."

Rosaline distracted herself by glancing over his shoulder at the prone, unmoving McGrath. "What should we do about him?"

The Duke snorted. "Nothing. Let him wake up with a mouthful of dirt."

With that, he began to make his way towards the house.

It was slow going, but the Duke was very sure of foot; he avoided every rabbit den, every pocket of mud. Soon, they exited the enclosed garden and found themselves in the wide, green expanse of the lawn, silver and damp under the moon. From the branches of the ancient oaks, from the distant woods, came the persistent, sharp chatter of nightingales pouring their hearts into the evening air, joined by the low coo of the owls. Still trembling from her residual fear, Rosaline looked up at the stars, wondering who might be watching, or listening. She thought, then, of her mother, draped in light and golden warmth, nodding her approval from the shadow of the moon as the Duke's fist found its home. She thought of her mother smiling to see her now, every bit the damsel in distress she had sworn never to be.

As they drew nearer to the house, Rosaline could hear the sounds of the ball, which seemed to be in full swing. "It is strange to think," she mumbled, breaking the silence between them, "that an hour ago—"

"Oh, I don't know, Rosaline, this is not so very different from a waltz—"

A grin broke to the surface, but she did not look at him. They passed beneath the veranda, where she heard Miss Brown's unmistakable shriek of laughter. "Seems we are missing a joke."

"I think I can live without it."

They soon reached the front of the house, just a dozen feet from the circular drive. Torches burned at intervals of three feet, and now, she could see the details of the Duke's face that she'd missed before — the muss of his hair, the smear of mud across his cheek. The Duke paused at the edge of the lawn, then gently lowered her to the ground. "I have to go and find your driver," he said, glancing across the sea of carriages. "And Lord Devon—"

"No!" Rosaline gasped, seizing him by the sleeve, forcing him to one knee. "No, just tell your driver to wait for the Princes and take them home, this is Charlotte's night—"

The Duke frowned at her, but before he could elaborate, the

front doors of the house burst open, throwing them into a halo of bright, amber light.

A sudden silence fell, and Rosaline could only squint up at the vague blur of the crowd before someone — Miss Brown, she thought — let out a shriek.

The crowd swarmed down the stairs at once, and then Rosaline realized what a scene they must have made — the Duke, his clothing torn and mussed, dirt on his face, and Rosaline, covered in mud and scratches, her shoes and gloves missing, her ankle the size of the moon, and her dress destroyed. She looked out at the sea of faces before them, wondering if this was Purgatory.

"What on earth!" An older woman led the charge, and Rosaline recognized her as one of the mothers — the Marchioness Camden. The matriarch of the season. "Look at the state of you! What happened? What are you two doing out here, alone?! Explain yourselves, at once!"

The Duke shot Rosaline a look, and she began to tremble, feeling as if the earth were collapsing down upon her. Then, to her mounting horror, he mouthed the words, "Trust me."

With the feeling that she was jumping off a cliff, Rosaline nodded.

The Duke flashed the Marchioness an easy grin, and Rosaline could have sworn she heard some of the women shudder and sigh. "It is entirely my fault, Lady Camden. I asked Miss Bailey to accompany me on a walk in the garden. But she met with a rabbit den, turned her ankle, and fell into a thicket of brambles. I did not want to leave her alone while I fetched assistance — instead, I did my best to help her back to the house."

There was a sudden movement in the crowd, and Rosaline looked up in time to see Charlotte and Cadogan's confused faces. Charlotte gave a great gasp and hurried forward, pushing past several gawking debutantes and sweeping down upon her like an angel, Cadogan in her shadow.

For a second, none of it felt real. Charlotte knelt in front of her, shielding her from prying eyes. Her hands fluttered over Rosaline's arms, and Rosaline clung to her, feeling rather faint.

"How strange," Charlotte murmured, a frown creasing her forehead. Her fingers traced one of the scratches in a silent question, and Rosaline shook her head.

"A walk in the garden?" the Marchioness was saying, incredulity dripping from every word. "Unaccompanied, Your Grace? Why not with her chaperone?"

"Because," the Duke replied, with a bite of impatience, "I needed to ask her something, something important. I did not want to be overheard."

"Ask her something?" repeated the Marchioness, and a ripple of surprise went through the crowd. Whispers broke out like a rash, snaking from mouth to mouth in a ceaseless tide. "Do you mean to say—?"

"Yes." The Duke's voice was steady, firm. He looked at Rosaline. "I do."

Something inside her shattered and went numb. She stared at him, and he stared back, but his expression did not waver.

There was a sudden silence, then utter pandemonium broke out — shrieks of excitement, wails of disappointment, and everything in between. But Rosaline heard none of it, felt none of it. The world had shrunk to the distance between her and the Duke, and he reached out, put his free hand to where her fingers were still fastened onto his sleeve.

Engaged, was the whisper, the cry, that tore through the crowd. *Engaged, engaged, engaged*—

"Rosaline." The Duke's voice was low enough to be for her and her alone. "I need to go and get the carriage—"

"Don't be stupid," said Cadogan — he evidently had sharp ears. "Allow me." With that, he marched off towards the crowd of drivers, who had gathered to see what the commotion was.

His absence gave Charlotte the opportunity to look Rosaline

in the eye and show a glimmer of honest concern. "What happened?" she breathed. "What *truly* happened, Rosaline? A woman who had just accepted a proposal would not be so distraught."

Rosaline hiccuped a laugh and tightened her grip on Charlotte's wrist. Her skin was still buzzing with shock and exhilaration.

"We cannot discuss it here," murmured the Duke. "We need to get her home, and quickly. She can barely walk."

Charlotte looked at him, and Rosaline could see the debate happening inside her angelic head — to fight him on it, or to let it pass. Evidently, she made up her mind, for she returned her attention to Rosaline and said, "If you are injured, we should contact your father."

"No." Rosaline's voice was ragged with pain. "No, he would only worry—"

"That is an excellent idea, Lady Prince." The Duke gave Rosaline a pointed look. "And there is no better doctor than the Royal Physician himself."

A fresh sob caught in Rosaline's throat. God, even just the thought of seeing him—

The Duke gave her hand a squeeze. His skin was hot against her own, and she brushed the pad of her thumb against the callouses that were becoming more and more familiar. Rosaline felt her heart slow, even as her stomach turned over.

I need a three course meal, she thought suddenly. *And a custard tart—*

Cadogan came running over. "Your carriage is ready, Miss Bailey. Why don't you go with Charlotte, and Prongs and Lord Devon will follow?"

"Good." The Duke gave a nod. "Take yours to the palace, get her father."

Cadogan clapped a hand to the Duke's shoulder. "Excellent idea."

"Where is Lord Devon, anyway?"

"Asleep," came Charlotte's soft reply. "In the library."

"Right." The Duke knelt beside Rosaline, and once again looked her in the eye. "Let's get you into the carriage."

"Do *not*," she growled, "*pick me up.*" When they were alone was one thing, but in front of the whole of London society was quite another.

He grinned at that, a real grin. "Very well." He and Charlotte each braced an arm around Rosaline's middle, and together, they helped her stand up.

It was a painful, difficult few minutes, but eventually, Rosaline ended up inside the Princes' carriage and fell into her seat, biting back a groan as she accidentally bumped her foot against the door. Charlotte shot her a worried look, but said nothing.

"Make haste," the Duke barked to the driver. "And avoid potholes." He turned to her again, captured her hand. "I will be right behind you, Rosaline. I promise. I will see you soon."

She tried to swallow and found that she couldn't. Behind him, the crowd had seethed and even grown, swarming to catch a final look at her. "Soon," she echoed.

The Duke stepped away, and Charlotte climbed in. The door slammed shut, and the carriage heaved into motion. Rosaline rocked with it, bracing herself on the edge of the window, and closed her eyes, wishing with all her might that she could turn back time and never leave that damned tennis court.

৩৯১৩

WHEN THEY ARRIVED BACK AT PRINCE MANOR, COMPLETE chaos broke out with surprising speed.

"I am *fine*," Rosaline insisted, *again*. "Truly, I am—"

"If you say 'fine' one more time—" spat Mrs. Randolph, blocking her exit from the carriage, "I will personally shove your head into a bucket of cold water—"

"Look at the state of her!" shrieked Lisette, from behind Mrs. Randolph. "She needs a hot bath, and sleep—"

"Everyone," Charlotte announced, looking out the carriage window, "the cavalry has arrived—"

A sudden gasp and Mrs. Randolph's stunned expression were the only warnings Rosaline had of the Duke's arrival. "Out of my way," he barked, and they scattered — his voice, though heated, was an instant balm, and Rosaline hated herself for thinking it. He stepped into view, poked his head into the carriage, and there he was, the same as he had been not a half hour before. "Well, now." The corner of his mouth twitched, irritation seemingly forgotten. "Ready to go inside?"

Rosaline slumped over with relief. Her whole body ached, her head buzzed with exhaustion, her dress itched against her sweaty skin, and her ankle was so tender she could hardly dream of walking. She wanted to sleep for a year. "Yes, thank you. But do not—"

"Carry you, I know, though I think Lisette would enjoy it—"

"She would fall into an instantaneous coma." Rosaline leaned heavily against his arm, then lowered herself to the floor and scooted down the carriage steps. "It would be a medical marvel."

"Reason enough for you, I think."

A small crowd of Prince staff had formed in the drive — Rosaline counted no less than a dozen faces, and her own face heated with mortification. Some were carrying candles and lanterns, others towels and blankets. She clung to the Duke and kept her eyes on the ground, trying not to think about what the town's gossip would be like by the following morning.

"What is your footman's name?"

Rosaline glanced at the Duke in surprise. "That's Benny."

He nodded. "Benny," he said loudly. "Fetch Miss Bailey a bucket of very cold water, the coldest you can find. Bring it to the—"

"The Blue Room," she said.

"The Blue Room," the Duke repeated. "And Lisette—"

Lisette hurried forward. "*Oui, monsieur*—"

"Get Miss Bailey a change of clothes, hot water, some fresh towels, and a screen. She cannot walk upstairs for the time being."

"Of course, Your Grace—"

Both she and Benny hurried inside. Rosaline and the Duke had reached the edge of the drive, and she paused, confronting reality. She had forgotten about the front steps.

"Very well," she mumbled to the Duke. "You may carry me."

He almost smiled. "No need to sound so disappointed."

And when he lifted her, for the second time that evening, Rosaline had to stop herself from wrapping her arms around his neck and burying her face in his shoulder. As she glanced behind them, she saw Charlotte and Lord Devon's matching looks of concern, Mrs. Randolph's mixed expression of outrage and anxiety. They were all staring at her as she was carried into the Manor, and she looked away, heat rushing to her face.

Once they were inside the foyer, the Duke lowered her back to the ground and helped her hobble into the half-darkness of the Blue Room. Rosaline collapsed onto one of the sofas, and the Duke frowned when she let out a gasp of pain.

"Do you think it is broken?"

Yes, Rosaline wanted to say. *Everything is broken.* "Truthfully, I am not sure. Ankles can be tricky, Your Grace."

Something shifted in his face, and he sat down beside her, took her hand. "I think," he said, his voice low, "that we have much to talk about."

Her heart skipped a beat as she remembered, with frightening clarity, that in the eyes of London society, they were engaged to be married. "Yes, I suppose so."

He looked at her, his gaze full of concern and sincerity, but before he could reply, the door burst open and a flock of servants rushed into the room, headed by Lisette and Benny, wielding a dressing suite and a bucket, respectively.

The Duke was on his feet at once. "I suppose I should—"

"No," Rosaline said quickly, feeling a stab of panic, "do not leave—"

"I will be just across the hall," he assured her, stepping back as Benny deposited the bucket at her feet. "In the drawing room."

"All right," she managed, but then Lisette swooped down upon her and effectively ended the conversation. She did not see the Duke exit; one minute, he was there, and the next, he was gone.

Lisette looked right at her and said in French, "*What the fuck happened to you?*"

Rosaline sighed. "Not now, Lis—"

"No," snapped Lisette. "I know what it looks like to fall into a hedge, and this is not that. And the Duke is too worried." She took hold of Rosaline's arm and said, "Mattie, help—"

Mattie closed and locked the door after Benny's exit, and together, she and Lisette helped Rosaline limp behind the dressing screen. She leaned on an armchair while Lisette and Mattie attacked her dress and decided that this was as good a time as any to stare Death in the face.

"I suppose I should begin with this morning," said Rosaline. "I had a visitor."

Lisette paused, then continued her work.

"Lieutenant McGrath came to call." Ignoring Lisette's pointed silence, Rosaline plowed on. "He asked for my hand in marriage, and became quite cruel when I refused."

"*Quoi!*" Lisette straightened up and stared Rosaline in the face. "You mean to say—?!"

"Yes." Rosaline took a slow breath and closed her eyes. "If Randolph had not been there, I dare say the Lieutenant would've become physical. His anger is quick to violence, which he proved this evening."

Something like horror welled in Lisette's eyes. "*Ma chère—*"

"He was there, at the Black and White Ball." For a moment, she was transported back into that terrifying, clarifying moment, and she shivered just as her stays cracked open. "He and the

Duke, they have a past. McGrath was only using me to get to my inheritance, and to him, the idea of using me in a tug-of-war with the Duke was the height of entertainment." She tried to take another breath and found it sticking in her throat. "I went into the garden alone, little fool that I am. He cornered me, and made it clear that my refusal meant nothing to him. He was going to have what he wanted, no matter the cost."

Both Lisette and Mattie had stopped working. They were very quiet and still. Then, Mattie put her hand to Rosaline's bare shoulder, and that was enough.

"But you fought him," said Lisette, her gaze finding the red, raised scratches on Rosaline's arms, the tangles in her hair.

"Yes." Rosaline leaned away, and managed to pull off her shift. She stared down at her naked body, at the streaks of mud and tears in her stockings, at her ankle, which was twice its normal size and almost purple, and felt none of it. "It was not enough, Lisette. If the Duke hadn't found us in time…"

The ominous silence said the rest. Lisette reached out, took her hand. "But he did find you. And I assume he put the Lieutenant in his proper place?"

"A grave, you mean?" Mattie bit out.

Rosaline almost smiled. "Yes," she said. "He was very brave. And he helped me get back to the house, and into the carriage."

Lisette gave her a thoughtful look. "You were seen," she said. "That is why you concocted this outrageous story about falling into a bush."

"Yes," Rosaline managed. "In part, yes."

Lisette nodded. "Well, then." She dipped the corner of a towel into a basin of what Rosaline realized was warm water and soap, then smiled. "Let's get you cleaned up, *ma chère*."

Rosaline closed her eyes and nodded, and for the first time that evening, felt a complete, overwhelming wave of relief flood her body, leaving her drifting on an ocean of rose-scented water, her mind filled with the bright warmth of a blue gaze.

26

Rosaline, her face flushed and damp from her bath, looked up when she heard a knock at the door. "Come in."

She was expecting to see her father, but no — it was the Duke, and, somewhat to her surprise, he carried a plate heavy with food. She could see cold roasted chicken, cheese, bread, and a freshly-cut apple. She could also see that he'd taken the opportunity to tidy up — gone was the streak of mud, he'd taken off his jacket, and his hair was somewhat more reasonable.

"I managed to sneak past the others," the Duke said, closing the door behind him. He paused beside the couch, looked her right in the eye. "How are you?"

"Better. This helps." She nodded at the bucket of cold water, into which she had plunged her foot not ten minutes before. It took the edge off the pain, dulled her exhaustion.

The Duke nodded, but worry still creased his features. "I thought you'd like something to eat," he said, handing her the plate and a napkin. His gaze snagged beside her hip. "Forgive me, I did not think to bring an offering for your familiar."

Rosaline smiled, ignoring the tingle of foreboding low in her stomach. She had not expected to be alone with the Duke again so soon. "I can share." She pushed her fingers through the cat's belly fur and got a low little purr in response.

The Duke sat down in the nearest armchair, and a small part of her wished that he'd instead taken a seat beside her. "The bow suits him. Does he have a name?"

"Oberon," she replied. "He joined the household just yesterday. I found him in the garden, half-drowned and miserable."

The Duke smiled and put his hands in his lap. It was only then that she noticed—

"*Hal.*" Rosaline sat up with a gasp, sloshing some of the water out of the bucket and nearly knocking her plate to the ground. She reached for his hands. "I did not realize—"

"Oh, it's—" He seemed quite flustered, but he allowed her to take his hand. "I am used to it, it's just a part of fighting—"

She grazed a finger over his swollen knuckles, over a cut that had clotted but was still an angry red. His right hand was even worse. "And to think I let you *carry* me— How on earth did I not notice—?"

"Rosaline." His voice was low, careful, and when she looked up, his gaze was warm, tender. "I am fine, truly. And you had far more pressing concerns."

She bit her lip and looked back down at his hands. His lovely, broad hands. An unexpected surge of emotion caught in her throat, and she found her fingers curling between his. His skin was warmer than usual, and when his fingers curled in return, entwining with hers, she could not deny that it was the most comforting feeling in the world.

"Rosaline," the Duke said again, even more gentle. "We must discuss what happened this evening. Before your father arrives."

"Yes," she said, her throat thick. "Where should we begin?"

"We should begin," he said, "with what you know about Lieutenant McGrath, and your connection to him."

A blush surged up her neck, but there was no escaping it now, any of it. She remembered her conviction, her determination to never tell the Duke what she knew, to never reveal that she was privy to his greatest shame, his greatest regret. It had been a fool's dream, to think that she might escape his acquaintance without surrendering to the unsaid. If she had the energy for it, she probably would have cried. "I do not want," Rosaline said, "to lose your good opinion, Your Grace, nor do I want you to believe that I—"

"As to my good opinion," said the Duke, "you need never worry, on that score. As for the rest, I would never believe anything of you that I did not see with my own two eyes, or that you did not confirm yourself." He seemed to hesitate, then to take a leap. "Earlier this evening, I asked you to trust me, and you did so at once, without question. You must know that the feeling is mutual, Rosaline."

A weight seemed to vanish from her chest, and she nodded, forcing herself to reach for a piece of cheese. If she was going to tell him everything, she would need all the energy she could get.

It took a long time. As Rosaline spoke, she watched his face — the face that she knew so well now, but not well enough to parse its many hidden emotions. The Duke's expression was an impassive mask, save for a constant shade of concern, of careful attention. He never showed anger, betrayal, or even surprise, but then, she supposed, if he'd known McGrath his whole life, perhaps there were very few surprises left.

She did her best to tell the entire story in chronological order — from her first few meetings with McGrath, to his absence, to the masquerade ball, to her meeting the Captain, and the truths that had come to light as a result of her contact with Constable Morris.

Here, the Duke finally showed a reaction. The corner of his mouth twitched as he toyed with a bit of bread she'd forced him to take from her plate. "Sounds like you've made a friend," he said. "Bill Morris is a good man. And a brilliant detective."

Rosaline found herself smiling. "You won't get him or the Captain into trouble, will you? For telling me the truth?"

"Not in the least," the Duke replied. "Besides, as Bill said, everything he told you was a matter of public record. Given another of your page-boy outfits and a note from a gentleman employer, it was nothing you could not find yourself in the Public Record Office."

"I know that, but..." For a moment, the right words eluded her. "It felt... intrusive, to learn so much of what you had experienced without your knowledge. I almost feel I have to apologize."

The grin he gave her was sudden, dazzling. "No apology needed. Please, continue."

"Well, I—" Rosaline's heart throbbed in her throat. "I realized that McGrath's pursuit of me was somewhat surprising, given my public attachment to you. He must have known the risk of you telling me the truth. And, he only told me of his supposed woes once he'd learned my name, and who my father was."

The Duke frowned, then a glimmer of realization crossed his features. "You believe McGrath's interest in you became strategic."

She nodded. "I spoke to my father. He informed me that my dowry would be substantial, and that I was due an inheritance from my mother's estate once I reached the age of twenty-five. The first fact, McGrath would have assumed from my father's position in the Royal household. The second, he could have learned from looking up my mother's will, or simply discovering her maiden name. Altogether, the money would be no mean sum, and if we were wed—"

His frown deepened. "Surely that possibility never arose?"

"Actually, he..." Rosaline cleared her throat and ignored her blush. "He proposed to me just this morning. And he did not take it well when I refused him."

The Duke stood up suddenly, and she could see it now, the anger seething off his shoulders in waves. He began to pace the short distance between the armchair and the windows, trying to regain his control. "That slimy, foul—"

"I made the mistake of assuming that I had injured his pride," she went on. "Which I thought might prevent him from making further overtures. But when he cornered me in the garden, I realized that he was a man without conscience or empathy."

"So he—" The Duke's jaw worked. "He tried to force a match."

"By putting my virtue into doubt, yes."

"I—" He halted by the windows, his back to her. "I need a moment."

Silence fell, and something about the image of the Duke, silhouetted against the gauzy white curtains, bathed in the dim yellow light of the candelabras, stirred a feeling deep within her. She wanted to close the distance between them, run a hand along the back of his arm, his shoulders, press her body against his and murmur into his ear until his temper faded, until he relaxed and leaned into her weight, turning his head to capture her in that deep blue gaze, closing the distance between them, pressing his lips to—

A blush flooded her chest, her neck, and Rosaline quickly stuffed the remains of her chicken into her mouth, her heart pounding.

The Duke turned to face her, and she could see the anger still boiling under his skin. "He didn't, did he?" When she failed to reply, he winced and added, "He did not—?"

"No," she said quickly. "You had excellent timing."

He shook his head. "Not excellent enough. Your ankle, your arms—"

"It is still better," she said, "than the alternative."

For a moment, he simply looked at her, and it was as if an ocean had erupted beneath their feet — one of them would have to be brave enough to cross it.

"I cannot apologize enough," the Duke said, his voice low, "for allowing that monster to come within spitting distance of you."

Something within her cracked. "No, Hal— you did not know, and I did not tell you. His attentions, they..." Rosaline gave a hollow laugh. "No one had ever said such things to me before, not like—" *Not like they meant it,* she did not say. *Not like it was real.* "And I was foolish enough to think that he could not possibly have an ulterior motive—"

The Duke, it seemed, could be brave enough for the both of them. He crossed the room and took a seat beside her on the couch. He was far enough away from her to maintain a proper distance, yet close enough that she could feel the heat of his body, see the streaks of dirt on his trousers. He'd undone the topmost button of his shirt, exposing a thin, elusive triangle of surprisingly tanned skin.

Just like I imagined, Rosaline thought. She had the sudden urge to press her mouth to it.

"You are anything but a fool, Rosaline," he said fiercely. "When the time came, you were clever enough to doubt him, and to put him in his place regardless of the consequences. He made the grave, enduring error of underestimating you, and assuming that you would give in without a fight." The corner of his mouth twitched, and something in his expression softened. "Had he caught even a glimpse of you at the boxing match, he would have known otherwise."

Rosaline sighed, but could not help smiling in return. "You exaggerate." Her gaze dropped to the space between them — less than a foot — and the space where his hand, his lovely, bruised hand, rested against the cushions. Her fingers itched with the urge to take it, to press a kiss to his palm and tell him, again and again, that it was not his fault. "I do not want you to feel responsible for what happened."

"But I am responsible." The Duke's voice was bitter, dry. "To a certain degree. Had I shelved my pride, or my concern for my own reputation, I might have exposed him for what he was and prevented his presence at the season."

Rosaline shook her head. "You forget, Your Grace, that he has connections of his own. As Constable Morris pointed out, McGrath has somehow managed to obtain a commission, and we both know he could not have paid for it himself. He must have friends — or enemies — in high places, and that could have been enough to shield him from exposure, regardless of the facts. For all we know, he might have found a way to use your claims against you, and in doing so, gain half of London as his ally."

"See?" The corner of his mouth twitched again. "Even when I think I have all the answers, you find some way of surprising me."

The breath caught in Rosaline's throat.

"You look at the world," he went on, "and see the invisible strings that propel us across its stage. You hear the unspoken and uncover the hidden." The Duke shook his head, and she found herself falling into his ocean blue gaze. "You are unlike anyone I have ever known."

Rosaline tried and failed to take a breath. The distance between them had shrunk, and she could see his freckles, darker now from his time in the country. She could see the exhaustion beneath his eyes, the ceaseless energy that rivaled it. She could see the way his gaze dipped, the way he watched her, the way he reached for her.

His finger brushed the edge of her cheek and she fought back a shiver. His touch was warm, careful, fleeting. And when Rosaline met his gaze, she could see her own yearning reflected back at her, could see the exhilaration and impatience that threatened to break free at any moment, and when the Duke — when *Hal* — leaned in, she could not stop herself from giving in to the inevitable, her heart thundering in her ears as she—

The door burst open and Rosaline whirled around to face—

"Father," she managed. Behind her, she heard the Duke scramble to his feet.

"Yes," said Sir Ian. His expression was flat, restrained, but she could tell that he was livid with anger, and having a difficult time concealing it. He glared at the Duke. "You, I believe, were on your way out."

"No," said Rosaline at once. "No, Father, he was just—"

"I would *like*," barked Sir Ian, "to speak to my daughter alone!"

"Of course, sir," came the Duke's smooth reply. To his credit, he did not sound in the least bit caught out. "I apologize—"

"I am sure you do." Sir Ian knelt by Rosaline's side, reaching for her foot. The Duke shot Rosaline a glance that said all too much and yet not enough. "It is late," Sir Ian went on. "You should get home, Your Grace."

For a moment, Rosaline could actually see the Duke consider not obeying such an order. But then he nodded, reluctance evident in every line of his body. "I should indeed." He inclined his head towards them both. "Good evening, Sir Ian, Miss Bailey, Oberon." His gaze stuck on Rosaline for longer than it needed to, and for a moment, she could imagine the unsaid—

I will return. As soon as possible, I will return.

"Good evening," Rosaline said, wishing with all her might that her father had had slightly better timing. The Duke left the room, and once the door had closed behind him, she turned on her father and smacked his arm. "Your rudeness—"

"—was completely justified, given the circumstances." He was inspecting her foot, his hand braced against her arch. "Did I hear him mention an Oberon?"

Rosaline rolled her eyes and sank back into the cushions. "Might I introduce you to my new companion?"

Her father frowned and finally looked away from her ankle. He stared at the cat, who was dozing beside her, and shook his head. "What happened to you, Rosaline?" His gaze found hers, and she could see the concern, the sorrow. "Are you all right?"

She nodded. "I am fine, Father. With no small thanks to the Duke."

"Do not dodge the question." He pressed against the bottom of her foot, bending the joint slightly. She winced, but the pain was manageable. "What happened?"

"It is as Cadogan said." She glanced at him as he took hold of her foot and wiggled it a little, further testing the joint. "What did he tell you?"

Sir Ian's frown deepened. "Very little. I got the impression that even he did not know the details." His free hand tapped around her joint, then the top of her foot. "Is it numb?"

"No. But very tender."

He nodded, then gently lowered her foot to the ground. "I believe it is just a sprain. A very bad sprain, but we will keep a close eye on it, and if it does not improve, we shall take further action. In the meantime, you need to keep it elevated, and only walk when necessary." He gave her a stern look. "And when you do walk, you are to walk properly, as best as you can. None of this limping nonsense." Now that his practiced gaze had seen to the worst, it flickered over the scratches on her arms, the swelling, aching area on her jaw, where McGrath's hand had caught her by surprise.

For several moments, neither of them said a word. But Rosaline could tell that he was thinking quickly. Her father had spent much of his childhood in a Glasgow tenement, and he knew what it looked like when a woman had been attacked by a man.

"Do you know him?" The question was low, brittle. "Do you know his name?"

"Yes," breathed Rosaline, reaching for his hand. "As does the Duke."

Sir Ian made an aborted movement, then gripped her hand and bent his head. "We must tell someone," he said, his voice strangled with anger. "This is not to be borne—"

"Father." Even just the idea of having to go through all this again made her want to weep from exhaustion as much as anything else. "It is not so simple."

"You were *attacked*—"

"Father," she said again, squeezing his hand. "I will tell you everything, I swear, I just— I am so worn out—"

"Of course." Rosaline could hear his reluctance, but he pressed a kiss to her hand, and she put her palm to his cheek. He offered her something close to a smile. "We can discuss it tomorrow. Or the next day, whenever you feel up to it."

Rosaline smiled then, and felt an unexpected surge of tears prick at her eyes. "Thank you," she managed, surprised by her own relief.

"My Honeybee," he murmured, then shook his head. "I shall stay here for the night. Lord knows that Hieronymus is not hurting for the room. The King can go without me for a few hours," he added, upon seeing her expression. "Some things are more important."

"You worry too much."

Her father shrugged, and for a moment, she could see his age, his exhaustion. "Or I worry just enough." He stood up. "I shall have a bed brought in for you. It'll certainly be easier than trying to get you up those stairs."

Rosaline nodded, her gaze drifting to the windows. Outside, the cool summer night continued to unspool, and for a moment, she felt as if she were floating, caught in a reality, a time, that was not her own.

❧

Madam Kensington's High Society Papers, No. 35

WELL, MY LOVELIES — ONE HARDLY KNOWS WHERE TO BEGIN!

It seems that a sudden fever for Precious Gems has swept through the town — in less than twenty-four hours, our Star and Sapphire have found themselves stolen away by the greatest force of all — Love, and her twin, Marriage. The Star and her Pup have made their attachment formal, sealed with a certain Namesake that blinded and froze most of the attendees at last night's Black and White Ball. But who could have been more surprised than I, dear readers, when a flurry of activity brought our attention to the east entrance, where we found none other than the Sapphire — a little dusted-up, but still sparkling — and her delightful Recluse — appearing as if from thin air, as rumpled and delicious as always — huddled in a questionable attitude. Our Sapphire is perhaps not so sure of foot, or just a poor judge of discretion. But this did not dissuade our favorite Recluse, who made it plain that he must have her, brambles or no; what else could explain his sudden return, apart from love, rapturous love?

And so it seems, my darlings, we have yet another young rogue who has been felled by Cupid's touch! Our sparkling Jewels have been snatched up, just as we knew they would be, and we have a pair of August weddings to look forward to...

ROSALINE SLEPT DEEPLY AND AT LENGTH, UNDISTURBED BY MAN or beast until her eyes drifted open to a soft, gray morning damp with rain. She was warm, but not stifling, and her hand went to the cat's belly — he was curled up with her underneath the blankets, his back pressed against her stomach, snoring lightly. She smiled, nuzzling into her pillow. Around her, the Blue Room was quiet, peaceful, true to its name in the lack of sunshine. Rosaline felt snug and utterly at peace.

As the moments slipped past, she became aware of her body, of the aches and pains that began to wake just as she did. Her ankle had dulled its ferocious edge; she knew better than to try to move her foot, which she had kept out from beneath the blanket for fear of it getting twisted and tangled. Her shoulders were sore, as were her hands, her neck, her lower back. Her scalp was still tender where McGrath had yanked at her hair, her jaw ached, and though some of the scratches along her arms had faded, she could trace them with the tip of her finger, see where he had drawn a bit of blood to the surface. *A scar nobly got,* she thought, *is a good livery of honor*.

A snuffling noise drew her attention, and she looked across the room to see a small, blonde lump curled up on one of the sofas. Charlotte, in her nightgown, fast asleep and snoring, lilac circles of exhaustion under her eyes. For a moment, a wave of affection overcame her; Rosaline could only stare at her best friend, who, it seemed, had slipped into the room in the middle of the night, just to keep her company.

The previous evening had ended in the small hours. Rosaline could not remember getting into her chaise lounge, could not remember falling asleep, but she could remember saying good-night to her father, and the kiss he'd pressed to her forehead. She hadn't seen Charlotte or Cadogan since her arrival back at Prince Manor, but she had overheard the occasional rumble of their conversation, their hurried goodbye on the front steps, the sound of Cadogan's carriage bearing him into the London streets. Now, Rosaline felt yet another pang of guilt at spoiling what should have been Charlotte and Cadogan's special evening, their shining moment to bask in the delight of their match, their love, but no, it had all been ruined—

A quiet *click* announced the turn of the doorknob. She watched as the door cracked, then slowly swung open to reveal—

"Lis," Rosaline whispered, smiling. "*Bonjour*—"

But something was wrong. Lisette was not smiling — in fact, she was looking at Rosaline in this awful, wide-eyed way, and she hurried to Rosaline's side, pressing a bit of crumpled paper into her hands— "Your father," she whispered. "He has just seen—"

Rosaline's stomach went cold. She sat up, dislodging Oberon, who grumbled and jumped off the lounge, then tore open the all-too-familiar society gossip rag. As she took in the words before her, as their black lines swam and danced in her vision, a sickening dread began to curl through her stomach and into her mouth, and she could not believe, could not *think*—

"Where is my daughter?!" came her father's booming shout from down the hall, shattering the silence of the morning. "Is she still—?"

"*Vite, vite*—" Lisette tugged Rosaline off the lounge just as Charlotte woke up and turned to look at them, sleepy and confused. "It is a short drop from the window into the flower bed, and you can sneak around the back—"

"On a sprained ankle, Lis?" Rosaline hissed back, scrambling for her dressing gown. Her face was hot, a cold sweat had broken out on the back of her neck, and she could not handle this, she could not—

The door burst open and in marched her father, as livid as she had ever seen him. Behind him was Lord Devon, looking very worried and very uncomfortable all at once.

"Explain yourself!" Sir Ian was not yelling, not yet, but anger was rolling off him in waves. She could practically feel it. "Tell me how, in the course of our entire conversation last night, you failed to mention the fact of your engagement to the Duke of St. Albans?!"

"Father," she tried. "Father, I—"

"Perhaps I have gone soft in the brain," he continued, "because even though you are apparently engaged to be *married*, I do not happen to remember your charming fiancé asking me for my permission. Or even introducing himself, for that matter. One would think, given that I have just the sole daughter, that I would remember such a remarkable event, especially when she had assured me that she would never, *could* never marry, and would do all she could to avoid it!"

"I was going to tell you," Rosaline pleaded, hot tears stinging her eyes. "Today, I was going to tell you today, I swear—"

"Enough!" Sir Ian stared at her, and something in her twisted at the look of betrayal in his face. "Rosaline, you lied to me. You lied to me even while you were telling the truth. I had thought we were closer than this. Close enough to—"

"We are!" The tears spilled down her cheeks and Rosaline fought to keep her voice steady. "We are, Father, and you cannot take the word of a gossip rag as fact—"

"True." His expression did not change, and he gestured at Lord Devon. "Which is why I asked Hieronymus. He confirmed the news, and the events mentioned in Madam Kensington's delightful article." Sir Ian shook his head, and some of the fight seemed to go out of him. "I am almost at a loss for words."

"Don't be!" Rosaline bit her lip, aching to scream the truth regardless of the consequences. "Father, please, you must— we can talk—"

He turned away from her. "I cannot give my consent to this match. Nor can I look at you for another moment." A pause, then — "I think we both need some time, Rosaline."

"Father," she tried again, swallowing a sob. "*Father*—"

But he left, the front door slamming shut behind him, and she was surrendered to a ringing, hollow silence and the stares of her three companions. It was Charlotte who moved first, getting off the sofa and reaching for her— "Rosaline, he is just upset, he will—"

"No," Rosaline bit out, stepping away from her. She could not stand this for a moment longer — the collapse of her entire world, one piece at a time. She tore her blanket from the lounge and fled the room, hardly feeling the pain of her ankle as she hobbled down the hall, through the drawing room, and into the garden, where she disappeared into the rain.

❧ 27 ❧

Several hours later found Rosaline curled up on the wicker bench, watching the rain as it fell, thinned, stopped, and fell again. Not once had the sun broken through the deep gray cloud cover, and the whole world was soggy, dull, cold. But she felt none of it, cared about none of it. The blanket was enough to keep her warm, and the cool air soothed the hot skin of her ankle.

Once her tears had dried, a peculiar, aching emptiness had taken root in her stomach. It kept Rosaline company as she turned the events of the day through her head, as she relived each of her father's accusations, as she revisited the years of memories they had built together before coming back to London, before she had jeopardized his trust and tested the bonds of their relationship as she never had before.

Again, she tried to imagine a different outcome to the events of the Black and White Ball. Again, she retraced her own steps, wondering where she might have done something different, where she might have prevented her father's outburst, his feeling of betrayal. But what could she have said? *Father, I have been pretending with the Duke this entire time, and our engagement is just as false as our attachment?* She would sound mad, selfish, utterly unconcerned with their family's reputation. Her father would never look at her the same way, never trust her the same way—

Rosaline let out a low groan, and Oberon's ear twitched where he lay across the surface of the table, less than a foot away. He was pretending to sleep, and doing a poor job of it; she could see a thin slit of one very yellow eye, watching her. He was the only one who had invaded her solitude, a little more than an hour after she'd run out of the Blue Room. She had every confidence that her lack of interruption was Charlotte's doing — Charlotte would know that Rosaline did not want to see anyone, did not want to hear whatever it was that Lisette, Randolph, or even Charlotte herself would have to say—

She heard the shuffle of a footstep and glanced up, a rebuke ready on her lips, only to find the Duke, trimmed and pressed now in the light of a new day, standing beside the house and watching her with an unmistakable expression of worry.

Rosaline looked at him for a moment, then sighed and looked away. She could not bring herself to care that she, in contrast, was still in her night things, her face raw and swollen from crying, her hair in a loose braid that spilled over her shoulder and down her chest. It seemed that the universe was just determined to be unkind today. "You should not be here, Your Grace. Our reputations have already been pushed to their limit."

"I do not care." He paused for a moment, then seemed to muster his courage. He came over to her, sitting at the other end of the bench. She caught a whiff of his soap and fought off a responding shiver. "I had to see you. Charlotte helped me sneak in."

"I would ask how," she said, "but I think it is probably better that I do not know."

"Rosaline." His voice was low, pleading. "We cannot afford to be at each other's throats, not now. You must tell me what happened after I left yesterday evening, and why you are—" The Duke glanced around the garden. "You should not be alone."

"Perhaps solitude is the only thing I crave at the moment." She sighed, pulling the blanket tighter around her body. "My father found out about our engagement this morning."

The Duke's eyebrows said everything. "Ah," he managed.

"Exactly. And given that he was unaware of the... circumstances... of our attachment, he thinks the worst of me, and of you." Rosaline took a deep breath, forcing back the lump in her throat. "He is quite angry with me. Angry enough to forget, for the time being, that I was attacked. Funny, how men seem to be incapable of entertaining more than one complex truth at a time."

"Rosaline," the Duke said, "your father loves you more than—"

"Does he?" she bit out, not caring if it sounded cruel. "It seems that his love has its contingencies. He did not even allow me to explain myself."

"I am certain, then, that he was acting in the heat of anger. You must give him the benefit of the doubt. Anyone who knew you, Rosaline, truly knew you, would be surprised to learn of you accepting a proposal of marriage. He just needs time—"

"Speaking of time, Your Grace, how long are we meant to allow this false engagement to endure?" It was easier if she did not look at him. "If we let it go too long, we will find our wedding planned for us. I'm sure Mrs. Randolph is very keen—"

"Ten days."

His ready reply fell on her with all the weight of an iron feather. So he had thought about it; perhaps he'd had the plan in his head at the very same moment he'd asked her to trust him. He did not need her input, her voice. She nodded. "Very well. And what is to be the cause for our separation? Shall we make it a public spectacle, just like our engagement?"

There was a loaded pause. When the Duke finally spoke, his voice was low, careful. "Rosaline, I understand that you are angry, that you are upset, and you have every right to be. But you must believe that I am not trying to hurt you, to reopen the wounds you have already suffered."

A flush of shame heated her face. She still did not look at him.

"We can let it be a whisper," said the Duke. "A whisper that grows into a story, that grows into one of Madam Kensington's lovely articles. We can bolster it with a few public moments, for the sake of consistency. And our... attachment..." The word seemed to stick in his throat. "Can end. And we shall return to our separate orbits, masquerading as jilted, unhappy lovers."

Rosaline almost smiled. "That would make Charlotte and Cadogan's wedding very tense, indeed. What would the headlines read? *Best man and maid of honor unable to so much as look at each other; insults traded over cake, champagne flutes thrown across the ballroom.*"

"Good God," he said. "We are quite a violent couple."

"It would be fun, though. I've always wanted to purposefully break a glass."

"I am sure we could find you a better target," the Duke replied, "than my head."

"Perish the thought, Your Grace."

A silence fell, and the rain fell with it. Rosaline watched a squirrel take its risk and scamper across the lawn and up into the oak, where it disappeared among the branches. She wondered when the Duke would leave, and when she would see him again.

A small sound — the sound of him shifting closer. The edge of his leg slipped into her peripheral vision, and for a moment, she stared at his black leather boots, unable to imagine looking him in the face.

"We must speak to your father," said the Duke. "The both of us. Together."

She scoffed. "Oh, must we?"

"Yes." The Duke's voice was firm. "He must know the truth of the matter. About us, and about McGrath."

"He would never agree to it."

"Then we do not wait for his permission." His airy confidence almost made her grin. "An ambush can do a world of good for a gentleman's health."

Rosaline shook her head in exasperation as well as surrender. "Fine," she said. "The day after tomorrow, perhaps. Though how you plan to corner him is quite beyond me."

"I have a few ideas. But you need not worry about it."

She nodded, and again they lapsed into silence. Her stomach roiled at the thought of facing her father, of having to restrain herself from saying everything she thought and felt about the way he'd spoken to her, berated her as if she were no more than a child—

The Duke's bruised hand, warm and gentle against her own. She looked up at him in astonishment, tears clouding her vision, and she realized then how close he was — hardly a foot away. It was an echo from the night before, and he was looking at her, waiting.

"I," Rosaline managed, the tears spilling down her face, "I am not crying."

"No," said the Duke. His eyes were infinite pools of cobalt, and he looked so concerned, so sad. "No, you are not."

A sob caught in her throat, and something seemed to break. The next thing she knew, he was tucking her in against his shoulder, wrapping his arm around her, pulling her against his side. She buried her face in the crook of his neck, so overcome that she could hardly process the way he felt, solid and warm, and he smelled so lovely—

The Duke did not say a word. But it was as if she'd been given a dose of medicine — heat pooled in her stomach, spreading out into her body, bringing with it a wave of calm, and Rosaline wondered how he'd known to do this, how he'd known what she needed without even asking — and if she opened her eyes, she could see part of his neck, just above his collar, and it was so strange, so exhilarating, to be so close to his bare skin, to look but not touch—

Rosaline closed her eyes and curled into his side, thinking that perhaps she could survive never seeing him again, so long as she had this.

⚜

CHARLOTTE FINISHED HER BRAID AND TWIRLED THE END, contemplative. "You are very skilled," she said, "at keeping secrets."

Rosaline winced, pushing a hand through Oberon's fur. "I am sorry for not telling you sooner, Charlotte. But it was imperative that no one discovered our ruse—"

"No, I quite understand." And Charlotte flashed her a small smile to confirm it. "You are a marvelous actress, Rosaline. It was quite easy to believe that your feelings for the Duke were genuine. You two always had such natural conversation, and seemed quite happy in each other's presence. Anyone would have believed it in a second, which, I suppose, is why it worked."

Rosaline's heart throbbed once in her throat. "He and I are friends, Charlotte. Just very good friends. We understand one another, and enjoy spending time together."

"But it did not begin that way," Charlotte pointed out. "Though I suppose it was the best outcome for you both. If you had to pretend together, it would surely be easier if you did not hate one another."

"I could not hate him," Rosaline said. "Not for all the money in the world."

Charlotte put a hand to her arm. "Indeed. He did a very kind thing, helping you avoid the suitors of London."

They were on Charlotte's window seat, looking out on a pale, sunny morning. It was the day after Rosaline's fight with her father, a day after the Duke had held her until she'd stopped shaking, until she'd felt that she could hardly look him in the eye for fear of him seeing too much of the truth written in her face. She still felt raw, but the pain and fatigue had dulled somewhat, eased by time, a good night's sleep, and the memory of the Duke's arm around her.

Her ankle had improved; she kept it elevated and wrapped tightly in a cloth bandage, which had given her the support she'd needed to make her way upstairs. Tonight, she would sleep in her own bed, and tomorrow, if she was feeling up to it, she would have a proper bath.

Rosaline looked down at where Oberon's front paw pressed into her thigh, and for a moment, could not believe that this was her reality. "It was not only for my sake. The Duke needed to escape the mothers, and our delightful fellow debutantes."

"Yes, they all seemed very keen to get to know the Reclusive Duke." Charlotte smiled again, then shook her head. "It is strange to think that you are engaged to someone you will not marry."

"I know," Rosaline replied, with feeling. "But, dear Charlotte, at least the same cannot be said about you!" She took Charlotte's hand, gave it a squeeze. "Come, we must discuss the details."

Charlotte blushed, but her smile grew. "It is early yet, Rosaline, very little has been decided—"

"Then you must tell me what *has* been decided." *To hell with wallowing*, Rosaline thought. Now, she needed to be Charlotte's sister, her maid of honor. "I am sure Cadogan's great aunt has plenty of ideas."

"She does," Charlotte agreed. "Chief among them that she would like us to use their house for the reception. It is bigger than ours, and the ballroom has a legendary floor."

"So she is pleased, then, with the match?" The day before, while Rosaline had hidden away, Charlotte had gone to tea with Cadogan and his great aunt.

"I believe so. She was quite intimidating, in her own way, and she asked me lots of questions. But she seemed satisfied with my answers, and she even gave me the tiara she wore at her own wedding."

Rosaline stared at her. "Goodness, Charlotte. You seem to have made the best first impression in history."

Charlotte chuckled. "You exaggerate." She stood up and went over to her dresser, then came back with a black velvet box in hand. "I am nervous about wearing it. What if it were to fall, to break? It's irreplaceable." With that, she opened the lid, and Rosaline gaped as the tiara was revealed to the light.

"Charlotte," she breathed, her hand hovering over the diamonds. "It's exquisite."

"I know." Charlotte was a study in nervous energy. "But can you imagine if something were to happen? She would spend the rest of her years cursing me—"

Rosaline grinned at her. "Charlotte, you underestimate your own grace. If it were me, I would run a serious risk of tripping, but you move like a swan."

"You flatter me." Charlotte sighed and closed the lid. "I will have to practice walking in my dress while wearing it. Perhaps even dancing, if you would oblige me."

"Of course. Have you decided, then? About your dress?"

Charlotte frowned. "What do you mean?"

Rosaline took a breath — she'd have to do this carefully. "I thought perhaps you had your mother's dress. Or her veil."

For several moments, Charlotte said nothing. She just looked at Rosaline, her expression unchanged. "Well," she eventually said. "I do have them."

"But you do not know where they are?"

"I do not know," Charlotte said, "if I want to wear them."

"Oh." Rosaline nodded. "The dress does not fit?"

"No, it—" Charlotte looked down at her hands. "I am quite my mother's equal, in height and in figure."

"Charlotte." Rosaline took her hand, and waited until Charlotte met her gaze. "You do not need to consider it, if it would be too much—"

Charlotte's eyes widened. "No, that is not—" Suddenly, she smiled, and it was a sheepish one. "Perhaps a demonstration will do more than words ever could." With that, she slid off the window seat and went over to her closet, disappearing from Rosaline's view.

For a minute or two, Rosaline heard nothing, apart from a very determined rustling. She frowned. "Do not go to too much trouble, Charlotte—"

"No trouble at all," came Charlotte's airy reply. "This requires a presentation of the highest order. Now, close your eyes."

"Very well." And Rosaline did so, putting a hand over her eyes for good measure.

The rustling paused, then grew louder as Charlotte exited her closet. "Well," came Charlotte's voice. "Open your eyes."

Rosaline did, and immediately had to clap her hand over her mouth. She stared, in equal parts amusement and horror, at the delightful monstrosity that Charlotte was wearing. "Yellow," was the only thing she could bring herself to say, and the word echoed into her hand.

Charlotte grinned, adding to the illusion that she was a giant, benevolent sun. "Indeed." She swayed back and forth, and the taffeta swished ominously. "My mother had a great aptitude for color, you see."

That was the understatement of the century. It was like looking at an open wound — Rosaline could not stop staring at the dress, nor could she bring herself to look away. There were *bows*. "But for a wedding—?"

"She believed that yellow was good luck," Charlotte replied. "My father's suit was cut in a matching color, and his wig was dusted with yellow as well." She shook her head. "This was before the French skirmish, you see, and theirs was not the only colorful wedding. But if they'd dressed like this ten years ago, they would have been lampooned in the streets as well as the papers."

Rosaline's mind was churning through the math. "Charlotte, how long were your parents married?"

"They knew within ten minutes of meeting each other that they wanted to marry." Charlotte twirled on the spot and her dress ballooned accordingly, tripling in size. "She was seventeen, and he was eighteen. And they were not in any rush to have children."

Something seemed to stick in Rosaline's throat. "Really?"

Charlotte nodded. "It was not a popular decision at the time, but my mother wanted to wait. They spent several years traveling before they settled in London." She glanced at Rosaline. "Strange to think, is it not, that I am older than she was the last time she wore this dress?"

Rosaline nodded. She wondered, then, if her mother's wedding dress still existed, stored away somewhere like a secret. "But I am sure she could not imagine a better husband for you, Charlotte. If she could see you now, she would not be able to speak for happiness."

Charlotte smiled, and Rosaline did not miss the tears shining in her eyes. "I think," she said, "I might take a small piece of the train, and sew it into the lining of my dress."

"That," said Rosaline, "is a wonderful idea."

"And I shall have a bouquet of peonies," Charlotte added, giving another twirl. "They were her favorite as well as mine."

Rosaline grinned. "Peonies it is."

28

"This," said Rosaline, glancing around at the various landscapes hanging on the walls, "is probably a terrible idea."

"Give me some credit," said the Duke, eye-to-eye with her father's prized skeleton. It was mounted on a metal frame, its bones wired together. One could even see the nick in the ribs that betrayed the cause for its demise. "Sneaking into a royal palace is no mean feat."

"Your use of the word 'sneaking' does not bolster my confidence." She sat in the nearest armchair with a sigh, wincing and putting her injured foot up on the armrest. Her ankle was still too swollen to fit into any of her shoes; she was wearing a pair of boots she'd borrowed from Benny. They were well-worn and soft in the sole, and they looked very odd when paired with her muslin dress. "I see you've met Archibald."

"Is that his name?" The Duke tapped the skeleton's chin. "Suits him."

"My father gave me the honor," Rosaline replied. "In return for reciting at least four of Shakespeare's sonnets from memory. I recited seven."

The Duke looked at her. "And how old were you?"

She shrugged. "Five or six."

Before he could reply, the door to her father's chambers opened and in walked the man himself. Rosaline bit back a wave of apprehension as he halted, looked at her, then at the Duke, and let out a low growl of frustration.

"Good afternoon, Sir Ian," said the Duke, smooth as butter. He did not react when Sir Ian slammed the door shut in reply. "I thought we might have a discussion."

"Did you?" Sir Ian bit out. The glare he gave the Duke was murderous. "And where was this consideration when you asked for my daughter's hand?"

"Father," said Rosaline. "We would not invade your privacy were it not of the utmost urgency and importance."

His gaze landed on her and he frowned. "Are you well?"

"I am fine," Rosaline replied. "But it is time that you heard the truth. The entire truth. Which is why the Duke and I came here today."

Her father stared at her for a moment, then went alarmingly pale. He stumbled over to the nearest chair and sat down on a pile of books and papers, but did not seem to notice or care. "I am not ready," he choked out, "to be a grandfather."

"No!" Rosaline's face flooded with heat, and she could not look at the Duke. "No, Father, you have the wrong idea—"

"Sir Ian," managed the Duke, "I would never—"

"Stop talking, Hal—"

"I will *not* stop talking, am I really thought to be that much of a rake?" He turned on Sir Ian, indignant. "Do I really give the impression that I run around the country—"

"Not the point!" Rosaline said loudly. She still could not look at him. "Father, you need to know that the engagement between this so-called rake and myself is a fabrication. A falsehood. A complete *lie*. An invention to protect me from something far, far worse than matrimony."

A sudden silence fell, and her father stared at her, the color returning to his face. For several moments, they simply looked at one another, unmoving, until her father stood up and went over to a small wooden chest. He opened the lid, withdrew a bottle, and poured a healthy measure. He brought the bottle and his glass over to his favorite armchair — she recognized it from his study in Paris — and sat down. "Continue," said Sir Ian, and proceeded to take a large gulp of Scotch.

And Rosaline did just that.

She spent the next twenty minutes carefully reconstructing the whole of her acquaintance with the Duke, though she omitted some of the more colorful parts, including the boxing match. The words fell from her mouth in an easy, fluid rhythm, and she built a reality in which she and the Duke were no more than reluctant allies with a surprisingly strong friendship and not so much as a hint of romance. She almost believed it herself, almost believed that she had never dreamt of kissing him, had never imagined what it might be like to wake up and find the Duke asleep beside her, his bare chest pressed against her shoulder — and had never once pictured what he might look like in the library of his own home, toying with her hair until she tired of the more earthly delights.

Rosaline almost believed it. Almost.

Next came the Black and White Ball, and her encounter with McGrath. She spared no detail — her father took each word as it came, and though it pained him to hear it, she could tell that he was relieved — relieved that nothing worse had happened, relieved that all that had come of it was a sprained ankle and a false engagement. Relieved that she had escaped, that she had had someone there who had wanted to help her for no reason other than it being the right thing to do.

At the end of it, her father was staring at her in a mixture of horror and incredulity. Sir Ian's gaze found the Duke. "I suppose I should apologize," he said, his voice thick. "And thank you, for saving my daughter's life as well as her reputation."

"No need," said the Duke. "After all, that rogue was only present during the season because I valued my reputation above the safety of others. Had I been honest about his past, he would not have been allowed within ten feet of Kensington."

"The Duke censures himself too harshly," said Rosaline. "He did not learn of McGrath's presence in London until it was too late. And, it happened to be the same night that the Duke was forced to return to the country on an urgent personal matter. There was little he could do from such a distance."

Sir Ian shook his head. "Even if you had put an announcement in the *Times*, Your Grace, it might have only encouraged your peers to take sides. They would have seen it as entertainment."

Rosaline alone caught the flash of surprise on the Duke's face — he had not expected her father to speak so plainly.

"At any rate," Sir Ian continued, "this... engagement of yours. A week, you said?"

"Yes," said Rosaline. "Roughly."

After a moment, he nodded. "I suppose it makes sense." But his reluctance was plain even from across the room. "But you do not—?"

"No," she said at once, her cheeks flaming.

Her father nodded again, not looking at her. "Who else knows about this?"

"Only Lisette, Charlotte, and Cadogan know the truth," said Rosaline, glancing at the Duke for confirmation. He nodded — he'd told her on the journey over that he'd brought Cadogan up to speed the night before. "Mrs. Randolph and Lord Devon know the popular story — that the Duke proposed, and I fell into a bush."

Her father exhaled, and it was almost a chuckle. "Now that I would believe. You do not have the gift of balance, my dear." He glanced at her. "How has Randolph been treating you?"

"Mostly the same," Rosaline replied. "She is quite angry that I made such an apparent fool out of myself in public, but she's so pleased I matched with a Duke that she's seen fit to overlook my shortcomings."

"And she has not noticed the cat yet," said the Duke. "Which helps."

"And do you need me to..." Sir Ian winced. "To do anything? To bolster your charade?"

"A disapproving prospective father-in-law would make for some delightful gossip," said the Duke, "but we already have a plan."

"Of course you do," muttered Sir Ian. He stood up, pacing the short distance between his chair and the dormant fireplace. "Seems we would all be at a loss without my daughter's plans." Then, he paused and looked right at the Duke. "And what of this lowlife, McGrath? Has he been seen since your altercation?"

Something swooped in Rosaline's stomach — he had just voiced the very question she had been unable to bring herself to ask. She, too, looked at the Duke, at the shift in his face as he said, "He has vanished, as best I can tell. No one has caught a glimpse of him since that night."

"How do you know?" she said, before she knew she was saying it.

He met her gaze, inscrutable. "I have many friends."

But Sir Ian was shaking his head. "I know men like this. They disappear only when they are nearest to hand. He will be back, you realize. And what is your plan then, Your Grace, should he begin making claims about my daughter?"

The Duke's gaze snapped to her father's like a whip. "That," he said, his voice simmering, "will not happen."

"I wish I shared your confidence." Sir Ian sat down again with a sigh. "But I suppose we have to tackle each problem as it comes. One must try to subdue the enemy without fighting."

"But in the midst of chaos," replied the Duke, "there is also opportunity."

Rosaline turned to look at him so quickly she felt something crack in her neck. Had he really just—?

The Duke did not notice her reaction. "The hustle and bustle of the London season offers a seemingly perfect shield for a man trying to escape notice. But McGrath will not be able to set a foot out of doors without us knowing about it. Of this I am quite confident."

"Confidence," returned her father, "is simply arrogance writ large."

The corner of the Duke's mouth twitched, as did his hands — he was once again impatient, and Rosaline could hardly believe she *recognized it.* "Not," he replied, "when I own half the eyes and ears of London." He turned to Rosaline. "I believe your time is running short. Perhaps we should—?"

"Yes." She hauled herself upright without a single ounce of grace and winced as she put her weight on her foot. "Father, I am going to revoke your medical license. My foot appears to be hanging on its last hinge."

"Nonsense." Sir Ian came over to her and brushed a kiss to her cheek. "Tighten the wrappings, keep it elevated, and try to eat some fish."

Her nose wrinkled. "Fish?"

"I'll write a note to Hieronymus." Sir Ian gave the Duke a nod, his approval obvious though reluctant. "Your methods were unorthodox, but I appreciate your courage in coming here today. Both of you." He twinkled at Rosaline, and she smiled in return. "But if you break into my chambers again, I shall set the Queen's spaniels on you."

As the Duke opened the door and looked out into the hall, Sir Ian took Rosaline's hand and lowered his voice. "I must apologize to you." He shook his head "The things I said—"

"You had every right to be surprised," she replied. "I just did not expect you to be angry."

"Nor should you have. But it was a shock, and I... I was upset with myself, for not being able to protect you from that monster. Your engagement was just another reminder of how much you are growing up, how much of your life I am not privy to, not anymore."

Rosaline swallowed a wave of emotion. "Father—"

He squeezed her hand. "It is no matter. But I can admit, Honeybee, that when it comes to you, I am not particularly adept at keeping a level head."

"Even so, Father." She shot him a pointed look. "You will find your temper tested more than once before we see this through."

He gave a rueful sigh. "I suppose you are right." But then he smiled. "You seem to have found yourself a most admirable shield."

She glanced at the Duke and smiled in return. "More of a partner in crime."

"We must hurry," muttered the Duke, once Rosaline joined him in the hall. She could practically see the energy jumping through his frame as he glanced up and down the corridor. "Charlotte only guaranteed us an hour."

"What did you mean?" she hissed, bracing herself on the wall as she tried to rush along behind him. "When you said you owned half the eyes and ears of London?"

"Oh." The Duke offered her a sudden, sharp grin. "I only said that to sound impressive. But I suppose it is not far from the truth."

Rosaline frowned at the back of his head. "And what is the truth?"

The Duke seemed to hesitate before he said, "My time on the East End has allowed me to develop... friendships, with all sorts of people. And their children are often in need of things like shoes, sweaters, and chocolates." He shrugged. "In return, they keep an eye on what I ask them to keep an eye on. They seem quite adamant about it, actually."

For a wild, blinding moment, Rosaline wanted nothing more than to push him up against the nearest wall and kiss him until she could not breathe.

Oblivious, the Duke halted by the doorway to the inner courtyard, glancing around for any observers. "They will inform me of any whispers or sightings." He looked her right in the eye. "You have nothing to fear."

Rosaline managed one pathetic, shaky breath before she nodded in reply. His gaze held her, as if on a tightrope, for another blistering moment, then he turned and led her into the courtyard, where his coach was waiting.

"And what," she said, once she'd found her voice again, "is the point of it all?"

"What do you mean?"

"If you have people watching for him, and waiting for him..." When the Duke did not finish her thought, she stopped a few feet shy of the carriage. The Duke stopped as well, close enough that she could reach out and touch him, and she met his gaze without flinching. "Does that mean you have a plan?"

"Oh." He nodded, easy as a breeze. "Of course I have a plan."

Rosaline raised an eyebrow. "What is it?"

"Simple." His mouth twisted into a smirk, and something inside her twisted in reply. "I will remove McGrath from the country, or from this mortal coil. Whichever comes first." He turned back to the carriage. "Come on, let me help you up—"

Merde, thought Rosaline, her face burning and far too many things happening in her stomach. How she would survive the next twenty minutes in an enclosed space with the Duke of St. Albans was one of God's finest mysteries.

SEVERAL HOURS LATER, ROSALINE LOOKED UP WHEN SHE HEARD the sound of the front door and took a deep breath, steeling herself. A rumble of voices, footsteps echoing in the hall, and then the door to the drawing room opened and Benny appeared.

"Miss Bailey." He seemed quite excited. "The Duke of St. Albans."

She nodded. "Let him through."

The Duke came into the room, looking much the same as he had earlier that day. But her stomach did not seem to know the difference. He nodded at her. "Miss Bailey."

"Your Grace."

Benny departed, leaving the door ajar, and she knew he was going to fetch Mrs. Randolph. They would have to be quick.

"You took your time, Your Grace," she spat, just as they'd agreed.

The Duke grinned, delighted, and burst out with — "You cannot expect me to rearrange my entire schedule to accommodate your whims, Miss Bailey—"

"Whims?" she repeated, loud enough for anyone in the hall to hear. "How dare you imply that our engagement is anything less than your utmost priority—"

"How could I?" He, too, began to raise his voice. "When you go out of your way to remind me of the exact opposite?"

She scoffed, the sound echoing around the room. "And if I did not remind you, Your Grace, you would forget it within the day."

"What are you saying?" he fired back. "Are you saying that you want me to be some sort of sniveling puppet you can tug around to your heart's content? Someone who waits on you hand and foot?"

Sniveling puppet? she mouthed at him, and he shrugged. "Perhaps that would be preferable to the current scenario. You would finally listen to me, would you not?"

He let out a loud groan of exasperation, and she had to bite her lip to keep herself from laughing. "How can I listen to someone so obtuse, so unaware of their own selfish nature?"

"I could say the same to you!"

Suddenly, the Duke closed the distance between them, took her hand, and squeezed it. "This was fun," he whispered. "Same time tomorrow?"

She nodded, and he returned to the opposite end of the room just in time to loudly proclaim, "I cannot speak to you when you are in this sort of state. I shall leave at once." He gave her a wink, then put on his best scowl and stormed out of the room, the door swinging open behind him. Rosaline heard the distinct sound of half the kitchen staff skittering out of his way.

A moment later, Mrs. Randolph came marching in like a thunderstorm. She stared at Rosaline, then at the space previously occupied by the Duke, just as the front door slammed shut. "What on earth," she said, "just happened?"

Rosaline made her chin wobble and her voice thin as she said, "I cannot discuss it, Mrs. Randolph, it was just too awful—"

Mrs. Randolph said nothing, then her gaze caught on the sole occupant of the sofa. "Is that a cat?"

৩৵৩

"Lovely, Charlotte." Rosaline beamed at her friend in the mirror. "You shall have the finest trousseau in all of London."

"You flatter me," Charlotte replied, though she beamed in return. She looked radiant in her blue nightgown and its matching dressing gown. "I imagine every bride looks like the happiest bride in the world." She shot Rosaline a quick, cheeky look. "Except for you, perhaps."

Rosaline grinned, but then their modiste reappeared, preventing her from replying. She sipped her tea while Madam D'Amboise knelt at Charlotte's feet and began pinning the hem. The shop was busy — the lull of the season always loosened purse strings, especially once the engagements began and desperation swept through the mothers like an epidemic. Anything to make their daughters stand out, to make them more noticeable, more enviable, more like the wives they so wanted to be.

She and Charlotte were ensconced in their own private nook near the back of the shop, but Rosaline had noticed that her presence had caused some whispering and poorly-hidden stares. She could feel the gazes raking over her body, over her determinedly naked finger, and she could hear the silent questions.

Where is her ring? I thought they were engaged—

Perhaps she will only wear one after the ceremony—

Did you hear? Apparently, they were arguing in Sloane Square yesterday—

She said nothing, thought nothing. Hid her smile in her tea, even as an ugly, dark feeling curled through her belly. A feeling that made her wish none of it was true, that she and the Duke—

"I truly cannot stomach lace," sighed Charlotte, now wearing a pale peach gown that made her complexion sing. Her finger danced along the lace edging. "But I suppose if it is the fashion—"

Madam D'Amboise tutted and smirked. "I have a feeling Mademoiselle would enjoy French lace. Chantilly can be breathtaking, not like this—" She flicked at the lace trim.

"It is an option worth exploring, Charlotte," said Rosaline. "Madam D'Amboise is quite right."

Charlotte smiled. "Very well, then. Show me what lace can be."

Madam D'Amboise nodded, and as she passed Rosaline on the way to her shelves of fabrics, an unmistakable, coy smirk danced over her face. "*Perhaps,*" she said in French, "*you, too, will have Chantilly lace on your gowns. We can begin your fittings today, if you like.*"

"No," said Rosaline loudly, not missing the way a few other young ladies' heads whipped round in surprise. "No, I think not."

Madam D'Amboise paused to give her a look of bewildered

concern. Charlotte glanced at Rosaline in the mirror, paying close attention but hiding it well.

"What do you mean?" said Madam D'Amboise, now in English, her voice low.

"What I *mean*," said Rosaline, "is that I will likely not have need for a trousseau. Not now, not ever. So there is hardly a point to me trying anything on." She cleared her throat loudly. "Let us continue with Charlotte. After all, she is the bride to be."

There was a loaded pause, then Madam D'Amboise nodded and returned to her work, and the other customers went back to their browsing. Rosaline met Charlotte's gaze in the mirror, ready to share a secret grin, and was surprised to find her friend looking at her with something like sorrow in her beautiful blue eyes.

❦ 29 ❦

Less than two days later, Charlotte returned to Prince Manor with one hand much the heavier.

Rosaline gaped and grabbed Charlotte's hand, staring at the enormous ring. "Pearls and diamonds, Charlotte, how incredible!" And it matched her engagement gift perfectly.

"I know!" Charlotte beamed, still blushing with joy. "I could hardly believe it. The Earl said it was his mother's. He just had to have the band reshaped."

"Charlotte..." Rosaline found herself speechless. She looked at her friend, at her sister, and could not believe that they were here, where neither of them had ever thought they'd be. "I am so, so happy for you."

"Thank you." Charlotte squeezed her hand. They were in the Blue Room, and the light from the windows glowed around her like a halo.

Rosaline smiled. "Little stars for a Star."

"Stop it," Charlotte began, bursting into laughter, but before Rosaline could reply, Mrs. Randolph came into the room, slack-jawed and a funny shade of green.

Both Charlotte and Rosaline fell silent and stared at her —

they had never seen her like this before. "Mrs. Randolph," said Rosaline, "are you well? Has something happened?"

"Yes," Mrs. Randolph managed, wobbling a little on her feet. "Yes, I—" She seemed to collect herself, glancing down at a card in her hands. "Miss Bailey, you have— you have been summoned."

An eerie silence fell. Rosaline continued to stare at her, then glanced at Charlotte, who seemed equally puzzled. "Is that supposed to mean something to me, Mrs. Randolph?"

Mrs. Randolph pushed the card at her in lieu of explanation.

Rosaline looked down at the card, and realized that she was holding a piece of royal stationery. Her legs went numb and she had to force herself to read the brief, curt note. This done, she read it again. And again.

Then, Rosaline found her way over to the nearest armchair and sank down into it, her hands shaking.

"What?" said Charlotte. "What is it?"

"The Queen," Rosaline managed, the words sticking like thorns in her throat. "She wants to see me, personally."

Charlotte gasped and snatched the note out of her hand, falling upon it like a woman possessed. "But she— why would she—?"

"That," said Mrs. Randolph, a hand pressed to her stomach, "is my question precisely." She gave Rosaline her usual pointed glare. "Miss Bailey?"

She knows, thought Rosaline. It was the only explanation. The Queen knew something — some scrap of information, some piece of the true story, and she wanted to dig at it, to question Rosaline, to demand answers. *But why would she care? What am I to her?*

She realized a moment later that Charlotte and Mrs. Randolph were waiting for her reply. "I do not know," said Rosaline, which was partially true. "But I suppose I shall soon find out."

"Soon?" echoed Mrs. Randolph with a scoff. "You barely have enough time to become presentable, let alone ready to face the

Queen." She took Rosaline by the arm and pulled her out of the chair, then turned to Charlotte. "You had better come along, Lady Charlotte. We will need all the help we can get."

❦

ROSALINE COULD HARDLY BREATHE AS ST. JAMES'S PALACE appeared in the windows of her carriage. It had been little more than a week since she'd visited her father, but now the building seemed cold, imperious, an impression strengthened by the sudden cloud cover that had swallowed the sun. Her heart in her throat, her mind turned through the events of the past few days, through the different fights she had had with the Duke in public as well as private. By now, the entire peerage — if not all of London — knew that her engagement with the Duke was on rocky ground, that it would likely not survive the fortnight. Everybody knew it; many of the mothers were already scheming, trying to find the best way of throwing their daughters at the Duke without raising suspicion. Everybody knew it, so it stood to reason that the Queen knew it as well. But why would she care?

The carriage drew to a halt in the internal courtyard, and Rosaline disembarked amidst a cloud of apprehension. She worked to keep the fear from showing on her face as the royal footman led her into the building.

The palace was silent, empty. Imperious in its red brick might. It was a long walk to the throne room. Long enough for her resolve to waver, long enough that Rosaline began to wonder what would become of her, if she said something the Queen did not want to hear. *No point in worrying*, she reminded herself, *not when you don't even know what it is she wants.*

Rosaline was led into a passage, then down a short hall, and finally, to a small chamber outside a set of enormous, gilded double doors. The walls around her were papered in a sumptuous, bloody red, and she tried not to think much of it.

"Wait here, Miss Bailey," said the footman, then, somewhat to her surprise, he left.

Her solitude was sudden, overwhelming. Every small movement seemed to echo in the silence, and she turned slowly on the spot, taking in the paintings, the decorations, the furniture. Everything about this place was so deliberate, so calculated. She wondered if the hunting scene depicted on the tapestry was meant to induce fear or awe. Or both.

There came a clatter of footsteps, and she whirled round in time to see none other than—

"Your Grace!" Oh, but Rosaline was so glad to see him, even if she had no idea— "What are you doing here?"

"I received a summons." And the Duke seemed rather windswept — like her, he had probably rushed to get here in time. "I assume you received the same?"

"Yes," she said, her heart thudding. "Yes, but I have no idea—"

"Nor I," he replied, a touch grim. She could tell that the drama and mystery of the whole occasion had worn his patience thin — this was not a man who liked to be toyed with. Then he looked at her, and seemed to slow down. "You look rather lovely."

Her cheeks burned. "Thank you, but don't start."

He almost smiled. "Was it very terrible?"

"I thought Mrs. Randolph was going to cry."

Before the Duke could reply, there came a loud thudding noise from behind the double doors, and they swung open to reveal the throne room. "The Duke of St. Albans," boomed a loud voice, "and Miss Rosaline Bailey."

Rosaline's heart rocketed into her throat, and it was all she could do to walk in without tripping over her own feet. Her and the Duke's footsteps echoed around the narrow room, bouncing between the blood-red walls, nestling in the ornate velvet canopy suspended above the royal head. Apart from the throne, there was very little furniture — a bench, a few armchairs, a couple paintings and vases scattered around the room. But the space was dominated by the long, open wooden floor, and for a moment, it felt as if she were crossing a wide, solid ocean.

A familiar dark gaze burned into her from the throne, and it distracted her from the presence of other individuals. But then, she realized that the people by the windows were not courtiers at all — one of them was her own father. Sir Ian was standing between two other men, neither of whom she recognized, and he was watching her closely. Rosaline stared back at him, but she could not say anything, could not—

Beside her, the Duke halted, and she did the same. They were six feet in front of the throne, and the Duke swept into a low bow. "Your Majesty."

Rosaline bent into a curtsy. "Your Majesty."

"Lovebirds," said the Queen, and Rosaline could practically hear her father's wince. "Thank you ever so much for obliging me on this fine summer day."

A light rain began to patter at the windows.

"I am sure you are well aware," the Queen continued, "why I asked you here today."

The silence that followed was pained, pointed.

"Are you not?" she prodded.

"Actually, Your Majesty," said the Duke, "we have no idea why you summoned us here, let alone together."

"Ah." Her smile was wide, smug. "Well, as you know, I take a great interest in our annual season. It is so diverting, you see, to predict matches and to run the odds, as it were. So you can imagine my delight when news broke of your engagement."

A cold jolt of fear liquified Rosaline's stomach — she had been right. For a moment, she could not breathe. But she was brought back to reality when one of the men standing by her father scoffed. No one acknowledged it.

"I knew both your mothers," the Queen went on. "And I believe I owe it to their memory and their friendship to demand to know what on earth you were thinking by creating this *mess*."

With that, she flung a handful of papers onto the floor in front of the throne.

Rosaline's heart sank as she took in the familiar sight of Madam Kensington's publication. She recognized these editions as the issues from the past week, each one featuring another installment in the ongoing catastrophe of her and the Duke's fractured engagement.

A Certain Couple seems to be encountering choppy waters... Reports of raised voices, visits cut short, and slamming doors... Seen again exchanging Words in front of the fountain, tempers flaring as hot as this July day... Our Sapphire was overheard dismissing the need for a trousseau — one can only wonder at her cynicism, though perhaps there is something deeper at play...

"I can admit," said the Queen, "that some couples are not made for matrimony, let alone for engagement. I can acknowledge that such mistakes are made every year and are either amended and forgotten or allowed to play out over a lifetime. And if you were one of those couples, I would not give these reports a second thought. However..." She gave them each a sharp look. "Having seen you both with my own eyes, having known your mothers, especially Miss Bailey's, and having questioned other members of the peerage, I have come to the opposite conclusion — you are *not* one of those couples. And so, I ask you, what are you playing at?"

"Ma'am," began the Duke, much to Rosaline's relief — she had no idea what to say. "It is as simple as you put it. If our engagement is falling apart, then it is because we are not well suited to one another—"

"Do not toy with me, Your Grace." Her voice cut like a knife. "I know you, I know your family. This—" she pointed at the pile of Madam Kensington— "is not your style."

"Perhaps matrimony," he replied, "is not my style."

"What the Duke means," broke in one of the men beside Sir Ian, the one who had scoffed before, "but stated rather inelegantly, is that he is set against marriage. He has been that way ever since he was—"

"Perhaps the Duke should say what he means, Lord Black-wood." The Queen arched her eyebrow, and Rosaline's world tilted — that was the Duke's *godfather.* "Marriage is one thing, my lord, and love is quite another." Finally, her gaze drifted to Rosaline. "I would be most surprised if the Duke had declared himself immune to both."

A heavy silence fell, and the air in the room seemed to change, seemed to become charged with something new, something inde-scribable. Rosaline could not bring herself to look at the Duke, but could see that his godfather was staring at him in shock. Why, she could not think.

"I refute," the Duke managed, "your implication, ma'am."

"But you do not deny it," the Queen fired back. She straight-ened up, as if settling in for the strike. "What would your mother think, if she knew what you were doing to yourself?"

"What I am doing?" repeated the Duke, with genuine heat — he was actually *raising his voice to the Queen.* "Perhaps you can enlighten me, ma'am, as to what, precisely, it is that I am doing?"

"Lying to yourself. Preventing yourself from entertaining the greatest happiness—"

"I am doing nothing of the sort," retorted the Duke, and finally, Rosaline summoned the courage to glance at him. His chin was out, his back was straight, and his eyes were flashing — he was at war, and it suited him. "If you understood the situation—"

"And what situation is that?" pressed the Queen, exasperated. "God, the number of young rakes I've seen kick up a fuss at the idea of getting married, all because they think it is nothing short of the end of the world—"

"Not the end of my world," cut in the Duke, "but of hers."

Another silence — this one loaded with equal parts astonish-ment and anger. Rosaline could feel her father's gaze on the side of her face. It was a welcome distraction from the way the Queen was staring at her in utter confusion.

"The end of hers," repeated the Duke, the words raw in his throat, "because Miss Bailey does not wish to be wed, and I would never presume to change that."

Rosaline stared at him, her mind finally catching up with her body. Her breath sizzled in her chest, and she could not believe, could not think—

"Well," said the Queen, "That is rather a noble—"

"Your Majesty."

Every pair of the eyes in the room snapped to Rosaline, and she ignored them all, except for one. "Your Majesty," she said, "might I beg a minute of the Duke's time?"

The Queen frowned. "I suppose—"

"Alone." With that, Rosaline seized the Duke's arm and tugged him back down the length of the room, towards the double doors. She caught movement beside the throne and snapped, "If any of you come within ten feet of me, I swear to God I will put you through that window. Even you, Father."

The three men quickly took a step back. Then the Duke's godfather grinned and said, "Oh, I *like* her."

Rosaline ignored this and continued marching down the room, the Duke barely keeping pace beside her.

"Rosaline—" He stumbled but caught himself. "Rosaline, what the hell—"

"Shut up," she gritted out, sweaty and angry and *ready.* "Just—"

They reached the doors. She hauled one open, shoved the Duke into the antechamber, and slammed the door shut behind her. Now, they were alone, and all was quiet.

Rosaline whirled round, tossed a stray piece of hair out of her face, looked the Duke in the eye, and said, "When, exactly, did you fall in love with me?"

An ominous silence fell. He looked catastrophic in the pale

gray light. "Well," he managed, a few moments later, "well I suppose—"

"You!" Rosaline snarled, lunging for the nearest armchair. She flung one cushion at him, then another. "You rampallian! You canker-blossom!"

"Rosaline! Rosaline, for God's sake—!"

She landed on the sofa and grabbed two more cushions, lobbing them at his head. "You are a boil, a plague sore—!"

"Rosaline, are you really yelling at me in Shakespeare—?!"

"You!" The last cushion hit the floor, and she sagged against the back of the sofa, her knees on the seat. She stared up at the Duke, the fight going out of her in an instant. "You weren't supposed to do that, Your Grace."

The Duke looked at her, and took a tentative couple of steps closer. He was less than a foot away, only the back of the sofa between them, and she could see the amber along with the honesty in his eyes. "Rosaline." He smiled, and it made her tremble. "Can you blame me?"

"Yes," she said, even as she reached for him, grabbed his lapels, "yes, I can—" And with that, she pulled him down and pressed her mouth to his.

For a moment, shock left him motionless, long enough for Rosaline to begin to panic, but then, it was as if he was hit by a bolt of lightning. The Duke — *Hal* — melted, groaned into her mouth, one hand going to her waist, the other nestling below her jaw, and the feeling of his skin on hers was so perfect, so acute, that her mouth fell open on a gasp and he licked his way in. It was like dying and dancing all at once, her body alive with heat, with need, and she grabbed at him, her hands tangling in his hair, her tongue pressing against his, and they battled for it, drunk with the feeling of *finally*, and Hal broke away to press his mouth to her cheek, her chin, her neck—

Rosaline jumped, a jolt of *something* going through her, and he made a muffled, strangled noise against her collarbone, his hand raking dangerously high along her waist, his thumb pressing at the lower curve of her—

"Hal," she somehow managed to say. "Hal, we have to—"

"I know," he bit out, his teeth grazing the side of her throat.

"Hal, you must tell me—"

"I thought you already knew—"

"Hal," she pleaded, pulling him even closer. "You have to tell me why you will not marry."

He paused. Then, he pressed his mouth dangerously low on her chest, making her shudder against him. Hal pulled back to look at her, his eyes dark, his cheeks ruddy. "What does it matter, if you will not marry, either?"

"Well." Rosaline bit her lip, carded a hand through his soft, supple hair. Now that she could, she feared she would never stop. "Perhaps I am reconsidering my position on the matter."

His grin was sudden, mischievous. "Oh, are you?"

"Perhaps," she repeated, a blush flooding her face. "But I gave you my reason, at the very beginning. You never gave me yours."

For several moments, he said nothing. But he cupped the back of her head, pressed his thumb against the bolt of her jaw, and watched her shiver.

"You said," she went on. "At the Denison Ball, you said you had no desire to marry. Is it because you do not wish for children—?"

"No," the Duke said, his voice low. "Nothing like that."

"Then tell me," she replied, with an edge of impatience. "Tell me, or prove that you never trusted me at all."

He looked at her for another moment, then stepped away with a sigh. His hands fell to his sides, and she watched as he began to pace, the rain-filled window looming behind him. "It is not," he said, pushing a hand through his hair, "that simple."

Rosaline stood up from the sofa. "Neither was rescuing me from McGrath, and yet."

"Rosaline." And there was something desperate in the word.

"What you ask of me is more than I could freely give. What you ask," he repeated, "has an answer that would potentially put you, and your father, in serious danger. Do not ask me to do that, not to you."

"Take a look around, Hal." Rosaline gestured at the paintings, the tapestries, all of them full of people who looked nothing like her. "My father and I are always in danger. We are accustomed to it by now. And you speak of risk," she added, heat flooding her neck. "There are a few moments in life that are worth it. This is one of those moments."

The Duke looked at her, a wave of emotion passing over his features, but said nothing.

Rosaline frowned. "Is it a source of shame? Are you worried that it would change my opinion of you, the way I—"

"No," he said, at once. "Shame has nothing to do with it."

She nodded. "Then you will tell me. If not today, then soon." Something inside her trembled. "Hal, we—" Something caught in her throat, and she told herself to be brave. "The Queen was right. We owe it to ourselves, do we not?"

He smiled, then, sudden and dazzling, and nodded. "I suppose we do."

Rosaline could not help smiling back, her heart bursting. "Well, then." She brushed off her dress and tucked a loose strand of hair back into her bun. "We should—"

But the Duke shook his head, striding towards her across the room. "They can wait another minute, Miss Bailey."

"Hal," she began, her skin buzzing— "Hal, we are in the *palace*—"

"It's seen worse." He closed in on her and pushed her up against the wall, fastening his mouth to hers.

It was all Rosaline could do not to explode on the spot. It was as if she were transported out of her own body, watching as the world trembled and shifted around her. But it was overwhelming — *he* was overwhelming. Hal's mouth on hers, hot and persistent, building a liquid heat that roared under her skin, surging to a tidal wave in her belly, her lower back— his arms, wrapped around her, holding her together— his torso, his hips, pressing against her as she tangled her hands in his hair, dragged her nails across his shoulders, fought for breath— she wondered if she was melting into the wall, leaving an impression of her body, entangled with his—

"For what it is worth," he murmured, nipping at the swell of her breast before soothing it with his tongue, "I could die here, quite happily—"

"You," she managed, almost dizzy with exhilaration, "exaggerate—"

"Not at all," he said, so matter-of-factly she almost laughed. Hal sighed, nuzzling the space between her breasts. "Do you know what torture it's been, seeing you in these dresses, and not being allowed to—?"

"Behave," Rosaline hissed, though she smiled. She knew. She knew he'd been looking—

"Whoever decided that women have to wear these things must be a masochist, or trying to give every young man in London a neck injury—"

"Be quiet," she told him, and tugged his face back up to hers.

Several lovely, languid moments later, Hal broke their kiss, panting for air. He looked disastrous. "I think," he said, "that if I do not step away now—"

"Give yourself some credit," Rosaline said, likewise short of breath. "We could never get me out of this dress by ourselves."

She'd expected him to grin, but he winced and closed his eyes. "The last thing I need is to think about you not wearing a dress."

"Sorry." With that, Rosaline slipped out of his arms and took a few steps away. She glanced down at her arms, her hands, at the body that was the same but felt completely different. Her face was almost numb with delight. She looked back at him.

The Duke met her gaze. "Give me two days. I will send you word."

"Very well." Rosaline straightened her back, cleared her throat, and opened the double doors, ignoring the Duke's muttered oath.

The throne room fell silent. The Queen and her companions stared at Rosaline as she marched a few yards into the room and halted.

"Give us some time, Your Majesty." She dipped into a deep curtsy. "Thank you for your concern. It has been quite... clarifying."

"Has it?" The Queen's face was impassive, save for a glimmer of sly satisfaction. "I trust, Miss Bailey, that you will not allow him to make a fool of himself."

Rosaline almost smiled. "Not if I can help it, Your Majesty." She curtsied again, and, ignoring her father's pointed look and Lord Blackwood's gleeful grin, marched back out of the throne room.

The Duke had collected himself and was staring at her with an expression of utter shock. "You fiend."

Rosaline nodded, then leaned in and brushed a kiss to his cheek. "Two days. You would do well to steer clear of me until then."

His eyebrow twitched. "Why is that?"

"Because, Your Grace. I might do something untoward."

With that, Rosaline swept from the room, and the Duke's answering bark of laughter was enough to bring a grin to her face.

❧ 30 ❧

Rosaline slipped in through the front door of Prince Manor and gently closed it behind her. There was no sign of Benny — perhaps the gossip hour in the kitchen had been too distracting for anyone to hear the carriage on the front drive. She was surprised not to see Mrs. Randolph waiting to pounce on her for details of her royal audience, but that feeling was fleeting, replaced by the giddy euphoria that had swept through her body the moment she'd left the Duke's line of sight.

Rosaline could not help it — she grinned like an idiot, her face glowing with heat, and leaned against the nearest wall. Out of everything she could have imagined, she had never thought it would feel like that to kiss and be kissed, to have someone she loved pressed against her, devouring her, telling her how wonderful it was to *feel* her—

Because it was the truth, even if she hadn't said it to him yet. She loved Hal, loved him in a way that was breathless and easier than falling asleep, in a way that was endless and bountiful, and not in spite of his flaws, but because his flaws were not the end nor the beginning of his character. She put one hand to her neck, where his mouth had been not an hour before, and slid down to the floor, her other hand going to her chest, where she could feel her heart thundering like a racehorse's. The memory of his mouth alone was enough to make her knees turn to liquid, make her mind churn and imagine the decadent, the impossible—

She could not tell him. Not yet. It would be a terrible thing to confess your love to someone you could not marry.

But she had a feeling that whatever the Duke had to tell her would not cause her to waver. Rosaline was intelligent enough to know that their attachment was unlike anything she could have ever imagined, that together, they could build a life that was their own — unique and complete, all at once.

But what would he tell her? And why did he need two days to prepare whatever it was he needed to prepare? The entire thing was completely bizarre. And it would eat at her, she was sure of it, until the very moment he told her the truth.

Rosaline grinned again, rubbing her cheek. She could still remember the way he'd felt against her body, full of energy and desperate yearning—

The sound of footsteps echoed down the hall, and she looked up in time to meet Lisette's startled expression.

Lisette took one look at her and smirked. "*Viens ici*, Charlotte!" she called over her shoulder. "Our Sapphire has returned, and I think she has just been kissed."

Charlotte's gasp rattled the paintings. "What?!" She came hurtling down the stairs, or as close to hurtling as Charlotte Prince could get, and skidded to a halt in the hall. "Is it true, Rosaline? Was it the Duke? Oh, tell me it was the Duke!"

For a moment, Rosaline could only stare at them. But then her heart squeezed tight and she nodded, pressing her hands to her mouth to stifle the most ludicrous giggle.

Charlotte let out a squeal and came running down the hall, dropping to her knees and sliding the last few feet until she collided with Rosaline, nearly knocking her to the ground. They both collapsed into delirious laughter, clinging to each other for support, and it was at this moment that Mrs. Randolph decided to appear at the foot of the stairs.

"What on earth?" Her frown was as menacing as her speech as she glared at the end of the hall. "Lady Charlotte, we do not fling ourselves onto the floor—"

"Be at ease," interjected Lisette, rolling her eyes. "They were only celebrating Miss Bailey's triumph at court."

Mrs. Randolph showed unmistakable surprise. "Triumph? Really?" She turned to Rosaline, who was reminded of a panting dog. "What did she say? The Queen?"

Rosaline swallowed, feeling true nerves for the first time since she was in the antechamber with the Duke. "She merely wanted to... express her concern. About my engagement to the Duke," she quickly added, when Mrs. Randolph turned an alarming shade of puce.

"What... what..." Mrs. Randolph seemed to teeter, and put a hand to the wall to catch herself. "How could she possibly find fault with such a wonderful match?"

"Not the match," Rosaline replied, "but the fractured state of our engagement. It was the verbal equivalent of knocking our heads together."

Charlotte gasped. "The Duke was at the palace?"

"Yes." Rosaline did not blush.

"Well?" Mrs. Randolph stared at her. "Did it work?"

Rosaline smiled. "It is too early to say." But she squeezed Charlotte's hand, hoping that the signal was clear — there was more to the story.

Mrs. Randolph scoffed. "If you lose the match, Miss Bailey, you shall have no one to blame but yourself, mark my words. Now." She drew herself up, her color returning to normal. "I must go see about supper. And where on earth is that footman?" With that, she marched off towards the kitchen, and the moment she was out of earshot, Lisette came running over to Rosaline and Charlotte.

"Quick, you must tell us everything—" Lisette flung open the door to the Blue Room and ushered them both in. "*Vite, vite*—"

Rosaline collapsed onto the nearest sofa, and Charlotte and Lisette sat down on either side of her, eager and ready, like two hounds poised for the chase.

"Start at the beginning," said Lisette. "Spare no detail."

Rosaline took a shuddering breath and did just that. She told them about getting to the palace, the empty, quiet, intimidating halls, about hardly having a clue why she was there until she saw the Duke. She told them about the throne room, about the Queen's blistering remarks and Lord Blackwood's attempt to deflect them on his godson's behalf. About the Duke saying that he would never jeopardize her ideas about her own future, regardless of his own feelings, and about not understanding all the implications of his statement until it was almost too late. She told them about interrupting the Queen — eliciting a series of gasps — and dragging the Duke from the throne room to answer some of her questions.

"And did you?" Lisette smirked. "Question him?"

Rosaline grinned, her face flooding red-hot and her stomach bursting into butterflies. "Yes," she said. "Most thoroughly."

Charlotte and Lisette burst into squeals, bouncing in their seats. Charlotte flung her arms around Rosaline's shoulders and pulled her into a fierce hug. Lisette, meanwhile, was not done.

"And what did he say?" she said. "He must have said—"

"He loves me." And Rosaline felt giddy at hearing it aloud. "Quite a lot."

Another round of squeals, and Lisette squeezed her so hard that for a moment, she could not breathe.

"So?" said Charlotte, grinning. "Does this mean that the great Rosaline Bailey will find herself wed before the end of the summer?"

Here, suddenly, a lump in her throat. "Well," Rosaline said. "Perhaps. I will know for certain in two days."

"Two days?" Charlotte's grin melted into a frown. "Whatever do you mean?"

Rosaline quickly explained the situation, and Lisette and Charlotte exchanged looks of complete bemusement. "When he said he would never marry," said Charlotte, "I assumed it to be for the usual reasons, bachelor pride and all that nonsense."

"I know," Rosaline agreed. "But no, it seems to be something serious indeed."

"Perhaps he is a criminal," said Lisette. "Perhaps he only masquerades as a Duke, and lives a second life as a notorious gang leader on the streets of London."

Rosaline rolled her eyes. "Don't be ridiculous."

"It is not *ridiculous*," Lisette replied with a sniff. "It would explain why he did not kill McGrath. Such a deed would draw the wrong type of attention, no?"

"Or he did not kill McGrath because the act itself would weigh on him for the rest of his life." Rosaline let out her breath and shook her head. "Waiting will be the most difficult part."

"I can help, on that score." Charlotte smiled at her. "There is plenty to keep us busy."

"Oh, yes, the wedding—"

"Not just mine," said Charlotte. "Katherine's, as well."

God, Rosaline had completely forgotten—

"The invitation came while you were at the palace." Charlotte stood up and went to the writing desk, where she pulled out a few papers. "Along with a letter from Katherine. She's asked you to be her maid of honor, Rosaline." She winked. "Seems you are quite popular for that employment."

"Oh, gosh." Rosaline took the invitation from her and quickly scanned the details. The wedding was soon — two weeks away. "What about you, Charlotte?"

"I am a mere bridesmaid, along with half her cousins, apparently." Charlotte looked over Katherine's letter. "There are six of us in total."

"Good Lord." Mrs. Knight's hand was becoming obvious. Charlotte, in contrast, had insisted upon a small wedding, with only Rosaline in the bridal party. "What of the groomsmen? Do we know any of them?"

"A mixture of brothers and cousins, and I do not recall ever making their acquaintance — the Knight family keeps to the country." Charlotte shot her another wink. "Lucas is the best man. The Duke will have to watch out."

Rosaline blushed, and Lisette decided to chime in. "Why is that?"

"Because Lucas Knight is a determined rake and a flirt," said Rosaline, sinking back into the cushions. "He can hardly pass through London without causing some scandal or other."

"Oh." Lisette's eyebrows threatened to reach the ceiling. "It seems we will have some... how do you say, drama, before this wedding is over."

"Only if Lucas Knight decides to cause trouble," Rosaline replied. "I can handle him."

Lisette flashed her a grin. "Of that I have no doubt."

Rosaline ignored her. "What is expected of us, Charlotte?"

"We, along with the rest of the bridal party, have a dress fitting at the Knights' London house tomorrow afternoon. A light tea will be provided." Charlotte scanned the rest of Katherine's letter. "There is the rehearsal, of course, but that is not for another ten days. And here is something else that is interesting." She glanced up at Rosaline. "Katherine mentions that her beloved is to be wed on the same day."

Rosaline sat up. "What?" Her gaze darted around the room. "Where is the paper?"

"My father has it, I'm afraid. Not that it would do much good, if the announcement was printed earlier in the week." Charlotte sighed and returned Katherine's letter to the desk. "Though perhaps we should not be so keen to uncover her beloved's identity."

"Perhaps," Rosaline agreed. "I suppose we shall find out soon enough."

⚜

KATHERINE'S BRIDESMAID DRESSES WERE IN A LIGHT, CREAMY lilac, and Rosaline could not shake the feeling that she looked like a foxglove.

"Lovely," said Mrs. Knight, smiling at her. "Just lovely."

Rosaline smiled in return, trying not to wobble where she stood on the podium. The modiste — who was looking more harried by the moment — pinned her hem with ferocious speed, giving her time to glance around the room.

Charlotte stood near the sofa with Katherine and Amanda, one of the cousins. They were all still in their dresses, the pins twinkling in the light from the windows, and sharing what looked to be a good joke. The entire bridal party was in the drawing room, which was abuzz with activity and gaiety, and every once in a while, there came a loud thud from the dining room, followed by a cheer.

"My brothers," Katherine had told them, upon first occurrence of this extraordinary sound. "It's something of a drinking game. They always play it whenever they're stuck inside."

Curiosity had gotten the better of Rosaline, and, apparently, a few of the cousins. When her pins were finally done, she wandered over to the group of ladies and into quite the conversation.

"—not everyone, just one of us—"

"Yes, we could draw straws—"

"Honestly," said Katherine, "it is no fun at all—"

"We shall be the judge of that!"

"Indeed." Amanda held up a handful of long matches. "Come on, then!"

Everything was fine until Rosaline drew the short straw. She stared at it, her stomach flopping over, and began to realize just what she'd gotten herself into.

"Quick," whispered Laura, another cousin. "Before they see—" She, Charlotte, and Amanda shoved Rosaline out of the drawing room and into the hall, just in time for another burst of noise from the dining room.

Rosaline stumbled and turned on the bridesmaids. "You are absolute beasts—"

"Straw's a straw, Rosaline." Amanda grinned. "Enjoy yourself." With that, she closed the door, leaving Rosaline alone in the empty hall.

For several moments, Rosaline just stood there, staring at the door to the dining room. Here she was, again — testing the limits of her reputation. Why did she keep doing this, *how* did she keep doing this? One could only tempt Fate a certain number of times—

She shook her head, muttered an oath, marched down the hall, and knocked loudly on the dining room door.

A sudden silence fell in the room, and a wave of apprehension overcame her as she waited, heart pounding, wondering if this was an enormous mistake—

The door opened, revealing a handsome young man with Katherine's enormous dark eyes, a pile of curly brown hair, a thin scar above his left eyebrow, and a wide, impressive chest. He was older than her, and he carried an unmistakable air of self-assurance. Lucas Knight smirked, leaning against the door frame. "Gents," he called over his shoulder, to a wave of jeers, "looks like a little Turtledove lost its way."

Rosaline took a breath and steeled herself. "The Turtledove would like a drink."

His smirk widened into a grin. "Does she know that each drink comes with a price?"

"Yes, and she welcomes it."

A loud chorus of "Ohhhh!" Lucas held the door open, letting her into the room.

It seemed to be a gentlemen's club, writ small. The air was thick with cigar smoke and the scent of liquor, and the room was packed with young men, all of them looking at her. Some were grinning, some were unimpressed, and some were too drunk to know the difference.

"Right." Rosaline turned to Lucas. "What's the game?"

He nodded at the dining table, which was enormous and covered in a random assortment of dishes, glasses, and other breakables. "To run the length of the table without breaking a single object. Each object broken requires another drink. You jump down, take a foil—" He pointed to a row of the same— "and drive it home in dear old Bonaparte." This was an effigy of Napoleon, built out of rough burlap and what looked to be Mrs. Knight's nice pillows. "Then, you must drink."

Much easier than she'd expected. Her heart beating loudly in her ears, Rosaline nodded and kicked off her shoes. "I hope you have Scotch." With that, she gathered her skirts and climbed up onto the nearest dining chair, ignoring the dozen helping hands, then up onto the table.

The men seemed very short from such a height, and they were all watching her, some cheering, some booing. Rosaline took a breath, looked down at the winding path before her, and took her first step.

It was a lot like dancing. She wove between the objects, taking small, careful steps, mindful not to put too much weight on her newly-healed ankle. The noise around her had dulled to a roar, and before she knew it, she'd reached the end of the table. Rosaline leaped down, grabbed a foil, shoved it into Napoleon's feathered gut, then turned around and reached for the bottle of Scotch.

The bottle was half-full, and it sloshed eagerly into her mouth. The first gulp burned like fire, but she was used to it —

she took another few gulps, then slammed the bottle back down just as the room erupted into a cascade of cheers, yells, and applause.

Grinning, she made her way back to the door, where Lucas was waiting by her shoes, looking like he'd been clubbed over the head. The gentlemen parted around her like the Red Sea, their cheers and whistles deafening, and she had to laugh, giddy from the liquor and the ridiculousness of it all.

Rosaline picked up her shoes and smirked at Lucas. "Thanks," she said. "Just what I needed." With that, she turned and exited the room, leaving the door open behind her.

"Well, gents." Lucas's voice echoed into the hall. "I think I'm in love."

⚜

Rosaline glanced out the window just as the Duke's carriage slowed and turned onto a wide road lined with flowering trees. Her heart throbbed with anticipation, anticipation that had been building ever since that morning, when she'd received a note stamped with the Cunningham family crest and a flurry of the Duke's handwriting.

> *Carriage will come for you at two o'clock.*
> *For you, in my respect, are all the world.*
> *H.*

The carriage drew to a halt, and Rosaline could not keep herself from staring at the Duke's London residence. It was smaller than she'd imagined, smaller even than Prince Manor. It was built in a handsome, pale red brick, with cheerful windows and a dark blue front door. But unlike many of the wealthy houses in Kensington, it opened directly onto the road, with no sign of a garden. Almost numb with nerves, she took the footman's hand

and allowed herself to be led across the sidewalk, up the front stairs, and into the entrance hall.

The decorations were simple, in a series of cream and olive tones that contrasted the dark furniture. But there was no sign of the Duke as the butler greeted her and gestured to the nearest set of doors, which appeared to lead to the drawing room.

"The Duke will join you shortly, Miss Bailey."

"Thank you," she said, a touch breathless, and went in.

The drawing room was light, airy, but a tad stale — she could tell it was not often used, and when it was, it was treated with the greatest reluctance and respect. The furniture gleamed, a symphony of polished dark wood and rich, but tasteful, uphol-stery. In the corner was a pianoforte, and above the fireplace was a portrait. A rather lovely portrait, of a young, beautiful couple — the woman, a redhead with lots of freckles and a serene expres-sion; the man, floppy-haired but handsome with a curl of mischief in his mouth. They were breathtaking.

A few minutes later, Rosaline heard a telltale footfall, and turned around just as the Duke entered the drawing room. Her heart jumped at the sight of him — rumpled, dressed in rather casual clothing, cuffs rolled to his elbows, and a red smear on one cheek.

"Miss Bailey." He halted, then quickly closed the door behind him. He looked as nervous as she felt. "Apologies for my tardiness, I was somewhat delayed."

She tried to smile. "Not to worry, Your Grace." She glanced at the open door behind her, then at him — he nodded, and she quickly closed it. "You have her smile, you know."

He cracked said smile, and she realized that the red smear was not blood — it looked pink, and sticky. "Yes, everyone says. And his hair."

"And his hair," Rosaline echoed. "Well. Shall we?"

"Yes." He gestured to the couch. "Take a seat."

She did just that, while he took the nearest armchair. They

were alone, and her body throbbed with the urge to take advantage of it. But not now.

"You brought something?" The Duke nodded to the hatbox in her hands.

"Yes." She did not blush. "That comes later. We should start with—"

"Indeed." He leaned forward, bracing himself on his knees, and his forearms— "I have to begin with a story."

Rosaline settled back into the cushions, forcing herself to relax. "Then begin."

The Duke sighed, and for a moment, looked years older. "Some thirty years ago, a girl was born in Belfast. She grew up poor and hungry, and saw the way the English treated her brethren. She began to think, to dream about the Ireland that could be. She was not alone. And when the French people took arms against their sovereign, the Irish began to plan. They, too, would rise against their English oppressors, and do whatever it took to win."

She frowned. "Are you talking of the—?"

"The Society of United Irishmen, yes."

"I did not know they accepted women into their ranks."

He almost smiled. "This woman was the exception to the rule, which tells you everything you need to know about her determination and her intelligence. She was far too valuable for them to turn aside. And as the movement grew, spreading across Ireland with unprecedented speed, she began to attract attention — the wrong type of attention. As you know, the English government began a campaign of brutal, incessant oppression, including torture and violence and burning houses to the ground." The Duke sighed again. "And into this mess entered an English soldier who forsook his country and joined the Irish cause."

Rosaline's hand went to her mouth before she could stop herself.

"The soldier had fallen in love with her, of course, but it was more than that — he saw what his King was doing to Ireland and disagreed. He wanted his life to mean more, he wanted to be more than just another English foot soldier condemned to Irish mud. He joined the United Irishmen just as they began preparing for an insurrection, and when the time came in 1798, he was at her side."

"But, the rebellion—"

"Yes." The Duke nodded. "Did not go according to plan. The woman and the soldier managed to escape, to rely on those loyal to the cause for food, shelter, a place to stay the night or work for a few days. And so the next couple years passed in this fashion — they lived as vagabonds, on borrowed time, as the United Kingdom came to be. Eventually, they made contact with their old comrades, and began, again, to plan, but, at the same time, to live as good and simple people. They were able to nurture their love, and from that love came a child." But it was as if he'd uttered a death sentence. "A few years later, the woman found out that she was being followed by no less than three different English spies — they were watching her, waiting to see if she would again make an attempt at rebellion. She and the man — living and married under assumed names — took their child and went on the run. Within the next two years, they traveled the length and depth of Ireland, doing their best to stay one step ahead of their pursuers.

"And finally, a light at the end of the tunnel. They secured passage to England, into the lion's den, but sometimes, the best place to hide from your enemy is directly under his nose — the woman's pursuers never dreamed that she would have the audacity to set foot on English soil. It would be dangerous, but they had the assurance of a life, a profession, in a small country town, where they could hide and raise their child in peace." He paused, as if weighing his words. "They became separated at the docks. The soldier watched the English spies kill his wife in broad daylight. But it was too late — he could not reach her, and he still had their son with him. What else could he do, but see the child safely home?"

A pit of emotion had opened in Rosaline's stomach, but she was still confused — what did this have to do with anything?

"Out of grief, and fear for his son's safety, the man decided that he could not remain in England. He left for a life in America, where he remains to this day."

Rosaline stared at him. "And what of his son?"

The Duke finally looked up at her, his gaze piercing, pleading. Then he straightened up and called out, "Come on, then!"

31

The drawing room door burst open, and in came a small hurricane on two legs. Rosaline stared in utter shock as the hurricane — a young boy with tousled, sandy blond hair, pale skin, and dark eyes — halted in front of her and stared back.

"Hal." He glanced at the Duke. "There's a lady."

Rosaline almost laughed. The Duke gave a sheepish grin. "Jamie, meet Miss Bailey. Miss Bailey, meet Jamie. Miss Bailey wanted to play a game with you, Jamie."

"Really?" Jamie was already relaxing, cheeky as anything. His voice had a light, almost unnoticeable, Irish lilt. "I thought I wasn't allowed to play with anyone except you."

"I have made a special allowance for Miss Bailey." The Duke cut her a quick glance. "Just this once, unless she sees fit to return."

Jamie grinned, and she caught the streaks of red at the corners of his mouth — strawberry jam. It matched the pink smear on the Duke's face, conjuring quite the image of Jamie's afternoon tea, and she again had to fight the urge to laugh. Instead, she leaned forward, meeting Jamie's gaze, and smiled. "What shall we play?"

"Rebels and Indians," the boy promptly replied. He bent down to retrieve something from beneath the sofa, which gave Rosaline enough time to look at the Duke and mouth, "*Rebels?*"

The Duke rolled his eyes but grinned. "Americans. You can thank my godfather for that one, he thinks it a most delightful joke."

Jamie straightened up, saving Rosaline a reply. He was clutching two bows and four arrows, all of them fashioned out of what appeared to be tree branches and twine. He handed her one of the bows and put on a very serious expression. "I think I saw two Rebels in the hall."

Rosaline nodded, equally serious, and took off her gloves. "Then we must catch them."

She spent the next half an hour shadowing Jamie through "Queen Mary's Land" and "Louey-sana," brushing aside invisible trees and vines as they stalked — and occasionally shot at — those pesky blue-coated Rebels.

Jamie was an utter delight, a completely unspoiled child, with an imagination that rivaled Rosaline's own at that age. And he was content to take her through the entire ground floor of the Cunningham household, along with the kitchen, where the staff either ignored him or joined in, even falling to the floor in a parody of injury. He was well-loved, Rosaline noticed, by everyone who tended to him, and not just because he was the ward of their master.

"Jamie," she said to him at one point, when they were in the front hall, "why don't we go looking for Rebels outside? It's a beautiful day."

He turned and gave her a very solemn look. "I cannot go outside," he said. "Not in London. I can only go outside when I'm in the country."

"Oh." Something flailed inside her chest. "Oh, I am sorry—"

Jamie shrugged. "Outside's better in the country, anyway." And with that, he resumed his stalking, slowly getting nearer and nearer to the drawing room.

The Duke was still in his armchair, but his posture was completely different. Now, he was slumped back into the seat, his knees splayed wide, and he blinked at them as they came into the room — Rosaline got the feeling he'd been close to nodding off.

"Well?" he said to Jamie. "How did she do?"

Jamie nodded. "Very well."

"Good." The Duke's smile was easy, lopsided. Rosaline stamped down the urge to kiss it. "Now, Jamie, I believe your tutor is waiting."

Jamie stuck out his tongue, but gave Rosaline a little bow. "It was a pleasure to make your acquaintance, Miss," he said, an obviously rehearsed but sweet line.

She smiled and curtsied. "Likewise, Jamie."

He shot her a final grin, then turned and ran out of the room — she heard him go thundering upstairs, but he slowed down when he reached the landing. Soon enough, all was quiet, or as quiet as it had been, before Jamie's entrance.

Rosaline took a breath, then returned her gaze to the Duke. He was watching her, still at ease, as if he were daring her to climb onto his lap. She was half tempted to do so, but she cleared her throat, breaking the silence. "So you are his—?"

"Godfather," replied the Duke. "And his legal guardian, until he comes of age."

"And the man in Ireland?"

"One of my father and Lord Blackwood's closest friends. They were like brothers."

She hummed. "It must be difficult, him being so far away from his son."

"It is. We hope, one day, to be reunited, but there always seems to be some war or other going on. Makes crossing an ocean rather difficult."

"And Jamie is what, six?"

"Just turned seven."

"What an age to be without a mother."

"I quite agree."

"Then I am perplexed, Your Grace." When he frowned, she added, "I would have expected you to want a wife right away, rather than to avoid one at all costs."

"It is not that simple." Here, he threatened to brood. "You can imagine that the offspring of two of Ireland's most wanted political dissidents — one of whom is branded a traitor to the Crown — must be kept very hidden, indeed. He would be worth quite a ransom, to the right buyer."

Rosaline's eyebrows flew up her forehead. "Are you serious?"

He nodded. "Perfectly. That is why I keep him in the country for most of the year."

Suddenly, the two-day delay made sense — he had had to send for Jamie, arrange to have him smuggled into the city.

"There," the Duke continued, "he is secluded and protected. He is watched day and night, whether he knows it or not. I pay through the nose for discretion, for absolute secrecy, and I've been blessed with a very loyal staff. They know Jamie as my godson, a boy lifted from difficult circumstances. But they do not know his parentage."

"And you stay with him. In the country."

"For most of the year, yes. Except when I lose bets, apparently."

"And so the riddle of the Recluse has been solved. You weren't ill-tempered, you were protecting your ward." A thought occurred to her. "And Cadogan, the Captain—"

"They know nothing." The Duke looked right at her. "You are the only one, apart from myself and Lord Blackwood. And my staff, I suppose."

Well. That was... She sat down on the sofa, a touch dizzy — he'd said he trusted her, and here was the undeniable proof. "And even if you had tried to—"

"Perhaps I'm sentimental, but it never occurred to me to try to pass Jamie off as my bastard." The Duke's voice was wry, without judgment. "That alone would be difficult enough to explain, given my age, not to mention quite the tarnish on my family's good name."

"And he looks nothing like you." Rosaline met his gaze. "This was a test."

It was several moments before he responded. "Of sorts."

"What does that—?"

"I wanted to see how you would react to Jamie, how he would react to you. If you were serious, about..." The silence filled in the word for them. "You deserve to know what you would be getting into."

"Motherhood," said Rosaline, the word foreign and familiar all at once.

"Of a kind," the Duke replied. "I occupy the blurred space between parent and guardian, just as my godfather did for me. It is not a role made for everyone." He paused, seeming to weigh his words. "I would understand, if you did not find it fitting for yourself."

"No, I—" But again, her head spun. "I suppose it is rather a lot to consider."

He nodded, dropping his gaze. "If you need time—"

"No." Rosaline's voice was firm. She shook her head. "I came here expecting — goodness, I did not know what to expect. But I have to tell you, Your Grace, that this was quite the opposite of what I had imagined, and I mean that in the best possible way." Her hand began to shake, but she stilled it — this was not the moment for nerves. This was the moment to be brave, to be honest. "And while I did not see myself becoming a mother for several years, if at all, I would be quite willing to begin that journey with Jamie. By your side, if you would have me."

The air between them flickered and changed. It was as if they were inches apart instead of several feet.

"You realize," said the Duke, his voice low, "that you would be putting yourself, and your father, into considerable danger. It is a fact of life for everyone who is attached to that young boy, even if he is not aware of it."

"I know," she replied, her heart beating once, painfully, in her throat. "It is worth it. And my father would say the same thing."

"Would he." The Duke's voice was noncommittal — she could not tell if he was being sarcastic or not. "What is in the hatbox?"

Thrown a little, Rosaline looked down at said hatbox and blushed. "Proof."

"Proof?"

"Of a kind." She reached for it, ran her fingers along the edge of the lid. "The other day, you made some things clear, when we were in the Queen's antechamber."

"Did I?" He was teasing now.

"Yes." Her face burned. "You did. And I believe that I owe you the same." Rosaline took off the lid, then put the box on the end table. She could not bear to hand it to him.

The Duke watched her for a moment, then sat up and reached for the box. He looked down, smiled, and pushed his hand through its contents. "You kept them."

"Yes. All of them."

Before him was a pile of papers and cards — every single note he'd tucked into her flowers, and every letter he'd sent her while he was in the country. Rosaline could not remember how many times she'd read and reread them, just to relive those wonderful, private moments when she'd found herself surprised by his ability to know her, even when he hardly knew her at all.

"Look," she said. "On the back."

The Duke picked up one of the notes — from the first bouquet he'd sent her — turned it over, and read aloud, " 'Today, the Duke called me beautiful for the first time. Unclear if he meant it.' " His gaze darted to hers, and he smiled in a small, delightful way. "I did."

Rosaline took an unsteady breath. The room was very warm. "*A Midsummer Night's Dream*. What made you choose it?"

The Duke shrugged. "That was our first meeting."

She frowned. "Our second, technically."

"Our first meeting when I was not behaving like an ass," he amended. "I had never met a woman who carried a book about her person, even while wearing a ballgown. And not just any book. The Bard himself." He winked at her. "You're quite memorable."

Rosaline sighed. "In that moment, I'd so hoped you had not noticed which book it was."

"Why not?"

"Because, Hal. It is my favorite."

His hand stilled, and when he looked at her, there was a crease between his brows. "I thought you said— when we were in the tennis court—"

Of course he remembers, she thought. "I lied. I did not want you to know the truth — that you had unwittingly constructed a false romance using some of my favorite words. That you had discovered something personal about me, something deeply personal that I had never dreamed of telling you, not while we were..."

"Pretending," he finished for her. When she said nothing, Hal let out a breath and slid off his seat, dropping to his knees.

Rosaline's heart rocketed into her mouth as he moved closer to her. God, he looked incredible like this — tousled, worn out but still brimming with energy, confident and careful—

"But we're no longer pretending, are we, Rosaline?" Hal was kneeling at her feet now, looking up at her with all the open warmth and love she could feel spilling out of her own heart.

"No," she managed, breathless.

"No," he agreed. His eyes were very, very blue. "You must know how deeply, and how ardently, I adore you. How I love you in ways I did not know were possible."

"And I love you," she returned, the emotion welling in her throat. "Just as well, Hal."

"Then perhaps I need to ask you something."

"Do you?" Even now, it was difficult to believe. "Are you certain?"

"Rosaline." Hal smiled, and it was like the sun coming out from behind the clouds. "I have never been more certain in my entire life."

"Then ask me."

"Miss Rosaline Bailey." Hal took her hand, and the heat of his skin almost unmade her. "Would you do me the greatest happiness, and consent to becoming my wife?"

"Yes," she said at once, unexpected tears brimming in her eyes. "Yes, of course—"

Hal beamed at her, his joy effusive, and reached for her, but she was already meeting him halfway, wrapping her arms around him, swallowing a ridiculous sob as she kissed him, artless and wet, but it did not matter, none of it mattered—

He chuckled against her mouth, pulled away. "As usual, the Queen was right."

"Sod the Queen," Rosaline said at once. "We now have to replace a false engagement with a real one."

He hummed, and she could feel it where her hand rested on his chest. "I believe I have something that might help." Hal reached for the end table and opened a drawer. He fished out a small, black leather box, and Rosaline's heart flew into her mouth.

"Hal." She took his hand, covering the box from view. "You must speak to my father."

"I will," he replied. "This very night."

"Another ambush?"

"Of course." And something cheeky showed in his face. "Would you at least try it on?"

A part of her wondered if her heart would survive the hour. "Yes," she said, and withdrew her hand. "Yes, I will."

Hal opened the box, but kept it facing towards him. "It is a family heirloom," he said. "And if you do not like it, we can swap it for another. My grandmother was very fond of jewelry." With that, he propped the open box on her knee and looked up at her, waiting.

Rosaline could not breathe. She could not think. "Hal—" She reached out, her fingers hovering above the ring. "It's— it's—"

"Is it too much?"

"Well—" Trembling, she pulled the ring out of its slot and held it up. "It is quite stunning."

"It is your equal, then." He bent down, brushed a kiss to her knee. "Try it on."

She obeyed, sliding the ring home on the fourth finger of her left hand. There, it twinkled up at her — a sapphire, nestled in a coronet of diamonds. It was quite breathtaking. And it was one of the most enormous jewels she had ever seen.

"There is a matching necklace." Hal was busy at her ankles, and it took her a few moments to realize he was sliding his hand up her leg, gently nudging her skirts out of the way. "And earrings." His mouth, warm and teasing on her knee through the fabric of her stockings. "And a bracelet."

"Good Heavens," she managed, carding a hand through his hair. He flashed her a grin, and some part of her liquified. "If I wore all that, I would be quite weighed down."

His hand came to rest on the lower part of her thigh, and he grazed his thumb across her leg, sending a jolt of heat to her belly. He was only a few inches away from her inner thigh, from the place where the stockings ended and— "I think it would suit you." He went to her other thigh, mouthing at the thin fabric. "I think you will make quite a breathtaking Duchess."

"Duchess," she repeated, almost dizzy at the idea that would soon become her reality.

Hal nodded, letting out a puff of air as he pushed her skirts even further up her legs — now, half of her thighs were showing, and her heart was beating in her ears. He looked up at her, and the unbridled heat in his gaze made her shiver. "I like the way you look," he said, "in my ring."

He surged forward, capturing her mouth in an open-mouthed kiss, sliding his tongue along her bottom lip until she shuddered and moaned, her hands tangling in his hair as she pulled him even closer, and his hands were on her, one at the side of her neck and the other at her waist, holding her together even as she felt like she was falling apart—

Time melted, and she forgot everything — forgot where they were, that they could be caught at any moment, that she had to be home in less than an hour — except the feeling of his hands on her body, his mouth on her neck— She gasped at the feeling, found it within her to say, "You know, you have strawberry jam on your cheek—"

He groaned, but not with pleasure. "That little rodent—"

Rosaline laughed. She twisted her fingers into his hair and pulled him away from her neck — he surfaced with a wet, ruddy mouth and an expression of discontent. "Allow me," she said, then kissed her way from his cheek to his jaw, and finally to the streak of jam. Hardly able to believe her own daring, she mouthed at it, then licked it away, and sucked a kiss at the corner of his mouth.

Hal made an unintelligible noise and surged against her, biting a hot line of kisses into her breast, and she let out a sound that was neither a gasp nor a moan, but something in between—

The door opened. "Your Grace—"

Hal broke away from her and caught himself on the cushions. "What," he spat.

"You asked me to inform you when it was four o'clock, sir." His butler's voice was carefully neutral. "It is now four o'clock."

"Yes, thank you, yes."

"My pleasure, sir," came the reply, followed by the sound of the butler departing, but not, she noticed, of the door closing.

Like her, Hal's face was flushed, though with pleasure or

embarrassment she could not tell. He looked at her, thumbed the ring on her left hand. "You should go."

"Yes, I should." But Rosaline could not bring herself to move just yet. "Are we really doing this, Hal?"

"I hope so." His voice was wry. "Unless you are having second thoughts?"

"No," she said at once. "Never."

He smiled, brushing a kiss to her hand. "I will call on you tomorrow. One o'clock."

"Very well," she said, and they shared one final, tender kiss before she gathered her things and left, feeling as if she were floating on air.

༄༅

A FEW HOURS AFTER SHE'D FALLEN ASLEEP, ROSALINE WAS woken by Benny's voice from the doorway of her bedroom. "Miss Bailey. Your father."

She was awake in an instant, and tugged on her dressing gown before she slipped downstairs, the house silent and gray around her. Benny was barefoot and in his pajamas, though he'd put on his livery coat, and his hair was a catastrophe.

"Were you abed?" she whispered.

"Mostly." He smiled. "It is no trouble. Though I hope there is nothing the matter."

"No," she replied, though it was possible that that was a complete lie. "Where is he?"

"Drawing room."

"Thank you, Benny."

Rosaline could hear the crickets outside as she entered the drawing room, which was dark save for the light from a few candles on the mantelpiece. Her father had his back to her, but he turned when he heard the door close.

"Rosaline." His voice gave nothing away. "I had the strangest conversation this evening."

"I know." She tried to take a breath. "And?"

"Answer me this." He looked her dead in the eye. "You love him?"

"Yes," she said. "With everything I am."

"And this is not some further farce or pretension?"

"No."

"And you trust him? You trust that he loves you?"

"Absolutely."

"And this is what you want?" Something about his expression was tentative.

"More than anything." Rosaline began to walk towards him. She'd removed the ring before returning to Prince Manor, and had only replaced it after getting into bed. It was one thing to tell Charlotte and Lisette that the engagement was still on, but announcing it to the entire staff and half the neighbors was another. Now, she held up her hand, the jewel answer enough.

His eyebrows flickered. "Good Lord."

"I am more serious about this than I have been about anything else," she told him. "I want a life with him so badly I ache."

"I see." Sir Ian nodded. "Well, if I had to surrender my daughter to anyone, he is the best candidate I could have hoped for."

Rosaline grinned. "Was he impertinent?"

"Yes, while trying to be deferential. It was quite amusing." Sir Ian's face softened. "But he was very firm on one point."

This was news to her. "Which is?"

"That your dowry, and your inheritance, are to be yours, and yours alone. They will remain separate from the estate, and his own finances. Though he made it clear," her father added, "that he would support you, and that you could do what you liked with your own money."

Rosaline stared at him, her ears ringing with surprise. "Truly?"

Sir Ian nodded. "He is a good man, Rosaline. A very good man."

A truthful understatement, if she had ever heard one. "I am very fortunate to have found him, Father. Was that the extent of your conversation?"

"Well..." He seemed to mull over something. "Do not ask me how, but the Duke and I ended up at a pub with the Earl Cadogan and some friend of theirs, a Lord Martel—"

Rosaline swallowed a burst of laughter. "Really?"

"I am beginning to suspect that I rather enjoyed myself. Do not tell the Duke, though."

This explained Sir Ian's arriving at the Princes' later than she'd expected. "I would not dream of it, Father."

He was silent for a moment, then he reached for her, took her hand. "I would never have imagined that our return to London would have brought such unexpected results. But I am thrilled to see you happy, Honeybee. And so would your mother."

Sudden tears pricked her eyes, and she beamed. "Thank you, Father."

"Of course." He brushed a kiss to her hand. "Now run off back to bed. You must begin planning a wedding tomorrow."

And Rosaline did just that.

32

Rosaline woke to her curtains rasping open and Lisette singing like a cuckoo. She blinked as sunshine beamed into the room, illuminating a world that was completely the same and yet utterly different, then smiled and sat up. "*Bonjour.*"

"*Bonjour*, my future Duchess—"

"Let us leave the pleasantries aside, we have no time to lose." Mrs. Randolph came bustling in, not unlike a bulldog with a disappointing bit of prey clamped between its teeth. "Come, you must have some breakfast before we are due at the modiste."

Rosaline frowned. "The modiste?"

"Yes, for Lady Charlotte." Mrs. Randolph tched, picking up a loose pair of stockings and handing them to Lisette. "Perhaps we might even dare to have you fitted for wedding gown as well, should you ever decide to return to your senses."

Rosaline bit back a smile and slid out of bed, wishing she was still wearing her ring — the look on Randolph's face would have been worth spoiling the surprise. "As long as we are back in time for three o'clock." She went over to her pitcher and basin. "The Duke will be visiting."

"Very well." Mrs. Randolph's frustration was evident. She huffed and cast one final glance around the room. "Dress her well, Lisette. Perhaps we can shock the man into setting a date." With that, she swept from the room, no doubt on her way to fawn over the future Lady Cadogan.

Lisette's expression was sly. "*If only she knew*." She caught Rosaline's eye, and they both began to giggle.

NOT FIVE MINUTES HAD PASSED SINCE ROSALINE AND Charlotte's return to Prince Manor when a horse sounded on the drive. Rosaline looked up from their tea tray, buttered scone in hand, and felt a spasm of nerves deep in her stomach.

Charlotte caught her eye and smirked. "Well. At least he is punctual."

"My goodness." Mrs. Randolph, for once, looked rather on the back foot. She glanced at the clock. "On the dot of the hour. And he rode here himself."

Rosaline stuffed the scone into her mouth, her heart pounding. This was it. It was happening. In just a few short minutes—

What would happen, exactly? She did not know; they had not discussed it in detail the day before. Would he bend his knee in front of everybody? No, that would be redundant — the act itself had already occurred, it was the follow-through that they needed, and one afternoon passing without raised voices or other incidents would not be enough. She listened to the sound of boots hitting the gravel, then the steps, the bell ringing, the door opening, a murmur of conversation, footsteps in the hall—

Benny, in the doorway. "Miss Bailey, Miss Prince. The Duke of St. Albans."

"Yes," Rosaline managed, stamping down the urge to charge into the hall. "Send him in."

The Duke came striding into the room, and something inside

her melted. He was windswept, his breeches spattered with mud, his hair wild, his face alive with energy. His gaze found hers at once and the corner of his mouth twitched — it was small, but it was enough.

"Ladies." The Duke nodded at Charlotte, Rosaline, and Mrs. Randolph in turn. "Mrs. Randolph. How are you on this fine day?"

She seemed to quiver. "Very— very well, Your Grace, you are much too kind to inquire—"

"Not at all," he replied. "You must forgive my abrupt entrance, but I find myself in something of a hurry."

"Oh?" Mrs. Randolph looked from him to Rosaline and back again. "I suppose it is understandable, given the... situation—"

"Perhaps," the Duke quickly said. "But I believe I left something here the other day, something important. Something I need to give to Miss Bailey." And he looked right at her and winked.

Rosaline nodded, slipping her hand into her pocket. She slid her thumb through the band of the ring, then gave a swift jerk, breaking the stitch holding it in place. No one had noticed a thing — she used her thumb to push the ring onto her fourth finger and took her hand back out of her pocket. "Yes," she said, closing the distance between them. "I believe I found it, Your Grace." And she reached out for his hand, allowing the ring to catch the light.

Charlotte actually gasped, clapping her hand over her mouth. Mrs. Randolph stared at Rosaline's hand, going very red, then very pale.

"Ah," she managed. "Ah... what a... what a beautiful..."

And with that, Mrs. Randolph slumped onto the floor in a dead faint.

For a moment, Rosaline, Charlotte, and the Duke could only share a startled, horrified look. Then, as one, all three of them burst into action.

"Quick, Rosaline, there are smelling salts in the desk—"

"Would it be so terrible?" Rosaline hissed, tapping Mrs.

Randolph's flat, lifeless cheeks. "If we were to leave her to revive herself?"

"No," Charlotte replied, sliding a cushion beneath Mrs. Randolph's head. "In fact, I am sure half the staff would applaud us. But if my father were to hear of it—"

"I have an idea." The Duke met their gazes. "And I think it might buy you both some goodwill from our dear Dragon."

"Then do it," said Rosaline. "Whatever it is, do it at once—"

"Very well. Fetch me the smelling salts."

Rosaline obeyed, and when she handed them over, the Duke looked up at her from where he knelt beside Mrs. Randolph's head. "I want you to know," he said, "that I love you very, very much, and do this only for the sake of—"

"Just do it, Hal!"

He cleared his throat, and, to her simultaneous horror and delight, braced his arm beneath Mrs. Randolph's shoulders, propping her up against his leg. He uncapped the jar of salts, and held it beneath her nose.

It took only a few moments. Mrs. Randolph twitched, then shuddered and blinked awake. "Oh!" She stared up at the Duke, who was smiling at her as if she'd just won the Derby, and seemed to nearly faint again. "Oh, Your Grace—!"

"Welcome back." His voice was rich, amused. "You gave us all quite a fright."

Charlotte gripped Rosaline's hand hard enough to stop the blood. Rosaline herself was having a difficult time containing a spasm of hysterical laughter.

"Oh, I—" Mrs. Randolph could not look away from him. "You are too kind, I do suffer from the occasional nervous complaint. It is no matter... no matter at all, I find it soon passes... though it does feel quite odd, such strange spasms and flutterings all over my body..."

"It is no trouble," he replied. "You did have rather a shock just then."

"Yes, I— Yes, I did..." Mrs. Randolph finally seemed to remember that she and the Duke were not alone. Her head wobbled, as if on a stick, as she turned to look at Rosaline and Charlotte. Her gaze fastened on Rosaline's left hand, and her face flushed red again. "I would never have dreamt— it is such a beautiful jewel, Your Grace—"

"Lady Charlotte will fetch you a glass of water," said the Duke. Charlotte obeyed at once, flying out of the room, but Rosaline caught the unmistakable sound of a stifled snort.

"Yes," said Rosaline, biting her tongue. "Yes, a glass of water is just what you need. Or perhaps you'd like a cup of tea, Mrs. Randolph?"

But Randolph was not paying attention to a word Rosaline said. She was staring at the Duke, her eyes glassy and reminiscent of a puppy. "Such a gentleman," she murmured, bringing a hand to her ample bosom. "Such a lovely, caring gentleman—"

The Duke chuckled. "You flatter me, my good lady. But perhaps we should move you to a more comfortable location?"

"Oh, I would not dream of imposing upon you like that, Your Grace—"

"Nonsense." The Duke shot Rosaline a pointed look, and she knelt beside Mrs. Randolph, taking her by the arm. "Now," said the Duke. "On three—"

It took some effort, and lots of slow, careful steps, but together, Rosaline and the Duke managed to get Mrs. Randolph onto the nearest sofa. "Thank you, Your Grace," simpered Mrs. Randolph, "thank you—"

"What good timing," said the Duke loudly as the door opened. "Here is Lady Charlotte with your water—"

Charlotte appeared, glass in hand, her face conspicuously red. She said nothing as she handed the glass to Mrs. Randolph, and the moment she rejoined Rosaline, Rosaline swatted at her arm. "Pull yourself together," she hissed, and Charlotte trembled, a wheeze catching in her throat.

"Thank you, my dear!" Mrs. Randolph sipped at her water, her gaze still wandering to Rosaline's left hand. "I feel quite refreshed."

"Nonetheless," said the Duke, "the ladies and I should leave you to your rest, and I myself have an appointment with my tailor. Seems he wants to fit me for a rather matrimonial suit."

Rosaline's heart leapt into her throat, and Mrs. Randolph let out a little gasp. "Oh, yes, it is all terribly exciting — we shall have to have Miss Bailey taken to the modiste right away — Oh, there is so much to plan, so many invitations, so many details—"

As if sensing danger, Charlotte's hand curled into Rosaline's skirts and she began to gently pull Rosaline towards the door, away from the sofa.

"Then I bid you a very good afternoon, Mrs. Randolph, and a swift recovery." The Duke cleared his throat and turned to Charlotte and Rosaline. "If the ladies might show me out?"

"Of course, Your Grace," said Charlotte, and she tugged Rosaline out of the room, the Duke hot on their heels.

When they were in the foyer, with the door to the Blue Room safely shut behind them, Charlotte and Rosaline surrendered, bursting into silent laughter.

"Hal," wheezed Rosaline, bent double, tears in her eyes. "That was wonderful—"

"Such a *gentleman*," gushed Charlotte, in a near-perfect imitation of Mrs. Randolph's saccharine voice. "Truly, never met another one like you—"

"Calm yourselves," said the Duke, but he was grinning. "It worked, did it not?"

"Perhaps too well, Your Grace." Rosaline struggled for breath. "You shall find yourself with another admirer."

"Fiend." The Duke pressed a kiss to her forehead.

Meanwhile, Charlotte had slumped against the wall, her face the color of a tomato as she fought for air. Benny chose this perfect moment to appear.

"What's happened?" He looked from Charlotte to Rosaline and back again. "What on earth's the matter?"

"Please escort Lady Charlotte to the kitchen," said the Duke. "She's had a bit of a shock, nothing that a splash of brandy won't cure."

Benny nodded, taking Charlotte by the arm. As they made their way down the hall, Rosaline simpered, "Such strange spasms and flutterings all over me—"

The Duke shook his head, wrapping an arm around her middle. "If you do not watch your tongue," he murmured into her ear, "I shall give you spasms and flutterings of another kind entirely."

A jolt of heat whipped through Rosaline's stomach, bringing her back to earth. She managed a coy smile, wrapping her arm around him in turn. "Why, Your Grace, we are not even married yet—"

He let out a sigh. "Do not remind me."

"Then allow me to spare your sanity..." She stepped out of his embrace and reached for her purse, which she'd left on the table in the entryway. After checking that they were indeed alone, she took out a small, wooden object. "The modiste is next door to a toy shop. I could not resist. Do you think Jamie would like it?"

He looked down at the horse figurine and smiled. "He would. Though I'm afraid you'll have to wait to give it to him until after the wedding."

"Oh." Rosaline frowned at him. "He returned to the country so soon?"

The Duke nodded. "I never keep him in London longer than necessary."

"I see." Rosaline returned the figurine to her purse and tied it shut. "Just as well, the horse was only one part of a much larger set."

The Duke's smile widened and he shook his head. "You will spoil him rotten."

"Not rotten," she smiled back. "But just enough."

The Duke quickly glanced down the hall, then swooped in and kissed her. Rosaline sighed into his mouth, slipping her fingers between his jacket and his shirt. His body was deliciously warm through the fabric — enough to make her melt.

"I wish I could stay." Hal pressed a kiss to her jaw, her cheek. "But my tailor is on the warpath."

"Seams and buttons do not sew themselves, Your Grace."

"The devil seems far too keen to see me wed." He gave a rueful sigh and pulled away, straightening his glasses. "Lots of talk about how formidable she must be."

"Who?"

"The woman who won me over." He kissed her cheek again. "Now, off with you."

Rosaline sighed, then remembered something very important. "Charlotte had the idea of us getting married on the same day, and sharing the reception. What do you think?"

"I think," said the Duke, pulling on his riding gloves, "that if we had more people like Lady Charlotte running the government, Napoleon's reign would have ended before it began."

She grinned. "Is that a yes?"

"Of course." He captured her hand, squeezed it. "Whatever you like best, Rosaline."

She sighed again, but with exaggeration. "What I would like best is to blow past all of this nonsense and run away to Alban Hollow."

"Do not tempt me. I have a fresh horse." He squeezed her hand again. "Until tomorrow?"

"Yes," she said, even if it seemed an eternity away. "Until tomorrow."

✺ 33 ✺

Madam Kensington's High Society Papers, No. 42

Goodness me, my dears, it seems we have left the rough and stormy seas and found ourselves in the balmy Bay of Love! I am certain you all know who we may credit for the sudden change of outlook — who among us could ignore the Tempest as it swept through the town, flapping our sails and forcing our eye? True, some considered the Tempest to be quite a good omen, a sign that the Overlooked might steal their chance, might step into the light and make their bid for one of the most generous titles in the land. But it was not meant to last — the Tempest blew over almost as soon as it appeared, settling quite happily into the fine lines of matrimony and questions of lace and *hors d'oeuvres*. One can only hope that it will be smooth sailing from here on out.

You may be wondering, my darling readers, why I can speak on these matters with such confidence. Why, anyone who had happened to pass through Kensington Gardens yesterday after-noon would have to be quite the imbecile to miss the delightful, open-air picnic beside the pond, not to mention the Accessories featured at the table. One could see them — particularly the fresh, azure addition — from at least fifty feet away. They dazzle, they blind, and they match our Star and Sapphire so wonderfully it does make one wonder if, perhaps, our Suitors are rather more clever than they might appear...

৩৵৩

"YES, LILIES, I THINK, AND TULIPS, AND ROSES, PILES OF ROSES— and of course there must be peonies, though Rosaline would prefer a bouquet of—"

"Charlotte," said Rosaline, unable to hold back a smile. "You must occasionally take a breath."

"This is one of few moments where I actually agree with Miss Bailey," said Mrs. Randolph. "You cannot allow your excitement to overtake your sensibility."

Charlotte scoffed, but continued to smile and twirl around the room. From the armchair, Oberon watched her with a level of attention he usually reserved for flies and mice. "What use is there in sensibility when our weddings are but two weeks away? There is still so much to decide—"

"True enough," Rosaline replied, feeling a sudden jolt of nerves. Not that she could change anything; the marriage licenses were acquired, Katherine was set to march down her own aisle in two days' time, and Rosaline had even gotten the Duke to express an opinion on his preferred flavor of cake. The madness, it seemed, would only continue. "At least we do not have to worry about hosting the reception, Charlotte."

Cadogan's great aunt, the Dowager Countess of Lichfield, had taken to the idea of a shared wedding in remarkable stride. Within days, she had sent out a new flurry of invitations, doubled the menu, and hired an extra dozen wait staff. She had also insisted upon meeting Rosaline, which was an afternoon tea that Rosaline would not likely forget anytime soon.

The Dowager Countess of Lichfield was as tiny as her great-nephew was tall, and they shared the same warm brown eyes. Though unlike Cadogan, the Dowager's gaze was sharp, merciless beneath her thin, wrinkled eyelids.

After half an hour, she'd looked Rosaline dead in the eye and said, "You are more than a match for him. The Duke, I mean."

Rosaline's mouth had gone dry. "My lady, you flatter me—"

"He shall have his hands full with you." The Dowager's eyebrow twitched. "And I think you have plans, yes? You know what it means to be a Duchess, what you will be able to build."

Rosaline nodded. "Yes."

"Good." The Dowager thumped the end of her cane on the floor. "I look forward to seeing you at the helm of Alban Hollow."

And that had marked the end of their brief introduction.

Now, as the days grew shorter and shorter, as the fateful date itself approached, Rosaline could not help feeling as if she were floating on a cloud, destined to watch the insanity unspool around her, seeing but not touching, guided from step to step, choice to choice.

Then, a carriage sounded on the drive. A large carriage, with two footmen.

"Good Heavens." Mrs. Randolph went to the window. "I do not recognize it. Were we expecting—?"

Rosaline looked to Charlotte, who shook her head. "No," said Rosaline. "We were not."

The horses sputtering, the footman's feet on the gravel, a knock at the front door. The turn of the lock, the squeal of the hinge, Benny's low, patient voice, sounding first in the foyer, then at the door to the Blue Room.

"Miss Bailey." There was something different, something wary, in his face. "You have visitors. From the noble house of ——."

Rosaline's blood went searing cold. The room around her became very quiet.

Charlotte turned to stare at her. "Your mother's—?"

Rosaline nodded, clasping her hands together to keep them from shaking. "What is it they want, Benny?"

"An audience, Miss Bailey. With you."

Rosaline forced herself to take a slow breath, then nodded again. "Very well. I will see them in the drawing room. There is no need to call for tea, they will not be staying long."

"Miss Bailey!" Mrs. Randolph's reproach was hesitant, for once — even for her, these were untested waters. "This is your family. You must extend even—"

"They are my relatives, Mrs. Randolph," Rosaline corrected her. "Not my family. After you, Benny." And without a second look, she swept from the room.

Once she was in the drawing room, running a practiced eye over its surfaces, checking for dust, for tears, for anything out of place, Rosaline allowed herself a single moment of panic. She had no idea — had not heard from them since the funeral, not since going to France. She could hardly remember her grandmother — the cold, imperious woman who had never so much as entertained the idea of love — or her aunts and their snide, thin noses. She could, however, remember the names they had called her father when he wasn't in the room.

"You," she whispered to her reflection in the window, "are stronger than they are." And with that, she turned at the sound of Benny in the doorway.

"Miss Bailey." He looked uneasy and worried all at once. "May I present the Duchess of —— and her daughters, the Viscountess ——, the Baroness ——, and the Lady ——."

"Thank you, Benny."

He stepped to the side, and behind him came Rosaline's worst nightmare.

First was her grandmother, a tall, stately, elderly woman with opaque white hair, a classical nose, and a dark, intimidating gaze. She looked Rosaline up and down, her expression impassive. Rosaline's aunts filed in behind her, each one coated in fine silk and a tasteful amount of jewels, looking much as they had the last time she'd seen them; age had tried and failed to touch them. Each carried an echo of her mother's face, but none of her mother's kindness.

"*Grandmother.*" Rosaline dipped into a deep curtsy, dropping her gaze. "*Aunt Céline. Aunt Gabrielle. Aunt Aubergine.*"

"*Must you insist upon using that vile nickname?*" said her grandmother in French, her voice just as dry and sharp as Rosaline remembered. "*At least you still speak French, though with a very provincial accent—*"

"*Would you care to sit down?*" said Rosaline, straightening up. "*Though perhaps not. I cannot imagine you will be staying long.*"

"*Insolent girl.*" Her grandmother's eyes sparkled. "*How dare you address me in such a manner?*"

"*She always had her father's ill temper,*" chimed Aunt Gabrielle. Her black hair gleamed in the light from the windows. "*Is it any surprise?*"

"*We will take a seat, thank you.*" Her grandmother took the nearest armchair, and her aunts took the sofa. Seeing them sit together in a row rather reminded Rosaline of a line of pigeons. "*We are here to congratulate you,*" her grandmother went on, "*on your upcoming nuptials.*"

This threw Rosaline for all of two seconds. Then, she recovered, smiled, and sat down opposite her grandmother. "*How very kind of you.*"

"*Yes, we were all surprised to hear the news. No one ever expected you to make such a match, let alone to such an old and noble family.*" Something like warmth crept into her tone. "*It is a remarkable achievement, even for a ——.*"

"*We were also surprised not to receive an invitation.*" This came from Aunt Céline, the eldest of the three. Her neck was so long and thin it rather reminded Rosaline of a praying mantis. "*Surely you can agree that this would be a mistake worth rectifying.*"

"*I did not invite you,*" replied Rosaline, "*because I assumed you would not care to come.*"

"*You see, Mother?*" Aunt Aubergine's lip curled. "*It is just as I told you. She has no respect, no regard at all for our family.*"

Her grandmother ignored this. "*Why would you assume that, my dear?*"

"*Because I had not heard from you in over a decade. And I must admit,*" Rosaline added, steeling herself, "*that I am surprised to see you now.*"

"*This is the beauty of weddings,*" her grandmother replied. "*They bridge divides, reignite old friendships. They remind one... of a sense of duty.*"

A brief silence fell, and Rosaline held her grandmother's gaze, her mind churning as it calculated, adjusted, and calculated again. "*There is no need,*" she eventually said, "*to make such a pretense about friendship and duty. I know the true reason you came here today.*"

A dangerous little smirk flitted across her grandmother's face. "*And what is that?*"

"*All you have ever cared about, Grandmother, all you have ever truly cared about, is the family's reputation, and what you can do to further increase your own power, your prestige, your foothold in this country. To you, my alliance with the Cunningham family is just another opportunity, and one that comes with a sizable inheritance.*"

"*Bite your tongue!*" spat Aunt Gabrielle. "*How dare you—!*"

"*This is the height of insult.*" Aunt Aubergine seemed to swell, her cheeks gaining the color that had lent her her famous nickname.

"*To think that you would speak this way to your own family,*" said Aunt Céline, her voice brittle. "*Your mother's only surviving relatives—*"

Her grandmother did not react, but held up a hand, silencing the others. "*You give your opinion quite readily and assuredly for such a young woman. This arrogance, no doubt, is the result of your father's influence."*

"And because I inherited my mother's mind, her ability to think for herself. You must realize that you have played a very obvious hand — why else would you be interested in me now, when you've been all too content to ignore my existence for years? The answer is obvious — power, and money, two things that your family always needs." Rosaline paused for breath, her heart thudding in her chest. *"You are guests in this country, and you know that if you were to return to France, you would risk your lives. You have to do whatever it takes to secure your position, and what better way of doing that then entwining yourselves with every noble family in Britain? An alliance with me would only further cement your position, would only bring you closer to the throne.*

"You think yourself entitled to my friendship, my regard, perhaps even my inheritance. But you forget that I am no longer a little girl you can chastise and send from the room. You can control me no more than you could control my mother, who built a beautiful, incredible life in spite of your disapproval." Rosaline stood up. *"And now, I must ask you to leave."*

A ringing silence fell. Her grandmother and aunts all stared at her, mute with astonishment and, she was certain, horror. After several long, tense moments, her grandmother stood up and gave her a cold look.

"News of our reception today will not reflect kindly upon you, Rosaline. Is that how you mean to begin your tenure as Duchess?"

"Rumor is a pipe blown by surmises, jealousies, and conjectures." Rosaline raised an eyebrow. "Anyone can play upon it, and its music says more about the composer than the subject." She lowered her voice and switched back to French. *"Do not forget, grandmother, that my father and I inherited all of my mother's files and letters upon her death. It would be a shame if the Queen were to learn what certain members of the peerage had said about her favorite Physician, and to what lengths they may have gone to try to sabotage his career."*

Here, finally, a reaction. Her grandmother's face twitched, and something ugly, something bestial, flickered through her expression. She turned to her daughters. "Come. We must depart. These insults are not to be borne."

All three of them stood up, flashing Rosaline looks of utter contempt. Her grandmother led them from the room, and they each filed out behind her. Then, to Rosaline's astonishment, Céline stopped and turned to her, flashing her a genuine smile.

"*Congratulations, Rosaline. You will make a beautiful bride, and a wonderful Duchess.*" She pressed something small and cold into Rosaline's hand. "*It was your mother's. She would want you to have it.*" Then she was gone, disappearing from the room, and a few moments later, Rosaline heard the front door open and close, followed by the distant clatter of the carriage.

Heart thumping, Rosaline looked down at the object in her hand, a wave of emotion building in her chest. It was a silver rattle, intricately carved, its handle dented on one side. She smiled, unable to shake the image of her mother as an infant, banging the rattle on a table or a chair in her determination to be heard.

So it seemed that at least one of her aunts had something resembling a heart. Rosaline filed away the information for later thought, slipped the rattle into her pocket, and left the room.

❧

"OUCH, CHARLOTTE! THAT WAS MY FOOT—"

"Sorry, sorry, I cannot see for—"

"You have a *candle*, Charlotte—"

"*Mon Dieu*," said Lisette, once they managed to get Rosaline's bedroom door open. She was standing by the changing screen, unimpressed. "You two are like bulls in an elephant shop."

Charlotte staggered in, Rosaline just behind. Charlotte was giggling. "She found us!"

"You are not nearly as quiet as you think." Lisette raised an eyebrow at them. "I can see it was a merry reception."

"Yes," said Rosaline, stifling a hiccup. Her face was very warm, and she could not feel her feet. "Mrs. Knight throws an excellent party."

This was perhaps a severe understatement. It was one of the best parties Rosaline had attended during her entire time in London. Everything — the food, the wine, the guests, the music — had been of the best quality, but not ostentatious. Katherine's brothers were quite practiced in the art of entertainment, and were nothing short of superb hosts. In many ways, the reception had been a very casual affair, where gaiety and laughter ruled the halls, overlooking the conventional boundaries of station and etiquette.

The wedding, in contrast, had been stuffy and dull. Though Rosaline had recognized the glimmer of friendship, of warmth, between Katherine and Mr. Heath. Happiness, it seemed, was to be a part of their equation, even if it was for a more complicated reason than usual.

It had been impossible, of course, not to spend the entire ceremony imagining her own wedding. Rosaline had run the pad of her thumb across the band of her engagement ring over and over again, wondering what it would be like to stand at an identical altar before a God she did not believe in, making an oath that would change her life forever. It was a daunting, though not frightening, prospect. When once she had feared marriage and all its potential constraints, now she was excited for it, ready beyond words to leap into this next great adventure.

At the reception, Rosaline had set aside propriety in favor of eating her way through several helpings of *canapés* and *hors d'oeuvres*, furnished by countless healthy measures of wine (encouraged in part by the Duke, who seemed to delight in getting her to giggle). She had even consumed a reasonable portion of a sumptuous wedding cake that, she feared, would put her own to shame.

And the dancing. Hours upon hours of dancing, even though now, Rosaline could hardly remember when she'd had the time for it, between greeting the reams of guests and keeping one eye on Katherine, who was easily overwhelmed by the attention.

Then, of course, there had been the moment of reckoning, just when Charlotte had raised a fresh glass of wine to her lips.

"—yes, apparently this was quite a banner day for the young ladies of London," Katherine's aunt was saying, loud enough to be heard by half the room. "Not just one wedding, but two! The other being a Lady Alwyn to a Lord Oswalt, a most sumptuous specimen—"

Charlotte inhaled half her wine just as Rosaline's heart bounced into her mouth. She quickly let out a loud, false sneeze, to cover Charlotte's spluttering. The Duke stared at both of them, utterly bemused, as half the room turned to look at the source of the extraordinary noise.

"My apologies," Rosaline said quickly, her face burning, and gave another terrific sneeze. "It must be— the flowers—"

With that, she seized hold of Charlotte's arm and pulled her into the next room, the Duke a step behind. Katherine had watched them leave, a glimmer of panic evident in her expression.

"Oh, my Lord—" Charlotte was trembling, a smear of wine in the corner of her mouth. "It was Rebecca the whole time—"

Rosaline nodded, then shook her head. "I know, Charlotte, but we cannot—"

The Duke was frowning. "What on earth are you talking about?"

But there was no time — they were already being approached by two more of Katherine's aunts. "Later," Rosaline murmured, then brushed a kiss to his stubbled cheek. He met her gaze, his eyes bright with interest, then nodded, putting on a fresh smile.

In that moment, she'd realized that they'd already begun to develop their own personal vocabulary, a way of speaking to each other without saying a single word.

Now, Lisette came over to Rosaline and Charlotte. "How was Lucas Knight? Did he behave?"

"Hardly." Rosaline began to giggle and Charlotte snorted, leaning back against the wall. "But the Duke was very gallant. He was determined to protect me."

"I am not surprised." Lisette bent down and tugged off Rosaline's shoes. "Come, we must get you changed."

Rosaline glanced down at her, wobbling as fresh blood rushed to her toes. "Why the hurry?"

Lisette met her gaze. "Because, my girls, very soon, you both will be wed. And before that happens, there are some things you need to know." With that, she moved on to Charlotte's feet.

Rosaline and Charlotte traded a glance, their giggles evaporating into thin air. "What do you mean, Lis?" said Rosaline.

"I mean," said Lisette, "that this could well be the last time I get you both alone, without that awful Dragon breathing down my neck." She pulled off Charlotte's shoes and Charlotte stumbled, setting the candle down hard on Rosaline's dresser. "I must take advantage of it."

"To do what?" Rosaline was frowning. "Lis, it is late, we are both well into our cups—"

"Precisely." Lisette straightened up and faced them both, arms akimbo, expression bright with determination. "That is the best time to discuss matters of the marriage bed."

Charlotte let out a very strange sound, then clapped her hand to her mouth. Rosaline, meanwhile, had gone as red as a beet.

"Lis," she tried. "Surely that is not necessary—"

Lisette snorted. "Maybe not for you, *ma chère*, but certainly for this one." She gave them both a stern look. "There are things you need to know, things that a creature like Randolph would never dream of mentioning. Things of pleasure, of satisfaction, that have nothing to do with child-making, and everything to do with taking what *you* want. With knowing your body as well as your lover's."

Charlotte once again made her very strange sound, and Rosaline felt a funny jolt around her middle. Suddenly, her mind was awash with all the moments she'd stolen with the Duke, when she'd wanted him to reach and keep reaching, touching parts of her that had never been touched. Her mind returned to the dull, wet, keen ache between her legs that had persisted for weeks, which even her own hand could not fully satisfy in the dark, quiet depths of the night, leaving her yearning, wanting more.

"Fine." Rosaline swallowed and nudged Charlotte towards the changing screen. "Come on. Let's get it over with."

And as she slipped out of her stockings, Rosaline could not help feeling thankful that once again, Lisette could be brave enough for all of them.

❄ 34 ❄

Later, when Rosaline thought back to her and Charlotte's wedding day, she found that she remembered little of the ceremonies, and even the morning of was a bit of a blur.

She'd hardly slept at all and was too nervous to eat breakfast, much to Lisette's chagrin and in spite of several dire warnings in brittle, humorless French. Finally, after a few hours of preparations, Rosaline found it within herself to scarf down a bit of toast and a single soft-boiled egg. But even this small amount of food twisted and curdled in her stomach as she was draped in her maid of honor gown.

"So beautiful," sobbed Mrs. Randolph from the corner. Charlotte and Rosaline exchanged a wide, alarmed glance. "My lovely girls, what a joy to see you—"

Charlotte's ceremony would occur first, followed by a quick costume change, then Rosaline's ceremony. Madam D'Amboise had had a stroke of her usual genius. She'd prepared them both a set of new, unique petticoats that fit the silhouette of both their wedding gown and their maid of honor gown. All Rosaline and

Charlotte had to do was step into a nearby chamber and switch their outer layer. Perhaps, Rosaline reflected, this was a lot of show for the space of a mere hour, but, she thought, as she faced herself in the mirror, it did not matter. It was what she and Charlotte wanted, and after all, it would look rather ridiculous to have two women dressed in white before the altar.

When Charlotte took her vows, she cried. So did Rosaline, and even Lord Devon looked rather watery. Sir Ian gripped Lord Devon's shoulder, his mouth twisted with emotion. Across the aisle, Lord Blackwood was grinning, and beside him, the Dowager Countesses McDunn and Lichfield were watching with twin, enigmatic smiles. When the registration had been signed, the small congregation burst into furious applause, and Cadogan kissed his bride, his smile as bright as the sun.

Then, for the first time since their arrival, Rosaline caught the Duke's gaze. He was grinning, then he let out a whistle, and he winked at her. *Soon*, he seemed to say. *Soon, this will be us.*

Once they were alone, Rosaline took Charlotte's hand, her mouth numb, and said, "How does it feel, Charlotte?"

"Magical," Charlotte whispered, her face bright with joy. "Utterly magical."

For the first time in her life, Lisette fumbled with Rosaline's dress. She muffled a sob, then threw her arms around Rosaline, managing a feeble, "*Ma chère*—"

"*I know*," Rosaline whispered back, clinging to her, and for a moment, the years disappeared, and she was twelve again, burying her face in Lisette's chest on one of those long, miserable nights when she could hardly breathe for grief. "*But I will always be the same, Lisette, nothing will change*—"

"*Some things will change*," Lisette corrected her with a smile. "*But not the important things.*"

When Rosaline stepped out of the chamber, her father turned to her, and a deep, unfiltered emotion flickered across his face. He took an unsteady, shuddering breath, and, to her horror, clapped a hand to his mouth, tears shining in his eyes.

"Oh, Father—" She gripped his arm, put a hand to his shoulder. "He is a very good man—"

"No, that isn't—" Sir Ian took a forceful breath. "I just— I wish she could see you—"

Emotion welled thick in Rosaline's throat, and she blinked away tears as she nodded. "I know. I do, too. But I think she is here, don't you? Watching through the stained glass?"

Sir Ian nodded, smiling, brushing away a loose tear. "You are right. She is always here." He looked her in the eye, tucked her hand into the crook of his arm. "Well, Honeybee. Shall we?"

And when the music swelled, when she took her first step into the aisle, Rosaline watched as the Duke — as *Hal* — turned to look at her, and his face erupted into a wide, beautiful grin, shining and elated, and she could not help beaming back at him, her body exploding with joy.

She felt the whisper of her veil as her father lifted it away, the brief kiss he pressed to her cheek before he stepped aside. Then, her world narrowed to the nearby warmth of the Duke's body, mere inches away, the curve of his smile, which she could see even in her periphery. And she did not hear a single word of the sermon.

But when it came time to speak her vows, she did so in a clear, unwavering voice, holding the Duke's gaze, pouring all of her devotion, all of her love, into the few, simple words. And he drank them in, seeming to hear the unsaid, squeezing her hand as he returned the favor, his voice rich and equally steady, enveloping her in a cloud of sanctity, clarity.

Her new ring was simple, cold, delightful against her skin. And when she slid his ring home, the Duke grinned down at his own hand, almost as if he could not believe it was happening.

The next thing Rosaline remembered was signing the register, getting a splash of ink on her fingers as she ceased forever to be Rosaline Bailey and became instead Rosaline Cunningham, the Duchess of St. Albans.

Then, the church exploded with cheers, but she felt, heard, saw very little of it. She had eyes only for the Duke, for Hal, for her *husband*, as he pressed his mouth to her hand and whispered, "Here we go."

৩৯৩

THE RECEPTION WAS ABSOLUTE CHAOS. ROSALINE FELT AS IF SHE were watching it all from a distance, as she smiled and greeted person after person, people she had seen but never met, names that were familiar but not well known. It seemed that everyone in London had merited an invitation, and Cadogan's great aunt had been all too willing to oblige.

But she hardly noticed the stares, the smiles, the occasional jealous looks. Her awareness was limited to the sparse inch between the Duke's arm and her own, the occasional brush of his elbow against hers. Occasionally, her thoughts would drift to the inevitable moment that they would be alone, fully alone, and she would shiver with anticipation.

She watched as her father, Lord Blackwood, and the Dowager Countess McDunn drank, spoke, and laughed together in a small, exclusive corner of the enormous room. She had a brief hope that her father would not embarrass her too terribly, but then was distracted by the arrival of a very familiar Rodent.

"The new Mr. and Mrs. Cunningham." Martel's smirk could cut glass. "What a delight."

"Behave," the Duke chided him.

"When have I not?" Martel returned, then he turned to the person beside him. "I do not believe you've been formally introduced. Duchess, this is my wife, Lady Martel."

She was stunning as ever, still dressed in that signature

emerald green, and her dark head bobbed as she curtsied. "An honor, Your Grace."

Something trembled in Rosaline's stomach — she still was not used to her new title. "Likewise, Lady Martel."

"Congratulations to you both," Lady Martel replied. "I do hope we can look forward to many splendid *soirées* at Alban Hollow."

"Perhaps," the Duke replied. "The ballroom has been gathering dust."

Lady Martel gave a light, trilling chuckle. "But now, Your Grace, you have something to celebrate. And that makes all the difference."

"And do not think," added Martel, "that I've forgotten about that wine cellar of yours."

The Duke nodded. "I'll have to drag you out feet-first."

Martel smirked. "Good to know we have an understanding. Duke, Duchess." He inclined his head once again, then he and his wife drifted into the crowd.

"We have many interesting supper parties in our future," the Duke murmured in Rosaline's ear, making her shiver. Then he leaned away, swiping a handful of *canapés* from a passing tray. "God, I am famished."

"Me, too," said Rosaline, startled by the sudden realization. She stole two of his *canapés*. "I've hardly eaten a thing today."

His glance was sharp, knowing. "Nervous?"

"Perhaps," she allowed, making quick work of one of the *canapés*. Thankfully, they'd reached a break in the guests.

"So was I," the Duke replied, somewhat to her surprise. He turned away again, swiping two glasses of champagne and handing one to her. "I'll have to see if I can bribe one of the footmen to bring me something more potable." He winced down at his glass, then drained it in one go.

Rosaline watched, delighted. "Steady on—"

"Lousy stuff." But the Duke traded his empty glass for a full one. "Whose idea was it?"

"The French," she replied. "A group of Benedictine monks, I believe."

The Duke nodded, draining his glass again. "I'll have to have a word with them."

"Will you?" Rosaline sipped her own champagne — it was a good one, in spite of the Duke's censure. "I'd love to see that."

He smiled at her, his eyes shining in the reflected light of the chandeliers, and she could not help smiling back, her stomach fuzzy with joy.

And then, she remembered that they were husband and wife.

Rosaline leaned in, mere inches from his ear. "How long must we stay?"

The Duke let out a low chuckle. "Another hour, at least. And if you think we can make a quiet exit—"

"Why not?" she countered, her gaze flitting across the room to where Lord and Lady Cadogan were holding court. They seemed to float on air, London's Golden Couple, laughing and shining in the wide circle of guests. "They are the center of attention, not us."

The Duke raised an eyebrow. "You do us a disservice, Duchess. But in this particular matter, I do not think I mind."

She grinned, feeling a keen jolt of *something* at hearing her title on his lips. "Though I would like a piece of cake."

He gave an exaggerated groan. "I will make you a cake with my own two hands, Rosaline, if it means we can get to the carriage—"

"Such agreeable terms." Rosaline leaned in, brushed a kiss to his cheek. "Escaping this party. You, covered in flour, wearing only an apron."

To her utter delight, the Duke flushed red and turned to stare at her, stunned. Then, he shifted so that he was standing just behind her, his hand at her waist and his mouth hot at her ear. "Fiend."

"And legally yours," she replied, flashing her ring at him as she took another sip of champagne. It was a welcome distraction from the heat tingling down her back. She looked across the vast room and sighed. "Very well. *Canapés*, then the rounds, then we—"

"Sneak away," he murmured, brushing a kiss to her neck. "With a bottle of wine."

"Not champagne," Rosaline added, reaching for the nearest footman. She flashed him a smile. "Be a dear and leave the tray."

The poor man stared at her for a moment, then nodded, handing the tray of *canapés* to the Duke. The Duke shook his head and smiled. "I will never be bored."

"No, dear husband," Rosaline replied, taking three *canapés*. "You will not."

As they made their way around the room, stopping and speaking to everyone they were expected to stop and speak to, Rosaline noticed, perhaps more than she ever had before, the difference between the Duke as she knew him and the Duke as the rest of London knew him. He trod the thin line between geniality and detachment, haughty and approachable all at once. Too quickly, she recognized the shades she had seen on display the first night they'd met, the coldness that often threatened to bury the rest of his nature, and she saw it for what it was — a defense mechanism, borne, perhaps, of inheriting his title so young, of always fearing that someone was trying to get something out of him. Of feeling a need to keep everyone at a distance, to protect the unseen ward at his side from every possible threat.

Rosaline understood him, now. And she did her best to balance it, smiling and laughing, softening where he remained unyielding. And it seemed to work.

Some time later, she felt a hand on her shoulder. Rosaline turned, and found herself faced with none other than Lord Blackwood. He was smiling.

"Hal," he said, "might I steal your delightful wife for a moment?"

Something interesting showed in the Duke's expression — apprehension.

Lord Blackwood scoffed. "Come along, I promise to behave."

"All right." But the Duke still seemed reluctant. He kissed her on the cheek. "I'll go see about that bottle of wine."

Lord Blackwood watched his godson depart. "I have never seen him so happy, you know."

Rosaline blushed. "You exaggerate."

His glance was sharp. "Not in the least. I could not have imagined a better match for him."

"Lord Blackwood," she began, "you flatter me—"

"Your reputation precedes you, Duchess, as does your father's good word. And not just anybody can get away with interrupting the Queen." His smile had turned into a smirk. "I look forward to us spending more time together. It will be good to have another reader in the family."

She smiled. "Yes, I look forward to it."

"Stop hogging the Duchess, Lord Blackwood." The Dowager Countess McDunn swept in with her usual faint smile. "It is terribly poor form. Congratulations are in order, I think, Duchess."

"Thank you, my Lady." Rosaline bowed her head.

"All's well that ends well, my dear." The Dowager twinkled. "After your honeymoon, you must come to the country house. My library is even larger than the one at Alban Hollow."

Rosaline's skin tingled. "I would enjoy that immensely, Lady McDunn."

The Dowager leaned in, dropping her voice. "And if you were to sneak away now, Lord Blackwood and I would provide a most acceptable distraction."

Rosaline took her hand, feeling a rush of relief. "Oh, thank you— thank you—"

"Not at all, my dear, and your father is waiting by the door."

With that, the Dowager and Lord Blackwood turned away, then began a loud discussion about the Exchequer, drawing the attention of half the room. Rosaline slipped away, darting through the crowd until she reached—

"Charlotte!" Rosaline squeezed her hand. "The Duke and I are leaving—"

"Oh, yes!" Charlotte smiled at her. "Get away while you can!"

"You do not mind—?"

Charlotte laughed. "Not at all. This is to be my future, after all. I need the practice."

Rosaline looked at her, at the delightful, odd, clever woman who had become one of her closest, dearest confidants. It was almost impossible to remember the women they'd been just a few months before — they had changed so much, had grown in ways she had not known possible.

And until that moment, she had not realized how much she would miss Charlotte.

"Oh!" Charlotte gave a quiet chuckle and returned Rosaline's sudden embrace, squeezing her tightly. "We will be together again soon—"

"I know." Rosaline pressed a kiss to her cheek. "But I shall miss you, Charlotte."

Charlotte sparkled. "And I you."

"You must tell your husband goodbye from both of us."

"Of course, and the same to yours!"

No one noticed as Rosaline slipped back across the room, stuffing a few *vol-au-vents* into a napkin. Her father was indeed waiting by the door, and he smiled when he saw her. "Quite the right idea, I think."

She sighed and reached for him. "Father—"

"None of that, now." He hugged her. "You have a great journey ahead. And I do not mean just from here to Somerset." When he pulled away, his eyes were shining. "Just promise that you'll write. And come and visit your poor Papa every once in a while."

"Of course!" Rosaline kissed his cheek, fighting back tears. The last time they'd said goodbye, it was in France, when all of this had been but a distant possibility. "And you will come to stay. The Duke insists."

Sir Ian smiled and nodded. "One day." He nudged her towards the hall. "Now go, while you still can."

Rosaline gave him a final wave, then she darted out into the hall, where she nearly ran straight into the Duke, who caught her just in time.

"Good Heavens." He had a fresh bottle of wine in one hand. "Is this to become a habit?"

"We can leave, Hal, they're all covering for us—"

Hal stared at her. "Really?"

Rosaline grinned. "Yes, yes, but we have to leave now, before the guests notice—"

He took her hand at once. "Come on, then."

They darted through the mansion, the sounds of the party echoing around them, following them like invisible shadows. But soon enough, they made it to the front, where the Duke's carriage sat ready and waiting in the cool, early evening air.

"Damn." Hal held up the bottle, panting. "Forgot a corkscrew."

"No matter." Rosaline handed him the *vol-au-vents* and took the bottle. She walked up to the carriage, smiled at the driver, and said, "Fair warning."

With that, she smacked the bottom of the bottle against the side of the carriage. Out popped the cork, followed by a glug of wine. She took a quick swig, then turned to Hal and smiled.

"Christ." He looked a bit dazed. "If I had not already married you—"

"Yes, yes." Rosaline swept up into the carriage. "No time to waste, husband."

"Make haste," Hal said to the driver. "In case they send after us." He leapt into the carriage and slammed the door shut behind him. There was a sudden jolt, and they were off — Rosaline fell into his lap, the wine sloshing onto the floor, and they both burst into laughter, dizzy with their success.

❧ 35 ❧

It is a truth universally acknowledged that one cannot get from London to Somerset in a single night — at least, not in a carriage. Which, of course, Rosaline had known long before her wedding day. The plans had been made quite clear; she and the Duke were to spend the night in a small inn several hours outside of London, then continue on to Alban Hollow in the morning. Lisette had already traveled ahead with the Duke's servants, along with Oberon and the rest of Rosaline's luggage.

These were all facts that Rosaline technically knew. Whether she remembered them was another question entirely.

The carriage rolled to a stop, and the Duke surfaced from her neck.

"Damn." The glow of the lantern outside the inn shone through the windows, highlighting the disastrous scruff of his hair, the wet curve of his mouth. At some point, the first half-dozen buttons on his shirt had come undone. "I'd forgotten."

"Me too." Rosaline was panting, buzzing, a touch sweaty. Her hands were on his bare chest, her nails grazing the fine hair scattered across it.

A loud thump sounded above their heads, followed by the helpful warning of the driver. "We've arrived, Your Grace!"

"Shit." The Duke sat up, scooting away from her. He started fastening his buttons. "I suppose we'd better—"

"Yes.' Rosaline sat up as well, brushing her hair out of her face. It was a lost cause — she pulled out the last few pins, letting her curls spill down her shoulders and over her chest.

"That," said the Duke, "was not helpful."

They disembarked, and were met with a jovial innkeeper sporting impressive mutton chops. "Your Grace!" He bowed to the Duke. "Delightful to see you, as always!"

The Duke smiled. "Same to you, Nigel. Might I introduce you to my wife?"

Every part of Rosaline burned to hear the word. Not that there was any doubt — she was still in her white gown.

"An absolute pleasure!" Nigel's bow deepened. "Your usual room is prepared, Your Grace, unless you and the Duchess would like some supper?"

"No," said the Duke quickly — too quickly. Rosaline stifled a giggle and he set his jaw. "It was a long journey, and we are quite exhausted."

"Ah." Nigel gave a sage nod. "I completely understand, Your Grace, follow me—"

The inn was busy, but not packed, and warm with cheer. The bar spilled into the garden, and Rosaline caught sight of all sorts of town and country people, happily mingling around pitchers of beer and bottles of wine. Some of them looked up as she and the Duke passed, but she tried to ignore it. The less attention they drew, the better.

Nigel led them up a steep, rickety flight of stairs and onto a wide landing. He went down a short hall, then opened a heavy wooden door. "There you have it, Your Grace, same as always."

It was a large, comfortable room with an equally large four-poster bed. A pair of armchairs squatted before the empty hearth, and the paneled walls were dotted with paintings and even a mounted stag's head. The windows opened onto the back lawn, and the soft rumble of conversation floated up on the sweet summer breeze.

"Lovely," said Rosaline, just as their driver arrived with their luggage.

Nigel beamed. "Thank you, Your Grace. Will you be requiring a maid?"

"Not tonight," she replied. "But tomorrow morning, I will."

It took a few more moments for everything else to be settled, but finally, the door closed, and she and the Duke were alone once again.

He looked right at her, and she trembled from the heat of his gaze. "Finally."

She smiled. "I cannot get used to being addressed as 'Duchess.' "

"Give it time." Hal's gaze dropped to her chest. "Now, how on earth—?"

"It is quite simple." Rosaline ran a finger along her *décolletage,* and his eyes followed it. "But you will have to help me."

He swallowed. "All right."

Gone was the heady, burning urgency of the carriage — yes, desperation still lingered, a fine hum beneath their skin, but when Hal approached her, she could see that he was nervous, that he knew this moment would be different, had to be different, than all other moments that had come before it. He moved to stand behind her, his hand grazing her hip.

Rosaline undid the waistband of her gown and let it fall away, leaving her in her petticoat. Hal's touch, when it came, was hesitant, gentle, and she felt every brush of his fingers as they slid along the dip of her neck, the back of her arms, the hollow of her throat.

She could not see him, but she had never been more aware of his presence — his mouth was plush, warm, unhurried as it traced the boundaries of her skin, the notches of her spine. When he unlaced her stays, his hands went to grasp her hips, and she nearly whimpered from the feeling, from knowing that his skin was almost on hers.

Her stays fell to the floor with a mute thud, and this, somehow, seemed to break the tension. Suddenly, one of Hal's hands was slipping beneath the waistband of her pantalettes, and the other slid up over her chemise to her breast, cradling it, his thumb grazing over her nipple. Rosaline bit out a gasp, surging against him as his mouth went to her neck.

Hal hummed, and she could feel it where his chest pressed against her back. "To think I get to have you, just like this, for the rest of our lives—"

Rosaline managed a breathless chuckle, a surge of liquid heat curling around her, nestling between her legs. She ached for the hand at her hip to slip lower. "Well, I have to get dressed sometimes, Your Grace—"

"Nonsense." He squeezed her breast again, thumbing at her nipple as he kissed along her neck. "You never have to leave the bed."

A groan caught in Rosaline's throat, and she finally turned to face him, pressing up against his body. He looked down at her, and the unbridled heat of his gaze made her tremble. Rosaline could feel him now, a thick pressure against her belly, and her head spun a little. "I think we are entirely too clothed."

Hal smiled, his hands going to her hips, sliding up her back. "Do your worst."

Rosaline reached for his shirt, and as she unbuttoned it, she dragged her mouth against his chest, listening to the way his breath caught in return. She had to admire his body, the lean, sure weight of it, broad but nimble, and she took note of the few fading bruises from his recent sparring. When she reached the waistband of his trousers, Rosaline did not hesitate. She undid the fastenings, and slipped her hand inside.

Hal shuddered, stifling a moan in her neck, his hand digging into her bum. She smiled with triumph, not that he could see.

He felt... warm, stiff, but still soft to the touch. And somewhat larger than she'd expected. Rosaline slid her hand along his length, taking a mental note of how it felt, then squeezed. He shuddered again, and she tipped her head back to murmur, "You must tell me, Hal, what you want—"

"I want to touch you," he bit out, his hand tangling in her hair. "I want to feel you—"

Rosaline smiled, feeling a surge of exhilaration. "We need not hurry, then." She slid her hand back up his chest, and tugged his shirt off.

Suddenly, his hands were at the band of her pantalettes, pulling them down and away, then his hands tangled in her chemise, grazing her bare skin. Rosaline's stomach jumped at the feeling, and she fumbled at his trousers, desperate, but then his mouth was on hers, and she forgot what she was doing, where she was. He kissed her with a ferocity she had never imagined, and her head spun, the world blurring around her. Rosaline came back to earth when her legs bumped into the mattress, and she fell back onto the bed with a huff.

Hal looked down at her, golden and shadowed in the light of the few candles. His trousers had slid a few inches down his legs, and she could see him now, pressing over the edge of the fabric. Just as she'd imagined, all those weeks ago.

To Rosaline's fascination and surprise, her mouth watered, and, her heart thumping in her ears, she propped herself up on an elbow. She reached for the hem of her chemise, slowly pulling it up her legs, exposing inch after inch of bare skin.

Hal watched, and his eyes seemed to darken. Then he shoved a hand through his hair and bit out, "Rosaline, you are testing my conviction."

She raised an eyebrow. "Whatever do you mean?"

"I did not intend," he began, then, as her hem fluttered above her thighs, seemed to lose his train of thought. "To take you in a bed that was not our own."

"Oh." Heat bloomed across her face, but not from embarrassment. "Hal, that's very—"

"If you say romantic, I shall pitch a fit." He sank to his knees and put his hand to her calf, his mouth to her ankle. It tickled.

Rosaline smiled and slid her hem even further up. Now, it hid very little. "There is still plenty we can do."

Hal hummed, his mouth trailing up her leg. "I love it when you test my sanity."

She began to reply, but then he curled over the bed, pressing an open-mouthed kiss to her bare thigh, and the words caught in her throat just as her hand caught against the bedding. The reality of the moment began to sink in as he came towards her, intent and gorgeous in the low light. Rosaline slid her hand along his shoulder, cupping the back of his head. Hal looked up at her as his hands tangled in her chemise, finally pulling it up and away.

The feeling of his breath on her skin was almost enough to unmake her. He nuzzled at her inner thigh and murmured, "I must confess, I've devoted a considerable amount of thought to this in particular."

Butterflies exploded in her stomach and she had to smile. "Really?"

"Perhaps more than a young man should." Hal's mouth found its way to and over her hip, along her belly. "That dress you wore to the opera was sheer torture. I wanted nothing more than to sneak you into an empty box and put my head beneath your skirts." His free hand traced the line of her body until he reached her breast. He thumbed at her nipple just as he pressed a kiss to her sex, and Rosaline shuddered from her head to her toes. Her nerves tingled with delight, zipping across her skin in a wild, frenetic pattern, and she wondered if this would be where she met her end, here, between his hands and his mouth.

His gaze found hers, and she swallowed. "You will tell me," he murmured, "what feels—?"

"*Oui*," she managed, then remembered that his French was terrible and this was not the time for a miscommunication. "There is— well, obviously, there is the place where you—"

"Right." He kissed her inner thigh again.

"But at the top, here." She fluttered a hand over the area she meant. "That is where you should devote the majority of your attention."

The corner of his mouth twitched, and for a moment, she caught it, that flash of mischief he so rarely indulged. "Should I?"

"Yes." Rosaline pushed her fingers through his hair, making it even more wild. "But you will doubtless find a way to entertain both areas at once."

"Oh, believe me." His attention was already returning to the areas in question. "I intend to get a lot of practice."

When he first licked her, it was tentative, exploratory, and Rosaline bit her lip. She could not help but wonder what would happen if this was terrible, if he— *Oh.* She let out a gasp and met Hal's gaze, and he looked far too smug. "Do that again."

She could've sworn he smirked. "Yes, dear."

Over the next several minutes, she discovered that her husband was a very quick learner. He needed the occasional nudge in the right direction, yes, but his dedication was literally breathtaking. And he was full of surprises.

Hal's tongue flicked over her clit until she trembled, his fingers digging into her hip as she twitched against him, floating on that burning edge between too little and too much. He worked his way down, licking over her folds, dipping inside her, then, to her astonishment, he fastened his mouth to her clit and sucked.

Pleasure exploded across her body, and Rosaline let out a moan, arching into his grip. Hal rocked with her, and when she managed a breathless, "My breast— please—" he obeyed at once, his thumb flicking over her nipple, and it was so much, it was—

He hummed, apparently quite pleased with himself, and she could feel it vibrate against her skin. It only deepened the moment, the intensity of the way his mouth felt, wet and supple. And when he lapped at her, gentle and almost not enough, she finally broke, pleasure surging through her in a warm, unhurried rush.

Hal pulled away and she quivered as he pressed a line of kisses to her thigh. Her entire body tingled with it, and her skin was so sensitive she could feel every grain of his stubble. Rosaline expected him to say something, but he remained silent, and she could only lie there, incoherent, as he wiped his mouth on the sheet and kissed his way up her body.

When he reached her chest, his chin grazed the swell of her breast and he finally said, "Was that all right?"

Rosaline nodded, tangling her hands in his hair. Hal grinned, leaning into her touch, and put his mouth to her nipple.

She choked on a moan, her back arching against the comforter, a fresh twinge of pleasure jolting to her belly. She'd known, of course, that her breasts were sensitive, but this was—

Hal hummed again, his hand going to her other breast, and he gave her nipple another flick of his tongue before he pulled away to kiss her, wet and artless, and she kissed him back, her entire body alive with the heat of *finally*, and he felt so good against her, warm and heavy in the best possible way, a steady reminder that this was to be her future, her reality—

Hall pulled away and buried his face between her breasts with a sigh. "I stand by my previous statement." A sloppy, sucking kiss, with just a hint of teeth, below her nipple. "I could die here, quite happily."

Rosaline managed a chuckle, squirming against him. "You are ridiculous."

He sighed again, rolling his hips, grinding down into the mattress. "Merely honest."

"Then tell me." Her fingers caught in his hair, and she tilted his head back until she could look him in the eye. "You were surprisingly adept at that, Hal. And yet you claim to have never been with a woman."

"I claim it because it is true," he replied, raising an eyebrow. Then, to her delight, he looked rather sheepish. "I may have... read something. And heard a few things."

"Read something?" she repeated, her heartbeat quickening in its usual traitorous way.

"You know what I mean. We all read books we are told not to read." Another sucking kiss, on her other breast. "And you know what gentlemen's clubs are like, some of the men say the most foul stuff—"

"And they bring in groups of women," Rosaline said. "For your entertainment."

Hal met her gaze. "I never. Neither did Cadogan."

She grazed her fingernails across his scalp, pressed her thumb against his jaw. "Why not?"

It was the very question she'd been too nervous to ask, before now.

"It felt too impersonal." He winced. "And there was too much risk. With Jamie."

She nodded. "I understand."

Hal watched her, and something in his expression quickened. "What about you?" His hand, unseen, sliding up the inside of her leg. His thumb grazed the narrow, damp skin just beside her opening. "You seem very... knowledgeable." As if to prove it, he tapped once on her clit.

Rosaline tried to take a breath. "It is as you said. I am French, am I not?"

He laughed then, and smacked a kiss to her neck. "Cheeky."

"And, well." She cleared her throat. "The Romans were very explicit writers."

"You must read some of it to me," he said. His fingers grazed through the thin curls of hair around her sex, teasing. "In Latin."

426

"Hal, you *know* Latin."

"No, I don't," he replied at once, before sucking at her nipple with a ferocity that made her see stars. "I pretended to know Latin. There is a big difference."

Rosaline tried to take a breath, grinding against his hand, chasing the scant pleasure. "You will need to improve your French. So we may speak together in secret."

"Go on, then." He flashed her that cheeky grin. "Teach me."

"Fine." A jolt of apprehension snaked through her belly, and she smiled. "*Répète après moi.*"

"*Répète après moi,*" he parroted.

"*Je veux faire l'amour.*"

"*Je veux faire l'amour.*"

Rosaline rolled her hips against him again, and he pressed his thumb to her clit. "*Je veux te faire brûler de plaisir.*"

"*Je veux te faire,*" he tried, then shook his head. "Sorry."

She repeated it, and he stumbled through the words, uncertain.

"Good." The word was little more than an exhale as she circled her hips. "Now, you say to me, *Je veux que tu m'avales tout entier.*"

Hal did his best, and she could see the question in his eyes.

"And now I say, *Tout pour toi, mon amour.*" With that, she pulled him into a deep kiss, sucking on his tongue until he grunted into her mouth.

"Rosaline—" He grazed his teeth against her neck, pressed his length against her hip. "What did I say?"

"You will see." She wrapped her arms around him, hooked her foot behind his knee, and rolled them to the side. Hal fell back onto the covers with a gasp, and his hands were on her in an instant, grabbing her like he was worried she would fall onto the ceiling, and she whimpered, grinding down on his thigh, feeling as if it might actually happen.

Rosaline made short work of his trousers, only pulling away

long enough to ensure that they fell to the floor. She knelt between his thighs and looked down at him, at the taut muscles of his legs and their light dusting of dark hair, and realized, again, just how lucky she was.

Hal took a shaky breath, his hands skating against hers, his finger brushing her cheek. "I know that look. I fear that look."

"I don't know what you mean." She reached for his length. It was stiff, curved up towards his belly, shining at the tip. She squeezed, and his breath caught.

"It's the same look you had— when you came up to me at the match—"

Rosaline raised an eyebrow. "Oh?"

"Yes," he bit out, his head falling back to the covers. "Impudence. Mischief."

She smiled. "Then let me assure you, dear husband, of my good intentions." She leaned forward, and pressed her mouth to the tip of his length. He let out a slow hiss, followed by a short, mangled swear word.

Tentative, Rosaline opened her mouth and sucked at him, trying to remember all of Lisette's advice. She worried briefly about grazing him with her teeth, and squeezed the root of his length, watching as he twitched and moaned. Swirling her tongue, she began to move up and down, taking what she could, feeling her jaw ache in response.

It was slow at first, but Rosaline began to get used to the weight of him in her mouth, against her tongue, and the way he tasted, bitter and clean — it reminded her of the air before the dawn, sharp and still — and she tried to remember every sound Hal made, the way his fingers tangled in her hair, knowing that they would repeat this, but never relive it. The way he felt, the way he tasted — it made something pool and churn between her legs, a feeling that was difficult to ignore, and every part of her wanted to climb up his body and sink down onto him, let him impale her and keep her suspended in the air until she quivered and fell apart, but no, not yet — they could come to that eventually, but here, now, this was about the beginning, not the middle, and—

"God." His whole body twitched, his cock sinking deeper into her mouth, and the air around them seemed to crackle. "God, Rosaline—"

And that was all the warning she had before he spilled down her throat. Rosaline automatically swallowed, surprised by the salty, bitter taste, and pulled away, panting. Her body ached from kneeling, her skin was livid with chambered pleasure, and her mouth was almost numb, but something in her felt utterly alive, and somehow at peace. She lay down beside him, hooking her leg over his stomach, and ground her cunt against his hip.

Just like that, he went from stunned with pleasure to brittle with tension. Hal's hands tangled in her hair and he pulled her head back to mouth at her throat. "God, you feel incredible, utterly incredible—"

"Talk to me," she managed, her face on fire, her mouth blurry. "Tell me—"

"What I would do to you?" Hal finished for her, grazing his teeth along her clavicle. "We would need all night—"

Rosaline moaned and gave in, slipping a hand between her legs. She did not know why, but something about hearing his voice—

Hal noticed, and stilled for only a moment before he returned his mouth to her ear. "You never told me," he murmured, "that you touched yourself."

Something caught in her throat. She tried to speak, but could not.

"Had I known that," he continued, his voice hot liquid against her neck, "I might have told you what to think about, to imagine that your hands were mine. I would have stroked myself and imagined you doing the same, in your own bed, in the dark."

Her entire body was on fire, was burning into the mattress—

"Did you think about me?" Hal's voice was nothing but a purr. "Did you think about my fingers, my mouth? Did you think about me sinking into you, about how I would feel inside you—?"

"Yes," she managed, and that was it, the heat built at the small of her back, ready and merciless, and all she could say was, "Yes, I did—"

Her orgasm was instant, blinding, and it rattled through her like a shock. Hal reached for her, kissed her through it, his mouth gentle and plush, his hands on her hips, in her hair. And when she finally opened her eyes, it was to meet his familiar blue gaze.

"Is it true?" He brushed another kiss to her nose. "What you said?"

She managed a nod. "Your letters... when you wrote to me in London..." Rosaline cleared her throat. "Hal, you were very clear."

"Yes, but—" Hal shook his head, his face still flushed with pleasure. "I wish I had *known*." And in that moment, he suddenly looked so vulnerable. "I would have..."

Rosaline let the words hang in the air until she could not stand to watch them fall. "You would have what, Hal? You were determined not to marry."

"I was," he agreed. "Until I met you."

She smiled, warmth spilling through her belly, into her chest. "But surely knowing a bit of scandalous information about your new acquaintance would not have changed that."

He smiled in return, but his expression still held that glimmer of vulnerability, of honesty. "It might have. Though sometimes, I thought you could hardly stand me."

She stared at him. "Really?"

"Yes. Especially at the beginning." He toyed with a piece of her hair. "I found myself drawn to you in a way I had never been drawn to anyone. You were not like the other people in London. You wanted nothing from me, and you were not intimidated by my status, my rudeness. And you were kind. Our closeness... it was not something I had expected."

"Nor I," Rosaline replied, and it was the truth. She ran a hand over Hal's chest, reveling in the smooth muscles, the unruly dusting of hair. He felt more real than anything else in the world. "And it almost got the better of us a few times, did it not?"

The corner of his mouth twitched. "I suppose so. The tennis court—"

"I cannot tell you," she murmured, sliding her fingers through his hair, brushing a kiss to his mouth, "how much I regretted our interruption—"

Hal huffed, almost smiling. "Ironically, I went to the Eventide Ball determined not to find myself in a compromising situation with you."

"Did you?" Rosaline smirked and nudged him with her hips. "Why is that?"

His hand went to her waist, and he thumbed at the curve of her belly. "I knew... that my feelings for you were growing from a friendship into something more. I did not want to risk losing what we had built, losing you. And I feared that if we were left alone together, that I..."

She hummed, and her mind began to turn. "Is that why you were in such a strop at the end of the boxing match?"

Hal did smile then, pressing a kiss to her cheek. "You do not miss a thing. One day, you must tell me how you manage it."

"And now you must tell me why," she pressed. "At the time, I could not understand what had happened."

"Seeing you there, in your disguise..." He shook his head. "It made me realize that you were even more stubborn and more clever than I'd originally thought. And when we embraced..." He squeezed her again now, in an echo of the moment. "I did not know what to do. I wanted to kiss you so badly I thought I would explode. But I could not, for more reasons than one, and so I resolved to keep my distance. Not that it did much good."

Rosaline sighed happily. "Well, now you can kiss me as much as you'd like." To prove it, she fastened her mouth to his and ran her tongue along his teeth. And then, to her surprise, she had to pull away and yawn widely enough to crack her jaw.

Hal grinned. "My goodness. I think they heard that in Yorkshire."

"You beast." But then another yawn rendered her speechless.

"We have had a long day." He stroked her back, kissed her neck. "Shall we, my love?"

Rosaline smiled, a fresh burst of sparks going off in her belly. "Yes, we shall."

She had hardly ever shared a room with anyone before, and it was strange to go through the motions of washing and preparing herself for bed with another person present. Hal made himself useful by rummaging through their luggage for their night things. Rosaline slid into her nightgown while Hal threw on a night shirt, and his hair made a fresh attempt to defy gravity. He looked positively scrumptious.

"I do not usually bother, but since we are among the public..." He sat down on the bed, watching her. "What are you doing?"

She glanced at him over her shoulder. "What does it look like I'm doing?"

"It smells nice. What is it?"

"Rose-hip oil." Rosaline had reached the ends of her hair now — she took a few more drops of oil and rubbed them in, then shook her hair out and began to braid it. "I have to do this every few nights, especially if I wear a complicated style."

He shook his head. "I do not know how you ladies put up with it."

"Lots of patience," Rosaline replied, twisting the end of her braid. "And the occasional *éclair*."

When she finally climbed into bed, her stomach tangled and frothed with excitement. She grinned at Hal, giddy, and slid under the blanket, nudging her feet into his. He smiled back at her, floppy, artless against the sheets, and she could not believe that he was hers and hers alone. She turned to blow out the last candle, then paused.

"Rosaline?" His voice was already heavy with sleep. "What is it?"

"I always wish for something before I blow out the candle," she replied. "But tonight, I cannot think of anything to wish for."

Hal was silent for several long, languid moments. "Wish for good weather," he mumbled. "And good roads." His hand, at the small of her back. "I cannot wait to get you home."

Rosaline smiled, looked down into the flame, and made her wish.

36

Madam Kensington's High Society Papers, No. 50

Well, well, well... I must confess, my darlings, how superbly satisfying it is for me to see my predictions come to absolute and complete fruition. When the season began, I had only the vaguest of notions about who might be the most eye-catching, the most notorious, the most scandalous. Some of these notions were correct, others were not, and some were only the tip of the iceberg. Of course, when the Queen bestowed her favors, that led most of us — or anyone with a functioning pair of eyes — in the right direction. Lady Love seemed destined to smile upon our leading ladies, remaining a steadfast companion even through the turbulent waters...

But enough speculation — I am sure you are all foaming at the mouth for details of the Joint Nuptials. And what an exclusive ticket! I personally was unable to gain access to the ceremonies, but several witnesses can attest to their utter splendor and riveting romance. Our Star and Sapphire shone brighter than they ever have before, draped in lavishing white silk, their fresh gold bands twinkling on their merry little fingers. Their reception was no less resplendent, and one can hardly recall a more uproarious party — it certainly put many of the season's *soirées* to shame. There was drinking, dancing, piles of flowers and available gentlemen, and at the center of it all, the Star, and her beloved Pup, already transmuting into glorious, iridescent Gold.

And what of the Sapphire, you may ask? Well, it seems that she and her Recluse were not made for crowds... Not even two hours into their own reception, they vanished, and the sound of carriage wheels driven at full speed echoed around Kensington...

ঔৣৣ৵

WHEN ROSALINE WOKE, IT WAS TO A BLISTERING HOT FOOT tangled between her own, and a long, heavy arm thrown across her chest. She smiled into her pillow, and a fresh wave of butterflies burst into her belly. *This,* she thought, *has to be the best feeling in the world.*

A fresh dewy sunshine was spilling into the room, brightening the dark furnishings and creating an unmistakable feeling of peace. It had to be midmorning, at the very earliest. She'd slept deeply, much to her own surprise — Rosaline had expected to have more trouble sharing a bed, especially with a man, but perhaps she'd been too exhausted to care. At least Hal did not snore, or if he did, it was not loud enough to trouble her. Now, he was still breathing deeply, and she could feel it puffing against the back of her neck. Rosaline sighed with happiness, let her eyes slip shut again, and wriggled a touch closer to him, determined to revel in this moment for as long as she could. He really was like a furnace.

A few minutes later, Hal let out a snuffling noise and yawned — he was waking up. And then, to her surprise and delight, he pulled her even closer, bringing her body flush with his. An obvious weight pressed into her bum. He put his mouth to her neck, and his hand slid along the line of her body, grazing the swell of her breast through her nightgown. He hummed, and left a trail of wet kisses on her shoulder.

Rosaline smiled, her face heating with delight. "Good morning."

"Morning," he mumbled, mostly into her skin. "How did you sleep?"

"Very well." She could not ignore what his attentions were doing to her body — her limbs were still soft with sleep, but her belly churned with renewed heat. She reached over her own shoulder, tangling her hand in his hair. "And you?"

"The same." Now, he was mouthing at her neck. "I must admit, it is exceedingly wonderful to wake up with you in my bed."

"Is it?" But she could already tell that he agreed with her — his hand had gone from her breast to the hem of her nightgown, sliding up her thigh to the edge of her sex. She thrilled at the feeling. Hal had always been physically affectionate, especially after their engagement, but this was unlike anything she'd imagined. She could not believe how eager he was to touch her, feel her, whenever he could.

"I am beginning to think..." He paused, trailing his nose from her neck down to her shoulder blade. "That perhaps we shall not leave this bed today."

"*Hal.*" But she did not stop his hand from slipping between her legs, his fingers nudging against her. "You know we must reach Alban Hollow by nightfall at the very latest. You promised Jamie!"

He hummed, sucking on the spot below her ear. "That was before I found you to be so obliging, my love. Care to divulge the subject of your dreams?"

Rosaline bit out an exaggerated sigh, her eyes slipping shut as his fingers brushed her clit. "Surely you can guess."

She could feel his smile. "I suppose I can." His fingers, now moving in a lazy circle. "Perhaps later this afternoon we can recreate them."

The thought alone was enough to make her shudder and press against him with a sigh of absolute yearning. His hand skated up to her breast, squeezing it as if he were afraid she would slip away. But before they could go any further, there came a knock at the door.

"Good morning, Your Graces!" The maid, and a young, enthusiastic one at that. "I have your breakfast here, and your driver says that your horses will be ready within the hour."

Hal muffled his groan in his pillow and sat up. "You should have wished for incompetent staff. Or some calamity that would trap us in this room for several hours."

Rosaline rolled over and smiled at him. "Need I remind you that we will be alone together for the entire carriage ride?"

"I suppose," he groused, and she had to bite back her laugh. He was actually *grumpy* about this. Hal cleared his throat and called out, "Very well, you may enter."

The door opened and in came the maid, smiling, her cheeks rosy. Rosaline's guess had been correct — the girl couldn't have been older than sixteen. This lack of experience was only confirmed when she caught sight of Hal and Rosaline, cuddled up next to each other.

The maid stumbled on her way to the table, almost dropping the breakfast tray. She put it down as fast as she could, then turned to face them, though she could not bring herself to look them in the eye, and instead fastened her gaze upon the rug. "I'm to assist you this morning, Your Grace. I mean—" Her blush intensified. "I mean for the Duchess, of course, not that I would ever presume to—"

Hal chuckled, a low, dark sound, and for a moment, Rosaline feared the girl would faint. It was understandable — the sight of the Duke in his nightshirt, slumped and rumpled, his hair tousled beyond belief, his eyes lazy with sleep and satisfaction, would be enough to unmake any reasonable woman.

"That sounds lovely," Rosaline said, offering a smile. "Come back in a quarter of an hour."

The maid nodded. "Yes, Duchess. Thank you, Duchess." And she bobbed a quick spasm of a curtsy before she fled, closing the door behind her.

Rosaline smacked Hal's arm. "You were no help at all."

He was grinning. "I don't know what you mean, my love. Though I do wish she'd brought the tray to the bed."

Rosaline snorted. "If she'd had to come within two feet of us, she would have exploded on the spot." There was nothing for it — she could smell the tea and the bacon, and her stomach rumbled in response. She slid out of bed and stretched, reaching for the sunlit ceiling. She did not miss the way Hal watched her, his gaze smoldering. "Come. We need our strength."

"I suppose you're right." Hal let out a sigh and followed her lead, getting out of bed. He looked absolutely delicious, and when he stretched, his shirt hiked up his torso, hinting at what she had felt in bed. Rosaline fumbled with the tea pot and nearly spilled it on her toes. He noticed, and smirked at her.

They ate quickly, not even bothering to sit down. Rosaline took her toast over to the window, where she looked out on the land that had been dark and obscured the previous night. It was stunning, simple in its beauty, rolling green fields intercut by dark seams of blackish forests. She could see a nearby field of sheep, and the air carried the tang of manure and fresh grass.

"Is this what it's like?" she said. "At Alban Hollow?"

"Yes, but infinitely more beautiful." Hal downed the rest of his tea in a single gulp. "I had better get dressed, and leave you to the mercy of your new friend."

She shot him a smile. "If you must."

True to his word, Hal dressed quickly, shaved, and made a valiant attempt at his hair. "I will meet you at the carriage." He crossed the room, pressed a quick kiss to her mouth. She sighed into it, aching for more. The corner of his mouth twitched. "Try to hurry."

"I will," Rosaline promised.

The maid, bless her soul, was punctual, and still blushing. Her name was Sandra, and she did quite well with Rosaline's dress, but paled when faced with her hair.

"Do not worry." Rosaline smiled at her. "We shall tackle it together."

Between the two of them, they managed two braids woven into a single strand, then twisted and pinned above the nape of her neck. Sandra stepped away, staring at it in awe.

"Well done, indeed!" Rosaline squeezed Sandra's wrist, and Sandra's blush deepened. "And in record time." She stood up and gathered the things she'd prepared for the carriage ride. The driver appeared for their luggage, and, to Rosaline's surprise, Sandra cleared her throat.

"Your Grace, I just wanted to say..." The poor thing was beginning to resemble a beet. "You and the Duke make a very lovely couple."

Something curled tight around Rosaline's heart. "You are far too kind." She gave Sandra's wrist another squeeze. "I hope we shall meet again."

The girl smiled. "I'd like that, Your Grace."

The Duke was outside the inn, leaning against their carriage, all floppy and gorgeous. The moment he saw her, he broke into a grin. "You are more beautiful each day."

Rosaline hummed, almost smiling. "And you are setting quite a high standard for yourself, *ma puce*. You will run out of compliments before our first anniversary."

"Do not doubt my creativity." He opened the door of the carriage for her and raised an eyebrow. "Off to the races."

After saying their goodbyes to an obsequious Nigel, they climbed into the carriage and were off. Within minutes they were back on the main road, and the hills began to roll away beneath their feet. Once they were out of anyone's sight, Hal snaked a hand around Rosaline's waist and pulled her back against his chest. Now, they were ensconced in the corner of the seat, not far from where they'd begun the previous night's activities, and his hand was sliding dangerously low.

Rosaline smirked at him. "I see how you plan to entertain yourself."

"Well, I hope it would entertain both of us." He brushed a kiss to the corner of her mouth. "Why, did you have other ideas?"

She gave a very put-upon sigh. "Actually, yes." Rosaline reached for her bag, and produced two volumes — one, a reader on Ancient Greek, and the other, a short novel.

His eyebrows flickered. "Goodness. I should have known." Hal brushed his finger across the cover of the novel. "You can read in the carriage?"

"Yes. I know, I am lucky. You cannot?"

Hal shook his head. "It makes me ill. That is part of the reason why I so hate riding around in a carriage. There is nothing for me to do."

Rosaline felt a stab of sympathy for him — Hal brimmed with a natural energy that was not suited to such close quarters. She reached into her bag and produced a deck of cards. "Would this help?"

"Worth a try." He took the deck, brushed a kiss to her nose. Then, his expression sobered. "Are you ready? To go home?"

Rosaline looked at him for a moment, then beamed. "Yes."

OVER THE NEXT SEVERAL HOURS, ROSALINE REALIZED THAT SHE would have to learn how to share a carriage with her husband, because it was certainly an acquired taste.

Her guess that he would not take well to prolonged periods of stasis turned out to be quite correct. The deck of cards amused him for no more than half an hour, and he could only sit still for a few minutes at a time. Soon, he began to fidget, which was enough to distract her from her book.

Rosaline snapped the Ancient Greek reader shut and said, "What if I read to you?"

He stared at her. "Really?"

"Yes, really." She traded the grammatical text for the novel — she'd made little progress as it was. "Does Cadogan likewise struggle to sit still for long periods of time?"

"No," Hal replied, with an easy grin. "He usually has a book on plants, or a plant itself, if you can believe it. Charlotte will not find herself quite so encumbered as you."

The other newlyweds were on their way to a month-long honeymoon in the Lake District. Rosaline had been slightly jealous when Charlotte announced it, but there was nothing she could do — Hal did not want to leave Jamie alone for so long, or allow such distance between them. "One day," he'd said to her, after kissing her breathless in one of the few stolen moments they'd had before the wedding, "when the wars are done, I shall take you to France."

" 'Encumbered' is the wrong word, Hal." Though she did feel guilty for making her irritation that obvious. "Come, I think you will enjoy this one."

He settled back onto the corner, his leg nudging into hers. "I'm all ears."

Rosaline lost track of time as she read to him. After a while, she noticed that he was watching her with this sweet, sly expression that almost went beyond her powers of description. It made her blush, and she stammered through her words. He absolutely noticed, but it was a while before he did anything about it.

When she reached the end of a chapter, Hal's hand went to the book, tugging it out of her grasp. "I love," he murmured, "your voice." And he kissed her, gentle at first but building to something determined and filthy. When his tongue grazed the roof of her mouth, Rosaline let out a gasp and surged against him, her tongue tangling with his. He held her, clung to her, one hand squeezing her bum and the other cupping the back of her head. His fingers slid beneath the twist of her hair and his nails dragged at her scalp — shivers cascaded down her back, and Rosaline fought the urge to climb into his mouth.

It was just like the night before, but sharper, keener now that they'd been together, watched one another shudder and fall apart. Now that Rosaline knew how he tasted, how he felt, how his hands would shake when she touched him, she yearned for it in a way that was more acute, more intense, than it had ever been before.

It's a lot like pastry, she thought. *Once you have one, you want them all.*

The minutes melted, and before long, Hal's shirt was undone and his hand had found its way beneath her skirts. His fingers tangled in her pantalettes and he broke away to groan against her cheek. "Fuck," he bit out, and the word almost startled her. "I swear to God Himself, Rosaline, these infernal things are to be banned the moment we set foot in Alban Hollow—"

She grinned, sucking briefly on his lower lip. "What you are suggesting is quite rakish indeed, Hal Cunningham. Me, waltzing around *en plein air?*"

"Precisely." Hal fell back against the cushions with a sigh. "It would be so much more convenient. For us both."

Her stomach flipped at his implication, and she tingled down to her toes. "I shall consider it. I will admit, they are quite cumbersome in high summer — they make one rather inclined to perspiration."

He winced and closed his eyes. To her utter surprise and delight, she felt his length twitch where it was pressed against her thigh.

"Hal." Rosaline's voice was faint with disbelief, and she waited until he cracked open an eye. "Do you enjoy the thought of me... exerting myself?"

For several moments, he said nothing. Then, he nodded, a blush snaking up his neck. "When we were on the tennis court," he muttered, "you were almost impossible to resist."

Something like triumph surged in Rosaline's belly — she loved learning things like this about him, now that they could speak freely. "Duly noted." She shifted a little, rested her hand upon his length, and gave it a squeeze through his trousers. "How would you like to pass the time, husband?"

Hal made a strangled sort of noise and took her wrist, gently pushing her away. "You," he managed, "are to sit on the seat opposite, and keep your hands to yourself."

She smirked. "Am I?'

"Yes." Hal kissed her once, briefly. "Because you are not to lay a finger on me until I can do the same to you."

Rosaline sat back with a sigh. "Spoilsport." But she picked up the novel and switched seats, taking the untouched couch opposite Hal's. "How much longer?"

He glanced out the window, his profile a wonderful compliment to his half-bare chest. "Another two hours, I think."

"Very well." She cracked open the book and cleared her throat. "Chapter three."

❧ 37 ❧

They paused only to eat a few light sandwiches provided by the dutiful Nigel, and not once did the horses tire of their task. Rosaline watched as Somerset grew and surged around them, sleepy and tucked up into its own ceaseless patchwork of wheat and grass and apple trees. She watched a set of cows approach and recede; she watched the villages grow and dissolve. She watched the words on the page, felt them as she read them aloud, and, it seemed, before too long, Hal sat up from where he'd been splayed across his seat, his eyes bright and alert.

"We're here," he said, and his grin was dazzling. He began doing up his shirt.

They passed quite suddenly into a dense forest, the light turning a heavy grayish green, but before Rosaline became accustomed to it, they burst back into the sunlight, and crossed the outer boundaries of the village, Alban Glen. It was a small village, but full of energy — as they passed the blacksmith's and turned onto the main road, Rosaline was astonished to see the street lined with people. They were all cheering, waving handkerchiefs and ribbons, and tossing rice and flowers upon the carriage as it passed.

"Say hello." Hal was still grinning.

Mute with surprise, Rosaline waved at the crowd, inciting a roar and a heavy rain of rice.

"What is this?" She stared at a hand-painted banner lined with flowers — *Welcome home, Duchess!*

"It seems that news of our marriage has spread." Hal raised an eyebrow at her. "They wish to greet the woman who won over the sworn bachelor."

Rosaline had no words for that. But she waved again, and smiled when the villagers cheered and clapped. It felt profoundly odd, but, she supposed, it was something else she had to get used to.

Alban Hollow was a mere ten minutes outside the village. Rosaline watched, breathless, as they turned off the main road and onto a long drive lined with cherry trees. The branches were heavy with the last of their crop, but the blossoms in the spring had to have been beautiful.

"My mother planted them," said Hal. "And the tenants and villagers are permitted to harvest the fruit whenever they'd like."

"How lovely." Rosaline shifted closer to the window, desperate to take in every detail of Hal's home. *My home now*, she thought, and her heart thudded. The drive curved, switching to gravel, and the trees ended, replaced by a sprawling green lawn. As she watched, a wide, flat pond appeared, dotted by lily pads and bordered by thick, flowering shrubs. Behind the pond loomed the house itself, and Rosaline couldn't help herself — she gaped at the sight of it.

Alban Hollow was a formidable building, three stories of pale yellow brick with turrets at the corners and a wide veranda along the front. It reminded her of a fortress — austere, with little ornamentation, squatting with a determined aspect and impressive windows. It was absolutely enormous. There had to be at least fifty rooms. A faint tingling kicked up at the base of

Rosaline's neck, and for a moment, she felt a bit faint — this was all hers, now.

The main entrance was at the side of the building. They passed through some trees, the pond disappearing from view, and onto a drive shaped in a wide half-circle. To her further surprise, they were not alone. The entire staff was waiting outside the house, and once they saw the carriage, they burst into cheers, tossing rice and flowers into the air, just like the villagers. A laugh bubbled up out of Rosaline's throat before she could stop herself, and Hal grinned as the carriage drew to a halt.

"How lovely!"

"Yes." Hal took her hand, gave it a squeeze. "They are very excited to meet you."

"Well." Rosaline managed a quivering breath and stuffed her books into her bag. "Best foot forward."

A footman rushed over and opened the door. Hal flashed her another grin and said, "Come on, then." He hopped down from the carriage and held out his hand, waiting.

Rosaline took another breath and forced herself to move, clasping his hand and stepping out onto the drive.

The cheers and applause surged, and a fresh rain of rice fell upon her and Hal's shoulders. Chuckling, he gave her a little tug, bringing her closer to the staff. They were all beaming, and Rosaline stared out at the cluster of friendly faces — the butler, the same man she'd encountered in London, was watching the others with an austere, impassive face. Then she caught sight of Lisette, wearing her new uniform and standing beside the other maids, grinning fit to burst, and felt a wave of absolute relief.

"You are too kind!" Hal's words brought them all to silence. "Everyone, I am most proud to introduce you all to my wife, Rosaline." A wave of fresh, excited whispering, and Rosaline blushed. "Be sure to give the library a very thorough dusting. I have no doubt that is where she will be spending much of her time." He looked to his butler. "Brooks, anything to report?"

"No, Your Grace. Master Jamie is excited to see you."

"Your Grace." This came from a woman older than the rest of the maids, and not wearing an apron. She had a kind face, and she smiled at Rosaline. "I was hoping I might steal the Duchess today, to give her a tour of the estate."

"A splendid idea, Mrs. Andrews, but perhaps we should wait for tomorrow." Hal brushed a kiss to Rosaline's cheek, eliciting a stifled gasp from the maids. "I am not certain I'd like to share her just yet."

Before anyone could reply, there came the sound of small running feet, then a surprisingly loud bellow of, "Hal!"

Hal dropped to one knee just as Jamie came flying down the drive and into his arms. Hal burst into laughter and swung the boy up into the air, and Rosaline felt something very distinct settle into her chest.

Oh, she somehow thought. *Oh, no—*

Rosaline cleared her throat and approached them, smiling. "Hello, Jamie, remember me?"

"Yes!" The boy was just as she'd left him — floppy hair, big eyes, eager and shy all at once. He smiled back at her from where he sprawled over Hal's shoulder, and her stomach turned to goo. "You helped me hunt the Rebels."

"I did." On impulse, she reached for his hand and kissed it. "Guess what, Jamie? There might be something in my trunk with your name on it."

His eyes lit up, and Hal let out a low chuckle. "Like a cat to catnip."

"Jamie!" This new voice boomed across the circle, and it belonged to the largest person she'd ever seen in real life. The man came lumbering towards them, hand raised in apology. He had a lot of hair and an enormous beard, above which twinkled a pair of kind, dark eyes. "Sorry, Hal. He knows he's got his tutor."

"That's all right." Hal smacked a kiss to Jamie's head and

Rosaline, along with the maids, almost fainted. "Hamish, this is Rosaline. Rosaline, Hamish."

Hamish beamed down at her. "It's a real pleasure, Duchess. I've heard so much about you."

"Not too much, I hope. We must have tea and venture to separate truth from fiction."

"Oh, that'd be smashing!" Hamish turned to his charge and gave him a stern look. "But now, I must return Master Jamie to his tutor."

Jamie pouted, and for a brief, terrifying moment, Rosaline wanted to give him the world.

Hal patted him on the back. "Come on, Jamie, it'll be all right. We'll have supper together later this evening."

Jamie's pout disappeared. "With Rosaline?"

"Yes, with Rosaline." And Hal flashed her a wink.

"All right!" Jamie jumped out of Hal's arms. "See you later!" With that, he ran off towards the house.

Hamish rolled his eyes but grinned. "That's me done for. Nice meeting you, Duchess." And he set off in pursuit of his charge.

"Hamish is Jamie's shadow," Hal said to Rosaline in an undertone. "They're together most hours of the day."

"He's lovely." But now that they were alone again, the air seemed to crackle with tension, and heat curled around Rosaline's torso, pooling at the base of her spine.

Hal seemed to be thinking along the same lines. He cleared his throat. "Brooks?"

The butler snapped to attention. "Yes, Your Grace?"

"Clear a path. Tradition must be observed."

And that was how Rosaline found herself carried over the threshold of Alban Hollow.

She buried her laugh in the crook of Hal's neck. "This is ridiculous—"

But then she looked up at the ceiling, and her words died in her throat.

Above them was an intricate, sprawling mural of gods and goddesses — she recognized Athena, Apollo, Zeus, and the level of detail was breathtaking. The hall itself was lined in shining creamy tile, and the walls were dotted with landscapes that had actual character. It was one of the grandest places she'd ever been in, including the Queen's favorite palace.

Hal's voice, in her ear. "I would show you around, but I think we are only concerned with the staircase, yes?"

"Yes," Rosaline managed, as he lowered her feet to the ground. She took his hand.

Hal grinned, and again, that jolt of heat between her legs. "Let us fly."

They ran down the hall, their laughter echoing against the walls, and up an enormous flight of marble stairs. He led her around a corner, down a hall, and around another corner. Everywhere Rosaline looked, she saw further evidence of the Hollow's simple elegance, but she barely had a moment to pay attention to it. Hal halted before an enormous pair of doors, panting a little, his hair mussed and his expression flushed.

"This," he said, "is our room." He nodded to the matching pair of doors just down the hall. "Those are your personal chambers and dressing room, should you ever require them."

"Oh." But of course, that was the expectation. Rosaline reached out, and opened the door to their shared chambers.

They were enormous and beautiful, bathed in the rich sunlight of the perfect summer's day. The windows were open, and the thin white curtains billowed in the breeze. She walked in, taking note of the simple furnishings — a writing table, armchairs before the fireplace, a small, well-stocked bookcase. And, of course, the huge four-poster bed.

The furniture was all made of a dark, shining wood, and there was a conspicuous lack of the more indulgent forms of decoration. Very little was plastered in gold, and, to her relief, there were not any portraits of old family members looming on the walls. In the corner, she spotted her own trunk, which was filled to the brim with books, and felt a brief wave of gratitude for Lisette, who had followed her instructions precisely.

Behind her, Hal closed the door, and her skin tingled in response.

"I think," he said, turning to face her, "before we find ourselves beyond the help of coherent language, we should ensure that we understand one another."

She met his gaze. "Yes?"

A haze of red appeared on Hal's cheekbones. "You do not... want children, for the time being, correct?"

Rosaline swallowed, her mouth dry. "Ideally. I think it would be... too soon."

He nodded, reached for his boots. He tugged one off, then the other, and reached for his socks. "There are certain precautions we can take. Are you aware of them?"

"I believe so." Rosaline toed off her own shoes. "Lisette has been dosing me with a particular tea, and when we..." A blush heated her own face, and she reached for her hair, tugging out the pins and undoing all of Sandra's hard work. She gave a quick toss of her head, then raked her fingers through the braids. "You can..."

Hal sort of smiled. "Pull away." His hands twitched, as if he wanted to reach for her. "Is that... acceptable?"

She nodded. "Yes," she managed. "Yes, it is—"

He was on her in an instant, licking into her mouth, his hands tangling in her dress. A gasp caught in Rosaline's throat, and she reached for her own skirts, desperation squealing under her skin. Hal groaned, his breath hot on her cheek. "Fucking layers—"

Rosaline almost laughed. "I know, I'm sorry—"

"I was serious," he said, tugging at her petticoat, "about those infernal leggings—"

"Well, since I am on my honeymoon..." She sucked a kiss to his cheek. "I believe an exception can be made."

Hal responded with a growl, tugging her petticoat up and over her head, and she heard a few stitches pop, but did not care, because his mouth was on her neck and his hands were— She shoved his shirt off his shoulders, fumbled with the fastenings on his trousers as his fingers tangled with the laces on her stays. In moments, they fell to the floor.

"You," Rosaline managed, "are becoming quite good at that—"

Hal made equally short work of her pantalettes and chemise, and the second she was bare, he pressed a dozen kisses to one breast, squeezing the other, muffling a sigh against her skin. She shuddered at the feeling, her hand grazing the heated length into his trousers, and he shuddered in return, then wrapped his arms around her and pushed her back onto the bed.

Rosaline bounced once on the mattress, and it was an echo from the night before, only now, she was in her stockings instead of her chemise. She had to grin as Hal, staring at her chest, undid his trousers and shoved them onto the floor. His swollen cock sprang free, thick and shining at the tip, and then his hands were on her again, tearing off her stockings and throwing them into the corner, leaving her naked, flushed, on top of the bed.

He fell upon her like a jungle cat, his mouth hot and ruthless as he tongued at her breasts and sucked at her neck. It was all she could do to cling onto him, her nails digging into his back, kissing whatever part of him she could reach. Eventually, he kissed the skin below her ear and managed, "Tell me what to— I don't want to hurt you—"

Every part of her quivered. "Perhaps you should... You could start with your mouth."

Rosaline could feel his grin. "Oh, could I?" But Hal pulled away, grabbed her hips, and shoved her even further up the bed.

Rosaline's brain switched off. Hal's grin became a smirk, and for a moment, she could hardly believe that they were here, now, together, and he shifted down the bed, lifted one of her legs, pressing a kiss to her ankle before spreading her leg wide, laying her bare. He hummed, then closed the distance, pressing his mouth to her damp and swollen sex.

"My goodness." Hal gave a dark, liquid chuckle. "You are quite obliging." He squeezed her thigh, and she knew what it meant — *Tell me.*

Rosaline managed to take a breath. "Since— since we kissed in the carriage—"

He made a sound that was not quite a groan and not quite a growl, then licked a stripe up her sex and lapped at her clit, humming as she twitched and shuddered against the sheets. His hands came up, his fingers digging into her thighs, and it was a reminder of his own need, his infatuation with her body. Rosaline tangled her fingers in his hair, her skin buzzing, and tried something new — she rocked against him, circling her hips, pushing his tongue in a neat, dizzying circle. The movement, the succulent heat of his mouth, sent fresh tendrils of pleasure raking down her legs, up her back, sharp and merciless.

She chased it, that endless crackle of pleasure, gasping when he broke away to suck at her, thumb at her nipple. She grabbed his hand and managed, "Use your fingers— inside—"

It would be a good idea, Lisette had told her. Especially for the first time.

Hal's gaze snapped to hers, a silent question forming between his brows. Rosaline nodded, feeling, for a split second, the briefest flash of nerves. She'd done it a couple of times before, but always tentatively, and never very deep. She'd always found herself more than satiated by touching merely the outside of her sex.

Until now. Now, Rosaline recognized the keen, endless ache that would not be satisfied by mouths or hands alone. Though the previous night had been wonderful, she knew that what she wanted had little to no equivalent, and her nerves were outpaced by her determination, her desperation to learn how it would feel to be filled and stretched.

Hal broke away and for a moment, she could not tell what he

was doing. But he brought a finger to his mouth and sucked on it briefly, then lapped at her clit while the tip of his finger slid slowly into her body.

It felt much the same as her own finger had felt, except a touch thicker, perhaps. Rosaline wiggled her hips, and his finger slid deeper, up to his final knuckle. It felt... fine, and wonderful all at once. His gaze found hers again as his tongue circled, and she nodded, feeling a fresh spasm of pleasure between her hips.

"More," Rosaline breathed.

His finger withdrew, then was joined by a second. Hal stroked her for a moment, wetting his touch, then slowly breached her again, muffling a moan against her thigh as his fingers sank in. Rosaline trembled and circled her hips. It felt— it felt— it was good, but not enough.

"Hal," she managed, and waited until he surfaced, his face ruddy, his mouth slack and shining. "Can you try— circling, and perhaps— if you bend them up a little, you may find— *Oh!*" A shudder tore through her, borne of surprise as much as anything else. "Oh, that's—"

He pulled away to smirk, then gave her a lick, his fingers steadily shifting inside her body. Sparks and fissures burst down her legs, and then, to her astonishment, he pressed his thumb directly onto her clit while he bit a line of sloppy kisses along her leg. His fingers worked in and out of her, building a steady, ceaseless rhythm, and for a moment, it was so easy to imagine the real thing, to imagine him, heavy and thick, sliding into her—

Rosaline tangled her fingers in Hal's hair, yanked him towards her. Her chest was on fire, and a numb tingling had built at the base of her spine. "Kiss me, kiss me—"

Hal licked into her mouth, sucking on her bottom lip, his fingers never ceasing their relentless task. She did her best to kiss him back, her mouth loose and sloppy with unspent moans, and it was so much, it was—

He kissed her while she came undone, shivering and shaking

against the covers. Pleasure washed over her like a cool tide, dancing across her skin in wave after wave of tingling delight. Rosaline had the brief illusion of falling backwards, and when she finally returned to herself, after several long moments, she opened her eyes to see him looking at her, smug and adoring.

His fingers had stilled, but as Hal spoke, they shifted, teasing her oversensitive skin. "Well. That appears to have worked."

Rosaline shook anew, gripping the wrist of his occupied hand. "Give me... a moment." She cleared her throat and blinked a few times. The room remained unchanged, still full of light and fresh air and all the promise of a new home. The air between them was thick, salty.

Then he moaned in her ear, shifting to rut against her hip. His length dragged over her skin, heavy and slick. "You feel..." Hal's voice was unsteady. "God, you feel—"

Rosaline moaned in reply, because she knew what he meant — she was surprised at her own body, at the way it had opened, wet and pleading, to his touch. Even now, when everything still felt tender, raw from pleasure, she wanted it, wanted it *now*— "How..." The question tangled in her throat. "How do you want me?"

Hal trembled, then mouthed at her neck and murmured, "Like this, unless—"

She nodded, feeling another jolt of nerves, coupled with exhilaration.

He brushed a kiss to her mouth. "I make no promises about my stamina."

A startled laugh burst out of her. "Do not worry." She kissed him back. "We will have plenty of time to improve it."

Hal pulled away, smiling, but something in his face showed the keen, unstoppable need that was seething in her own belly. He shifted down her body, and she parted her legs for him. Hal took one of her knees in hand, gently bending it until her foot rested flat on the bed. "I think," he murmured, "it might be better if—"

"Oh." Rosaline did the same with her other leg, and for a moment, it felt a bit undignified, lying there, knees bent, legs spread apart, but he was looking at her as if she were the world's greatest treasure, and when he bent down and kissed her, it was slow, sweet.

"I love you." He nuzzled her chin, his eyes bright. "You know that?"

"Yes," she managed. "And I you."

He nodded, as if answering an unspoken question, and his hands went to her hips, his thumbs rubbing circles into the notches of her bones. He knelt between her legs, bit his lip, and leaned forward.

At first, it felt as if a finger were nudging at her again, and the head of his cock bumped against her clit, then her inner thigh, and Rosaline swallowed as Hal let out a muffled curse and shifted again. This time, he entered her, and they both let out equally brutal moans.

And then, because Hal was a gentleman, he waited.

It felt... different. She could feel him throbbing inside her, and she was almost dizzy with it, with the surreal reality of the way he felt, hot and thick and unlike anything she could have imagined. Rosaline took a few breaths, then nodded.

Hal sank the rest of his length into her, a second moan punching out of him, and her back arched as her mouth fell open, because *God—*

Once again, he was touching parts of her that had never been touched before. That thought alone was almost enough to unmake her.

They were chest-to-chest now, and he braced himself on the mattress, his mouth grazing her forehead. She reached up, tangled one hand in his hair and gripped his formidable backside with the other. Biting a line of kisses into his jaw, she hissed, "Move."

Hal obeyed at once, pulling out of her only to sink back in, another moan tearing out of him, and his eyes slid shut, his lovely face flushed and sweaty, and she kissed him, moved with him as he began to speed up, setting a steady pace that grounded her, flattened her, overwhelmed her, and she could feel every burning inch of him, and it did not hurt — her body was opening in a way it had never opened before, and it was wonderful, all of it, and a sob caught in her throat—

"Oh—" Hal shuddered, hard enough that she felt it in her hips, her thighs, and a sudden blush blossomed across his chest. "Oh, Rosaline, I can't—"

"It's all right." She carded her hand through his hair, brushed a kiss to his chin.

He let out a guttural groan and thrust once, twice, before he pulled out and collapsed on top of her, spilling across her belly. She clung to him, murmured in his ear, waited as he slowly came back to himself.

This, of course, was signaled when he ducked his head and began nuzzling at her breasts.

Rosaline almost giggled, tugging gently at his hair. "You are insatiable."

"Can you blame me?" Hal kissed a long, winding trail around one breast, then settled between them, looking up at her with those bright, devastating eyes. "Are you..." His hesitation was obvious. "Was that...?"

She sighed, rolling her hips against him. "That was perfect, Hal. I mean it."

He smiled, then it disappeared. "Did I... did I hurt you?"

"No," she replied honestly. "Not at all. In fact..." She rolled her hips again. "I still find myself quite... obliging."

Hal let out a laugh, his stubbled chin grazing her breastbone. "I need a minute."

Rosaline smiled. "I suppose that's acceptable." She sighed, loving the way his mouth fluttered over her skin, the edge of his teeth catching on her nipple, and her eyes slipped shut.

She began to catalog the feelings and sensations that were still new to her, at least in this context. A fine sheen of sweat had materialized across her skin as well as Hal's, and wherever they touched, they clung together like limpets. Her legs were slightly numb, as if they had come apart from her body and only just returned to their original place. The rest of her body felt fuzzy, muted and oversensitive all at once, the last tingles of pleasure still fizzing out in the corners of her limbs. She looked down at Hal, and noticed, for the first time, that he had a dark mole behind his left shoulder, along with a smattering of freckles across his back. They suited him, somehow, and it renewed her smile.

Now that the intensity of the moment had passed, now that she had a floppy, satiated husband sprawled across her, something rather like utter content had settled along her back, against her neck, below her hips. It was a heavy, pleasant weight, not unlike Hal himself, and he was so warm, so soft and wonderful. He hummed, kissing the skin just above her breast, thumbing at one of her ribs in a way that should have tickled but didn't.

I could lie here forever, thought Rosaline, and it was the last thing she thought before she fell into a light, supple doze.

38

When Rosaline woke, the sun had shifted, and so had her husband. He was still sprawled on top of her, but now he was fast asleep. Hal's face was tucked in beside her neck, his arm thrown across her chest, his leg curled over her hip. He was snoring gently, his face slack and utterly at peace, and Rosaline had to smile, reaching up to card her fingers through his hair.

His seed had dried to a thick jelly, adhering his leg to her stomach. With a finger of her free hand, Rosaline grazed the edge of it, watching with interest as it pulled at her skin. This was all so new to her, still. It was strange to think that this streaky, white substance held half of the key to life, that so little could cause so much change. And it seemed that one had to remove it before it dried — she would need a damp cloth to scrub it away.

Her body still felt lax, pleasantly heavy. She shifted a little, wiggling her hips, and blushed to find that her sex was wet and swollen, dormant but not slumbering.

Rosaline was still getting used to it, this newfound freedom to indulge her attraction as much as she liked. When she'd imagined marriage in the past, it had never included *this*. Rosaline had to wonder if this would be what the entire honeymoon was like... relaxed, unhurried, untroubled by some of the more conventional concerns of time and place and everything in between. And how would it compare to their marriage? She'd heard so many horrifying tales of the flame of passion snuffing out over time — such a possibility seemed hardly imaginable.

As Hal slept on, Rosaline looked up at the intricate scrollwork on the ceiling and began reviewing a mental catalog of her personal library. Doubtless, she would soon devote some time to unpacking the trunk in the corner, and would have to determine which volumes would reside here, or in her chambers, and which ones would find their new home in the family library.

"There is plenty of room," Hal had told her only a few days before. "When my godfather took up residence, he went through the collection with a vengeance and trimmed what he referred to as the 'decaying fat.' I know," he'd added, as she'd stifled a snort of laughter, "but you shall have the freedom to add to it as you will."

And she would, in time. Already, Rosaline's mind churned with the possibilities. Her new title afforded her even greater freedom than she'd had before. She could hire a new tutor, *two* new tutors. She could purchase as many books as she liked, subscribe to magazines and serials, invest in young authors struggling to make ends meet. She could open a salon, a place where the women of England — perhaps the women with whom she'd spent the season — could discuss matters of serious importance, and teach each other whatever they could not learn themselves.

And then, they could begin to dream. Of the right to vote.

Rosaline's mind was so overrun with plans and facts and figures that she almost did not notice it when Hal sighed and stirred, nuzzling her arm. He began to kiss her shoulder before his eyes even opened, and it was so simple, so lovely a gesture, that her heart thudded with joy.

"I believe," he mumbled, "that I just proved something."

"Oh?" She had to smile, tugging gently at his disastrous hair. "And what is that?"

"It was only a theory." His mouth, trailing along her arm. "Until now."

"Well? Don't hold me in suspense."

Hal glanced up at her, and she shivered from the unending heat of his gaze. "That I can hear you thinking."

Something squeezed tight around her chest, and Rosaline gave him a playful shove. "You are *incorrigible—*"

Hal caught her arm, slid his own around her back, and pressed her down into the sheets. "Yes, I am." With that, he licked into her mouth, determined and filthy.

Rosaline let out a moan, unashamed of the way she rutted against him. It was as if he'd flicked a switch in her body, taking it from dormant to alive with the mere skill of his mouth, his hands, his presence. And she did not care, not even for a moment, if she seemed desperate, or loose, or any of the other ridiculous things men liked to call women — she'd waited long enough for this, and she was determined to have it.

He kissed her until she could hardly breathe, and when he broke away, it was to chuckle against her neck. "Goodness me, am I always to find you this... eager?" His hand slid across her sex, a gentle, ridiculous tease.

"Perhaps," Rosaline managed, trailing a line of kisses down his neck. "If you give me good enough reason."

"And what would be a good reason?" Hal lapped at her breast, squeezed her thigh. His swollen cock bumped against her hip. "That you should be naked, with a hand to yourself, in this very bed, at five o'clock every afternoon?"

The thought alone made something new and hot twist in her gut, but she hummed, pretending to speculate. "That might be difficult, if we are to entertain guests."

"Well, if you did not obey..." His teeth, grazing the line of her chest, just as two of his fingers curled at her entrance, there but not moving. "You might find yourself in terrible trouble."

Again, something twisted in her gut, and Rosaline smiled. "Would I? And what trouble would that be?"

He actually seemed to consider the question, giving her a look that was all challenge. "Perhaps when I sought to pleasure you... you would find yourself brought most determinedly to the edge, but never permitted to cross it."

A ringing silence fell as she stared at him, speechless, her face on fire.

And an expression of absolute surprise crossed Hal's face as he looked down at where his fingers lingered at the edge of her body, finding them suddenly rather damp. When he looked back up at her, his face still slack with astonishment, he said, "My God, I did not think—" But he was silenced when she yanked him down into a searing kiss and used her other hand to shove his up and forward, moaning as his fingers finally slid home.

Kissing turned into loose, ceaseless bites as he shifted, getting properly between her legs. Rosaline wrapped her legs around his torso, beginning to get a feel for how her body could move and respond, how she could guide him where she wanted him. And when she dug her nails into his shoulders and her heels into the small of his back, the message was unmistakable.

Hal huffed a weak, broken laugh against her jaw. "You will be the end of me—"

"Yes, but not yet—" she bit out, rolling her hips against his hand. "Please—"

"Very well." And he was smiling when he brushed a kiss to her cheek. "Anything for my lovely, temperate wife."

"You," she hissed, "will suffer for that later."

"Will I?" Hal replied, but before she could say anything else, he removed his fingers and slid into her with one single, fluid motion. His balls bumped against her thigh, and they both gasped as he bottomed out, filling her just as keenly, just as astutely, as he had before. It was a moment both more real and more unreal than Rosaline could ever have imagined.

She made a keen sort of moan, twitching her hips. Hal let out that broken laugh once again, his mouth grazing her jaw, her neck. One of his hands drifted to her breast, and she shook against him as he began to move, her eyes slipping shut as all of her awareness came to focus upon the succulent, singular feeling of his being inside her.

Hal hitched himself up onto one elbow, and a fresh jolt of pleasure whipped through her as the slope of his pelvis was brought into contact with her sex, creating a delightful, fleeting friction. A desperate sort of sound surfaced from her throat, and Rosaline's hips twitched again, seeking that little spark of ecstasy, of abandon. And within minutes, Hal began to tremble, his mouth stuttering against her cheek.

"Rosaline, I—" He shook his head. "I'm much too close—"

She opened her eyes, took a breath, and shot him a cheeky grin. "Then, by all means, seek another form of entertainment."

It was as if he'd been waiting for such permission. Hal pulled away, sliding out of her, and Rosaline frowned, a little confused, but all that vanished when he took hold of her hips, shoved her up into the pillows, and fastened his mouth to her sex.

It was all Rosaline could do to keep from turning into pure liquid. She writhed against him — he was too much, pulling her towards that unstoppable ivory edge with a precision that was dizzying. He set a ruthless, punishing pace, his hand fumbling for her breast, and Rosaline's hands found a pillow, shoving it on top of her face, because she could not handle it, could not—

Her orgasm hit like a lightning bolt, there and gone within an instant, leaving her with a numb mouth, watery eyes, and feeling as if she'd been fired from a cannon. Her exhalation was lost to the down, and she shoved the pillow out of the way just in time to meet Hal's gaze. He was still crouching between her legs, his eyes bright and coy, and he tongued a line of kisses into her thigh, his mouth wet against her skin. Something about the way he looked — smug, determined — sent butterflies through her stomach and down to her hips, but before she could say anything, do anything, he was on his knees, parting her legs, and once again sinking into her.

Now, Rosaline was the one shaking. She was still too sensitive, and she could feel every inch of him as he drove into her, fast and messy and artless, his hips stuttering as he let out a moan. He was sweating now, but so was she, and his chest glistened in the late afternoon sun. Now, for the first time, Rosaline became aware of the way they sounded — the slick slap of skin on skin, his panting, his moaning, the little sounds that were falling out of her own mouth, into the pillows — and it was positively lewd. But something about it was so delicious that she almost smiled, and she rolled her hips, meeting him halfway.

That did it. Hal grunted, gave one, two, three more thrusts before he pulled away, falling into the sheets and burying his face beside her hip, muffling his final groan.

Rosaline did not know how long they lay there like that, panting into the warm, salty air. Her hand found its way to his hair; his found its way to her thigh. They were not looking at each other — Hal still had his face buried in the sheets — but Rosaline found that they did not need to. This was utter bliss. Lying there, sated and warm and still tingling with spent pleasure, overflowing with the love that she'd only just begun to allow herself to feel. She was sticky, yes, and breathless, and she was certain that her hair was an absolute nightmare, but none of that mattered, because it had to be one of the best feelings in the world. Being here, being with him in the most complete, overwhelming way she could imagine. Even the possibility of moving seemed like a sin.

Hal's voice, muffled. "Are you still with me?"

"Yes, I think so." She brushed her fingers along the back of his neck. "Are you?"

"Not sure," came his reply. "I haven't decided yet." A few moments later he surfaced, and he looked an absolute wreck — his face and chest flushed, a haze of sweat along his hairline, his eyes hooded and almost sleepy. Hal smiled at her, and she melted. "Goodness. Perhaps we should get cleaned up."

"Perhaps," Rosaline echoed. He kissed her leg, then slid off the bed and went over to the dressing table, where there was a pitcher and a basin. She could not help enjoying the view — he really did have the most fantastic arse.

Hal poured some water into the basin, soaked a washcloth. He swiped it over his face and the back of his neck, then brought it over to the bed. He climbed up, smirking down at her, then proceeded to spend the next few minutes wiping her and kissing her in turn. Soon, the sticky mess from earlier was gone, and she hummed as he pressed his mouth to her throat and threw the towel over his shoulder.

"At this rate," said Rosaline, "we shall go through quite a few sets of sheets."

"Sacrifices must be made," Hal replied. "Hungry?"

"Actually, yes." And she was surprised to admit it. "But supper is not—"

He flashed her a grin. "Who said anything about supper?" He rolled over, reached for the bedside table, and produced a round metal tin. He popped the lid, and several different scents drifted into the air — vanilla, chocolate, ginger.

"Hal!" She was laughing now. "You keep a secret stash of biscuits?"

"Of course," he said, unruffled. He took one of each and held out the tin.

The biscuits were lovely, and they certainly took the edge off her hunger. "Have you always done this?"

"Eaten while naked? Well, I must admit—"

"No, Hal!" She gave him a playful shove. "Kept food in your chambers."

"Oh." Hal put on a mock-thoughtful expression. "I came into the habit at Eton, I suppose. Their meals were somewhat... lacking."

"Now that, I believe. But I would think that young, well-off gentlemen would be more than capable of patronizing the local eateries?"

He shrugged, took another biscuit. "I'm frugal by nature, and our cook was always happy to indulge me. When I was at school, they only had to feed my godfather, which I imagine got rather dull. And," he added, "the nights at Cambridge can be long indeed, without a little chocolate."

For a moment, she just smiled at him, delighting in this new knowledge. But more importantly — "What was it like? University?"

Hal gave her a knowing look. "If I tell you, will you chop off your hair, secure a false beard, and run away to one?"

"I haven't decided yet." She poked him in the belly. "Tell me."

So he did, weaving a rich tapestry of his life as a student, living in a drafty tower with Cadogan just next door, getting lost in the library and falling asleep on his books, sitting through lectures that were dull and tutorials that were thrilling. Sneaking out in the warmer months to drink wine by the river, hunting for ghosts on All Hallows' Eve. Passing his exams and drowning in champagne, whether he wanted it or not.

"Magic," she whispered. "It sounds like pure magic."

Hal smiled, but it was sullied by a flash of guilt. "I wish..." He shook his head. "I wish you could go."

She kissed his hand, his cheek. "I make do."

"I know." He brushed a few crumbs from her shoulder. "You know... You know that now, as Duchess, you may spend your time as you like?"

"Yes." Rosaline squeezed his hand. "I know."

"I do not want you to feel trapped, ever." And his gaze was so bright, so earnest, as it found her own. "I do not want you think that just because we are married, that you—"

"I know," she murmured, reaching for him, brushing a kiss to his concerned mouth. "I know, my love, you need not worry—"

But before he could reply, they were surprised by the arrival of Oberon, who chose that moment to leap onto the bed, give them an unamused look, and pad over to Hal.

"Hello!" Rosaline ran a hand down the cat's back, and his tail quirked in reply. "How on earth did you find your way in here?"

"The house is full of secret passages," said Hal. "He undoubtedly availed himself of one."

In reply, Oberon let out a little chirp and climbed onto Hal's chest. Hal froze as the cat leaned in and sniffed his face, then, apparently satisfied, lay down right where he was, his face mere inches from Hal's nose. A low, rumbling purr soon emanated from Oberon's chest, his tail swishing across Hal's belly.

Hal stared at the cat, then at Rosaline, who was trying not to laugh. "What do I do?"

"Pet him," she said. "Go on."

Hal hesitated, then did so, running his fingers through Oberon's fur. The purr intensified, and Hal's eyes widened with surprise. "He smells like fish."

"You can thank your cook for that," Rosaline replied. "Looks like he's settled right in."

"That makes two of you, then?" Hal glanced at her, showing her just the barest glimpse of nerves. And when she smiled and nodded, his face broke into a brilliant glow, like the sunset on a perfect summer's day.

⚜

"I CANNOT FATHOM," HAL WAS SAYING, "HOW YOU DO THIS every day."

"It is not so terrible," Rosaline replied, slipping on her petticoat. She'd forgone her stockings and pantalettes, and it was delightful to let her body breathe. Hal was equally dressed down, wearing only a pair of loose trousers and a shirt. "Especially without the pantalettes." She gave him a wink, and he smirked.

"So tell me," she continued, once they were on their way down the hall. In her arms was a meticulously-wrapped box tied with a bright green ribbon. "What are the expectations of a Duchess at meal times? Doubtless, I will find myself quite overwhelmed by the set table, and will require smelling salts as well as tutelage in the finer art of cutting my own meat."

Hal shook his head, then he grabbed her, his fingers dancing across her waist, and she let out a squeal, trying to shove him away using only her elbow. "You are such a menace."

"Tell me," she pressed, kissing his cheek. "Even a general likes to know the lay of the land before a battle."

"You make it sound as if every meal is to be some sort of test."

"Is it not?" Rosaline countered as they rounded a corner. "How would it look if the new Duchess was flummoxed by her own silverware? I have to prove myself worthy of my new title, in every possible way."

Hal gave her a pointed look. "I trust we owe that directive to a certain Randolph."

"Perhaps."

He nodded. "Then I think it is best to adopt the rule we applied to the rest of her wisdom. To take it with a grain of salt, or ignore it altogether."

"*Hal.*" And now she did feel a wave of nerves. "I do not want to make a fool of myself. That would hardly be a good beginning in my new home."

"Rosaline." He gave her another pointed look. "I think you overestimate the formality of this household."

That took a moment to sink in, and when it did, she frowned. "What do you mean?"

Hal smiled. They had reached the top of the main staircase,

and as they began their descent, he put his hand to the small of her back. "Do you think, in many households, it is common for a child to leap into the arms of an adult in full view of the staff?"

"Well... I suppose not."

"Growing up," Hal continued, "I saw the way things were in other families. Lawrence hardly ever even saw his father, let alone spoke to him, and when they did speak, it was brutal to watch." He shook his head. "All I had ever known was the way *I* grew up, surrounded by love and affection in equal measure. My godfather made a point of spending as much time with me as possible, and he took a great interest in my hobbies, my education. Even when I was away at school, he would write several times a week, and visit me every term." They had reached the bottom of the stairs, and even now, at the brink of dusk, the entrance hall sparkled. "When it came time for me to shoulder my own responsibilities, I made a decision. I wanted to give Jamie the same upbringing, the same level of care." He shrugged. "So we do things a little differently here at Alban Hollow. You'll see what I mean soon enough."

"Oh." Rosaline tried to process everything he'd just said, and he led her down a different hall, past what appeared to be an enormous drawing room. "But what about the formal suppers?"

Hal smiled. "With any luck, those will be few and far between. And if it's any consolation, it is impossible for your table manners to be any worse than mine. But," he added, when she shot him a frown, "if you're concerned about using the wrong fork, I'm sure Mrs. Andrews will be more than happy to show you the basics."

Rosaline glanced around as he led her down another hall. "Where are we?"

"Well, as you probably guessed, most of the ground floor is meant to be used for entertaining. But the west wing is reserved for our own personal use." He reached for the nearest door, held it open for her. "After you."

Rosaline stepped into a parlor that was large by London standards but small compared to most of the rooms they'd passed on the way. Like their bedroom, the furnishings and decorations were simple, and even included a dining table with four chairs. She quickly noticed that the room was a bit messy, dotted with all sorts of toys, books, and even a few items of children's clothing. A smile broke through as she went over to the nearest couch and deposited Jamie's present. "I think I can tell who uses this room the most."

"Can you?" Hal smirked, wandering over to the French doors, which opened onto a small, west-facing veranda. Beyond it, the grounds stretched in a brief lull before erupting into a cluster of woods — the pond at the front of the house was not in view. "Wait until you see his bedroom. I've been on him to keep it tidy, but he never listens."

Rosaline noted that he did not expect the maids to pick up the slack, and she hid a smile. "Where is the rascal?"

Hal nodded out the open French door, just as a welcome breeze drifted in. "On his way. Hamish looks thoroughly worn out." He shook his head. "The man deserves an entire barrel of ale."

Rosaline had wandered over to the little bookshelf, but now, she glanced at him. "Hal, you said earlier that Hamish was Jamie's shadow. But what, exactly, does that mean?"

He shot her a careful look in return. "For lack of a better word, Hamish is Jamie's bodyguard. He is there when I cannot be, and in case the worst happens."

"Really?" She stared at him, her mouth dry. "Do you honestly expect—?"

"Always." Hal nodded, then returned his gaze to the veranda. "It's the best way I can ensure his safety, since I refuse to keep the poor boy locked inside the house. I pity the man who tries to best Hamish."

And Rosaline agreed. Hamish was like a brick wall with legs.

"Oh." Hal broke into a sudden grin. "Incoming—"

And then, suddenly, there came the familiar thunder of

running feet, followed by a sudden blur of tawny hair and green breeches. Hal wheezed at the impact, but managed to catch Jamie, hitching the boy onto his hip. Jamie had a streak of mud across one cheek and was grinning from ear to ear.

"We found owls," said the boy. "In the old elm at the top of the hill."

"Did you?" Hal shot Hamish a glance as he came lumbering through the French doors, definitely looking a little winded. "How many?"

Jamie seemed to think for a moment, his mouth pursed in concentration. "At least a hundred. They were all sleeping, like this." He drew his arms into his sides and squeezed his eyes shut, then let out a muffled "hoo."

Hal bit his lip, and Rosaline could tell that he was stifling a laugh. "You know, Jamie, I think you'd make an excellent owl. Perhaps we should loan you out, and you could spend the night in a tree."

Jamie opened his eyes and began to giggle, shoving at Hal's shoulder. "No, Hal, I don't have any wings! I'd fall off!"

"Not if you rigged yourself a little tent," Hal replied, ruffling his hair. "Now, what do we say to Hamish?"

"Goodnight, Hamish," said Jamie. "Thanks for looking after me."

Hamish chuckled. "My pleasure, you little monster. And if you'll excuse me, Your Graces, I believe there's a steak and kidney calling my name."

"Of course," Hal replied. "Goodnight, Hamish."

"Yes, goodnight," Rosaline added, and she shot him a smile as he left the room.

Jamie, meanwhile, had noticed the parcel sitting on the couch. His eyes were comically wide, and Hal shot Rosaline a knowing look.

"Supper first," said Hal, pressing a small button mounted on the nearest wall. "And we have to get that mud off your face."

Jamie nodded, his attention still fixed on his present as Hal carried him over to a side table, where a basin and pitcher of water stood at the ready. Hal dampened a small towel, then held it out to Rosaline, his eyes forming a silent question.

Rosaline nodded and crossed the room, taking the towel and meeting Jamie's gaze. "Now, Jamie, may I clean your face?"

"All right," he said, though he seemed skeptical. But he remained still as she wiped the mud away, and when she was finished, he flashed her a tentative smile. "Marcus told me that you and Hal are married now."

"Yes," Rosaline replied, mock-thoughtful. "I suppose we are, since I can remember signing a bit of paper and putting on a ring."

"So does that mean you're going to live here?" Jamie went on, his hand curling into the lapel of Hal's shirt. Hal, who was grinning at her, all devilish and knowing. "With us?"

"I think so," Rosaline replied. "If that's all right with you."

Jamie smiled, and it was just a touch shy. "Yes."

Before she could reply, the door opened, and Brooks appeared with a cart full of covered dishes, flatware, and silverware. "Your Graces." He managed to sound endearing and disapproving all at once. "Dinner is served."

"Yes!" Jamie jumped out of Hal's arms and ran over to the table. As Brooks wheeled the cart over, Jamie produced an enormous volume of the encyclopedia, and slid it onto the seat of what Rosaline presumed to be his chair. This done, he climbed up and waited, smiling, feet swinging.

"We eat most of our meals in here," Hal said to her, answering an unspoken question. "I hate the dining room. We'd be twenty feet apart, end to end."

"I cannot blame you," Rosaline replied, putting aside the washcloth. "It's rather cozy in here."

"And we usually take breakfast on the veranda," Hal continued. His hand slipped around her waist, and he pulled her close. "Weather obliging."

"You know, *ma puce*, I just have to be sure— we are married, yes?"

He rolled his eyes, then grinned and kissed her temple. "Yes, my love. Come, let's eat."

39

They sat down to a cold meal of potato salad, smoked salmon, and greens. Rosaline watched, impressed, as Jamie steadily worked his way through his food. She would never have dreamed that a seven-year-old would enjoy smoked salmon, let alone hold a knife and fork properly.

As they ate, Jamie told them all about his day, and everything he'd been up to while Hal had been busy getting married in London. Rosaline heard about his tutors, a Miss Vector and a Mr. Raghorn, and made a mental note to shadow some of his lessons. Jamie was already learning Latin and French, along with arithmetic, reading and writing, and even astronomy. Hal, it seemed, devoted a considerable amount of time to Jamie's education as well, but the more physical, practical tasks, such as fencing and horseback riding. Now, Rosaline was beginning to see just how irritating it must have been for Hal to trade the countryside for the city — at Alban Hollow, his entire day revolved around Jamie, and leaving that behind must have been quite a shock.

The bond between them was obvious, even tangible, and its depth impressed and intimidated her all at once. Sometimes, it was difficult for her to imagine how she would fit into the picture, but then Jamie would flash her a smile, or Hal would brush her hand with his, and her heart would steady, reassured. Even if she did not quite fit in now, she would soon.

The moment Jamie cleared his plate, he began shooting furtive glances at his gift, but Hal pretended not to notice until he and Rosaline were likewise finished. "All right," Hal finally said, pouring himself a fresh glass of wine, "have at it."

Jamie leapt out of his chair and darted across the room. Within seconds, he'd torn off the ribbon and had the paper in shreds. "Wow!" He clutched at the case of figurines — a full set of horses, soldiers, and cannons. "They even have faces!"

Rosaline laughed, and Hal grinned, shaking his head. "What do you say to Rosaline?"

"Thank you!" And to her surprise, Jamie came running over and threw his arms around her. Rosaline barely managed to embrace him in return before he ran off again, back to his soldiers.

"Jamie, you can take them into the garden tomorrow," said Hal, clearly fending off the question before it was asked. "But tonight, you need to keep them inside."

"All right." Jamie was already busy lining up his soldiers, and sticking a few of them onto horseback. He lifted one of the cannons, spinning its wheels.

Hal flashed Rosaline a smirk and said, "We have a good quarter of an hour before he remembers that we're here." His finger stroked the curve of her hand. "So tell me. How are you?"

"Very well," she replied, sinking back into her chair. "Hal, this..." She shook her head. "This is wonderful."

His smirk took on a self-deprecating edge. "You should wait until you see him in a bad mood. You might feel differently then."

"Possibly," Rosaline allowed. "But I can see why you prefer to spend your time here. London simply pales by comparison."

"I think," he said, "that you are trying to get on my good side."

Rosaline smiled. "Is it working?" She let her gaze drift back to

Jamie, and her thoughts sobered somewhat. Hal apparently noticed.

"I know he and I seem close," he said in an undertone. "But it was not always this way. The first few months were especially difficult. It took him two weeks to even eat a meal with me."

"Really?" It was hard to imagine.

He nodded. "Really. He blamed me for his father leaving, not that I fault him for it."

"Do you ever hear from Jamie's father?"

"Sometimes. But you know what the post is like coming across the water, and the war does not help any. The correspondence that does get through is shaky at best — his father cannot be too detailed, for our safety as well as his."

"Do you even know where he is?"

"New York, last we heard." Hal shook his head. "It must be dismal."

"Careful, your bias is showing."

"No, I mean." He flashed her a smile. "I mean... a foreign country, a big city, all alone, with your child halfway across the world..." He shook his head again. "I cannot imagine it."

Something inside her quivered. "Well, with any luck, it won't last much longer. Will it?"

"It's impossible to say. Treason is not a crime taken lightly."

"Nor is the matter of the little one's heart." Rosaline sighed, took a sip of wine. "At least it's a beautiful evening."

"It is," Hal agreed, squeezing her hand. "And we must savor it."

ROSALINE DID NOT SEE LISETTE UNTIL IT CAME TIME TO prepare for bed. Hal showed her the shared door between their room and her personal chambers, told her how to ring the bell. Her chambers were lovely, airy, scented with a fresh bunch of gardenias, but Rosaline couldn't help feeling a little nervous as she went over to the button and pressed it for the very first time.

Just a few minutes later, a hidden door opened by the bed and Lisette appeared, smirking like a cat who'd caught a mouse. "Well, well, well…"

Rosaline grinned at her, unable to hide it. *"Bon soir."*

"Good evening to you as well, Your Grace." Lisette dipped into an exaggerated curtsy. *"You look incredibly well."* She raised an eyebrow. *"Care to divulge the details?"*

"Not just yet," Rosaline replied, fidgeting a little where she stood. *"I can hardly believe that I'm here, that we're here."*

"I know, my dear, I know." Lisette came over, took Rosaline's hands in hers, and squeezed them. She pressed her forehead to Rosaline's, and Rosaline closed her eyes, took a breath. *"But where else would we be?"*

"Nowhere," breathed Rosaline. *"Nowhere could be more perfect, more beautiful."* She pulled away. *"Have they explained about Jamie?"*

Lisette scoffed. *"Of course. I should have known there was a child involved — didn't I say that the Duke had his secrets?"*

"But not quite so scandalous as you imagined," Rosaline teased, then glanced around the room again. *"I cannot believe that this is all mine."*

"But it is, my dear. Just as it should be. Now, do you want to change?"

"Yes, please."

Lisette nodded, crossed over to what Rosaline realized was a closet. She disappeared inside, then reappeared with one of Rosaline's nightgowns from her trousseau.

"Oh." Rosaline glanced at the closet door. "I had not realized that my clothing—"

"All unpacked today," Lisette replied, hanging the nightgown over the changing screen. *"Except for what you took with you to the inn. And I did not dare touch your books, I can remember all too well what happened the last time."* She winked.

Rosaline huffed, blushing at the memory. "*You did not alphabetize them, and I was in a bad mood that day.*"

"*Do not worry, I already warned the other maids not to touch them, on pain of a verbal smack.*" But Lisette winked again, then reached for her. "*Come, let us get you out of that dress.*"

Rosaline complied, still blushing, and said, "*I am not wearing pantalettes. Or stockings.*"

"*I know,*" Lisette replied, a touch smug. "*After all these years, my dear, I can tell when you are and when you are not.*"

Once Rosaline was down to her chemise, feeling the prickle of the cool evening air, she blurted, "And that should... continue."

A silence fell. Lisette shot her a cunning look, then smirked, hand on one hip. "Oh, really?"

"Yes," Rosaline managed. "Just... for now."

Lisette hummed. "*Very well. Wish I could say that I was surprised, but to me, it makes sense. No man in his right mind would want anything between himself and you.*"

"Lis!" Rosaline's blush deepened, and she tugged off her chemise. "*You give me too much credit, as usual.*"

Lisette scoffed, handing her the nightgown. "*Do not be ridiculous. Have you seen yourself?*"

"Well, I—" And to her horror, Rosaline felt genuine emotion prickle at her throat. "*I know that I look... that my body is different, from most of these other English girls.*" Unbidden, the image of Charlotte's tiny, light little body floated into her mind.

Lisette scoffed again. "*Because unlike them, you actually eat your food.*"

"*A part of me did worry,*" Rosaline said, before she could stop herself. "*That he would not... like it. I know,*" she added, when Lisette shot her a look of incredulity, "*it is utterly ridiculous, but still, it was a passing thought.*"

"*The Duke is a good man, my dear, in more ways than you might think.*" Lisette seemed to sit on her words before she said them. "*Has he shown any reluctance to touch you, when you are alone together?*"

"No," Rosaline said at once. "Just the opposite." Even now, she could feel the ghost of Hal's hands on her hips, her waist. "*He cannot seem to help himself.*"

Lisette gave her a sudden, genuine smile. "*Just as it should be.*" She reached out, put her hand to Rosaline's cheek. "*Remember, my dear, comparison is the thief of joy.*"

"*I know,*" Rosaline replied, and felt something quieten in her, something that she had not known was in uproar.

The rest of her toilet did not take long. She washed her face, cleaned her teeth, and Lisette braided her hair. Soon enough, the time came for her to return to their shared chambers.

"*You can ring for me whenever you'd like,*" Lisette said, gathering all of Rosaline's discarded clothing. "*But if it is the middle of the night, it might take a while to rouse me.*"

Rosaline shook her head. "I cannot get used to the whole bell business."

"*Soon it will feel like second nature,*" Lisette replied. "*Anything you want, at the push of a button.*"

"*Don't, that sounds so horribly spoilt.*"

Lisette laughed. "*Perhaps you deserve to be spoilt, for a little while.*" She leaned in, brushed a kiss to Rosaline's cheek. "*Have a good night in your new home.*"

Rosaline kissed her back. "*Thank you, Lis, for everything. And the new uniform suits you.*"

Lisette winked at her. "*I know.*"

When Rosaline slipped back into her and Hal's bedroom, she was surprised to find him already in bed, though not beneath the covers. And, to her delight, he was naked.

"Hello." Hal smiled at her, all sleepy and soft. "You look lovely."

Her nightgown was one of Madam D'Amboise's signature creations — pale blue silk, thin straps, the neckline edging dangerously low. It felt deliciously cool and supple against her skin, perfect for sharing a bed with a furnace like Hal. Rosaline turned on the spot, flashing him a glimpse of where the night-gown dipped low, exposing half of her back.

"Good Lord." He looked a bit dazed, and she was delighted to see a certain part of him twitch and begin to take interest. "Do all your nightgowns look like that?"

She sighed, going over to her side of the bed, not missing the way his eyes remained glued to her breasts. The silk left very little to the imagination, and she knew exactly what he could see. "I am afraid the winter ones are rather more practical."

Hal shook his head. "I cannot decide what I like more. You, in bed, naked, or you, in bed, dressed like this." He reached for her, brushed a finger against her breast.

Rosaline smiled. "You will have plenty of time to make up your mind."

"Come here."

She obeyed, but took her time about it, slowly sliding in beside him. Then his hands were on her, tugging her even closer, pressing into the curve of her waist. Rosaline smiled into his hair as he mouthed at her neck. "What about you? Where's your nightshirt?"

"I told you last night," Hal replied, his words a hum against her skin. "I don't usually wear one, unless I am expecting company."

"Oh." She'd thought he'd been joking. But now she flushed with the knowledge, going hot all over. "Even in winter?"

She could feel his smile. "All right, sometimes, if it is very cold."

"I see." Rosaline reached up, tangled her fingers in his hair. "I suppose that's... acceptable."

"Is it?" His hands skated over her body, tangling in the silk. Hal thumbed at the lowest curve of her breast, teasing and silent, then reached around to trace a line up her bare shoulder blade, his touch gentle and rough all at once.

Rosaline sighed, then shivered. "Why is it that you have calluses? Are they from boxing?"

His hand stilled, then resumed, rubbing circles into her skin. "I am not sure. It could be that, or from riding. I don't usually wear gloves. They get very hot and irritating." The circle became a figure eight, then turned back into a circle. "Does it trouble you?"

"No." She shivered again. "The opposite."

Hal chuckled, brushed a kiss to her nose. "I am glad to hear it." And when he kissed her, it was sweet, simple, leaving her aching for more.

For a long while, all they did was kiss each other, and touch each other, putting hand to muscle and skin and bone. Rosaline discovered a sensitive spot below Hal's left ear, and learned how his clavicle felt beneath her mouth. Perhaps it was absurd, after all that they'd done, to feel that she'd only just begun to learn him, to connect the contours of his body to the dozens of anatomical figures she'd memorized over the course of her life.

"I want to learn you," she breathed against his stubbled cheek. "I want to know everything."

For a spare, fleeting moment, Hal trembled, but then he squeezed her, brushed a line of kisses down her jaw. "I could say the same to you."

Rosaline smiled. "What do you mean?"

"Well, we did not grow up together." One of her straps had slipped down her arm, and Hal's gaze found the space where her chest dipped and her breast swelled. His thumb followed its path, brushing a feather-light touch to the bare, sensitive skin. "And I know so little about your life in France."

She tried to take a breath. He could be quite distracting. "There is not much to know."

"I disagree." He was watching his own hand where it pressed, gently, into her skin.

"We could make a promise."

"A promise?"

"An agreement," she amended. "At the end of each day, when we are lying here, in bed, we must tell each other something. It can be a story, or even a secret, something we've never told anyone else."

His gaze found hers, bright and knowing. "Have many secrets, do you?"

"I do not think so," Rosaline replied. "I'm certain you have more."

"You overestimate me." His mouth, now, dipping to the space where her skin met silk. He tongued at the fabric, and she shivered, aching for more. "I'm very dull."

"Then so am I."

"I shall be the judge of that. Go on, then." Hal nosed at her nipple. "Tell me a secret."

Rosaline had to take a moment to actually think — he was getting very good at shutting off her brain. "I won a lot of money at the boxing match."

He glanced up at her, surprised. "Did you really?"

"Yes." She'd collected her winnings in a small, furtive moment before Hal, Edward, and Lawrence had descended upon the poor bookie, then tucked the bills into one of her many pockets. She hadn't told anyone at the time, except Lisette and Charlotte. "I kept it hidden under my bed, beneath a loose floorboard. I thought, perhaps..."

Hal raised an eyebrow, again brushed his thumb over her skin. "Go on."

Rosaline bit her lip. "I can be... rather... dramatic."

"And?"

A part of her wanted to give him hell for not denying it, but she pressed on. "I had a few things stashed under that floorboard. In case I felt the need to make a quick escape."

Delight flashed across his face. "You thought of running away?"

"Only sometimes," she said. "When Randolph made things truly dull."

"I cannot blame you. What did you do with the money? Don't tell me I should start checking under the furniture in here."

Rosaline rolled her eyes. "No. I gave it away."

Both of his eyebrows went up. "You *gave it away?* To whom?"

"To Katherine. As a wedding gift."

Now he just seemed lost. "Why? She is quite well-off, and Mr. Heath—"

"It wasn't really for her." Her heart was throbbing in her ears, but she tried to ignore it. "It was for her and Rebecca. To buy themselves a cottage, wherever they'd like. So that they could be together, separate from everyone else, away from prying eyes."

For several long moments, Hal stared at her, and she felt as if she could see the gears turning in his brain as he fully caught up. "That is a great kindness, Rosaline."

She blushed. "Well, it's not as if I needed the money."

He smiled, a small, tender thing. "My point stands." And he leaned forward, kissing her on the mouth, simple and slow.

"Your turn," she mumbled against his cheek.

"No, I cannot top your story—"

"Tell me, Hal—"

"Fine." He sat up, tugged his pillow away from the headboard. "I carve my initials into every bed I ever sleep in."

Rosaline stared at the bottom of the headboard, where, true to his word the initials HJC were roughly carved into the lowest beam. She turned to stare at him, and he offered a sheepish smile in return. "Did you—? At the inn?"

"No," he said. "I don't bother if it is only one night. But my childhood bed, my bed at Eton, at Cambridge, London... I don't know, I have always done it."

"How odd." She reached for his pillow, tugged him back down into the covers. "Perhaps I shall have to copy you."

Hal grinned, brushed a kiss to her nose. "I would love that.

But for now..." He glanced behind him, at the darkened windows. "Shall we sleep?"

"Yes."

"Do you want the candle?"

Rosaline nodded, but before he could move, she rolled on top of him, pressing him down into the sheets.

"God—" he wheezed. "My stomach—"

Ignoring him, Rosaline went nose-to-nose with the flame, paused, then blew it out.

In the darkness: "What did you wish for?"

"Rain."

40

Rosaline woke early, coming slowly out of her dream into the still, gray-blue light of the pre-dawn. She sighed into her pillow, about to turn over and find her way back to sleep, but then she felt it, the hand skating up between her parted legs, squeezing her thigh, her bum. His mouth, plush and warm from sleep, grazing the back of her neck, her shoulder.

Rosaline mumbled something, leaning back into his touch. Hal made a sound of satisfaction, sucking a kiss into her neck, and his fingers teased at her inner thighs.

They did not speak, because they did not need to. They moved together in a silent, rolling agreement, one that was familiar and yet very new.

When he put his mouth to her, it was light, gentle. He lapped at her clit, tongued at her entrance, and she shook against him, a whimper breaking in her throat. But then he shifted away, his tongue brushing over her, waiting until she squirmed and hitched her hips to finally return his mouth to where she most needed it. His fingers skimmed over her silk nightgown, dancing and ticklish, until he reached her breast. Hal grazed his thumb across her nipple, his fingers around the curve of her breast, and it was too much and not enough all at once.

He brought her to the edge in a slow, heady swell of delight, a fall so gradual that she almost did not notice it was happening. When it finally broke, Rosaline shook and gasped, pleasure rolling through her on a slow-moving wave, and it surged again and again until it faded and ebbed, until all she could do was lie there, dazed and sleepy, while his mouth suckled at her thigh.

Hal shifted up the bed, kissing his way from her stomach to her breasts, her neck. He pushed her nightgown up to her hips, and buried his cock in her with a broken moan. The sound seemed to shatter the silence of the morning, and she watched him bite his lip, his jaw clenching with the effort of keeping silent. He braced himself above her, the muscles livid in his arms, and fucked her at a slow, unhurried pace.

Her stomach turned to jelly. Rosaline tangled her fingers in his hair, mouthed at his chest, desperate to touch him, to feel him with every inch of her body. Hal moved so slowly it was almost like he was ghosting through her, real and unreal all at once.

It did not take long for him to unravel, muffling his groan against her neck as he collapsed into the sheets beside her. Rosaline let out a mumble, rolling towards him, wrapping her arms around his sweaty body. Her nightgown tangled against his skin, and her head was so heavy, her body throbbing with spent and chambered pleasure. She nuzzled his chin, and her eyes slid shut. She could feel his heart pounding beneath her arm, and wondered, distantly, if the beat would echo through the room, down the halls, into the endless labyrinth of the estate. Would it be trapped between the doors and the windows, knocking into eternity like a ghost?

His mouth, hazy and dry, against her forehead. His hand, skating across the small of her back, hugging her close. And it was here, with her cheek pressed to his chest, and her head pillowed on soft, forgiving down, that she fell asleep.

ROSALINE WOKE SEVERAL HOURS LATER TO THE PATTER OF A light rainfall and her husband's breath on her neck. She blinked, focusing on the curtain rods mounted a dozen feet above her, and noticed that the ends were carved into decorative griffin heads. An odd, though somehow fitting, choice.

In spite of the rain, the air was warm, made warmer still by the blazing heat of Hal's body, pressed against her like a second shadow. Sweat hazed over her, in spite of the silk, and though she was loath to do it, Rosaline shifted, untangling herself from his embrace, turning to brush a kiss to his forehead. "Hal. We fell asleep."

He made a muffled sort of sound and frowned against her shoulder. "As we bloody well should. Have you heard of a honeymoon?"

Rosaline bit back a surprised laugh. She was still unaccustomed to how grumpy he could be in the morning. "*On peut avoir une lune de miel et encore manger le petit déjeuner.*"

"No." He pulled back, burying his face in the pillows before he surfaced to frown at her. "I thought we discussed this. No French before noon."

She did laugh then. "*Je ne crois pas que nous ayons discuté de quoi que ce soit du genre.*"

"Duchess!" he said, loud enough for half the servants to hear, but he was grinning. "You must honor and obey your husband!"

Still laughing, Rosaline just said, "*Si je ne le fais pas?*"

"Insubordination," said Hal, mock-affronted, leaning in to kiss her once, twice, thrice. "Insubordination, in my own home."

Then, her stomach growled, and they both heard it. Hal sat up with a sigh, and his hair threatened to break a gravitational record. He had sheet creases up the right side of his torso, his eyes were still mussed with sleep, and the light dusting of hair on his chest, his thighs, seemed darker than usual in the pale light.

Every part of her body wanted to tug him back into the pillows, but that would have to wait.

"Very well," he said. "I suppose we can get something to eat."

Rosaline glanced at the clock on the bedside table. "*Mon Dieu*, it's quarter to eleven!"

"Then Jamie will already be at his lessons," said Hal, unaffected. "We can ring for trays and eat in here. We will see him this afternoon."

"But won't they——?" Rosaline stopped short, then blushed when he raised an eyebrow.

After a moment, he said, "Go on."

"If we ask them to bring us... won't they know... that we..."

Hal looked at her, then slowly broke into a grin. "Rosaline. As astonishing as it may seem, the servants do, in fact, know that we are married."

"Still." If only she would stop blushing! Rosaline slid out of bed, padded over to the dressing screen, where she pulled on her robe. "I find it embarrassing."

"You know it is traditional for married women to take their breakfast in bed? I am supposed to breakfast on my own downstairs."

"Oh." Rosaline paused, and sat back down on the bed. "I do not think I would like that."

"No?"

"No," she agreed. "I would prefer to breakfast with you and Jamie."

Hal smiled. "We can tell Lisette when you ring for her."

Rosaline swallowed, hard. "Must it be... Lisette?"

"Considering that she is your lady's maid, yes, she will be the one who answers."

She looked at him for a moment, then shook her head and stood up again, going over to the nearest bell pull. "On your own head be it."

Lisette was wearing her tiniest smirk when she appeared at

the hidden door in the wall. "Your Graces." Behind her, Oberon came waltzing into the room. "How may I be of assistance?"

"We would like breakfast, Lisette," said Rosaline. "In... here."

"Very good, *ma chère*."

"Lots of bacon," added Hal, who, much to her relief, had gone back under the covers. Oberon jumped up and wandered over to him, purring.

"Understood, Your Grace." Lisette curtsied. "I will make haste." She shot Rosaline a final look before leaving the room, the hidden door closing silently behind her.

Rosaline met Hal's gaze. "I shall never hear the end of it."

❧

"AND THIS," SAID MRS. ANDREWS, TURNING A CORNER, "IS THE East Wing. It is mostly bedrooms for guests, but traditionally, the children of the family live here, at the end."

"Oh!" Rosaline glanced between the three nearest doors. "Does one of these bedrooms belong to Jamie?"

"Yes, Your Grace, would you like to—?"

"Very much!"

Mrs. Andrews smiled and walked two doors down. "He is with Miss Vector, so I am sure he won't object." She opened the door, and Rosaline went in.

It was a small room, simply furnished, but Hal had been quite correct in his estimates of his godson's untidiness — there was a light clutter of toys and books scattered across the floor, the bed was unmade, and the desk was covered in piles of drawings and various jam jars full of insects.

Rosaline leaned down to peer at a praying mantis and said, "Jamie has never mentioned this particular hobby."

"Oh, yes," said Mrs. Andrews. "Master Jamie is very fond of the local flora and fauna. For better or for worse."

Rosaline recalled the conversation about owls the night

before. She'd have to find some good books, or perhaps a collection of drawings. She could do the theoretical, but the practical did not seem particularly appealing. "Legs," she muttered, glancing at a jar housing an enormous brown spider, and shuddered.

As they exited the room, Mrs. Andrews glanced at her and said, "The nursery is just two doors down, if you would like to see it."

Rosaline stopped short for a moment, then nodded. "Yes, I would."

The small room was lily-white and serene. A bassinet stood in the corner, opposite a small bed. Rosaline turned slowly on the spot, taking in the rocking chair, the china basin and matching pitcher, the hand-sewn quilt. It was impossible not to imagine a miniature Hal, all legs and piles of hair, running around the room, laughing and wreaking havoc until he flopped onto the bed, worn-out but happy. It was even easier to imagine a little girl with Rosaline's curls and Hal's blue eyes chasing the little boy, screaming with delight as she landed on top of her brother, breathless and brilliant with energy.

Rosaline paused beside the wooden chest at the foot of the bed. She bent down to lift the lid, gazing down at the neatly-stacked piles of knitwear and fluffy towels, grazing her finger along a line of delicate pearl buttons.

"Beautiful, are they not?" Mrs. Andrews was smiling. "The late Duchess was ever so skilled."

Rosaline glanced up at her, surprised. "She made these?"

"Oh, yes! The doctors put her on bedrest the last two months, so she kept herself busy. The Duke wore them all, but, of course, by the time he outgrew them..."

"I see." Something was fluttering beneath Rosaline's heart, but she ignored it and closed the lid. "They are wonderful."

"Yes, I suppose they are." Mrs. Andrews gave her a careful look. "It would be a joy to see this room have some use again."

Rosaline managed a smile. "With luck, Mrs. Andrews. With luck."

The tour ended shortly after that, and they ended up back near the main entrance, their footsteps echoing against the pristine marble floors. Rosaline couldn't help looking down at the vague reflection of her figure in the polished stone. "Gosh, this must be terrible to mop."

Mrs. Andrews paused, but only for the briefest moment. "Yes, Your Grace. Most of the time, we use the side and back entrance, to save ourselves the trouble. If the Duke rides in wet conditions, he comes to the kitchen and takes off his boots in the mudroom. He really is quite thoughtful. But the Hollow has not hosted an event larger than a small dinner party for the past two decades, so we have never had much cause to clean it, apart from the usual."

Rosaline took this in with a nod. "By the way," she added as they reached the front door, "I would prefer it if you and the rest of the staff would refer to me as 'my lady.' There is no need to be quite so formal all the time. We can save 'Duchess' and 'Your Grace' for special occasions."

Once again, Mrs. Andrews did a fantastic job of hiding her surprise. "Of course, my lady. That is very kind of you."

Rosaline smiled at her, and was glad to see the older woman smile tentatively at her in return. "I would like us to be friends, Mrs. Andrews. As you can probably tell, I am quite a fish out of water. I have a lot to learn, and I should be glad of your guidance."

"You undersell yourself, my lady," said Mrs. Andrews, and she took a step closer, dropping her voice. "You are doing very well already."

Rosaline beamed, squeezing Mrs. Andrews' arm. "Oh, you are kind. I look forward to learning whatever you can teach me. And is Lisette... adapting?"

Mrs. Andrews nodded. "She does good work, and she learns quickly. She told me that she has only ever worked for your family, which, I must admit, shows a remarkable level of dedication."

"Yes, we were her first posting as a housemaid. But my father really hired her to be my *au pair*, and since he was often away from home, she became more of a sister to me than anything else."

Mrs. Andrews smiled. "That is lovely, my lady."

"Yes," said Rosaline, "I suppose it is." Then, she heard something out on the drive — something rather like the clatter of hooves — and, after trading a look of confusion with Mrs. Andrews, opened the front door.

"What perfect timing!" Hal was grinning from where he sat astride a beautiful black horse. He was dressed casually in a pair of breeches and a thin shirt, and he wore a pair of faded riding boots. Beside him was another horse, this one slightly smaller, with a bay dun coat. It was outfitted with a saddle and bridle, and Hal had the reins in hand. The bay horse turned to look at Rosaline with dark, expectant eyes.

"Hal!" Rosaline frowned, bemused. "What is this?"

"Since the rain cleared up," he said, "I thought we should take advantage of the fine weather. Would you like to see the estate?"

Rosaline turned to Mrs. Andrews. "Is our tour complete?"

"Yes, my lady."

"Perfect. We shall continue my education in hosting tomorrow. I would love to see the kitchen."

"Of course, my lady. I will inform the cook accordingly." Mrs. Andrews leaned in once again, with a glimmer of mischief in her eyes. "Enjoy your tour of the estate."

Rosaline smiled at her, then bounded down the steps and went up to the horse, hand aloft. The horse sniffed at her, and, as she stroked its nose, let out a whinny.

"She is beautiful," Rosaline said, tangling her fingers in the mare's jet-black mane. "Does she have a name?"

"She is a wedding present to you from my godfather," said Hal with a smile. "So the name is left to your discretion."

She stared up at him. "What? A horse? Hal, that is far too generous—"

"Not to him," he replied. "I had to convince him not to buy you a whole new library. Do you need assistance?"

"No, thank you. She is the perfect height." Rosaline took the reins from him, and in one quick, fluid movement, climbed atop the horse. She adjusted her dress and situated herself side-saddle.

Hal shook his head and grinned. "When you said you were a practiced rider—"

"Well, it has been a while. Not since I left France. But our house in Provence bordered a farm that kept horses. I learned how to ride as soon as I learned how to ask the farmer if he could teach me."

"How kind of him." Hal turned his horse, and she copied him. "We'll head north, you should be able to see much of the land from there."

They set out at a walk, and Rosaline couldn't hold back a grin at the familiar feeling of the horse's body rocking beneath her. She had enjoyed London, in the end, but it had not given her this freedom, this ability to go where she pleased, to roam the countryside for hours on end.

The immediate land around Alban Hollow consisted of a flat and well-tended lawn, interrupted by wild hedges and clusters of trees. She noticed a seething, though trimmed, garden around the back of the house, bordered by another grove of cherry trees and what looked like a cluster of apple trees. "Does the house keep a kitchen garden?"

"Yes," Hal replied. "And several of our tenants provide us with dairy and vegetables, in exchange for a discount on their lease. It is all run quite smoothly." He shot her a wink.

Rosaline rolled her eyes but smiled. "Yes, I am sure it is. When do I get to meet the estate manager? He must be fearsome indeed."

"The day after tomorrow. He is in Glastonbury on business."

"It was very kind of him to agree to steering the ship on his own whilst you wile away on your honeymoon."

Hal bit out a laugh. "You forget, my dear, that he had most of the summer to prepare himself for my continued absence. Though he was rather astonished to hear that I had found myself engaged and married."

"You speak as if it were an occurrence of chance," Rosaline teased, and her horse let out a nicker of agreement. "Rather than one of choice."

"Not at all. It was the easiest decision I have ever made." Hal flashed her that smile, that cunning, delightful smile, and a blush surged up her neck.

Rosaline smiled in return, then had to look away and take a long, deep breath. There was very little she could do to him from atop a horse.

Hal took them due north, through a small burst of trees, up the curve of a hill. They broke through the tree line, and below them unrolled a seemingly endless stretch of land; she saw a few dozen acres of wheat, then a herd of sheep and cattle grazing. She turned her attention further east, and saw another parcel of land, this one likewise devoted to sheep and what appeared to be several acres of dark, leafy vegetables.

"This," said Hal, nodding to the first farm, "is the Jenkins tenancy. The one you're looking at belongs to the Morrises."

"Oh! As in the Captain Morris!"

"And the Bow-Street Runner," he pointed out, giving her that sly look again.

"They must miss their sons," said Rosaline, ignoring the way a blush surged up her neck. "It must be lonely, to go from having a household of six children to a household of only one."

Hal nodded. "They would quite like to meet you, if you are willing."

"I would love that," she said, and it was the truth. "Though it is a shame that we don't have Captain Morris in tow."

"Christmas," he said. "If he isn't sent to the Continent."

She looked at him in surprise. "Is that a possibility?"

Hal pursed his lips in thought, and his horse let out a huff. "Considering his injury, I would say not, though these wars have hardly followed any pattern of logic." He shifted, turning his horse, and said, "Come this way. There is something I want to show you."

Rosaline followed him, and as they passed through the sparse trees, she said, "Even if my horse is nameless, yours must have some type of moniker."

Hal gave his horse a hearty few pats on the neck. "This is Nimbus," he said, his tone warm with affection. "I cannot bring him to London with me, so I always make a point of giving him some exercise when I return."

"Is there a reason why you must keep him here at the Hollow?"

He shot her a sheepish sort of look. "The stables in London are rather compact, and he has to have his own stall. He cannot be kept with the other horses."

Rosaline raised an eyebrow. "He sounds very spoilt."

"It is not for his own sake," said Hal. "He pesters the other horses. Chases them. Nibbles on their hindquarters. You would not be so amused," he added, as she snorted with laughter, "if you had seen animals twice his size run away from him in abject terror."

"Good grief!" She was still giggling. "But he behaves himself here?"

"For the most part. We have a mule in the stables who maintains the rule of law."

"A mule?!"

"You can laugh, but it works. The mule is his God."

Hal led them through the woods, skirting the edge of the Hollow's lawn. They were now parallel to the house, and she could see the edge of the roof through the treetops. The sunlight splashed down on them in friendly, golden dapples, and the air was warm but not humid. She'd left the bottom half of her hair loose, and her curls fluttered in the breeze. It was a delightful change from the rainy morning, and Rosaline took a deep breath, relishing the cool tang of mud and leaves decaying underfoot. Autumn was coming, but for the moment, she was happy to savor these mellow end-days of summer.

They cut across part of the lawn, and Rosaline realized that they were approaching the southern drive up to the house. But they passed once again into a parcel of wild, untamed woods. She was just beginning to wonder where they were going when Hal went ahead and halted some ten feet in front of her. "Here," he called out, and she drew even with his horse, bemused.

In front of them, a two-story building burst out of the under-growth, in the midst of a sudden clearing. The sun beamed down upon its mellow golden brick, and its twin pillars were dotted with curling ivy. The windows were dirty, and the front steps were caked in dust and decaying leaves, but beneath the surface, she could see a grandeur, a beauty, that was undeniable. Rosaline guessed that the building was at least a hundred years old, if not older.

41

"Hal," Rosaline breathed, staring up at the edifice. "What is it?"

"That," he said, swinging himself down from Nimbus and landing with a thud, "is a question with several answers." Hal led Nimbus over to the nearest tree, and tied him to the lowest branch. "Come and have a look."

Rosaline did the same with her horse, and joined Hal where he stood in front of the building, looking up at the towering columns.

"This building has served many purposes over the years," he said. "First, it was a chapel. Then it became a gallery. In my parents' time, my mother used it as her studio. She painted," he added, when Rosaline shot him a questioning look. "You have seen some of her work in the entrance hall."

Rosaline stared at him, the images of those beautiful landscapes flashing in her mind's eye. "Hal, she was a brilliant artist."

He smiled. "So, I decided that it was only fitting that it should return to use under the tenure of its new Duchess." Hal reached for her, squeezing her hand. "You may use it however you wish. The staff and some of the farmers are more than happy to lend a hand in restoring it to its former glory. And we can clear the land, connect it to the main drive, if you so wish."

Rosaline shook her head, overcome with emotion. It fizzed in her stomach like champagne, bursting down her arms and through her feet. Unbidden, the thought of establishing a school for the local girls returned to her mind, and she wrapped her arms around his neck, putting everything she felt into a kiss that left them both breathless and dizzy.

"Goodness," Hal managed, dancing a line of kisses along her jaw, down her neck. "Perhaps I should have shown it to you sooner—"

Rosaline responded by kissing him again, sweeping her tongue through his mouth and grabbing every inch of him she could reach. Within moments, what had begun as a trickle of yearning became a wave of desperation, and she clung to him, moaning into his mouth when his hands tangled in her skirts, at her waist.

"What," he bit out, before he bit at the shell of her ear, "has gotten into you?"

Rosaline said nothing, unable to put what she was feeling into any series of coherent words. It was too much, it was too over-whelming — to see this, to have a physical expression of his love for her, his devotion to her independence, and to know that he was hers, that they were only at the very beginning of this journey. She kissed him instead, raking her tongue across his teeth, rolling against his body until she felt it, the tell-tale nudge digging into her hip. Hal's breath caught, and he broke away to pant against her neck. Around them, the birds screamed.

Rosaline settled for kissing his jaw, raking a hand up his back, tangling it in his hair. Hal let out a broken laugh, followed by a groan when she rubbed his length through the fabric of his trousers, intent and ruthless.

"Rosaline—" he managed, his hands gripping her hips hard enough to bruise. "We cannot— we're out in the open—"

She noticed that Hal did not pretend to mistake her intentions. It only made a fresh surge of pleasure, blinding-hot, tear through her, simmering in her gut. "Then follow me, Your Grace."

Rosaline stepped away, took his hand, and led him back into the forest. She had no plan, only a vague idea of what she wanted. She would do anything to touch him, to feel him, to make him gasp. So she walked up to an enormous tree, leaned back against it, and pulled him towards her.

One of Hal's hands went to her neck, cupping her jaw, and the other tangled in her skirts, yanking them up and out of the way. His other hand, hot and dry, gripped her thigh and lifted it until she bent her knee, hitching her leg around his hips. Then his mouth, wet and searching as he licked into her mouth and sucked on her tongue. A moan broke in her throat, and Rosaline clutched at him, tearing at the buttons on his shirt until she forced them open and tugged his shirt down his shoulders, getting one hand on his chest while the other fumbled for the fastening on his trousers. Hal grunted against her mouth, and the hand on her jaw tightened, his nails grazing her cheek, leaving a burning cold in their wake. Rosaline's heartbeat thundered through her body like a shockwave, and it was just them, the trees, the birds, the distant rustling of the undergrowth. Then the whole world tilted and fell still because his hand reached the space between her legs and he tapped her clit with his thumb.

Her focus shrank to the sparse distance between their bodies, the air they shared as they panted against each other's mouths. She kissed him, sloppy and uncaring, aching for more. Sweat hazed over her arms, at the small of her back, and she could feel the dampness between her legs, just inches away from his hand, but he wasn't, he wouldn't, and it was infuriating—

"You are quite eager." Hal's murmur broke over the skin of her neck and she shook with it, her hips twitching beneath his hand. As if complying, he again tapped her with his thumb, sending a jolt through her belly. "Tell me what you—"

"You," she managed, and it came out in a whimper. Rosaline

squeezed her eyes shut, her fingers digging into his bare shoulder. "All of you—"

Hal muttered an oath, his mouth dropping to skim over her breasts, her clavicle. She finally managed to get his trousers undone, and he swore again, louder, when she squeezed his cock, giving it a few firm, teasing strokes.

"Duchess," he finally bit out, his head tipping back. He looked like a god, all bare-chested and gleaming in the golden light of the afternoon. "We are in a forest—"

Rosaline took a great gulp of air. "Do I look like I care?"

He let out a groan and dove in for another kiss, grunting as her hand twisted and squeezed.

"Now," she murmured against his lips, and he nodded, his hand fumbling once again at her skirts. "Don't be gentle."

Hal stepped away, his face livid with lust, and grabbed her hips, hitching her up against the tree. The bark dug into her skull, her shoulders, her back, but she did not care, she just clung to his shoulders as he shoved his trousers out of the way, tangled a hand in her hair, hitched up her leg, and sank into her in one fluid, burning movement.

A gasp broke and died in Rosaline's throat and she shuddered, overwhelmed, but barely had time to adjust before he began fucking into her, steady and ruthless, his breath puffing against her cheek, her neck. It was tight, controlled, and the angle was tricky, he was only halfway inside her, but it was good, so good, and his pelvis brushed against her clit, rough and sudden, and she let out a moan, keening, her nails digging into his skin, catching in the fabric of his shirt. She could come undone like this, wanton and standing in a grove of ancient trees, she could—

Hal's hips stuttered and he slid out of her with a curse. "The angle," he said, frustration bleeding through the heavy timber of his voice as he shifted against her, his cock bumping her inner thigh. "It isn't—"

Rosaline swallowed hard, and gently nudged him away. Hal

stepped back, looking perplexed, and she gathered her skirts, then turned around. Rosaline bent over, bracing herself against the tree, and spread her legs.

"Oh—" His voice broke, and his hand, hot as a brand, fumbled at the curve of her bum. "Oh, you will be the death of me—"

But he wasted no time. Again, Hal gripped her hips hard enough to bruise, and thrust into her once, twice, testing her until she moaned. Then, his voice ragged, he said, "Touch yourself."

Rosaline fumbled to obey, fighting a short war with her dress as she tried to get her hand where she needed it. When she finally did, with the scent of earth and leaves in her nose, he abandoned all pretension and began to fuck her, fast enough that her brain went silent and her throat tightened with suppressed moans. Then his hand, shifting from her hip to her hair, tangling in it and tugging at her curls until her back bowed and her neck arched, her mouth falling open as pleasure ripped through her, endless and devastating.

It did not take long.

"Oh—" was all the warning she gave as sparks jolted in her legs, up her back, down her neck. "Oh, Hal—"

His hips stuttered, but he kept going and going until she burst, pleasure showering through her body, white spots bursting in her vision as her body shook like an earthquake. Rosaline barely noticed when he pulled away and muffled a groan in the small of her back, his mouth dry and his forehead sweaty.

Rosaline shifted against him as the forest came back into focus. The branches twitched, the insects hummed, and she had to swallow a few times before she said, "Your hair... it tickles."

"Sorry," Hal mumbled, but he kept one hand on her hip as he pulled them both upright. Rosaline swayed, feeling drunk, and allowed herself to be led back into the clearing, where Hal lay down in the grass, bringing her with him.

For several long, gorgeous minutes, they lay there with their eyes closed, her forehead tucked under his chin, her hand on his stomach, his at her waist. Rosaline catalogued the warmth of the sun on her face, her chest, the stickiness of his skin against hers, the plush heat of the grass and the dirt against her back. The area between her legs was a slick mess, but she barely noticed it, instead paying attention to the rise and fall of Hal's chest, the shade of the stubble on his chin.

Finally, he huffed a chuckle and said, "I was correct, in what I said before. You will be the death of me. Or almost, anyway."

"That," Rosaline said, "makes no sense."

Hal's chuckle became a laugh and he rolled over to press a kiss to her neck, her cheek. "Of course it does, my love. So, are we to make a habit of this?"

"Ask me after Lisette sees the state of my shoes," she replied, glancing down at the offending articles, which were now caked in mud. "Though I could always wear boots."

Hal hummed, still kissing her neck. His hand slid her skirts up her leg, dancing over the bare, sensitive skin. She smiled, and captured his hand in hers. "Behave. We shall have to go back to the house at some point, and I would prefer to be clothed."

"Nonsense," he muttered, the word muffled against her skin.

Rosaline brought his hand to her mouth and kissed his knuckles. "Thank you for my gift, Hal. I cannot tell you what it means to me."

"In fact, I think you just did," he said, followed by a loud "Ow!" when she smacked his arm.

They untied their horses, climbed up, and made their way back to the house, taking a long route that brought them under the cherry trees of the front drive. After continuing west, where he showed her another neighboring tenancy, they shifted north, then east. Soon, they were drawing even with the western wing of the house, and Rosaline could see the terrace and the French doors where Jamie had come barreling in the previous night.

As if on cue, the air was rent by a shriek of delight, followed by a huge splash, then a rumble of deep laughter.

Rosaline turned to frown at Hal, but he was grinning. "We are just in time." He clicked his tongue, and Nimbus continued on down the hill. Bemused, Rosaline followed, taking a moment to double-check her dress and remove a leaf from her hair.

A footman came running up to them as they approached the front of the house, and Hal hopped down first, handing the reins to the footman. Hal offered Rosaline his hand and helped her down from her horse, who nuzzled at his elbow.

Hal smiled at Rosaline, reaching out to tuck a curl behind her ear. He looked just as rumpled as she felt, and his eyes sparkled with their shared secret. "Thought of a name yet?"

"Titania," said Rosaline, smiling back at him. "It is quite fitting, don't you think?"

"We have to introduce her to Oberon," he replied, but before she could reply, there came another shriek, followed by a splash, and another rumble of laughter. Hal took her hand, then led her around the front of the house, below the front terrace.

A wonderful scene erupted before Rosaline's eyes. Hamish was standing at the edge of the pond, knee deep in water, and some ten feet away, Jamie was splashing about like a fish, making his way back to Hamish. As soon as he saw them, he stopped and let out a shout: "Hamish! It's Hal!"

"Well, hello, Your Grace," said Hamish, raising a hand in greeting. "And, er— Your Grace."

Rosaline chuckled. "It is all right Hamish, there is no need for such formality. You may address me as Lady Cunningham."

Hal squeezed her hand as Hamish replied with, "Thank you, my lady, that's very kind."

"Oh, our new Duchess is most gracious," came another voice from the terrace above. "We shall all have to be on our best behavior."

"Marcus?" blurted Hal, shading his eyes as he squinted up at the terrace. "We did not expect you until this evening!"

"I was impatient," Lord Blackwood replied, making his way to the railing. He stepped into view, and he looked as handsome as ever, rakish and with a chambered grin. "One can hardly blame me for wanting to see the new Duchess in action."

"You flatter me, my lord," said Rosaline.

"For the love of God, call me Marcus," he said.

"We seem to have interrupted a very important physics lesson," said Hal, reaching for his boot. "Hamish, would you care to demonstrate?"

"Certainly," said Hamish with a grin. Jamie came barreling over to the edge of the pool, leapt into Hamish's arms, and was immediately thrown into the air, though which he sailed like a hawk, letting out another ear-splitting shriek before he landed in the depths of the pond with an enormous splash.

"Excellent," said Hal, now barefoot and unbuttoning his shirt. Rosaline blushed and made a point of looking away, unable to shake the memories that were only an hour old. "Jamie, may I?"

"Yes, Hal!" came the delighted shriek.

Hal bit back a grin, then leaned in and brushed a kiss to her cheek. "Excuse me, my love."

Rosaline smiled. "Have fun."

Hal waded into the pond, and once he was hip-deep, he dove in like a swan. Rosaline watched him disappear beneath the water before she turned and headed up the wide, sloping steps that opened onto the terrace.

Marcus was still leaning against the stone railing, glass of wine in hand. He looked tired, but his eyes were bright and he seemed to be hiding a smile.

"There's another glass on the table, along with the bottle," he said, which was an understatement. The table had been set, though informally, for six, and contained several covered platters of cold food.

Rosaline went over and poured herself a glass of wine. After glancing at Marcus' rolled-up sleeves and bare feet, she kicked off her muddy shoes and joined him at the railing just as Hal burst out of the water with Jamie on his shoulders.

"This is somewhat of a ritual," said Marcus, raising an eyebrow. "Any sunny day in the summer, and you will find them here. In the winter, they ice-skate."

"I think it is wonderful," she said, taking a sip of her wine. "I so enjoy seeing a family make actual use of their property."

"So do I," he said. "I can tell you it was hardly a part of my own upbringing. And if I had ever dared to turn up barefoot or with my sleeves rolled to the elbow, my mother would have disowned me on the spot."

"Hal did tell me that you made a point of disregarding the more traditional methods when you were raising him. I must tell you, I find that quite admirable."

Marcus did smile then, and his eyes crinkled at the corners. "That is kind of him, though I must admit it was a survival tactic more than anything else."

Rosaline cocked her head to one side. "May I ask what you mean?"

Marcus let out a sigh, and she realized, then, that she could see something she had not noticed in London — that he carried something with him, something invisible but heavy. It weighed on him like a cloak, followed him like a second shadow. "When Hal lost his parents, I lost the two people who were, by that point, what I considered to be the last remaining members of my family, two people who meant more to me than— they were all I had, you see, and by then, I had lost so much already that losing them..." Marcus shook his head and gave a rueful smile. "Did Hal tell you that it took me a while to shoulder my duties as godfather?"

She swallowed. "A bit."

"Again, he does me a kindness." Marcus took a sip of wine. "I spent the first few years after their deaths drinking my way across the Continent, mostly Italy, though there are a few Frenchflavored blurs that were perhaps more hedonistic than I would like to admit. But it got to me, in the end." He looked at her. "I had to face it. And I realized that as difficult as it was for me, it would be even more difficult for him, for Hal. And that if his father could see the mess I'd made of myself, he would smack me upside the head and tell me I was a fool, and a coward. So I came back to Alban Hollow. And I made a promise to myself. That Hal would not grow up as I had grown up. That he would know every ounce of kindness and love that his parents would have been capable of bestowing. And I will admit," he added, rueful once again, "that I see much of his parents in him. Too much, sometimes. Whether or not that explains anything..."

As his voice trailed off, Hal and Jamie burst out of the water once again, sending a wave surging against Hamish's legs. They were all laughing, but a weight inside Rosaline was sinking, and sinking fast.

Marcus noticed, and something glimmered in his eyes. "Have I spoken out of turn?"

"No," she said at once, but not too quickly. "Though I must likewise admit to some surprise at your trust in me."

"Why should you be surprised?" He polished off his glass and wandered over to the bottle. "I saw you face the Queen, remember. And you swore yourself to lifelong secrecy to protect a boy you had never met and therefore had no reason to protect."

"I did meet him," she said, "though I suppose it was after Hal had told me." Rosaline frowned, then shook her head, forcing herself to return to the point she'd forgotten to make. "Marcus, why did you tell me all of this?"

Marcus turned around, and she was surprised to find that the glimmer in his eyes had hardened, turning them into dull, obsidian chips. "Because," he said. "History repeats itself." And he shot a pointed look at where Hal and Jamie were splashing about like dolphins.

Rosaline looked at them, then back at him. "I do not understand," she said. "Hal told me that Jamie's father was one of your closest friends, one of the late Duke's closest friends—"

"And so he was," said Marcus. "But unlike Hal's parents, he is living, and he is one of the most dangerous, most resourceful, and most loyal people on the planet. And you would be a fool to think that he is no longer your concern." He took another sip of wine. "When Charles and Lily died, I was not the only one who lost a brother and a sister. But, where one of us ran off to the Continent, the other ran off and joined the army." Marcus looked at her again, and she saw something then, a shadow of a hunted beast. "Jamie may need someone to protect him, and I do not mean in the way that Hamish protects him." He almost smiled. "Hal loves Jamie, but he forgets that Jamie is not his son, or his brother, and that everything could change based on the whim of a single man. That leaves Hal vulnerable, which, now, leaves you vulnerable as well."

Rosaline could only stare at him, at a complete loss for words. And Brooks chose that precise moment to step onto the veranda and clear his throat.

"Dinner will be served in five minutes," he announced, loud enough that his voice boomed down onto the pond. "And shall be served outside, per the Duke's request."

"I will take supper in my room, Brooks," said Marcus, and he gave Rosaline a final nod. "Have a good evening, Duchess. Please excuse me." With that, he disappeared into the house, leaving Rosaline with a churning mind, and no idea what to make of it all.

42

T he following month was one of the happiest of Rosaline's life. She could hardly remember a time more peaceful, more filled with laughter, more buoyant with love.

As the weeks passed, she saw more and more of the estate, and finally met Mr. Randall Merrywether, the manager. He was tall, leonine, and his skin was even darker than her father's. After taking her hand and offering her an enigmatic smile that rivaled Charlotte's, he said, "Welcome to Alban Hollow. Our little estate is already much improved by your warmhearted presence."

"Mr. Merrywether." Rosaline smiled at him. "You are kind, and I so appreciate your flexibility with regard to the Duke's honeymoon."

"Not at all," Mr. Merrywether replied, then showed the faintest glimmer of a smile. "Besides, it is easier to balance the books if he does not have the first pass at them."

"I heard that," said Hal, indignant.

"In any case," said Rosaline to Mr. Merrywether, "you certainly know what you're doing. And we would love to have you join us for supper sometime."

His smile did show then. "My lady, it would be an honor."

Not once did any of them mention the McGraths, much to her relief.

She also met Miss Vector and Mr. Raghorn, and sat in on some of Jamie's lessons. In the evenings, after the plates had been cleared away and the wine was congealing in the bottom of her glass, Jamie would sit in Rosaline's lap while she read to him, his hair tickling her nose as he slumped against her and fell asleep. In those moments, Rosaline would look down at him and smile, then look up and meet Hal's gaze. Sometimes, his eyes were hooded and sleepy; other times, they were awake and bright, knowing. *One day*, he would say to her, without saying anything. *One day*.

Jamie came out of his shell slowly, like a snail, testing her and meeting her in equal measure. He had a warm, even temperament that rarely spiked in displeasure or anger, and when it did—

"But I don't *want it!*" Jamie's lower lip wobbled as he glared up at Hal, his small hands clenched into determined fists. "Take it away!"

"Jamie." Hal was frustrated, she could tell, but doing an excellent job of hiding it. "It is just a cup of warm milk, and if you cannot sleep—"

"I'm not tired!" came his shriek, which only confirmed the opposite.

Rosaline watched from where she stood, half-hidden behind the door frame, as Hal let out a sigh and slumped over, pushing a hand through his hair. And then, she had an idea.

"Jamie." Rosaline stepped into his bedroom. "I am not tired, either, in spite of the late hour, and I was going to try to find some buried treasure. Would you like to help me?"

Jamie stared at her for a few moments, frowning, then rubbed at his sleepy eyes. "I s'pose." Behind him, Hal frowned at her and mouthed, *What?*

Rosaline nodded. "Good." She held out her hand, and after doing some thinking, Jamie reached out and took it.

Rosaline led the boy back to her and Hal's bedroom, Hal following a few paces behind. Once they'd reached it, she gave Jamie a seat beside hers at the desk, and picked up her quill.

"Now," said Rosaline, ignoring Hal as he came in and shut the door. "I assume you've heard of the Dread Pirate Bartholomew?"

"No," said Jamie, suspicious.

Rosaline gaped at him. "Then aren't you a lucky one! He is one of the most infamous, the most bloodthirsty scoundrels to ever sail the seven seas, and when he buries his treasure, he leaves behind messages written in code." With that, she pulled her most recent geometrical proof out from beneath a book and laid it in front of him.

Jamie's eyes went as wide as saucers. "Oh."

"Yes," said Rosaline, her voice hushed. "Whoever can decipher the code will discover the location of his buried treasure. Does that not sound wonderful?"

"It does," came Jamie's reply.

Rosaline gave a nod. "Excellent. Then anchors aweigh."

She began to explain her proof aloud, noticing but not remarking when Jamie slumped in his seat, pillowing his head on the desk. He put in a valiant effort, but within five minutes, he crawled into her lap and tucked his head under her chin. Rosaline continued her work, wrapped her free arm around him, and said nothing. A few minutes after that, Jamie was sound asleep, his breath puffing against her chest.

Rosaline smiled, put down her quill, and leaned back in her chair. She finally looked over her shoulder to Hal, who was seated by the fireplace with an open, discarded book in his lap. He was watching her, his expression hinting at smugness.

"Piece of cake," she murmured, carding her fingers through Jamie's hair.

"Only you would try geometry." Hal closed his book and stood up, stretching like a lion. She caught a glimpse of his bare stomach and fought off a shiver. "Shall I take him back to his room?"

"I suppose." She glanced down at Jamie's slack, peaceful face and said, "Or... would it be so terrible, if he were to stay?"

After a moment, she mustered the courage to look up and meet Hal's gaze again. He was smiling, in that small, subtle way, and he nodded.

As she slipped into bed, Rosaline could not deny the way her heart fluttered at the sight of Hal and Jamie, already curled up beneath the sheets. Hal was still awake, and he watched her as she lay down beside Jamie. The boy murmured, and Rosaline rubbed a gentle circle into his back.

"We should not get him into the habit," Hal whispered.

"I know," said Rosaline, and her thoughts returned to Marcus' warning. *Everything could change.* "But once in a while it could not hurt."

⚜

SUMMER GAVE ITS LAST GASP IN MID-SEPTEMBER, WHEN A single day became the hottest the county had seen in twenty years. By late evening, the heat had become so unbearable that Rosaline sat up in bed and said, "Follow me. I have had enough."

Hal did not ask a single question as he followed her through the dark and empty manor. She led him into the kitchen, then the mudroom, where she unearthed and lit a large lantern.

The garden was full of fireflies and crickets, and the water of the pond was cool, luscious against her sweaty skin. Rosaline let out a gasp as she slipped in up to her neck, flashing Hal a smile when he joined her. The water lapped around his bare chest, and in the light of the full moon, she could only see the edges of his body, the dark sparkle of his eyes.

"One of your better ideas, I think." His hands, sliding around her waist.

Rosaline bit her lip, clutching at his shoulders. "Tell me a secret."

Hal hummed, pressing a kiss to her cheek, her temple. "Do you have any idea," he murmured, "how difficult it was for me not to kiss you that morning? When I came to see you before I left London?"

A smile broke through before she could stop it. "But you did kiss me, dear husband, if we are to follow a literal interpretation of the word."

"Fiend." He dipped his head, licked a stripe up her neck, holding her as she shuddered.

"It feels—" Rosaline managed, "like another world, does it not?"

"London?" His teeth, grazing her clavicle.

"London, the season, all of it."

"It is another world." Hal kissed his way back up her neck, along her jaw. "And I am thrilled to have left it all behind."

"All of it?" she teased, reaching down to squeeze his bum. "I thought we had some wonderful moments, but if you wish to expunge the record—"

He gave a loud sigh, the water lapping around him. "Very well, not all of it."

"I wanted you to kiss me that morning, when you said farewell. Why did you not?"

Hal looked at her, and even in the near-darkness, she could feel the heat of his gaze. Their clothing billowed and floated around them, the water swirling around her legs. "Because," he said. "If I had, I would not have been able to bring myself to leave you."

A thrill of delight rippled through her, and Rosaline clung to him, burying her smile against his stubbled cheek. Even now, being able to touch him, to kiss him, in this intimate way felt like a forbidden privilege. She could remember too clearly, how, just a few months before, the touch of his bare hand to her arm had been enough to send her reeling. How she had ached for it, yearned for an excuse to brush against him — the feeling remained, but had deepened, intensified. There was a newfound comfort to his touches, a type of sanctuary, where there had once been nerves.

"Your turn." His hand slid up her back, splayed between her shoulder blades.

Rosaline took a deep, controlled breath, and smiled. "Very well. But you must release me."

Hal dropped his arms and stepped away.

Rosaline nudged her toes into the mud and straightened her back. Around her, the insects hummed, and a few frogs let out their throttling grunts. She took another breath, then began to sing.

The song was nothing special, just a simple aria, but it was one Rosaline knew so well she could sing it in her sleep and hear it in her dreams. A blush flooded her cheeks — it had been so long since she'd sung in front of anyone, and Hal was looking at her with a warmth, a reverence, that was palpable, even in the darkness. She did not sing for long, just a minute or two, but when she stopped, taking a deep breath, he reached for her at once, pulling her close.

"I had no idea." His voice came in a murmur, and he thumbed at her waist. "Did your mother—?"

"Yes," said Rosaline. "She was my first teacher. As I got older, I had lessons with an instructor, but after her death, it was... it was a while before I sang again."

"You are incredible," he said. "Whatever's next, an aptitude for juggling fire?"

She laughed. "It is merely a hidden talent, Hal, not a hidden side of my personality—"

Hal kissed her, his arms wrapping around her body. Rosaline sighed into him, melting against his chest, and they passed several lovely moments in silence.

"I hope you will sing again," he said. One of the frogs croaked in agreement. "Whenever you like, but hopefully, within my earshot."

She smiled. "I shall give it due consideration."

"Oh, will you?" said Hal, his voice rich with amusement. And Rosaline was not expecting it when he stepped away and smacked the surface of the pond, sending a huge splatter of water cascading over her chest.

Rosaline let out a shriek and immediately returned fire. The grounds echoed with their laughter and the sound of splashing water; on the bank nearby, the frogs continued to croak.

❦

THE LIBRARY AT ALBAN HOLLOW WAS ONE OF THE LARGEST AND best that Rosaline had ever seen — it easily outranked the one at her father's Paris house, and was surprisingly cozy, given its size. It was difficult for her not to spend her entire day within its loving confines, but now that Hal had resumed his duties for the estate, she had more time to herself.

Rosaline could not spend each day shadowing Jamie, as much as she might want to. True, the "house" — as Hal and the staff insisted upon calling it — was large enough that she could spend the better part of a day wandering its rooms and never find the end of it. But even she had to tire of looking at paintings and sculptures and everything in-between. And while the grounds were extensive, and she could request Titania whenever she liked, there was something a touch lonely about wandering the cold fields day after day, watching the rain and breathing in the fog that settled above the grass and between the trees.

So, more often than not, she found herself in the company of Marcus, who would spend hours each day reading in a squishy red leather armchair beside the library fireplace. "Anything and everything," he told her, with the ghost of a wink. "But most recently, the Ottomans."

A week after her and Hal's midnight dip in the pond, Rosaline was sitting alone in the library, tucked into one of the window seats with a new novel and a cup of tea. Marcus had gone to Glastonbury, and Jamie was exploring the woods with Hamish before his afternoon lessons. Outside, the early morning frost was still melting, and she could see where the edges of the trees began to curl and bleed into yellow and orange. Autumn was fast approaching, and Rosaline could not help but smile — she could hardly wait to see the Hollow in all its seasons.

A sound at the door surprised her, and she looked up to see Hal coming into the room. He looked trim but rumpled, still wearing his outdoor jacket, and he was almost smiling.

"Thought I might find you here," he said, his voice a low rumble. He closed the door, but not all the way — it hovered just a few inches from the latch.

Rosaline smiled at him. "It is a reasonable guess. I thought you had a meeting with that farmer — Benson?"

Hal had slipped out of bed earlier than usual that morning, brushing a kiss to the back of her neck. She'd reached for him, half-asleep, and had woken an hour or two later with her hand still outstretched, tangled in the sheets.

"Several meetings with several farmers," he corrected her, crossing the room. "But I have a spare few minutes before I am spoken for again." Hal bent down, kissed her. His teeth grazed her lower lip and she hummed, tangling a hand in his hair.

"Then I am most honored, Your Grace, to be afforded a piece of your precious time."

Hal grinned but did not reply as he sat down by her feet. Then his hand on her ankle, his thumb pressing into her calf as he nudged her legs apart.

Rosaline's stomach leapt into her mouth, and the book slid

from her lap down onto the seat. "Hal—" she managed, her heart thudding in her face. "You cannot be serious—"

Again, he did not reply. But he shifted, caging her with his legs. Hal watched his own hands as they slid her skirts up her legs, the fabric tickling her bare skin. Rosaline still went without stockings and pantalettes, but those days of freedom were numbered, with the weather changing. Perhaps he'd been aware of this, perhaps he'd decided that he ought to take advantage of it while he still could. Because, she knew, Hal was nothing if not diligent.

"Hal," Rosaline tried again, ignoring the jolt of heat that burned between her legs. "Hal, you have a meeting with a tenant, and we— we are in the *library*—"

He finally looked up at her, but again said nothing. His hand, skating up her inner thigh, settling a bare inch from her entrance. He thumbed at the skin, then settled between her legs.

Oh. Another jolt, from Rosaline's belly to her groin, and her stomach trembled. "Hal, the door, you left the door—"

Hal looked up at her once more, and the heat in his eyes made her shiver. "Then you shall have to be quiet, my dear."

Rosaline choked on a gasp as he pulled her skirts up and out of the way, letting them pool over her stomach. Then his mouth, wet and hot and determined, licking a stripe up the center of her sex, pausing to circle and tease her clit.

Rosaline was already trembling, her blood flooding hot and cold as it roared around her body. She glanced over her shoulder at the door, a fleeting wave of panic passing through her, but then he lapped at her again, steady and relentless, and she clung to him with a stifled moan, squeezing his face with her thighs, just as he liked it.

Pleasure whipped through her, ebbing and tangling in tandem with his tongue, and he went after her with a precision that was breathtaking. Sometimes, Hal liked to tease her, to kiss her and pull away, mouthing at her leg or at her belly until she squirmed with desperation, but now, he did not pause, did not hesitate to lick at her until she shook with it.

He shifted, and the angle was too much, it— Rosaline stuffed her wrist into her mouth, muffling a deep groan that burst out of her, catching in her throat, but she could hardly see, could hardly think, could only feel his mouth, his tongue, and his hands, his fingers digging into the flesh of her thighs, the curve of her hip, and it was too much, it was—

A muffled growl, deep in his throat, and Hal shifted again, and then his mouth fastened to her clit and he sucked and sucked until—

Rosaline broke in a sudden, ripping current as pleasure poured through her body. She shook against him, her moans high and muffled against the skin of her arm, stars bursting through her body in a rippling cascade. A velvety blackness swept over her, and the room faded away.

Slowly, almost painfully, her awareness began to return. Rosaline realized her eyes were half-closed, and the room around her was blurred. Her hips still tingled, and her mouth was wet, slack, from being shoved against her arm. There were even teeth marks in her forearm, and she looked, almost shocked, at where redness was blooming beneath the surface of her skin. Thoughts fired and misfired in Rosaline's mind, and she realized that she felt drunk.

Hal was kissing her thigh, light and gentle, but then, as she watched, he pulled away, putting her skirts back into place. He wiped a hand across his mouth, smirked at her, and, without saying a word, stood up and left.

❧ 43 ❧

Hal closed the library door behind him, and Rosaline stared at the dark, paneled wood, her head throbbing from a rich tangle of emotions. *What just happened?* she asked herself, even though the evidence of her slick inner thighs and her hazy, fluttering body needed no explanation. But it was so impossible, to difficult to believe that he had just walked in here, left the door open, and had—

Rosaline blinked a few times and cleared her throat. It took her several moments to sit up, and when she did, she stared into the middle distance and, between one moment and the next, decided to take her revenge. If her husband could take what he wanted whenever he wanted it, and leave her aching for more, then so could she.

Her mind began to turn, but she quickly realized that her plan required a certain degree of patience. Hal was not often alone during the day, and she could hardly pounce on him in front of Randall or the tenants. No, she would have to wait. And she would have to find something else to occupy her in the meantime.

Rosaline left behind her book and her cup of tea and made her way back to her private chambers. Thankfully, Lisette was nowhere in sight, but she had left a fresh pitcher of water, along with a new pile of clean towels.

A half hour later, Rosaline was feeling refreshed and much more put-together. She'd even attempted to tame her hair, twisting it into a long braid and weaving a new purple ribbon between the strands. As she considered herself in the looking-glass, she could not help but feel the weight of change — how different she looked now, compared to the Rosaline who had arrived at the London docks. Different, but better.

With the day still stretching ahead of her, empty and waiting, she gathered a few letters from her personal desk — one from Charlotte, one from her father — and began to make her way back to the library, where she would compose her replies. But she was only halfway there, passing through one of the bright, sunlit halls, when the sound of hurrying footsteps overtook her.

Rosaline frowned as Elsie, one of the housemaids, came running up to her from the direction of the library. Elsie was red-faced and panting, clutching a stitch in her side. "Good grief, Elsie, what on earth is the matter?"

"There you are, my lady," Elsie managed, followed by a quick curtsy. "We've been looking everywhere for you. You have a visitor at the door."

Rosaline could not help it — she stared at her. "A visitor?"

Elsie nodded, her cap bobbing precariously on her head. "He has a letter for you, and he is most determined to speak with you personally."

Something in Rosaline's chest broke and fell, swooping down through her stomach to her feet. But she could not show it, and she could not panic until she knew— *It cannot be,* she thought, *McGrath would not dare—* She swallowed and said, "Can you tell me anything about this... man?"

If Elsie thought her request puzzling, she did not show it. "He is a most interesting character, my lady." She took another great gulp of air. "He has a wooden leg, and he wears an eyepatch. And," she added, with a sheepish look, "he has a somewhat disagreeable temperament. Brooks did not want to let him inside the house without your permission."

Rosaline's panic had vanished, replaced by an overwhelming sense of confusion. This person was no one she had ever met before, to her knowledge. But she could hardly turn him away without finding out what he wanted. "Very well," she said, tucking the letters into her pocket. "Take me to him."

Brooks had ushered the visitor into an antechamber off the side of the main drawing room, and he was looking a little more flustered than usual when he met Rosaline just outside the door.

"I must caution you, my lady," Brooks muttered to her in a rumbling undertone. "He is a most impertinent individual. I am happy to dismiss him at once."

Rosaline raised an eyebrow. "Do you think he would comply with such a dismissal?"

Brooks seemed to swell. "Perhaps not. He did threaten to..." His neck turned purple. "Box my ears and send me packing if I would prevent him from reaching his target."

For an absurd moment, Rosaline wanted to laugh. But she nodded and took a deep breath, steeling herself. "It is time I spoke to him. Let me in, Brooks."

When she entered the antechamber, Rosaline found herself faced with a gnarled old stump of a man. He was tall and broad, but his wide, imposing features were marred with deep scars and, true to Elsie's word, a black cloth eyepatch. His remaining eye was a soft, clear brown, and his curling hair hung to his shoulders in shades of blond and gray. He wore a thick, beaten overcoat, and a heavy staff took most of his weight. Her eyes were immediately drawn to his wooden leg, but she forced herself to meet his lopsided gaze.

"Good morning, sir," she said, hoping her voice did not tremble. "How may I be of assistance?"

"Your Grace." The man's voice erupted in a low, gravelly rumble, and he inclined his head. "My name is Archimedes Smith, and I come at the request of the Dowager Countess McDunn."

This statement so floored her that for a moment, all Rosaline could do was stare at him. When she finally gathered herself, she said, "I am afraid I need more of an explanation, Mr. Smith."

The corner of his lopsided mouth twitched, and for a moment, it was all too easy to imagine him threatening to box Brooks's ears. "It is all in this letter," he said, holding out a sealed envelope. "Peruse it at your leisure."

Rosaline took the envelope, her eyes briefly fixing on the McDunn seal before she tore it open. She read the short letter within seconds, then read it again. And again.

Finally, she looked up at him and said, "I do not understand."

"Really?" Smith limped over to the nearest armchair, and sat down with a sigh of relief. He hitched his false leg up onto the nearest footstool, utterly at ease. "The Dowager Countess is known for speaking quite plainly."

"Then you are... to be my tutor?"

"In ancient Greek, yes."

All too quickly, Rosaline remembered the Dowager's words at their first meeting — *There may be someone*, Lady McDunn had whispered, *I shall have to see if he is still in retirement.* Undoubtedly, this was the very man himself, considering her with a petulant sort of look.

"How kind of her." Overwhelmed, Rosaline sat down across from Smith. "I had no idea that she would..."

"That much is plain," he said with a nod. "I thought perhaps she might write to you in advance of my arrival, but she does enjoy a good surprise, even if she is not there to witness it."

"You know her well, then?"

Again, that twitch of a smile. "As well as anyone can know the

Dowager, yes. She was once a student of my colleague's, and our acquaintance goes back many a year."

Still feeling rather dazed, Rosaline glanced down at the letter and said, "Mr. Smith, I trust the Dowager's recommendation on any matter, but perhaps you might tell me a little about your qualifications?"

"Two degrees," he said. "One from Oxford, one from Cambridge. I am the ranking authority on Herodotus and Thucydides, and more recently, on Socrates. I have spent more time in Greece and the Mediterranean than I have in England, and I have lectured at universities across the Continent. At least, I did, until our Mr. Bonaparte decided to tempt Fate. Since then, I have found myself somewhat prematurely retired." Smith tilted his head to one side, and his clear blue eye seemed to look right through her. "I understand you have an interest in reading Homer."

"Yes," she managed. "And the tragedians."

"And you have experience, yes? With ancient languages?"

"Latin," Rosaline said. "But I am fluent in French and Italian, and I know a little Spanish and Arabic. One of my old tutors was—"

He nodded, thumping his staff on the floor. "Then we shall begin this very afternoon. The alphabet first, and the letters, with a brief overview of grammatical structures."

"But," she tried, her head spinning again, "we have not decided where you are to reside, nor have we discussed your rate—"

Smith hauled himself to his feet with a stifled grunt. "Do not trouble yourself, Your Grace. The Dowager has booked me a set of rooms in the village, and she is taking care of everything else."

Rosaline stood up as well. "But that is— I cannot allow—"

"Your Grace." And he raised an eyebrow. "As the Greeks would say, do not look a gift horse in the mouth."

"And the Trojans would say the precise opposite," she fired back.

Smith ignored this and turned towards the door, his staff thudding against the floor with every odd step. "We are to meet every day, your schedule permitting. We shall begin at ten o'clock sharp each morning and finish at two. You are to complete your assignments in your own time, with some allowances for..." He glanced around at the furnishings and muttered something under his breath, followed by: "Your... duties."

"I—"

"Now, I shall return to the village," he went on, "and settle my matters. I will reappear at two this afternoon, and in the meantime, you can decide where you would like us to work."

Rosaline could only nod.

Smith nodded in return. "See you this afternoon, Duchess." With that, he lumbered out of the room, straight past Brooks, and, she presumed, out the front door.

Rosaline slumped back down into her chair, and looked up when Brooks came into the room, his face still ruddy with suppressed insult.

"Well, my lady?" he said. "Did you find out what he wanted?"

"His name is Archimedes Smith, and he is to be my tutor," Rosaline said, hardly believing it herself. "A gift from the Dowager Countess McDunn. So you had best get used to his presence."

For a brief moment, Brooks could not hide his surprise.

"We shall have to work out a system," she went on. "So that he does not see Jamie."

"Of course, my lady." Brooks nodded. "Is there anything else?"

"Send one of the maids to the small study with the necessary cleaning supplies, along with a fresh tray of tea." Rosaline paused to take a breath. "This afternoon, I go to war."

LATER THAT EVENING, ROSALINE MADE HER WAY DOWN THE corridor towards the north end of the ground floor. Dusk had fallen, the evening purplish and chilly, and many of the candles at this end of the household remained unlit. For a brief moment, she felt like a ghost, a shade, wandering between the worlds, underneath the fabric of reality. But then, a familiar door appeared in front of her, and she smirked, her stomach jumping with anticipation.

Hal looked up when the door opened, and he smiled when he saw the cause for his interruption. His personal study was the image of organization, save for the occasional, scattered pile of notes and maps and diagrams. It was a snug, homey sort of room, with warm wooden furnishings and an enormous globe in one corner. It felt like him, and Rosaline could not ignore a familiar flutter of affection as she crossed the room towards his desk.

"To what do I owe the pleasure?" said Hal, putting down his quill. He'd taken off his jacket and left the top button of his shirt undone, exposing that familiar triangle of warm, golden skin. His hair was half-vertical, and he was creased, rumpled, from hours of work. He glanced at the darkened windows behind him and muttered an oath. "I had not realized the time — is it really so late?" Hal looked back at her, and now he was frowning. "Why did no one ring me for supper?"

"Jamie and Marcus ate early," Rosaline replied. "And you and I will take supper on trays in our room."

Hal raised his eyebrows. "And why is that?"

"No particular reason," she said with a shrug. She'd reached the desk, and she circled his chair, then braced herself on the arm rest and lowered herself onto his lap, straddling his legs. His hands immediately went to her hips. "I thought you might be tired."

"Did you," he said, his voice warm, amused.

Rosaline nodded. "You have had a long day." Then her hand,

slipping low and squeezing. "You have been hard at work." Another squeeze, and she felt him begin to swell.

Hal's entire body tightened, and his smile vanished, replaced by an expression of shock. "Rosaline," he muttered, his glance darting at the door, which she had left ajar. "Not here—"

She did not reply, but only squeezed again. Then, in a flash, she had his trousers undone and her hand on his cock. She twisted, squeezed, and twisted, and his head fell back as he groaned, a flush spreading up his neck.

"Rosaline." His fingers were digging into her hips. "The door—"

"Oh." Rosaline tilted her head to one side and pumped his cock. "Did I leave it open?"

Hal bit out a mangled curse, his thighs tensing beneath her. "Someone could—"

"And what would they see?" she countered, her heart thudding in her throat. "A wife, sitting in her husband's lap. Hardly the most scandalous thing in the world."

He choked on a disgruntled laugh. "They'd see your hand, and my—"

"Would they?" With that, Rosaline raised herself up, shifted her skirts, steadied him with her hand, and sank down onto his cock.

Hal groaned loud enough for it to echo down the hall, and even she found her resolve tested as he filled her, hot and pulsing. Rosaline wrapped her arms around his shoulders, tangled her hands in his hair, and tugged his head back until he looked at her, his eyes bright and desperate. "You see," she murmured, slowly rolling her hips until he trembled. "Nothing out of the ordinary."

"Rosaline," he said again, his voice vicious with lust. "The *door*—"

She kissed his cheek, his neck, and his hands slid up her back. "Then you had best control yourself, Your Grace, lest anyone come running."

Hal buried his face in her breasts, his mouth burning and wet against her bare skin. He muffled a moan in her cleavage as she circled her hips again and sighed when his cock grazed against something that sent sparks through her belly. "Have you—" he managed, his tongue laving over her breast, "have you been like this since—?"

"No," Rosaline said, surprised at how steady her voice was. "No, but I did take the time to... prepare myself."

He moaned again, his teeth digging into her breast. A wave of pleasure overcame her, and she felt her nipples harden and rub against the fabric of her dress.

Hal noticed, and he paused for a moment. His hand slid from her back to her waist, then up to her breast. His thumb circled and pressed, and she twitched against him. "God," he muttered, pinching her nipple between two of his fingers. "You took off your stays."

"Perhaps," Rosaline managed, swallowing a gasp. She clenched her thighs around his legs and began to ride him in earnest, setting a slow, steady pace as she raised and lowered herself back onto his cock.

Once again, his entire body went brittle, and his hands returned to her hips, moving with her as she rocked against him. Then his mouth, snaking a line of wet kisses across her breasts and down to her nipple. Hal sucked at her through the fabric of her dress, held her as she bucked against him, pleasure ricocheting through her body.

But Rosaline could not lose focus. She'd come in here with an agenda, and she could not allow herself to be distracted. So, even as his teeth grazed her nipple through the wet, tender fabric, she rolled her hips and did something she had never done before.

Hal gave a full-body twitch, burying a desperate groan between her breasts. "What," he managed, "what was—"

"Oh," said Rosaline, unconcerned. "This?" She did it again, clenching around him, and he let out another groan, this one even more broken than the last. "Shhh," she whispered, tugging at his hair. "Quiet now."

"Rosaline," he bit out, the word almost lost against her skin. "If you continue to— I will not last—"

In response, she did it again, loving the way he shuddered in return, his teeth latching onto her other nipple. *Focus*, she reminded herself as she shook with it, pleasure burning slow and deep in her lower back.

She fucked him slowly, deeply, her hands on his shoulders and in his hair. She held him as his hips stuttered and broke against her, as his mouth found new patterns across her breasts, and soon enough, he began to tremble, his fingers digging into her hips hard enough to bruise.

"I'm—" Hal managed, the word high and desperate. "Oh Rosaline, I'm—"

Rosaline pulled off of him just in time, and he buried his face in her breasts as he came with a muffled grunt, his body shaking and twitching, spilling between her legs. She leaned against him, her chest heaving, pleasure still trapped under her skin, sweat hazed over her body, but she barely had a moment to recover before he raised his head, his eyes sleepy and determined.

Without saying a word, Hal gently pushed her off his lap. Her legs wobbled like jelly as she stood up, and he did the same, tucking his spent cock back into his trousers and fastening them shut. "Come on," he bit out, grabbing her hand and marching towards the nearest bookcase, which she knew was a hidden door to a staircase that would take them to the hall of their personal chambers. "I am not finished with you yet."

Rosaline could only grin and allow herself to be led up into the cool, plush darkness.

"I USED TO SPEND MUCH OF MY TIME AT ROSINGS PARK," HAL was saying as the carriage rolled through a small cluster of trees. "Whenever Ed would oblige me."

Rosaline smiled at him, turning away from the window. "Then we are returning to the scene of many a bachelor crime."

He shook his head. "You do paint me in quite a cruel picture, my love."

She laughed. "Not in the least. Though I am quite excited to see your second home."

The carriage slowed, then turned onto a wide gravel drive. It took them through another small cluster of trees, then along a stretch of land bordered by thick hedges. Eventually, the house — enormous, imperial, built in a hefty, pale brick — burst into view. Their carriage curled around the circular drive and came to a halt before the front door.

"Are you excited?" Hal asked her as the butler approached the carriage.

Rosaline grinned, her heart leaping. "Does a leopard have spots?"

Their feet barely met gravel before a pale blue blur came bursting out of the front door, and Rosaline found herself tackled by a small, slight fairy of a woman.

"Charlotte!" she squealed, squeezing her friend tightly in return. "What a warm welcome!"

"I am so very glad to see you!" came Charlotte's earnest reply, and she broke away to beam into Rosaline's face and take her hands. "It feels like an age!"

Edward appeared behind her, grinning fit to burst, and greeted Hal with a firm handshake. "Welcome to Rosings Park. You are a sight for sore eyes!"

"As are you," said Rosaline, clinging to Charlotte like a limpet. "You both look very well."

"So do you," said Charlotte, and she flashed Rosaline a wink. "Marriage seems to suit us."

"Indeed, my love," said Edward. He brushed a kiss to Rosaline's cheek, and Hal did the same to Charlotte. "You had excellent timing. Why don't we begin with a tour of the grounds?"

"Perfect," said Rosaline, linking her arm with Charlotte's. And when she met Hal's gaze, his eyes warm with mirth, she realized that there was nowhere else she would rather be.

❦ 44 ❧

"**G**oodness, Charlotte," Rosaline was saying as she bent her face towards another rose bush. "I had no idea there were so many varieties."

Charlotte smiled at her. A few yards away, Edward and Hal were facing the nearest hill and discussing something to do with the land. "That one," she said, "is one of Edward's newest hybrids. He perfected it just last year." She joined Rosaline and took a rose in hand. "It has greater resilience to the colder weather, which means that it blooms longer and with more radiant color."

"The color is spectacular," Rosaline agreed. It was a brilliant, sunny orange.

Charlotte hummed, dipping her head to inhale the fresh, delightful scent. "He is determined," she said, "to create a variety that can bloom throughout the winter. It is a fool's errand, but he is no fool. I think he is more courageous than anything."

Rosaline cut her a sly look, then glanced at where the men remained at a distance, still absorbed in their own conversation. "You have not said, Charlotte... How was your honeymoon? In truth," she added.

For a moment, Charlotte did nothing, then she straightened

up and flashed Rosaline a wicked grin. "It was sheer bliss," she whispered, a fresh blush rising in her cheeks. "Lisette certainly knew what she was talking about. And what about you?" She nudged Rosaline with her elbow.

Surprisingly, horribly, Rosaline found herself blushing as well. "Yes," she managed, a giggle catching in her throat. "We have been... quite happy."

She and Charlotte clung to each other, fighting back a wave of hysterical laughter, and Hal noticed. "Trading secrets?" he called out. "In plain view?"

"We would not dream of it, my love," Rosaline called back, dabbing at the corners of her eyes. "Charlotte was just giving me a recipe for—"

"Royal Jelly," muttered Charlotte.

"Royal Jelly," Rosaline announced at a volume that rattled the trees. Charlotte gave a great snort and bent double, nearly taking Rosaline to the ground.

Edward shook his head at them, but he was grinning. "I think our wives have already been at the wine," he said to Hal.

"Undoubtedly," said Hal, dry as a bone. "We should join them."

Edward pulled out his watch. "You are not wrong. It is time that we change for supper."

"Must we?" said Rosaline. "It is only the four of us, and who would know the difference?"

"Very well," said Edward, still grinning. "I suppose it shall give the staff something to discuss over their evening meal."

"That's the spirit," said Hal, clapping him on the shoulder. "What are we if not destined for infamy?"

They all laughed, but something prickled down Rosaline's back, and goosebumps erupted across her arms. She ignored the feeling and joined the others as they wove their way back through the rose garden towards the house. And what a house it was.

"It certainly rivals Alban Hollow," Rosaline said to Charlotte.

Their arms, linked at the elbows, bumped along in time with their strides. "Charlotte, in truth, you are the mistress of quite a remarkable estate."

"As are you, if the rumors are to be believed." Charlotte turned her smile upon the edifice looming above them. "Rosaline, it feels like home. And the gardens are better than anything I could have imagined." She glanced over her shoulder at Edward. "He had the staff put in all these new plants while we were gone — my favorites — and some of them were in bloom when we returned. It was one of the kindest gifts I have ever received."

Rosaline smiled and nudged her. "And to think that you were worried, once, about what it would mean to marry him."

Charlotte let out a light, mercurial laugh. "I know, is it not amusing? I feel quite the fool now."

As they passed into the entrance hall, the butler looked up and stood at attention. "Shall I ring the gong, my lord?"

"That won't be necessary, Smith," said Edward. "We shall take supper as we are."

Rosaline watched as, like Brooks, Smith struggled to comprehend such a drastic change in routine. Finally, he seemed to force it down his throat. "Yes, my lord. I shall inform the cook accordingly. Will you still take drinks in the drawing room?"

"Yes," said Edward, "but we are happy to serve ourselves."

Smith then went positively purple. But he nodded, gave a slight bow, and went on his way.

Once he was out of earshot, Rosaline said, "Poor man. You did not make it easy."

Edward shrugged, unbuttoning his jacket. "Even a sleeping tiger needs its cage rattled."

"Brave last words," said Hal with a laugh, but before anyone could reply, there came the loud, urgent clatter of wheels on the drive, followed by the familiar sound of horses pulling to a sudden stop.

They all looked at each other in astonishment. Hal turned to Edward. "Were you expecting anyone?"

"No," said Edward with a frown. "No, otherwise Smith—"

The front door was still open, and, to Rosaline's astute shock, in came none other than Lord Blackwood. His clothing was a mess, his hair was wild, and he was as pale as a sheet. His gaze met hers, and in that instant, her heart went ice-cold and plummeted to her feet.

"Marcus?" said Hal, finding his voice before she could find hers. "What on earth—?"

"Forgive the intrusion, my lord," Marcus said to Edward, his voice hard and stilted. "But I come on a matter of the utmost importance." He turned to Hal. "I must speak with you and Rosaline."

"Of course," said Hal, meeting Rosaline's gaze. She nodded, and went to his side. "Ed, might we use the—?"

"Certainly," said Edward, though he was still frowning, his concern evident.

Marcus led them into the drawing room and shut the door behind them, pausing to check that it was firmly shut and locked before he turned to both of them. He looked even paler now in the direct candlelight, and his hands were shaking. "I will not mince words," he said, his voice flat. "Jamie has been taken."

For a brief, quiet moment, the world tilted. Rosaline rocked with it, her heart pounding in her skull, but she clenched her fist, determined not to fall, not now.

"Or, he's run away," Marcus continued, a muscle jumping in his jaw. "Either way, he's gone."

Hal was silent for several long, gut-wrenching moments. She could see the tension building, livid, in his shoulders, though his expression remained unchanged. Then, finally, he turned to her. "I must go at once—"

"Hal, *we*—" she said, reaching for his hand, squeezing it. "We must go—"

"No, one of us must stay, must—"

"If you say 'Keep up appearances,' I will throttle you—"

"But Charlotte and Edward cannot know—"

"They will not ask," Rosaline said, swallowing hard. "You know that, Hal, especially if you tell them it is something important."

He looked at her, and for a second, she could see it, could see the instant that he decided to give in rather than to fight. He turned back to Marcus. "We will ride back with you. They'll return our luggage to our carriage and send it back with our driver."

Marcus nodded, reached for the door. No more needed to be said.

Edward and Charlotte were waiting for them, pale and concerned, in the entrance hall. Rosaline mustered an apologetic smile and reached for her friend. "It is an emergency, I'm afraid, and we must leave at once."

"What is it?" said Edward, looking right at Hal, who shook his head.

But Charlotte had taken it all in stride. "Of course you must go. We shall retrieve your luggage and send it on with your other carriage."

Rosaline pulled her into a brief, desperate hug. "Thank you," she murmured, and Charlotte squeezed her tight. Emotion welled in her throat until she almost choked on it, but she forced it down and pulled away, joining Hal and Marcus by the door. "Another time," Rosaline said as she put on her cloak, and the last thing she saw was Edward's nod and Charlotte's soft smile.

The instant they were alone in the carriage and on their way out of Rosings Park, Hal looked right at Marcus and said, "What happened?"

Above them, the lantern swayed, and the yellowish circle of light hovered over Marcus' features like a firefly. "He was out in the garden," said Marcus, "with Hamish. Just a few yards from the house. As Hamish describes it, between one moment and the next, he was knocked unconscious by an unseen intruder. When he came to, he was face-down in the grass, and he can estimate now that he was unconscious for the better part of half an hour. Jamie had disappeared, and there were signs..." He broke off, glancing at Rosaline. "There were signs of a struggle."

Something lurched in Rosaline's stomach and she gripped Hal's hand hard enough to turn her own knuckles white. "Is Hamish all right?" she managed to say. "Did you send for the—?"

"The surgeon is with him now," Marcus replied, "and it seems that he was hit with nothing less than a cricket bat."

"Has there been a search?" said Hal, his voice low and even. "Of the house? And the grounds?"

Marcus nodded. "It is in progress as we speak, but nothing yet."

"And no one saw anything?" Hal went on. "Nothing in the garden, nothing in the—?"

"Not that we can make out," said Marcus. "But Brooks is still in the process of questioning the staff. He may have more answers by the time we return."

For a brief moment, Rosaline almost asked if someone had informed the local authorities, but then she remembered the scope of their circumstances. They were on their own. They could not ask for help, not even—

"If..." Hal began, then he paused, as if steeling himself. "If what we suspect is true, and Jamie was indeed taken, we will need to broaden the search. London, even Brighton and Bristol and Manchester. God, Edinburgh." He scrubbed a hand through his hair, and for a second, Rosaline could see her own panic and sadness mirrored in his face. "We will have to requisition the staff. Brooks can stay at the house, but the footmen, and Merrywether—"

"One problem at a time," said Marcus, his voice gentle. "And whoever took Jamie would be at a similar disadvantage — they, too, are limited to horseback. Besides, smuggling a child is no mean feat."

"But who?" Rosaline found her voice again. "Who would take him? Surely it would have to be someone who knew him, who was aware of his existence. How else would they know where he was, and that Hamish would be with him?"

Marcus shook his head. "We have to hope that Brooks' questioning will yield more answers than we have at present."

"You cannot think—" she began— "someone on the staff?"

"It is the best explanation," said Hal, a new, hard edge to his voice. She looked at him, and his eyes flashed with anger. "Someone could have learned about his past, his parentage. When we return to the house, Marcus, we have to send riders. We have to find out—"

"Already done," said Marcus. "One apiece to Glastonbury, Somerton, Bridgwater, and Wedmore."

Hal gave a nod, and with that, they lapsed into a shared, hollow silence. Rosaline could practically hear them all thinking the worst, imagining the worst. Her own mind churned with images of Jamie being flung over a stranger's shoulder while he cried, or worse, while he slumped, overcome by some sort of drug. She fought off a shudder, curling into Hal's side. A soft squeeze on her shoulder was all the indication he gave that he was aware of her presence; he was mute, his jaw clenched, his entire body tense with anger. Rosaline was certain that some of his rage was self-directed — she knew Hal would blame himself for this, and for any of the resulting events, for the remainder of his life.

Although it was a short carriage ride back to Alban Hollow, it seemed to stretch into infinity. The sky was just beginning to darken as their carriage drew to a halt before the entrance, and the wheels had hardly stopped moving before Hal launched himself out of his seat. Rosaline and Marcus hastened to follow him.

Alban Hollow was quiet — abnormally quiet.

"I will fetch Brooks," said Marcus, heading for the hidden staircase that would take him to the basement. "Hal, they're keeping Hamish in the Yellow Room—"

Hal nodded. "I'll see to him. Meet me in the drawing room in ten minutes." He looked at Rosaline, his eyes full of all the emotions he could not name, squeezed her hand, and they parted ways.

As Rosaline trod the familiar path to the western wing of the house, a prickling dread crept up over her shoulders. She shivered, holding her cloak close against her body, and tried not to remember that morning, when she and Jamie had raced each other to breakfast down this very hall. It was tempting to ring for Lisette, just to have someone to keep her company, but she did not want to interrupt Brooks' questioning. And perhaps Lisette, in her usual clever way, was keeping a sharp ear and a warm shoulder for some of the more talkative servants. No, it was better to keep her downstairs. Sighing, Rosaline reached for the door to the drawing room and went in.

The room was shadowed — no one had been in to light the fire, or the candles. The familiar, empty furniture seemed to sing with the unsaid, with the obvious, and she shivered again before she went over to the fireplace.

Soon enough, the flames roared to life, and Rosaline closed her eyes as the heat washed over her. It had been a while since she'd built her own fire, and she'd forgotten how soothing the ritual could be. But when she opened her eyes, Jamie was still gone, the air still chilled with his absence. She swallowed a sob and held a candle to the flames, then straightened up and turned around.

And then, fear, pure and cold, jolting through her. Because sitting in the armchair across from her was a man, and he was pointing a pistol at her.

❧ 45 ❧

The man was thin, middle-aged, with pointed features made all the sharper by the haggard state of his body and his long, unkempt hair. But he too seemed badly startled, almost as if she'd surprised *him*. When he spoke, it was in a voice as thin and ragged as his clothes. "My God. I thought you were a maid."

"Hardly." Rosaline was shocked by how steady her voice was, even as her heart thundered in her ears. "If I was, my response to you would be the same. Who are you, and why are you pointing a pistol at me?"

"Who are *you?*" he countered, then looked around the room. "This is Alban Hollow, is it not?"

"It is." Too late, Rosaline realized she could have lied.

"Strange." The man returned his piercing gray eyes to her, and he frowned. "Charles and Lily never had a daughter. Or a niece."

Charles and Lily? "Who are you?" she demanded, in spite of the pistol. "Why are you here?"

But he ignored this. "Where is he?" And when she did not reply: "Where is my son?"

With all the weight of the tide pulling away from the shore, realization slotted, deep and sudden, into her mind. "Jamie?" Rosaline managed. "Are you Jamie's father?"

But before the man could reply, the door opened, and Hal entered the room. "Hamish is doing well, he insisted upon staying awake until we returned, but now, he should be able to rest."

"Hal—" she said, the word catching in her throat. Jamie's father watched her, unruffled. Hal would not see him unless—

Hal shut the door and made his way over to her. "A few days of bedrest and he should be—" Here, finally, he halted, taking in her expression. Then, he turned to face the man, and immediately stepped between Rosaline and the pistol.

For several long moments, the only sound in the room was the hiss and crackle of the fire.

"Hello, Hal." The man's voice was calm, soft.

"Titus." Hal's voice was hard as stone. "May I ask why you are pointing a weapon at my wife?"

Rosaline's heart beat a tattoo in her ears. Her free hand clung to Hal's hip.

"Your wife?" The man — Titus — repeated, again unable to mask his surprise. "I had no idea you wed."

"My question stands," said Hal, "and has now become a demand. Put down the pistol."

Something flickered in Titus' expression, something tough and dark. He stood up, shaky but determined, and Rosaline noticed that he favored his left leg. His grip on the pistol did not falter once. "Where is my son?"

"Titus," Hal began, but before he could continue, the door opened, and Marcus and Brooks entered the room.

Unlike Hal, they saw Titus immediately, and Rosaline watched, dumbfounded, as a series of emotions surged over Marcus' face: shock, confusion, and finally, an anger as deep and threatening as a thunderstorm.

"You," Marcus growled. In a flash, he'd slammed the door shut and locked it. His burning gaze was fixed on Titus. "Get away from them."

"Marcus," said Titus, and there was something pleading about the word. "Where is my son?"

"Why are you brandishing a weapon at Lily and Charles' only child?" Marcus spat at him in return. "And more to the point, what the hell are you doing here?"

Titus' jaw worked, and he fumbled for his pocket. "I received a letter—"

"A letter?" said Marcus. He and Hal traded a look, but neither of them moved.

Titus held a scrap of paper aloft. "From Jamie. Claiming that he'd left Alban Hollow, and had gone to stay with a new family in Brighton."

This announcement was so astonishing that neither Rosaline, Hal, nor Marcus said a word.

"Forgive me," Titus went on, "but I was a little surprised to discover that my son had been foisted off on some stranger's family. To say that I was suspicious, and worried, would be an understatement. Rather than send a reply, and be left waiting for months, I bought passage on the next ship out of New York to get some answers myself."

"With a pistol," Marcus pointed out. Behind him, Brooks glowered at Titus.

Titus let out a broken, gut-wrenching laugh. "I am a desperate man, Marcus, and as you know, a desperate man does desperate things." But then, finally, he lowered the pistol.

Rosaline released a breath she hadn't known she was holding, put the candle down on the mantelpiece, and clung to Hal, relief seeping through her veins. He turned to her at once, his hands at her shoulders, her neck, cupping her head. She pressed a kiss to his palm, and he let out a sigh, brushing a kiss to her forehead.

But now, they had a very different problem. And as she looked into Hal's eyes, she could see her own resolve reflected back at her — they could not tell Titus that Jamie was missing, not yet. Not until he'd surrendered his weapon, at the very least.

"Let me see that letter," said Hal, turning to Titus. "You received it just before you left?"

"Yes." Titus handed him the paper. "What is today, the twenty-second? Almost two months to the day." And as the words left his mouth, Rosaline noticed, once again, just how exhausted he looked. She ached to offer him something to eat and a bed for the night, but she knew that he would not accept it.

Hal scanned the letter, and without saying a word, held it out to Rosaline. One glance was all she needed to confirm her suspicions. And when she again met Hal's gaze, she heard the unsaid — they had to get the pistol away from Titus.

"Titus," said Rosaline, and he jumped, as if he'd forgotten that she was there. "Would you care to take a seat?"

He shot her a manic grin. "No, I would not." Behind him, Marcus continued to glare daggers.

"Sit down, Titus," said Hal, the words soft but an order nonetheless.

Titus stared at him for a moment, as if weighing his options. But eventually, he complied, and sat back down in the armchair, the pistol lolling at his side.

Hal held out his hand. "Your weapon."

Titus' eyes flashed. "Stop wasting time and just tell me — where is my son?"

"I will," said Hal. "But not with a loaded weapon in the room."

How do you know, Rosaline wanted to ask, even if it seemed redundant. *How do you know if the pistol is loaded?* Titus could easily have held her at gunpoint without any ammunition — she would not have known the difference.

For a long moment, Titus and Hal just looked at each other.

The air was as tense as a fresh rope, and once again, Rosaline could feel her pulse in her throat. And when Titus sighed and held out the pistol handle-first, she clung to the edge of the mantelpiece, fighting off a wave of dizzy relief.

Hal took the pistol went over to the nearest bureau. He locked the pistol in a drawer and pocketed the key.

As if answering an unspoken signal, Marcus bit out, "Brooks. Would you gather the remaining footmen and station them at the exits to this room, both indoors and out? We cannot have Mr. Wolfe making a quick escape." Another hard glare at Titus, this one edged with fury.

Rosaline expected Brooks to bluster and stammer, but to her astonishment, he did neither. Though, she remembered, this was not Titus' first visit to Alban Hollow. "Certainly, my lord."

"Come back once they're sorted," Marcus continued. "So you can tell us your findings."

"Yes, my lord." Brooks left the room, and Marcus closed and locked the door after him.

"That," said Titus in his thin voice, "was hardly necessary."

"We," snarled Marcus, "are the ones who will decide what is necessary when you bring a weapon into our home!"

"Marcus," intoned Hal, raising a placating hand. "Control yourself." He looked at Titus, his gaze wary but full of understanding. "Titus," he said, "first, I feel it is important to tell you that, to our collective knowledge, Jamie has never written you a letter."

For a moment, Titus could only stare at him. "What— what do you mean?"

"Furthermore," Hal continued, gesturing to the letter in Rosaline's hands, "that is not Jamie's handwriting."

"Here," said Rosaline, going over to the nearest desk. She opened the top drawer, and found what she'd left there that morning — a piece of paper with a draft of Jamie's report on frogs and toads. She handed it to Titus, who frowned at it. "Whoever wrote that letter tried very hard to make their handwriting look like a child's, but I think we can assume it was not written by Jamie."

"Who, incidentally," said Hal, "is not in Brighton."

"But that..." Titus scrubbed a hand across his stubbed jaw, through his lank hair. "That is not the first letter I've received from him."

Then came a silence so sudden and so unnerving that one could have heard a pin drop.

After several moments, Hal managed to say, "What?"

"I have received three letters," said Titus, still staring at Jamie's report. "This being the third. The first two I received one after another, and they were nothing, mere trifles. Stories about the woods and the pond. No more than a few sentences." He met Hal's gaze. "I had no reason to believe that those letters were sent to me by anyone other than my son."

Hal frowned. "I see. And these were sent to you, personally? Not," he added, "through a post office or a place of work?"

"No," Titus agreed. "And I was under the impression that you and Marcus were the only ones who knew of my location?"

"So were we, until now." Hal's voice was grim.

"But why?" Titus went on. He still clung to the piece of paper like a lifeline. "Why would someone do such a thing? And why would they lie to me about Jamie's location?"

Hal exchanged a look with Rosaline, and across the room, Marcus' expression rippled with an emotion she could not name. "Titus," said Hal. "We have to tell you something. Something about Jamie."

"Hal," snapped Marcus. "May I speak to you and Rosaline in the hall?"

"Marcus," said Hal, "we are not going to discuss Titus and his child when the man himself is standing right in front of us."

"Titus deserves to know," said Rosaline. "Time is of the

essence, and we cannot waste any more of it solely because of a grudge."

Marcus raised his eyebrows, as if warding off a blow. "A grudge?" he repeated, his shoulders hitching with insult. "You do not know what it is of which you speak so *lightly*—"

"Titus," said Hal, ignoring his godfather. He looked the man dead in the eye and said, "Titus, earlier this afternoon, Jamie was kidnapped."

Another ringing silence fell as Titus just stared at him, speechless. But Hal did not let it last for long.

"Neither Rosaline nor I were here at the time, and Jamie's absence was not noticed until about a half-hour after he was taken from the property. We have already sent riders to the four nearest towns," Hal went on, "looking for anything out of the ordinary, and for any information about travelers passing through. Whoever did this knew where Jamie was, and was unafraid of hurting Hamish, his minder. As far as we can tell, this was planned well in advance. It is possible that the perpetrators colluded with members of the staff, and—" There came a knock at the door, and Marcus let Brooks into the room, then locked the door once again.

"Brooks," said Hal. "Excellent timing. I was just explaining the events of this afternoon to Mr. Wolfe. Perhaps, now, you might tell us your findings."

"Of course, my lord." Brooks cleared his throat, and drew himself up to his full height. "I have questioned all members of the staff as a group, and in turn questioned several of them individually."

Suddenly, Titus lurched out of his chair and began to pace. He said nothing, but he again pushed a hand through his hair, and while his expression was flat, Rosaline could see the agony that was tearing him apart.

Brooks leveled one of his trademark disapproving looks at Titus. "I believe," Brooks went on, "that most of the staff was unaware of any plot to remove Mr. Jamie from his home."

"Most?" Marcus repeated, raising an eyebrow. "You mean—?"

Brooks nodded. "Yes, sir, I believe that I might have found a possible informant. Or, at the very least, I have narrowed the pool of suspects to one person. My only concern, my lords, is that if I make my suspicions clear without enough evidence, she may find a way to warn her accomplices."

"Or she could run," said Hal. "Before giving us any information."

"She has not done so yet," Marcus pointed out. "Perhaps she is not as clever as we might imagine. Or she is simply arrogant."

"In any case," said Hal, "we cannot draw further conclusions without hearing from the four riders." He checked his pocket watch. "What time did they leave, Brooks?"

"Shortly before Lord Blackwood departed for Rosings Park," Brooks replied. "Little more than an hour and a half ago."

Rosaline's head spun. Had it really only been an hour?

Hal gave a nod. "Then we have nothing to do but wait." He looked to Titus, trying to make eye contact with him. Titus ignored him, and continued to pace. "Titus," he said, to little effect. "We will find Jamie, and we will bring him back."

Titus let out a strangled sort of laugh, and said nothing.

"In the meantime, Brooks," said Hal, "no members of staff are to exit the building. Please have the cook prepare a plate of tea and sandwiches for Mr. Wolfe—"

Titus let out another strangled, derisive laugh.

"Which he can supplement with Scotch from the sideboard," Hal continued, undeterred. "And please send Lisette and Dobson up to our personal chambers — the my wife and I will require assistance with packing."

"Packing?" said Rosaline with a frown.

Hal nodded and squeezed her hand. "We are going to follow

him, Rosaline. We are going to follow him, and we are going to bring him home."

And his words were so determined, so full of love, that she had to believe it.

"I will remain in the drawing room," said Marcus, his voice brittle. "To ensure that Mr. Wolfe behaves himself."

"Behave myself?" barked Titus suddenly, making Rosaline jump. "My son has been kidnapped from what you promised me would be the safest place on earth, and—"

"He was never safe, Wolfe, not once!" Marcus barked back, with equal vehemence. His eyes flashed, his shoulders rippled, and Rosaline had never seen him so angry. "He was never given the privilege of safety, thanks to you and your recklessness!"

"Gentlemen!" Hal glared at both of them. "Control yourselves, for Jamie's sake if no one else's. We are nothing if we are not level-headed, and we do not have time to air your personal grievances. Bring this nonsense to an end at once." He took a breath, his nostrils flaring. "I shall rejoin you in a quarter of an hour. In the meantime, I do not want to hear so much as a shout from these chambers. Have I made myself clear?"

For several tense moments, neither of them moved. Then Titus gave a nod, and Marcus did the same. They did not look at each other.

Once they were in the hall, Rosaline clung to Hal's arm and said, "You said to me, when I met Jamie, that there were people willing to pay a small fortune for the son of a traitor—"

"There are, and that is why I believe he has been taken," said Hal. Now that he no longer had to control himself, she could see the anger, ceaseless and turgid, writhing under his skin.

"Do you think that the people who wrote to Titus are the same people who—?"

"Yes," he said at once. "I believe they have orchestrated this entire scenario. Why limit yourself to collecting one bounty if you could have two?"

For a moment, something heavier and far more terrifying than fear swept through her stomach, sinking down to her hips, her feet, and it was all Rosaline could do to keep walking. "But who?" she managed. "Who would want—?"

Hal let out a bitter chuckle. "Agents of the King, my love. Perhaps even some unknown figures in the military. I believe Titus' commanding officer is still alive, and he would not be the first soldier to hold a grudge."

They hurried up the steps, and Rosaline's heart continued to beat a steady drum in her ears. "I cannot bear it," she muttered, her words echoing down the empty hall. "I cannot bear the thought of Jamie—"

"Me either." Hal's hand, squeezing hers. His touch was hot and sweaty, and for some reason, it calmed her.

"Can I ask why it is that Titus and Marcus seem so... at odds?"

"You can ask," Hal replied as they turned a corner. "But whether I can answer—"

"I thought they were friends," she pressed. "Your parents' closest friends—"

"They were— are." Hal cleared his throat. "You recall that Marcus did not react well to their deaths? He found solace in drink," he went on, when she nodded. "Titus... found a different path altogether."

Rosaline stared at him. "Is that when he joined the army?"

Hal nodded. "As far as I know, yes. Whether their deaths explain his later actions, I could not tell you for certain."

They'd reached their chambers. Lisette and Dobson, Hal's valet, were standing at the ready. Their faces, usually so warm and cheerful, were pale and drawn.

"*Ma chère*—" Lisette came to Rosaline at once, drawing her into a hug. "*I cannot believe*—"

"*I know.*" Rosaline clung to her with trembling hands. "*Do you know anything?*"

"*Very little.*" Lisette pulled away and met her gaze, her mouth set into a determined line. "*I do not know what Brooks has told you, but you must be sure to question Elsie.*"

Rosaline stared at her. "*Elsie?*"

Lisette nodded, glancing at where Hal and Dobson were engaged in their own hurried conversation. "*She is not as clever as she thinks, and she would not dare to try and leave tonight, not with guards at every exit. But she knows something.*" She squeezed Rosaline's hands, in an echo of Hal's own actions. "*You must make her confess.*"

"*Lisette, I cannot make anyone do anything—*"

"*Yes, you can.*" Lisette leaned in close. "*You are the Duchess of St. Albans, second only to the Queen of England. You can do whatever you bloody well please.*"

"*You have too much faith in me—*"

"*No.*" Lisette's voice was fierce. "*I have just enough.*" She stepped away and gave Rosaline's hand another squeeze. "Now, tell me what to pack."

"The usual, I suppose, though—" Rosaline bit her lip. "Lisette, it sounds preposterous, but I would love to have a pair of trousers."

Lisette barely even blinked, though she did suck her teeth. "*I knew that day at the boxing match would have its consequences. Where,*" she said in English, loud enough for Hal and Dobson to hear, "am I going to find a pair of trousers?"

"Here," said Hal, going over to the nearest closet. He emerged with two dark pairs of trousers and handed them to Lisette. "They're from my Eton days, and one of them has a hole in the pocket. Dobson won't mind, will you, Dobson?"

"Not at all, my lord," said Dobson.

"Will that do?" Hal said to Lisette.

She nodded, casting a careful eye over the trousers. "Thank you, my lord."

"Dare I ask?" said Hal, turning to Rosaline now.

Rosaline smiled at him, or rather, tried to. "Where you go, I shall go."

Hal shook his head, but he brushed a kiss to her cheek nonetheless.

☙

Rosaline approached the drawing room, now dressed in a heavier-weight, plain muslin gown with her hair in a simple braid and not a scrap of jewelry on her body, save for her wedding band. *Incognito*, Hal had said as he put on a wrinkled shirt with a torn sleeve. *Rank only gets in the way, unless people are feeling less than talkative.*

Hal was still with Brooks, arranging the details of their proposed transport, and she was alone as she made her way down the hall. They were expecting at least one of the riders any moment now, and they had to ready themselves for news, any news—

As Rosaline drew even with the drawing room, she overheard the unmistakable rumble of raised voices from within. But something, whether curiosity or instinct, made her pause and put her ear to the door, rather than burst through it and demand civility.

"—need to trust Hal, he is his father's son and he—"

"How can anyone speak to me on matters of trust on a night like tonight?" Titus' voice was brutal with sorrow.

"How can you speak on matters of trust at all?" Marcus countered, and Rosaline could hear it clearly now, the hurt that had previously lingered beneath the surface of his voice. "Last I remember, you were unconcerned with its confines, its promises."

Titus sighed, and when he spoke, it was pleading. "Marcus... not now, not tonight."

"Not tonight," Marcus echoed. "Or any night, apparently. Not the night that you left without a word, not the night that you came here begging for help, for solace, not even the night before you left for America—"

"Do not." Titus' voice was brittle, now, with the unsaid. "You have no idea—"

"Oh, but I do. You are the one, Titus. You are the one who left."

"You were gone," Titus bit out. "You were gone the moment they died, even if your body was still here—"

"You mean to say that I deserved it?" Marcus' voice gained a taunting edge. "I deserved to be left alone, in *our bed*—"

Rosaline jerked away from the door and clamped a hand to her mouth, stifling a squeak of surprise. Her heart beat a tattoo in her ears, but she gathered herself, managing to take a quiet breath before she returned her ear to the door.

"And what am I supposed to think?" Marcus, again. "You have a son, Titus, a *son*. Where does that leave me?"

"He has nothing to do with you, *Ireland* has nothing to do with you—"

"You married a woman, Titus! You took a *wife!*" The word was strangled in Marcus' mouth, and Rosaline's stomach twisted with sympathy. "Do you understand what that means, what it means to *me?*"

Then, to her combined surprise and dismay, Hal appeared and frowned when he saw her hunched against the door. "What are you—?"

Rosaline shushed him, took him by the arm. "I will tell you later," she whispered.

Hal shook his head. "Never a dull moment." Then, he knocked loudly on the door and entered, Rosaline a step behind him.

She hadn't known what to expect, but Titus and Marcus were turned away from each other in an attitude that suggested a quick, hasty separation. Rosaline's heart clanged against her ribs, and as she watched, they both schooled their expressions, hiding the raging hurt that she'd heard so clearly in their voices.

"The riders should be here any moment," said Hal. He strode over to the center of the room, where Rosaline saw the tea tray left for Titus, its contents barely touched. "Once they give us their reports, we should be able to—"

"If the people who wrote to Wolfe are the same people who took Jamie," said Marcus, "then the riders may be in far greater danger than we realize."

"I agree," said Hal. "But we must track them down regardless."

"I think Wolfe should stay here," said Marcus, ignoring Titus' answering scowl. "If things do not go as planned, then we should hedge our bets—"

"You are *speaking*," snarled Titus, "of my *son*. And," he said, rounding on Hal, "leaving a highly-trained soldier behind on a rescue mission may be one of the most idiotic ideas I have ever heard."

Hal fixed him with a cool look. "A highly-trained soldier is hardly much use without a square meal and a good rest."

Titus looked at him for a moment, then let out a forced breath, went over to the tea tray, and took a large, pointed bite of his ham sandwich.

Hal gave an approving nod. "We have to assume that Jamie has been taken to a large city, perhaps for transport to another destination. My money's on London, but as soon as we have a lead, we can leave Alban Hollow in pursuit."

"It is a very daring plan," said Titus between bites. "Especially if they catch wind of our pursuit — they may flee, or put Jamie into hiding."

"Which is why we are not to take any unnecessary risks," Hal replied. "We can travel on horseback or in the small carriage, whichever you think is most suitable."

"Four would be a squeeze in that carriage," said Marcus with a frown. "Five, if we find Jamie."

"*When* we find Jamie, you and I can switch to horseback, if necessary," Hal replied.

But before Marcus could say anything, there came a great scuffle from the front of the house, and a moment later, the drawing room door opened and Brooks appeared. "My lord," he said, "one of the riders—"

"Let him in at once," said Hal. Both Marcus and Titus straightened up, like dogs scenting a rabbit.

One of the footmen — Dawes, Rosaline remembered, who was from a nearby farm — came striding into the room, windswept and wide-eyed. "Good evening, my lord—"

Hal swatted away the greeting with an impatient hand. "Come, come, we do not have time for all that nonsense, tell us what you found—"

"I was dispatched to Somerton, my lord," Dawes went on. "Once there, I questioned the local proprietors, without trying to draw attention to myself, and I'm afraid I..." He swallowed. "I'm afraid I have nothing to report."

It was silent for a moment, then Hal turned to Titus. "It seems they did not ride south. That is some comfort, at least." He nodded at Dawes. "Thank you, Dawes, now go downstairs and get a warm bowl of soup before you go to bed."

Dawes nodded. "Thank you, my lord." He bowed his head and left the room.

Unable to stand it, Rosaline sank onto the nearest sofa, twisting her skirts in her hand. Hal seemed so calm, so collected, not showing an inch of the impatience that was screaming under her skin, desperate to burst out. Even the solace of a book held no temptation for her.

Then, somewhat to her surprise, Marcus sat down beside her and offered her a grim smile. "There is nothing so terrible as waiting."

Rosaline sighed. "You are quite right." And when he took her hand, she leaned into his shoulder, grateful for his presence.

Over the course of the next half-hour, they received the riders from Bridgwater and Wedmore, neither of whom had any news. Each of these announcements only caused Rosaline's heart to sink lower and lower, but Hal was determined in his optimism.

"They did not ride west, and they did not ride north," he said. "Not to Wales, nor to Plymouth. This leaves but one option—"

Even if London seemed the most logical conclusion, Rosaline's heart withered at the prospect of trying to track down Jamie in that enormous, seething city. Just the image of him holed away in some squat hovel of the East End made her want to scream.

Is he cold? she could not keep herself from wondering. *Is he hungry? Is he frightened?* Perhaps that final thought was nothing short of ludicrous — Jamie had to be afraid, even if his kidnappers shared a scrap of decency among them.

When, finally, the last rider burst into the room — Baxter, she remembered, from the stables — and said, "My lords, they've gone to Glastonbury."

It was as if the room had been struck by lightning. Rosaline and Marcus were on their feet at once, and Hal rounded on Baxter. "Really?" he said. "You are certain?"

Baxter nodded. "They may have left by now, but two men were staying at the Carriage Arms, and when they returned this evening, they had a parcel over one shoulder. I assume—"

"Yes," breathed Hal. "That has to be him. Did the landlord say where they were—?"

"East," said Baxter, his chest heaving, his eyes bright. "To London."

Titus swore, but Hal did not relent. "And did he have a description of the men? Anything at all?"

"A bit," Baxter replied. "One was quite dark, and he had a scar along one cheek. The other was..." He blushed. "Well, to use the proprietor's words, a pretty-boy. He was quite tall, and he had blond hair, parted to one side, though he tried to hide it by wearing a hat."

The air seemed to vanish from the room. Rosaline wobbled on her feet, and she clung to Marcus' arm, wondering if here, now, she would faint for the first time in her life. And when Hal turned to meet her gaze, his own full of simultaneous horror and understanding, she knew that they were both back in that garden, under the moonlight, the smell of mud fresh in their noses.

"Brooks." Hal's voice was brittle with anger. "I believe it is time we questioned that housemaid."

❦ 46 ❦

"Hal," Rosaline whispered, darting a glance over the edge of the screen, "is this not a bit of a gamble?"

"Absolutely," he whispered back from where he was hunched beside her. "But if Lisette's read of this woman is as accurate as I imagine, it is less of a gamble and more of a surety."

"I need a drink," muttered Marcus. He was sitting on the floor opposite Hal, arms wrapped around his knees, looking rather dismal.

Rosaline hummed. "Unfortunately, the Scotch is on the other side of this screen—"

"Quiet," hissed Hal. "I can hear Brooks."

A moment later, the door to the drawing room opened, and Rosaline heard, rather than watched, three people enter the room. One of them immediately let out a gasp.

Mrs. Andrews: "Are you quite well, Elsie?"

"Yes." The maid cleared her throat, but even then, her voice was still wobbly with shock. "Yes, thank you."

"Right, I shall leave you to it." Brooks, now. "I will be just outside the door."

"Thank you, Mr. Brooks." Mrs. Andrews, again. The door opened and closed.

"I do not understand." Elsie now. "I thought the Duke—"

"I am sure the Duke will join us in a moment."

"But he—"

"Yes?"

Silence.

When Elsie spoke, Rosaline again heard the wobble of her resolve giving way. "That... that man—"

"Oh, him?" Mrs. Andrews' voice was airy, unconcerned. "Pay him no mind, he is here to mend the flue."

Even to Rosaline's ears, it sounded absurd, especially given how late it was. But Elsie did not have the benefit of such resolve. Then Titus gave a very obligatory rattle of his tools. It was a stroke of genius on Brooks' part — Titus' clothes were so filthy that anyone would believe him to be in the trade of chimneys.

"Are you sure?"

"Quite certain." Mrs. Andrews was frustrated now. "I hope you will not insist upon pestering the Duke with such absurd questions."

"No, I— I— I would not dream of it." But Rosaline could hear the concern and the panic warring equally in her voice. "Is this man local? I don't believe I've ever—"

"Ask him yourself, Elsie."

Mrs. Andrews could've had a second life on the stage, Rosaline thought. Beside her, Hal had tensed, and even seemed to stop breathing. She put a hand to his shoulder.

"S–sir? Excuse me?"

"Good evening to you, Miss." Titus' Welsh accent was liquid and perfect. She wondered, then, if that was where he was originally from.

"Good evening. Do you hail from the village?"

"Aye, Miss, though I do most of my business in Somerton."

"Really?" Elsie's voice pitched higher. Rosaline did not dare to breathe. "I grew up just two miles from here, and I've got a mind for faces. Never forget a face, me. And I don't recall yours."

"I don't know what to say to that, Miss." Titus' voice was mild. "I work on chimneys the whole county over."

"Do you?" A sharp edge, now. "What did you say your name was?"

"Robert Taylor, Miss."

"Taylor?"

"Yes."

"From Somerton?"

"Yes."

"I've never heard of a Taylor from Somerton, or from anywhere around here."

"I can't help you there, Miss." Titus really did sound baffled. "My name is Robert Taylor, and I grew up on Honeysuckle Row—"

"Stop lying."

Those two words were icy-sharp and deadly with anger. Rosaline could tell, through the silence, that Elsie had shocked even herself.

"Elsie!" Mrs. Andrews, now. "How dare you address this man—"

"That's all right, Mrs. Andrews," said Titus, mild and unaffected. "The young lady is just confused."

"Am I?" Elsie bit out. "The Richards family lives on Honeysuckle Row, always have. This man's a liar, and a pretender. You should throw him out at once."

"Elsie! Control yourself!"

Titus, again: "Really, Miss, I don't know—"

"Yes, you do!" Elsie sounded almost tearful. "Just stop it, stop lying!"

"My name is Robert Taylor, Miss, and I—"

"You were supposed to go to Brighton!"

A sudden, deadly silence. Rosaline's heart throbbed against

her ribs, and her head clanged in reply. She met Hal's gaze and recognized the triumph, the conviction, in his eyes. Then he cleared his throat and stepped out from behind the screen. In the space of an instant, she watched him transform, shouldering the invisible cloak of his rank that always hung in the air, ready, waiting.

"Thank you, Mrs. Andrews. That should be sufficient."

Rosaline followed him, and after a beat, his face expressionless, so did Marcus.

They formed quite a tableau — on one side of the room, she, Hal, and Marcus, facing down the housemaid and the supposed chimney sweep. Between them, Mrs. Andrews held her ground, giving Elsie a look that would turn flesh to stone.

Elsie was standing not three feet from Titus, her hands clenched into fists, blotches of color high on her pale cheeks. "Your— Your Grace." She trembled, then seemed to swallow her fear. "You set me up."

"You helped a criminal kidnap my ward," the Duke replied, as smooth and cold as ice. Titus was looking at Elsie, and Rosaline could not parse his expression at all. He betrayed not one hint of emotion. "You," the Duke continued, "still have sunk to greater depths than I."

"Explain yourself," Mrs. Andrews said to Elsie, her voice cutting and determined. "You have been given steady, good employment, at a respectable home. What on earth made you throw all that away, and put a child at risk?"

Elsie ignored her, and she met the Duke's gaze directly. "You call *him* a criminal," she spat, "and extend this man, a traitor, every accommodation, you let his *offspring* live under your roof—"

The Duke's eyes flashed. "I hardly think you are in any position to cast the first stone."

Him, Rosaline thought, a jolt of energy prickling down her spine. *She said it. She said 'him'*— But she could not bring herself to speak, not yet. She wanted to see how well Elsie would spin the web of her own doom.

"You said this man—" the Duke gestured to Titus— "was supposed to go to Brighton. Where, I presume, your associates were lying in wait at the address given in the letter."

Elsie's coloring deepened. "You know *nothing.*"

"But why separate them?" the Duke continued. "Why not bait him to go to London, where, no doubt, you planned to take Jamie?"

"Because that is not where his command is stationed," said Marcus. Everyone turned to look at him, and he gave Elsie a hard glare. "You were going to take this man to his commanding officer."

"He is a deserter," hissed Elsie, the veins standing livid in her neck. "And he should be treated as such. A court-martial is the least of what he has coming to him, and as for that mongrel of a son—"

The words had barely left her mouth before Titus lunged at her, fastening his hands around her throat.

The room exploded. Mrs. Andrews let out a little scream, and the Duke immediately made a grab for Titus, but Marcus got there first, wrangling Titus until his hands broke free of Elsie's throat. Elsie fell to her knees, coughing and spluttering, and Marcus dragged Titus into the corner, pinning one arm behind his back, his mouth at Titus' ear as he muttered an endless stream of words that Rosaline could not and did not want to hear. Titus only stared, his eyes bulging, his face deathly pale, at the stooped, hunched woman before him. For an instant, Rosaline felt a true, undeniable ripple of fear.

She could see, now, the man that had broken the line and taken up the mantle of revolution.

Elsie gave a great, rattling cough. "You see— you see what he is."

It seemed that everyone had reached their breaking point.

Rage flickered across the Duke's features, and he took a long, careful breath as he stared down at her. "Get up," he spat. "Now. Or you shall have to contend with far worse than a vengeful father."

After a few moments, Elsie finally shifted, her skirts rustling against the wooden floor.

Mrs. Andrews went to her side, her jaw set and her expression grim, and she gripped Elsie's elbow, helping her up from the floor. As soon as she was standing, Elsie shook off Mrs. Andrew's hand without so much as a glance.

The Duke met Elsie's gaze and she returned it with an unbelievable degree of arrogance. "Tell us who took the boy, and where."

Elsie smiled. "You will not find him."

"I think you would be surprised to learn what I am capable of," the Duke replied.

Elsie sneered, and Mrs. Andrews balked. Rosaline herself was having a difficult time reconciling this version of Elsie with the one she'd known before — the cheerful, sweet housemaid who was never quite in the right place at the right time.

But then, Rosaline remembered McGrath. She remembered his kind eyes, his ready hand, his attentive nature. It was all a show, of course, but an effective one. He would not have been able to get anywhere near Alban Hollow without sounding the alarm, and the villagers were so loyal they never would have agreed to help him, unless—

Something stirred in Rosaline's memory, and before she could stop herself, Rosaline looked at Elsie and said, "Elsie, how is your uncle?"

For just a split second, Elsie blinked and stared at her, looking as if she'd just seen a ghost. But she quickly schooled her expression and stuck out her chin. "I don't see what—"

"Elsie comes to us from a very strained background," Rosaline said, glancing first at Marcus and Titus, then back at the Duke.

"Her family had fallen on difficult times, and she and her mother were forced to work to support her younger siblings. The estate was able to give her a livelihood, and her family was glad for it." She returned her gaze to Elsie and, to her surprise, felt nothing but compassion. "Her father, you see, passed away several years ago, and her uncle is in debtors' prison."

"My God." The Duke's words were hardly audible. "That's how he did it. That's how McGrath got to her."

Here, thought Rosaline. *Here, now, is where the dam breaks.*

Indignation flashed across Elsie's face. "He did not *get* to me—"

"Then he must have promised you something." Rosaline watched Elsie carefully, and noticed that she did not deny McGrath's involvement. "He certainly promised me the world."

"He didn't promise you nothing," Elsie snapped, her temper flaring once again. "You tricked him, you made him think you loved him, when it was all just a game—"

"And I suppose when he tried to force himself on me, that, too, was just a game."

"Lies," spat Elsie. "Filthy lies—"

Ah, Rosaline thought. *He told her all he could.* "I have nothing to gain by lying, Elsie. He had everything to gain." She took a few steps closer to the girl, feeling as if she were approaching a wild animal. "You are smart, Elsie, smart enough to know that if what McGrath wanted was money, there are far easier ways of finding it. Easier than tricking a deserter back to his native land and easier than kidnapping an innocent child. You know that McGrath is motivated by vengeance, that he is determined to hurt the Duke and anyone connected to him. That is what this is about. Not money, but who can deal the deadlier blow."

Elsie looked at her, but, to Rosaline's dismay, did not seem to waver.

"We are talking of a child, Elsie." Rosaline's voice shook, but she ignored it. "A child who insisted on helping you carry the laundry and who chased you around the kitchen. Why on earth should you want to hurt him, to cause him suffering?"

Elsie continued to look at her, and said nothing.

"You are mistaken, Rosaline," said Marcus. "This woman is incapable of feeling emotion, let alone sympathy." He took a slow breath, his grip still firm around Titus' arms. "There is no entreaty you can make that would force her to listen to her own conscience."

With that, Rosaline stepped away, and the emotion that had been clouding her gaze slid back down her throat. "I see." She turned to Mrs. Andrews. "Please fetch Mr. Brooks."

Mrs. Andrews nodded. "At once, my Lady." She left the room.

Elsie looked at Rosaline, a silent question in her eyes, but Rosaline ignored it and turned to the Duke. "Are any of the constables nearby?"

The Duke nodded. "I can have two of them brought to the house."

"And the magistrate?"

"He is near Somerton, but he can wait until morning."

Brooks entered the room. "My lady?"

"Brooks," said Rosaline. "I know we have made many demands upon our staff this evening, and I am afraid that will have to continue. Elsie will be spending the night in the spare room in the basement, and until the constables arrive, we will need two men stationed outside her door."

Brooks nodded. "Understood, my lady."

Rosaline ignored the way Elsie was staring at her and said, "In the morning, the magistrate will escort her to the county jail, where she will be kept until her hearing."

"But you—" Elsie suddenly burst out. "You can't—"

Rosaline rounded on her. "I can and I most certainly will. You are to be charged with conspiracy, aiding and abetting a criminal, and most certainly with kidnapping a child. And not just any child, but the ward of one of the most important men in Britain."

She closed in on Elsie. "You will be flayed alive. Each and every one of your missteps will see the light of day, and if you think McGrath will come running to your side, you are sorely mistaken. You will break your mother's heart, and she and your siblings will have to watch you endure the suffering and embarrassment of a public trial."

"As will the Duke," Elsie fired back. "I'll sing like a canary about that boy and his father, about the Duke being a traitor to King and country—"

"Go ahead," Rosaline said coolly. "The magistrate is sure to trust the word of a housemaid over that of a Duke, a Lord, a Dowager Countess, and, as you may have forgotten, a Duchess."

Elsie stared at her, and the enormity of her situation seemed to sink in. She began to tremble, and Rosaline steeled her heart.

"No man is worth this," Rosaline went on. "McGrath is hardly worth more than a fleeting glance. Whatever he has promised you, he cannot fulfill it. What did he tell you to do, Elsie? Once Jamie was taken?"

It was several long moments before Elsie spoke. She blinked, her eyes glassy. "I was to wait a week, then take the post coaches and meet him in Gretna Green."

Rosaline's heart jumped. A week, even if it was a lie, could imply that whatever McGrath had lying in wait for Jamie would be quickly resolved. "I can assure you," she said, "McGrath never had any intention of meeting you in Gretna Green, Elsie."

Elsie's lip trembled. "You do not *know* that."

"He certainly failed to account for Titus' natural distrust," said the Duke. "Had Titus taken the bait and gone to Brighton, as you'd planned, your deception might never have been discovered. Did McGrath truly believe that your actions would escape our notice?"

"I suppose." But Elsie's certainty seemed to waver.

"He did not require much from her," Rosaline said to the Duke. "He simply needed to know where Jamie would be, and when. And perhaps for her to provide a distraction to ensure that Jamie's absence would go unnoticed for as long as possible." She gave a sniff. "To him, she is completely disposable, unnecessary once her use has been met."

Elsie's eyes flashed, but before she spoke—

"Tell us, Elsie." The Duke gave her a hard look. "Help yourself, and tell us what you know."

"And why should I?" she spat. "Either way, you will clap me in irons."

"The irons are at the magistrate's discretion," the Duke replied. "But if you help us, if you help me find Jamie, I give you my word that I shall advocate for leniency in your treatment and sentencing. I cannot promise the same if you refuse."

Elsie looked at him, and she seemed to be thinking hard. She glanced around the room, her eyes darting from person to person. The disappointment on Brooks's face alone made Rosaline's stomach quiver. "What assurance do I have?" she finally said to the Duke. "That you would keep your word?"

"The assurance," barked Marcus, "that you are dealing with people who would never dream of taking a child away from his family, no matter how great the incentive."

"Marcus," cautioned Rosaline, but her concern was unnecessary.

"Fine." Elsie's throat worked. "Just... my mother cannot lose what little work she has. And my brother... he's always wanted to have a tenancy."

The Duke gave a nod. "They will be provided for, regardless of your own fate."

"You should have thought of your family, Elsie," Brooks rumbled. "Before betraying your employer."

Elsie ignored him, looking right at the Duke. "Callum promised me ten percent. Ten percent, all to myself."

The Duke nodded again. "You need not worry."

Privately, Rosaline thought that Elsie had well and truly been tricked. McGrath parting with ten percent of anything was impossible to imagine. He likely had had no intention of meeting her anywhere, and would have ensured that when she arrived in Gretna Green, she would find herself introduced to any number of characters who would have sealed her fate and guaranteed his own protection.

"I do not know much." Elsie watched as Rosaline hurried over to the nearest desk and got out a bit of paper, ink, and a quill. "But he is taking the boy to London." She shook her head. "They may have a different final destination, but I think it unlikely. Callum always got very excited when he spoke of London. It might have something to do with the Major."

"The Major?" said the Duke.

Elsie nodded. "The man who purchased Callum's commission."

Rosaline continued to scribble, her mind churning. That certainly answered a few questions, but why would such a high-ranking officer purchase the commission of a man who had to be a stranger, and a known criminal at that?

"I had wondered how he'd managed to climb the ranks so quickly, given his utter lack of income and his family history. And now I come to find out it has nothing to do with talent, or personal sacrifice." The Duke gave her a grim smile. "Tell me what you know about this Major."

"His name is McNally," said Elsie. "He and his wife... they are vile people, Your Grace. McNally is wealthy, and powerful, and he is the reason Callum was able to participate in the season."

Something floated to the surface of Rosaline's memory — a shrill, sickly laugh echoing through the ballroom, a saccharine call of *Lieeuuu-tenant!* She remembered McGrath's grimace at the summons, which, for all she knew, had not been part of his act. "If McNally is as elevated as you claim, why should he take any interest in a commoner with a ruined father, let alone offer to pay his way through the army?"

Elsie shrugged. "That, I do not know."

"Do you know where he lives?" said the Duke. "McNally?"

Elsie shook her head. "I would guess somewhere near Kensington. But Callum was never specific." Here she blushed and looked at the floor, and Rosaline guessed that she was realizing the lengths to which McGrath had gone to make sure she would never find him.

The Duke turned to Brooks. "Brooks— in the library—"

"At once, my lord." Brooks left the room.

"Did McGrath ever mention anything else, anyone else?" the Duke pressed. "Anywhere he might have taken Jamie, to keep him out of sight?"

Elsie again shook her head. "There is a tavern, near the cathedral. The Bear's Head, I think. He often mentioned staying there, or drinking there. If Callum is not with McNally, he might be there. But Callum, he... he likes finery." She looked at Rosaline. "He might not be able to deny himself the comfort of a proper household, especially if he and McNally are working together."

"Might they be?" said the Duke.

"If McNally needs the money," Elsie replied. "Though why he would, I cannot think."

"The wealthiest people often harbor the greatest secrets," the Duke replied, his face drawn. "Today's events have only proven the truth of that statement." He turned to Rosaline, Marcus, and Titus. Marcus still had Titus in a firm grip, and though he had remained silent, Titus' face was livid with anger. "We can leave for London at once, and change horses along the way. Marcus, would you—?"

"I will remain here," said Marcus, and Rosaline did not miss the way Titus' expression flickered, surprise darting across his features. "The house cannot stay empty, and someone will need to answer the magistrate's questions, and to vouch for the girl."

Elsie lowered her gaze to the floor.

Hal gave a nod. "Very well. But Titus is to come with us. He knows London better than anyone I've ever met, and it is his son after all. Can you lend him a fresh change of clothes? Unfortunately, he will not have time to bathe—"

"Of course," said Marcus, but his voice was stiff with reluctance. He and Titus did not look at each other; in fact, Marcus' gaze returned to Elsie. "I have some questions of my own."

The Duke seemed surprised; he turned to Mrs. Andrews, who nodded. "By all means."

"I'm assuming that this McGrath or one of his associates was the one who wrote to Titus under Jamie's name. How on earth," said Marcus, "did you find his address?"

Elsie looked up, and a strange look of pride crossed her features. "In the Duke's study, my lord."

The Duke stared at her, dumbfounded. "I burnt it," he said. "I memorized the address and I burnt the papers—"

"Not all of them," Elsie replied. "One had fallen behind the top drawer of your desk, and was lying underneath the leg."

Mrs. Andrews stifled a gasp. "You searched my lord's desk?"

Elsie ignored her, and so did Marcus.

"You knew him," Marcus said, and Titus, too, stared at Elsie. "You knew this man as soon as you saw him, in spite of his... rough appearance." He cleared his throat, almost as if he were embarrassed by his own acknowledgment of Titus' present state. "How on earth did you know what Titus Wolfe looked like?"

Elsie looked from Marcus to Titus and back again. "In the attic," she said, "there is a painting—"

"My God." For a moment, Marcus looked decades older. "I'd forgotten."

A shade like a ghost passed over Titus' face — he went gray, and his gaze traveled somewhere miles away. The Duke frowned at both of them.

They were interrupted by Brooks entering the room. "I have a London address for McNally, my lord," he said, holding a piece of paper aloft. "It is not much, but it is something."

"Excellent. We are to leave at once."

What followed then was a hustle and bustle unlike anything Rosaline could have imagined. A footman was sent to retrieve some clothing for Titus, and Mrs. Andrews whisked away to fetch a pitcher of water and a basin, along with a fresh razor and a towel. Titus, finally released, turned away from the room to face the fire, silent and brooding. Beside him, Marcus was a portrait of chambered nerves — worry was writ large across his face, and even Rosaline could see that he was aching to reach for Titus, to speak to him. She said nothing, and kept her head bent over her work. Now, she was writing a letter to the magistrate, which she and the Duke would sign and leave with Marcus.

Once that was done, Rosaline locked the sealed envelope into the top drawer of the desk, then went over to Marcus and slipped the key into his hand. He gave her a nod and reentered the conversation between the Duke and Brooks.

Rosaline, meanwhile, went over to Elsie, who had backed into the far corner and stood waiting, her jaw clenched, her gaze fixed on the floor.

"Thank you," Rosaline said to her in a low voice. "For telling us the truth."

Elsie said nothing, but a muscle twitched in her jaw.

"How long, Elsie?" When the girl did not reply, Rosaline continued: "How long did he... court you?"

Elsie's head snapped up, and a fresh wave of color overcame her features. It was several moments before she spoke. "A year."

Something jolted in Rosaline's stomach. And she had an awful feeling— "There was a break-in here, at Alban Hollow, a few months ago. Was that... Elsie, was that McGrath's doing?"

Nothing, not even surprise, showed in Elsie's face. "Yes. Though it was not him, exactly. It was his associate. It was their..." Elsie shifted, and her gaze dropped again. "It was their first attempt to take the boy. Callum thought it might be easier, if the Duke was not here."

"But he was wrong," Rosaline managed, suddenly feeling quite dizzy.

Elsie nodded. "He was... he was angry." She let out a sigh. "That is why he decided that, when he tried again, he would do it himself."

"So McGrath was here." The dizziness surged. Before, Rosaline had assumed that McGrath had gotten someone else to do his dirty work. But now, the confirmation that he had been here, on their property, near her *home*, made nausea roil through her belly, up into her chest. She closed her eyes for a moment, and took a deep breath. When she opened them again, Elsie was watching her. "The magistrate is a fair man. If you are honest with him, he will show you mercy."

Then, somewhat to her surprise, Elsie bit her lip and shifted her weight from foot to foot. The color rose again in her face. "Duchess, there... there is something you should know. Something else, I mean."

Rosaline frowned at her. "Yes?"

"There is..." Elsie steeled herself, and took a shaky breath. "There is a reason why I insisted upon Callum marrying me. There is a reason why I would not tell him how to get to Jamie unless he promised."

It took several moments for Rosaline's overwhelmed mind to put the pieces together. When it finally did, she fought the urge to grab Elsie's arm. "How far along are you?"

❦ 47 ❧

The color drained from Elsie's face. She would not look Rosaline in the eye. "Three months," she whispered.

"Good Lord." It made sense now, why Elsie had insisted that McGrath would not abandon her. Rosaline glanced at the others, but they had not heard a thing. They were still busy figuring out the details of their trip. "You must let me tell Lord Blackwood, at the very least. The magistrate needs to know—"

"I just want the child to be safe, and loved." Elsie's voice was almost empty of emotion. "Even if I am to be condemned—"

"We— the Duke and I— would never allow an innocent child to suffer, Elsie, regardless of the actions of its parents."

"Yes, I... I know that."

Rosaline felt a sudden surge of sympathy for this wretched girl. It was a difficult situation, to be sure, and it was possible that Elsie's condition was the result of a forced union. Even if Elsie had willingly conspired to steal a child, she was, in her own way, another victim of McGrath's endless, greedy, vengeful ambition.

"Do not worry," Rosaline whispered, just as Brooks nodded and left the room once again. "We will help you, Elsie."

Elsie nodded, and, to Rosaline's astonishment, her chin wobbled. "Thank you, Duchess."

Rosaline turned away, and rejoined her husband.

"All settled," he said to her. "We will ride through the night, changing horses where we can, and we will have to open the London house ourselves. No servants," he added. "I do not want any more eyes on this situation than we already have. Our driver will stay at an inn."

Rosaline nodded, her mind churning with the handful of recipes Lisette had attempted to teach her during those long, rain-filled autumn evenings in Provence. "We shall make do."

"Titus," said the Duke, and the man in question merely lifted his head in reply. "Get changed, and make yourself presentable. We are leaving in ten minutes."

For several moments, Titus did not move. Then, finally, he complied, picking up Marcus' spare clothing from where it lay on the couch. Mrs. Andrews approached him, hesitant, but with a friendly, warm expression.

"Mr. Wolfe, I've put the water and shaving equipment in the next room, if you'd like to follow me."

When Titus spoke, his voice was soft and mellow, his Welsh lilt quiet but present nonetheless. "Thank you, Mrs. Andrews, but I do remember my way around." He glanced at her, and his hooded eyes showed a spark of warmth. "How is your sister?"

Rosaline could only stare as Mrs. Andrews beamed at him and nodded. "Very well, thank you for asking."

"Of course," Titus replied. He did not look at any of them again before he left the room.

Once the door had shut behind him, Marcus let out a great, rattling breath. The Duke shot him a look.

"I know." The Duke's voice was low. "He looks awful."

Marcus turned to Mrs. Andrews. "Mrs. Andrews, is there any way you could—?"

Mrs. Andrews nodded. "There is already a picnic basket in the carriage. Mr. Partridge—" the cook— "packed plenty of sandwiches and fruit and cold meat."

Before Marcus could reply, there came a loud clatter from the hall. Rosaline and the Duke traded a look — they knew that sound. Running feet.

Coates, one of the footmen, came stumbling into the room, breathless. He turned to the Duke. "My lord— there is a— there is a carriage—"

The Duke stared at him. "What?!"

"We couldn't—" Coates wheezed, clutching a stitch in his side. "We couldn't stop them—"

"Get ahold of yourself, boy," muttered Mrs. Andrews, going over to him. But she'd hardly laid a hand on his arm before the doors burst open and in marched none other than—

Rosaline gasped. "Charlotte?!"

"Edward?!" The Duke sounded just as astonished as she.

"We've come to help," said Edward. "And we brought your carriage back."

Charlotte swept over and took Rosaline's hands in her own. She and Edward were likewise dressed in plain, warm traveling clothes, and her hair was pulled back into a single plait. "We saw the other carriage out front. Are you leaving?"

Rosaline could only stare at her, speechless.

"Help?" the Duke repeated. "What do you mean, 'help?'"

"In whatever way you need," Edward replied. For the first time, Rosaline noticed that he carried a rapier — a genuine, honest-to-God rapier with a golden pommel — at his hip. He was looking at Hal, guileless, concerned.

Several tense, quiet moments passed, in which the Duke and the Earl Cadogan simply stared at one another. Then, suddenly, the Duke rounded on his godfather.

"*Marcus!*"

"What?" Marcus replied, unaffected. "Someone outside the family had to know. I told them before I left London."

Rosaline began to tremble. Charlotte noticed, and her grip tightened.

The Duke swore loudly and at length. "If we were not quite literally running short on time, I would throttle you—"

Marcus crossed the room, took his godson by the hand, and muttered something. The Duke frowned, then grimaced, then nodded. Rosaline ached to know what was passing between them.

"We assumed it had to be about your ward," said Edward, "given the way you left so abruptly. How bad is it?"

"As bad as it could be," said the Duke, grim. "Someone has kidnapped the boy. Taken him to London, we believe, where any number of—"

"Do you know who took him?" said Edward.

The Duke nodded. "McGrath."

Charlotte let out a low gasp, and a muscle twitched in Edward's jaw before he spat, "*Bastard*—"

"We have a lead," the Duke went on. "But perhaps I could explain everything—"

"In the carriage, yes," Edward finished for him. He glanced around the room. "Will it seat six?"

"Five," the Duke corrected him. "Marcus is staying behind."

Edward nodded. "Then Brooks—?"

"Is also staying behind." The Duke licked his lips, showing just a hint of nerves.

A beat.

"Five." Edward frowned. "Who—?"

Then, the door behind them opened, and in walked Titus.

He looked a little better now, and though he and Marcus were of a height, he was thinner, lankier, and the clothing hung loosely about his frame. He'd clearly availed himself of the warm water — his stubble was gone, and his skin was scrubbed pink and clean. His long hair was scraped back into a low ponytail, tied with a bit of torn ribbon, leaving his face open and sharp, and Rosaline could not help staring at him.

She was not the only one. Marcus himself looked a little dumbstruck. Edward, meanwhile, shifted his hand to rest on his pommel.

"Ed," said the Duke in a low voice. "Meet Titus Wolfe, Jamie's father. He joins us," he added, "as a result of very fortunate, if accidental, timing."

Titus looked from Edward, to the Duke, to Charlotte, and back again. He said nothing.

Edward relaxed and nodded. "Pleasure to meet you, sir." He walked up to Titus, unconcerned, and held out his hand. "My name is Edward, and my wife, Charlotte, stands beside Rosaline."

Charlotte smiled and waved. "Hello, Mr. Wolfe."

Titus merely looked at both of them, then shook Edward's hand. "I gather you are to be a member of the rescue party?"

"The Lord Cadogan is most obliging," said Marcus.

"Cadogan?" Titus looked at Edward with a new understanding. "I knew your parents. They were wonderful people."

Edward's ears went pink and he nodded, then turned to Hal. "The carriage. Will it seat five?"

"Yes," said the Duke, with a hint of impatience. "We should leave as soon as possible."

"We are ready," said Charlotte, squeezing Rosaline's hand again. Rosaline could only nod, still stricken speechless by the events of the past few minutes.

"My lord!" Brooks arrived, red-faced and puffing, at the door, glaring at Edward. "I see you've received our visitors—"

The Duke nodded. "They are coming with us, Brooks."

Brooks looked at him for a moment, then seemed to gather himself. "In any event," he rumbled, "the room in the basement is ready."

As one, everyone glanced at Elsie, who had remained silent in her corner. She did not react to the news, but made her way to the door, her gaze fixed on the floor.

Here, finally, Rosaline regained her voice. "Elsie." She stepped away from Charlotte and went to the girl, putting a hand to her shoulder. "It will be all right," she murmured. "Just tell the truth."

Elsie met her gaze and nodded, then followed Mrs. Andrews out of the room and down the hall, where they disappeared into the shadows.

When Rosaline went back to Charlotte, she could see the question in her friend's eyes, but she ignored it. There would be time enough to explain on the way to London.

"Well, then." The Duke looked around at all of them. "Let us fly."

They all bade Marcus farewell, and though they did not speak to one another, Rosaline did not miss the look Titus and Marcus traded — barbed, cold, but edged with longing.

After their goodbyes, the travelers all moved towards the front of the house. Her thoughts whirling, her feet still unsteady from the revelations of the past hour, Rosaline did not notice Titus' presence behind her until they all went out into the cold, black night, their breath fogging in the air before them. Torchlight flickered, amber and red, over the glossy black exterior of the estate's largest carriage, and Rosaline gulped at the enormity of the task before them.

Titus came to stand beside her as Charlotte and Edward climbed into the carriage. He was wearing a borrowed coat, and its sharp collar made him look a little bestial in the moonlight. "Your name is Rosaline?" he said in his low, quiet voice.

With a jolt, Rosaline realized they were never formally introduced. She turned to him and said, "Yes, Mr. Wolfe. My name is Rosaline."

"As in *Romeo and Juliet?*"

In spite of herself, in spite of everything, she smiled. "My mother loved Shakespeare."

He nodded. "I am sorry we met like this."

"As am I." She had to say something, she had to. "Mr. Wolfe, you have to know—"

"Titus," he said, still in that quiet, lilting voice. "Call me Titus, please."

"Titus," she said. "I love your son as I would my own. I would do anything for him."

For a bare, split second, the emotion showed in his face, then it was gone. He nodded. "You are a very kind woman."

Rosaline had no idea what to say to that. Instead, she turned away, took Hal's hand, and clambered into the carriage.

Charlotte and Edward sat opposite, and Titus took the seat beside Hal. Charlotte and Edward were holding hands, and seeing it made Rosaline smile.

The seating arrangements did make things a bit snug, along with the picnic basket taking up half the floor. Above them, the single lantern swayed as the footman closed the door.

"Perhaps we should extinguish that," said Edward. "If we are to be traveling at a hasty speed. Besides," he added, with a glance at all of them, "we should try to get some rest. There will be enough time to discuss everything later."

To Rosaline, the idea of falling asleep was unimaginable — her nerves still jangled with stress and sorrow, and her stomach roiled with unease. But sitting in the dark would perhaps be easier than sitting and staring at one another, too miserable and worried to speak.

Hal was the one who stood up. He looked at his friend, and said, "Thank you, Ed. You did not have to come."

"Yes, I did," Edward said at once. "Put out the light, Hal."

They plunged into a sudden darkness, and Rosaline blinked at the shadowy figures across from her, Hal's hand finding hers and weaving their fingers together. She squeezed her eyes shut, and rocked with the carriage as it set off, the gravel crunching under its relentless wheels.

This will pass, she thought. *It has to.*

Somewhere between Glastonbury and Shepton Mallet, Rosaline fell into a light, rolling doze. She woke only when the carriage drew to a stop, and sat there, blinking, her eyes muddy with confusion, at the figure shifting beside her.

Hal's hand at her arm, his mouth at her ear. "We are at Westbury, to change the horses." He brushed a kiss to her forehead, and she leaned into it with a sigh. "Would you like to stretch your legs?"

Rosaline shook her head, burrowing further in against his chest. She heard and felt him let out an amused huff, and he wrapped an arm around her shoulders. Once again, she slipped into a light doze, and the carriage rocked back into motion.

Rosaline dreamt of running through wet grass, in tandem with a cat, a fish, a wolf, until she was breathless and reeling, and when she woke, her tongue was thick and her head was muzzy. The carriage had stopped once again, and a warm, orange glow was spilling through the windows, throwing streaks of light across Charlotte and Edward's faces.

Slowly, Rosaline realized that they were outside a tavern. Across from her, Charlotte and Edward shifted, making for the door.

"Five minutes," Edward whispered.

Rosaline felt Hal nod, and Charlotte flashed her a smile before she and her husband disembarked. There was a muffled shout, and the sound of feet hitting mud.

It was a few moments before Titus spoke. "How much do they know?"

Hal let out a breath. "Marcus told me that he did not give them much information, just that the child is my ward for the time being. You, supposedly, have quite a few enemies from your time in the military, and your child might be worth something to those enemies. Jamie stays with me as a matter of safety." Hal paused. "They do not know why you should have enemies, of course, but they did not question it, bless them."

Titus seemed to mull this over. "Cadogan is his parents' child, and no mistake."

"He is," Hal agreed. "In a way, I suppose I am glad that Marcus told them. Edward will be very useful to have in London."

"From the earlier conversation," said Titus, "I gather that you and your wife know the man who took my son."

A tense silence fell, and the breath froze in Rosaline's lungs. Hal must have felt her stiffen — he squeezed her hand again, asking a silent question.

"Yes," Rosaline managed, her stomach rolling once again. "We do."

"Does the name McGrath mean anything to you, Titus?" said Hal.

Another pause. "A little," said Titus. "Was there a McGrath at Alban Hollow?"

As Hal quickly detailed the history of the McGrath family, Rosaline closed her eyes once again and willed her mind elsewhere. Since she could not read, she settled for conjugating the Greek verbs that Smith had assigned her the week before. It was almost enough to drown out the conversation happening to her left.

"The maid mentioned that this man was present at the season," Titus was saying. "Rosaline, is that how you—?"

She nodded, opening her eyes. "He did his best to court me, and when I rejected his advances, he tried to... well, let us say that Hal got there right in the nick of time, and thank God he knows how to throw a punch."

"I see." Titus' voice was stiff. "Perhaps you were too merciful, Hal."

Hal let out a bitter laugh. "Trust me, I regret it now."

Charlotte and Edward reappeared, and once they clambered back into the carriage, Edward took one look at them and said, "If we are all awake, perhaps you could tell us everything you know."

"And the maid," said Charlotte, glancing at Rosaline. "What did she have to do with it?"

Rosaline sighed, and settled in against Hal's side. They were in for a very long night.

⊙※⊙

THEY ARRIVED IN LONDON SHORTLY AFTER EIGHT O'CLOCK IN the morning, when the early hustle and bustle of the city was beginning to kick into high gear. Rosaline could not deny a feeling of absolute relief as she disembarked from the carriage, wincing at the aches in her hips, her back.

It was impossible for her to deny the wave of memories brought on by seeing the Cunningham town home for the first time since their wedding. Rosaline's mind flooded with images of that fateful day when she and Hal had put aside all pretense and confessed their true feelings. Meeting Jamie, learning the truth. Seeing her ring for the first time, feeling his hands on her legs, his mouth on her skin.

Rosaline shook her head, coming back to the present.

The carriage had brought them to the street behind the house, to avoid attracting attention. Hal led them through the alley to the kitchen entrance, and she followed him into the quiet, cold basement, hoping that this small deception would guarantee no one in London noticing the return of two of its most prominent couples.

The five of them moved as one into the silent house, where all of the furniture was covered in thick white sheets. For a moment, it felt as if Rosaline had wandered into a ghostly and unforgiving past. In spite of the familiarity, and the assurance of being back in home territory, Rosaline shivered, and turned to meet Charlotte's gaze as they stepped into the front hall.

"Lovely." Charlotte almost smiled, then made straight for the drawing room. "Let's see about getting a fire going."

Once all of their luggage had been brought inside, the driver left to board the carriage and find an inn. The five of them gathered in the drawing room, watched closely by the late Duke and Duchess as they removed the sheets from each piece of furniture and built a large, roaring fire. Rosaline could not help shivering again as the heat washed over her and spilled out into the room — it was difficult to ignore the memories of Jamie darting between the furniture, toy bow in hand, roaring with delight.

"What is our plan of attack?" said Edward, turning to Hal.

"First, I need to make contact with my associates," Hal replied. In spite of his near-sleepless night, he was alert, tensed, ready to act. "They were watching McGrath for me, and I need to find out what they know about his movements."

Titus' hands twitched as he looked at Hal. "Surely our first step should be to go to this man's house, this McNally—"

"Yes, but before we do, I want to be sure I have all the information I can get about McGrath. If we play our hand too early, he may take Jamie and hide him somewhere else."

Titus said nothing, merely looked at him for another moment before he turned away, his hands now clenched into fists. Rosaline could not imagine what he was feeling — her own impatience, worry, and fear must have been the smallest taste of his anguish.

"I shall accompany you," said Edward. "None of us should travel alone."

Hal nodded, going over to his trunk. "We'll take hackneys." He opened the lid and rifled through its contents. Out came two woolen caps, and he threw one of them to Edward. "You'll have to leave the sword."

Edward shrugged, putting on his cap. "It is no matter. I have a knife in my boot."

Rosaline gaped at him, but Hal did not seem surprised. He turned to her and Charlotte. "We will be back within two hours. In the meantime, do whatever you can to settle in, but remain out of sight. No one can know that we are here."

Rosaline nodded. "We will be waiting."

Hal looked at her, and for a moment, they were the only two people in the room. He reached for her hand and squeezed it, his eyes telling her everything he could not say aloud. Rosaline looked back at him, her heart catching in her throat, then he and Edward left, their steps echoing through the hall as they made their way to the kitchen.

Charlotte turned to her with a shadow of her enigmatic smile. "Well, then. Let us get to work."

❦ 48 ❧

Just as Rosaline had never imagined that she would become a wife, she had never imagined that she would find herself in the unique position of performing a wide array of domestic tasks. And Charlotte, it seemed, was similarly stumped by the challenge at hand.

"I suppose the linens should come first," said Charlotte, frowning at the list on which she and Rosaline had spent the past ten minutes. They were both hunched over the desk in the drawing room, and Rosaline's neck was beginning to ache afresh. "Do you know how many bedrooms there are upstairs?"

"Three, I think." Rosaline then frowned as well. "No, four."

"Five," came a quiet intonation from behind them. "And three rooms in the attic for the servants."

They both turned to Titus, who was standing near the fireplace. With a jolt, Rosaline realized that he must have spent countless days and nights here in his youth.

"There is a linen cupboard at the top of the stairs," Titus went on. "Brooks always ensures it is fully stocked before the family leaves for the country."

"Oh," said Rosaline. "Oh, how fortunate."

But he was not finished. "You should get the fire going in the kitchen, and set several pots of water on to boil. And you will need to sort through the larder that Mr. Partridge so obligingly packed for us, to ensure that we eat the perishables first. The bedrooms will need to be aired out before the fires are lit, and you can save the linens until last." He turned to look out the shaded window. "We will need a hot meal before we need to rest."

Rosaline and Charlotte stared at him, then traded a glance. All too late, Rosaline remembered that they were dealing with a seasoned soldier, and a man more than accustomed to making a home wherever he happened to land. She stood up and held out the quill. "Tell us what to do. Please."

Within the next two hours, the house was in fighting shape and Rosaline had learned more than she'd ever expected to learn about making a home. Rooms were aired, fires were built, sheets were changed, coverings were removed, candles were trimmed, lanterns were filled, clothes were put away. And Titus' suspicions about the picnic basket were correct — Mr. Partridge had packed them far more than a simple assortment of sandwiches and fruit. They had bacon, eggs, butter, cold roast beef, fresh bread, an enormous hunk of cheese, two dozen apples, roasted walnuts, two tins of biscuits, and even a cake.

Once the food was put away, Titus and Rosaline emerged from the larder to find Charlotte standing over the stove, staring down into a frying pan.

"How does one know when the butter is hot enough?"

"It foams, I think." Rosaline joined her. "Charlotte! There must be half a pound in here—"

"Why, how much is one meant to use?"

"Not that much!" Rosaline grabbed a spare dish and a spoon. She hurriedly scooped the softened butter out of the pan, splashing some of it across the hob — it sizzled and smoked. "I thought you were going to make bacon!"

Charlotte looked at her, sheepish. "Do you not need butter to fry bacon?"

Rosaline almost smiled, in spite of everything. "No, Charlotte—"

Titus reached for a clean pan and gently nudged the two of them away from the stove. "Pass the bacon, please, Rosaline."

The eggs had just come out of the pan when they heard the lock turn in the kitchen door. Rosaline leapt to her feet as Hal and Edward entered the room, sodden but with bright, keen expressions. They looked so different, in their rough overcoats and flat caps, and they certainly did not look like who they really were.

"Ah, brilliant!" Hal shed his hat and coat and Edward did the same. "We're starving."

"And we come with news," said Edward, accepting a kiss from Charlotte. "My goodness, what a marvelous meal!"

"We take none of the credit," Rosaline said. She hung their coats and hats on the set of pegs just behind the larder. "It was all Titus. We would be quite lost without him."

"Your charming wife exaggerates," Titus replied, sliding a fresh pot of tea onto the table. "Now, tell us everything."

As they ate, Hal told them about his and Edward's excursion. They'd not gone as far as Rosaline imagined — only to an alley behind St. Paul's — and they'd quickly made contact with one of Hal's informants.

"Apparently, McGrath got to London not long before we did," Hal was saying as he cut into his second fried egg. "He must have ridden like a lunatic."

"What of Jamie?" said Titus.

Hal nodded. "He had Jamie with him. There are rumors flying around about an important child coming into the city. Yes," he added, at Titus' startled look, "it seems that McGrath's actions are no secret."

"Is that not odd, even amongst criminals?" said Charlotte. "To announce yourself and your quarry? I would think he'd prefer to avoid detection."

"Not if he wants certain people to hear the news," Edward replied. "People who might be able to give him a better price than the one he's already been offered."

Rosaline fought off a shudder, and Hal squeezed her hand.

"But this man, McGrath," said Titus. "Is there any word of his location?"

Hal and Edward traded a look before Hal spoke. "Our suspicions appear to be correct. All of the whispers indicate that McGrath is staying at the McNally town residence. But..." And here, Hal shot Titus a look. "It seems that he is alone."

Titus muttered an oath and stood up from the table. He began to pace, his expression drawn with frustration.

"Whatever do you mean?" Rosaline managed, her food curdling in her stomach.

"Jamie is not with McGrath," said Edward. "As far as we know."

"But you could be wrong," said Charlotte. "Your informants—"

"They have never been wrong before," Hal replied. "And besides, I agree with them. McGrath is an idiot, but not such an idiot to leave himself that vulnerable. By keeping Jamie in a separate location, he minimizes the chances of someone hurting him to get to Jamie."

"So where is he?" said Rosaline. "Did your informants—?"

"No," Hal replied grimly. "But they are now making their inquiries. We should have something by tomorrow morning."

"But Jamie could be gone by then!" Titus burst out. Privately, Rosaline agreed.

"I know," Hal said. "And I wish I had better tidings on that score. But," he added, "I may have found something else that will help." He checked the clock on the wall. "It should be here in a few hours."

Titus shot him a glare. "What else could possibly help?"

"Information," said Hal. "We know some things about McGrath, but not everything. He is greedy and self-interested, but not fond of hard work. Why would he go to all this trouble to get you back into the country, *and* to kidnap your child? We have been assuming it to be merely an act of revenge, but I believe there is something more at work."

Titus paused mid-stride, realization drifting over his features. "You think McGrath is not acting alone?"

"I think he is doing someone else's bidding," Hal replied. "A person who is motivated by something other than a long-standing grudge and a bruised pride."

"But who?" said Titus. "And what would a complete stranger want to do with my son?"

"We have a hunch," Edward replied. "But we need to gather more answers before we can pursue this line of inquiry."

"And who do you think it is?" said Rosaline. "This invisible puppeteer?"

"Major McNally," said Hal, meeting her gaze.

Rosaline frowned. "What would he stand to gain from any of it?"

"It is impossible for us to know," said Hal. "Without asking a few questions."

"But consider it," said Edward. "Any association between him and a character like McGrath cannot be the result of an innocent introduction. I would not be surprised if one was blackmailing the other."

"At the very least," Hal added with a nod.

Titus shot Hal a look of exasperation. "But that may have nothing to do with Jamie."

"Or it might have everything to do with Jamie." Hal's gaze was bright, unrelenting in its conviction. "We cannot know until we pursue every lead we have at our mercy."

"Nor can you make a casual inquiry into the personal habits of one of His Majesty's finest Majors," Titus fired back. "Not without drawing undue attention to yourself, which I thought you were determined to avoid."

"I agree with you," said Hal, and Titus' expression flickered with surprise. "And I believe I have found a way around the issue."

"What is it?" said Rosaline, too curious to restrain herself.

"The help of a friend," he replied, a glimmer in his eyes. "With a familiar face."

❦

IT WAS NEARLY FOUR O'CLOCK, THE STREETS SLICK WITH RAIN and grit, when there came a quiet, careful knock at the kitchen door. Rosaline surfaced from the deep throes of her thoughts and watched as Hal stood up from the kitchen table, making for the door.

The afternoon had dragged like wheels through mud, and the five of them had sat, brooding and mostly silent, in the warm, cozy kitchen. It was better than sitting in the drawing room, Titus said, just in case anyone saw the light from the street. But light in the servants' hall could mean any number of things, and would not turn as many heads. Rosaline had to admit that it made sense, even as she began to loathe the hard stone walls and the way they trapped her, comforting and maddening all at once. She ached to put on a pair of boots, throw open the front door, and pound the streets of the unforgiving city until she found Jamie and took him home.

Like her, Hal had been silent, lost in his own thoughts. There was little they could do while they waited, and as the dim gray light deepened into early evening, Rosaline felt as if a shroud were descending over the household. It made her shiver and wish that she had something, anything, to distract her.

Edward, it seemed, was just as restless as she. He retrieved his sword and worked his way through drill after drill at the other end of the kitchen, facing off an invisible enemy in front of one of the workstations. Charlotte watched him, her gaze distant but lively, and more than once, Rosaline wondered how she did it, how she took a near-sleepless night under her wing and still managed to look like a painting.

Titus had ignored all of them, brooding into the fire whenever he stopped pacing or checking the locks and windows. Rosaline could see, now, where Jamie got some of his energy. And again, she caught shades of the revolutionary, the soldier who was accustomed to being on his feet, on the move, never able to rest. She ached with sympathy, with pity, with worry, and it hung like a ball of lead in her stomach.

When they heard the knock, Rosaline and Charlotte sat up straight and Edward paused in the middle of some complicated footwork. They all stared at the door, as if unable to believe that it was real, frozen in a tableau of fear and worry. But then Hal moved, breaking the spell.

He paused with his hand on the doorknob, put his knuckle to the wood and rapped a quick, uneven rhythm. A moment later, there came a reply in the form of three quick taps and, apparently satisfied, Hal turned the locks and opened the door.

Captain Morris stepped over the threshold, huddled into a long black coat and a cap that had seen better days. He was dressed in civilian clothing, and even took on a hunched posture that showed none of his years of military training. He nodded at all of them, his gaze lingering on Titus, and took off his hat.

Rosaline stared at him in bemusement. "Captain?"

"Lovely to see you again, Miss Bailey— though I suppose it is 'Duchess' now." He stepped towards her, took her hand. "I wish we met under better circumstances." He turned to Edward and closed the distance between them — they clasped forearms, and Edward smiled. "Ed, you look terrible."

"So do you." Edward clapped him on the back. "Perhaps it is high time that you returned to the country."

"I should be so lucky," the Captain replied. He turned to Charlotte. "I've not had the pleasure."

After Edward had made the introductions, Charlotte gasped and said, "Oh, of course! You are Captain Morris from the Dowager Countess' dinner party!"

Captain Morris cut Rosaline an amused look. "I see my reputation precedes me."

"I hate to break apart this charming reunion," said Titus, brittle, "but who is this man?"

"Oh, of course." Hal stepped forward. "Titus, this is Captain Ronald Morris. He grew up in Alban Hollow and he's known McGrath, one way or another, for years."

"McGrath?" said the Captain with a frown. "That is why you asked me here?"

"You did not know?" Rosaline asked him.

"No," Hal replied on behalf of his friend. "My note had to be very vague."

"Cryptic, more like." Captain Morris hung up his cloak and said, "I suppose there must be a reason why four of England's noblest are crowded into a London cellar, and it cannot be a good one."

"No," Rosaline agreed. "Perhaps you should sit down."

Their last pot of tea was still warm, and Rosaline put together a fresh plate of biscuits. She and the others had not touched anything since their late breakfast, but unlike them, Captain Morris' appetite was not deadened by fear and worry. He ate three biscuits in quick succession, followed by a cup of tea — black, since they did not have any milk — then looked to Hal and Edward and said, "Tell me everything, and quickly."

Hal and Edward did just that, and Captain Morris listened, his bright eyes darting from one friend to another as they spoke. He said little, letting them reach the end of the sorry tale before he asked them any questions.

"Blimey." He raised his brow at Hal. "You know how to keep a secret, and no mistake. I'll bear that in mind."

Hal said nothing, but Edward shook his head and said, "*Ron.*"

"Right, sorry." Captain Morris held up a biscuit-dusted hand in apology. "And you, Mr. Wolfe. You are the boy's father?"

"Yes." Titus' voice was dry and cracked.

Something in the air shifted, and Rosaline knew what it was — Hal and Edward, who had mentioned very little about Titus, were bracing themselves. She could understand why they would want to offer as few details as possible about Titus' history, but, she thought, surely they could not expect to avoid it altogether—

"Do you have any enemies?"

A very pointed silence fell, and Rosaline could feel her heart in her throat as she, along with the others, turned to look at Titus. Something like a smile threatened in the corner of his mouth before he said, "Yes, plenty."

"Then perhaps McGrath is working with one of them. He can be resourceful, when backed into a corner." Captain Morris looked at Hal. "And you have heard nothing since your return to the city?" When Hal frowned, he added, "No threatening letters, no note of ransom?"

"No," Hal said at once, and Rosaline reeled at the thought of receiving such a letter. "Nothing like that."

Captain Morris nodded, considering. "Then perhaps it is not just a question of money."

"That is what we thought," said Rosaline. "But it seems that the Major keeps McGrath quite comfortable. He had that surgery in Edinburgh, and Dr. Knox charges a premium."

"Yes," said Hal to the Captain. "What do you know of McGrath's relationship with this Major McNally? It seems very odd."

"I do not know much," Captain Morris replied with a frown. "Though it is an open secret that the Major paid for McGrath's commission."

"Is that not strange?" said Edward. "And uncommon?"

Captain Morris shrugged. "It depends. If the Major were an old family friend, or a relative, then no, but we all know that not to be the case."

"That is precisely what gives us cause to think that Major McNally must be involved in some way," said Hal. His gaze was fixed on the Captain's. "Is there anything you can tell us about McNally's personal habits? His debts?"

"Anything that would give us some clue as to what a man of his status would want with a stranger's child?" added Edward.

Captain Morris's frown deepened. "Nothing of any substance."

Rosaline swallowed hard, emotion welling in her throat. She could not bear this — another idea, another lead, drying up before their very eyes—

"However," Captain Morris added, "I may know someone who does."

Both Hal and Edward perked up, like hounds scenting a rabbit. She could practically hear Titus holding his breath.

"He is not terribly... personable." Captain Morris winced and reached for another biscuit, as if on reflex. "I cannot guarantee his compliance."

"That does not matter," said Hal. "When can we speak with him?"

"Er... well." Another biscuit. "Perhaps you should let me—"

"Ron." Edward, now. "We do not have time to accommodate your friend's proclivities. Let us speak with him—"

"My *acquaintance* is like a fickle woman." Captain Morris shook his head, missing Rosaline's glare. "He must be wooed."

Hal leaned back in his chair, understanding flashing in his gaze. "How much?"

Captain Morris darted him a glance. "At least twenty."

Charlotte and Edward shared a look of alarm, but Hal nodded. "When can we speak to him?"

"I... well." Captain Morris surrendered with a sigh. "You will have to meet me down the dodgy end of Clamhurst Lane, next to the tobacco stand. I will take you to him. If he speaks to you at all, he will not do so without my introduction."

"Delightful," Hal replied, heading for the small desk in the corner. He retrieved a spare sheet of paper and a pencil. "When you say the dodgy end of Clamhurst, I assume you mean—?"

"Yes." Captain Morris nodded, scribbling an address on the paper. "Is it any surprise?"

"I am coming with you," said Titus, his jaw set, his expression firm.

"As am I," Rosaline said at once.

"No," said Hal, meeting her gaze. "Trust me, you do not want—"

"I am *coming with you,*" Rosaline repeated, gritting her teeth. "It is not a question."

Captain Morris, whose face had been getting red, put up a hand. "Actually, it might be a question. This place... it is nowhere that a respectable woman should be seen, Duchess."

Rosaline sniffed. "Then it is just as well that I will not appear as a woman."

"Oh, God," Hal muttered, while Edward stared at her. It was a parody of the moment at the boxing match. "Rosaline, it will be dangerous—"

"That hardly matters!" she fired back. "This is about Jamie, Hal. After everything, you cannot expect me to sit back and wait."

"Nor I," said Titus, stepping forward. "And I warn you, I have yet to encounter a lock I could not pick. Restraining me would take time, and energy."

Hal looked at him for a moment, incredulous, then returned to the task at hand. "Rosaline, I cannot guarantee your safety—"

"That is a risk I am all too happy to take," Rosaline replied, heat rushing to her face. "If it means getting us one step closer to Jamie."

"But your being there might not change anything," Hal said. "It might just—"

"Or, it might make all the difference. You forget how useful I can be, Your Grace, when faced with a recalcitrant foe."

A pointed silence fell. Captain Morris had gone completely pink and was staring at the ceiling. Edward broke it by clearing his throat.

"I shall remain here, with Charlotte. You will all need a strong cup of tea by the time you return."

❧ 49 ❧

Several hours later, Rosaline slipped out of an alley and onto a cobblestone street, one step behind Hal as he wove between the fog and the smoke. Dust hung in the air, gritty and foul, mired in the leftover funk of raw sewage and decades of spilt liquor, and it clung to the back of her throat. She fought the urge to gag, drawing her kerchief further up over her nose, and dodged a puddle with a dead rat clinging to its shoreline.

Night had descended upon the city in one grim, sweeping measure, leaving the streets cold and dismal as the hour chimed closer and closer to midnight. Every breath hung in the air, every exhalation brought a fresh wave of shivers, and every scent, especially the sewage, was magnified by the spectacular brutality of the coal-black sky hovering above them, trapped behind clouds of greenish, lingering smog. Rosaline felt as if she were an ant, skittering through the corridors and valleys of an unseen empire — the endless afternoon, the hours of waiting and pacing and worrying, had fallen away, replaced only by the sheer exhilaration of facing London in the dark.

"Ready?"

Hal's speech was a mere breath. Rosaline nodded in reply.

The tobacco stall appeared before them, a looming hulk out of the gray shadows. Beside it, a hunched figure looked up at their approach.

"Well?" Hal said, casting a quick glance around them.

"He'll see you," Captain Morris replied. He stepped aside as a drunk woman dressed in red stumbled down the road, a bearded sailor in tow. They were braying like donkeys. "But he's in his cups already."

"Brilliant," Hal muttered.

Captain Morris led them down another alley, around a sharp corner, and back to Clamhurst Lane.

Here, a pub seemed to erupt from the earth itself — its walls were so stooped, so caked in muck, that Rosaline wondered that it had not yet succumbed to the river. It seethed with patrons, more braying women and leering men, all of them cherry-red with drink. Some type of music spilled from deep within its bowels, along with screams, shouts, cackles of delight and dismay. She fought a shiver, and was reassured by Titus' presence behind her — close enough to protect her, but not so close as to crowd her or appear solicitous.

Not that anyone would recognize Rosaline for what she was. Trousers, an old shirt and coat, a cap over her braided hair, and ashes smeared across her cheeks had done enough to transform her into a common street urchin. Here, she could be invisible at best and a nuisance at worst. As they pushed their way into the pub, Rosaline could only hope for the former.

Inside, the pub was like a stomach — dark, gloomy, thick with the fug of body heat and sour sweat, undercut by the bitter tang of the house ale and whatever else had been pounded into the dirt floor. Rosaline dodged a barmaid wielding a handful of flagons, and narrowly avoided a swinging fist. She kept to Hal's heels as they ventured further into the gloom, the air catching in her chest.

They slowed near an empty back corner, where a pile of rags twitched and shuddered atop a rickety table. As she watched, Captain Morris cleared his throat, seemed to say a silent prayer, then extended a hand and tapped the pile of rags.

"Nick?" With no reply, Captain Morris cleared his throat. "Nick?"

The pile of rags twitched and shuddered. Then it shifted to show one bleary, bloodshot, sunken eye. "Morris."

Rosaline could practically feel the whiskey in the word, but the Captain, blessedly, did not react. "Nick, I've brought some people to talk to you. Remember?"

Nick said nothing, but his doleful eye spoke volumes.

"Ah, right." Captain Morris turned to Hal, pained, and took something from his hand. "Will this do?"

It was a ream of banknotes, neatly folded. After a few moments, the pile of rags twitched, and an aged, smudged hand appeared. It took the banknotes and returned them to unseen depths. "Well," came the dry, reedy voice. "Let us proceed."

The rags shifted again, and Nick sat up. His tufted head wobbled on its neck, perched precariously atop a filthy, wrinkled ruff, such as that of an actor. Rosaline could see now that the rags were actually the long-misused dregs of an officer's uniform, and that an empty sheath for a sword hung on his threadbare belt. Hal sat down beside him, but Titus remained standing, and after a moment, so did Rosaline.

"Tell me." Hal's voice was barely audible over the roar of the pub.

Nick offered him something close to a smile, his face creased with age and dirt. His eyes were dark and gloomy. "Are we to dispose of the pleasantries quite so early?"

"Yes." Hal's voice was hard, and Captain Morris winced. "I met your terms, and now you must meet mine."

Nick sighed, reaching for his half-empty glass of whiskey.

"How dreadfully dull. What is it you want to know? What makes that mongrel McGrath tick?"

"Not quite." Hal watched Nick carefully. "But what is his connection to Major McNally?"

"Ah, that." Nick tapped his nose. "A tale not so easily told. But I shall do my best." He cast a look over one shoulder, then another, then said, "Major McNally... is not terribly skilled at covering his tracks."

This odd pronouncement hung in the air for several moments before Hal poked at it. "What do you mean?"

"Let us just say that he does not adhere to the more refined inclinations of the male sex." Nick poured himself a fresh measure of whiskey, and though his hand shook, he spilled none of the liquor. "And he gets sloppy. He allowed himself to be caught. And by none other than that charming young idiot, McGrath."

Rosaline stared at the man, hardly able to believe what she was hearing. She was aware of Titus tensing like a hound behind her, determined to catch every last word.

"It was luck more than anything, which McGrath seems to have in spades." A glug of whiskey down Nick's throat, and a gasp like a man fighting for air. "A trick of the timing, I think he called it. Five minutes later, and McGrath never would have found the boy, never would have caught so much as a scent." He shrugged. "*C'est la vie.* And McGrath may be an idiot, but he knows value when he sees it. And he saw it then, when he learned what Major McNally was doing to the local boys — he saw the potential. For himself, of course." The rest of the whiskey disappeared.

Tension swelled, thick and lethal, in the air. Rosaline took a careful step back, bringing herself a scarce few inches from Titus' body.

"The price of his silence, of course, was the commission. Something that would elevate him beyond the rank of a dismal private destined to shine boots for the rest of eternity." Nick smiled down into his glass. "He is clever, that one. As a rat. But even he could not reach the perfect agreement. There is always a price to pay. And McNally's, apart from silence, was the affability of his wife. Oh, yes," he added, with seeming relish. "He needed something to distract her. Or rather, *someone.*"

Once again, Rosaline remembered that horrible, echoing call — *Lieeuuu-tenant!* It did make sense, even in its own twisted way. With his wife otherwise occupied, McNally would have greater freedom, and the assurance of a fellow officer's word to explain his absences.

"Is McNally in the habit of taking children?" said Hal, his voice low.

Nick shrugged. "How should I know? But what I can tell you, beyond any doubt, is that he is not the only one of his kind."

"Are you certain?"

"Of course," Nick barked, impatience rattling him thin. Rosaline jumped, her heart pounding, and watched his head wobble like a top above his ruff. "Cut one away and three more grow in its place, or something... something..." All at once, the fight seemed to leak out of him. He reached for the bottle and filled his glass.

"Where do they..." Hal paused, as if fighting with the words. "Does it all happen here, in London?"

Nick snorted, the whiskey splashing onto his fingers. "You must be thick, boy, if you think creatures of this sort would ever limit themselves."

"And how do you know about this?" Hal's look was powerful, unrelenting. "How can I know that what you are saying might be true?"

"Ah." Nick tapped his nose again, smirking like a schoolboy. "You will simply have to trust in old Lucky-Neck Nick."

"Lucky-Neck?" said Rosaline, before she could stop herself. "What do you mean?"

A dead silence fell, save for the rumble and the roar of the pub around them. Rosaline could only meet Nick's gaze head-on as it found its way to hers, creeping like a beetle. He looked at her for a moment, then smiled.

"Like this.'

A hand came up and tugged the ruff away from his neck. From beneath it sprouted a thick, roped cord of ugly red tissue, warped and curdled into itself. Rosaline stared at it, unable to breathe, unable to think, because this man had had his neck sliced open and had *lived*.

"Nice, isn't it?" Nick grinned, took another drink, and the neck disappeared back behind the ruff. "I, too, have your friend to thank for that."

Hal was frowning. "What do you mean?"

"McGrath and McNally realized I had caught on to their little game. They attempted to buy me off, but in those days, I had better morals and less of a disposition towards whiskey." He snorted. "I should have surrendered. It would have cost less. One night, our camp was beset upon by thieves, rogues. Hired by McGrath, no doubt. We did all we could to fight them off, but they tore through our stores. McGrath and McNally told everyone who would listen that I was to blame for the incident — I had betrayed the garrison, had let enemies in under the cover of night to the end of making a quick profit. My protests fell on deaf ears. I was dishonorably discharged, and McGrath was ordered to remove me from camp, accompanied by a host of our finest soldiers. A scuffle broke out, and..." Nick gestured to his neck, and Rosaline fought the urge to grab her own and assure herself of its presence. "How I lived, I do not know. I would not call it a blessing, in any case."

"Then you truly have no cause to lie," said Hal. "You hate him as much as we do."

"Perhaps." Nick gave a shrug. "Have you gotten your money's worth yet?"

"Almost," Hal replied, unaffected by his crudeness. "Tell me where I can find them."

"Now that, I could not tell you." Nick finished his glass, the whiskey surging at the corners of his mouth. "But it would not be at the Major's house here in town. He has learned from his mistakes — never to indulge when in familiar territory."

"Is there anything?" A glimmer of impatience, now. "Anywhere you might think of—"

"God in Heaven, what do you take me for?" Nick scowled, his head swaying on its delicate perch. It was several moments before he relented. "There is a place... not far from here. Near the river. A boarding house, of sorts. I have heard whispers that that is where one may go if one desires an unconventional indulgence."

Rosaline could practically feel the anger pouring off of Titus. But none of it showed on his blank, attentive face.

"Where is it?" said Hal.

Nick rattled off a list of directions, though they adhered to no logic that Rosaline could discern. When he'd finished speaking he lurched to his feet, bottle in hand.

"Best of luck to you all," he mumbled, his body wobbling in tandem with his head. He swung his near-empty bottle wide. "Should you require further assistance, do not hesitate to call on your dear friend, Lucky-Neck—"

It happened so quickly that Rosaline almost missed it. Nick lost his balance and fell to the ground, his bottle smacking another man on the side of his head. The man let out a roar and grabbed Nick by what remained of his shirt — Hal and Captain Morris were at Nick's side in an instant, tugging him away, but then the man swung a fist, clipping Captain Morris on the jaw, and from there, the room exploded.

Rosaline found herself pulled backwards and away from the fray, crowded into a far corner behind Titus. She could barely see over his shoulders, but the noise was incredible — she caught a glimpse of Captain Morris bellowing like a bull and tackling another man to the ground, then of Hal — *Hal* — trading blows with not one but two sweaty, red-faced men. He was yelling, and there was blood on his shirt, and—

"Rosaline!" Titus stumbled when she smacked against him, then pushed her back into the corner. "You cannot—"

"Then help him, Titus!" She was trembling, her stomach flooding hot and cold. "For God's sake, help them!"

Infuriatingly, he hesitated. "But you—"

"I swear to you, I will not move from this spot if you would just *help them*—"

Titus muttered an oath, then turned to look at her. "One move—"

"Go!" she shouted, and now, finally, he obeyed.

But they were still outnumbered — it was Titus, Hal, Nick, and Captain Morris against a dozen men, and those men had the confidence imparted by hours or even years of consuming hard liquor. The men were brutal, inelegant fighters, but what they lacked in ability they made up for in sheer determination—

"Behind you!" Rosaline shrieked — or, rather, yelled, in an attempt to disguise her voice. "Hal, behind you!"

He whirled around just in time to duck a punch and hit another man in the stomach. Beside him, Titus grappled with two men, kicking and elbowing, and Nick seemed to be gnawing on somebody's leg. Captain Morris had another man in a headlock and was dodging blows to his pate, and around them, the pub was screaming and jeering, mouths were frothing with bets and cheers, mugs and beer were flying through the air—

Then, Rosaline watched, horrified, as someone got an arm around Hal's neck. He choked and flailed, taken by surprise, and then everything hazed over. Rosaline forgot who she was, where she was. Between one moment and the next, she found herself charging across the floor, jumping onto the hooligan's back, clinging onto his shoulders, and dragging him away from her husband.

He let out a roar, stumbling backwards, and Rosaline held on for dear life, the room swaying ominously around her — but it worked. He let go of Hal, who stumbled free and, once he saw what was happening, grabbed Captain Morris. Together, they hurled themselves forward, and managed to remove her. Rosaline fell to the ground, but immediately leapt to her feet and aimed a kick at another man's leg.

"Wolfe!" Hal roared, smacking someone upside the head. "Get her out of here!"

Ten minutes later, Rosaline looked up as two disheveled figures appeared in the dim, damp light of the alley. She hurried forward, her face numb with worry. "Are you hurt?"

But her question answered itself — Hal had one arm wrapped around Captain Morris's shoulders, and the cuts stood out in stark relief on his unnervingly pale face. He gave her a feeble grimace, and she reached for him, her heart rocketing into her mouth.

Rosaline turned to Captain Morris. "What happened?"

The Captain's swollen face twitched as he winced. "He took a hard fall, Duchess. It is his shoulder, I think—"

Her hands raked over the arm hanging limp at Hal's side, confirming what her mind had already told her — dislocated.

Rosaline squeezed her eyes shut and swallowed hard. "We need a doctor."

"No," said Hal. "No one can know I am in London—"

"This is not up for debate, Hal, your arm needs to be returned to its *socket*—"

"What about your father?" said Captain Morris. His eye seemed to be swelling shut even as he looked at her. "Couldn't he help?"

Rosaline shook her head, remembering her last letter from him. "He is not in London. He is at Windsor."

"Damn. A colleague, perhaps?"

"No doctors," said Hal again.

"Then what, pray tell, is your solution?" she demanded, ignoring the tremor in her voice.

It was several moments before Hal looked up. His gaze was steady, determined, showing none of the pain that had to be pouring through his body. "You are."

The breath disappeared from her lungs. Rosaline stared at her husband, unable to process the words he'd just spoken. Behind her, she heard Titus shift where he stood — though whether out of nerves or agreement, she could not tell.

"You have lost your mind."

"I have not." Hal grimaced and leaned more of his weight against the Captain. "You can recite the bones of the body, Rosaline. You know treatments and tinctures. You know how to stitch a wound, how to set a broken bone. You certainly know how to relocate a shoulder."

"Theory," she bit out, "is very different from practice, Hal—"

"I trust you," he said, easy as breathing. He shifted again, proffering his injured shoulder. "Come, we must get home."

Rosaline stared at it and gulped. This was unthinkable, unimaginable—

Then, Titus spoke: "I have faith in you, Rosaline."

"As do I," said the Captain. He gave her a nod. "Brace him against me."

Rosaline nodded, mute with fear, but when she raised her hands, they did not shake.

NONE OF THEM SPOKE AS ROSALINE, TITUS, AND HAL approached the darkened house, having parted ways with Captain Morris a few streets earlier. He had to return to his post, to report to his superiors, to find some explanation for his appearance. "I shall say I was beset by a group of hooligans," he'd told them with a lopsided grin, highlighting his split lip. "It will be a blemish to my pride, but there are worse things." He'd given them all a nod. "Send me a message when you find him, should you need any further help."

On their way back to the house, Hal had already found one of his informants and passed on the address from Nick. "Watch it," had been his gruff order. "Like a hawk."

Rosaline had made him a makeshift sling out of their kerchiefs tied end-to-end, but she'd have to replace it as soon as they were inside. As far as she could tell, she had not done any permanent damage to his arm, but it would be some time before they knew for certain.

Edward answered the door after hearing the secret knock, and gaped at the sight of Hal and Titus. "God in Heaven, what—?"

"Not with the door open," Hal muttered, pushing past him into the kitchen. Rosaline and Titus followed him, and now that she was back in the close, cozy warmth, Rosaline felt something within her come undone.

She sat down hard at the table and began to shiver. Charlotte was at her side in an instant, frowning but not saying a word, and put a hand to her shoulder.

Edward closed and locked the door, pausing to glance out into the back alley. "The Captain?"

"Gone home." Hal sat down across from Rosaline, casting her a worried glance. "I know we look a sight, but I promise it was well worth it."

"Your arm, Hal," said Charlotte, with an air of realization. Rosaline said nothing, but continued to shiver.

Edward looked at Hal, then at Titus, then at Rosaline, and reached for the kettle. He poured a fresh pot of tea and slid it into the middle of the table. "Tell us everything."

Later, when they were lying in bed, tucked beneath several blankets and surrounded by the velvety dark, Rosaline rubbed the tip of her nose against Hal's bare chest and whispered, "None of it felt real."

He hummed, and she could feel it in her throat. His uninjured arm squeezed her close, and his hand drifted over her hair. "You were marvelous."

She blushed. "Do not be ridiculous, I did nothing—"

"You saved a poor man's arm. And you fought like a cornered badger."

"I suppose you mean that as a compliment?"

"Of course." His mouth, grazing her forehead. "What was it you gave me to drink?"

"A tincture of willow bark and poppy." Rosaline frowned at him. "Why?"

"It..." Hal let out a sigh. "I believe it is working."

Rosaline traced a finger along the edge of his new sling. She'd made it out of an old bed sheet cut into strips, using the fabric to bind his arm snugly against his body and create a line of support beneath his shoulder blade. It was something she'd seen in one of her father's field notebooks, once, and a part of her could hardly believe that she remembered the construction in such great detail.

"You should tell your father." Hal's voice was hazy with sleep, and it was as if he'd heard her thoughts. "He would be proud."

She pressed a kiss to his uninjured shoulder. "That I performed unlicensed and unsupervised medical care? I think not."

"No, I think he would." His hand, tangling in her hair anew. "I am... I am sorry for putting you on the spot like that."

Her heart skipped a beat. "It's all right," she murmured, kissing him again.

"No, I..." He sighed again. "I should have just... gone to a doctor."

"Hal, even without the risk, it likely would have been at least two hours before we found a suitable surgeon. And not many would answer a midnight house call from two ruffians claiming to be members of the gentry. No, it..." Now she sighed as well. "It was for the best. I just..." Rosaline cleared her throat. "I do not enjoy hurting you."

"Who said it hurt?" he teased. "I do not think it hurt—"

She rolled her eyes, pressing her cheek to his chest. "*Hal.*"

They lapsed into silence, and for a minute, all was quiet, save for the occasional creak of the house settling, or a far-off cry in the street.

"I never asked," she murmured. "What happened to Nick?"

"Nick?" said Hal, as if surprised. "Oh, he... put up a fair fight, then I believe he... he went over a table, considered getting up, and went to sleep instead. And he will probably remain there until morning."

Rosaline blinked into the darkness. "Oh."

"An example to us all."

It was several minutes before Rosaline worked up the courage to say, "Hal, are we going to find him? I cannot shake the feeling that all this has been for nothing. If what Nick said is true, then Jamie..." She forced back the lump in her throat. "Jamie is destined for something terrible indeed."

"No," said Hal, and she caught the barest glimmer of ferocity. "He is not. We will find him. And soon."

Rosaline squeezed her eyes shut. "How can you be so certain?"

"I do not know," he replied. "But I am."

"Did you see..." Rosaline bit her lip, swallowed a sob. "Titus..."

Hal squeezed her shoulder. "It will pass, Rosaline. All of it will pass. If nothing else, believe that. Believe me."

And she forced herself to nod, burrowing into his side.

"Tomorrow." His voice was thick with sleep. "Tomorrow, we will have answers."

For a brief moment, as she drifted into an uneasy and dreamless sleep, Rosaline allowed herself to believe it.

᪐ 50 ᪐

One day passed, then another, with little news about McGrath or Jamie. Rosaline could not remember a longer two days in her entire life, not even the ones she had spent traveling from France to England. The waiting, the wondering, the yearning — it was unbearable, and it weighed on her like an iron chained to her ankle. But she was not alone in her misery, and the others' company gave her the smallest shred of comfort.

Edward passed the time by practicing more of his drills, reading, or coaxing Hal into card games. His unwavering kindness softened Hal's palpable frustration, which occasionally flared, but, for the most part, was restrained, like a caged animal, silent and tense. Hal's injured arm did not help the situation — Rosaline knew it was painful, and she continued to make tinctures of willow bark, but she likewise knew that Hal was more frustrated by how the injury limited him. The bruises and cuts to his face began to heal as well, but slowly. The purple and blue shades mottling his skin made her heart twist with something between anxiety and empathy, and when they were in bed, she would brush a fingertip over his cheeks, his chin, wondering how it felt, wondering if he would always carry a scar on his cheekbone.

Titus bore the worst of it. When he wasn't pacing the length of the house, he sat brooding, staring into the kitchen fire, his face flat with outrage, anger, worry. Though on occasion, his emotions manifested themselves most suddenly and powerfully—

"Let me out." Titus struggled against Edward. It was the morning of the third day after the fight at the pub, and tensions were running high. "Or I swear—"

"You know I cannot!" Hal gave him a hard shove away from the front door, but it did had little effect. "Titus, you cannot believe that it will do any good for you to—"

"To what?! To try and find my child, my son—?!" Titus had barely raised his voice, but it was as if he were yelling. He writhed, but Edward had his arms in a firm grip. It was an echo of that fateful evening just a few days prior, with Edward in Marcus' place. Behind him, Charlotte watched, hand at her mouth, aghast.

"If we act too quickly, and without due cause, they could move Jamie, and he would be lost to us forever!" Hal had his good arm raised, in defense as well as in supplication, and Rosaline ached as she looked at him, knowing how much it pained him to have to turn on a member of his own family— "Titus, I beg you to see sense!"

"What sense is there!" Titus' voice was mangled with despair. "What sense is there in us sitting here while they could be doing God-knows-what to my child—?!"

"We know they do not have him, not yet," Hal said. Rosaline watched his chest heave as he attempted to calm himself. "They have not removed him from the boarding house. We know McGrath has been meeting people all over the city." His words were familiar — they'd gone over this a half-dozen times already. "We have every reason to believe—"

"Yes," Titus spat, lurching against Edward. "Yes, I bloody well know what you would like us all to believe—"

"Titus!" Hal snapped. "We have to wait until they try to move him. You know that would give us our best chance of—"

"What chance!" Titus' face rippled with agony. "What chance!"

Rosaline stood up from the table and said, "Titus knows the plan as well as any of us, Hal. But he *feels* something rather different." She turned to Edward, and gave him a pointed look until he released Titus. "Titus, why don't you step outside with me?"

Hal bristled, and his eyes flashed in the dull glow of the kitchen fire. "Rosaline, I do not think—"

"Titus is more than aware of my ability to knock him to the ground," Rosaline replied, reaching for her shawl. "He saw me in fine fettle the other night, did he not?"

"Yes," said Hal, almost with reluctance. "I suppose—"

"We will be fine." Rosaline went over to the back door and unlocked it, then turned to Titus. "Well?"

Autumn had settled into the bones of the city with all the insistence of an ague. Rosaline shivered at the damp, hazy air, and crossed the minuscule courtyard behind the house. Titus hovered in the doorway, watching her, almost puzzled.

Several silent moments passed before she glanced at him over her shoulder and said, "By all means." She nodded at the gap in the wall, which would take him into the alley, then the street.

Titus stared at her.

"Go ahead, Titus," Rosaline went on, "if you truly believe that Hal's instincts are wrong, that he is not doing everything he can to protect your son and secure his well-being."

Titus' throat worked. After a moment, he looked away. "I would not... you know very well that is not what I meant."

Rosaline let out a sigh, grazing a finger through the moss lining the brick wall. It was different out here, with nothing between her and the air, her skin and the stone. "You are Jamie's father. If you think that seeking him out on your own would be for the best, then perhaps we should defer to you." When he remained silent, she added, "Titus, none of us have even the faintest idea of what we are doing. We are following instructions, and instincts. It is natural that we should disagree."

Titus moved then, crossing the cobblestones, making for the gap in the brick. But then, at the last second, he hesitated. It was several moments before he spoke, and when he did, it was as if a shade had passed across his face. "I do see the logic of it. Moving in one, as a group. And if we wait until Jamie himself is..." He shook his head, then shifted to lean against the brick. He looked even older in profile.

Rosaline nodded. "It is a gamble, in its own way."

They lapsed into silence, and Rosaline could not help wondering if Jamie would one day have Titus' lovely pointed nose, or if it would be his mother's. *The invisible woman*, she thought, which turned her thoughts to the conversation she'd overheard between Marcus and Titus. And perhaps it was because she and Titus said so little to one another over the past few days, or because she could not bear not knowing, but something curled up her throat and pushed the words out of her mouth — "I could not help but notice your strained relationship with Lord Blackwood."

She had to give him credit — he barely reacted, but she caught the flicker of panic, of grief, all the same. "Yes," he said. "We... did not part on good terms."

"I understand. From what Hal tells me, it was a tense situation indeed."

Titus gave a jerky nod, but said no more. For a moment, she truly thought he would step through the passage in the wall and be gone. But he did not.

Rosaline watched Titus but tried to appear as if she were not watching him. "I imagine you missed... England... terribly."

"Yes, I... I did." He gave an aborted shrug. "Ireland is not so very different. More wild, perhaps, in its land, but the climate..."

Why, she ached to ask him. *Why did you desert?* But a part of her felt as if she already knew the answer. Because, somehow,

Rosaline knew she would have done the same. "Lord Blackwood can be very proud," she said instead. "He is never keen to admit his faults."

A ghost of a smile. "Are any of us?"

Rosaline bit her lip. She had to tread carefully. "I promise you that as angry as he may have seemed... He was very glad to see you."

Titus let out an indignant bark of laughter, loud enough to make her jump. "Was he indeed? I must have missed that part of his blistering tirade."

Rosaline trembled, tucking a loose bit of hair behind her ear. "Apart from Hal, you are all he has left, Titus. I hope," she quickly added, "you might forgive me speaking so plainly. But I do think that if you were to leave Lord Blackwood again, he would be most... inconsolable."

She held her breath as Titus stilled, his gaze drifting somewhere into the distance.

"Believe me, Titus." Rosaline steeled herself. "You should not leave him again. You cannot." She swallowed. "However you may classify his reaction the other day, I promise you it was only the result of something bigger, something more painful. And you cannot compound that pain, Titus."

He turned to look at her, and she forced herself to hold his gaze. Naked surprise showed in his features — an understanding had passed between them; she was sure of it. A part of her almost expected him to roar at her in fury, or even threaten to strike her — this was uncharted territory for both of them, and she knew that Titus did not like being backed into a corner.

"But he—" Titus spoke in a whisper. "I broke—" His face twisted, and Rosaline wanted to reach for him. "We were... we were so lost, after Charles and Lily. We hurt each other, without meaning to. And then I..." He shook his head. "I should never have left. I am not sure I can be forgiven, Rosaline."

She did reach for him then, laying her hand on his arm. "Perhaps he should be the one to decide, Titus. And you will have to decide if you can forgive him, as well."

Before Titus could reply, there came the sound of running feet, and they both turned just as a filthy, red-cheeked youth came bursting into the courtyard, clutching a stitch in his side.

Rosaline, Titus, and the child all stared at one another, then Rosaline turned and bolted for the kitchen. She knew what this meant.

"Hal—" she managed, tearing open the door. "Hal, there is news—"

He was up from the table in an instant, meeting the child halfway. He knelt so that they were eye-to-eye, and gripped the child's arm. "Tell me," he said.

"McGrath has left the manor house," wheezed the child. "He takes a hackney, and a bag. We think he means to—"

"Yes, yes, of course." Hal scrubbed a hand through his hair, darting a look at all of them. This was real. This was happening. He returned his attention to the child. "What about the others, did you—?"

The child nodded. "Yes sir, all of them—"

"Good." Hal passed the child a biscuit and stood up. Even with his arm strapped to his side and his face blotchy with injury, he still looked like a young general called to action. "We must go at once. We cannot spare a single minute."

Rosaline's heart was pounding as she and Charlotte scrambled into their coats. She caught a glimpse of Titus doing the same, and of Edward strapping his rapier to his side. She helped Hal into his coat, buttoning a single button down the front to keep his arm tucked away. They all swarmed into the courtyard, and Edward locked the kitchen door as Hal turned to the child and said, "What do you think? Should we try to catch them via carriage, or on foot?"

The child screwed up his mouth in consideration — he looked like an accountant weighing his options. "There's a big accident down the end of Hyde Park, traffic's backed up for miles. He'll be slow in his hackney, so you might as well—"

"Thank you!" Hal squeezed the boy's shoulder, turned to the others, and said, "It's just over a mile. We'll catch him."

What then followed was a hectic, mad dash through the streets of London.

Hal led them down streets, across thoroughfares, and along alleys. He followed a path indiscernible to Rosaline's eye, and it was all she could do to keep up with him and the others. She was just grateful that she and Charlotte had had the foresight to wear boots instead of their usual shoes, which would have been useless against the clotted, half-frozen mud of the streets. The breath caught in Rosaline's chest, tore at her lungs, but she kept moving, kept dodging merchants and street vendors and servants doing the day's shopping. Mud splashed up over her feet, catching in her hem and, she was certain, staining her stockings, but none of it mattered. All that mattered was the air surging in and out of her chest, the city streaking past her. *Please*, she somehow had the capacity to think. *Please, let us find him, let us get to him in time*—

Their plan was a shaky one at best, but they'd had to account for any number of variables that would remain unknown until they arrived at the boardinghouse. Rosaline's crowded brain churned and flipped through all of their ideas, everything they'd discussed in the hours and minutes they'd spent sitting, pacing, standing in that stone kitchen. She felt ready, more than ready, to see Jamie, to find him, to bring him home, but the reality of being here, in the street, the ground under her shoes and the wind tearing through her hair, was something very different, something grim and promising all at once. She almost choked with it, with the burning need to *know*, to have the answer to the problem before she'd faced it, fought with it, put it to pen and paper and made it *talk*—

They all came to halt before a wide thoroughfare, a quarter of a mile away from their destination, and Hal shot her a blazing look over his shoulder. His gaze said everything Rosaline was feeling, it carried the weight, the surging fury and exhilaration, the feeling of *almost*— they were almost there, they were almost—

Finally, a gap in the traffic, and they all darted across the road. Rosaline could hear herself panting, she could hear Charlotte's gasp when she ran through a puddle, the cold filthy water splashing across her hem, she could even hear the muted *clink* of Edward's rapier at his side, and she clung to it, all of it, feeling and knowing that in a few moments, whatever happened would change everything, shift the entire course of her life, like a ship tilting along the line of a broken compass, billowing and capsizing on an infinite ocean—

Rosaline blinked back tears as they passed shops, pubs, residences, darting around carriages and horses and piles of mucky, stale rubbish. She could not lose herself, not now, not when they were so close, when they would know—

"Here!"

Hal's order came in a low, pervasive throttle, and the five of them immediately drew to a halt. Her ears ringing, her chest fuzzy with exertion, Rosaline stood, panting and numb, staring at the soot-stained building not twenty feet away. Here it was. The place they'd only heard about, never seen, carried to them on the whispers of children.

The boarding house was squat, dirty, but not so squalid that she could not imagine Jamie surviving there for a few days. It was not the best, yes, but it was not the worst—

"Rosaline!" Titus tugged her out of the street, up against the nearest building. Rosaline's mouth fell open as her back hit brick, but a moment later, she realized that she'd been standing out there alone, in plain view, staring up at the boarding house, and there was a carriage, a hackney, devoid of its passenger, lingering just a few feet from the front door—

Here, she and the others were out of sight, obscured by the lingering traffic and pedestrians. They could see the building, but they would not be readily visible to anyone exiting it. Rosaline understood the advantage it gave them, even if it left them further away from Jamie.

Charlotte's hand found hers and squeezed it. Beside her, Edward and Hal were likewise plastered against the brick, their chests heaving but silent as they too stared at the hackney.

"Any moment now," Hal breathed. "Any moment—"

Edward finally broke his focus to glance around, mutter an oath. "God in Heaven, where are they—?"

"They will be here," said Hal, and even as her stomach swooped with anxiety, Rosaline had to believe him, he sounded so certain. "They will be here."

"And if they are not?" said Titus, his voice hard. "What then?"

Hal let out a long, slow breath. His face was flushed and his hair was everywhere, but he carried all the assurance, all the determination, that Rosaline wished she could feel. "Then," he said, his voice still low, "we shall find a way to corner McGrath ourselves."

Rosaline gulped, sucking in the cold, dusty air. Her dress clung to her lower back, her thighs, her underarms, and she was on fire, burning like an ember, desperate—

"I cannot do it," muttered Titus, clenching and unclenching his hands, his eyes wild. "I cannot just stand here while—"

But they did not have long to wait. Within five minutes, they caught movement in the dim, tiny windows of the ground floor, then the front door opened and Rosaline's stomach dropped to her feet because there he was, McGrath — grinning, wearing a hat and civilian clothing, and in his arms, *in his arms*—

"He's asleep," she whispered to Titus, clinging to his arm, keeping him from launching himself away from the wall. "Titus, he's just asleep—"

Jamie looked somber in slumber, and even from their distance, she could see the shadows under his eyes, the fitful stir of his limbs. *Not asleep*, her rattled mind told her. *Not asleep but drugged*—

It made sense — how else would McGrath control a child? But it still made something within her boil and churn with outrage, with pure, fitful anger—

"Hal," Titus bit out as they watched McGrath approach the hackney and deposit Jamie in the seat. "Hal, how much longer—"

"Just one moment," Hal replied, his eyes fixed on the scene. "Just when he has Jamie out of reach—"

The five of them watched with bated breath as McGrath draped a blanket over Jamie and stepped away, apparently satisfied. Rosaline could see his smug look even from this distance, and she wanted nothing more in the world to break ranks, charge across the road, and smack him clean across the face—

Rosaline had wondered, before, if she would be frightened when she saw him again. If just the sight of him would be enough to throttle her back in time, back to those fateful moments in the hidden garden, his hands tearing at her, his whiskey-soaked breath catching in her mouth — she'd wondered if fear, cold and ruthless, would undo her, leave her shaking and unable to move.

But now, she no longer wondered. Now Rosaline knew that what she felt was anger, clear and pure, racing through her and surging in her belly.

And she was ready for whatever might come next.

"Now," said Hal, and, as agreed, he and Edward stepped away from the building and out into the road, making a direct line for McGrath.

Rosaline watched, holding her breath, as they got closer and closer. McGrath, oblivious as anything, did not notice that anything was amiss until they were within a few feet of him. He turned, saw Hal and Edward, and in the space of an instant, his body stiffened, his eyes flashed, and his hand went to his hip where, she guessed, he had some sort of weapon stowed out of sight.

An unspoken message seemed to travel the length of the street. Traffic congealed or redirected as everyone began to take notice of the three men standing at odds, staring each other down. It looked like a duel, Rosaline realized — a duel before the pistols.

Everything went quiet, or perhaps it was just her imagination. McGrath's attention was still entirely focused on Hal and Edward — he did not seem to notice where she, Charlotte, and Titus remained hunched in the shadows of the building opposite. Then, McGrath shifted closer to the hackney, getting between Jamie and Hal.

"Well, McGrath." Hal spoke first, and his tone was almost affable. "Seems you've expanded your field of expertise since last we met."

McGrath said nothing, but she saw the way he tensed, irritated.

"Come now," said Edward, easy and unconcerned. "Give us the boy, and no harm will come to you."

McGrath snickered then, raising an eyebrow at Hal. "It seems you've got yourself a new guard dog, Cunningham. What, too cowardly to fight your own battles?"

"No," Hal replied. "I simply tired of beating you. It is time someone else had a chance."

Something ugly flashed across McGrath's face, but he stifled it and continued to grin. "What's this pup going to do to me?" He shifted again, getting closer to the hackney. He did not notice the driver turning and frowning at the situation playing out before him. "You cannot have the boy, you know."

"I can understand the greed," said Hal, ignoring him. "I can understand why you might be tempted to kidnap my ward. I can understand your partnership with McNally, filthy though it is. I can even understand why you hesitated upon your return to the city, waiting until you found the most lucrative option to suit your desires." He took a step closer. "But what I cannot understand is how you learned of Jamie's existence in the first place. Was it

Elsie? Or did you approach her after you were made aware of the fact?"

McGrath's resolve seemed to flicker. "Elsie?" He looked to Hal, then Edward, clearly rattled by the revelation that his informant had broken her silence.

"Just tell us," said Edward. "Or we shall force it out of you."

McGrath snorted, recovering. "You talk a good game there, pup, but you don't seem to understand. You will not win."

"And what about this boy's father?" Hal went on. "Elsie told us of that plot as well. Why go to all the trouble of tricking him overseas, only to kill him?"

McGrath snorted again. "You truly are ignorant, Cunningham—"

"Then enlighten me," Hal replied, spreading his good arm wide. Rosaline did not miss the way McGrath's gaze darted to Hal's injury, which was obvious, even though it remained obscured by his coat. "Why not, if you are so convinced of your own success? What have you got to lose, Callum?"

McGrath smirked. "The regiment will not kill him, Cunningham. Do try not to be so vulgar. No," he continued, with a hint of swagger. "He's far more useful alive."

Rosaline nudged Titus, and he took the cue without any hesitation. He stepped into the street and approached the three men, determined and impertinent. "Am I?" he said, loud enough for McGrath to hear. "What a revelation."

McGrath stared at him, unable to mask the blank surprise flooding his features. "Impossible," he managed. "You were— you were meant to go to—"

"Brighton?" Titus supplied for him, coming to stand between Edward and Hal. "Yes, so I gathered. But I made a stop along the way."

"McGrath's men must not have gotten word to him that the plan fell through," Charlotte whispered. She was watching them as closely as Rosaline, and her grip was firm around Rosaline's hand. "I wonder why."

Rosaline sniffed. "Too frightened of the consequences, perhaps. Not telling him anything gave them the chance they needed to get away, find new employment."

"Give it up, boy." Titus' voice brooked no debate. "Return my son to me."

McGrath's throat worked, but that was the only sign he gave of his worry. "Not a chance," he said, and his right hand shifted to withdraw a dagger. The driver's eyes widened.

The others tensed, and Edward's hand went to his pommel. "Come now," he said, his voice level and affable. "No need for that."

"Oh, I think there is." McGrath took another step back, and it made no sense to Rosaline — he was allowing himself to be backed into a corner. "I have worked too hard and too long for this deal to fall through—"

"If Wolfe was meant to remain alive," said Hal, much to everyone's surprise, "why bother with Jamie? You would receive a hefty bounty on Wolfe alone, and it would have been far less trouble than traveling with a reluctant child."

McGrath growled. "Drop it, Cunningham—"

"Actually," said Titus, with the mild interest of an affable school teacher, "I would like an answer as well."

"I bet you would, you traitor—"

Hal clicked his tongue. "And to think we were getting along so well—"

"Shut up!" roared McGrath, and he leapt into the hackney, bracing himself on the roof. "Driver—!"

The poor man was trembling, but he hastened to comply, snapping the reins, and the cab lurched forward, Rosaline's heart lurching with it. Her face went numb as the men jolted into action, taking off after the cab, and after a split second of disbelief, Charlotte pulled her into the road. They both broke into a run, and Rosaline's heart throbbed in her ears, her chest, her hands— *Not now*, she somehow thought, *not yet, it's too soon*—

Traffic was light, and the hackney began to pick up speed, but they kept pace with it, people scattering around them as they realized what was happening. "Give it up!" McGrath roared, lurching as the hackney hit a dip. "You'll never outrun us!"

"No!" Hal shouted in return. "But you'll never make it past the blockade!"

Rosaline could actually see McGrath frown in confusion. "The what?" Then he turned around and found the road blocked by a company of the 44th Regiment of Foot, led by Captain Morris on horseback.

S everal things happened at once. First, the hackney driver
yanked on the reins in an attempt to halt the carriage
before it crashed into the soldiers. The horse let out a
scream of terror, and it reared up onto its hind legs. Captain
Morris quickly moved aside, but it was too late — the carriage
rolled belly-up, throwing the driver and McGrath down into the
mud. The hackney horse returned to earth, then reared again, and
the strained traces finally gave way, snapping loudly enough that
Rosaline thought someone had broken a bone. They all watched,
astonished, as the carriage tottered, its shaft pointing right up
into the air, then slowly fell to one side with a loud, unmistakable
crunch.

For a moment, the five of them stood there, speechless, then
one of the soldiers leapt forward and grabbed the reins of the
horse, getting it under control. Hal and Titus ran for the carriage,
Rosaline hot on their heels, her head pounding, her eyes swimming with tears, because this couldn't be happening— *all this, just
to have Jamie killed in a carriage accident*—

Rosaline swallowed a sob and fell to her knees beside the front
of the coach, grabbing Hal's shoulder. Titus was already tugging at

the fastenings on the wooden flap, and they gave way within seconds. He dove into the cab and resurfaced a moment later with Jamie in his arms. Jamie — whole, uninjured.

Rosaline was so relieved to see him that, for a moment, it took all of her willpower not to faint. Her head swam as she looked at him, as she clutched at Hal and heard his sudden, relieved sigh, and then she realized that Jamie wasn't moving.

"Titus." Rosaline's voice was deadly with fear. Her nails dug into Hal's coat. "Titus—"

"He is breathing," said Titus, but he sounded more puzzled than anxious. He gave Jamie a bit of a shake. "Jamie? Jamie?"

"He is likely drugged," said Rosaline, wiping away the tears that had begun to slide freely down her cheeks. "But we have to check that there is nothing else—"

"I— I—" Titus was staring down at his child, at a loss. "I have no idea—"

"Rosaline." Hal nudged her forward. "You know what to look for."

Rosaline trembled but obeyed. She clambered into the basin of the coach, catching her dress on the latch doors, and began to examine Jamie.

He bore no injuries that she could readily see, and she pressed her fingers against his shins, his knees, his elbows. Rosaline could feel nothing that gave her any indication of internal injury — no fractures, no swelling — and as she nudged her thumbs against his small, thin ribs, she bit back another sob. *What if he never wakes up?* her treacherous brain whispered to her. "He seems fine," she forced herself to say. Rosaline moved on to his skull, and she found the smallest bump above his temple, where he had likely knocked his head when the carriage tipped over.

The feeling of the bump under her fingers grounded her in some way, and she looked up at Titus, who was still holding his son. "He hit his head," she managed, fresh tears leaking down her face. "But it seems mild, he's done worse to himself running around the woods." Then, she took Jamie's hand and gently pinched the skin near his wrist.

Titus shot her a frown. Rosaline met his gaze again, wiped her nose, and said, "He is a little dehydrated, perhaps, but he is not feverish. It might take a while before he wakes, depending on what he was dosed with."

Titus looked at her for a moment, then turned to glare at, she presumed, McGrath. She could see it, the rage pooling under his skin, and she did not think she could stop him if—

"Hal!" Captain Morris came running up, his face twisted with worry. He still had the cut on his lip, a bruise around his eye. "Is the child safe?"

"Yes!" Hal replied, laying his hand on the small of Rosaline's back. She leant back into its ready warmth. "Yes, but we cannot revive him—"

Captain Morris frowned, then turned to face the crowd that had formed in the street. "Water!" he yelled. "Has anyone got water?!"

Someone came running forward, and a flask was passed into the hackney. Rosaline tipped a little into her own mouth and swallowed, just to check that it was clean, then leaned forward over Jamie and tilted the flask, letting a thin trickle fall over his lips. She paused and watched, but moment after moment passed with no change.

Titus groaned, and Captain Morris, who had been watching the whole thing, said, "Something stronger." He stepped away, turning to the crowd, and bellowed, "Has anyone got something stronger?!"

"No," Rosaline tried, without success. "No, Captain—"

"Here." This was a new voice — brisk, dry. A man appeared beside the Captain — a man with the Captain's red hair and freckles, though he was lankier, taller, with a scar on his chin. "I always carry something about my person."

The Captain rolled his eyes and accepted the man's flask,

pushing it into Rosaline's hands, but she was too distracted by the man to notice.

"Bill," said Hal, confirming her suspicions. "Glad you could make it."

"Wouldn't miss it for the world," Bill Morris replied, unperturbed. He was dressed in gray and black, and he had a grim, sharp sort of look about him. He gave Rosaline a nod. "Duchess, so glad to finally make your acquaintance in person."

Rosaline stared at him, dazed. She'd known, of course, that if all went according to plan, he would be there, but seeing him for herself, the man who'd told her the truth about McGrath, weighed heavily indeed. "The— the pleasure is all mine—"

Titus made a strangled noise. "My *child*—"

"Oh, yes, sorry—" Rosaline bent over Jamie, opened the flask, and tipped a little of the liquid — whiskey, she realized — into her cupped hand. She dipped a finger into it, then traced her finger over Jamie's upper lip, letting some of the alcohol slip into his mouth.

They all waited with bated breath as several moments passed without change. Then, to Rosaline's absolute relief, Jamie's face twisted and he spluttered awake.

"Urgh!" He rubbed his face, getting more of the liquor in his nose, and began to snort and splutter all over again. Titus clutched at him, speechless with joy, beaming at his son with all of the wonder of a new parent.

"Hal!" Jamie wailed, his eyes screwed shut. "Make it stop!"

"Here, Jamie," said Hal, and his voice contained every emotion threatening to burst out of Rosaline's chest. He passed Rosaline the flask of water, and she took it, splashing some across Jamie's face.

"*Urgh!*" Jamie twisted away from her, tucking himself against Titus' chest, then froze when he realized that his face was pressed into the body of someone who was not Hal. After a few tense moments, he slowly pulled away and blinked up at his father.

Rosaline held her breath, but she need not have worried.

"Papa." Jamie's lip wobbled, even after he rubbed at his face to hide it. "I thought you were with the Rebels."

"No," said Titus at once, his voice breaking. "No, not anymore."

Jamie looked at him for another moment, then, just when Rosaline thought she might burst, flung himself onto his father, wrapping his arms around Titus' neck. Titus let out a bolt of laughter and clung to him, looking younger and happier than ever.

A fresh wave of tears cascaded down Rosaline's face, and Captain Morris began to clap and cheer. The crowd joined in, and even Bill cracked a smile and clapped along.

Rosaline grabbed Hal, nearly overwhelmed with emotion. She could hardly speak, could not even begin to describe—

"I know." He kissed her ear, her temple, and gave her a squeeze with his good arm. "But it is not over yet." He pulled away, and she saw something like resolve in his eyes. "I still want answers. Do you?"

Rosaline looked at Hal, and for a moment, wanted nothing more than to walk away and leave everything where it was. She would be happy to never think of this again in her life. But he was right. They needed answers if they were to ever have a good night's sleep again. She nodded. "Yes."

Hal helped her to her feet, and together, they walked away from the carriage and around its other side. Rosaline had hardly spared a thought for McGrath since the crash, but now she saw quite a tableau.

There was indeed a huge crowd of spectators, held at bay by the soldiers, and some half-dozen feet from the carriage lay McGrath, mutinous, propped up on an elbow and held at sword-point by none other than Edward.

"Ah, Hal!" Edward turned and flashed them a smile, as if nothing were amiss. "I gather that Jamie is quite well?"

"Yes," said Hal. "Yes, thank God."

Then, Rosaline saw where Charlotte was — bent over the hackney driver, tending to his bleeding head wound and administering what looked like gin and tea in equal measure. The driver stared up at her, besotted and dazed, but she carried on her work with all the professionalism of a field nurse. People were watching her, confused but impressed, and Rosaline had to smile at her friend's gumption. *Incredible*, she thought, *that I once thought her daft*.

"If you had been reasonable," Hal said, addressing McGrath, "we might have avoided this whole mess."

McGrath merely glared up at him, his face ruddy with anger.

"You may as well tell us now," Hal continued as Bill made his way over, notebook in hand. "You will have to repeat it all before the magistrate, anyway."

"You cannot charge me with anything," McGrath spat. "I've never seen that child before in my life—"

"Nice try," said Bill, raising an eyebrow.

"And do not think you've escaped punishment for your other crimes," said Hal, his voice brittle. "Attacking my wife the least among them."

"I did no such thing," McGrath replied. "She—"

"Is a Duchess now," said Rosaline coolly, stepping forward. "And can crush you under the heel of her shoe."

McGrath ignored her. He glanced around at his captors, and seemed to realize that he was out of options.

"Why kidnap Jamie?" Hal asked him, once again. "If you already had—"

"Because, you imbecile," McGrath snapped, "the plan was never to kill Wolfe, though he more than deserved it for what he did."

"Bold words," said Bill. "Considering you yourself are also a deserter."

McGrath's color deepened, and for a moment, Rosaline feared he would stop speaking. But something, perhaps his own self-absorption, now driven to self-hatred, spurred him on. "They wanted Wolfe alive. He has unique information about the Irish rebels that could prove invaluable to the right authorities." He slotted a look at the overturned carriage, where Titus and Jamie were still hidden from view. "Having control over the boy meant they stood a greater chance of getting his father to cooperate."

Rosaline heard the implication before he'd finished speaking. So Titus would have been tortured, and shown that his lack of compliance would have resulted in unimaginable horrors for his son. But that still did not explain—

"Then why send them, or take them, to different cities?" said Hal with a frown. "If you needed one to guarantee the other?"

"Because he found himself a better deal," said Bill, cocking his head to one side as he considered McGrath. "Or rather, because he realized he could use Jamie to make some money for him before the boy was ever required to see his father. Is that correct, McGrath?" When McGrath did not reply, Bill turned to Hal and said, "McGrath is his father's son, and no mistake. Always knowing how to make the most out of a gamble."

Hal was staring at McGrath, and for a moment, Rosaline could see all the revulsion, all the fury, that he had thus far kept hidden from view. "How did you know?" His voice was low, mangled. "How did you find out about Jamie?"

McGrath smirked then, as if he were amused by the question. "I knew there was a reason you kept yourself tucked away in that damn estate. Something more than your inability to keep company with other people. I just had to find out what it was. So I convinced that little housemaid to turn traitor, to both our advantages."

"To yours and yours alone," Rosaline spat. "You left her ruined, McGrath, do not dare to pretend otherwise. Though I suppose your testimony will be quite useful in her trial. Once the magistrate learns what sort of creature you are, he will not hesitate to grant her clemency."

His eyebrows flickered. "I did not coerce her. Everything she did was of her own free will."

"Indeed," Rosaline allowed. "But she did so under the false pretense of love. And that, you cretin, is perhaps the worst coercion of them all."

"Constable," said Hal, turning to Bill. "Are we to release this man to your custody, or has the army taken precedence?"

"Not sure," Bill replied, looking over his shoulder as Captain Morris approached their group. "Tell me, brother, what would His Majesty want?"

"McGrath is to come with us first," Captain Morris replied. "He will be court-martialed, then he and McNally are to be remanded to the general courts to be tried for kidnapping, conspiracy, and any number of other charges. But," he added with a shrug, "you and your men are welcome to visit him at any time."

McGrath was staring at Captain Morris in shock, and the Captain noticed.

"Yes," the Captain went on, flashing McGrath a smirk. "The Major was taken into custody shortly after you left his residence. He is not saying much yet, but you never know how he might respond to the right sort of pressure." He turned to Hal. "Prongs, my men and I will get this mess cleared away. You need not concern yourself with anything further."

For some reason, hearing those words lifted an invisible weight from Rosaline's shoulders, and when she met Hal's gaze, she smiled.

As Captain Morris approached McGrath, wielding a short length of rope, McGrath sat up and scowled at Edward. "You can get that out of my face."

"Can I?" said Edward lightly, then with a twitch of his hand, he sliced open McGrath's cheek with the point of his rapier.

It was a thin cut, barely enough to bleed, but McGrath let out a snarl of fury and scrambled in the mud, trying to get to his feet.

Edward grinned. "Do not bother. I bested you at swords when

we were twelve, and I can do it again." He wiped off the blade on his sleeve, then sheathed the sword and turned to Charlotte. "Ready, my love?"

"Yes!" She gave the hackney driver a farewell pat on the shoulder and hurried over, wiping her hands on her filthy skirts. Her face was ablaze with energy, and she beamed at them all. "I must admit, I did not think it would all go off without a hitch."

Rosaline could not help it — she let out a laugh. She could, now that it was all over.

"We were lucky," said Hal, so fervent because it was true. There could have been any number of outcomes, and their success was only due to Hal and Titus' clever estimates of McGrath's reactions. "We were very lucky."

They all watched Captain Morris bind McGrath at the wrists and hand him off to some of his soldiers, who seemed very keen to take him away. Then Titus appeared, still carrying Jamie, and for a moment, Rosaline wondered how he had the strength — New York had not been kind to him, nor had the crossing, and the past few days had been trying indeed. But Titus seemed unaffected, propelled only by his relief and his happiness at seeing his son again. Jamie still seemed bleary, what little she could see of him — he had his arms wrapped around Titus' neck and his head tucked in against Titus' shoulder. His feet dangled, unshod, in the air, and her heart twisted as she looked at his filthy soles.

A bath, she resolved. *A good strong bath, before anything else.* Then Rosaline remembered that they would have to haul in and heat the water themselves, and smiled at the image.

"Now," Hal said to Bill and Captain Morris as Titus and Jamie joined them. "Do you require anything more from us?"

"Not at present," said Bill, with a nod from his brother. "Though you may want to write to your solicitor. This will take some time to sort out, and it is possible that McGrath is only the beginning of something much bigger."

"Understood," said Hal.

There was an awkward pause, and it took Rosaline several moments to figure out why — Bill and Captain Morris kept glancing at Titus, who looked back at them, his expression mild and unassuming.

"And, uh, well." Captain Morris gave a cough. "All that talk of... desertion, and the Irish rebels, and, well, the implications of treason." He laughed then, unnatural and high. "Even if we could prove that you were who McGrath claimed you to be... Bill and I... neither of us heard anything. Nor did any of my men."

"No," confirmed Bill, pocketing his notebook. "Not a word."

"Right, Ed?" prodded Captain Morris.

Edward nodded. "Right."

"I do not believe I have met this gentleman," Captain Morris went on, offering his hand to Titus with a wink. "What is your name, good sir?"

Titus took the Captain's hand with a sly smile. "Taylor," he said. "Robert Taylor."

"Robert Taylor," Captain Morris echoed. "Pleasure to meet you. Allow me to be the first to congratulate you on your reunion with your son."

Titus grinned then, a real, genuine grin, and it was like the sun coming out from behind a cloud. Rosaline found Hal's arm and squeezed it, unable to hold back her own smile. "Thank you," said Titus. "But the pleasure is all mine."

"Are you staying in London, then?" said Captain Morris to Hal.

"Not for longer than a day or two," Hal replied, and the others nodded their agreement. In any case, they were almost out of food. "It is best that we return to Alban Hollow as soon as we can."

"I understand. But drop me a line before you leave."

"Of course." Hal took Captain Morris's forearm. "Thank you, Ron. And thank you, Bill. I cannot thank you both enough. You saved the boy's life."

Captain Morris waved his thanks aside. "Anytime." He

stepped away, dipped his head to Rosaline, then Charlotte. "Ladies, always a delight."

Bill flashed them an almost-smile. "Nice meeting you all. Will be in touch."

With that, the two Morrises turned away, and as Rosaline watched, Bill reached out to ruffle his brother's hair. The Captain shoved him off and returned to the men currently trying to dismantle the carriage — she could see that the back of his neck was pink, and had to stifle a giggle.

Hal took her hand, and she met his gaze. Above them, the clouds shifted, and sunshine burst across the road. Rosaline lifted her face to it, relishing the muted warmth on her skin, feeling as if she could float into the sky. But it was wonderful just to stand here, surrounded by her friends, her family, and feel the future open before her, unencumbered and full of joy.

"Well, my love?" Hal squeezed her hand and smiled. "Home?"

"Yes." Rosaline nodded. "Home."

ACKNOWLEDGEMENTS FROM
THE AUTHOR

Thank you to my beta readers, B. and D. If it weren't for you, this story wouldn't exist. I owe you infinitely many orders of Pad Thai.

Endless gratitude to Mya Saracho for bringing Rosaline and Hal to life.

Thank you to Jennifer Shore, for answering all the questions in the known world.

Thank you to everyone who has supported my writing, both published and unpublished, whether it be through kudos, comments, DMs, or mood-boards. I don't have the words to express what it means to me.

Thank you to my family for your unwavering support over the years, for introducing me to the works of William Shakespeare, and for keeping me fed and watered.

The next installment of this series will feature Katherine and Rebecca's love story. Follow me on social media for all the updates on its release.

ABOUT THE AUTHOR

E.B. Neal lives in Cincinnati, Ohio.

You can find more about E.B. Neal at:
www.authorebneal.com

 twitter.com/ebnealwrites
 tiktok.com/ebneal_writes
instagram.com/ebneal_writes

ABOUT THE COVER ARTIST

Mya Saracho creates queered, body positive art under the name A. LoveUnlaced. They began in various fandoms and now create a mix of original art and fan art. They live with their two wonderful spouses and a gremlin cosplaying as a dog.

You can find more from Mya at:
https://aloveunlaced.carrd.co/

twitter.com/A_LoveUnlaced

instagram.com/a.loveunlaced

Printed in Great Britain
by Amazon